V.C. Andrews® Books

**The Dollanganger
Family**
Flowers in the Attic
Petals on the Wind
If There Be Thorns
Seeds of Yesterday
Garden of Shadows
Christopher's Diary:
　Secrets of Foxworth
Christopher's Diary:
　Echoes of
　Dollanganger
Secret Brother

The Audrina Series
My Sweet Audrina
Whitefern

The Casteel Family
Heaven
Dark Angel
Fallen Hearts
Gates of Paradise
Web of Dreams

The Cutler Family
Dawn
Secrets of the Morning
Twilight's Child
Midnight Whispers
Darkest Hour

The Landry Family
Ruby
Pearl in the Mist
All That Glitters
Hidden Jewel
Tarnished Gold

The Logan Family
Melody
Heart Song
Unfinished Symphony
Music in the Night
Olivia

The Orphans Series
Butterfly
Crystal
Brooke
Raven
Runaways

**The Wildflowers
Series**
Misty
Star
Jade
Cat
Into the Garden

The Hudson Family
Rain
Lightning Strikes
Eye of the Storm
The End of the
　Rainbow

The Shooting Stars
Cinnamon
Ice
Rose
Honey
Falling Stars

The De Beers Family
"Dark Seed"
Willow
Wicked Forest
Twisted Roots
Into the Woods
Hidden Leaves

**The Broken Wings
Series**
Broken Wings
Midnight Flight

The Gemini Series
Celeste
Black Cat
Child of Darkness

The Shadows Series
April Shadows
Girl in the Shadows

**The Early Spring
Series**
Broken Flower
Scattered Leaves

The Secrets Series
Secrets in the Attic
Secrets in the Shadows

The Delia Series
Delia's Crossing
Delia's Heart
Delia's Gift

**The Heavenstone
Series**
The Heavenstone
　Secrets
Secret Whispers

The March Family
Family Storms
Cloudburst

The Kindred Series
Daughter of Darkness
Daughter of Light

The Forbidden Series
The Forbidden Sister
"The Forbidden
　Heart"
Roxy's Story

The Mirror Sisters
The Mirror Sisters
Broken Glass
Shattered Memories

**The House of Secrets
Series**
House of Secrets
Echoes in the Walls

The Girls of Spindrift
Bittersweet Dreams
"Corliss"
"Donna"
"Mayfair"
"Spindrift"

Stand-alone Novels
Gods of Green
　Mountain
Into the Darkness
Capturing Angels
The Unwelcomed
　Child
Sage's Eyes
The Silhouette Girl

My Sweet Audrina

and

Whitefern

V.C. Andrews®

G

GALLERY BOOKS

New York   London   Toronto   Sydney   New Delhi

G

Gallery Books
An Imprint of Simon & Schuster, Inc.
1230 Avenue of the Americas
New York, NY 10020

Following the death of Virginia Andrews, the Andrews family worked with a carefully selected writer to organize and complete Virginia Andrews's stories and to create additional novels, of which this is one, inspired by her storytelling genius.

First Gallery Books trade paperback edition May 2019

V.C. ANDREWS® and VIRGINIA ANDREWS® are registered trademarks of Vanda Productions, LLC

GALLERY BOOKS and colophon are registered trademarks of Simon & Schuster, Inc.

For information about special discounts for bulk purchases, please contact Simon & Schuster Special Sales at 1-866-506-1949 or business@simonandschuster.com.

Manufactured in the United States of America

10 9 8 7 6 5 4 3 2 1

Library of Congress Cataloging-in-Publication Data is available.

ISBN 978-1-9821-0665-2

MY SWEET AUDRINA

For Ann Patty, my editor

For Anita and Humphrey,
my agents, with gratitude

PART 1

Whitefern

There was something strange about the house where I grew up. There were shadows in the corners and whispers on the stairs and time was as irrelevant as honesty. Though how I knew that I couldn't say.

There was a war going on in our house, a silent war that sounded no guns, and the bodies that fell were only wishes that died and the bullets were only words and the blood that spilled was always called pride.

Though I'd never been to school—and I was seven years old and it was high time I was in school—it seemed I knew all about the Civil War. Around me the Civil War was still being waged, and though the future might stretch ahead for billions of years, it was still the war we'd never forget, for our pride had been injured, and our passions were lingering on. We'd lost the battle better won by the opposite side. Maybe that's why it still kept hurting.

Momma and my aunt Ellsbeth always said that men liked violent discussions about wars better than any other topic, but if there were other wars of any importance at all, they were never discussed in our house. Papa would read any book, see any movie, cut out any magazine photo that represented that war between brothers, even though his ancestors had fought against my maternal ones. He was Yankee born, but a Southerner by preference. At the dinner table he'd recount the plots of the long novels he read about General Robert E. Lee and give grisly accounts of all the bloody battles. And if most of what he read charmed me, it did not charm either my aunt, who preferred the television, or my mother, who preferred to read her own books, claiming Papa left out the best parts, which weren't fit for young ears to hear.

That meant my ears, and my cousin Vera's ears. Though most of the world believed Vera to be my sister, I knew she was my unmarried aunt's illegitimate daughter—and that we had to shield her from the scorn of society by pretending she was my legitimate older sister. I did have a legitimate older sister, too, but she had died before I was born. Her name was also Audrina, and even though she had been dead a long time, still she lingered on. My papa never forgot the first and best Audrina, and still hoped that someday I would be as special as she was.

My cousin Vera liked people to think she was my sister. I didn't know her true age, for she refused to tell me that. Nobody in our house ever revealed their ages. Only my age was talked about all the time. It was Vera's boast that she could be any age she wanted to be—ten, twelve, fifteen, and even twenty. With a few elegant and sophisticated postures, truly she did change her manner and expression. She could look very mature—or very childlike—depending on her mood. She liked to ridicule me because I was so uncertain about time. Often Vera told me I'd hatched full blown from a giant ostrich egg at the age of seven. She always said that I had inherited that bird's famous habit of sticking its head in the sand and pretending nothing in the world was wrong. She didn't know about my dreams and the ugliness they gave me.

From the very beginning, I knew Vera was my enemy even when she pretended to be my friend. Though I wanted her for my friend in the worst way, I knew she hated me. She was jealous because I was an Audrina and she wasn't. Oh, how I wanted Vera to like and admire me, as sometimes I really liked and admired her. I envied her, too, because she was normal and didn't have to try to be like someone who was dead. No one seemed to care if Vera wasn't special. No one except Vera. Vera was fond of telling me that I wasn't really special, either, I was merely strange. To tell the truth, I thought there was something strange about me, too. I seemed to be unable to recall anything about my early childhood. I couldn't remember anything about the past—what I had done the week or even the day before. I didn't know how I had learned the things I knew, or why I seemed to know some things I shouldn't.

The many clocks scattered throughout our giant house confused me even more. The grandfather clocks in the halls chimed out different hours; the cuckoos in their wooden Swiss clocks popped in and out of small ornate doors, each contradicting all the others;

the fancy French clock in my parents' bedroom had stopped long ago at midnight or noon, and a Chinese clock ran backwards. To my great distress, though I searched everywhere, there were no calendars in our house, not even old ones. And the newspapers never came on the day they were due. Our only magazines were old ones, stacked in closets, hidden in the attic. Nobody threw anything away in our house. It was kept, saved for our descendents, so they could sell it one day and make a fortune.

Much of my insecurity had to do with the first Audrina, who had died exactly nine years before I was born. She had died mysteriously in the woods after cruel and heartless boys had spoiled her in some indescribable way, and because of her, I was never supposed to enter the woods, even to go to school. And the woods were all around us, almost smothering us. They embraced us on three sides, the River Lyle on the fourth. To go anywhere we had to travel through the woods.

Everywhere in our home photographs of the First and Best Audrina were scattered. On Papa's desk, there were three framed portraits of her, at age one, two and three. There was not one single baby picture of me, not one, and that hurt. The First Audrina had been a beautiful little girl, and when I looked at her photographs, I felt oddly haunted, wanting to be her so badly I ached inside. I wanted to be her so I'd feel as loved, as special as everyone said she had been; and then again, contrarily, I wanted more than anything to be myself, and on my own merits gain the love I felt denied me.

Oh, the tales Papa could tell me about the wonders of his first daughter, and everyone he told made me know I was not the Best Audrina, not the perfect and special one—only the second and the inferior one.

My parents kept the first Audrina's bedroom like a shrine for a dead princess. It was left exactly as it had been on the day she met her fate, which was never explained in detail to me. That room was so full of toys it seemed more a playroom than a bedroom. Momma herself cleaned that room, and she hated housework. Just to see *her* room made me realize nothing had been too good for *her,* while my bedroom lacked toy shelves, and her vast array of playthings. I felt cheated, cheated of a real childhood. Audrina the First and Best had stolen my youth, and everyone talked so much about her that I couldn't remember anything about me. I believed it was because of her that my memory was so full of holes.

Papa would try to fill those holes by putting me in her rocking chair and making me rock and sing until I became "the empty pitcher that would fill with everything."

He wanted me to fill with her memories and capture her special powers since she was dead and didn't need them anymore.

And as if one ghost weren't enough, we had a second who came every Tuesday at four. "Teatime," we called Aunt Mercy Marie's day. There she'd sit on the piano, in her black and white photograph in a silver frame, her fat face beaming a vacuous smile, her pale blue eyes staring out as if she could see us, when she couldn't. She was dead, and yet undead, just like my dead sister.

My aunt and my mother would speak for Aunt Mercy Marie, and through her they would let loose all the venom they held back and saved for "teatimes." Strangely enough, my cousin Vera enjoyed these Tuesday teatimes so much she'd find any reason to play hookey from school, just to be there and hear all the ugly things my mother and her half sister could say to one another. They were Whitefern sisters, and once upon a far ago time, that had meant something wonderful. Now it meant something sad, but they would never tell me exactly what.

Long ago the Whitefern family had been the most notable family in our Tidewater section of Virginia, giving the country senators and vice presidents. But we'd fallen out of favor not just with the villagers, but also with everyone, and we were no longer honored, or even respected.

Our house was far from the nearest city of any size.

Whitefern Village was fifteen miles down a lonely country road, but we seldom went there. It was as if long ago some secret war had been declared, and we in our castle (as Papa liked to call our home) were hated by the "serfs" in the lowlands. If anyplace in our vicinity could be called "highlands" it was the slight hill on which Whitefern sat.

Papa had to drive thirty miles to and from his stock-brokerage office. All the friends we had lived in the city. Our nearest neighbors were twelve miles away as a car drove, five as a crow flew. Papa drove our only car to work, leaving all of us without transportation. So often my aunt Ellsbeth would bemoan the day she'd sold her small car to buy the TV set.

My aunt, who'd never been married, loved her portable television set with a twelve-inch screen. She seldom allowed me to watch, though her daughter, Vera, could watch as much as she liked when she was home from school. That was another thing I couldn't understand: why Vera was allowed to go to school when I couldn't go. School was dangerous for me, but not for Vera.

Naturally I presumed there had to be something terribly wrong with me. My parents had to hide me away to keep me safe, if not from outsiders, then from myself. That was the scariest thought of all.

At the age of seven, while other children boarded yellow buses and rode off giggling and having fun, I sat down at the kitchen table and was taught how to read, write, add and subtract by my mother, who played the piano beautifully but was not good at teaching anything but how to play the piano. Fortunately, or maybe not, my aunt Ellsbeth was there to help. She had once been a grade-school teacher with ready slaps to deliver any boy who dared to call her a nasty name. Just one slap too many, and the parents had seen that my aunt was fired. Though she tried for many a year to find another teaching position, the word was out. My aunt had a ferocious temper and a ready hand.

Aunt Ellsbeth, like her daughter, Vera, also had

ready comments to criticize our way of living. According to my aunt we were all as "antediluvian" as the house in which we lived. "Out of sync with the rest of the world," she'd say.

In my dreams of home, Whitefern loomed up high and white against a dark and stormy sky, frightening to behold. It threatened in the night, but in the day it welcomed me with open arms. I had a habit of sitting outside on the lawn and admiring the grandness of Whitefern. It was a gingerbread Victorian house of many frills, with its white paint peeling, its dark blinds loose and crooked. It had three stories, with an attic and a basement toward the back half of the house where the spacious lawn inclined toward the River Lyle. As I stared at that house, I thought I had much in common with it. We were both antediluvian and "out of sync."

Our windows were myriad, many of them beautiful stained glass. The shutters, about to fall off, were so darkly red they appeared black from a distance, like dried blood. From the outside the most marvelous thing of all were the balustrades on all the many porches, balconies and verandas, designed to look like stylized woodferns.

In the very center of the dark roof was a round cupola with a copper roof now turned green from tarnish. It formed a point that was topped by a golden ball whose gold leaf was coming off bit by bit each time it rained. The cupola was about fourteen feet in diameter, and every single one of its many windows was made of leaded stained glass with scenes to represent the angels of life and death.

Inside and out, ferns cascaded everywhere from wicker stands. There were other plants, but the ferns seemed to steal what moisture there was in the air so soon all other plants died.

On stealthy, timid feet I played my small lonely games in the great foyer where the stained glass from the double front doors threw colorful patterns on the floor. Rapier-sharp colors sometimes, stabbing into my brain and punching holes there. I also had little rhymes Vera had taught me that I said to protect myself from the colors:

Step on black, live forever in a shack.
Step on green, never be clean.
Step on blue, work will never be through.
Step on yellow, hear the world bellow.
Step on red, soon be dead.

Just so I wouldn't have to step on any color, I stole along near the walls, keeping to the shadows, listening to the clocks ticking away the wrong times and the silly cuckoos going crazy in the night. When the wind blew hard, the shutters banged and the floors creaked, the furnace in the basement coughed, sputtered, groaned, and the wind chimes in the cupola tinkled, tinkled.

Yet in the daytime there were things so wondrously grand in our house that I felt like Alice lost in a house of jewels. Art deco lamps and *objets d'art* were scattered hither and yon. Tiffany lamps rose up to throw more colors, to pattern the walls. Crystal prisms dangled from lamp shades, from wall sconces, from chandeliers, from gas lamps, catching colors, refracting rainbows that flashed like lightning whenever sunlight managed to steal through the lace curtains.

We had a fireplace in every room. There were eight of marble, many of elegantly carved wood and none were made of brick. Brick was not elegant enough for our type of house that seemed to despise simplicity.

Our ceilings were high, and carved with elaborate designs, making frames for biblical or romantic scenes. In the olden days people had, or so it seemed to my young eyes, either too many clothes on, or too little that wanted to stay in place. I wondered why the biblical scenes usually had more flesh showing than the ones where people were decidedly wicked. One could hardly believe those near-naked people were sincerely trying to follow where God would lead them.

Bare bosoms of impressive proportions protruded brazenly in every room of our house but mine. George Washington and Thomas Jefferson and several other dead-eyed presidents gazed day after day at the naked lady lying on a chaise across the way as she forever dropped grapes into her gaping mouth. Naked baby boys flew about shamelessly shooting aimless arrows. But the men always modestly hid their maleness behind some strategically placed leaf or graceful flow of drapery. Women were not so apt to hide what they had, I'd often thought as I gazed at them. They looked shy, but acted bold. Aunt Ellsbeth had come up behind me once and explained bitterly that since most artists were men, it was only natural for them to delight in "exploiting" the nude female figure.

"Don't judge women by what you see in paintings and statues. Judge them only by what you yourself know about the women in your life. The day any man understands any woman will be the day the world comes to an end. Men are hateful, contrary creatures who say they want goddesses to put on pedestals. Once they have them up there, they rip off the halo, tear off the gown, slice off the wings so they can't fly and then kick the pedestal away so the woman falls at his feet and he can scream out as he kicks her, tramp!—or worse."

To hear my aunt Ellsbeth talk one would think she'd been married a dozen or more times, and one thousand men had disappointed her. As far as I knew, only one man had.

Our furniture had many styles, all of them fancy. It seemed each chair, each table, each sofa, lamp, pillow, hassock, desk was in competition, trying to outdo the others. Although Aunt Ellsbeth complained about the furniture, Momma would catch hold of my hand and lead me reverently from room to room, explaining that this table was a "Renaissance Revival" centerpiece, made by Berkey and Gay, Grand Rapids, Michigan.

"All antiques, Audrina. All worth their weight in gold. The bed in my room is five hundred years old. Once kings and queens slept behind its curtains."

Behind us my aunt would snort her contempt and disbelief.

Other people had electricity in all their rooms; we had electricity only in our kitchen and bathrooms. In other rooms we used gas lamps because Momma thought them more flattering to her complexion. My aunt thought them a pain in— (But I wasn't supposed to use some of the words my aunt said readily.) Even more than gas lamps, Momma loved candles burning, and logs in the fireplace snapping and crackling and making shadows dance on the dark paneled walls. Our kitchen stuck out like a sore thumb with all its modern gadgets that made life bearable for Momma, who hated any kind of hard work but loved cooking the gourmet meals my father had to have.

The room we all favored most was the Roman Revival Salon. On its royal-purple velvet lounging chaise with the gold cording tarnished and falling off where it wasn't fastened by fancy tassels, Momma would lie dressed in some filmy negligee, or a soft summer dress. She didn't seem to notice that the stuffing was coming out and the springs poked through in a few places. Sprawled elegantly on that chaise, she'd read her romances and occasionally lift her eyes to stare dreamily off into space. I guessed she was imagining herself in the arms of the handsome lover on the colorful cover of her paperback novel. I told myself bravely that someday I was going to have the nerve to read novels like that, wicked and beautiful at the same time—though how I knew they were wicked books I couldn't say, since I'd never read one. But almost-naked people on the cover seemed awfully wicked.

Papa's huge round home office, directly under the

cupola, held thousands of old-old books, and many fine editions of classics that nobody read but me and Aunt Ellsbeth. Papa said he didn't have time to read them, but he kept on adding to our leather-bound collection as if hoping all his friends would think he read them. Momma hid her paperbacks in her bedroom closets and pretended that she, too, loved the high-minded tales printed on fine paper and bound with beautiful leather.

Some of those classic books contained very wicked material, according to my cousin Vera, who always informed me about what was, or was not, wicked.

I liked to watch Momma lying on her couch. Behind her was a concert-sized grand piano that her father had given her when she had won a gold metal in a music competition. Many a time she'd told me she could have gone on to play in all the best concert halls, but Papa hadn't wanted a professional musician for his wife. "Don't expect to have too many talents, Audrina. Men won't approve if it's likely you'll earn more money than they do." Downward her hand would drift. Without even looking, she would cleverly find the very piece of chocolate she wanted and pop it into her mouth. My father often warned her about eating too much chocolate and becoming fat, but she never did.

My mother was tall, curvy where she should be and slender in all the places a woman should be. My papa often told me she was the greatest beauty on the East Coast and had been the catch of the season at her debutante ball. Many a handsome and rich man had asked for my momma's hand in marriage, but it had been Damian Jonathan Adare who had swept my mother off her feet with his dashing dark good looks and his winning charm. "He towered over every other man in my life, Audrina," my mother would tell me. "When your father came back from the sea, all the girls went gaga just to have him in the room. I felt so lucky when he had eyes only for me." Then she'd frown as if remembering some other girl Papa might have "had eyes for."

Vera liked to joke that my father had married my mother only because he admired her hair color so much. "Witchy hair," Vera called Momma's hair and mine. "Chameleon hair," Papa often called it. It was strange hair, and at times I believed Vera was right. Our hair didn't know which color it was supposed to be, and was, instead, all colors. Flaxen blond, with gold, auburn, bright red, chestnut brown, copper and even some white. Papa loved the strange prismlike color of our hair. I believed he'd ordered God to give me the kind of hair I had; if He hadn't, Papa might have sent me back. For the first Audrina also had chameleon hair.

My papa, six foot five and weighing well over two hundred pounds, was the tallest man I had ever seen, though Vera was always telling me there were many men who were taller, especially basketball players. Papa's hair was the darkest black, looking blue sometimes in the sunlight. He had beautiful almond-shaped eyes, so brown they appeared black, and his lashes were so long and thick they appeared false, even though they weren't. I knew; I'd tried to pull them off after I saw Momma glue some false ones on. His eyes were slick as oil, scary and wonderful, especially when they glittered. He had smooth, soft skin that often appeared ruddy in the winters, and richly bronze in the summers. When Momma was displeased with Papa and his selfish ways of spending more on himself than on her, she'd call him a dandy and a fop, though what those words meant I didn't know. I suspected she meant that my huge, powerful papa cared more about clothes than he cared about principles.

He feared growing old, especially feared losing his hair. He checked his hairbrush each day, almost counting the hairs he found there. He saw the dentist four times a year. He flossed his teeth so often Momma grew disgusted. His doctor checked him over as much as the dentist did. He fretted about minor flaws no one would ever notice but him, such as thick, horny toenails he had difficulty clipping. Yet when he smiled, his charm was irresistible.

Principles were another thing I didn't understand, except Momma often said that Papa lacked them. Again I vaguely guessed she meant Papa wanted what he wanted, and no one had better get in his way and try to prevent him from taking what he had to have. Yet, sometimes when he was with me, and he was tender and loving, he'd give me my way. But only sometimes. There were other times—terrible other times.

It had been agreed when my aunt came back to live here when Vera was only one year old that she would do all the housework in exchange for her board and keep, while my mother did the cooking. Unreasonably, my aunt wanted to do the cooking (which she considered easier) instead of the housework, but no one could eat anything my aunt prepared. Momma despised housework, but she could throw anything into a pot or bowl without measuring and it would come out tasting divine. Papa said she was a "creative" cook, because she had an artist's mind, while Ellie (as only he called her) was born to be some man's slave. How my aunt glared when he said mean things like that.

My aunt was a fearsome woman. Tall, lean and mean was my father's description. "It's no wonder no man wants to marry you," my father often teased my aunt. "You've got the tongue of a shrew." Not only did she have a sharp tongue, as mean for me as for Vera, but she also had her golden rule about sparing the rod and spoiling the child. Neither Vera nor I were spared when she was in charge. Fortunately my parents seldom left us alone with her. In some ways, it seemed my aunt disliked her daughter even more than she disliked me. It had always been my belief that women were born to be loving mothers. Then, when I gave that more thought, I couldn't remember how I had arrived at that conclusion.

Momma *liked* for my aunt to chastise Vera, so then she could open her arms wide and welcome Vera into them, saying time and again to Vera, "It's all right, I'll love you even if your own mother can't."

"That's the weakness of being you, Lucietta," said my aunt sharply. "You can give love to anything."

As if her own daughter, Vera, was less than human.

Never would my aunt Ellsbeth name the man who was Vera's father. "He was a cheat and a liar. I don't *want* to remember his name," she'd say with scorn.

It was so difficult to understand what was going on in our house. Treacherous undercurrents, like the rivers that ran into the sea that wasn't so very far away.

It was true my aunt was tall, her face was long and she was skinny, even if she did eat three times more than my mother. Sometimes when Papa said cruel things to my aunt, her already thin lips would purse together to become a fine line. Her nostrils would flare, her hands would tighten into fists, as if she'd like to belt him one if she only had the nerve.

Maybe it was Aunt Ellsbeth who kept our city friends from coming more often. There had to be some reason why they came only when we threw a party. Then, Momma said, our "friends" popped out of the woodwork like insects come to feast on the picnic. Papa adored all parties until they were over. Then, for one reason or another, he would jump on Momma and punish her for some trivial thing he called a "social error," such as looking at a handsome man for too long, or dancing with him too many times. Oh, it was difficult being a wife, I could tell. One never knew just what to do, or how friendly to be. Momma was expected to play the piano to entertain while people danced or sang. But she wasn't supposed to play so well that some people cried and told her later that she'd been a fool to marry and give up her musical career.

No casual callers ever came to our doors. No

salesmen were allowed either. Signs were posted everywhere: "No Solicitors Allowed," and "Beware of
the Dog," and "Keep Off, This is Private Property.
Trespassers will be Prosecuted."

I often went to bed feeling unhappy with my life,
feeling an undercurrent that was pulling my feet from
under me, and I was floundering, floundering, bound
to sink and drown. It seemed I heard a voice whispering, telling me there were rivers to cross and places
to go, but I'd never go anywhere. There were people
to know and fun to have, but I wouldn't experience
any of that. I woke up and heard the tinkle of the
whispering wind chimes telling me over and over that
I belonged where I was, and here I would stay forevermore, and nothing I did would matter in the long
run. Shivering, I hugged my arms over my thin chest.
In my ears I heard Papa's voice, saying over and over
again, "This is where you belong, safe with Papa, safe
in your home."

Why did I have to have an older sister dead and
in her grave at the age of nine? Why did I have to be
named after a dead girl? It seemed peculiar, unnatural.
I hated the First Audrina, the Best Audrina, the Good
and Perfect and Never Wrong Audrina. Yet I had to
replace her if ever I was to win a permanent place in
Papa's heart. I hated the ritual of visiting her grave
every Sunday after church services and putting flowers
there bought from a florist, as if the flowers from our
yard weren't good enough.

In the morning I ran to Papa and right away he
picked me up and held me close as the grandfather

clocks in the hallways relentlessly ticked on. All about us the house was as silent as a grave, as if waiting for death to come and take us all, as it had taken the First and Best Audrina. Oh, how I hated and envied my older dead sister. How cursed I felt to bear her name.

"Where is everyone?" I whispered, glancing around fearfully.

"Out in the yard," he said, hugging me closer. "It's Saturday, my love. I know time isn't important to you, but it is to me. Time is never important to special people with unusual gifts. Yet for me the weekend hours are the best ones. I knew you'd be frightened to find yourself alone in an empty house, so I stayed inside while the rest went out to harvest the rewards of their planting."

"Papa, why can't I remember every day like other people? I don't remember last year, or the year before—why?"

"We are all victims of dual heritages," he said softly, stroking my hair and gently rocking me back and forth in the rocker that my great-great-great-grandmother had used to nurse her twelve children in. "Each child inherits genes from both parents, and that determines his or her hair color, eye color and personality traits. Babies come into the world to be controlled by those genes and by the particular environment that surrounds them. You are still waiting to fill with your dead sister's gifts. When you do, all that is good and beautiful in this world will belong to you, as it belonged to her. While you and I wait for that marvelous day when your empty pitcher is filled, I am doing my damnedest to give you the very best."

At that moment my aunt and mother came into the kitchen, trailed by Vera, who carried a basket of freshly picked butter beans.

Aunt Ellsbeth must have overheard most of what Papa had just said, because she remarked sarcastically, "You should have been a philosopher instead of a stockbroker, Damian. Then maybe someone would care to listen to your words of wisdom."

I stared at her, dredging up from my treacherous memory something I might or might not have dreamed. It could even be a dream that belonged to the First Audrina, who'd been so clever, so beautiful and so everlastingly perfect. But before I could capture any illusive memory, all were gone, gone.

I sighed, unhappy with myself, unhappy with the adults who ruled me, with the cousin who insisted she was really my only sister because she wanted to steal my place, when already my place had been stolen by the First and Best Audrina, who was a dead Audrina.

And now I was supposed to act like her, talk like her and be everything that she'd been . . . and where was the real me supposed to go?

Sunday came, and as soon as the church services were over, Papa drove, as he always did, straight to the family cemetery near our house where the name Whitefern was engraved on a huge arching gateway through which we slowly drove. Beyond the archway the cemetery itself had to be approached on foot. We were all dressed in our best, and bearing expensive flowers. Papa tugged me from the car. I resisted, hating that grave we had to visit and that dead girl who stole everyone's love from me.

It seemed this was the first time I could clearly remember the words Papa must have said many times before. "There she lies, my first Audrina." Sorrowfully, he stared down at the flat grave with the slender white-marble headstone bearing my very own name, but her birth and death dates. I wondered when my parents would recover from the shock of her mysterious death. It seemed to me that if sixteen years hadn't healed their shock, maybe ninety wouldn't, either. I couldn't bear to look at that tombstone, so I stared up into my papa's handsome face so high above. This was the kind of perspective I would never have once I grew up, seeing his strong, square chin from underneath, next his heavy pouting lower lip, then his flaring nostrils and the fringe of his long lower dark lashes meeting with the upper ones as he blinked back his tears. It was just like looking up at God.

He seemed so powerful, so much in control. He smiled at me again. "My first Audrina is in that grave, dead at nine years of age. That wonderful, special Audrina—just as you are wonderful and special. Never doubt for one moment that you aren't just as wonderful and gifted as she was. Believe in what Papa tells you and you will never go wrong."

I swallowed. Visiting this grave and hearing about this Audrina always made my throat hurt. Of course I wasn't wonderful or special, yet how could I tell him that when he seemed so convinced? In my childish way I figured my value to him depended on just how special and wonderful I turned out to be later on.

"Oh, Papa," cried Vera, stumbling over to his side and clutching at his hand. "I loved her so much, so very much. She was so sweet and wonderful and special. And so beautiful. I don't think in a million years there will ever be another like your First Audrina." She flashed a wicked smile my way to tell me again that never would I be as pretty as the First and Best and Most Perfect Audrina. "And she was so brilliant in school, too. It's terrible the way she died, really awful. I'd be so ashamed if that happened to me, so ashamed I'd rather be dead."

"Shut up!" roared Papa in a voice so mighty that the ducks on the river flew away. He hurried then to put his pot of flowers on that grave, and then he seized my hand and pulled me toward his car.

Momma began to cry.

Already I knew Vera was right. Whatever wonderful specialness the First Audrina had possessed was buried in the grave with her.

In the Cupola

Not wanted, not worthy, not pretty and not special enough were the words I thought as I went up the stairs and into the attic. I wished the First Audrina had never been born. I had to wade through the clutter of old dusty junk before I came to the rusty, iron, spiraling stairs that would take me through a square opening in the floor that once had a rickety iron guardrail that someday Papa was going to replace.

In that octagon room there was a rectangular Turkish rug, all crimsons, golds and blues. Each day I visited I combed that fringe with my fingers, as Papa often raked through his dark hair with his fingers when he was enraged or frustrated. There were no furnishings in the cupola, only a pillow for me to sit on. The sunlight through the stained-glass windows fell upon the carpet in swirls like bright peacock feathers and confused the designs with patterns of colored light. My legs and arms were patterned, too, like impermanent tattoos. High above, dangling down from the apex of the pointed roof, were long rectangles of painted glass—Chinese wind chimes that hung from scarlet silken cords. They hung so high the wind never made them move, yet I often heard them tinkle, tinkle. If just one time they would sway for me while I watched, then I could believe I wasn't crazy.

I fell down on the cushion on the rug and began to play with the old paper dolls that I kept lined up around the walls. Each one was named after someone I knew, but since I didn't know too many people, many of the paper dolls had the same names. But only one was named Audrina. It seemed I could vaguely remember once there had been men and boy dolls, but now I had only girls and ladies.

I was so absorbed in my thoughts that I didn't hear a sound until suddenly a voice asked, "Are you thinking about me, sweet Audrina?"

My head jerked around. There stood Vera in the haunted, colored lights of the cupola. Her straight hair was a pale apricot color unlike any other color I'd ever seen, but that wasn't unusual in our family. Her eyes very dark, like her mother's, like my father's.

The colors refracted from the many windows cast myriad colored lights on the floor, tattooed patterns on her face, so I'm sure my eyes were lit up just like hers, like many-faceted jewels. The cupola was a magic place.

"Are you listening to me, Audrina?" she asked, her voice whispery and scary. "Why do you just sit there and not answer? Have you lost your vocal cords as well as your memory?"

I hated her being in the cupola. This was my own special, private room for trying to figure out what I couldn't remember as I moved the dolls about and pretended they were my family. Truthfully, I was putting the dolls through the years of my life, trying in this way to reconstruct and dredge up the secret that eluded me. Someday, some wonderful day, I hoped to retrieve from those dolls all I couldn't recall so that I'd be made whole, and just as wonderful as that dead sister ever was.

Vera's left arm had just come out of a cast. She moved it gingerly as she stepped into my little sanctuary.

Despite my off-and-on dislike for Vera, I felt sorry she could break her arm just by banging it against something hard. According to her she'd had eleven broken bones, and I'd never had any. Little brushes against a table and her wrist fractured. A slighter bump and huge purple bruises came to mar her skin for weeks. If she fell off her bed onto a soft, padded carpet she still broke a leg, an ankle, a forearm, something.

"Does your arm still hurt?"

"Don't look at me with pity!" ordered Vera, limping into the cupola, then scrunching down on her heels in an awkward way. Her dark eyes bore holes into me. "I have fragile bones, small, delicate bones, and if they break easily, it's because I have more blue blood than you do."

She could have her blue blood if it meant broken bones twice a year. Sometimes when she was so mean to me I thought God was punishing her. And sometimes I felt guilty because my bones were tough and refused to break even when I occasionally fell.

Oh, I wondered again, if the First, Best and Most Perfect Audrina had been as aristocratic as Vera.

"And of course my arm hurts!" shrilled Vera, her dark eyes flashing with reds, greens and blues. "It hurts like hell!" Her voice turned plaintive as she went on. "When your arm is broken it makes you feel so helpless. It's really worse than a broken leg because there are so many things you can't do for yourself. Since *you* don't eat much, I don't know why your bones don't break more easily than mine . . . but, of course, you must have peasant bones."

I didn't know what to say.

"There's a boy in my class who looks at me so sympathetically, and he carries my books, and talks to me, and asks me all kinds of questions. He's so hand-some you just wouldn't believe it. His name is Arden Lowe. Isn't that an unusual and romantic name for a boy? Audrina, I think he's got a case on me . . . and he's kissed me twice in the cloakroom."

"What's a cloakroom?"

"My, are you stupid! Holes in the belfry with bats flying 'round, that's Papa's sweet Audrina." She gig-gled as she tossed her challenge. I didn't want to fight, so she went on to tell me more about her boyfriend named Arden Lowe. "His eyes are amber colored, the prettiest eyes you ever saw. When you get real close, you can see little flecks of green in his eyes. His hair is dark brown with reddish highlights when the sun hits it. He's smart, too. He's a year older than me, but that doesn't mean he's dumb, it just means he's traveled around so much he fell behind in his schoolwork." She sighed and looked dreamy.

"How old is Arden Lowe?"

"Yesterday I was twenty, so Arden was younger, naturally. He doesn't have my kind of talent for being any age I want to be. I guess he's eleven, and kind of a baby when I'm twenty, but such a good-looking baby."

She smiled at me, but I knew darn well she couldn't be more than . . . than twelve? I went back to my dolls.

"Audrina, you love those dolls more than you do me."

"No, I don't . . ." But I wasn't really too sure even as I said that.

"Then give me the *boy* and *men* dolls."

"All the boy and men dolls are gone," I answered in a funny, tight voice that made Vera open her eyes wide.

"Where did all the male dolls go, Audrina?" she whispered in the weirdest kind of knowing voice that made me shiver.

"I don't know," I whispered back, somehow afraid. I quickly glanced around with scared eyes. Tinkle-tinkle sounded the chimes above as they dangled perfectly still. I shrank tighter inside. "I thought you took them."

"You're a baa . . . ad girl, Audrina, a really wicked girl. Someday you'll find out exactly how bad, and when you do, you'll want to die." She giggled and drew away.

What was wrong with me that she'd want to hurt me time and again? Or was something wrong with her? Like my mother and her sister . . . were we going to repeat history over and over?

Vera's pale, pasty face grinned at me wickedly, seeming to represent all evil. When she turned her head the colors came to play upon her skin and her apricot hair turned red, then blue streaked with violet. "Give me all your dolls, even if the best ones have gone on to hell." She reached to seize up half a dozen of the closest dolls.

Moving lightning fast, I snatched those dolls from her hands. Then, jumping to my feet, I ran about gathering up all the other dolls. Vera crawled to rake my legs with her long fingernails, always filed to sharp points. Still I managed to hold her off with one foot against her shoulder as I gathered up the last handful of dolls and costumes. With both hands full now, I shoved her with my foot so that she fell backward, and I was off and running down the spiraling stairs at breakneck speed, sure she couldn't catch me. Yet I heard her right behind me, screaming out my name, ordering me to stop. "If I fall it will be your fault, your fault!" She added a few filthy names, which had no meaning for me at all.

"You don't love me, Audrina," I heard her wail. Her hard-soled shoes made clunking noises on the metal stairs. "If you really loved me like a sister, you'd do what I want and give me everything I want to make up for all the pain I have to suffer." I heard her stop and gasp for breath. "Audrina, don't you dare hide those dolls! Don't you dare! They belong to me just as much as they belong to you!"

No, they didn't. I'd been the one to find them in an

old trunk. There was a rule about finders being keepers, and I believed in rules, old adages, maxims. They were tried and tested by time that knew so much more about everything than I did.

It was easy to duck out of sight as Vera tediously, clumsily clambered down the steep and narrow stairs. Under a loose floorboard I stuffed the dolls and all. their colorful Edwardian costumes that took them to many an important social function. That's when I heard Vera scream.

Oh, golly! She'd fallen again. I ran to where she lay in a crumpled heap. Her left leg was buckled under her in a grotesque way. It was the leg she'd broken twice before. I cringed to see a bit of jagged bone protruding through her torn flesh, which was gushing blood.

"It's your fault," she moaned, in so much agony her pretty face was twisted and ugly. "It's your fault for not giving me what I wanted. Always your fault, everything bad that happens to me, your fault. Somebody should give me what I want sometime."

"I'll give you the dolls now," I said weakly, prepared to give her anything she demanded now that she was hurt. "I'll run for your mother and mine first—"

"I don't want your damned dolls now!" she cried. "Just get out and leave me alone! But for you I would have had everything. Someday you're going to pay for all that you've stolen from me, Audrina. I'm supposed to be the first and best, not you!"

It made me feel sick to back off and leave her alone like she was, broken and in pain, that left leg gushing blood. Then I noticed her left arm was lying there in a peculiar position, too. Oh, dear Lord. It had broken again. Now she'd have a broken arm, and a broken leg. But even so, God had not taught Vera anything about humility, as I'd been taught, and taught well . . .

How did I know that?

Flying down the stairs I bumped into Papa. "Haven't I told you to stay out of the cupola?" he barked, grabbing hold of my arm and trying to prevent me from reaching my mother. "Don't go up there until I have that guardrail put back. You could fall and hurt yourself."

I didn't want to be the one to tell Papa about Vera's broken bones. Yet I had to, since he refused to let go of my arm. "She's up there bleeding, Papa. Great gobs of blood, and if you don't let go of me and call an ambulance, she might die."

"I doubt it," he said; still, he did bellow out to Momma, "Call for the ambulance, Lucky. Vera has broken her bones again. My health insurance will cancel my plan if this keeps up."

Still, when it came down to the nitty-gritty, Papa was the one who calmed Vera's fears and sat beside her in the ambulance and held her hand as he wiped away her tears. And on a stretcher, in an ambulance that knew her well, Vera was again on her way to the closest hospital to have yet another cast put on her arm, and on her leg, too.

I stood near the front door and watched the ambulance disappear around the bend of our long drive. Both my mother and my aunt refused to go to the hospital again and suffer through all the long hours of waiting and watching that shriveled leg being again put into a cast. The last time she'd broken her leg, Vera's doctor said that if she broke it again, the leg might not grow as long as the other.

"Don't look so worried, darling," comforted Momma. "It wasn't your fault. We have warned Vera time and again not to climb those spiraling stairs. That's why we tell you not to go up there, knowing she'll follow sooner or later to check on what you're doing. And doctors always give you the most dire predictions, thinking how grateful you'll feel when they don't come true. Vera's leg will grow to match the other . . . though God knows how she manages to break the same one over and over again so consistently."

Aunt Ellsbeth said nothing at all. It seemed her daughter's broken bones didn't concern her nearly as much as hunting throughout the house for an old vacuum cleaner, which she finally found in the closet under the back stairs. She headed toward the family dining room, where six presidents hung to stare at the naked lady eating grapes.

"Is there anything I can do to help, Aunt Ellsbeth?" I asked.

"No!" snapped my aunt. "You don't know how to do anything right, and in the end you only make more work. Why the devil didn't you give Vera the paper dolls when she asked for them?"

"Because she'd only tear them up."

My aunt snorted, glared at me, at my mother, whose arms were around me, and then she tugged the vacuum down the hall and disappeared.

"Momma," I whispered, "why does Vera always lie? She told Papa I pushed her down the stairs, but I wasn't even near her. I was in the attic, hiding the dolls, while she was coming down the stairs. She fell in school, and even then she said I pushed her. Momma, why would she say that when I've never been to school? Why can't I go to school? Did the First Audrina go to school?"

"Yes, of course she went," said Momma, sounding as if a frog had caught in her throat. "Vera is a very unhappy girl, and that's why she lies. Her mother gives her very little attention, and Vera knows you receive a great deal. But it's hard to love such a mean, hateful girl, although we all try our best. There's a cruel streak in Vera that worries me greatly. I'm so afraid she'll do something to hurt you, to hurt us all." Her lovely violet eyes stared off into space. "It's too bad your aunt didn't stay away. We didn't need her and Vera to complicate our lives more."

"How old is Vera, Momma?"

"How old has she told you she is?"

"Sometimes Vera says she's ten, sometimes she says she's twelve, and sometimes she's sixteen, or twenty. Momma, she laughs like she's mocking me . . . because I really don't know how old *I* am."

"Of course you know you are seven. Haven't we told you that over and over again?"

"But I can't remember my seventh birthday. Did you give me a birthday party? Does Vera have birthday parties? I can't remember one."

"Vera is three years older than you are," said

Momma quickly. "We can't afford to have birthday parties anymore. Not because we can't spend the money—but you know why birthday parties bring back tragic memories. Neither your father nor I can bear to think of birthday parties anymore, so we all stopped having birthdays and have chosen to stay the age we like best. I'm going to stay thirty-two." She giggled and kissed me again. "That's a lovely age to be, not too young and not too old."

But I was serious and sick of evasions. "Then Vera didn't know my dead sister, did she? She says she did, but how could she have when she's only three years older than me?"

Again my mother looked distressed. "In a way she did know her. You see, we've talked so much about her. Perhaps we talk too much about her."

And so it went, as always, evasions but no revelations, at least not the kind I really wanted, the kind I could believe in.

"When can I go to school?" I asked.

"Someday," murmured Momma, "someday soon . . ."

"But Momma," I persisted, following her into the kitchen and helping her chop vegetables for the salad, "I don't fall and break my bones like Vera. So I'd be safer in school than she is."

"No, you don't fall," she said in a tight voice. "I suppose I should be grateful for that—but you have other ways of hurting yourself, don't you?"

Did I?

Papa's Dream

Before darkness could steal the last rosy glow of dusk, Papa was home from the hospital and carrying Vera into the Roman Revival Salon. As if Vera weighed only a feather, even with a hip-length cast on her left leg, and a fresh cast on her left arm, too, Papa tenderly deposited Vera on the purple velvet couch that my mother loved to keep for herself. Vera appeared very happy with the large box of chocolates she'd half eaten on her ride home from the hospital. She didn't offer the box to me, though I stood there longing to have just one. Then I saw that Papa had also bought her a new jigsaw puzzle to put together with her good right arm. "It's all right, honey," he said to me. "I brought you chocolates and a puzzle too. But you should be grateful you don't have to fall and break *your* bones just to gain some attention."

Immediately Vera threw away her puzzle and shoved the chocolates from the table to the floor. "Now, now," soothed Papa, picking up the boxes and handing them back to her. "Your puzzle is very large, Audrina's is very small. You have a two-pound box of candy. Audrina's box weighs only one pound."

Happy again, Vera smirked my way. "Thank you, Papa. You're so good to me." She stretched her arms forth, wanting him to kiss her. I cringed inside, hating her for calling him Papa, when he wasn't her father, but mine. I resented the kiss he put on her cheek, resented, too, that huge box of candy, that larger puzzle that had prettier colors than the one Papa gave me.

Unable to bear watching longer, I wandered away to sit on the back veranda and stare at the moon that was coming up over the dark water. It was a quarter moon, what Papa called a horned moon, and I thought I could see the profile of the man in the moon, old and withered looking. The wind through the summer leaves had a lonesome sound, telling me that soon the leaves would die, and winter would come, and I hadn't enjoyed summer at all. I had vague memories of happier, hotter summers, and yet I couldn't pull them out to clearly view them. I put a round piece of chocolate in my mouth, even though we had yet to eat dinner. This August seemed more like October, really it did.

As if he heard me calling, Papa came to sit next to me. He sniffed the wind as he always did, an old habit, he'd told me many times, left over from his days in the Navy.

"Papa, why are the geese flying south when it's summer? I thought they only flew south in late autumn."

"I guess the geese know more about the weather than we do, and they're trying to tell us something." His hand lightly brushed over my hair.

I started to put another piece of candy in my mouth when he said, "Don't eat but one of those." His voice was softer when he spoke to me, kinder, as if my sensitivities were as eggshell fragile as Vera's bones. "I saw you looking jealous when I kissed Vera. You resented the gifts I gave her. Somebody has to pamper her when she's suffering. And you know only you are the light of my life, the heart of my heart."

· "You loved the First Audrina better," I choked. "I'm never gonna catch her gift, Papa, no matter how many times I rock in that chair. Why do I have to have her gift? Why can't you take me like I am?"

With his arm about my shoulders he explained again that he only wanted to give me confidence in myself. "There's magic to be had in that chair, Audrina. I *do* love you for what you are, I just want to give you a little extra something that she no longer needs. If you can use what she used to have, why not? Then your Swiss cheese memory would fill to over-flowing, and I'd rejoice for you."

I didn't believe there was a gift to be gained from that chair. It was all another lie that gave me as much terror as it seemed to give him hope. His voice took on a pleading tone. "I need someone to believe in me wholeheartedly, Audrina. I need from you the trust that she gave me. That's the only gift I want you to recover. Her gift for having faith in me, in yourself. Your mother loves me, I know that. But she doesn't believe in me. Now that my First Audrina is gone, I'm depending on you to give me what once made me feel clean and wonderful. Need me as she needed me. Trust me as she trusted me. For when you expect only the best, that's what you will get."

That wasn't true! I yanked away from his embrace. "No, Papa. If *she* expected only the best, and was so trusting of you, why did she go into the woods against your orders? Was she expecting the best the day she was found dead under the golden raintree?"

"Who told you that?" he asked sharply.

"I don't know!" I cried, unsettled to hear my own words. I didn't even know what a golden raintree was. His face bowed down into my hair as his hand gripped my shoulder so hard it hurt. When he finally found something he could say, he sounded miles and miles away, like the warm place those geese were going to. "In some ways you're right. Perhaps your mother and I should have given her more explicit warnings. As it was, we were embarrassed and didn't tell our First Audrina enough. But none of it was her fault."

"None of what, Papa?"

"Dinnertime," sang out Momma, as if she'd been listening and knew exactly when to interrupt our conversation. My aunt was already at the round table in the family dining room, glowering as Papa carried Vera into the room. Vera glowered back. The only time my aunt seemed to like her daughter was when she was out of sight. When Papa was around she could be so cruel to Vera even I winced. She wasn't as cruel to me. Mostly she treated me with indifference, unless I somehow managed to irritate her, which was often.

Papa hugged Vera before he went to sit at the head of the table. "Feeling better, honey?"

"Yes, Papa," she said with a bright smile. "I feel fine now."

The minute she said that, Papa beamed a broad smile my way. He gave me a conspiratorial wink that I'm sure Vera saw. She dropped her eyes and stared down at her plate, refusing to pick up her fork and eat. "I'm not hungry," she said when my mother tried to coax her.

"Eat now," ordered Aunt Ellsbeth, "or you won't eat anything until breakfast. Damian, you should have known better than to give the children candy before dinner."

"Ellie, you give me a pain in a certain part of my anatomy I won't mention in front of my daughter. Vera will not die of malnutrition. Tomorrow she'll stuff herself as she stuffed herself before her fall."

He reached to squeeze Vera's pale long fingers. "Go on, darling, eat. Show your mother you can hold twice as much as she can."

Vera began to cry.

How awful of Papa to be so cruel! After dinner, just like Momma did, I ran upstairs, threw myself on my bed and really bawled. I wanted a simple life with firm ground beneath my feet. All I had was quicksand. I wanted parents who were honest, consistent from day to day, not so changeable I couldn't depend on their love to last for longer than a few minutes.

An hour later, the corridor resounded with Papa's heavy tread. He didn't bother to knock, just threw open the door so hard the latch banged into the plastered wall and made another nick. There was a key in the lock which I never dared to use, fearful he would kick my door down if I did. Papa strode to my room wearing a new suit he'd changed into since dinner-time, telling me he and Momma were going out. He'd showered and shaved again, and his hair fell in soft waves perfectly molded to his skull. He sat on my bed, caught my hand in his, allowing me to see his square, large nails that were buffed so much they shone.

Minutes passed as he just sat there holding my hand, which felt lost in the hugeness of his. The night birds in the trees outside my bedroom window twittered sleepily. The little clock on my night table said twelve o'clock, but it wasn't the real time. I knew he and Momma wouldn't go out at midnight. I heard a boat whistle in the distance, a ship putting out to sea.

"Well," he said at long last, "what have I done this time to wound your fragile ego?"

"You don't have to be nice to Vera one minute and nasty to her the next. And I didn't push Vera down the steps." My voice sounded faltering, and this was certainly not the kind of confident speech that would make anyone believe me.

"I know you didn't push her," he said somewhat impatiently. "You didn't have to tell me you didn't. Audrina, never confess to a crime until you are accused." In the gloomy dimness his dark ebony eyes glittered. He frightened me.

"Your mother and I are going to spend the evening with friends in the city. You don't have to rock in the chair tonight. Just be a good girl and fall into dreamless sleep."

Did he think I could control my dreams? "How old am I, Papa? The rocking chair has never told me that."

He'd left my bed to head for the door, and in the open doorway he paused to glance back at me. The hall gas lamps shimmered on his thick, dark hair. "You are seven, soon to be eight."

"How soon to be eight?"

"Soon enough." He came back and sat down. "How old do you want to be?" he asked.

"Only as old as I'm supposed to be."

"You'd make a good lawyer, Audrina. You never give me a straight answer."

Neither did he. I was catching his habits. "Papa, tell me again why I can't remember exactly what I did last year, and the year before."

He sighed heavily, as he always did when I asked too many questions. "My sweetheart, how many times do I have to tell you? You are a special kind of girl, with talents so extraordinary that you don't realize the passing of time. You walk alone in your own space."

I already knew that. "I don't like my own space, Papa. It's lonely where I walk. I want to go to school like Vera does. I want to ride on that yellow school bus. I want friends to play with . . . and I can't remember ever having a birthday party."

"Can you remember Vera's birthday parties?"

"No."

"That's because we don't celebrate birthdays in this house. It's much healthier to forget about time and live as if there were no clocks and no calendars. That way you never grow old."

His story was so much like Momma's . . . too

much. Time did matter, birthdays, too; both mattered more than he said.

He said good night and closed the door, leaving me to lie on my bed and wonder.

One night screams woke me up. My screams. I was sitting up, clawing at the sheet, covering myself up to my chin. In the long corridor I heard the pounding of Papa's bare feet as he came running. On the side of my bed he perched to hold me in his arms, smoothing my tousled hair, hushing my piercing cries, telling me again and again that everything was all right. Nothing could harm me here. Soon I fell asleep, safe in his arms.

Morning light woke me, and Papa was in the doorway smiling broadly, almost as if he'd never left me alone. "Sunday morning, love, time to rise and shine. Put on your Sunday clothes and we'll be off."

I stared at him, sleepy-eyed and disoriented. Was it only last week that Vera broke her leg? Or was it much, much longer? It was a question I put to Papa.

"Darling, you see what I mean? It's December now. In five days it will be Christmas. Don't tell me you've forgotten."

But I had. Time had such agility when it came to fleeting past me. Oh, God . . . what Vera said about me had to be true. I was vacant headed, forgetful, perhaps brainless.

"Papa," I called out nervously before he closed the door so I could dress for church. "Why do you and

Momma let everyone in church believe Vera is your daughter and not Aunt Ellsbeth's?"

"We don't have time for that kind of discussion now, Audrina. Besides, I've told you many times before how your aunt went away for almost two years, and came back with a one-year-old daughter. Of course, she was expecting to marry Vera's father. We couldn't let everyone know a Whitefern had given birth out of wedlock. Is it such a crime to pass Vera off as our own and save your aunt from disgrace? This isn't New York City, Audrina. We live in the Bible Belt, where good Christians are supposed to abide by the rules of the Lord."

Vera belonged to some nameless man and my father was generous and was doing the decent thing, and I was his one and only living daughter. Vera liked to pretend he was her father, but he wasn't. "I'm so glad I'm your only daughter . . . who's alive."

He stared at me blankly for a moment, his full lips thinning. I'd been told many a time that eyes were the windows of the soul, so I ignored his lips as I studied his dark, shuttered eyes. Something hard and suspicious rested in them. "Your mother hasn't said any differently, has she?"

"No, Papa, but Vera has."

Suddenly he laughed and hugged me so tight against his chest that my ribs ached afterwards. "What difference does it make what Vera says? Of course she wants me for her father. After all, I'm the only father she's ever known. And if all others think Vera is your mother's child, let them think what they will. There isn't a family anywhere without skeletons in its closets. Our skeletons are no worse than anyone else's. Besides, wouldn't the world be a boring place if everyone knew all there was to know about everyone? Mystery is the spice of life. That's what keeps people living on and on, hoping to uncover all the secrets they can."

I thought the world would be a better place without all the skeletons and mysteries. My world would be a perfect place if only everyone in my home knew how to be honest.

The Rocking Chair

Vera came to my room that night, soon after I'd climbed into bed, determined to have only happy thoughts before sleeping, hoping they'd lead to happy dreams. Hobbling with considerable skill on the crutches she'd grown accustomed to, she managed to carry things in a bookbag she'd slung over her shoulder—only this bookbag was different from any I'd seen before.

"Here," she said, tossing me the bag on the bed. "Educate yourself. Those two women in the kitchen will never teach you what I will."

I felt a little skeptical but happy, nevertheless, that she was interested in my education. I knew there were many things I was missing by not going to school. Shaking the bag's contents onto my bed, dozens of photographs cut from magazines fell to my bed in a ragged clump. I couldn't believe my eyes when I picked them up and started to separate them, staring all the time at pictures that showed naked men and women in lewd, weird embraces. The hateful things clung to my fingers, so tacky I plucked them free from one hand only to find them sticking to the other.

Then, to my consternation, I heard the heavy tread of Papa's feet as he came toward my room.

Vera had done this on purpose! She knew Papa came to my room each night around this time.

"I'm going," said Vera with a delighted grin. She hobbled toward the door of the bedroom that adjoined mine, planning to escape Papa. "Don't you dare tell him I was here if you know what's good for you."

But on her crutches she couldn't move fast enough. Papa threw open the door and glared at the two of us. "What's going on in here?" he asked.

With the guilty evidence stuck to my fingers, I hesitated and thus gave Vera the chance to dump all the crime in my lap. "I found that bookbag in a closet, and since it was monogrammed with *her* initials, I thought *this* Audrina should have it."

Scowling darkly, Papa came to me and tore the clippings from my fingers. He took one glance and howled in rage; then, whirling around, he thrust out his arm and sent Vera reeling to the floor—and she was already broken enough. Like someone demented and dying, Vera screamed out her rage. "It's hers! Why are you hitting me?"

Papa picked her up and held her as if she were some stiff-legged puppy from the gutter. He held her over my bed. "Now pick them up!" he ordered harshly. "My first Audrina would no more look at that filth than she'd tar and feather you—which I'll do if you don't stop tormenting me! Now you have to eat them," he added when she had them in her nervous, pale hand. I thought he was joking; so did she.

"I'm going to scream for my mother!" threatened Vera. "I'm hurt! I've got broken bones! I could die! You let me go, or tomorrow I'll go to the police and tell them you abuse me—"

"Eat them!" he bellowed. "You've coated them with glue, they shouldn't taste worse than your mother's cooking."

"Pa . . . pa," she wailed, "don't make me eat paper and glue!"

Snorting in disgust, he carried her out of the room. A few seconds later I heard her screaming as he applied his belt to her bare skin. I didn't truly know if he used his belt when she was naked, but ten to one she'd tell me he did. Vera could scream if a fly lit on her arm, so how could I know unless I got up and found out for myself? I never did because for some reason I was afraid what she said might be true.

Minutes passed while my heart raced. Eventually Vera's screams ebbed away, but still Papa didn't come.

Somewhere downstairs a clock chimed ten times, but that meant little. Every bone in my body ached, every muscle was tensed. I knew I'd have to sit in the rocking chair again tonight.

Finally, when I felt I could bear the suspense no longer, knowing I'd never fall asleep until I did what he'd force me to do, I heard a door close and soon heavy footfalls sounded in the corridor. Papa's tread was even, heavy, squeaking the old sagging floorboards.

Softly, he eased open my bedroom door and stepped inside. Quietly, he closed the door behind him. He loomed up in the night like some huge monster, casting a long shadow in the dimness of my moonlit room.

"Sooo," he drawled in his most beguiling southern voice, cultivated over the years from his clipped Yankee delivery, "now you've taken to looking at obscene photographs that will dirty your mind. That shames me, Audrina, really shames me."

"Not me, Papa," I said. "Vera brought them in here—but don't hit her again, please. You could break her other arm and leg, or maybe her neck. You shouldn't whip her when she's hurt."

"I don't whip her," he said harshly. "I just scolded her, and she started screaming that I didn't love her. God, how can anyone love someone who makes so much trouble? Even if Vera brought in those nasty pictures and gave them to you, you didn't have to look, did you?"

Didn't I?

"I thought better of you than that. Don't let Vera destroy the best that's in you."

"Why are boys dangerous for me and not for Vera, Papa?"

"Some girls are born to be what Vera is. Boys can sniff them out from miles away. That's why I don't bother about her. It wouldn't do any good. It's you I care about because it's you I love. I used to be a boy, and I know how boys think. I'm sorry to say most boys cannot be trusted. That's why you have to stay out of the woods, and close to home, and out of school, too. It's dangerous for a beautiful, sensitive girl like you. It's the kind of woman you'll grow up to be that will be the salvation of mankind. That's why I struggle to save you and protect you from contamination."

"But, but . . . Papa—"

"Don't protest, just accept the fact that parents worry. Adults are far wiser about the world, especially wise about their own flesh and blood. We know you are ultrasensitive. We want to spare you those unnecessary pains. We love you. We want to see you grow up healthy and happy, that's all."

He came to sit on the edge of my bed as I lay on my back, frozen and trying not to breathe. Tightly I squeezed my eyelids together. My lids parted a bit to peek and see if he believed I'd fallen asleep, so deeply asleep I might even be dead, and maybe in death I'd gain the nobility of the First and Best Audrina and would never have to sit in her chair again. But he leaned closer. I seized hold of the sheet and pulled it up high under my chin. Papa's ironlike hands closed down on my shoulders. His strong fingers digging into my tender skin made my eyes pop wide open and clash with his. Our gazes locked, and in a silent duel of wills we fought until my mind went vague, out of focus, and he was the winner again.

"Now, now," he soothed, beginning to stroke my hair, "it's not so bad, is it? You've done it before, and you can do it again. I know sooner or later you will catch the gift, if you are patient and keep trying. You can help me, Audrina."

"But—but," I stammered, wanting to make him stop. But he went on and on, inundating me with his needs, which had to be my needs too.

I was afraid. Still, my love for him made me an easy subject, willing to be cajoled, flattered and won over to feeling I had to be wanted just for my "gifts" when I had them.

"And all you have to do is dream, Audrina, just dream."

Dream, dream. That was the one thing I didn't want to do. Was he going to keep it up until I was an old lady, or would I be able to seize hold of the First Audrina's gift and satisfy Papa? Pray God the First and Best Audrina's gift would help me end up differently than she did. Why didn't he ever worry about that?

"Dream, Audrina, my love, my sweet. Shakespeare wrote about it: 'to sleep, perchance to dream.' To dream and know the truth. Come back and give me your dreams, Audrina, and make all your father's hopes for the future come true."

I stared at him sitting there on my bed. His dark eyes were no longer glittering and frightening, only pleading and full of love—how could I keep on resisting? He was my father. Fathers were supposed to know right from wrong. And I did owe him a great deal. "Yes, Papa," I whispered. "Just one more time. Won't just one more time be enough?"

"Perhaps it will be," he said, his smile lighting up his face.

Appearing happy, Papa led me by my hand down the hall, to the very end room. Once there, he released me and took out a large key to unlock her door. I felt a cold draft that made me shiver. It was the first Audrina's grave breathing on me.

I looked around as I always did, as if I'd never been here before. I couldn't say how many times I'd been here. This room seemed to be the one thing that filled all the holes in my memory, looming larger than any other experience. Yet each time I came it was a shock to hear the wind chimes in the cupola begin to softly tinkle, tinkle. Even in the dark, crystal-prism colors flashed behind my eyes. Perhaps I had seized hold of a memory—the memory of this all too familiar room. Perhaps I was beginning to benefit just from being here.

If it hadn't once been *her* room, I'd have wanted it for my own. It was huge, with a big tester bed under the fancy canopy. There were two giant dark armoires filled with all the pretty clothes that had once been hers, clothes they didn't want me to wear. Little shoes were lined up in neat rows, from one-year sizes to those a nine-year-old girl would wear. Some were scuffed and old, some were shiny and new. The dresses that hung above grew longer with each succeeding year.

Toy shelves lined the walls, full of everything any little girl could ever want. There were dolls from every foreign country dressed in native costumes. There were toy tea sets and dinner sets, picture books and storybooks, beach balls and bouncing balls, jumping ropes with fancy handles, jacks, boxes of games, puzzles and paint sets . . . oh, there was nothing they hadn't bought for the First, the Best and the Most Perfect Audrina—far more than they'd bought for me. On those dark and brooding shelves where the toys sat eternally grieving and waiting to be loved again were dozens of soft, plushy, pastel animals, all with dark button eyes that glinted and gleamed and seemed to follow my movements. Even baby rattles with small teeth marks were there, and worn-looking bronzed baby shoes in which she'd taken her first steps. They hadn't saved mine and had them bronzed, nor had they saved Vera's,

Beneath the wide windows covered by fussy white Priscilla curtains was a dollhouse. A child's toy table with four chairs was set and ready for a party that was never given. Fancy rugs were scattered about to make stepping stones across the room, compartmentalizing it into rooms within a room, or mazes within a maze.

Quietly as vandals we left the doorway and stole inside that room that breathlessly awaited us. My bedroom slippers were left in the hallway outside, as were his, to show our respect to this room where the perfect daughter had once reigned. The very way Papa had taught me to bow my head and lower my eyes and speak in reverent whispers once I was in this room instilled fear in me. Expectantly, he kept his eyes on me, as if waiting for her specialness to jump into my brain and fill my Swiss cheese memory with the First Audrina's gifts.

He kept watching me, waiting for something to happen, but when I only turned in circles, staring at one thing and then another, he grew impatient and gestured toward the only adult-sized chair in the room—the magic rocking chair with the lacy calla-lily back and the rose velvet cushion. I inched toward it reluctantly, holding my breath as I forced myself to sit. Once I had stiffly settled myself on the seat, he came to kneel at my side. Then began his ritual of kisses rained on my hair, my face, even my arms and hands, all meant to tell me that he loved *me* best. He murmured endearments in my ear, his breath hot and damp, and before I could protest, he bounded to his feet and raced from the room, slamming and locking the door behind him.

He'd never left me alone in here before!

"No, Papa!" I screamed, panic in my voice, terror all around me. "Come back! Don't make me stay in here by myself!"

"You're not alone," he called to me from the other side of the door. "God is with you and I am with you. I'll stay and wait right here, watching through the keyhole, listening, praying. Nothing but good can come from rocking in that chair. Believe that, Audrina; nothing but good will fill your brain and replace your lost memories."

I squeezed my eyes shut and heard the wind chimes clamoring louder, much louder now.

"Sweetheart, don't cry. There's nothing to be afraid of. Hold on to your faith in me and do as I say, and your future will shine more brightly than the sun above."

Beside the chair was one of the night tables that held a lamp and a Bible, *her* Bible. I snatched up the black leatherbound book and held it close against my heart. I told myself, as I'd told myself before, that there was nothing to be afraid of. The dead couldn't harm anyone. But if they couldn't—why was I so terrified?

I heard Papa's soft voice outside the locked door. "You do have her gifts, Audrina, you do. Even if you don't believe, I believe. And I'm the one who knows. I'm sure the reason our previous efforts have failed is because I stayed in the room with you. It's my presence that ruins your chances at succeeding. I know now it's solitude, loneliness, that makes the process begin. You've got to wash your mind free of anxieties. Feel no fear, no joy, no confusion. Expect nothing and everything will be given. Feel nothing but contentment to be alive, to be where you are and who you are. Ask nothing, receive everything. Sit there and let go of whatever makes you afraid or worried. Let contentment loosen your limbs and relax your mind, and if sleep wants to come, then let it come. Do you hear me? Are you listening? No confusion. No fear. For Papa is here."

All his words were familiar. Same old thing about not being afraid, when fear was almost choking me. "Papa," I wailed for one last time, "please don't make me . . ."

"Oh," he said heavily, sighing, "why do I have to force you? Why can't you just believe? Lean back in the rocker, put your head against the high back, hold the chair arms and begin to rock. Sing if it helps to wash your mind clean of fear, of worries, of desires and emotions. Sing and sing until you become an empty pitcher. Empty pitchers have room for many, many things, but full pitchers can hold no more . . ."

Oh, yes, I'd heard this before. I knew what he was doing. He was trying to turn me into the First Audrina—or maybe I was going to be the instrument through which he'd be able to communicate with her. I didn't want to be her. And if ever I was her, I'd hate him, hate him. Yet, he kept soothing me, cajoling me, and if I didn't want to stay in here all night, I'd have to do as he said.

First I stared around at the room again, memorizing again every detail. Little tickling sensations began to whisper, whisper, that I could be her, I was her, the dead Audrina, who was only bones in her grave. No, no, had to think the right thoughts and give to Papa what he had to have. I told myself this was only a bedroom filled with old toys. I saw a huge spider spinning a web from doll to doll. Momma didn't like housework, even cleaning this room. Though it appeared a spotless spic-and-span shrine, it wasn't anything but surface clean. For some reason that made me feel better—Momma was paying what Papa called "lip service" to reverent cleanliness. And Aunt Ellsbeth refused to clean this room.

Unconsciously I began to rock.

Into my head filtered an old, almost forgotten tune. The music and the lyrics played over and over again. The words lulled me, while the melody tingled my spine and slowed my pulse. Peace was coming unbidden to heavy my eyelids . . . and then vaguely I heard my frail voice singing:

Just a playroom, safe in my home,
Only a playroom, safe in my home,
Got no tears, no fears
And nowhere else to roam,

'Cause my papa wants me always to stay home,
Safe in my playroom, safe in my home.

The playroom of the First and Best Audrina. The Perfect Audrina who'd never given her parents the pain and the trouble I delivered daily. I didn't want to sing her song. But I couldn't stop. On and on I heard the singing, trying to keep my eyes open so they could see those elephants, bears and toy tigers on the toy shelves, all sweet and friendly looking until I glanced away. When I looked back, they were fiercely snarling.

The wallpaper was faded bluish violet, entwined with glittery silver threads to make spiderwebs on the walls. There were more spiders on the toys. A giant one began to weave more dolls together, and another came to rest in the eye socket of one doll that had hair somewhat the color of my own. How awful.

"Rock, Audrina, rock!" ordered Papa. "Make the floorboards creak. Make the gray mists come. Watch the walls dissolve, hear the wind chimes tinkle. They'll take you back, back to where you'll find all your memories, all the gifts that were hers. She doesn't need them where she is, but you do. So sing,

sing,
sing . . ."

Hypnotizing, like a singsong chant he, too, had to use, but he didn't know the words I was saying. Papa loves me, yes he does. Papa needs me, yes he does.

Jesus loves me, this I know,
For the Bible tells me so . . .

The shiny black button eyes of the plushy animals seemed to glitter and gleam with more knowledge than I'd ever have. Little pink or red tongues appeared ready to speak and tell me secrets Papa would never reveal. High above, the wind chimes were tinkling, and contentment was coming as I rocked and rocked and became more and more tranquil. Nothing wrong with me, for sooner or later I was going to be changed in some indefinable way for the better. . . .

I grew sleepy, sleepier, unreal feeling. The orangey light from the gas lamps shivered, caught silver and gold threads in the wallpaper. All the colors in the room began to move, to sparkle like diamonds suddenly caught fire. The music of the cupola wind chimes was in my brain dancing, dancing, telling me of happy playtimes up there, slyly whispering of one terrible time up there. Who was flashing that crystal prism in my eyes? How did the wind get into the house to blow my hair when the windows were all down and locked? Were there drafts in the cupola, and ghosts in the attic? What made the hair on my head move, what?

Way back near the sane side of me, I wanted to believe all of this was hopeless and I'd never become an "empty pitcher" that would fill with everything wonderful. I truly didn't want to be that First Audrina, even if she had been more beautiful, and more gifted, too. Still I rocked and sang, I couldn't stop.

Contentment was on the way, making me happier. My panicky heart slowed. My pulse stopped racing. The music I heard was beautiful as I heard behind me, or ahead of me, a man's voice singing.

Someone who needed me was calling; someone who was in the future waiting, and dreamily, unquestioningly, I fuzzily saw the walls open as the molecules slowly, slowly separated, opened, and formed such grainy pores I could drift through them without difficulty. I was outside in the night that swiftly changed into day.

Free! I was free of the playroom. Free of my papa. Free of Whitefern!

I was skipping merrily home from school on my own special day. And I was me. Happily I danced along a woodsy dirt path. I'd just left school, and I didn't question or wonder about this, even knowing I'd never been to school. Something wise was telling me I was inside the First and Most Wonderful Audrina, and I was going to know her as well as I knew myself. I *was* her, and she was me, and "we" were wearing a beautiful crepe de chine dress. I wore my best petticoat underneath it—the one with Irish lace and embroidered shamrocks near the hem.

It was my birthday and I was nine years old. That meant soon I'd be ten, and ten wasn't so far from being eleven, and when I was twelve all the magic of becoming a woman was close at hand.

I spun in circles to see my accordion-pleated skirt flair up to my waist. I inclined my head and spun some more to see my pretty petticoat.

Suddenly there was a noise on the path ahead. Someone giggled. Like black magic the sky abruptly turned dark. Lightning flashed. Thunder rolled deep and ominously.

I couldn't move. Like a statue of marble I stood frozen. My heart began to beat wildly like a jungle drum. Some sixth sense woke up and screamed that something awful was soon to happen.

Pain, my sixth sense was beating out, shame, terror and humiliation. Momma, Papa, help me! Don't let them hurt me! Don't let them do it! I went to Sunday school every week, didn't miss even when I had a cold. I'd earned my black Bible with my name on the cover emblazoned in gold, and I had a gold medal, too. Why hadn't the rocking chair warned me and told me how to escape! God, are you there? Are you seeing, God? Do something! Do anything! Help me!

Out of the bushes they jumped. Three of them. Run, run fast. They'd never catch me if I ran fast enough. My legs unlocked, they ran . . . but not fast enough.

Scream, scream loud and louder!

I fought with kicks and scratches, I butted my head back against the teeth of the boy who pinned my arms behind me.

God didn't hear me cry for help. Nobody heard. Scream, scream, and then scream again—until I could scream no more. Just feel the shame, the humiliation, the ruthless hands that ripped and tore and violated.

See the other boy who rose from behind the bushes and stood there paralyzed, staring at me with his hair pasted down on his forehead from the rain that came down hard now. See him run away!

My screams brought Papa flying into the room. "Darling, darling," he cried, falling to his knees so he could gather me into his arms. He cuddled me against his chest and stroked my back, my hair. "It's all right, I'm here. I'll always be here."

"You shouldn't have, shouldn't have," I choked, still trembling from the shock.

"What did you dream this time, my love?"

"Bad things. Same awful thing."

"Tell Papa everything. Let Papa take away the pain and shame. Do you know now why I warn you to stay out of the woods? That was your sister, Audrina, your dead sister. It doesn't have to happen to you. You're letting that scene into your head when all I want is for you to travel beyond the woods and take for yourself all the specialness she used to have. Did you see how happy she could be? How joyful and vibrant? Did you feel how wonderful it used to be for her when she stayed out of the woods? That's what I want for you. Oh, my sweet Audrina," he whispered with his face buried deep in my hair, "it won't always be that way. Someday when you sit down to rock and sing, you'll bypass the woods, forget the boys and find the beauty of being alive. Once you do, all the memories you've forgotten, the good things, will come flooding back and make you whole again."

He was telling me, with good intentions, that I wasn't whole now—and if that were so, what was I? Crazy?

"Tomorrow night we'll do this again. I don't think it was as bad this time as before. This time you pulled out of it and came back to me."

I knew I had to save myself from this room and this chair. Somehow I had to convince him I had gone on beyond the woods and had already found the gifts the First Audrina no longer needed.

Tenderly he tucked me into bed, and on his knees he said a prayer to send me safely into sweet dreams, asking the angels on high to protect me through the night. He kissed my cheek and said he loved me, and even as he closed the door behind him I was wondering how I could convince him not to make me go to that room and sit in that chair again. How could I hate what he did to me, and love the idea of being what he wanted? How did I preserve me—when he was trying to turn me into her?

For hours I lay on my back staring up at the ceiling, trying to find my past in all the fancy swirls in the overhead plaster. Papa had given me many clues as to what would make him happiest. Papa wanted lots and lots of money, for himself, for Momma, for me, too. He wanted to fix up this house and make it like new again. He had to fulfill all the promises he'd made Lucietta Lana Whitefern, the heiress every worthy man on the lower East Coast had wanted until she married him. What a catch my mother had been. If only she hadn't given birth to two Audrinas.

Tuesday Teatime

Christmas came and went, but I hardly remembered anything but a princess doll that had shown up under the tree, making Vera jealous, even though she often insisted she was much too old to play with dolls.

It scared me the way time moved along so swiftly, so that even before I knew what was happening, spring was on its way. Days were falling into the holes in my memory. Vera liked to torment me by saying that anyone who couldn't keep track of time was insane.

Today was Tuesday, and Aunt Mercy Marie would visit again, even though it seemed to me only yesterday that Mercy Marie had been brought out for teatime.

Papa was taking his time about leaving this Tuesday morning. He sat at the kitchen table expounding on life and all its complexities, while Vera and my aunt consumed pancakes as if they would never eat again. Soberly my mother was preparing the canapés and other treats for teatime.

"They were the best of times; they were the worst of times," began my papa, who loved to say that phrase over and over again. It seemed to grate on my mother's nerves as much as it did on mine. He made it an awesomely fearsome thing to even think beyond tomorrow.

On and on he went, making his time to be young seem so much better than any time I was likely to know. Life had been perfect when Papa was a boy; back then people had been nicer; houses had been constructed to last forever and not fall apart as they did nowadays. Dogs, too, had been better when he was a boy, really reliable, sure to bring back every hurled stick. Even the weather was better, not so hot in the summers, nor so cold in the winters, unless there was a blizzard. No blizzard now had a chance of equalling the freezing ferocity of the blizzards Papa had to trudge home from school in.

"Twenty miles," he boasted, "through the wind and snow, through the sleet and rain, through the hail and ice, nothing kept me home—even when I had pneumonia. When I was in high school on the football team and broke my leg, that didn't keep me from walking to school every day. I was hardy, determined to be well educated, to be the best there was."

Momma slammed down a dish so hard it cracked. "Damian, stop exaggerating." Her voice was harsh, impatient. "Can't you see what false notions you plant in your daughter's mind?"

"What other kind of notions have either one of you ever planted?" asked Aunt Ellsbeth sourly. "If Audrina grows up to be normal it will be a miracle."

"Amen to that," contributed Vera. She grinned at

me and then stuck out her tongue. Papa didn't notice, he was too busy shouting at my aunt.

"Normal? What is normal? In my opinion normal is only ordinary, mediocre. Life belongs to the rare exceptional individual who dares to be different."

"Damian, will you please stop expounding on your ideas to a child too young to understand that you are not an authority on anything except how to run your mouth all day long."

"Silence!" bellowed Papa. "I won't have my wife ridiculing me in front of my only child. Lucky, apologize immediately!"

Why was Aunt Ellsbeth smirking? It was my secret belief that my aunt loved to hear my parents argue. Vera made some gagging noise and then, with a great deal of difficulty, rose to her feet and limped toward the front hall. Soon she'd be boarding the school bus I'd sell my soul to ride on like every other child who wasn't as special as I was. Instead, I had to stay home, lonely for playmates, with the kind of adults who filled my head with hodgepodge notions and then stirred them up with a witch's stick of contradictions. No wonder I didn't know who I was, or which day of the week, month or even year it was. I didn't have any best or worst times. I lived, it seemed to me, in a theater, with the exception being the actors on stage were my family members and I, too, had a role to play— only I didn't know what it was.

All of a sudden, for no reason at all, I was looking around the kitchen and remembering a large orange cat who used to sleep near the old cast-iron stove.

"I wish Tweedle Dee would come home," I said wistfully. "I'm even lonelier since my cat went away."

Papa jolted. Momma stared at me. "Why, Tweedle Dee has been gone for a long, long time, Audrina." Her voice sounded strained, worried.

"Oh, yes," I said quickly, "I know that, but I want him to come home. Papa, you didn't take him to the city pound, did you? You wouldn't put my cat to sleep, would you—just because he makes you sneeze?"

He threw me a worried look, then forced a smile. "No, Audrina, I do the best I can to cater to all your needs, and if that cat had wanted to stay and make me sneeze myself to death, I would have suffered on in silence for your sake."

"Suffered, but not in silence," muttered my aunt.

I watched my parents embrace and kiss before Papa headed for the garage. "Have a good time at your tea party," he called back to Momma, "though I wish to heaven you'd let Mercy Marie stay dead. What we need is someone to live in that empty cottage we own; then you'd have a nice neighbor-woman to invite to your teas."

"Damian," called Momma sweetly, "you go out and have your fun, don't you? Since we're held captives here, at least let Ellie and me have ours."

He grunted and said no more, and soon I was at the front windows watching him drive away. His hand lifted in a salute before he drove out of sight. I didn't want him to go. I hated Tuesday teatime.

Teatime was supposed to begin at four, but since

Vera had started playing hooky to escape her last class in order to reach home by four, teatime had been moved up to three o'clock.

Wearing my best clothes, I sat ready and waiting for the ritual to begin. I was required to be there as part of my social education, and if Vera was incapacitated enough to stay home legitimately, then she was invited to the parties, too. I often thought Vera broke her bones just so she could stay home and hear what went on in our best front salon.

My tension built as I waited for Momma and my aunt to show up. First came Momma, dressed in her prettiest afternoon gown—a soft flowing wool crepe of a pretty coral color, with piping of violet to match her eye color. She wore a pearl choker and earrings with real diamonds and pearls to match the choker. It was heirloom Whitefern jewelry she'd told me many times would be mine one day. Her magnificent hair was swept up high, but a few loose curls dangled down to take away the severity and make her look elegant.

Next came my aunt in her best outfit, a dark navy-blue suit with a tailored white blouse. As always, she wore her dark glossy hair in a figure-eight knot low on the back of her neck. Tiny diamond studs were in her ears, and on her little finger she wore a ruby class ring. She looked very schoolmarmish.

"Ellie, will you let Mercy Marie in?" said Momma sweetly. Tuesday was the only day my mother was allowed to call her sister by her nickname. Only Papa could call my aunt Ellie any time he chose.

"Oh, dear, you are late," said Aunt Ellsbeth,

getting up to lift the piano lid and take from underneath the heavy silver frame that enclosed the photograph of a fat woman with a very sweet face. "Really, Mercy Marie, we expected you to arrive on time. You've always had the annoying habit of arriving late. To make an impression, I suppose. But dear, you'd make an impression even if you arrived early." Momma giggled as my aunt sat down and primly folded her hands in her lap. "The piano isn't too hard for you, dear, is it? But it is sturdy enough . . . I hope." Again Momma giggled, making me squirm uneasily, for I knew the worst was yet to come. "Yes, Mercy Marie, we do understand why you're always tardy. Running away from those passionate savages must be very exhausting. But you really should know it's been rumored about that you were cooked in a pot by a cannibal chief and eaten for dinner. Lucietta and I are delighted to see that was only a malicious rumor."

Carefully she crossed her legs and stared at that portrait on the piano, placed just where music sheets were usually stacked. It was part of Momma's role to get up and light the candles in the crystal candelabra while the fire snapped and crackled, and the gas lamps flickered and made the crystal prisms on the chandeliers catch colors and dart crazily about the room.

"Ellsbeth, my dear, my darling," said my mother for the dead woman who had to participate, even if her ghost was often rebellious, "is that the only suit you own? You wore it last week and the week before, and your hair, good God, why don't you change that hairstyle? It makes you look sixty."

Always Momma's voice was sickeningly sweet when she spoke for Aunt Mercy Marie.

"I like my hairstyle," said my aunt primly, watching my mother roll in the tea wagon loaded down with all the goodies Momma'd prepared earlier. "At least I don't try to look like a pampered mistress who spends all her time trying to please an egotistical sex maniac. Of course, I realize that's the only kind of man there is. That is exactly why I chose to stay single."

"I'm sure that's the only reason," said my mother in her own voice. Then she spoke for the photograph on the piano. "But Ellie, I remember a time when you were madly in love with an egotistical maniac. In love enough to go to bed with him and have his child. Too bad he only used you to satisfy his lust; too bad he never fell in love with you."

"Oh, him," said my aunt, snorting her disgust. "He was just a passing fancy. His animal magnetism drew me to him momentarily, but I had sense enough to forget him and move on to better things. I know he found another immediately. All men are alike—selfish, cruel, demanding. I know now he would have made the worst possible husband."

"Too bad you couldn't have found a wonderful man like Lucky's handsome Damian," said that sweet voice from the piano, as my mother sat down to nibble on a dainty sandwich.

I stared at the picture of a woman I didn't remember ever meeting, though Momma said I had known her when I was four. She appeared to be very wealthy. Diamonds hung from her ears, neck, studded her fingers. The fur trimming on her suit collar made her face seem to sit on her shoulders. Often I imagined that if she rose, she'd have fur about long, full sleeves and rimming the edge of her skirt, like a medieval queen.

Mercy Marie had traveled all the way to Africa in hopes of salvaging a few heathen souls and converting them to Christianity. Now she was part of the heathens, eaten, hopefully, after she was killed and cooked.

According to everything I'd learned from attending these teatimes, Aunt Mercy Marie once had a ridiculous fondness for cucumber and lettuce sandwiches made with the thinnest possible cheese bread. In order to do this, my mother had to bake the bread, trim off the crust and flatten the bread with her rolling pin. The bread was then cut with cookie cutters into fancy shapes.

"Really, Mercy Marie," said my aunt in her harsh way, "ham, cheese, chicken or tuna is not as tacky as you think We eat food like that all the time . . . don't we, Lucietta?"

Momma scowled. I hated to hear what she'd say next, something cruel and biting. "If Mercy Marie adores dainty cucumber and lettuce sandwiches, Ellie, why don't you let her eat a few, instead of hogging them all for yourself? Don't be such a pig. Learn to share."

"Lucietta, darling," spoke up the shrill voice from the piano, this time donated by my aunt, "please show your older sister the respect due her. You give her such tiny portions at mealtimes, she has to make up for your stinginess by eating the sandwiches I adore."

"Oh, Mercy, you are such a dear, so gracious. Of course I should know my sister's appetite can never be satisfied. A bottomless pit could hold no more than Ellie's stomach. Perhaps she tries *to* fill the great emptiness of her life with food. Perhaps for her it replaces love."

On and on went the memorial teatime, while the perfumed candles burned and the fire spat red sparks, and Aunt Ellie consumed all the sandwiches, even those with chicken liver pâté, which I liked very much—and so did Vera. I nibbled on a sandwich I hated. This kind always tasted like Aunt Mercy Marie might have: damp, grassy and soggy.

"Really, Lucietta," said Aunt Ellsbeth, using the voice of the dear departed, casting me a grievous look for so obviously disliking what Mercy Marie must have loved most. "You should do something about that child's appetite. She's nothing but skin and bones and huge haunted eyes. And that ridiculous mop of hair. Why does she look so spooked? From the looks of her some dry wind could blow her away—if she doesn't lose her mind first. Lucietta, what are you doing to that child?"

About this time I heard the squeak of the side door opening, and in a few seconds Vera crawled into the room. She hid herself behind a potted fern so our mothers wouldn't see her and put her finger to her lips when I looked her way. She had with her a huge medical encyclopedia that had cardboard front pieces made of both the female and male body—without clothes on.

I cringed. Behind me Vera giggled. I shrank into that small hiding place in my brain where I could feel safe and unafraid, but that place felt like a cage. I always felt caged when Aunt Mercy Marie's spiteful ghost came to our front salon. *She* was dead and unreal, but somehow or other she still made *me* feel like a shadow without substance. Not real in the same way other girls were real. My hand fluttered nervously to feel my "haunted" eyes, to touch my "gaunt" cheeks, for sooner or later she'd get around to mentioning those things, too.

"Mercy," spoke my mother chastisingly, "how can you be so insensitive in front of my daughter?" She stood, looking tall and willowy in her soft, flowing dress.

I stared at that dress, confused. Surely she'd walked into this room in something coral colored. How had it changed colors? Was it the light from the windows making it seem violet, green and blue? My head began to ache. Was it summer, spring, winter or fall? I wanted to run to the windows and check the trees, only they didn't lie.

Other things were said that I tried not to hear, and then Momma strode over to the piano and sat down to play all the hymns that Aunt Mercy Marie liked to sing. The minute my mother sat on her piano bench, something miraculous happened: she assumed a stage presence as if an audience of thousands would soon be applauding. Her long elegant fingers hovered over the keys dramatically, then down they came, banging out a commanding chord to demand your attention. "Rock

of Ages" she played, and then she was singing so
beautifully and sadly I wanted to cry. My aunt began
to sing, too, but I couldn't join in. Something inside
me was screaming, screaming. All this was false. God
wasn't up there. He didn't come when you needed
him . . . he never had and he never would.

Mamma saw my tears and abruptly changed pace.
This time her hymn was played in a rock style that
bounced through the room. "Won't you come to
the church in the wildwood, won't you come to the
church in the vale," she sang, rocking from side to
side, making her breasts jiggle.

My aunt began to eat cake again. Discouraged, my
mother left the piano and sat on the sofa.

"Momma," I asked in a small voice, "what's a
vale?"

"Lucietta, why don't you teach your child something of value?" asked that merciless voice on the
piano. When my head whipped around, trying to
catch Aunt Ellsbeth talking, she was sipping hot tea,
which I knew was heavily laced with bourbon, just
as Momma's tea was. Maybe it was the liquor that
made them so cruel. I didn't know if they had liked
Aunt Mercy Marie when she was alive, or if they had
despised her. I knew they liked to mock the way they
thought she'd been killed, as if they couldn't quite
believe Papa, who had explained to me more than once
that Aunt Mercy Marie might very well be alive and
the wife of some African chieftain.

"Fat women are prized in many primitive societ-
ies," he told me. "She just disappeared two weeks after

she arrived there to do her missionary work. Don't believe everything you hear, Audrina."

That was my worst problem—what to believe, and what not to believe.

Giggling, Momma poured a bit more tea into my aunt's cup and some into her own, and then she picked up a crystal bottle labeled "Bourbon" and filled the two cups. Then Momma spotted Vera. "Vera," she said, "would you like a cup of hot tea?"

Of course Vera did, but she scowled when no bourbon was added.

"What are you doing home from school so early?" shot out my aunt.

"The teachers had a meeting and let all the students off earlier than usual," said Vera quickly.

"Vera, be truthful in the presence of the living dead," giggled my mother, almost drunk by this time. Vera and I exchanged glances. This was one of the only times we could really communicate, when we both felt strange and baffled.

"What do *you* do for amusement, Ellie?" asked my mother in that high-pitched, sugary voice she used for Aunt Mercy Marie. "Certainly *you* must get bored, too, once in a while, living way out in the sticks, having no friends. You don't have a handsome husband to keep you warm and happy in your cold, lonely bed."

"Really, Mercy," responded my aunt, looking straight into those photograph eyes, "how could I possibly be bored when I live with such fascinating people as my sister and her stockbroker husband, who both adore fighting in their bedroom so much one of them screams. Truthfully, I feel rather safe in my lonely bed, without a handsome brute of a man who likes to wield his belt for a whip."

"Ellsbeth, how dare you tell my best friend such nonsense? Damian and I play games, that's all. It adds to his excitement and to mine." Momma smiled apologetically at the photograph. "Unfortunately, Ellsbeth knows nothing at all about the many ways of pleasing a man, or giving him what he likes."

My aunt snorted contemptuously. "Mercy, I'm sure you never allowed Horace to play those kind of sick sex games with you."

"If she had, she wouldn't be where she is now," giggled my momma.

Vera's eyes were as wide as mine. We both sat silent and motionless. I was sure both of them had forgotten we were there.

"Really, Mercy Marie, you do have to forgive my sister, who is a bit drunk. As I was saying a moment ago, I do live with such fascinating people there is never a dull moment. One daughter dies in the woods, another comes to take her place, and the fools give her the same name—"

"Ellsbeth," snapped my momma, bolting upright from her slouched position, "if you hate your sister and her husband so much, why don't you leave and take your daughter with you? Surely there must be some school somewhere that needs a teacher. You do have the kind of sharp tongue that could really keep children in their place."

"No," said my aunt calmly, still sipping her tea,

"I'll never leave this cluttery museum of junk. It's just as much mine as it is hers." She held her small finger in a crooked way I admired. Never could I manage to make mine stay like that for so long.

Odd how my aunt had such prissy manners and wore such unprissy clothes. My mother had very prissy clothes, and very unprissy mannerisms. While my aunt held her knees close together, my mother parted hers. While my aunt sat as straight as if she had a poker down her spine, my mother made herself into a rag and assumed sensual poses. They did everything to antagonize one another, and they succeeded.

During teatime I never contributed anything unless it was demanded of me, and Vera usually stayed just as quiet, hoping to hear more secrets. Vera had crawled around in back of a sofa, and there she sat with her lame leg stretched straight out, her other pulled up to her chin as she slowly leafed through that illustrated medical book that showed human anatomy. Just beneath the front cover was her cardboard man of many thick paper layers. In the first one he was just naked. When that cut-out man was turned over, he was shown with all his arteries painted red, his veins blue. Beneath that colorful plate was another man with all his vital organs showing. The last plate showed the skeleton, which didn't interest Vera at all. There was also a naked woman who could be viewed inside out, too, but she never held much interest for Vera. Long ago she had pulled the "fetus" from the womb, and in her schoolbooks she used that tabbed baby for a bookmark. Bit by bit Vera began taking the naked man apart, untabbing his numbered paper parts and studying them closely. Each organ could be fitted back into proper position when the tabs were stuck through the right numbered slots. In her left hand she clutched his male parts, even as she plucked out his heart and his liver, turning them over and over, before she again took that cardboard thing from her left hand and examined it in great detail.

How strangely men were made, I thought, as she put the man back together and he came out right. Then she started again to take him apart. I turned my eyes away.

By this time both my mother and Aunt Ellsbeth were more than a bit drunk.

"Is anything as wonderful as you thought it would be?"

Wistfully, Momma met my aunt's softened gaze. "I still love Damian, even if he hasn't lived up to his promises. Maybe I was only fooling myself anyway, thinking I was really good enough to be a concert pianist. Maybe I married to keep from finding out just how mediocre I really am.

"Lucietta, I don't believe that," said my aunt with surprising compassion. "You are a very gifted pianist and you know it as well as I do. You just let that man of yours put doubts in your head. How many times has Damian soothed you by saying you wouldn't have succeeded if you had gone on?"

"Lots and lots and lots of times," chanted my mother in a silly, drunken way that made me want to cry. "Don't talk to me about it anymore, Ellie. It

makes me feel too sorry for myself. Mr. Johanson
would be so disappointed in me. I hope he's dead and
never found out I amounted to nothing."

"Did you love him, Lucietta?" my aunt asked in a
kindly way.

I perked up. Vera looked up from her play with
the gross, naked man whose heart she was squeezing
in her hand.

Mr. Ingmar Johanson had been my mother's
music teacher when she was a young girl. "When I
was fifteen, and full of romantic notions, I thought
I loved him." Momma sighed heavily and rubbed
at a tear that trickled down her cheek. She turned
her head so that I saw her beautiful profile, and she
stared toward the windows where the winter sun
could only dimly filter in to pattern our Oriental
with faded patches of light.

"He was the first man to give me a real kiss . . .
boys in school had, but his was the first real kiss."

Weren't all kisses alike?

"Did you like his kisses?"

"Yes, Ellie, I liked them well enough. They filled
me with longing. Ingmar woke me up sexually and
then left me unfulfilled. Many a night I lay awake
then, and even now I wake up and wish I'd let him go
ahead and finish what he'd started, instead of saying
no and saving myself for Damian."

"No, Lucietta, you did the right thing. Damian
would never have married you if he'd even suspected
you weren't a virgin. He claims to be a modern man
with liberal ideas, but he's a Victorian at heart. You

know damn well he couldn't handle what happened to Audrina any better than she could . . ."

What did she mean? How could the First Audrina have handled anything when they found her dead in the woods? Suddenly Momma turned to see me half hidden behind the fern. She stared, as if she had to readjust some thoughts in her head before she spoke. "Audrina, why do you try to hide? Come out and sit in a chair like a lady. Why are you so quiet? Contribute something once in a while. No one enjoys a person who doesn't know how to make small talk."

"What was it the First Audrina couldn't handle any better than Papa?" I asked, getting to my feet and falling unladylike into a chair.

"Audrina, be careful with that cup of tea!"

"Momma, exactly what happened to my dead sister? What killed her—a snake?"

"That's not small talk," snapped Momma irritably. "Really, Audrina, we've told you all you need to know about your sister's accident in the woods. And remember, she would still be alive if she'd learned to obey the orders we gave her. I hope you will always keep that in mind when next you feel stubborn or rebellious and think being disobedient is a good way to get back at your parents, who try to do the best they can."

"Was the First Audrina hard to handle?" I asked with some hope of hearing she was less than perfect.

"Enough is enough," Momma said more gently. "Just remember, the woods are off limits."

"But Vera goes into the woods . . ."

Vera had risen and was standing behind the sofa,

smiling at my mother in a knowing way that told me she knew the cause of my older sister's death. Oh, oh, now, suddenly, I wished she hadn't overheard Momma's warning, for that gave Vera another weapon to use against me.

From the way the party died after that, it seemed I was never going to be a social success. Aunt Ellsbeth put the photograph away. Vera hobbled up to her room, carrying one part of that naked man with her, and I sat on alone in the Roman Revival room, realizing I couldn't ask direct questions and expect an answer. I had to learn how to be sneaky, like everyone else, or I would never know anything, not even the time of day.

Valentine's Day came that very week, and Vera limped home from school with a paper sack full of valentines from all her boyfriends. She came into my bedroom with a huge red satin heart that opened to reveal a delicious array of chocolates. "From the boy who loves me most," she said to me arrogantly, snatching the box away without offering me even one piece. "He's going to take me away from here one day, and marry me, too. It's in his eyes, his marvelous amber eyes. Soon he's going to move—well, never mind where he's going to move, but he loves me. I know he loves me . . ."

"How old did you say he was?"

"What difference does that make?" She sat on my bed and dipped into the candy box again, eyeing me in a funny way. "I can be ten, twelve, fourteen, sixteen, any age. For I have caught the magic of the First Audrina, the Best and Most Perfect, Most Beautiful Audrina. Mirror, mirror on the wall, who is the fairest Audrina of all, and the mirror says, *you* are, Vera, *you* are."

"You sound crazy," I said, backing away from her. "And you can't catch a gift that's meant only for girls with my name. Papa told me that."

"Oh, Papa would tell you anything, and you'd be stupid enough to believe. I'm never going to be that dumb. My mother was stupid enough to let some sweet-talking guy talk her into his bed, but that's not going to happen to me. When the seducing is done, it will be me who does it. And I know how. That medical book is teaching me all I need to know. Those stupid sex courses they teach in school don't give enough facts."

Soon all the chocolates were gone, and when they were, Vera gave me the empty red-satin heart. For some reason that red heart touched me. How nice of that boy to give Vera candy. I hadn't known Vera could inspire love in anyone, not when she couldn't inspire it even in her own mother.

Lions and Lambs

One day I heard the special-delivery man say to Momma, "Isn't this a lovely spring day?" or else I might not have known it was spring from the cold way it was. The trees hadn't budded out yet, and birds weren't singing. I rejoiced to know the season, if not the month, but I was too ashamed to try and ask what month it was and have people look at me with pity. It wasn't special to not know anything about the passing of time—it was crazy. Maybe that was why they were ashamed to tell me why the First Audrina had died. Maybe she'd been crazy, too.

Daring his scorn, I ran after the deliveryman and asked my silly question. "Why, it's the month of March, girl, come in like a lion. And soon it will go out like a lamb."

It was cold, the wind was wild, and that I could easily associate with a lion. The next day I woke up and the sun was out, squirrels and rabbits were gamboling on our lawn and all was right with the world, according to Papa and according to Momma.

Dinner ended the next night with Papa bellowing

at Vera, "Get out of the kitchen! I've been hearing tales about your getting caught cutting out dirty pictures in the drugstore. Any girl who's stealing like that has already proved there's fire beneath the smoke!"

"I didn't do anything, Papa!" Vera sobbed.

Later, in my room, she hurled at me, "God cursed me with fragile bones and you with a fragile brain, but between the two, I got the best deal." But then she was crying. "Papa doesn't love me like he loves you . . . I hate you, Audrina, really hate you."

I was baffled. I was Papa's child, naturally he loved me best. I tried to tell her this. "Oh, you," she screamed. "What do you know about anything? You're spoiled and pampered and babied like you're too good for the world . . . but in the end it will be me who comes out on top. You just wait and see!"

Decided on a course of action, I went to Papa, who seemed terribly excited about something. He paced the floor of the Roman Revival Salon, glancing from time to time at his wristwatch. But he wouldn't let me look when I tried to. "What do you want, Audrina?" he asked impatiently.

"I want to talk about Vera, Papa."

"I don't want to talk about Vera, Audrina."

I drew back. "Even if she's not your daughter, you shouldn't be so mean to her."

"What's she been telling you?" he asked suspiciously. "Has she been trying to explain why you have that dream?"

My eyes widened. I'd never told Vera about my worst nightmare. He was the only one who knew about my troubled dreams. I was sure he didn't want Momma to worry about them, too. And that dream was my curse and my shame; never would I tell Vera. My head moved from side to side as I kept backing away.

"Why are you acting afraid of your own father? Has that girl been filling your head with foul tales?"

"No, Papa."

"Don't lie to me, girl. I can tell when you lie, your eyes betray you."

The mean, uncaring mood he was in made me turn and run. I bumped into things like armed coat racks and umbrella stands and finally fell into a corner, where I stayed just to catch my breath. That's when I heard my aunt coming down the hall with my father at her side. "I don't care what you say, Ellie, I am doing the best I can to cure her. I am also doing the best I can for Vera, and that's not easy. God, why didn't you give birth to a child like my Audrina?"

"That is exactly what this house needs," answered my aunt coldly. "Another Audrina."

"You listen to me, Ellie, and listen well. You keep Vera away from my daughter! You keep reminding Vera each day of her life to keep her mouth shut or I'll have the skin from her back and the hair ripped from her scalp. If ever I find out Vera was somehow connected—"

"She wasn't! Of course she wasn't!"

Their voices faded away. I was left in the shadows, feeling sick and trying to figure out what all that meant. Vera had the secret of why I couldn't remember like

everyone else. I had to get Vera to tell me. But Vera
hated me. She'd never tell me anything. Somehow I
had to make Vera stop hating me. Somehow I had to
make her like me. Then maybe she'd tell me the secret
of myself.

The next morning at breakfast Momma was smiling and cheerful. "Guess what," she said as I sat down
to breakfast. "We're going to have neighbors. Your
father rented that small cottage where Mr. Willis used
to live before he died."

That name rang a familiar bell. Had I known Mr.
Willis?

"They're moving in today," Momma went on. "If
we weren't expecting your Aunt Mercy Marie, we
could stroll through the woods and welcome them.
June is such a lovely month."

I stared at her openmouthed. "Momma, the
deliveryman said yesterday it was March."

"No, darling, it's June. The last deliveryman to
come here came months ago." She sighed. "I wish I
had the department store deliver every day; then I'd
have something to look forward to besides Damian's
return home."

All the joy I should have felt at the prospect of
neighbors was spoiled by my disjointed memory. Vera
limped into the kitchen then, throwing me a mean
look before she fell into a chair and asked for bacon,
eggs, pancakes and doughnuts. "Did I hear you say
we're going to have neighbors, Momma?"

Momma? Why was she calling my mother that?
I shot my own mean glare her way. I tried not to let

Momma see. She looked tired, rather distraught as she began to make goose liver pâté for the party. Why did she go to so much trouble when that woman was dead, and only Aunt Ellsbeth would be there to eat the best of everything?

"I know who the new neighbors are," smirked Vera. "The boy who gave me a box of candy for Valentine's Day hinted he might be moving near us. He's eleven years old, but he's so big he looks like thirteen or fourteen."

My aunt stalked in, her long face grim and formidable. "He's too young for you, then," she snapped, making me wonder if Vera really was much older than I'd thought. Gosh, why couldn't I know anyone's age? They knew mine. "Don't you start fooling around with him, Vera, or Damian will kick us both out."

"I'm not afraid of Papa," said Vera smugly. "I know how to handle men. A kiss, a hug, a big smile and they melt."

"You are a manipulator, I know that. But leave that boy alone. Are you listening, Vera?"

"Yes, Mother," answered Vera in her most scornful voice. "Of course I am listening! Even the dead could listen! And I don't really want a boy who's only eleven. I hate living 'way out here in the sticks where there aren't any boys but the stupid ones in the village."

Papa came in next, wearing a new custom-fitted suit. He sat to tuck a napkin under his chin so nothing would spot his pure silk tie. If cleanliness was next to godliness, Papa was a god walking the earth.

"Is it really June, Papa?" I asked.

"Why do you ask?"

"It seems only yesterday it was March—that man who brought Momma's new dress said it was March."

"That was months ago, darling, months ago. Of course it's June. Look at the flowers in bloom, the green grass. Feel how hot it is. You don't get days like this in March."

Vera ate half her pancakes and then was up and heading for the foyer to pick up her schoolbooks. She'd failed her grade and had to spend eight weeks of her vacation going to summer school.

"Why are you following me?" she bit out.

I held fast to my determination to make Vera like me. "Why do you hate me, Vera?"

"I don't have time to list the reasons." Her voice was haughty. "Everyone in school thinks you're strange; they know you're crazy."

That surprised me. "How can they when they don't know me?"

Turning, she smiled. "I tell them all about you and your quirky ways, staying close to the shadows near the wall, and how you scream out each night. They know that you're so 'special' you don't even know which year, month or day of the week it is."

How disloyal to spread family secrets. Again wounded, my desire to have her like me weakened. I didn't really think she ever would. "I wish you wouldn't talk about me to people who might not understand."

"Understand what—that you're a nutty freak with

no memory? Really, they understand you perfectly, and nobody, absolutely nobody, would ever want to be your friend."

Something hard and heavy grew in my chest, making it ache. I sighed and turned away. "I just wanted to know what everybody else knows."

"That, my dear little sister, is totally impossible for someone with no brain."

I whirled about and shouted, "I'm not your sister! I'd rather be dead than be your sister!"

Long after she disappeared down the dirt road, I stood on the porch, thinking maybe I was crazy.

Again, at three, Aunt Mercy Marie came to sit on our piano. As always, my aunt and my mother took turns talking for her. The bourbon was poured into the steaming hot tea, and I was given my cup of cola with two cubes of ice. Momma told me to pretend it was hot tea. I sat uncomfortably in my very best white dress. Because Papa wasn't there, I was soon forgotten as those two women lit into each other, letting loose all the frustrations they had held in check all week.

"Ellsbeth," shrieked Momma after some insult about the house she loved, "the trouble with you is you're so damned jealous our father loved me better. You sit there and say ugly things about this house because you wish to God it belonged to you. Just as you cry your heart out each night, sleeping alone in your bed, or lying there restless and awake, jealous again because I always got what you wanted—when you could have had what I have if you'd kept your damned big mouth shut!"

"And you certainly know when to open *your* big mouth, Lucietta!" barked my aunt. "All your life wandering through this mausoleum and gushing about its beauty. Of course our father left this house to you and not to me. You made me want to vomit you were so sweet. You set out to rob me of everything I wanted. Even when my boyfriends came to call on me, you were there smiling and flirting. You even flirted with our father, flattering him so much you made me seem cold and indifferent. But I did all the work around here, and I still do! You prepare the meals and you think that's enough. Well, it's not enough! I do everything else. I'm sick and tired of being everybody's slave! And as if that's not enough, you're teaching your daughter your tricks!"

Highly indignant, my mother's beautiful face flamed red. "Just keep it up, Ellsbeth, and you won't have a roof over your head! I know what galls you, don't think I don't. You wish to God you had *everything* I do!"

"You're a fool. And you married a fool. Damian Adare only wanted what wealth he thought you'd inherit. But you never told him until it was too late for him to back out that our dear father hadn't paid his taxes or had one lick of repair work done on this house. You claim to love gaslight, but the truth of it is you know electric lights would show Damian just how shabby this house really is. The kitchen and this room dominate our lives. The kitchen is so bright when he steps in here he can hardly see—none of us can. In your place, I would have been honest, and if you call honesty a fault, then by God, you are flawless!"

"Ellsbeth," screamed a high voice from the piano, "stop being nasty to your beloved sister."

"Go cook yourself," yelled Aunt Ellsbeth.

"Mercy Marie," said my mother in her most arrogant, haughty voice, "I think you'd better leave now. Since my sister cannot be kind to a guest, or kind to my daughter, or kind to this house, or kind to anyone, not even to her own flesh and blood, I think there's no reason to go on having these teatimes. I say goodbye with reluctance, for I loved you and hate to think of you as dead. I can't bear to see people I love die. This has been my pitiful attempt to keep you alive." She didn't look at my aunt as she said, "Ellsbeth, kindly leave this room before you say something to make me hate you more." Momma appeared on the verge of tears as her voice broke. Had she forgotten this was only a pretend game? Was I just a pretend game for her, too, so she could keep the beloved first Audrina alive?

Wednesday morning came, and I was happy I'd written myself a note to remind me that Tuesday was yesterday. Now I had a grip on reality. It was Wednesday. I'd write that down tonight. At last I'd figured out a way to keep track of the days.

As I was passing by my parents' room on the way to the kitchen, my mother called me inside. She was brushing her long hair with an antique silver hairbrush. Papa was leaning close to the dresser mirror, making a knot in his tie. Ever so carefully he made the turns, the twists, the pull-throughs. "You tell her, Lucky," said Papa in a soft voice. He looked happy enough to burst. Momma turned to smile at me, too.

Eagerly I ran to be embraced and held against the soft swell of her breasts. "Sweetheart, you're always complaining about having no one to play with but Vera. But someone new is coming to take away your loneliness. Come November or early December, you are going to have what you've wanted for so long . . ."

School! They were going to send me to school! At last! At long last!

"Darling, haven't you told us many times you'd love a brother or sister? Well, you are going to have one or the other."

I didn't know what to say. Visions of happy school days vanished. Will-o'-the-wisp dreams never came true for me, never. Then, as I stood trembling in the circle of her arms and Papa came to softly stroke my hair, I felt a surge of unexpected happiness. A baby. A little brother or sister would surely set me free from all their demanding attention. Then maybe they'd want me out of the house and in school, learning how to do many things I didn't know about now. There was hope. There had to be hope.

Momma gave Papa a long, distressed look, full of unspoken meaning. "Damian, surely this time we'll have a boy, won't we?"

Why did she put it like that? Didn't she like girls?

"Keep calm, Lucky. The odds are with us. This time we'll have a boy." Papa smiled at me lovingly, as if he could read my thoughts in my wide eyes. "We already have one beautiful and special daughter, so God does owe us a son."

Yes, God did owe him a son after taking the First and Best Audrina and replacing her with only me.

On my knees that night beside my bed, I put my palms together under my chin, closed my eyes and prayed: "Lord above, even if my parents do want a boy, I really won't mind if you send them a girl. Just don't let her have violet eyes and chameleon hair like mine. Don't make her special. It's so awfully lonesome being special. I wish you'd made me only ordinary and given me a better memory. If the First and Best Audrina is up there with you, don't use her to model from, or Vera, either. Make this baby wonderful, but not so special it can't even go to school." I started to close out and say amen, but I added a postscript. "And Lord God, hurry up and let those neighbors move in. I need a friend, even if that boy does like Vera."

I kept a daily journal now to aid my faulty memory. That Thursday my aunt and my cousin were told the news I'd known for a full day. It made me feel special for my parents to confide something so important to me first. "Yes, Ellie, Lucky is pregnant again. Isn't that wonderful news? Of course, since we already have the daughter we asked for, now we're going to demand a son."

My aunt threw my mother a startled look. "Oh, my God," she responded dully. "Some people never learn."

Vera's pasty pallor sickened more. Panic seemed to fade her dark eyes as well. Then she caught me staring at her and she quickly straightened before she stood. "I'm leaving to visit a friend. I won't be home until dark."

She stood there waiting for someone to object, as surely everyone would if I were to say the same words, but no one said anything, almost as if they didn't care whether or not Vera ever came back. Looking surly, Vera limped from the kitchen. I jumped up to follow her out to the front porch. "Who are you going to visit?"

"None of your damned business!"

"We don't have any close neighbors, and it's a long walk to visit the McKennas."

"Never mind," she said, choking, tears in her eyes. "You just go back inside and hear about the new baby, and I'll visit my friend who could never stand you."

I watched her limp off down the dirt road, wondering where she could go. Maybe she wasn't going anywhere, but only looking for someplace to cry alone.

Back in the kitchen Papa was still talking. "They moved some of their things into the cottage last week, but they only started staying there yesterday. I haven't met them myself, but the realtor says they've lived in the village for several years and always paid their rent on time. And just think, Lucky, now you'll have a live woman to invite to your teas, and we can say goodbye to Mercy Marie. Though no doubt you two enjoy imitating her cruel wit very much, I want you to quit that game. It's not healthy for Audrina to witness something so bizarre. Besides, for all you know, Mercy Marie may be the fat wife of some African chief, and not dead at all."

Both my mother and aunt scoffed—they wanted to believe no man would want Mercy Marie.

"We're finished with teatimes," said Momma dully, as if she'd finished with all social life now that she was expecting a baby.

"Papa," I began tentatively as I sat at the table again, "when did I last see Aunt Mercy Marie alive?"

Leaning across the table, Papa kissed my cheek. Then he shifted his chair closer to mine so his arm could encircle my shoulders. My aunt got up to sit in the kitchen rocker where she knitted, knitted. In a second or so she was so angry with her knitting that she threw it down, picked up a feather duster and began to swipe at dusty tabletops in the adjoining room, keeping always close to the door so she could listen.

"It was years and years ago when you knew Mercy Marie; naturally you don't remember her. Sweetheart, stop troubling your brain with efforts to recall the past. Today is what counts, not yesterday. Memories are only important to the old who have already lived the best of their lives and have nothing to look forward to. You're only a child and your future stretches long and inviting before you. All the good things are ahead, not behind. You can't remember every detail of your early childhood, but neither can I. 'The best is yet to be,' some poet wrote, and I believe that. Papa's going to make sure you have only the best kind of future. Your gift is growing stronger and stronger, and you know why, don't you?"

The rocking chair. That chair was giving me the First and Best Audrina's brain and erasing all my memories. Oh, I hated her. Why couldn't she stay dead in her grave? I didn't want her life, I wanted my own. I pulled from Papa's embrace. "I'm going out into the yard to play, Papa."

"Don't go into the woods," he warned. Aunt Ellsbeth seemed drawn back into the kitchen. She swung that duster in such a threatening way it seemed she might whack Papa with it.

Momma turned her violet eyes on her sister and said mildly, "Really, Ellsbeth, you're flinging around more dust than you're picking up."

Once I was outside, Papa's words kept resounding in my head. He didn't really love me. He loved her, the First and the Best. The Most Perfect Audrina. For the rest of my life I had to live up to the standards she'd set. How could I be everything she'd been, when I was me?

I had been planning to slip through the woods and see our new neighbors, but my aunt called me back inside and kept me busy all morning helping her clean the house. Momma wasn't feeling well. Something called "morning sickness" had her running to the powder room often, and my aunt would look pleased when she did that, muttering to herself all the time about fools who risked the wrath of God.

Vera came limping home around three, looking hot, pale and exhausted. She threw me a scathing glance and stomped up the stairs. I decided I'd check on what she was doing before I stole through the woods to meet the new neighbors. I didn't want Vera to follow me. She'd be sure to tell Papa so I'd be punished.

Vera wasn't in her room. Nor was she in mine, prowling through my drawers in hopes of finding something to steal. I kept searching, hoping to surprise her. Instead, she surprised me.

Inside the First Audrina's room, which Papa usually kept locked except on the days Momma cleaned in there, Vera was seated in the rocking chair with the calla-lily back. The magic chair. Back and forth she was rocking, singsong chanting as Papa made me do so often. For some reason it made me furious to see her there. No wonder I wasn't "catching" the gift—Vera was trying to steal it!

"Get out of that chair!" I yelled.

Reluctantly she came back to herself, opening her large dark eyes that glittered just like Papa's. Her lips curled in a sneer. "You gonna make me, little girl?"

"Yes!" I stormed bravely, striding into the dreaded room and ready to defend my right to sit in that chair. Even though I didn't want the First and Best Audrina's gifts, I didn't want Vera to have them, either.

Before I could do a thing, Vera was out of the chair. "Now you hear this, Audrina Number Two! In the long run it's going to be me who takes the First Audrina's place. You don't have what she had, and you never will. Papa is trying and trying to make you over into what she was, but he's failing, and he's beginning to realize that. That's why he told me to start using this rocking chair. Because now he wants me to have the First Audrina's gifts."

I didn't believe her, yet something frail within me cracked and pained. She saw me weaken, saw me tremble. "Your mother doesn't love you nearly as much as she loved the First Audrina, either. She fakes love for you, Audrina, fakes it! Both your parents would see you dead if they could get back the girl they really loved."

"Stop saying things like that!"

"I'll never stop saying what needs to be said."

"Leave me alone, leave this room alone! You are a fake, Vera, the worst kind of fake!" Then, taking a wild swing, I tried to hit her. She chose to stand at that moment, and if she hadn't timed it so well, my fist would have missed her. As it was, it caught her smack on her jaw. She fell back on the rocking chair, which tipped over. Surely that fall didn't do as much damage as her loud howls of pain indicated . . .

Aunt Ellsbeth came on the run. "What have you done to my daughter?" she yelled, running to help Vera stand. Once she had Vera on her feet, she dashed back to me and slapped my face. Quickly I dodged her second blow. I heard Vera screaming, "Mother, help me! I can't breathe!"

"Of course you can breathe," snapped my aunt impatiently, but a trip to the emergency room proved Vera had four broken ribs. The ambulance men gave

Momma and my aunt funny looks, as if they suspected Vera couldn't possibly always be hurting herself. Then they looked at me and weakly smiled.

I was sent to bed without an evening meal. (Papa didn't come home until late because of some business meeting, and Momma retired early, leaving my aunt in charge.) All that night I heard Vera moaning, gasping and panting as she tried to sleep. Doubled over like an old crone, she came into my room in the middle of the night and shook her fist in my face. "Someday I'm going to bring down this house and everyone in it," she hissed in a deadly voice, "and you'll be the first I fell. Remember that if you never remember anything else, Second and Worst Audrina."

Arden Lowe

In the morning I was desperate to escape the house. Since Ellsbeth was tending to the wounded Vera, and Momma was staying in bed with her morning sickness, I had the first opportunity of my lifetime to steal away unobserved.

The woods were full of shadows. Just like the First Audrina, I was disobeying, but the sky above said there wasn't a chance of rain, and without the rain it couldn't happen again. Shimmering sun rays fell through the lacy green canopy of leaves to pattern the path ahead with golden spots of light. Birds were singing, squirrels were chasing each other, rabbits ran, and now that I was free from Whitefern I felt good, yet slightly uneasy. Still, if ever I was going to make friends of my own I had to make the first move and prove something if to no one but myself.

I was going to see the new family living in the gardener's cottage that hadn't been occupied for many years. I'd never seen this part of the woods, but still it seemed familiar. I stopped to stare down at the path, which branched off right and crookedly wandered forward, too. Deep inside some directing knowledge told me to turn right. Each little noise I heard made me freeze, listen, straining to hear the giggle I heard when I was in that rocking chair, reliving events that had happened to the First and Best, and were glued to that chair. Little whispers were in the summer leaves. Little butterflies of panic were fluttering in my head. I kept hearing all the warnings: "Dangerous in the woods. Unsafe in the woods. Death in the woods." Nervously I quickened my steps. I'd sing like the seven dwarfs used to whistle to make them unafraid . . . now why did I think that? That was *her* kind of thought.

I told myself as I hurried along that it was time I braved the world by myself, time indeed. I told myself each foot away from that house of dim corners and brooding whispers was making me feel better, happier. I wasn't weak, spoiled or unfit for the world. I was just as brave as any girl of . . . seven?

Something about the woods — something about the way the sun shone through the leaves. Colors were trying to speak to me, tell me what I couldn't remember. If I didn't stop thinking as I was, soon I'd be running and screaming, expecting the same thing to happen to me that had happened to her. I was the only Audrina left alive in the world. Truly I didn't have to be afraid. Lightning never struck twice in the same place.

On the very edge of a clearing, I came upon the cottage in the woods. It was a small white cottage with a red roof. I ducked to hide behind an old hickory tree when I saw a boy come out of the cottage door carrying a rake and a pail. He was tall and slim, and already I knew who he was. He was the one who'd given Vera the box of candy on Valentine's Day.

She had told me he was eleven, and in July he'd be twelve. The most popular boy in his class—studious, intelligent, quick-witted and fun—and he had a crush on Vera. That sort of proved he wasn't *too* brilliant. But from what my aunt was always saying, men were only grown-up little boys, and the male sex knew only what their eyes and glands told them, nothing else.

Watching him, I could tell he was a hard worker from the diligent way he set about cleaning up the yard, which was a wilderness of tangleweed, briars, Virginia crabgrass, spidergrass.

He wore faded blue jeans that fit skintight, as if he'd outgrown them or they'd shrunk. His thin old shirt might once have been bright blue, but now it was faded gray-white. From time to time he'd stop to rest, to look around and whistle in imitation of some bird. Then, after a few seconds, he was back to work, pulling up weeds and throwing them in his pail, which he dumped often in a huge trash can. This boy didn't scare me, even though Papa and that rocking chair had taught me to be terrified of what boys might do.

Suddenly he tore off the worn canvas gloves he wore, hurled them down and spun around, directly facing the tree I was hiding behind.

"Isn't it time you stopped hiding and watching?" he asked, turning to pick up his pail of weeds to empty it in the larger can. "Come on out and be friendly. I don't bite."

My tongue stayed glued to the roof of my mouth, though his voice was kind.

"I won't hurt you, if that's why you're afraid. I even know your name is Audrina Adelle Adare, the girl with the beautiful long hair that changes colors. All the boys in Whitefern Village talk about the White-fern girls and say you're the most beautiful one of all. Why don't you go to school like other girls? And why didn't you write me a note and thank me for that box of Valentine candy I sent you months and months ago? That was rude, you know, very rude not to even call on the phone . . ."

My breath caught. He'd given *me* the candy and not Vera? "I didn't know you knew me, and no one gave me the candy," I said in a small, hoarse voice. I wasn't sure even now that he'd send a totally unknown girl a box of expensive candy when Vera was pretty enough and already shaping into a woman.

"Sure I know you. That's why I wrote you that note with the candy. I see you all the time with your parents." He continued, "The trouble is, you never turn your head to see anyone. I'm in your sister's class in school. I asked her why you didn't go to school and she told me you were crazy, but I don't believe that. When people are crazy it shows in their eyes. I went into the drugstore and looked for the prettiest red satin heart of all. I hope Vera gave you at least one piece, since it was all yours."

Did he know Vera that well, enough to suspect she'd lie and eat it all? "Vera said you gave the box of candy to her."

"Aha!" he said. "That is exactly what my mom said when I told her you must be a very ungrateful kind of girl. And even if you didn't eat a piece, I hope you realize I did try to let you know there's one boy who thinks you are the prettiest girl he's ever seen."

"Thank you for the candy," I whispered.

"I deliver the morning and evening newspapers. It's the first time I've spent my hard-earned money on a gift for a girl."

"Why did you do it?"

He turned his head quickly, trying to catch a glimpse. Oh, his eyes were amber-colored. The sun was in them, making him almost blind, but showing me in detail what a pretty color they were, a lot lighter in shade than his hair. "I guess sometimes, Audrina, you can look at a girl and know right away you like her a lot. And when she never even looks your way, you've got to do something drastic. And then it didn't work."

Not knowing what to say, I said nothing. But I did move a little so he could see my face, while my body stayed safely hidden by the bushes.

"Darn if I can understand why you don't go to school."

How could I explain when I didn't understand? Unless it was like Aunt Ellsbeth said, that Papa wanted to keep me all for himself and "train" me.

"Since you haven't asked, I'll introduce myself. I'm Arden Nelson Lowe." Cautiously, he stepped closer to my hiding place, craning his neck in order to see me better. "I'm an *A* name, too, if that means anything, and I think it does."

"What do you think it means?" I asked, feeling perplexed. "And don't come any closer. If you do, I'll run."

"If you run, I'll only give chase and catch you," he said.

"I can run very fast," I warned.

"So can I."

"If you caught me, what would you do?"

He laughed and spun around in a circle. "I really don't know, except it would give me the chance to see you really close, and then I could find out if those eyes of yours are truly violet, or just dark blue."

"Would it matter?" I felt worried. My eye color was like my hair color—ambiguous. Strange eyes that could change color with my moods, from violet to dark, dark purple. Haunted eyes, said Aunt Ellsbeth, who was always telling me in indirect ways that I was weird.

"Nope, it wouldn't matter," he said.

"Arden," called a woman's voice, "who are you talking to?"

"Audrina," he called back. "You know, Mom, the youngest of those two girls who live in that big fancy house beyond the woods. She's awfully pretty, Mom, but shy. Never met such a shy girl before. She stays behind the bushes, ready to run if I come too close. She sure isn't like her sister, I can tell you that. Would you say that's the proper way to meet a boy?"

From inside the cottage his mother laughed gaily. "It may be exactly the right way to interest a boy like my son, who likes to solve mysteries."

I stretched my neck to see a beautiful dark-haired woman sitting at an open cottage window, showing from her waist up. She seemed to me as lovely as a movie star with all that long, blue-black curling hair tumbling down onto her shoulders. Her eyes were dark, her complexion as fair and flawless as porcelain.

"Audrina, you're welcome here whenever you care to visit," she called in a friendly, warm fashion. "My son is a fine and honorable boy who would never do a thing to harm you."

I felt breathless with happiness. I'd never had a friend before. I had disobeyed, like the First Audrina, and dared the woods . . . only to find friends. Maybe I wasn't as cursed as she'd been. The woods weren't going to destroy me, as they had her . . .

I started to speak, to step forward and show all of myself and brave meeting strangers on their own ground. Just as I was ready to reveal myself, out of the depths of the woods behind me came the sound of my name being called repeatedly, commandingly. The voice was distant and faint, but each time it sounded it was closer.

It was Papa! How did he know where to find me? What was he doing home from his office so early? Had Vera called him to tell him I wasn't in the house or yard? He'd punish me, I knew he would. Even if this wasn't the forbidden, worst part of the woods, he didn't want me out of sight from those who watched over me from morning until night.

"Goodbye, Arden," I called hastily, peeking from around the tree and waving. I waved again to his

106 V. C. Andrews

mother in the window. "Goodbye, Mrs. Lowe. I'm happy to have met you both, and thank you for wanting me to be your friend. I need friends, so I'll be back soon, I promise."

Arden smiled broadly. "See you soon, I hope."

I ran back toward Papa's voice, hoping he wouldn't guess where I'd been. I nearly collided with him as he came striding along the faint path. "Where've you been?" he demanded, seizing hold of my arm and swinging me halfway around him. "What are you running from?"

I stared up into his face. As always, he looked wonderfully handsome, clean, wearing a new three-piece stockbroker's suit, tailored to perfection. Even as he let go of my arm, he brushed away dried leaves that clung to his sleeve. He checked his trousers to see if the briars had snagged them, and, if they had, he might have treated me worse. As it was, his quick inspection found his new suit undamaged, so he could smile at me enough to take some of the fear from my heart. "I've been calling you for ten minutes. Audrina, haven't I told you repeatedly to stay out of the woods?"

"But Papa, it's such a beautiful day, and I wanted to see where the rabbits run to hide. I wanted to pick wild strawberries and blueberries and find forget-me-nots. I wanted lilies of the valley to put in my bedroom to make it smell pretty."

"You didn't follow this path all the way to the end, did you?" There was something peculiar in his dark, dark eyes, something that warned me not to tell him about meeting Arden Lowe and his mother.

"No, Papa. I remembered what I promised and stopped following the rabbit. Papa, rabbits run so very fast."

"Good," he said, snatching my hand again and spinning me around so I could do nothing but be dragged along as I tried to keep up with the stride of his exceptionally long legs. "I hope you never lie to me, Audrina. Liars come to no good end."

Nervously, I swallowed. "Why are you home so early, Papa?"

He looked backward to scowl. "I had a feeling about you this morning at breakfast. You looked so secretive. I sat in my office and wondered if you might not just get the notion to visit the new people who moved into that cottage. Now hear this, girl, you are never to go over there. Understand? We need the rent money, but they are not our social equals, so leave them alone."

It was terrible to have a father who could read your mind. I had to try again to make him see how much I needed friends. "But, Papa, I thought you said Momma could invite the new neighbor lady to Tuesday teas."

"No, not after what I found out about them. There are a lot of old sayings in this world, and most of them should be heeded. Birds of a feather flock together— and I don't want my bird flocking with those beneath her. Common people will steal your specialness and make you just a member of the herd. I want you to be a leader, one who stands out from the crowd. People are sheep, Audrina, stupid sheep, ready to follow the one who has the strength to be different. And you don't have to worry about having friends when our family is going to increase soon. Think of how much fun it will be to have a little brother or sister. Make that baby your best friend."

"Like Momma and her sister are friends?"

He threw me a hard look. "Audrina, your mother and her sister are to be pitied. They live in the same house, share the same meals but refuse to accept the best each could give the other. If only they'd break through that wall of resentment. But they never will. Each has her pride. Pride is a wonderful thing, though it can grow out of proportion. What you see each day is love turned inside out and turned into rivalry."

I didn't understand. Adults were still like the prism lights, changing colors constantly, confusing my thoughts.

"Sweetheart, promise you won't go into the woods again." I promised. He squeezed too hard on my fingers not to promise. He seemed satisfied and eased his pressure. "Now, here's what I want you to do. Your mother needs you now that she's not feeling well with this pregnancy. It goes that way sometimes. Try to help her as much as you can. And promise never to disappear and not let me know where you are."

But he wasn't going to let me go anywhere, not ever. Did he think I might run away?

"Oh, Papa," I cried, throwing my arms about him again. "I'll never leave you! I'll stay and take care of you when you grow old. I'll always love you, no matter what!"

He shook his head, looking sad. "You say that now, but you won't remember when you meet some young man you think you love. You'll forget me and think only of him. That's the way life is, the old have to make way for the young."

"No, Papa, you can stay with me even if I do marry . . . and I don't think I will."

"I hope not. Husbands have a way of not wanting parents around. Nobody wants old people around to clutter up their lives and create more expenses. That's why I have to make more and more money, to save for my old age and your mother's."

Staring up at him, I felt old age would never touch him. He was too strong, too vigorous for age to gray his hair and put wrinkles on his face and sag his jowls.

"Are old ladies unwanted, too?" I asked.

"Not your mother's kind," he said with a bitter smile. "Somebody would always want your mother. And if no man wants her, she'd turn to you . . . so be there when or if she needs you. Be there when I need you, too."

I shivered, not enjoying this kind of serious, grown-up talk when I had just met the first boy I could like. We neared the edge of the woods now, where the trees began to spread out and the lawn began. Papa was still talking.

"Sweet, there's an old lady at the house whom you've never met. Your mother and I both want a boy so much that we feel we can't wait until the birth to find out what sex we're going to have. And I've been told this lady, Mrs. Allismore, has a talent for predicting the sex of an unborn child."

As we neared the house, I paused to stare up at our grand old house that I saw as a stale and timeworn wedding cake; the cupola was where the bride and groom should have been but weren't. I saw the tall narrow windows as sinister, slotted eyes looking out. When I was inside, I saw the windows as looking inward, keeping an eye on everyone, especially me.

Papa tugged me on. A strange little black car was parked on the long curving drive that needed repaving. Weeds shot up in all the many cracks that I was careful to step over, not wanting to break my mother's back. I tried to pull my hand free from Papa's so I wouldn't have to be there and watch something that might be scary, but Papa pulled me through the front door, giving me no opportunity to run to my hideaway in the cupola. Once the doors were closed behind us, I was released. Adroitly, I avoided putting my feet on any rainbowed design the sun made through the stained-glass windows in the doors.

In the best of the front salons, my mother, Aunt Ellsbeth, Vera and an old, old woman were gathered together. Momma was lying on the purple velvet chaise. The old woman leaned above her. The moment she saw us come in, she took the wedding band from my mother's finger and tied it to a piece of string. Vera leaned closer, looking very interested. Slowly, slowly, that old woman began to swing the ring tied to a string over my mother's middle.

"If the ring swings vertically, it will be a boy," muttered the old woman. "If it swings in a circle, it will be a girl."

At first the ring moved erratically, terribly undecided; then it paused and changed course, and Papa began to smile. Soon his smile vanished as the ring tried to make a circle. Papa leaned forward and began to breathe heavily. Aunt Ellsbeth sat very tall and straight; her dark eyes held the same intense expectancy as Papa's eyes. Vera drifted closer, her ebony eyes wide. Momma lifted her head and craned her neck to see what was going on and why nothing was being decided. I swallowed over the lump that closed my throat. "What's wrong?" Momma asked in a worried way.

"You have to stay calm," croaked Mrs. Allismore. Her witchlike face screwed into a tiny wrinkled prune. Her miniscule mouth pursed into a crudely stitched buttonhole. Hours seemed to pass instead of seconds as that ring on the string kept changing directions, settling nothing. "Has your doctor mentioned twins?" asked the old crone with a perplexed frown.

"No," whispered Momma, appearing even more alarmed. "He said the last time I went that he heard only one heartbeat."

Papa reached to take her hand in his, then raised it to his cheek, rubbing it against his faint stubble. I could hear the slight raspy sound. Then he leaned to kiss Momma's cheek.

"Lucky, don't look so concerned. This is all

tomfoolery anyway. God will send us the right child; we don't have to worry."

Yet Momma insisted that Mrs. Allismore try for a while longer. Five excruciating minutes passed before the old woman grimly untied the string from the ring and handed Momma her wedding band. "Ma'am, I hate to say this, but what you're carrying is not male or female."

Momma let out a small terrified cry.

Never before had I seen Papa fly into such a rage. "Get out of here!" he yelled. "Look at my wife! You've scared her half to death." He shoved the old woman toward the door, and to my utter amazement he shoved a twenty-dollar bill into her hand. Why was he paying her so much money?

"It's fifty dollars, sir."

"It's twenty or nothing for a report like that," barked Papa, shoving her outside and locking the door behind her. When I entered the salon again, Vera had moved into the shadows to stare at Papa with hard eyes. She had a huge chunk of chocolate cake in her hands, left for me to eat for dinner dessert. . . and she'd eaten twice as much last night.

Catching my glare, she grinned and licked chocolate from her fingers. "All gone, now, sweet Audrina. None left for you, because you had to steal away. Where did you go, sweet Audrina?"

"Shut up!" ordered Papa, falling on his knees beside the couch where Momma lay crying. He tried to console her by saying it was a crackpot idea in the first place. Momma threw her arms about him and really bawled. "Damian, what could she have meant? Everyone says her predictions come true every time."

"Well, not this time."

Vera balled up the wax paper that had held her cake and shoved it into her pocket. "I believe Mrs. Allismore is one hundred percent right. Another freak is about to come into this Whitefern house. I can smell it in the air." With that she headed toward the foyer— but not quickly enough. In a bounding flash Papa was on his feet and she was over his knee. He yanked up her skirt and began to spank her so hard I could see through her transparent white nylon panties how red her buttocks grew. She screamed and fought him, trying to wiggle free, but in no way could she match his strength.

"Stop it, Damian!" screamed my mother and my aunt simultaneously. "That's enough, Damian," Momma finished, raising up on one elbow and looking very weak.

Ruthlessly, Papa shoved Vera off his lap so that she fell on the floor. She began to crawl away, trying to tug down her skirt and cover her panties. "How could you, Damian?" asked my aunt. "Vera is a young woman— much too old to be spanked. I wouldn't blame her if she never forgives you."

After that, we ate dinner. Everyone was so angry that only Vera and my aunt managed to clean their plates. Later that night I heard Momma sobbing in Papa's arms, still worried about her unborn baby.

"Damian, something is wrong with this baby. Sometimes it moves constantly, keeping me awake, and other times it doesn't move at all."

"Sssh," he comforted softly. "All babies are different. We're two healthy people. We'll have another healthy baby. That woman has no more divining power than I do."

What could have been a wonderful summer was spoiled because Vera insisted on following me everywhere. Time and again I tried to slip through the woods without Vera knowing, but she seemed to smell my thoughts and, like an Indian, she was on my trail. Though Arden's mother insisted that we call her Billie, this felt strange. When she kept insisting, finally I did. She was the only adult I'd ever met who was ready to share her adult knowledge with me in a way I could understand. I liked it best when I could steal over without Vera, who had a way of dominating all conversations. Every time we visited, we both went away wondering why Billie didn't invite us into her cottage. I was too polite to say anything. Vera was pretending to be mannerly, so she didn't mention it either.

One day I heard Arden tell Billie that Vera was twelve. I stared at him, feeling very strange. He knew more about Vera than I did. "Did she tell you that?" I asked.

"Gosh, no," he laughed. "Vera's got nutty ideas about telling her age. But she is listed on the school register, and I happen to know she's twelve." He gave me a shy smile. "Are you trying to tell me you don't know your own sister's correct age?"

Quickly I covered. "Of course I do. She says people have long memories, so she's going to pass around so many lies that no one will ever know years from now just what age she was this summer."

Despite Vera, I did have fun that summer. It seemed to me that Billie gave me three times the warmth she gave Vera, and as shameful as it seemed, she seemed more concerned about my welfare than my own mother did. But Momma wasn't feeling well, and I could forgive her. Dark circles appeared beneath her eyes. She walked with her hand supporting her back. She stopped playing the piano and even stopped reading her paperback romances. Every day she'd fall asleep on the purple chaise with the book on her swollen breasts. I loved her so much I'd stand and watch her sleeping, so afraid for her and the little baby that wasn't a boy or a girl. Vera was telling me all the time it was going to be a "neutered" baby of no sex, like a doll. "Nothing between its legs," she'd laugh. "That does happen sometimes. It's a fact. One of the bizarre things that nature can do. It's written about in medical books."

Monthly cramps that kept Vera in bed gave me my best times to run to Arden and Billie. Arden and I ate picnic lunches under the trees, spread on red and white checkered gingham tablecloths. I never felt afraid of him. When finally he did touch me, it was to feel my hair. I didn't mind that.

"When is your birthday?" he asked one day while

I was sprawled on my back, staring up through the tree above, trying to see the clouds and make them into sailing ships. "September the ninth," I answered unhappily. "I had an older sister who died exactly nine years before I was born. She had my very same name."

Until I'd said this, Arden had been busy hammering a dent out of some tiny wheel he meant to use on something. He stopped hammering and stared at me in a strange way. "An older sister? With your same name?"

"Yes. She was found dead in the woods, under a golden raintree, and because of that, I'm never supposed to come here."

"But you *are* here," he said in a strange voice. "How do you dare to come?"

I smiled. "I'd dare anything to visit Billie."

"To visit my mom? Why, that's very sweet, but what about me?"

That's when I turned on my side so he couldn't see my face. "Oh, I guess I can put up with you."

I turned to peek at him, and he was just sitting there cross-legged in his white shorts, his chest bare and glistening where sunlight hit it. "Well," he said, picking up the hammer and beginning to beat on that little wheel again, "I guess that tells me you've got a lot of growing up to do—or else it tells me you're quite a lot like your sister after all."

"She's not my sister, Arden, but my cousin. My parents only pretend she's theirs to save my aunt from the shame. My aunt went away and came back almost two years later. Vera was only one year old. My aunt was so sure the father of Vera would take one look at his baby and fall in love with her. It didn't happen that way. While my aunt was gone, he married someone else."

Arden didn't say one word. He just smiled to let me know he didn't care who Vera was.

Arden loved his mother more than I thought boys ever could. When she called him, he'd jump up to fly into the house. He'd hang up her wash and take it down. He carried out the garbage cans, something my papa would never do. Arden had strong principles about honesty, loyalty, about helping those who needed it, about devotion and dedication to duty, and he had something else he didn't talk about, but I noticed it anyway. He had an aesthetic eye that seemed to appreciate beauty more than most people did. He'd stop in the woods and work for hours to dig up a bit of quartz that looked like a huge pink diamond. "I'm going to have this made into a pendant for the girl I marry someday. I just don't know what form it ought to take. What do you think, Audrina?"

I felt envious of that girl he'd marry one day even as I took the quartz and turned it over. It had many strange convolutions, but in the center were colors so bright and clear it resembled a rose. "Why not a rose? Just the blossom full and open, not a bud."

"A rose blossom it will be, then," he said, tucking the quartz into his pocket. "Someday when I'm rich, I'm going to give the girl I love everything she's ever dreamed of wanting, and I'm going to do that for my mom, too." A shadow passed over his face. "The only thing is, money can't buy what my mom wants most."

"What's that? If that's not too personal to ask."

"It's personal, very personal." He grew silent, but that was all right. We could go for hours without speaking and still we managed to feel comfortable with each other. I lay on the grass watching him repair his bicycle, glancing at his mother in the window as she blended some mixture for a cake, and I thought this was the way real families were supposed to live, without shouting, arguing, fighting all the time. Shadows in the house put shadows in the mind. Out here under the sky and trees the shadows were only temporary. Whitefern was permanently, densely shadowed.

"Audrina," Arden said suddenly, still fiddling with the spokes of his bike, "what do you really think of me?"

I liked him more than I wanted to admit, but in no way did I want to tell him that. Why would a boy of twelve want to waste his time on a girl of seven? Surely Vera must appeal to him more. But I didn't want to ask this, either. "You are my first friend, Arden, and I guess I am very grateful you bother with me at all."

His eyes met mine briefly, and I saw something glistening in them like tears—why would he cry because I said that? "I'm going to have to tell you something one day, and you're not going to like me after I do."

"Don't ever tell me if that's what it will do. For I don't want to stop liking you, Arden."

He turned away then. What did he have to tell me that would make me dislike him? Did Arden too have a secret, just like everybody else?

One early morning I ran to meet Arden so he could teach me how to catch fish and bait the hook with live worms. Vera trailed along behind, though I'd tried to slip out unseen. I didn't like spearing the worms on the hook, so soon Arden was pulling out his kit of fancy flies and trying to show me how to cast from shore. He stood on a riverbank higher than most to demonstrate the right technique. Seated beside me, Vera leaned to whisper about Arden in his red swimming trunks, giggling and pointing to where all the little babies would come from.

"I don't believe one word of what you say," I whispered back, turning red and knowing perfectly well that what she said was true. Why did she make everything about boys seem so vulgar and gross? As much as I disliked Vera, she did have a way of digging up all the facts no one else wanted to talk about. I figured her interest in medical books was teaching her more about life than I'd ever find out on my own.

"I'll bet you and Arden have already played show and tell."

Laughing more, she explained what she meant. I slapped at her for even thinking we'd do that. "I hate you sometimes, Vera!"

"Hey, you two," called Arden, turning to hold up his catch. "This is a really big one. A bass, and big enough for all of us. Let's take it to Mom and she'll broil it for our lunch."

"Oh, Arden," exclaimed Vera, clasping her hands together and widening her dark eyes with awe. "I do believe that's the granddaddy fish all the fishing experts around here have been trying to catch for years and years. And to think you caught it. What a wonderful fisherman you are."

Usually Vera seemed to annoy Arden, but this time he smiled broadly, flattered by her praise. "Gosh, Vera, it just jumped on my line."

I hated him for falling for her stupid flattery, for not recognizing that Vera would say anything to make him look at her more than he looked at me. I jumped to my feet and ran to where I'd left my sundress. Behind concealing bushes I hoped to change from my swimming suit into my clothes. But my clothes were gone, even my sandals! Already my white bathing suit was on the ground, wet and muddy, and I was looking everywhere, thinking my clothes may have been blown away. "Vera, did you hide my clothes?"

At that instant, as I looked in another direction, I caught a glimpse of a quick hand that snatched up my discarded bathing suit. I recognized the ring on her finger. Vera's hand. I yelled at her and started to give chase, but Arden was out there and I didn't have on one stitch. "Arden," I cried, "stop Vera! She's stolen all my clothes and my bathing suit, too." Almost crying, I looked around for something I could use to conceal my nudity.

I heard Arden thrashing around in the bushes, calling Vera—and then he was coming my way, making plenty of noise. "Audrina, I can't find Vera. She can't run very fast, so she must be hiding. You can put on my shirt. It's long enough to cover you until you reach home."

Daring to peek, I saw him turn to head for where he'd left his clothes. "Hey!" he cried, "my clothes are gone, too! But it's all right, Audrina. You just stay where you are and I'll run home and ask Mom to loan you something of hers to wear home."

At that moment my father came running through the bushes, shoving them aside as he yelled at Arden, "Where's my daughter?" He looked wildly around, then riveted his threatening eyes on Arden again. "All right, young man—where is Audrina? What have you done to her?"

Shocked into momentary speechlessness, Arden shook his head, unable to say a word. Then, as my father advanced, his huge hands balling into fists, he found his voice. "Sir, she was here a moment ago. She must be on her way home."

"No," growled Papa, knitting his thick brows and scowling. "I would have passed her on the way if that were true. If she's not home, and she's not here, where else can she be? I know she visits you and your mother often. Vera told me that. Now where the hell is Audrina?"

There was an edge of panic in Arden's voice. "I really don't know, sir." He leaned over to pick up his catch of fish. "I was teaching Audrina how to fish. She doesn't like hurting the worms, so I was showing her how to cast with flies. Audrina caught two of these big ones, and Vera caught one. Here's the one I caught."

Papa's back was to me. If I dared, I might be able to sneak away and perhaps he'd never even see me.

Scrunching down, I began to steal away. Suddenly I was shoved from behind. I screamed as I fell face forward, directly into a briar bush.

Papa bellowed my name. He came charging my way, thrashing through the heavy underbrush, yelling to find me naked, screaming out his rage as he tore off" his expensive summer sports jacket and threw it over my shoulders. Spinning on his heel, he raced back to where Arden stood and seized him by the shoulders. Then brutally he began to shake him.

"Stop it, Papa!" I yelled. "Arden hasn't done anything wrong! We were only fishing, and wearing bathing suits so we wouldn't ruin our clothes. It was Vera who stole my sundress, and when I had my bathing suit off, she snatched that and ran."

"You took off your bathing suit?" roared Papa, his face so red he seemed ready to explode.

"Papa!" I screamed as my father made another menacing move. "Arden hasn't done anything wrong. He's the only friend I've ever had, and now you're punishing him for liking me!" I ran to where I could put myself between Arden and my father. He glared at me and tried to thrust me aside, but I clung to his arms, weighing him down. "I was changing clothes behind the bushes; Arden was still fishing. When Vera stole my clothes, and even my bathing suit, he offered to give me his shirt to wear, but she'd stolen his clothes, too. Just before you arrived he was going to run home and bring back something his mother would loan me to wear — and now you want to punish him for what Vera did."

Behind me, Arden jumped to his feet. "If you feel

such a need to punish someone, punish Vera. Audrina has never done one thing to make you ashamed of her. It's Vera who plays the dirty tricks. And for all I know she may have been the one to tell you what we planned to do today, hoping you'd presume the worst."

"And what is the worst?" asked Papa sarcastically even as he held me close at his side. His jacket almost slid off my shoulders to the ground. I made a desperate grab to hold it in place. I was trying to hide a bosom that didn't exist.

Papa's anger began to simmer down, but only a little. His fingers uncurled, though he kept tight hold on my shoulder. "Young man, I admire you for trying to protect my daughter, but she's misbehaved just by being here. Vera told me nothing. I haven't seen that wretch since last night at the dinner table. All I had to do was watch my Audrina's eyes this morning. They were shining so much at the breakfast table I immediately became suspicious." His smile was charming and evil too, as he turned to me. "You see, my love, there are no secrets you can keep from me. I can guess what's going on even without a tattletale like Vera. And if anyone should know better than to meet secretly with a boy in the woods, it should be you."

Papa grinned, put his hand flat on Arden's chest and thrust him away. "As for you, young man, if you want to keep that nice straight nose of yours unbroken, leave my daughter alone!"

Arden staggered backward from the hard shove, but he didn't fall.

"Goodbye, Arden," I called, tugging on Papa's

hand and trying to move him along before he pushed
Arden again.

Papa chose the most overgrown and difficult paths
home, where everything clawed at my face, my legs
and feet. After a while, he let go of my hand in order
to protect his own face from being whiplashed by the
low branches.

I was having great trouble keeping his jacket in
place. The neck was so large it kept slipping off my
shoulders. When I reached to pull it up on one shoulder, it slipped off the other. The sleeves dragged on
the ground, and several times I tripped and fell. Impatiently he waited for me to stand after the third fall,
and then he took the sleeves and wrapped them about
my neck like a heavy scarf.

Helplessly, I stared up at him, wondering how
he could be so mean to me. "Are you feeling sorry
for yourself now, darling? Do you regret your hasty
actions—deciding to risk your papa's disfavor to see a
boy who will only ruin you in the end? He's only a bit
of trash, not worthy of you."

"He's not trashy, Papa," I wailed, already beginning to itch and burn. My feet were full of cuts, my
legs scratched. "You don't know Arden."

"You don't know him either!" he bellowed. "Now
I'm going to show you something." Again he seized
my hand and pulled me along in a different direction.
On and on he dragged me until I gave up trying to resist. Finally he came to an abrupt halt.

"You see that tree?" he said, pointing to a splendid one, lush with golden leaves that trembled in the

gentle summer breeze. "That's a golden raintree." There was a small mound under the tree, covered with clover over which honey bees hovered, hummed and fingered for nectar. "That's where we found your older sister, sprawled there stone-cold dead. Only it was raining that day in September. Raining hard. The sky was dark with thunderclouds, and lightning flashed, so at first we thought she might have been struck by lightning. But there was evidence enough to prove it wasn't the work of God."

My heart was a wild frantic animal in my chest, thudding hard against my ribs, screaming and wanting to get out. "Now you listen to me, and listen carefully. Learn from the mistakes of others, Audrina. Learn before it's too late to save yourself. I don't want to find you dead there too."

The woods were closing in on me, smothering me. The trees wanted me, wanted me dead because I was another Audrina they wanted to claim for their own.

His lesson still not complete, heartlessly Papa dragged me onward. I was crying now, completely defeated, knowing he was right. I should never disobey, not ever. I should never have forgotten the other Audrina.

He was leading me to our family plot. I hated this place. I tried to sit down and resist, but Papa picked me up by the waist. Holding me rigid before him like a wooden doll, he stopped in front of the high, slender tombstone that seemed symbolic of a young girl. He said it again, as he'd said it a hundred or more times in the past, and just as before, his words made my blood chill and my spine turn mushy.

"There she lies, my First Audrina. That wonderful, special Audrina who used to look up to me as if I were God. She trusted me, believed in me, had faith in me. In all my life I never had another who gave me that kind of unquestioning love. But God chose to take her from me and replace her with you. There must be some meaning in all of this. It's up to you to make her death meaningful. I cannot bear to live with the knowledge that she may have died in vain. Audrina. You have to take on all the gifts of your dead sister, or I'm sure God will be angered, just as I am angered. You don't love me enough to believe I am doing the very best I can to protect you from the very thing that happened to her. And certainly you must have learned from the rocking chair about the boys in the woods on the day she died."

Staring up into his handsome face, which soon streaked with tears, I twisted in his arms so my arms went around his neck, and my face tucked down on his shoulder. "I'll do anything you want, Papa, as long as you let me see Arden and Billie once in a while. I'll sit in the rocking chair, and really try to fill with her gifts. I swear I'll cooperate as I never have before."

His strong arms embraced me. I felt his lips in my hair, and later he used his handkerchief to clean my dirty face before he kissed me. "It's a bargain. You can visit that boy and his mother once a week as long as you keep Vera with you, and make that boy escort you through the woods, and never go there after dark, or on a rainy day."

I didn't dare to ask for more.

Competition

The cemetery and the rocking chair had taught me their lessons. From now on I'd be the kind of girl Papa had to have in order to gain wealth and live happily. I knew he believed his way was the best way, and I couldn't judge for myself the right and wrong of most situations. And I wanted Papa to love me more than that hateful First Audrina that I wished had never been born, just as I'm sure Vera wished that I'd never been born.

"You'll never be as wonderful as your dead sister," stated Vera so firmly that it seemed indeed she must have known her. She was trying to press Papa's shirt to show him she could, but she was only managing to ruin it. The iron kept sticking and left burned places shaped like the iron. Even the steam holes showed. "The First Audrina could iron shirts like an expert," she said, bearing down hard on the iron. "And she was so neat with her hair. Your hair is always a windblown mess."

Vera's hair wasn't exactly terrific looking, either, the way it fell down into her face in wispy strings. The sun through the windows shone through her apricot hair and turned it gold on the ends and red near her scalp. Sun hair. Fire hair.

"I can't understand why they'd name someone as stupid as you are after such a brilliant girl. You can't do anything right," she went on. "What fools parents can be. Just because you happened to have her coloring, they thought you'd have to have her brains and personality, too. And you aren't nearly as pretty. And you're moody and dreary to be around." She turned down the heat on the iron, but it was already too late. Worry puckered her brow as she studied the burn marks and tried to figure out what to do. "Mom," she called, "if I burn Papa's shirt, what should I do?"

"Run for the woods," called back my aunt, who was glued to her TV set, which was showing an old movie.

"Stupid," Vera said to me, "go ask your mother what can be done to take out the scorched place on Papa's shirt."

"I'm too stupid to know what you mean," I said, still stirring my cereal around, sure that Papa would put me in that rocking chair again tonight, as he'd been doing two or three times a week, hoping the gifts were coming my way.

"Poor second-best Audrina," Vera continued. "Too dumb to even go to school. Nobody here wants the world to know how idiotic you are with your senile memory." She took from the cabinet a huge bottle of bleach, poured a little onto a sponge and dabbed at Papa's new pink shirt. The shape of the iron made an unsightly burn right where his coat wouldn't hide it.

I went over to see what she was doing. The bleach seemed to be working.

Papa stalked into the kitchen, bare-chested, cleanly shaven, his hair styled and ready to go. He paused near the ironing board to stare at Vera, who looked extremely pretty now that she was shaping up and slimming down in her waist. Then he was looking from me to her, then back again. Was he comparing me to her? What did he see that made him look undecided?

"What the devil are you doing to my shirt, Audrina?" he asked, catching his first glimpse of the ironing board.

"She was pressing it for you, Papa," spoke up Vera, moving in closer, as if to side with him. "And the silly girl was so busy picking on me she left the iron flat on your new shirt—"

"Oh, my God," he cried, grabbing up the shirt and inspecting it closely. He groaned again as he saw something I hadn't noticed until the light shone through it. Holes were appearing in the fading scorch mark. "Look what you've done!" he roared at me. "This shirt is one hundred percent silk. You've just cost me a hundred dollars." He saw the huge bottle of bleach then and groaned again. "You burn my shirt, then pour on bleach? Where was your common sense, girl, where?"

"Don't get excited," said Vera, running forward and snatching the shirt from his hands. "I'll repair this shirt for you, and you won't know it from new. After all, Audrina doesn't know how to do anything."

He glared at me, then turned doubtfully to her.

"How can you repair a shirt that's been eaten by bleach? It's gone, and I had planned to wear that to an important meeting." He hurled down his wine-colored tie, looked down at his light gray trousers, then started to leave the kitchen.

"Papa," I began, "I didn't burn your shirt."

"Don't lie to me," he said with disgust. "I saw you at the ironing board, and the bleach bottle wasn't a foot away. Besides, I don't think Vera would give a damn if my shirt was wrinkled. I naturally presumed you would be the one who knows how much I like to be turned out to perfection."

"I don't know how to press shirts, Papa. As Vera says all the time, I'm too stupid to do anything right."

"Papa, she's lying, and what's more, I told her to turn on the steam and use a press cloth, but she wouldn't listen. But you know how Audrina is."

He seemed ready to flare back when he noticed my look of despair. "All right, Vera. That's enough. If you can salvage this shirt I'll give you ten dollars." He smiled at her crookedly.

True to her word, that evening when Papa came home, Vera showed him his pink shirt. It looked brand-new. He took it from her hands, turned it over and over to look for patch stitches and could find none. "I don't believe my eyes," he said, and then laughed as he pulled out his wallet. He handed Vera ten dollars. "Honey, perhaps I've been misjudging you after all."

"I took it to a silk-mender, Papa," she said demurely, bowing down her head. "It cost me fifteen dollars, so that means I lost five of my savings."

He was listening attentively. If there was one kind of person my papa admired, it was one who knew how to save. "Where did you earn the money to save, Vera?"

"I run errands for old people. Help by shopping for their groceries," she said in a small, shy voice. "On Saturdays, I walk all the way to the village and do what I said. Sometimes I babysit, too."

My mouth gaped. Sure, once in a while Vera disappeared on Saturdays, but it was hard to picture her walking fifteen miles to and another fifteen fro. Papa was triply impressed, and pulled out another ten and gave that to her. "Now this shirt cost me a hundred and twenty, but it's better than throwing it away."

He didn't even look at me as he impulsively planted a resounding kiss on her cheek. "You surprise me, girl. I haven't always been nice to you. I thought you wouldn't care about my ruined shirt. I even thought you didn't love me."

"Oh, Papa," she said with her eyes gleaming, "I love you from the top of your hair to the tip of your toenails."

I hated her, really hated her for calling him Papa, when he was my father, not hers.

For some strange reason, he backed away from Vera, glancing down at his shoes as if to check the horny toenails that embarrassed him. He cleared his throat and looked disconcerted. "Well, it's an overdone compliment, but if it's genuine, I'm pleased and touched."

Stunned, I watched him leave the room without

once glancing my way. He didn't come in that night to tuck me into bed, or kiss my cheek, or hear my prayers, and if I dreamed of boys in the woods, I was pretty sure on this night he wouldn't come running to save me.

In the morning it was Vera who poured Papa's coffee, spelling Momma, who seemed wilted and looked very pale. She jumped up to put on three slices of toast and stood close to see that it didn't toast too long. He liked it golden on the outside, tender on the inside. Vera fried his bacon to perfection, and I didn't hear one complaint from him. When he finished eating, he thanked her for waiting on him, then got up to leave for work. Limping after him, Vera caught hold of his hand. "Papa, even though I know you're not my real father, can't we pretend you are . . . can't we, Papa?"

He seemed uncomfortable, as if not knowing what to say, and at the same time, touched. Papa belonged to me and Momma, not to Vera. I glanced at my aunt, who sat tight-lipped and grim, and I wished that both she and Vera would leave and go anywhere away from here.

Soon Papa left. I watched as his car turned off the dirt road that would take him onto the expressway and into town, where he'd have lunch with businessmen and call it work. To my surprise, he stopped momentarily at the mailbox on the corner where our private road forked off to meet the main road. I wondered why he hadn't picked up the mail last night. Had he been so eager to reach Momma and see how she fared that he'd forgotten again to check the mailbox?

When I reached our mailbox, I found the mail was still there. In fact, magazines and newspapers were bulging from the door, which wouldn't close.

It took some doing to stack my arms with all that was addressed to Papa. This was just what I needed. I would win Papa back. I knew what he wanted from me. I knew what Papa cared about most—money. I had to use my "gift" to make Papa money. Then he'd love me best forever. I was trying to read the front page of *The Wall Street Journal* even before I reached the kitchen to toss the mail on the table. I raced off to find the items I needed: a pencil and notepad, and a length of string and a straight pin.

In the closet under the back stairs was all the junk we wanted to keep and later throw out. It was there I found old copies of the *Journal.* I laid out the quote sheets and began to list the most active stocks, thinking two weeks should give me time span enough. Even as I worked I could hear Vera upstairs arguing with my aunt, who wanted her to help with the laundry. Vera wanted to go to the movies. She was meeting a friend.

"No!" yelled my aunt. "You're too young to start dating." Vera said something else I couldn't make out. "No, no, no!" I could hear very well. "Stop pleading. Once I say no I mean no—I'm not like some others around here who say no and later change their minds."

"You let me do as I want or I'll spill out all our family secrets in the middle of Main Street," shrilled Vera. "I'll stand there until everybody knows who my father is, and what you did—and the Whitefern name will go even farther down on the list of scoundrels!"

"Open your mouth about family secrets and you won't get one dime from me or from anyone else. If you behave yourself, there's a chance for us to profit sooner or later. You antagonize Damian and Lucietta. You're a thorn in both their sides, but it can pay off for both of us if you just try to behave yourself. I used to rue the day I conceived you. Many a time I wished I'd have had an abortion, but when you had Damian's shirt repaired and I saw how impressed he was, I regained some hope." Pleading came into her voice. "Audrina doesn't have to be the darling in this family, Vera. Remember all that's happened to her has given you a certain edge. Take advantage of it. You know how he is, and what he needs. Admire him. Respect him. Flatter him, and you'll become his favorite."

There was a long silence up there and some whispering I couldn't hear. That all too familiar lead ball came to reside in my chest again. They were plotting against me—and they knew what had happened to me when I didn't.

I had almost believed that my aunt liked me. Now I was hearing that she, too, was my enemy. I went back to the table to work with more determination to find just the right stock that would go up, up, up, and make Papa very, very, very rich.

I tied my little birthstone ring to the string, figuring I could do the same as Mrs. Allismore and predict which stock would be a winner. Papa was always saying trading stocks was not a science but an art, and what I was doing seemed very creative. I'd fastened a pin to the ring with a bit of thread to use it for a pointer. Twice it touched down on the same stock. I tried to force it to touch a third time. Three of anything was a magic number. But it refused to choose the same stock three times, even when I opened my eyes and tried to control the ring. It seemed to have some power of its own, faltering, indecisive, the same as Momma's wedding ring had been confused over her abdomen.

Just then I heard a loud howl. "Where are my diamond-stud earrings?" shouted Aunt Ellsbeth. "They're the only things my father left me of value, and my mother's own engagement ring. They're gone! Vera, did you steal my jewelry?"

"No," bellowed Vera. "Perhaps you misplaced them like you do everything else."

"It's been years since I wore that ring. You know I keep all my best jewelry locked in a box. Vera, don't lie. You're the only one who ever enters my bedroom. Now, where are those things?"

"Why don't you ask Audrina?"

"Her? Don't be ridiculous. That girl would never steal anything; she's got too much conscience. It's you who doesn't have any." She paused as I began to fold up the newspapers, my stock list put safely away. "Now I know what you did to restore Damian's one-hundred-dollar pink silk shirt," said my aunt scornfully. "You stole my earrings and ring, hocked them and bought him a new shirt. Damn you for doing that, Vera! No, you are not going to the movies. Not today, or any Saturday! Until the day you earn enough money to reclaim my jewelry, you stay home!"

I'd drifted to the bottom of the stairs to hear better; then I heard a thump, like someone falling. Then Vera came rushing down the stairs, with my aunt limping after her. "When I catch you, you're going to be locked in your room the remainder of this summer!"

Vera came flying in her best dress and new white shoes. I stood in her way. Brutally she shoved me aside and reached the front door before my aunt was down the back stairs. "Audrina, you can tell that beast of a woman that I hate her as much as I hate you, your mother, your father and this house! I'm going to the village, and when I get there I'm going to sell my body on the streets. I'm going to stand out before Papa's barbershop and yell 'Get your Whitefern daughter!' I'll yell it out so loud that the men in the city will hear, and they'll all come running! And I'll be the richest one yet!"

"You tramp!" yelled my aunt, running through the kitchen and heading for Vera. "You come back here! Don't you dare open that door and leave!"

But the door was opened and slammed shut before my aunt ran out to the porch. I stood looking out a window, watching Vera disappear around the bend. The village was fifteen miles away. The city was thirty. Was she going to hitchhike?

My aunt came and stood next to me. "Please don't tell your father what you overheard here. There are some things better left unsaid."

I nodded, feeling sorry for her. "Can I help?"

Stiffly, she shook her head. "Don't waken your

mother. She needs to rest. I'm going upstairs. You'll have to fix your own breakfast."

On Saturdays Momma liked to sleep late, and that gave my aunt her chance to stay in the little room off the dining room where she kept her television set. She loved to watch old movies and soap operas. They were the only entertainment she had.

My appetite had fled with Vera. I didn't doubt in the least that she would do just as she'd threatened. She'd destroy us all. I sat down and tried not to think of what Arden and his mother would think.

My mind was a workshop of miserable thoughts, wondering what made Papa the way he was, lovable and detestable, selfish yet giving. He needed someone nearby at all times, especially to watch him shave, and since Momma had to fix breakfast it was usually me who perched on the rim of the bathtub and listened to all the interesting things that went on in his brokerage office.

I asked many questions about the stock market, and what made stocks go up or down. "Demand," was his answer for high fliers. "Disappointment," was his explanation for those that went down. "Rumors of mergers and takeovers are great for sending stocks soaring but by the time the general public knows about those things, it's too late to get in. All the banks and big investors have bought and are ready to sell off to the poor unknowing investor who buys in at the top. When you've got the right connections, you know what's going on—if you don't have those connections, keep your money in the bank."

Bit by bit, I'd gained a great deal of knowledge about the market. It was Papa's way of teaching me, too, about arithmetic. I didn't think of money in cents but in eighths of points. I knew about triple tops that were sure to slide, and double bottoms that should take off. He'd showed me charts and how to read them, despite Momma ridiculing him about my being too young to understand. "Nonsense. A young brain is a quick brain; she understands much more than you do." Oh, yes, in some ways I loved my father very much, for if he couldn't restore my memory, he did give me hopes for my future. Someday he was going to own his own brokerage firm, and I'd be his manager. "With your gifts, we can't miss," was the way he put it. "Can't you just see it now, Audrina: D. J. Adare and Company."

Once again I went back to the most active lists and performed my string and ring trick, and again my pin pointer touched down twice on that same stock. Happiness swelled in my heart. I hadn't left it to Providence. Papa was going to make money when I gave him *this* dream.

And if this stock I'd chosen did go up, as by now I was fully expecting it would, then never again would I have to sit in that First and Best Audrina's rocking chair. I'd have her gift—or one even better. I knew Papa. It was money Papa wanted, and money he needed, and money was truly the one thing he didn't have enough of.

I raced upstairs to dress, sure that soon I'd have my memories back, too. Maybe the string-and-ring trick would work if I swung it over the Bible. I laughed as I sped on by the First Audrina's bedroom and hurried down to the kitchen, still tying my sash.

Momma was up and in the kitchen with blue curlers as fat as tin cans in her hair. "Audrina," she began in a weary voice, "would you mind watching the bacon while I whip the eggs?" Dark circles were under her eyes. "I tossed and turned all night. This baby is unusually restless. Just as I fell asleep toward dawn, your father's alarm went off, and he was up and talking ten miles a minute, trying to tell me not to worry about what that old woman said. He thinks I'm depressed, not tired, so he decided that he's going to invite twenty people over tonight to a party! Can you imagine anything more ridiculous? Here I am, in my sixth month, so tired I can hardly manage to get out of bed, and he thinks I need cheering up by preparing fancy little goodies for his friends. He tells me I'm bored, when he's the one who's bored. I wish to God he'd take up golf or tennis, or anything that would use up some of his energy and keep him away from home on the weekends."

Oh, oh, now I understood perfectly! Somehow that sixth sense Papa possessed had told him that today I had the gift—that had to be the real reason he wanted to celebrate. A hundred or more times he'd told me he'd celebrate with a party on the day my gift came to light. So it was true. I did have the gift now. Otherwise, the ring wouldn't have settled *twice* on the same stock, when nine others were listed there. I felt so good I wanted to shout.

"Where're Ellsbeth and Vera?" asked Momma.

I couldn't tell her about the argument and what Vera had threatened to do. Momma's maiden name was her most cherished possession. And if someone had picked Vera up, at this very moment she could be in the village shouting out all our secrets.

To think of Vera was to think of reality, and soon my confidence in my gift began to wane. All my life, or so it seemed, Papa had dumped all kinds of junk into my head about the supernatural, which he believed in and Momma didn't. I was convinced what he told me was true when I was with him, and convinced it wasn't true the moment he left the house.

"Where's Ellsbeth?" Momma asked.

"She tripped and fell, Momma."

"Cursed," murmured Momma, reaching to prod me into turning over the bacon. "A house of idiots, determined to make you and me idiots, too. Audrina, I don't want you to sit in that rocking chair anymore. The only gift your older dead sister had was an extraordinary amount of love and respect for her father, and that's what he misses. She believed every word he said. Every one of his crackpot notions she took seriously. Think for yourself, don't let him rule you. Just stay out of the woods— take that warning very seriously."

"But Momma," I began uncomfortably, "Arden Lowe lives in the gardener's cottage in the woods. He's my only friend. I'd want to die if I couldn't see him often."

"I know it's lonely for you without friends your

own age. But when the baby comes, you'll have a
friend. And you can invite Arden over here. And we'll
invite his mother to tea, and we won't let Aunt Mercy
Marie sit on the piano." I ran to hug her, feeling so
happy I could have burst.

"You like him a lot, don't you?"

"Yes, Momma. He never tells lies. He never breaks
a promise. He isn't so fussy he's afraid to get his hands
dirty, like Papa. We talk about real things, not like
the things Papa talks about so often. He told me once
he read somewhere that a coward dies many deaths.
He says that once he was so petrified he acted like a
coward, and he can never forgive himself. Momma, he
looks so troubled when he says that."

Pity filled her beautiful eyes. "Tell Arden that
sometimes it's better to run away and live to fight another day, for there is such a thing as odds too great."

I wanted to ask what she meant, but she had everything ready now to put on the table, and Papa wasn't
home, and my aunt was upstairs, and Vera . . . Lord
only knew what Vera was doing this minute.

"Set the table, darling, and stop looking worried. I
think Arden is a very noble-sounding name, and he's
living up to his name as best he can. Just try to love
your father as much as his first daughter did, and he'll
stop forcing you into the chair."

"Momma, when he comes home, I'm going to tell
him to cancel the party."

"You can't do that," she answered dully. "He's
driven into town to pick up party food and fresh flowers. As soon as his business meeting is over, he'll be

rushing back here. You see, your father never had parties when he was a boy, and now he uses any excuse to make up for that lack. Men stay children at heart, Audrina, remember that. No matter how old they become they manage to keep some boy inside them, always wanting what they wanted then, not realizing that when they were boys, they wanted to be manly instead of boyish. It's strange, isn't it? When I was a girl I wished we'd never have parties, for when we did have them I wasn't invited and I had to stay upstairs, dying to come down. I'd hide and watch and feel so unwanted. It wasn't until I was sixteen that I danced in my own house."

"Where did you dance?"

"We'd roll up the rugs and dance in the Roman Revival room or in the back parlor. Other times I'd steal out the window and meet a boyfriend who'd drive me to a dance. My mother would leave the back door unlocked so I could sneak back in and my father would never know. She'd come into my room when she heard me return and sit on my bed so I could tell her everything. That's the way it's going to be with us. When you're old enough to go to dances, I'll see that you go."

If my gift didn't set me free, maybe my mother would. "Did you have lots of boyfriends, Momma?"

"Yes, I guess I did." Wistfully, she stared over my head. "I used to promise myself I wouldn't marry until I was thirty. I wanted my musical career more than I wanted a husband and children—and look what I got."

"I'm sorry, Momma."

Then she was touching my hair lightly. "Darling, I'm sorry. I'm talking too much and making you feel guilty when it was I who made the choice. I fell in love with your father, and love has a way of brushing aside all other considerations. He swept me off my feet, and if he hadn't, I would probably have died of a broken heart anyway. But you be careful not to let love steal what aspirations you have for yourself. Though your father fills your head with silly ideas, in one he's perfectly right. You are special. You're gifted, too, even if you don't know what that gift is. Your father is a good man who just doesn't always do the right thing."

I stared up into her face, feeling more and more confused. First she said Papa gave me idiotic notions, and then she told me his craziest one about my being special was true.

Moments later, Papa was home with his sacks of groceries and florist's flowers. Vera came straggling after him. She looked dirty; her hair was a mess, and she'd been crying. "Momma," she sobbed, running to my mother and making me feel mean again because she was trying to claim not only my father but also my mother. "Papa pulled me into his car by my hair—look what he did to my hair, and I just set it last night."

"Don't comfort her, Lucky!" shouted Papa when he saw my mother's arms go protectively about Vera. He grabbed hold of Vera and shoved her into a kitchen chair so forcefully that she began to wail. "That smart-mouth was stumbling along the highway when I saw her. When I stopped and ordered her into the car, she told me she was going to become a whore and shame us all. Ellsbeth, if you don't know how to tame your daughter, then I'll use my own method."

I hadn't even noticed my aunt had slipped into the kitchen, wearing one of her plaid cotton housedresses that seemed so cheap and ordinary compared to the pretty clothes my mother wore.

"Vera, go upstairs and stay there until I tell you to come down again," barked Papa. "And no meals until you can apologize to all of us. You should be grateful you have a place at all in this household."

"I'll go, but I'll never be grateful!" Vera picked herself up and trudged out of the kitchen. "And I'll come downstairs when I get good and ready!"

Papa rushed forward.

"Momma, don't let him whip her!" I cried. "She'll only do something to hurt herself if he does." Vera always caused her own accidents soon after she had enraged Papa so much he had to punish her.

My mother sighed and looked more fatigued. "Yes, I guess you're right. Damian, let her go. She's been punished enough."

Why didn't my aunt speak up to defend her own daughter? Sometimes it seemed she disliked Vera as much as Papa did. Then I filled with guilt. At times I, too, absolutely hated Vera. The only time I liked her was when I pitied her.

Upstairs Vera was screaming at the top of her lungs. "Nobody loves me! Nobody cares! Don't you dare ever hit me again, Damian Adare! If you do, I'll tell! You know who I'll tell, and you'll be sorry, you will be!"

In a flash Papa was out of the chair and flying up the stairs. That stupid Vera kept right on screaming until he threw open her door, and then there was a thud. Next came the loudest and longest howl I'd heard her make yet—and her lifetime had a long record of howls and screams. My blood chilled. Another loud thump . . . and then total silence. All three of us left in the kitchen stared up at the ceiling, which was the floor of Vera's room. What had Papa done to Vera?

A few minutes later, Papa came back to the kitchen.

"What did you do to Vera?" asked Momma sharply, her eyes hard as she glared at him. "She's only a child, Damian. You don't have to be so harsh with a child."

"I didn't do a damn thing!" he roared. "I opened the door of her room. She backed off and tripped over a chair. She fell and started howling. She got up and started to run to hide in the closet where she put that lock on the inside, and darn if she didn't trip and fall again. I left her on the floor crying. You'd better go up, Ellie. She may have another broken bone."

Disbelievingly, I stared at Papa. If I had fallen, he'd have run to help me up. He'd have kissed me, held me, said a hundred loving things, and yet he did nothing for Vera but walk away. And only yesterday he'd been so nice to her. I looked at my aunt, almost holding my breath, wondering what she would do to Papa for being so heartless.

"After breakfast I'll go up," answered my aunt as she sat down again. "Another broken bone would spoil my appetite."

Momma rose to go upstairs and see to Vera. "Don't you dare!" ordered Papa. "You look tired enough to faint, and I want you well rested and pretty for the party tonight."

Shaken again, I got up and started for the stairs. Papa ordered me back, but I continued on, taking the steps three at a time. "I'm coming, Vera," I called.

Vera wasn't in her room lying on the floor with broken bones as I'd thought she'd be. I ran about, wondering where she could be. Then, to my utter amazement, I heard her singing in the First Audrina's bedroom.

Only a playroom, safe in my home,
Got no tears, no fears,
And nowhere else to roam,
'Cause my papa wants me always,
To stay home,
Safe in my playroom, safe in my home . . .

I thought I'd never heard such a pitiful tune, the sad way she sang it, as if she'd sell her soul to the devil to be me, and to be forced to sit in the chair I despised.

Reluctantly, I returned to the kitchen again, where an inexplicably jovial Papa was telling a grouchy Momma a party was indeed just the thing she needed to lift her spirits. "How's Vera?" Momma asked. I told her Vera was fine and not broken, though I didn't mention she was using the rocking chair and must have stolen that key from Papa's key ring.

"Didn't I tell you?" said Papa. "Lucky, as soon as

Audrina finishes her brunch the two of us are taking a stroll down to the river." He stood, and it seemed he deliberately tossed his linen napkin so it fell into his half-full coffee cup. Momma plucked his napkin from the cup and gave him an expressive you-have-again-proved-your-self-a-slob stare. But she didn't dare to reprimand him. It wouldn't have done any good. Papa did as he wanted and always would.

He led me by the hand to our back lawn, which gradually descended to the river. Its sparkling ripples made the day seem wondrously fine. He smiled at me and said, "Tomorrow's your ninth birthday, darling."

"Papa," I cried, staring at him, "how can tomorrow be my ninth birthday when I'm only seven today?"

Momentarily he seemed at a loss for words. As always when he lacked ready explanations, he caressed my hair, then lightly rubbed his curled fingers over my cheeks. "My sweet, haven't I told you many times that's why we don't send you to school? You are one of those rare individuals who has no sense of time at all." He spoke precisely, looking directly into my eyes as if to engrave his information. "We don't celebrate birthdays in our house because somehow it confuses your own special calendar. Two years ago, or one day short, you were seven years old."

What he said was impossible! Why hadn't he told me that I was eight years old and not seven? Was he deliberately trying to make me crazy? I put my hands over my ears to shut out anything else he had to say. My eyelids squeezed tightly together as I racked my brain to remember someone telling me I was eight years old. I couldn't remember anyone mentioning any age but seven.

"Audrina, honey, don't look so panicked. Don't try to remember. Just trust what Papa tells you. Tomorrow is your ninth birthday. Papa loves you, Momma loves you, and even shrew-tongue Ellie loves you if she'd dare to admit it. She can't because Vera is there, and Vera envies you. Vera could love you, too, if I showed her more affection. I'm going to try, really try to like that girl just so you won't have an enemy living in your own home."

I swallowed, feeling a sore throat coming on and tears filling my eyes. Something was weird about my life. No matter how many times Papa told me about my specialness, it wasn't natural to forget an entire year, it just couldn't be natural. I'd ask Arden. But then he'd know something awful was wrong with me and he wouldn't like me, either.

So it seemed I'd have to believe Papa. I told myself that I was only a child, and what difference did it make if I lost just one year in the process of growing up. And if time skipped past quicker than I could keep track of, what difference did it really make?

Sometimes unconscious fears tried to sneak out, whispering slyly, disturbing me, threatening my tentative acceptance. Inside my brain, colors were flashing and I felt the rocking motion of my body, to and fro, to and fro, singing voices whispering to me of birthday parties when I had been eight years old and I'd worn a white dress with ruffles tied round with a violet satin sash.

But what did rocking chair dreams mean, except that the First and Best Audrina had worn a ruffled white dress to her party. All those visions of birthday parties were her parties. Where could I go to find the truth? Who was there who was totally honest with me? There was no one who would tell me the truth because I might be hurt if they did.

Papa drew me down on the grassy slope beside him. The sun was high overhead and burning hot through my hair as I sat on and on with Papa. Every word he said washed clear images from my brain and replaced them with smeary blots. I watched the geese and the ducks that were using unseen paddle feet to swim like mad to where Momma liked to feed them. They had a fondness for eating her tulips and daffodils in the spring.

"Let's talk about what you dreamed last night," Papa said after we had been silent for a long time. "Last night I heard you moaning and groaning, and when I went to check on you, you were tossing in your bed, mumbling incoherently in your sleep."

Feeling panicky, I looked around to see a red-headed woodpecker working on one of our best old hickory trees. "Go 'way!" I cried. "Eat the worms on the camellia bushes!"

"Audrina," said Papa impatiently, "forget about the trees. The trees will be here long after you and I have come and gone. Tell me what you saw in the rocking chair."

If Papa believed in Mrs. Allismore's string-and-ring trick, it seemed only right that I could use the

same method to please him. I was about to speak and
tell him when I felt the hackles on my neck rise. Turning my head quickly, I glimpsed Vera in the room
where the rocking chair was. Still up there, still rocking. Let her rock on and on forever; there was no gift
but the one imagination concocted to please somebody who wanted magic in his life. And maybe in the
long run imagination was a special gift.

"Okay, darling. I'm not going to plead further. Just
tell me what you dreamed last night."

I spoke the name of the stock my pin had touched
on twice, and then twice again. Papa looked incredulous, then angry. Immediately from his reaction I
guessed I'd done the wrong thing.

"Audrina, did I ask you for a stock tip?" he asked
with annoyance. "No, I did not. I asked you to give
me your dreams. I'm trying to help you restore your
memory. Don't you realize yet that's why I put you in
the rocking chair? I've tried to make it seem your loss
of memory is natural, but it isn't. All I wanted you to
do was regain what you've forgotten."

I didn't believe him. I knew what he wanted. He
wanted me to turn into the First Audrina! That's why
he had all those books about black magic and psychic
powers hidden away in his study.

Pulling away, I stared back at the house again, terribly upset now. Back and forth Vera was still rocking.
Oh, God, suppose she had the only dream the chair
ever gave me? Would she scream? Would Papa go running to save her?

Or just suppose everything Papa had told me was

true, and there was a gift to be gained. Then, any second, she might replace me in his heart. Breathlessly I gushed, undecided no longer. "There I was, Papa, a grown-up woman, working in a huge place with business machines all around. They glowed, changed colors, talked in strange voices and sent messages through the air. I was up front instructing a large class how to use them. So that's why I thought—but, of course, I should have let you decide what it meant. The letters I told you were on all the machines, every last one, Papa."

IBM.

For a reward, his smile came tight and thin, though he did embrace me. "All right, you've tried to help me financially, but that's not what I wanted. Memories, Audrina, fill the holes in your brain with the *right* memories. We'll try the rocking chair again later and see if the next time doesn't skip the woods and put you down in the right place." I was about to cry, for I had had a funny dream about machines, and the pin had wanted to stop on those initials four times. "Don't cry, my love," he said, kissing me again. "I understand, and I might even put some money on that stock, even though it has had a thirty percent run-up and is due for a sell-off. Still," he went on thoughtfully, "it wouldn't hurt to wait for the profit-taking to end, and then buy in heavily before another climb. She is intuitive and her heart is pure even if—"

Jumping to my feet, I ran to escape his embarrassing ruminations. Now he was going to put money on that stock. What if it continued to go down after the profit-taking? Poor Momma was slaving in the kitchen, preparing for a stupid party she didn't need to have when she was feeling so rotten. I ran to a window where I could watch Papa still down by the river, standing now and skipping pebbles across the water as if he didn't have a care in the world.

Momma didn't say a word about tomorrow being my ninth birthday. Was that because tomorrow truly wasn't my birthday? I went to the closet under the back stairs and checked the newspapers. Tomorrow was September the ninth, and just like me, I forgot today was the eighth. Was reaching the age of nine really so meaningful? Yes, I decided as the day wore on and no one but Papa mentioned my birthday, reaching nine was dangerous.

The party began at nine-thirty, not long after I was sent to bed. The noise made by the crowd of twenty of Papa's best friends drifted up to me even though my room was far from the party rooms. I knew there were bankers down there, and lawyers, doctors and other affluent people with aspirations to become richer. They liked our parties; the food was elegant, the liquor plentiful and, the best thing of all, the moment Momma sat down to play the piano the party came alive. Because she was a musician, she drew other musicians who liked to perform with her, so that the doctors and lawyers would bring their teenage sons or daughters who knew how to play some musical instrument, with considerable skill. And together, with Momma as inspiration, they'd have a "jam session."

In my nightgown, on bare feet, I raced to peek

at her sitting on the piano bench. She was wearing a red silk gown that had a cowl neckline that drooped so low it showed more than Papa would approve. All the men gathered around the piano, leaning over Momma's shoulders, staring down into her bodice as they encouraged her to play on, play faster, put more jazz into what seemed to me jazzy enough. Her fingers flew; she bounced with the tempo that quickened. Smiling and laughing in response to whispers in her ear, Momma played with one hand and sipped the champagne her other hand held. She put down the empty glass, signaled a boy of about twenty to play his accordion, and they both began some wild version of a polka that no one could resist dancing to. According to Papa, Momma was all things to all people and true to no one, not even herself. If her audience wanted classical music, she gave them that; if they wanted popular ballads, she could give them those, too. If you asked her what kind of music she liked best, she'd answer, "I like all kinds." I thought it was wonderful to be so open-minded and so versatile. Aunt Ellsbeth didn't like any music that wasn't by Grieg.

From all the fun Momma seemed to be having, who would ever guess she'd complained all day about having to slave for people she didn't even like? "Really, Damian, you expect too much of me. I'm in my sixth month, really showing, and you want them to see me like this?"

"You're gorgeous and you know it, pregnant or not. You always look sensational when you put on your makeup and wear a bright color and smile."

"You told me this morning I looked awful." Fatigue had made her sound hoarse.

"And it worked, didn't it? You jumped out of bed, shampooed your hair, polished your nails, and I've never seen you look lovelier."

"Damian, Damian," my momma had whispered then, her voice choked with emotion, and then the door had banged shut. I'd stood alone in the hallway outside their bedroom, wondering what they did after Papa kicked the door.

All of the words exchanged between them echoed in my head as I watched Momma at the piano. She was so beautiful. My aunt looked dowdy in comparison in her print dress that seemed right for the kitchen but nowhere else.

I yelped from the pain of a pinch on my arm. There was Vera in her nightgown, and she was not supposed to come downstairs until Papa told her she could—and so far he hadn't. Vera never came near me that she didn't hurt me in some minor way. "Your mother is nothing but a big show-off," she whispered. "A woman as pregnant as she is shouldn't show herself." Yet, when I glanced at Vera, I saw admiration in her eyes as she, too, caught the rhythm of Momma's music.

"The First Audrina could play piano just like that," said Vera in my ear. "She could read music, too, and the watercolors she painted! You can't do anything in comparison."

"Neither can you!" I flared back, but I was hurt

again. "Good night, Vera. You'd better disappear when I do, or else Papa might see you and punish you again."

I headed back for my room. Halfway up the stairs, I looked back to see Vera still hiding behind the beaded portieres, clinging to them for balance as her feet shuffled in rhythm to the music; watching until the very end.

It wasn't until the noise below stopped that I was able to fall into a deep and dreamless sleep. It was my way to toss restlessly, and Vera's way to sleep soundly. I was wishing I had that knack when I drifted off, only to be awakened what seemed only seconds later. My parents were arguing violently.

No wonder Momma didn't like parties with Papa. Every time we had a party it ended this way. Lord, I prayed as I slipped out of bed, today is my ninth birthday and this isn't a good way for it to start. Please let it be like March and go out like a lamb.

Vera was already kneeling on the hall carpet, peeking through the keyhole. She held a cautioning finger before her lips and silently gestured for me to go away. I didn't like her spying on my parents and I refused to leave. Instead, I knelt beside her and tried to shove her away. Papa's strong voice came right through the solid oak door. "And in your condition, too, you danced like some cheap little tramp. You made a fool of yourself, Lucietta."

"Leave me alone, Damian!" cried Momma, as I must have heard her cry a hundred times or more. "You invite guests without telling me in advance. You go out and buy liquor we can't afford, and flowers, and champagne for them to drink, and even hand me a glass, and when I get drunk you become enraged. What am I supposed to do at a party? Sit around and watch you perform?"

"You never know how to do anything properly," Papa shouted. He had the kind of voice that could hurt your eardrums when he was angry, and a sweet soft voice to use when he wanted something from you. Why wasn't he considerate of Momma when she was so obviously in need of his understanding? Didn't he think at all of that little baby that might be hearing his rage?

Inside I was all aquiver, trembling with fear for Momma's health. Was this the way love went, on and off like an electric switch? I went back to my bedroom and pulled a down pillow over my ears, and still I could hear them fighting. Sickened, I didn't know what to do but get up again and go back to where Vera still leaned against the door. She, too, was trembling, but with suppressed laughter. Furious, I wanted to slap her.

"You flirted, Lucietta. Flirted and in your condition, too. You cuddled so close to that teenage piano player on the bench you seemed blended into one person. You jiggled! Your nipples could be seen."

"Shut up!" she yelled. My hands rose to cover my mouth. I wanted to scream out and stop them.

"Damian, you're a brute! An inconsiderate, selfish, contradictory boor. You want me to play, but you are enraged when you lose the spotlight. I've said it before, and I'll say it again and again: you have no talent but the ability to run your mouth! And you're jealous of mine."

Now she'd done it! He'd show her no mercy now. Slowly, slowly, as in a nightmare trance, I sank to my knees beside Vera. She allowed me to peek through the keyhole just in time to see his stinging slap wham against Momma's face. I cried out just as my mother did. Feeling her pain and humiliation as my own.

Vera started to laugh as she shoved me away and put her eye to the keyhole. "Audrina," she whispered, "he's taking off his belt. Now your mother is going to get what she deserves. And I'm glad, really glad! It's time he punished her—as he ought to punish you!"

Furiously I slapped at her, my rage as great as Papa's as I shoved her aside and clawed the door open. I fell into my parents' bedroom, tripping over Vera's sprawled form. Papa whirled around, shirtless, his trousers half unzipped. His face was a mask of rage. Momma was curled up on the bed, her arms hugged protectively over her protruding middle.

"What the hell are you two doing here?" roared Papa, throwing his belt to the floor and pointing to the door. "Get out! And don't you ever spy on us again!"

Jumping to my feet and trying to make my voice as powerful as his, I yelled, "Don't you dare hit my mother again, or use that belt to whip her! Don't you dare!"

He glared at me. His dark eyes were wild and wide. He reeked of liquor. As I glared back, my eyes wide and wild, too, he began to simmer down. He wiped his huge hand over his face, glanced at his reflection in a mirror and seemed shocked. "I'd never strike your mother, you should know that," he said weakly, as if afraid I'd seen, or ashamed that I'd seen, I didn't know which. Out in the hall Vera tittered. He spun around to yell, "How many times have I told you that this part of the house belongs to me? Get the hell out of here, Vera!"

"Oh, Papa, please don't yell at me. None of it was my fault. It was Audrina who came into my room and woke me out of a sound sleep and made me come with her. She's always spying through your keyhole, Papa, when she can't sleep."

His head snapped around. I could tell he considered me too honorable to spy. "Go to your room, Audrina," he ordered coldly. "And don't you ever spy on me again. I thought better of you than that. It may seem to you that I'm a brute, but that's only because I'm the only man in a house of women bent on destroying me. Even you try in your own way. Now, out! Both of you, out!"

"You won't hurt Momma?" I held my ground and waited for an answer, though he took a step forward.

"Of course I won't hurt Momma." Sarcasm was in his voice. "If I hit her and hurt her, then I'd have to pay her doctor's bills, wouldn't I? My son is inside her, and I am thinking of him."

Weakly my mother sat up to call me to her. Her arms opened as I approached. Her kisses felt wet on my face. "Do as your father says, darling. He won't hurt me. He's never really hurt me—in physical ways."

Undecided, I looked from her to Papa as he shoved Vera out of the room, delivering a hard slap to her bottom as he did. Then he turned to me. I, too, feared a slap, but he took me into his embrace. "I'm sorry I woke you up. When I drink too much I look in the mirrors and see a fool who doesn't know when to quit, and then I want to punish someone because I've failed myself."

I didn't understand any of that.

"Everything will be just fine. The party is over." There was a sob in his voice, pain in his eyes, shame, too. "Go back to bed and forget all you heard and saw here. I love you and I love your mother, and tonight has seen the last of my parties. No more, ever."

I lay on my bed torn with doubts about men, about marriage. I decided that night I'd never marry, not in one million years, not when all men could be like Papa, wonderful and terrible. Deceitful and lovable and cruel even when he loved, wielding the belt in private, screaming abuse, criticizing, stealing self-confidence and instilling self-loathing and a deep sense of shame for just being female.

Perhaps Aunt Ellsbeth was right. Men were king of the mountains, king of the woods, king of the home and office and everywhere—just because they were male.

The Nightmare in Daylight

That night when finally I fell into sleep I tossed and fretted and dreamed awful things, but I didn't dare whimper or scream for fear Papa would come flying into my room to question me.

From now on, no matter what went wrong in my life, I'd handle it all by myself. How could I forgive him even one slap on my mother's face?

Confusion was a daily state of mind for me, so why should I feel so depressed and disappointed by someone I loved when I'd known all along I could hate him, too? Baffled by my own contrariness, I somehow managed to slip into a light dream tortured by horrible visions of bony people ambling over a frail bridge into nowhere.

I willed myself to wake up and found tears had wet my pillow. I suspected the day would give me little pleasure, and the tears I'd cried without knowing would be tears for a very good reason.

Depression hung about me at dawn while I bathed, dressed and quietly crept down the stairs. The house was full of gloom; no sunlight came through the stained-glass windows. I didn't have to step over the colors, but I wished the colors back to make this day seem brighter and more ordinary. One glance out of a kitchen window showed me a murky dark sky that threatened rain. Morning mists hung heavy over the River Lyle. Distant foghorns sounded sad and mournful, and far away ships putting out to sea sent back melancholy goodbyes. The seagulls that always hung over the place where Momma fed the ducks and geese could be heard but not seen. Ghostly and muffled, their shrill, plaintive cries came to me and tickled goose bumps on my arms. On a day like this only awful things would happen.

Send out the sun, God, send out the light. It's my ninth birthday, God, and on this day the First and Best Audrina died in the woods.

I wanted the fog to lift, to tell me this birthday of mine was not foreboding terrible things ahead just because it was so dreary. I stood near the back stairs waiting to hear my mother's footfalls, or the sweet way she'd hum to herself as she dressed and moved about upstairs, her pretty satin mules clickety-clacking where the floors weren't covered by rugs. Hurry up and come down, Momma, I need to see you. She'd take away my fears.

I left the kitchen, which seemed so bleak without Momma moving around in there, and went into the formal dining room. All its twenty chairs were lined up along a huge rectangular table. That table made a wonderful dancing floor when no one was around, and often I took off my shoes to just slide up there.

But today the room was dreary and hardly a place for dancing. No one had pulled open the heavy green draperies to let in some light. Always Momma did that as soon as she reached the first floor. When I opened the draperies and looked around, the cheeriest room in the house still looked as grim as the others.

Somewhere there had to be a calendar to mark with a red circle this ninth birthday of mine. But I shouldn't want a red circle, for this had been *her* birthday, too. On this day she would have been eighteen years old. How young Momma must have been when she married Papa. Looking out the window, I saw the first few drops of rain begin to fall. Oh, dear God, did it always rain on September the ninth?

Work. Aunt Ellsbeth was always saying that when she was working she didn't have time to worry about anything. That's what I'd do. I'd fry the bacon, whip the eggs, make the omelettes, scrape the dishes after the meal, and Momma could sit and feel pleased about how well she'd trained me. If only Aunt Ellsbeth and Vera would keep their mouths shut.

I'd no sooner put the frying pan on the gas range, very intent on starting the bacon off in a cold pan so it wouldn't curl, when I was rudely shoved to one side. "What the devil do you think you're doing?" barked my aunt.

"Helping Momma."

Poor Aunt Ellsbeth couldn't cook worth a darn. Nobody wanted her in the kitchen unless she was there to scrub the floor or clean the windows.

"What nasty thoughts are in your head?" barked

my aunt, taking over the bacon. Right away she turned the heat up too high. She wouldn't listen if I told her she should keep the flames low.

I pulled out what I'd need for five place settings, watching my aunt as I did. A cup slipped from my hand and fell to break on the floor. I stood there frozen. It was Papa's favorite coffee mug. The only one he wanted to drink from. Now he'd have another reason to be angry with me.

My aunt threw me a disdainful glance. "Now look what you've done. You'd be a bigger help if you stayed out of the kitchen. That coffee mug was the last of a set given to your parents as a wedding gift. He's going to blow when he knows what you've done."

"What's idiot Audrina done this time?" asked Vera, limping into the kitchen, falling into a chair and putting her arms on the table so she could rest her head on them. "I'm still sleepy. This is the noisiest house; you can't ever get enough sleep."

Setting the table was the one thing I thought I could do correctly, and now my aunt was shouting something about using too many plates. "Three place settings, girl, that will be enough."

I turned to stare at her. "Why only three?"

She kept right on turning over the bacon. "Your mother's contractions began just before dawn. It seems all her children have to come just when I've finally fallen asleep."

"Do contractions mean Momma's baby is on the way?"

"Of course."

"But isn't the baby coming early?"

"That's the way it is sometimes. There's no way of predicting exactly when a baby will come. She's over six months, going on seven, so if the doctor can't stop the miscarriage, it has a chance to live anyway."

Oh, golly, I was hoping the baby would have plenty of time to be finished, with hair and little fingernails and toenails. "How long does it take for a baby to be born?" I asked timidly.

"No doubt it will take someone like Lucietta all day and most of tomorrow, knowing how she likes to make even the most simple and natural thing look very difficult and painful." Aunt Ellsbeth stretched her thin lips into a mean spinster smile. "Spoiled, all her life spoiled, just because she happened to be born prettier than most girls."

"Has Papa called to say Momma's having lots of pain? Did he say she was losing the baby?" I wanted to scream at her for saying so little, when it was my mother and my brother or sister involved. The heavy knot in my chest began to weigh more as it grew larger. The rain *was* forecasting trouble. The nightmare flitted in and out of my thoughts. Those bony people . . .

"Audrina is spoiled, too," Vera contributed, "and she isn't even the prettiest daughter."

I tried to swallow some awful stuff my aunt had thrown in a blender—a mixture she said would put meat on my gaunt bones and take the hollowness from my cheeks. Vera giggled when she said this.

The bacon was thrown down the garbage disposal, burned to such a dry crisp even my aunt wouldn't eat it. Grouchy and irritable, Vera complained about the omelettes my aunt had tried to make tasty. "Gee, it's sure going to be difficult to enjoy food now that Momma isn't here to cook the meals." Vera put great stress on Momma, just to watch her own mother wince. Aunt Ellsbeth tried to pretend she didn't hear the barb.

It was me who cleaned up the kitchen when my aunt went to watch TV, and me who swept the floor as Vera hurried off to finish dressing for school. As I polished the stove, I wondered if I was prettier than Vera, and if I was even half as beautiful as that First and Best Audrina had been. I pessimistically guessed I couldn't be from all the praise he gushed about her "radiant, transcendent, ethereal beauty."

"Now you stay home and out of the woods," warned my aunt from the other room when she heard the back door open. "It's raining. And the last thing your father said was to keep an eye on you and not let you wander off. If the rain stops, you can play in the backyard—but go no farther."

"What did he say about me?" asked Vera, all ready to hurry to where the school bus would pick her up. She wore a yellow rain slicker with a hood over her hair.

"Damian didn't mention you." How cold my aunt could make her voice when she wanted to. She didn't care much for her own bastard daughter. I smiled to myself, for it sounded so silly. Many a time I'd sneaked to peek at the television my aunt selfishly kept for her own viewing pleasure, and I knew those soap people were always having babies "out of wedlock."

"You can't trust Audrina when it comes to Arden Lowe," called Vera back hatefully. "You'd better lock the doors, bolt the windows or somehow she'll slip over to see him. You just wait and see, and sooner or later she's going to let him . . ."

"Let him what?" I asked, scowling at her.

"Vera," called my aunt, "not one more word out of you! Get out of here before you miss the bus."

Enviously I watched Vera stomp off toward the highway, making the water in every puddle splash. Just before she turned the bend, she looked my way and thumbed her nose. Vera disappeared, and still I stood on, thinking about Momma, hoping it wasn't hurting too much and that there wouldn't be a great loss of blood. All pain seemed to come with lots of blood, and lots of mental anguish, too. I already knew about that. Maybe that was the worst kind of pain, because nobody knew about it but you.

Why didn't Papa call home and talk to me? I wanted to know what was going on. I hung around the telephone so long that the rain went away, and the gloomy quiet house began to wear on my nerves.

When the rain ended, I walked down by the river where our backyard ended. In the weak sunlight under the pale, washed sky, I tossed pebbles into the river as I'd seen Papa do. A week without Momma's cooking was going to make me lose weight, and I was already skinny.

Papa didn't call all day long. I worried, fretted, paced the floor, went often to the windows. Vera trudged home, complaining she didn't like the vegetable stew Aunt Ellsbeth had prepared for dinner. Then I saw Arden come flying down our drive with a huge box fastened to his bike. I ran outside to meet him, afraid my aunt would report his visit to my father.

"Happy birthday!" he called, grinning as he left his bicycle and came running to me. "Haven't got but a second to stay—I've brought you something my mother made for you, and a little something from me, too."

Had I told him it was my birthday? I didn't think I had. I hadn't even known myself until yesterday. His eyes were warm and bright as I tore into the largest box. Inside was a wonderful violet dress with a white collar and cuffs. A small bouquet of silk violets was pinned at the neckline.

"Mom made it for you. She says she can measure anyone with her eyes. Do you like it? Do you think it will fit?"

Impulsively I threw my arms about him, so happy I wanted to cry. No one else had remembered my birthday. He seemed embarrassed and delighted with my reaction, then hastily handed me a smaller box. "It's nothing much, really, but you told me you had difficulty remembering and were keeping a dated journal. I looked everywhere to find you one to match the color of the dress Mom made you, but journals don't come in violet, so I bought you a white one with painted-on violets. And if you can slip over to our house around five, Mom's got a birthday cake all decorated just for you. If you can't come, I'll bring it to you."

I wiped my eyes and choked back my tears of gratitude. "Arden, the baby's coming today. My mother's been gone since before dawn, and we haven't heard one word. I'll come if Papa calls and tells me that Momma and the baby are okay. If he doesn't, I can't leave."

Gingerly, as if afraid I might scream or resist, he hugged me briefly, then let me go. "Don't look so worried. Babies are born every second of the day, millions of them. It's a natural thing. I'll bet your aunt forgot all about your birthday, didn't she?"

I nodded and ducked my head so he couldn't see the pain I felt. The pretty little diary he'd given me had a golden key to lock away my secrets. Oh, I had plenty of secrets, unknown even to me.

"I'll be waiting on the edge of the woods after I deliver the newspapers. I'll wait until the sun goes down, and if you don't show up, I'll bring your birthday cake here."

I couldn't let him do that. Papa would find out. "I'll come tomorrow for sure, and we can celebrate then. Thank Billie for this wonderful dress. I just love it. And thank you for the beautiful diary, it's just what I wanted. Don't wait at the edge of the woods. Terrible things happen in the woods, especially on this day. I don't want you there after dark."

The look he gave me seemed haunted, strange and full of something I didn't quite understand. "See you later, Audrina. I'm glad you're nine years old." Then he was gone and I was left feeling not so lonely and unhappy.

My aunt's dinner was so tasteless even she ate without much enthusiasm. Still Papa didn't call. "That's the kind of awful man he is," said Vera, "selfish and without regard for anyone's feelings but his own. I'll bet you right now he's in some bar, passing out cigars. And you can bet your bottom dollar, sweet Audrina, you won't be his favorite once he brings home that baby . . . girl or boy."

That night I flitted in and out of nightmares. I saw babies waiting to be born floating around on clouds, all of them crying to be my momma's child. I saw Papa use a huge baseball bat to knock all the girl babies out into the universe, and then he snatched one huge baby boy and called him "son." The brother I thought I wanted grew up overnight to be a giant who stepped on me — and Papa didn't even care.

I woke up to see my room pale and foggy. The sun was only a rosy glow on the horizon. Still tired, I fell again into dreams, and this time Momma came and hugged me, and told me I was the best and most wonderful daughter, and she'd be seeing me some day soon. "Be a good girl, obey Papa," she whispered as she kissed me. I didn't hear her words, only felt that's what she said. I watched her fade away, until she was part of one rose-colored cloud that shimmered like some of her fancy evening gowns.

Strange to wake up and know my parents weren't in our home. Even stranger to have dreamed about them. I never dreamed about anyone until they'd done something to hurt or disappoint me. I dreamed about Vera a great deal.

All that day was more of the same. My agitation grew so great I called Billie and told her to hold the birthday party, for Papa still hadn't called, and I had to be here when he did. "I understand, darlin'. Your cake will wait. And if need be, I'll make you a fresh one."

Around four my aunt called me into the kitchen. "Audrina," she began as she pulled out the blender, "your father telephoned while you were upstairs. The baby is born. She's been named Sylvia." Not once did she look my way, not once. I hated for people to talk to me without looking at me. Vera was busy for a change, peeling potatoes.

"Now you're in for it," she said with a mean grin. "He'll like her more than he does you, vacant head."

"Stop that, Vera! I don't ever want to hear you call Audrina that name again." It was the first time my aunt had ever defended me and I looked at her gratefully. "Vera, go upstairs and do your homework. Audrina can finish peeling the potatoes."

My gratitude vanished. Always I was doing Vera's chores. It was like having a wicked stepsister, and I was Cinderella. I glowered as Vera smirked. "I'm sorry to do that to you," said my aunt in what was for her a kind tone, "but I wanted to talk to you alone."

"Is Momma all right?" I asked cautiously.

"Audrina, I have more to tell you," said my aunt falteringly. Beyond the kitchen, I could see a lock of apricot-colored hair as Vera hid to eavesdrop.

"It's all right, Ellie," said Papa, who was just then coming into the kitchen from another doorway. He fell wearily into a chair. "I'll tell her in my own way."

He'd come so quickly and quietly out of nowhere that I stared at him as if at a stranger. I'd never seen him with so much beard stubble, never seen his clothes so rumpled. His eyes were red-rimmed and swollen, with dark circles underneath. He met my eyes briefly, then put his elbows on the table and bowed his head into his hands, covering his face as his shoulders trembled. Even more alarmed, I ran to him and tried to embrace him as he so often embraced me. "Papa, you look so tired." My heart seemed to have dropped into my shoes. Why was he trembling? Why did he hide his face? Was he so disappointed the baby was a girl that he just couldn't cope with the idea of another like me?

He shuddered before he lifted his head and lowered his hands and clenched them into fists. He struck the table several hard blows, making the vase of flowers topple over. Quickly my aunt was running to stand it upright again. She went for a sponge to mop up the water, as I ran to fill the vase with water again. "Papa, hurry! Tell me about Momma. It seems she's been gone a whole month."

His dark eyes were watery with unshed tears. He shook his head from side to side, with that same motion dogs used to throw off water. There was panic struggling to stay out of his eyes, and when he spoke I heard the heavy slowness of his words with dread. "Audrina, you're getting to be a big girl now." I stared at him, hating the way he'd begun. "Remember how you used to tell me about teatimes, and how Aunt Mercy Marie made life and death seem in a constant battle? Well, that's the way it is. Life and death are as much a part of our human experience as day and night, sleep and wakefulness. One is born, another dies. We lose, we gain. That's the only way you can look at life and stay sane."

"Papa," I sobbed, "don't you—"

"Oh, enough of this!" cried my aunt. "Damian, why don't you just come straight out and tell her? You can't always shield Audrina from the harshness of life. The longer you put it off, the harder it will be when finally she has to face up to the truth. Stop putting this daughter of yours into a world of fantasy."

He listened to her harsh words and her brusque, abrasive voice and looked at me regretfully. "I suppose you're right," he said with a sigh. One of those tears that glittered in his eyes slipped to the corner and trickled down his face. He reached to draw me into his arms, then lifted me onto his lap and cuddled me close against his chest. Then he had to clear his throat. "Sweetheart, this isn't easy for me to say. I've never had to give news like this to anyone, much less to the child of my heart. You may have heard in the past that your mother had a dreadful time delivering you."

Yes, yes, I had heard that before—but she'd had trouble with the First Audrina, too.

"She had an even worse time with Sylvia." He held me tighter, almost crushing my bones. "I think I explained to you some time ago how a baby comes through the mother's birth canal and out into the world." He hesitated, filling me with even more anxieties. "Poor Sylvia was caught in that canal—perhaps too long." Again he paused. My heart was beating so loud I could hear the thudding. Vera had stepped into the kitchen and was listening, too. Her dark, dark eyes seemed already knowing.

"Darling, hold fast to me now. I've got to say it, and you have to hear it. Your mother is gone, darling. Gone on to Heaven. . . . She died shortly before Sylvia was delivered."

I heard him say it, but I didn't believe him. No, no, it just couldn't be that way. I needed my mother. I had to have her, and God had already robbed Papa of his best Audrina. Was he so heartless he could hurt Papa again?

"No, Papa. My mother is too young and pretty to die." I sobbed. I was still a little girl. Who was going to help me grow up? I stared at him to see if he'd grin and wink and that would mean this was all some ugly trick dreamed up by Vera. I glanced at my aunt, who stood with her head bowed and her hands wringing out her apron that was spotlessly clean. Vera wore a peculiar look, as if she was just as stunned as I was. Papa's head bowed down on my shoulder then, and he was crying. Oh, he wouldn't cry if it weren't true!

I went numb inside and the tears in my brain flooded and washed my screams onto my face.

"I loved her, Audrina," sobbed my father. "Sometimes I wasn't all I should have been, but I loved her just the same. She gave up so much to marry me. I know that I kept her from the career she wanted, and I told myself daily that she wouldn't have amounted to anything, but she would have if I hadn't come into her life. She was turning down one man after another, determined to be a concert pianist, but I wouldn't let her refuse my proposal. I wanted her, and I got her, and then I told her she was only a mediocre musician, more to console myself than to console her. I wanted to be the center of her world, and she made me that. She gave so much of herself, trying to be all I wanted, even when what I wanted wasn't what she wanted. She taught herself how to please me, and for that I should have been grateful. I never told her I was grateful . . ." He broke then and had to dry his eyes and clear his throat again before he went on. "She gave me you, Audrina. She gave me other things, too, and now that it's too late, I realize I didn't appreciate her nearly enough."

Somewhere in my frozen panic I found visions of him standing above her wielding his belt. I heard her voice again, as she'd spoken on the last night I saw her alive. "He's never hurt me . . . physically." He must have hurt her emotionally. I felt rivers of hot tears flooding my eyes, melting my face. And why didn't Papa mention how she'd given him the best of all daughters, that dead daughter in the cemetery?

"No," Papa repeated, quaking all over and trying to drown me with his grief, "I didn't appreciate her nearly enough."

I was angry at Papa for starting that baby. Angry at God for taking her away. Angry at Vera and every-body else who had a mother when I didn't. Now I had only an aunt who hated me, and Vera wasn't one whit better, and Papa—what kind of love was his? Not the kind I really needed, the dependable, safe kind that never lied. Who would I have to confide in now? Not my aunt. She'd never want to hear what I needed to say, nor would she tell me all I needed to know about growing up. Who was there to teach me how to make a man love me? Papa's kind of love was so selfish and cruel.

Somehow I'd known since the moment I woke up this morning that something awful would happen. Something that was wise in me, all knowing, especially about tragedy, had prepared me in advance—and that's why I'd dreamed of her this morning. Perhaps she'd even come to me and said goodbye before she faded into a rose-colored cloud. Why did somebody always have to die on my birthday?

What if God took Papa, too, and I had only my aunt, who'd destroy the best in me?

"Where's the baby?" I asked in a thin, brittle voice.

"Darling, darling," began Papa, "it's going to be all right, really it is." Backing away and glaring at him, I could tell he was lying. His wide shoulders drooped. "All right, let me try to help you understand. Newborn babies are always frail. Especially those who are premature. Sylvia is very small, only three and a half pounds. She's not a finished baby like you were. No hair, no fingernails or toenails, so she needs a great deal of professional attention. It's not possible to give that to her here. She's in an incubator, Audrina, a heated glass case where the doctors and nurses can keep a vigilant watch over her. That's why Sylvia will have to stay in the hospital a while longer."

"I want to see her. You take me to the hospital so I can see her. Why, for all I know Momma might not have even had a baby but died from . . . from . . ." And so help me, as much as I wanted to tell him, I couldn't say he'd killed her.

"Sweetheart," he went on in his heavy flat voice, his dark eyes so tired, "Sylvia is a tiny, tiny baby. The nurses take care of her around the clock. They wear masks over their faces to keep her atmosphere sterile. Children your age carry many germs around; they wouldn't let you near her. She may not even live, so you must prepare yourself for her death, too."

Oh, God! If that happened, then Momma's death would be meaningless—if death could ever be meaningful. I told myself that Sylvia would live, for I was going to pray morning, noon and night until the day she came home to me and I'd be her mother.

"So little to have caused so much trouble and pain," murmured Papa wearily, once more putting his head onto his folded arms on the table. He closed his eyes and seemed to sleep. Aunt Ellsbeth hovered over him, seemingly wanting to console him and not knowing how to do it. Once she even started to touch his face, but quickly she snatched her hand away, and only her eyes lingered to caress him.

She was blaming him just as I was, I thought, never thinking perhaps Momma just wasn't built right to bear babies easily. Then, as if Papa felt my aunt hovering over him, he lifted his head and stared straight at her with some unspoken challenge in his tired but steadfast gaze.

"I hope you can afford to hire a nurse to take care of Sylvia when she comes home," said Aunt Ellsbeth in a flat, uncaring tone. Her dark eyes confronted him, challenged him right back. "If you think I'm going to throw away the rest of my life staying on here and taking care of two children who aren't mine—then think again, Damian Adare."

For long moments their dark eyes fought in a silent battle of wills, and only when her eyes dropped first did Papa answer. "You'll stay," he said tonelessly. She looked up then, meeting his steady gaze squarely, defiantly. "Yes, Ellie, you won't leave because you'll be mistress of Whitefern and all it contains."

Did he put some special emphasis on *all?* Perhaps it was only my imagination. And I did have a lively one, even at that time when I was in shock.

Vera slipped into my bedroom that night while I cried to whisper in my ear that Papa could have saved my mother's life if he hadn't wanted the baby. "But he didn't love your mother enough," she went on cruelly. "He wanted that baby he was positive would be his son. You can bet your bottom dollar if he'd guessed it would be only another girl like you, he would have told the doctors to let the baby go and save your mother."

"I don't believe you," I sobbed. "Papa didn't tell me there was any choice to make."

"Because he didn't want you to know. You see, he didn't even tell you your mother had a bad heart, and that's why she lay around so much on that purple sofa and on her bed. That's why she was always tired.

After you were born, her doctor told them that she shouldn't have another baby. So when Sylvia was caught in what your father calls the birth canal, he could have told the doctors to go ahead and save your mother's life and forget the baby. But he wanted that baby. He wanted a boy. All men want a son. That's why your mother is lying right this moment on a hard, cold slab in a huge refrigerator in the hospital morgue. And tomorrow morning early they will open the drawer and pull her out, and transfer her remains to a mortuary, where men will come and draw out all of her blood. They'll sew her lips and eyelids together so they won't open during the viewing of the deceased—and they will even stuff cotton into—"

"Vera!" roared my father, striding into the room and seizing her by her hair. "How dare you come into my daughter's room and fill her head with awful tales. What kind of sick mind do you have? What kind?"

It rained the day of my mother's funeral. It had been raining intermittently for three days. Our small family grouped under a drab canopy. The drizzle misted and ran in rivulets to drop on my mother's casket covered with a huge spray of red roses. Standing at the head of that casket was a cross of white roses with a violet ribbon that bore my name in gold. "To Momma, from your loving daughter, Audrina," it read. "Papa," I whispered, tugging on his sleeve, "who sent that cross for me?"

"I did," he whispered back. "The red roses that she loved best are from me, but I thought it more appropriate for white roses to represent a child's love for her mother. Our city friends sent all the other flowers."

I'd never seen so many beautiful flowers gathered together in such a dismal place. Around us somber-clothed people crowded with sorrowful faces, and still I felt so alone, even though I clung to Papa with one arm, and Arden on the other side kept tight hold of my hand.

"Dear friends," began the minister of the church we attended every Sunday, "we are gathered together on this rainy day to pay our last respects to a dear and beloved member of our society. A beautiful and talented lady who could light up a day like this with the sunshine of her presence. She graced our lives and made them better. Because she lived we are made richer. Because she was generous there are children in the village of Whitefern who had toys and new clothes under their Christmas trees when there would have been none. There was food on the tables of the poor because this lady cared . . ." On and on I heard of all the good deeds my mother had done. Never had she hinted that she contributed to any of the many charities the church sponsored.

And so many times my aunt had called my mother selfish and spoiled when she'd always been giving and wearing her old clothes she made look new. The wind began to blow, and I swear it felt like snow. Cold, I felt so cold. Clinging closer to Papa I squeezed hard on his gloved hand that gripped mine. I heard words then that I had known that minister would say sooner or later, even though this was my first funeral: "Yea, though I walk through the valley of the shadow of death, I will fear no evil, for thou art with me . . ."

It seemed I stood there forever with the rain coming down hard and splashing in the puddles it made. Behind my eyes I pictured my mother singing in her clear, soprano voice, "I come to the garden alone . . . while the dew is still on the roses . . ." and now I'd never hear her sing or play anything again.

Now that hydraulic lift was going to pick up her casket and lower her into the hole. I'd never see her again. "Papa!" I wailed, letting go of Arden and turning to press my face against his jacket front. "Don't let them put Momma down in that wet hole. Let's put her in one of those little houses made of marble."

How sad he looked. "I can't afford a marble mausoleum," he whispered back, telling me not to make a spectacle of myself. "But when we make it rich, we'll have a fine one designed, a temple for your mother—are you listening, Audrina?"

No, I wasn't listening with both ears. My mind was busy with thoughts as I fixed my eyes on the tombstone of the First and Best Audrina. Why weren't they putting my mother beside her? I asked Papa why. His square chin thrust forth. "I want to lie when I am dead between my wife and my daughter."

"Where will I lie, Papa?" I asked with pain in my heart that must have shone from my eyes. Even in death I didn't really belong anywhere.

"You'll know your place sooner or later," he answered in a tight voice. "Say no more, Audrina. The villagers are staring at you."

What he said made me gaze around at the White-fern villagers, who never came to call, who never spoke or waved when we drove through their streets. They hated us for too many reasons, said my father, even though none of what had been done in the past was our doing. Yet they came to see my mother buried. Were they the poor she'd fed and clothed and donated money to? If so, why weren't they crying, too? Still, I swallowed my tears, straightened my spine, raised my head in imitation of Papa and knew Momma would approve, wanting me to be brave and strong. "Cultured people never show their feelings; they save them for when they are alone."

Finally the funeral was over. The people drifted away to leave only our family ready to ride home in Papa's car. "I'm going to New York," I said to Papa as he held open the front passenger door for me to get in. "I've decided I'm going to be a concert pianist like Momma wanted to be. There's nothing, absolutely nothing that you can do to stop me."

Arden was right behind me, ready to climb into our car, too, and sit with Vera and my aunt in the backseat. "You don't know how to play the piano," Papa replied harshly. "When your mother was your age she'd been playing for years. You have not once put your hands on the keyboard. That surely indicates you are not drawn to music."

"Neither was she, Papa. She told me her parents forced her to take music lessons, until eventually she caught on. Then she began to like it very much. I'll like music, too, once I know how to play."

"Give Audrina her chance," said Arden, who'd clung to my other hand during the funeral. I was hurt because Billie hadn't come to see my mother buried.

"You stay out of this, young man," growled Papa, throwing Arden a hateful, mean look. "You're only a child, Audrina, and you don't know yet what's right for you. You have other gifts, gifts far more important than banging on the ivories."

I didn't believe for a minute that he really regretted making Momma only a wife and mother. Nor did I believe he'd let me escape him—but I was going to give it a try. I'd accomplish everything my mother had desired for herself when she was young and full of dreams. I'd make her dreams come true, rather than sitting on the rocking chair to make Papa's dreams come true.

"It's a foolish ambition," began Papa, still glaring at Arden, as if he hoped he'd drop dead and never bother me again.

"Now, wait a minute, Mr. Adare. Stop putting Audrina down. It's not a foolish ambition to want to fulfill her mother's dreams. Audrina is just the sensitive, feeling kind of person who'd make a great musician. And I know just the right teacher. His name is—"

"I don't want to hear his name!" stormed Papa. "Are you going to pay for her lessons, boy? For damned if I will. My wife's father spent a fortune, thinking his daughter would become world famous, and she failed to follow through."

Why, he was forgetting all he'd said the day Momma died. He didn't have any regrets! None at all!

"Because she married you, Papa!" I raged loud enough for the people still in the cemetery to turn their heads and stare our way. I blanched from their interested stares and moved my eyes to where that slender white headstone stood stark against the stormy sky. How disquieting to see your own name on a headstone.

"This is not the place to discuss careers," said Papa.

Once more he addressed Arden. "And you, young man, can stay out of my daughter's life from this day forward. She doesn't need you, or your advice."

"See you later," called Arden, waving to me and, in his own way, showing his defiance.

"That boy means nothing but trouble," grumbled Papa. Somehow or other, Vera had climbed over the backseat and sat between me and Papa, making him even more angry as she waved frantically to Arden when we passed him by.

Now that Momma was gone the house seemed empty, without a real heart, and Papa seemed to forget the rocking chair. It occurred to me one restless night that if Papa thought I could contact the First and Best Audrina by rocking and singing, perhaps I could communicate with Momma by doing the same thing. I wouldn't scream if I saw my mother again. The thought kept me from falling asleep. Did I dare steal into that room and rock all alone, without Papa in the hall outside? Yes, I had to grow up. Somebody had to teach me how to, and Momma surely would know her mistakes and tell me how to avoid them.

Silently I tiptoed down the hall, past Vera's room, where I could hear her radio playing. In the playroom I lit one dim lamp before I closed the door and looked around. It was not nearly so clean as it had been before Momma died. Aunt Ellsbeth said she had too much to do if she had to cook and clean and do the laundry as well. The few spiders that had scurried away to hide from Momma had reproduced and were clinging to the ceiling. Some were spinning webs between the lilies of the rocking chair. Feeling repulsed, I went to one of the two armoires and reached inside to find a baby dress. I yanked it off a hanger and dusted the rocking chair, then used the baby dress to shield my shoe before I squashed each spider dead. It was a messy, gruesome thing I'd never done before. Already I was growing stronger.

Trembling and weak, I sat gingerly in the chair, ready to jump out if anything bad happened. The house was so quiet I heard myself breathing. Relax, I had to relax. I had to become the empty pitcher that would fill with peace and contentment, and then Momma could come to me. As long as I thought of Momma and not that other Audrina, the boys in the woods wouldn't come.

It was one of Momma's songs I chose to sing.

> . . . and he walks with me,
> and he talks with me,
> and he tells me I am his own . . .

For the first time since Papa had forced me into this chair, it didn't terrify me, for Momma was waiting, as if she'd known I'd do this. Behind my closed lids I saw her, about nineteen, running in the fields of spring flowers, and I was a baby in her arms. I knew it was me and not the First Audrina, for around that little girl's neck was my birthstone ring on a golden chain. Then I was seeing Momma helping me tie my sash, teaching me how to form bows. Then, much to my surprise, she had me beside her on the piano bench and was showing me how to play the scales. I was older this time, and the ring once worn on a chain was on my index finger.

I came back from the playroom terribly excited. Nothing terrible had happened. And what was more, I'd found out a secret. A lost memory had filled one hole in my brain. Unknown to Papa, Momma had given me a few piano lessons.

That knowledge I carried back to my bed, hugged tight in my heart, for now I knew for certain. It had been my mother's desire to see me take her place, and find the career love had stolen from her.

PART 2

Music Begins Again

Life became very different in our house after Momma's death. I no longer went into the cupola to find peace and solitude. I sat in the once-dreaded rocking chair, where I could feel that Momma was near. Because life was opening up for me more and more, I paid little attention to Vera, who had difficulty climbing the stairs. When it rained she limped worse than when it was dry. Still, I couldn't help but notice she was beginning to be very concerned about her appearance. She washed her hair every day, curled it, polished her nails so often it seemed the house smelled constantly of polish remover. She pressed her slips, her dresses, and sometimes even her sweaters. Even her voice changed. She tried to speak softly and not shrilly as she used to do. I realized in many ways Vera was trying earnestly to imitate my mother's many charms—when I thought they belonged to me alone.

The fall days that had seen the last of my mother soon shortened into winter. Thanksgiving and Christmas were bleak celebrations that made my heart ache for Papa and me. Even Vera looked sad when she stared at Momma's empty chair at the foot of the table. When Papa was working I was alone in a house of enemies, a shadow of what I used to be when my mother lived. I clung to her memory desperately, trying to keep her image sharp in the vagueness of my nebulous memory. Never did I want anything about my mother to sink into those bottomless holes in my brain where all those awful forgotten memories struggled to reveal themselves.

Papa kept me almost a prisoner in our home, clinging to me with a kind of desperation that made me pity him, love him, hate him . . . and need him, too. I wasn't supposed to be seeing Arden at all, but quite frequently I managed to slip away to the cottage in the woods.

Whenever I had the chance, I was at the grand piano trying to figure out how to place my hands, how to make a tune come magically from the keys. For hours and hours I banged away before I began to sense the piano resented the sour, ugly noises I made. I couldn't play. Even if Momma had tried to teach me a long time ago, I hadn't inherited any of her talent, any more than I had inherited talent from the First and Best Audrina. Not gifted, not gifted, I went around tormenting myself.

"Audrina," Arden comforted me one day after I complained to him that I wasn't gifted, "no one magically, automatically knows how to play."

"Listen," I said, "I'll tell Papa I just have to have piano lessons. He'll pay for them if I plead hard enough."

"No doubt," he answered, looking away uneasily.

Then, hand in hand, we walked toward his cottage. Much to my disappointment, Billie stayed at the window but still didn't invite me inside the cottage. Arden and I sat on the back porch and talked to her through the open window. Flies could easily enter her house, and that would have driven my aunt crazy. Billie didn't seem worried about flies, but she did seem happy to see me again.

That very evening I approached Papa about music lessons. "I've heard you banging. If ever anyone needed lessons, it's you. Of course, your mother would have been thrilled. I'm thrilled, too." I couldn't believe he'd changed his mind so completely. He seemed lonely, bored, making me step closer to put my arms about him. Maybe, after all, Papa was going to try to let me be happy.

"I'm sorry for all the ugly things I said after Momma died, Papa. I don't hate you, or blame you for her death. If only you'd bring Sylvia home I'd feel she didn't die for nothing. Please bring Sylvia home soon."

"My darling," he said, looking far away, "I will. As soon as the doctors give the word, you'll have your baby sister."

I told myself that night that perhaps God did know what he was doing when he took away mothers and gave fathers a new daughter. Perhaps he had a good reason for doing what he did. Even if it did rob me of a mother I desperately needed, Sylvia wouldn't miss her because she'd have me and wouldn't know any better.

* * *

It was midsummer before the music teacher Arden knew came back from a long stay in New York City. Finally, one wonderful day Arden put me on the handlebars of his bike and rode me into Whitefern Village to meet Lamar Rensdale. He was tall and very thin, with a high, broad brow and wild, curly, chocolate-brown hair. His eye color matched his hair color exactly. He looked me up and down approvingly, smiled, then led me to his piano and asked me to demonstrate what I already knew. "Just fool around, like you said you've been doing," he said, standing behind my shoulder as Arden sat down to smile encouragingly.

"Not as bad as you told me," said Mr. Rensdale. "Your hands are small, but you can scale an octave. Did your mother play exceptionally well?"

That's the way it began. Of course, Papa knew that it was Arden who rode me to and from the village, but he didn't object. "But don't you play with him in the woods. You stay in view of his mother at all times. You are never to be alone with him. Never. You hear?"

"Now, listen here, Papa," I began, facing him squarely and struggling not to sound weak. "Arden is not the trashy, low-class kind of boy you think he is. We don't meet in the woods, but on the rim. His mother sits in the window and talks to us. We're seldom out of her sight. And she's so beautiful, Papa, really she is. Her hair is dark like yours, and her eyes are like Elizabeth Taylor's. Only Billie's eyes are even prettier. And you've always said no one had eyes prettier than Elizabeth Taylor's."

"Isn't that nice?" he said cynically, as if he didn't

believe any neighborhood woman could be as beautiful as a movie star. "Nobody is as beautiful as Elizabeth Taylor but Elizabeth Taylor. People are individuals, Audrina. Unique, each one of us. A miracle, each one of us—never to be duplicated, though this old world of ours may spin around another five to ten billion years. There will never be another Elizabeth Taylor, another Lucietta Lana Whitefern Adare, another you or another me. That's exactly why *you* are so special to me. If ever I am lucky enough to meet a woman as beautiful as your mother, and as warm and loving, then I will fall down on my knees and thank God. I may never find another like her, and I'm lonely, Audrina, so lonely."

He was lonely. It showed in his shadowed eyes, in his loss of appetite. "Papa, Billie is really beautiful. I haven't exaggerated."

"I don't care what she looks like," he said despondently. "I'm through with wives and married life. I'm devoting all my energies to taking care of you."

Oh, I didn't want him to devote all his energies to taking care of me! That meant he'd never give me any freedom. And that meant he'd spend all his time trying to turn me into the First and Best Audrina. And if he really believed there was only one of each person, why did he always want me to become *her?*

I stood before him, his hands still on my waist, and I couldn't speak up and say more. I could only nod and feel confusion whirling like a maelstrom in my brain.

Since Arden rode off every day to the village, I was

allowed five weekday lessons, which made me think I'd soon make up for lost time. For one solid hour I stayed with Lamar Rensdale and really tried to retain all he taught. According to Mr. Rensdale, I was an exceptional student with great natural ability. I wanted to believe he was telling the truth, not just flattering me just to keep me coming back and paying his fees. Arden would hurry back from delivering his evening newspapers to pick me up when my lessons were over.

Late one night eight months after Momma's death, I stole downstairs and again practiced on Momma's grand piano. Its tone was so wonderful, so true, much better than the cheap piano my teacher used. Before my music lessons I hadn't even noticed it had a tone. As I sat there in the dead of night playing my simple little piece, I closed my eyes and pretended I was Momma, and my fingers were as skilled as hers were, and I could pour into them all the nuances that she had. But it didn't sound wonderful. My music didn't send chills down my spine as hers had. Discouraged, I opened my eyes and decided I'd better keep a close eye on the music and not try to improvise. That's when I heard a small sound behind me. I whirled to confront Vera standing in the doorway. She smiled at me archly, making me squirm.

"You sure are wrapped up in music all of a sudden," she said. "What's he like, your Mr. Rensdale?"

"He's nice."

"I don't mean that, stupid. I heard the girls at my school say he's very young, handsome and sexy—and a bachelor."

Uneasily, I fidgeted. "I guess he is all of that, but he's too old for you, Vera. He wouldn't look at a kid like you."

"Nobody is too old for me—but everybody will be too old for you, sweet Audrina. By the time you escape Papa, you'll be creaky in the joints and wearing glasses to match your gray hair."

The worst of this was I knew every word she said was true. Papa was latching onto me more and more with each passing day. In all ways but bedroom ones, he was making me his wife. In fact, I listened to his stock market talk with far more tolerance and understanding than Momma ever had, and my aunt had no patience with that sort of "boring talk."

"I'm gonna make Papa give me music lessons, too," stated Vera, glaring hard at me, and I knew she'd give me hell if she didn't have her way.

The very next morning Vera was dressed in her most becoming clothes. Her strange, bright orange hair somehow flattered her very pale face, and her dark eyes were truly shocking. "You do everything for Audrina, and nothing at all for me," she said to Papa. "And it's my mother who cooks your meals and cleans your house and washes and irons, and you don't pay her anything. I want to study music, too. I'm every bit as sensitive and talented as Audrina."

He stared at her pale face until she flushed and turned half sideways, as she always did when she had something to conceal. "I need some beauty in my life, too," she said plaintively, casting down her dark eyes and tugging on a length of her apricot hair.

"Once a week for you," he said grimly. "You go to school and have lessons to learn. Audrina can have one class a day to keep her idle mind out of trouble." I thought surely Vera would object to this unbalanced arrangement, but oddly enough, she seemed satisfied.

I took Vera with me on Friday to introduce her to Mr. Rensdale. "Why, beauty must truly run in the Whitefern family, just as everyone in the village says," he said as he held out his hand and smiled. "I don't think I've ever met two prettier sisters."

It seemed to me Vera's fingers gripped his hand so that even when he wanted to stop shaking hands, she wouldn't let go. "Oh, I'm not nearly as pretty as Audrina," said Vera in a shy, small voice, fluttering her mascaraed eyelashes. "I only hope I'm half as talented."

I had to stare, really stare. This girl talking to Mr. Rensdale wasn't the Vera I knew. He liked her, I could tell that, and he was grateful for another student, especially one who flattered him and couldn't stop staring at him. Whenever she could, she was picking lint from his suit or brushing back that lock of hair that kept falling on his forehead.

On the way home she confided all she knew about him from her school friends. "He's very poor, a struggling artist, they say. I've heard he composes music in his spare time and hopes to sell his songs to some Broadway producer."

"I hope he does."

"You don't hope it nearly as much as I do," she said fervently.

* * *

The months passed so swiftly by without Sylvia coming home that I grew more and more apprehensive about my unseen little sister. I knew my father had taken my aunt to visit her several times, so she truly did exist, but not once did Papa allow me to go with him. He took me to the movies, to the zoo and, of course, to the First Audrina's grave, but Sylvia was still out of bounds.

Papa refused to bring Sylvia home no matter how much I pleaded. It was over a year now since my mother had died and Sylvia had been born.

"Surely she's weighing over five pounds by this time?"

"Yes, she weighs a bit more each time I see her." He said that reluctantly, as if he wished she didn't.

"Papa, she's not blind, without arms or legs— everything is there, isn't it?"

"Yes," he said in a heavy voice, "she's got the right parts where they should be, and all four limbs, same female equipment you have. But she's still not strong enough," Papa explained for the zillionth time. "She's not exactly normal, Audrina. But don't ask for more details until I'm ready to give them."

My thoughts about Sylvia kept me from feeling good. I longed for her as I dusted and pushed the vacuum. Vera couldn't vacuum because it made her short leg ache. She couldn't dust because she had little control of her hands and she dropped what she picked up. That also excused her from setting or clearing the table. I did every one of her chores. I even made all the beds, which was the one duty my aunt insisted Vera do. Perhaps because she was grateful, Vera seemed to like me more. Trustingly, I tried to treat her as a friend. "How's your music proceeding? I never hear you practicing like I do."

"That's because I practice at Lamar's," she said with a small insinuating smile. "I told him you wouldn't let me use your mother's piano, and he believed me." She giggled as I frowned and started to speak. "He's so handsome he sends chills over me."

"I guess he is, if you like his type."

"Not your type, huh? I think he's exceptionally handsome. He's told me all about himself, too. I'll bet he didn't tell you anything. He's twenty-five years old and graduated from the Juilliard School of Music. Right now he's composing a musical score for some play he's writing, too. He's sure he'll sell it to a producer he met when he lived in New York." She pressed forward to whisper. "I'm hoping and praying he does sell his musical and he'll take me with him."

"Oh, Vera, Papa would never let you go with him. You're too young."

"It's none of Papa's damn business what I do, is it? He's not my father and he doesn't own me like he owns you. And don't you dare tell him I've got designs on Lamar Rensdale. We're just as good as sisters . . . aren't we?" I needed her friendship and gladly promised not to tell Papa anything.

Wishes Come True

It was spring again. Momma had been dead for more than a year and a half. She was gone but far from forgotten. I pored over her gardening books and taught myself to care for her roses. Each rose petal reminded me of Momma with her creamy skin, her glorious hair, her rosy cheeks. In the backyard my Aunt Ellsbeth tended the onions, the cabbages, radishes, cucumbers and everything else she grew to eat. Things that grew and couldn't be eaten were valueless to my aunt.

Vera was sometimes hateful to me, sometimes nice to me. I didn't trust her even when I wanted to. Now that Vera had claimed the rocking chair, I avoided it as I had before, though Papa believed I still rocked in it, believed sooner or later the gift it had would be mine.

"How old did you say you were?" asked Mr. Rensdale one day after he'd explained again how I had to "feel" the music as well as learn to strike the right keys. For some odd reason tears began to streak my face, when long ago I'd learned to accept my unique plight.

"I don't know," I wailed. "No one tells me the truth. I've got a smeary memory full of half-seen images that whisper I might have gone to school, yet my father and my aunt say I never have. Sometimes I think I'm crazy and that's why they don't send me to school now."

He had a graceful way of rising, like a ribbon unfolding. Slowly he came to stand behind me. His hands, much smaller than my papa's, caressed my hair and then my back. "Go on, don't stop. I'd like to hear more of what goes on in your house. You confound me in so many ways, Audrina. You are so young, and so old. I look at you sometimes and see someone haunted. I'd like to take away that look. Let me help."

Just the tender way he spoke made me trust him, and out it all came, like a river bursting through the dam. All that confounded *me* came gushing out breathlessly, including Papa's insistence that I sit in that rocking chair and "catch" the gift that had once belonged to my dead sister. "I hate having her name! Why didn't they give me my own name?"

He made some compassionate sound. "Audrina is a beautiful name, and so right for you. Don't blame your parents for trying to hold on to what must have been an exceptional girl. Accept the fact that you, too, are exceptional, and maybe even more so . . ." But I thought I heard a something in his voice that said he knew more about me than I knew about me, and he pitied me, and wanted most of all to shield me from whatever it was I wasn't supposed to know. And it was that one thing I didn't know that I *had* to know.

Then, before I knew what to expect, he had his fingers under my chin and was looking deep into my eyes. It was strange to be so close to an adult man who wasn't my father.

I pulled away from him, a mixture of emotions stirring me into panic. I liked him, and yet I didn't want him to look at me in the way he was looking. I remembered Papa's warning about being alone with boys and men as flashing visions of the rainy day in the woods dazzled my eyes, making him seem a smeary vision of the past, too.

"What's wrong, Audrina?" he asked. "I didn't mean to frighten you. I just wanted to reassure you. You're not crazy, you're quite wonderful in your own special way. There's passion in your music and in your eyes, too, when you lower your guard. Nature is going to wake you up one day, Audrina; then the sleeping beauty inside you will come into her own. Don't smother her, Audrina. Let her come out. Give her a chance to set you free and your dead sister will haunt you no more."

Filling with hope, I stared at him pleadingly, unable to voice my needs. Still, he understood. "Audrina, if you want to go to school, I'll find a way to see that you go. It's against the state law to keep an underage child home unless that child is mentally or physically unable to attend. I'll talk to your father or your aunt . . . and you'll go to school, I promise."

I believed him. It was in his chocolate-brown eyes, he meant what he said. I know my eyes lit up with gratitude for Lamar Rensdale, who swore the very next day he'd visit my aunt. I warned him my father wasn't likely to listen to him.

*   *   *

Arden, Vera and I swam in the river that summer, fished and learned how to sail the small boat Papa had bought. Each month saw Papa just a little richer. Now he was making plans to fix up the house and restore it to its former grandeur. He talked so much about it without doing anything that I feared he never would. Anyway, it didn't matter now, for Momma was dead.

My aunt was not as grouchy as she had been; in fact, I often saw her looking rather happy. Papa no longer made sarcastic, cruel remarks about her long face and her skinny figure. He even complimented her new hairstyle and the makeup she'd begun to wear.

Papa still wouldn't tell me why he couldn't bring Sylvia home. I saved money from the allowance he gave me to buy Sylvia rattles and teething rings, but he never brought her home. Now she was too old for those things. He told me the hospital wouldn't let her have her own toys. I still didn't understand what was wrong with Sylvia.

Day by day Arden was growing taller. He was fifteen now, but seemed much older. He was beginning to plan for his future. "Now, please don't think this silly," he began in a tentative way, "but ever since I was a kid I've wanted to be an architect. At night I dream of the cities I'll build, functional and beautiful, too. I want to plan the landscaping, have trees in the middle of town. I'd make the highways multilevel so they won't take up so much ground space." He smiled at me. "Audrina, just you wait and see the kind of cities I build."

I wanted for Arden what he wanted for himself,

and many times I'd wondered why he bothered with me when so many older girls must have attracted his eyes. Why did he give me the feeling sometimes he was duty-bound to me and no other?

Arden had up days, and a few down days. He liked being outdoors more than he liked being in, and I told myself time and time again that's why we never went into his house. And Billie must be just the opposite, for she never came outside. In all the time I'd known Billie and Arden, not once had she invited me into their home. Of course, I couldn't invite Arden into my home, either, because of Papa, and maybe they were just retaliating. Vera often teased and said Billie didn't think I was good enough for her son, and not good enough for her house, either.

At the edge of the woods Arden and I paused to say goodbye. As the sun sank low over the horizon, Whitefern loomed up dark and lonely against a sky that was purple and shot through with crimson and orange. "What kind of sky is that?" I asked in a small whisper, holding tighter to his hand.

"A sailor's sky," he said in a low voice. "Signaling a better day tomorrow."

How like Arden to say that, even if it wasn't so. I looked from the house to the drive, and then I stared off in the direction of the family cemetery. I had to clear my throat before I could ask, "Arden . . . just how long have you known me?"

Why did he let go of my hand, blush and turn away? Was that such an awful question? Was I convincing him with such a question that I was truly crazy?

"Audrina," he said at long last, in the tightest of all possible voices, "I met you first when you said you were seven."

That wasn't the answer I wanted.

"Hey, stop frowning. Run on home so I can see you enter safely before I go."

From the doorway I looked back to see him waiting there. I waved, then waited for him to wave back. Reluctantly, I entered the gloominess of Whitefern.

Time had slowed down, and August really dragged. The sultry, sticky days made me wish for a vacation where it was cool, but we never went anywhere. Inside the house the high ceilings made it cooler than outside, but the dimness of the rooms made the stained-glass colors too brilliant, and the colors still tinkled the wind chimes that still tried to whisper secrets.

"Papa," I said in September when Vera was going back to school, "is Vera three years or four years older than me?"

"She's three, almost four years older," he said without thought, then gave me a strange look. "What age does she tell you she is?"

"It doesn't matter what she tells me, for she lies all the time, but she tells Arden she's older."

"Vera is fourteen," said Papa indifferently. "Her birthday is November the twelfth."

I marked that down as possibly true, knowing that birthdays in our house just didn't happen normally.

Knowing, too, that First Audrina's never-never party had spoiled all birthdays for everyone.

I did remember my eleventh birthday, for Arden gave me that piece of pink quartz he'd had made into a rose. It hung around my neck on a slender gold chain and made me feel very special. No one at my house gave me anything for my birthday—or even wished me a happy birthday.

I was still using my string-tied-to-the-ring trick and giving Papa my lists. Sometimes I found those lists in his office wastebasket, and sometimes I saw him stare at those lists for long, long moments, as if memorizing every stock I listed before he threw the list away.

In November I caught him doing this. "You wanted me to do something to help you, and when I do, you pretend I don't. Papa, why do you go to such trouble to convince me I'm special, then toss away my lists as if you don't believe I am."

"Because I'm a fool, Audrina. I want to gain by my own abilities, not by yours. And I've seen you perform your silly little trick by swinging the ring over the stocks. I want honest dreams, not contrived ones. I know when you're honest and when you're not. I'm going to make you what you should be if it takes me the rest of my life—and yours."

Chilled, I froze in position, frightened by his determined tone. "What is it you want me to be?"

"Like my First Audrina," he said resolutely.

Even colder, I backed away. Maybe he was the crazy one and not me. His dark, brooding eyes followed my every motion, as if commanding me to run to him now and love him as she'd loved him—and I couldn't do what he wanted. I didn't want to be her. I only wanted to be me.

I wandered into the front salon and found Vera sprawled again on Momma's purple chaise. Lately she had taken to lying around all the time on Momma's favorite chaise, reading those paperback romances Momma had adored. She said they were teaching her about life and loving. And it seemed they were, for certainly something besides medical books was putting sophistication in Vera's dark eyes, making them even harder and more brittle. Time and again she had told me that she was going to make herself so beautiful and charming that no man would notice her left leg was one inch shorter than her right.

"Vera," I asked, "why don't you have your shorter leg put in traction like your doctor advised? He said it would stretch out and be even with the other."

"But it would hurt. You know I can't stand pain, and I hate hospitals."

A fine nurse she was going to make. "Wouldn't the pain be worth the reward?"

She seemed to look inward and weigh the cure against the outcome. "I used to think so." Then, after more consideration, she said, "Now I've changed my mind. If I walked normally, then my mother would make me a slave, as she makes you one. Now I can live the life of luxury, like your mother did while my mother slaved until she dropped exhausted into bed." Meanly, she grinned. "I'm not stupid, idiot—or vacant-headed. I'm thinking all the time. And my game leg is going to stand me in better stead than both your normal ones."

There was no reasoning with Vera. It had to be her way or no way. Vera didn't want to do anything. When it suited her purpose, and often it did, she'd torment me with saying my mother had faked her incessant fatigue just to gain Papa's sympathy and her sister's free housemaid services.

As I ran the next afternoon to visit Arden, the wind blew leaves and scuttled them everywhere. Geese overhead were flying southward. Soon the snow would be falling. We were both bundled to our ears in heavy coats. Our breath came in small puffs of steam. What were we doing walking in the woods in freezing weather like this? Why couldn't we go into each other's houses like most people? I sighed as I stared at him, then lowered my eyes.

"Arden, you know why I can't invite you inside Whitefern. But I don't understand why Billie doesn't invite me inside your home. Does she think I'm not good enough for an indoor relationship?"

"I know what you're thinking, and I understand." He hung his head, looking more and more embarrassed. "You see, she's fixing up everything. Both of us are painting and wallpapering. She's sewing new slipcovers, making bedspreads, curtains. She's been working on our place ever since the day we moved in, but because she has to stop and sew for other people, ours gets done last. Our house isn't fine inside . . . not yet. One day soon, very soon, we'll be finished, and then you can come in and sit down and have a nice visit."

Thanksgiving, Christmas and New Year's came and went, and still Arden and Billie didn't think their home fine enough to invite me in. Workmen came to our house in droves to paint, wallpaper, remove old finishes, put on new stain, polish and redo the whole house. We had many, many rooms. The cottage had only five.

"Arden," I finally asked one day, "why is it taking the two of you so long to fix up your house? I don't care if it's pretty or not."

He had a habit of holding my hand and comparing it to his own hand size, just as a way to keep from meeting my eyes. His fingers were twice as long. Although it was a sweet sensation, I wanted him to meet my eyes and speak honestly. Yet he was evasive. "I have a father somewhere. He left when . . . when—" He stumbled, stammered, blushed, shuffled his feet and looked panic-stricken. "It's Mom . . ."

"She doesn't really like me."

"Of course she likes you!" He tugged me forward, as if he were going to drag me into his home whether or not his mother approved. "It's not easy to talk about, Audrina. Especially when she's asked me not to tell you anything. I said from the beginning we should be honest, and that would have saved us both a lot of embarrassment, but she wouldn't listen. I've seen you look at her, at me, and wonder what the heck was going on. I know your father doesn't want me in your life, so I don't question why I'm not invited inside Whitefern. Let's get it over with. It's time you knew."

It seemed all my life had been spent inside one house. I'd never been in another house—one without ghosts from the past. The cottage's small rooms couldn't be dim and frightening like our giant rooms, nor could they be full of faded splendor and decaying antiques. I was going to see, for the first time in my life, a small house, a cozy house, a normal house.

We reached the cottage where smoke limp as chiffon scarfs drifted heavenward. Seagulls were flying and sounding off, making the day seem very bleak. I came to an abrupt stop when Arden was about to pull me through the door. "Before we go in, answer one question. Just how long have we known each other? I've asked before, and you didn't give me a straight answer. This time I want the honest answer."

Such a simple question to make him shift his eyes away. "When I think backward, I can't remember when I didn't know you. Maybe I dreamed of you even before I met you. When I saw you in the woods, hiding behind the bushes and tree, it was like a dream coming true—that's the day I first knew you in reality. But I was born knowing you."

His words spread a magic shawl of comfort about my shoulders as with eyes locked and hands clasping he opened the cottage door and stood back to let me enter first.

This time I hadn't seen Billie at the window. Nor did I see her in the room I entered. Arden whispered, "I think my mom planned to postpone this day forever, so trust me as I trust you. Everything will work out fine."

That's all he said to prepare me. Many times I wondered afterwards why he didn't say much, much more.

Billie

Arden slammed the door behind us. Loud. Very loud. A warning to signal her. A few dead leaves had blown in with us. Quickly, I bent to pick them up. When I had them in my hand, I straightened to quickly glance around with a great deal of curiosity. The living room was very pretty, with bright chintzy fabrics covering the sofa and two comfortable-looking chairs. Compared to our huge rooms, it did look very small. The ceilings were hardly eight feet above the floor, giving me a claustrophobic feeling. Still, the room had a cozy charm our kind of rooms would never have, no matter how much money was spent to rejuvenate its lost splendor, or how many sofas and chairs were covered by chintz.

There were no shadows here, only clear, winter sunlight that poured in brilliantly. There were no stained-glass windows to dazzle my eyes and enchant me with unwanted spells.

"Mom," called Arden, "I've got Audrina with me. Come on out. You can't keep your secret forever."

I spun around to stare at him, the dead leaves forgotten in my hand. Secrets, secrets, everyone seemed to have secrets. I saw his anxiety, the nervous hands that he stuffed in his pockets as he looked back at me in apprehension. From the look in his eyes I knew that soon I would have to pass a test. God, I prayed, let me do this right—whatever it was.

"I'll be right out," called Billie from another room. She sounded as anxious as her son looked. Her usually warm voice had lost its welcoming tone. Now I felt uncomfortable and ready to turn and leave. Still I hesitated, seeing Arden narrow his eyes as he watched me closely. No, I wasn't going to run this time. I was going to stay and find out at least one secret.

Nervously Arden glanced toward what I presumed was Billie's bedroom door. He didn't ask me to sit down. Perhaps he even forgot I wore a heavy winter coat with a hood, for he didn't ask me to take off my coat. He was much too distracted by that closed door he kept watching. I shook off the hood but kept the coat on as I waited and waited, and waited some more. Arden hadn't removed his coat, either, as if he expected we wouldn't stay long.

Then, as he bowed his head and stared at his shoes, I noticed for the first time a wooden wall shelf that held dozens of gold medals with dates and names. Irresistibly drawn, I stepped closer. Oh, good golly day! Delighted, I whirled around to flash a happy smile at Arden.

"Arden! Billie used to be an ice-skating champion? How wonderful! Look at all these Olympic awards! How could you keep something so fantastic a secret for so long? Just wait until Papa hears about this."

Now what had I said wrong? He seemed even more embarrassed. Why, this was almost as good as Billie being Elizabeth Taylor. I could envision Billie gracefully skimming over the ice, wearing some skimpy little costume that glittered. She'd whirl and spin and do those things called double axels and never become dizzy. And in all the time I'd known her and Arden, they'd never boasted, never even hinted. She'd talked to me as if she was nobody special, and she was.

A small noise distracted me. I whirled around to see Billie, who must have waited until my back was turned, then swiftly hurried to sit in a chair. I stared. Why was she wearing such a full, long skirt in the middle of the afternoon? The gown she wore looked very expensive, as if she were going to attend some gala formal affair.

Her marvelous jet-black hair was piled high on her head in a mass of ringlets instead of just hanging loose down her back, and that alone made her look different. Her face was heavily painted, even garishly so. Her lashes were longer and thicker than I'd noticed before. And she must have put on every last piece of jewelry she owned. I smiled weakly, not knowing how to handle a situation like this. Without all that stage makeup she was stunningly beautiful. The fancy taffeta dress and heavy costume jewelry made her seem cheap, a fraud, someone I didn't even know. And worse, someone I didn't think I'd want to know.

"Mom," said Arden, a struggling smile trying to survive on his lips, "you didn't need to go to so much trouble."

No, Billie, you didn't. I liked you the way you looked before much better.

"Yes, I did—and Arden, you should have warned me, you know that."

I looked from one to the other, guessing something was dreadfully wrong. The vibrations between mother and son were so strong I quivered, sensing their anxieties because *I* was inside their house—where she didn't want me. Yet Arden was gazing at me with so much appeal; his eyes were pleading for me to notice nothing amiss. So I smiled and stepped over to shake her hand. I sat down and began a silly conversation. When she'd been at the window and I'd been on the ground outside, she'd been so easy to talk to. Now we were like strangers meeting for the first time. Soon I made some flimsy excuse about having to hurry home to help Aunt Ellsbeth.

"Won't you stay for dinner?" asked Arden. I flashed him a hurt look of reproach. At least Papa was direct with his hostility and didn't hide it behind the guise of friendship as Billie was doing. Gee, I thought childishly, feeling hot tears stinging the back of my eyes, our friendship was only for the outside, not indoors. It was just as Vera had told me—I wasn't respectable enough for Billie. Was I so crazy that people didn't want me in their houses? Again my eyes clashed with Arden's—mine accusing, his still pleading for understanding. Please, please, his eyes were begging. I decided to stay on long enough to find out what was making all of us so self-conscious.

There was something burning in the oven. Maybe

I was interrupting her cooking and she didn't like it. There wasn't enough for three and she didn't really want me to stay for dinner. It was such a little house that the kitchen seemed part of the living room. "Billie, I think I smell something burning in the oven. May I take it out for you?"

She blanched, shook her head, gave Arden a furtive signal before she weakly smiled at me. "No, thank you, Audrina. Arden can do all of that. But please do stay and have potluck with us." But the expression of anxiety she couldn't control gave lie to her words.

Really distressed and embarrassed now, I bowed my head. "Thank you for asking me. But, as you know, my father doesn't like for me to come through the woods and over here."

Arden glanced at me, then his mother, and said somberly, "Mom, this is getting to be a bit much. Can't *you* tell Audrina?"

She flushed, then paled. I didn't want to know now. All I wanted to do was escape. I stood to go.

Suddenly Billie gushed, "Oh, why not!" Flinging wide her slim, strongly muscled arms, she went on, "Audrina, my dear girl, you are now gazing upon what was once the world's Olympic ice-skating champion until I turned professional. That lasted about eighteen years. I had a glorious time, loving every moment of the excitement. Arden can tell you tales of how we lived out of trunks. We traveled all over the world entertaining people, and then one fateful day I fell on the ice because someone had lost a bobby pin. I could have broken my leg, but I only received a cut from my skate. That small cut should have healed in a week or so. But it didn't heal in six months because the doctors found out I had diabetes. Would you believe, my leg was rotting right before our eyes and there didn't seem to be anything the doctors could do to stop it. I hadn't been to a doctor all during my career. I suppose if I had known what kind of vicious disease I had, I might have given up skating much sooner. But as it was, I had my day, didn't I, son?"

"Yes, Mom. You had your day in the sun, and I'm happy you did." His eyes lit up with pride as he smiled. "I can close my eyes right now and see you skating, the star of the show. And I felt so proud, so very proud." He paused and glanced my way again. "Audrina, what my mother is trying to say and having so much difficulty with is—"

"I don't have any legs—that's what!" shrieked Billie.

I stared at her disbelievingly.

"Yes," she cried, "I was hoping you'd never find out. I wanted us to be friends. I wanted you to treat me like a normal human being and not like a freak."

So stunned by her information I felt sick, I stared at her face, trying not to look where her legs should be under all those rustling skirts. No legs? How did she get around? I wanted to get out, to run, to cry. For here was another beautiful, kind and wonderful woman whom God had punished—and somebody else Papa wouldn't approve of.

A dreadful silence filled the small room and spread throughout the whole cottage, almost as if time were standing still. We all hung on the brink of some chasm that would swallow Billie and forever separate Arden and me. Whatever I did or said, whatever expression was on my face this very moment, would tell them more than my words.

I didn't know what to do or what to say, or even what to think. I floundered helplessly, trying to grasp something that would give me the right words . . . and then I thought of my mother. Suppose, just suppose, that Momma had come home from the hospital with no legs. Would I have felt disgust, revulsion? Would I have been ashamed and embarrassed to have her seen? No, I'd have wanted her back, no matter what. I'd do anything to have Momma back, with or without legs. That's when I found my voice.

"You're the most beautiful woman with dark hair I've ever seen." I said it sincerely. "I'd say you were the most beautiful woman I've ever seen, but my mother was beautiful, too. If only I could have my mother again, I wouldn't care if she had legs or not—" I paused, flushed and felt guilty. For Momma would have cared. She wouldn't have been able to cope with her loss. She'd cry, hide herself away and probably die from the lack of wanting to live without her legs.

Admiration washed over me for Billie, who would live for Arden's sake, for her own, too, no matter what the circumstances. "I think, too, that you are the kindest, most generous woman I've ever known," I went on. "I've piled my problems on your shoulders and not once have you even hinted you had your own." Humbled and ashamed, again my head inclined. I had felt sorry for myself just because my memory was perforated with holes through which the secrets of my existence had been dropped.

Now that she'd told me a little, Billie was going to tell me everything. "My husband left me shortly after I came home from the second amputation two years ago." There was no bitterness in her voice. "My son waits on me; at least, he helps me with what I can't do myself. Although I'm pretty good about doing for myself, hey, Arden?"

"Yes, Mom, you're super. There's very little you can't do for yourself." He smiled at me, so proud of his mother.

"Of course, my ex-husband does send his piddling check once a month," added Billie.

"Dad will come back one day, Mom. I know he will."

"Sure he will. In a year of Sundays he'll come back."

I jumped up to run and kiss her heavily rouged cheek, then impulsively I hugged her close. Her strong arms closed about me almost automatically, as if she couldn't resist someone who loved and admired her, even though tears were streaming down her cheeks and black mascara ran in streaks. "I'm so sorry I burst in on you without warning," I choked, crying, too. "I'm sorry you lost your legs. But Billie, if you were still skating, and this may sound selfish, I'd never have known you or Arden. Fate brought you both to me." I smiled and brushed away my tears. "Papa says that fate is the captain of all our ships, only we don't know it."

"That's a fine way to put responsibility where it doesn't belong. Now get along home, Audrina, before your papa comes looking for you, and I'll see you another day. If you want to come back."

"Oh, I'll be back soon," I said with confidence.

That day Arden again walked me back through the woods.

I was full of admiration for Billie—and wonder, too. I wanted to know just how she managed to clean house and do the laundry when she had no legs. If only I could tell Vera all that Billie could do without legs, when she could hardly do anything with two. I wondered how I'd handle the day when finally I saw Billie without all those stiff, concealing skirts. For surely she couldn't wear so many clothes in the summer.

At the edge of the woods we said a hasty goodbye. Arden still had to deliver newspapers, and then bag groceries. It was likely he would never have enough sleep until he graduated from college. I watched him turn and race back home. He was so conscientious, so dedicated to his mother and helping her financially that I had less and less time with him. There was a price to pay for everything, I thought sadly, opening the side door and entering our house of shadows.

Sprawled on the purple chaise, Vera was busy reading another of the romances that filled Momma's closet shelves. She was so deeply engrossed she didn't pay much attention to me. I wanted to tell her about Billie, but for some reason held back, afraid she'd say something ugly. And it wouldn't make any difference if I told her how hard Billie worked. Vera thought work was for stupid people who didn't know any better. "My brains will see me through," she'd told me many times. As I watched her, and she was unaware of me, I saw the tip of her tongue moving back and forth on her lower lip. Her eyes appeared glassy; her breasts heaved upward and soon her hand was inside her blouse, caressing herself. Then she put the book aside, threw back her head and began to use her other hand under her skirts. I stared at what she was doing. "Vera! Stop that! It looks gross!"

"Go 'way," she murmured without opening her eyes. "What do you know about anything? You're a babe in the woods—or are you?"

Now that I was growing up, Papa would often take me to his brokerage firm, allowing me to watch and listen to learn all about what he did. I was his showpiece, replacing my mother, who'd often sat in the very chair he gave me beside his desk. Old men and women came to talk to me and to joke with Papa before they turned their conversations to financial talk Papa had taught me to understand. "My daughter is going to be my business partner one day," Papa proudly informed all newcomers who hadn't heard this a hundred times before. "With my kind of daughter, a man doesn't need a son."

He made me feel good on days like this, which ended with dinner in a fine restaurant and a movie afterward. On the city streets I saw legless beggars on little carts they shoved along, sometimes with gloved

hands. They used little things that looked like small
rubber-bottomed irons to grab at the sidewalks and
spare their hands the blisters. And before I'd never
noticed them, or if I had, I'd turned my eyes away and
pretended they didn't exist.

The very next day I had to say something to Billie
that I'd held back since the day I knew about her lack
of legs. "Billie, I've been looking at people in the city
who have no legs. So I won't be shocked if you don't
always wear those long skirts."

She scowled at me, then turned her head. She had
a lovely profile, classical and perfect. "I'll know when
you're ready to see me without my full, long skirts.
I'll tell by your eyes. And you're not ready yet. It's
not pretty, Audrina. Those men you see on the streets
wear trousers that they fold over so you don't see the
stumps. Once I had very beautiful legs; now I have
eight-inch stumps that even I can't look at without
feeling disgust." She sighed, shrugged, then gave me
a charming smile. "Sometimes my missing legs still
hurt. Phantom pain, the doctors call it. I wake up in
the night and feel my legs below me, hurting so badly
sometimes I can't help but call Arden, and he comes
running to give me some drug the doctor prescribes.
He won't let me keep it by my bedside, afraid I'll take
too much by accident. It makes my mind fuzzy so I
can't remember if I take one or even two pills. While
I wait for the pill to take effect, he sits by my bedside
and tells me silly stories to make me laugh. Sometimes
that boy of mine stays up all night just to entertain
me when the pains won't go away. God was good to

me the day he told me not to destroy the baby that might spoil my career. I thought twice and didn't have an abortion. If I had known long ago all the children I prevented would have been like Arden, perhaps I'd have had twelve children."

Did that mean she'd had many abortions? I didn't like to think she had. I convinced myself she meant she'd done something else to keep from having babies and giving up her career. I also knew even if she'd had a hundred sons, only one would be like Arden, devoted, responsible, a man even before he finished being a boy. He was never depressed or angry, just even and steady and always there when he was needed. Like Billie.

Overwhelmed with my thoughts, I got up to embrace Billie. I never was able to impulsively show affection to my aunt, when many times I wanted to. I needed Billie to be my substitute mother, especially when Aunt Ellsbeth always held me at arm's length. "All right, Billie, maybe I'm not ready yet to see you without your long skirts, but one day when I come over here and you don't have on your dressy clothes, I won't feel disgust. You'll look in my eyes and you'll see nothing but admiration and gratitude for being what you are and giving Arden to the world as well."

She laughed and put her strong arms around me before she looked deep into my eyes. There was sadness in her voice when she spoke next. "Don't go falling in love too soon, Audrina. Arden is my son, and I think he's perfect, but all mothers think their sons are perfect. You need someone special. I'd like to think that Arden is that special, for I'd never want him to disappoint you—but if at some point he does, remember that none of us is perfect. We all have our Achilles' heels, so to speak."

Then again, with a great deal of perception she was searching my eyes, and maybe my soul. "What troubles you so much, Audrina? Why all those shadows in such beautiful violet eyes?"

"I don't know." I held fast to her. "I guess I just hate being named after an older sister who died mysteriously at the age of nine. I wish like crazy I'd been the First Audrina, who was also the Best Audrina. My papa won't stop telling me how wonderful she was, and every word he says to praise her tells me I'm not living up to the standards she set. I feel cursed, and doubly cursed now that Momma died on *my* ninth birthday and Sylvia was born then, too. It's weird and not right for so much to happen when the ninth day of the ninth month comes around."

Soothingly, she held me, patiently listening until I finished. "Nonsense, that's all it is, plain nonsense. You're not haunted and not cursed, though your father should know better than to speak so often about a girl in her grave. From all that I hear my son say about you, if you were more perfect you'd have to wear a halo and sprout wings and stand on a pedestal of solid gold. Silly, isn't it, how men want women to look like angels and act like . . . well, never mind. You're too young to hear more."

Darn, there she went, stopping just when she was going to say something meaningful. Like Momma,

Aunt Ellsbeth and Mercy Marie, too, she grew embarrassed and left me hanging, still waiting for information that would never come.

One afternoon I was in the rocking chair, lazily drifting beyond the boys who waited in the woods to ravish.

I knew now that it was Papa's presence, even when he stayed in the hall, that had kept me from finding anything from the rocking chair but the terror in the woods. On my own, alone, I could fill the empty pitcher with contentment and peace, but with Papa anywhere nearby, I had to stand behind the rocking chair and pressure it hard with my hands to make the floorboards squeak. Only when he thought it was working would he leave.

This time I bypassed the school and headed toward somewhere wonderful when I heard an argument raging down by my aunt's bedroom. Reluctantly I gave up the vision of the First Audrina and came back to being only me. My aunt was shouting, "That girl needs to go to school, Damian! If you don't send her to school, someone is going to report you to the school authorities. You've told them you're hiring tutors to see that she's educated, and you're not. And she's not being neglected only educationally; she's abused in other ways, too. You have no right to force her to sit in that rocking chair!"

"I have the right to do anything I want with my own child!" he stormed back. "I rule this house, not you. Besides, she's not afraid of the rocking chair as she once was. She goes there willingly now. I told you that sooner or later the chair would work its miracle."

"I don't believe you. Even if she does sit there willingly, which I doubt, I want that girl to go to school. Every day I see her watching Vera, standing at the window, wanting what Vera has so badly I could almost cry for her. Hasn't she endured enough, Damian? Let her try again to find her place. Give her another chance. Please."

My heart was doing flip-flops. Did my aunt really care about me after all? Or had Lamar Rensdale found a way to convince her that I needed school if I was ever to grow up happy and normal?

My papa relented. I would be allowed to go to school.

Such a small normal thing to fill me with such overwhelming joy. When I had the chance, I whispered to my aunt while Vera pored over another romance, "Why, Aunt Ellsbeth? I didn't think you cared if I was ever formally educated."

She drew me into the kitchen and shut the door, as if she, too, didn't want Vera to hear. "I'm going to be totally honest, Audrina. And truth is something you are not likely to hear in this nuthouse from anyone but me. That man who teaches you to play the piano came here one day and pressured me into doing something to help you. He threatened to go to the school board and tell them about your situation; your father would have been fined or even sent to jail for keeping a minor out of school."

I couldn't believe it! Lamar Rensdale had fulfilled his promise, though it had taken him long enough. I laughed and spun around and almost hugged my aunt, but she backed off. I was left to run upstairs and in the rocking chair I began to sing, hoping to find Momma so I could tell her my good news.

Almost a Normal Life

Papa took me shopping so I'd be ready to attend school at the beginning of the midterm in February. All my Christmas gifts were school clothes—coats, shoes, even that raincoat like Vera's that I'd been wanting for years and years. It was exciting to select skirts and blouses, sweaters and jackets. Papa wouldn't allow me to buy the jeans other girls wore. "No pants for my daughter!" he stormed, letting the saleslady overhear. "They show too much. Now, you keep remembering to sit with your legs together and don't even look at the boys—do you hear me?"

His words were loud enough to inform the whole department store. I turned red and told him to lower his voice. Something ugly always came over Papa when he talked about boys.

When February finally rolled around, I was like a small child expecting the circus to keep me forever happy. There was no fear of the woods, for Papa would drive me in the mornings and I'd take the school bus home in the afternoons.

"You're going to loathe it," proclaimed Vera. "You

think it's going to be fun, that the teachers will care
if you learn, but they won't. You'll sit in a class with
thirty or thirty-five others, and soon enough you'll
find it's nothing but boredom—plain, dull monotony.
Without the boys there I would run away from home
and never come back."

Not once had she ever said this to me before.
When I couldn't go to school, she'd had glowing
reports of all her fun activities. Her friends she'd
numbered by the hundreds—now she was telling me
she had none. "Nobody likes a Whitefern, even if they
hide behind the name of Adare."

Papa told Vera to keep her big mouth shut. Hurriedly, I said good night, racing up the stairs and into
the playroom, where I could rock and tell Momma
about my life. Somewhere up there I was sure she was
listening, happy for me. And as I rocked, again the
walls seemed to dissolve and become porous, and the
First Audrina was running wild in a field of flowers,
laughing as a boy of about ten chased her. She whirled
to confront him when he tugged on her sash and it
came off in his hands. Who was he? Why did he stare
at the First Audrina like that? The scene faded and the
other Audrina was again in school, with a huge, ugly
boy with pimples seated behind her, and again, lock
by lock, he was dipping her long hair into his India-
ink bottle. It was during art class, and she didn't even
notice.

"Aud . . . dreen . . . na," chanted a frightening,
singsong voice that made me bolt back to myself. Vera
was in the doorway, glaring at me. "Get out of that

chair! You've got enough! You don't need her gift, too! Get out, and never sit there again—it's mine! I need her gift most."

I let her have the chair, thinking she was right. I didn't need that unknown gift. It hadn't kept her alive until she was eleven, like me. I was surviving, she hadn't, and for now that was gift enough.

Nervously I dressed for my first day in school the next morning. My skirt was deep periwinkle blue, made of some lightweight wool that would need dry cleaning. My hands trembled when I tied the black ribbon at the throat of my white blouse. "You look beautiful," said Papa at the door, smiling his approval.

Behind him Vera was standing, envy on her face. Her dark eyes scanned me from head to toe. "Oh, Papa," she said with scorn, "nobody dresses like that anymore. Everybody's going to laugh at overdressed Audrina." She glanced down at her outfit—faded blue jeans and a sweater. "I'm the one who's in style."

What she said did little to give me the confidence I needed. I wanted to fit in, not stand out like some oddity, yet Papa refused to let me wear anything but skirts, blouses, sweaters or dresses.

While Vera boarded the yellow bus for her high school, Papa drove me to my grade school and came with me to the principal's office. My entry into school had been prearranged, so there was nothing to it except I had to be shown where to go and told how to behave. The principal seemed to believe I'd been sick a long time. Sympathetically, she smiled. "You'll be just fine once you've learned your way around."

Panic seized me in a tight grip when Papa turned to leave. I felt six years old. Then I panicked more, for I didn't remember being six years old. Papa threw me a glance over his shoulder. "This is what you wanted, Audrina. What you've begged for, so if you can, enjoy it."

"You're a lovely girl," said the principal, striding off down a long corridor and indicating I was to follow. "Most of the children here are very well disciplined, but a few aren't. Your father says your aunt was a schoolteacher and has kept up your assignments. You should fit right into the fifth or sixth grade with no difficulty. We'll start you in the fifth so you won't feel overwhelmed, and if you do well there, we'll advance you higher." She gave me another warm smile. "Your father is a very handsome man and he thinks his daughter is absolutely brilliant. I'm sure he's the one who knows, too."

I looked around at all the children, who stared at me. Their clothes were very casual, just as Vera had warned. And yet Vera had told me the day before we shopped that the clothes I had on now were right for grade school. I should have known Vera would lie. The girls were all in jeans. None had ribbons in their hair. Furtively, I untied my ribbon and let it fall to the floor. "Hey!" called a boy from behind me. "You dropped your ribbon."

Several students had already dirtied it with their sneakers. Now I didn't know what to do with it but hide it away in my little purse.

"Girls, boys," said the principal, who strode to the

front of our classroom. "I want you all to meet Audrina Adare. Do what you can to make her feel welcome." She smiled at me, gestured toward an empty desk and left the room. As yet the teacher of this room hadn't shown up. I sat there with my notebook and new pencils and didn't know what to do. Somewhere far back in my brain was a hint that I needed books—the other students had books. In front of me sat a pretty girl with dark hair and blue eyes. She turned to smile. "Don't look so scared," she whispered. "You'll like our teacher. Her name is Miss Trible."

"I don't have any books," I whispered back.

"Oh, they'll give you books. More books than you'll want to lug home from school every day." She hesitated and looked me over again. "Hey, haven't you been to school before?"

For some reason I just couldn't say I hadn't been. I lied and said, "Yes, of course, but I was out for a while ... when ... when I broke my leg."

At last Vera had served some useful purpose. I could use her injuries and report on them faithfully. Soon all the girls were turning to hear about my broken bones that had kept me out of school until I was eleven years old.

When Miss Trible came into her class, she gave me the longest, strangest look. Her smile was tight. "Let us all stand to salute the flag," she said. "Then we'll have roll call, and each of you will answer 'Present.'"

Some boy behind me giggled. "Boy, what's wrong with her? She acts like we don't know what to expect."

I was excited, yet puzzled, worried, tense and

not too happy. I didn't think Miss Trible liked me. I thought groups of children in the halls at lunchtime were whispering about me. I didn't find it nearly as wonderful to talk to girls my own age as I'd thought. I felt so much older than all of them. And then, contrarily, I was like a first-grader, terrified of what to do if I needed the bathroom. Where was the bathroom?

The more I thought about the problem, the worse it became. Soon I needed to go so desperately I was in agony. I began to cross and uncross my legs. "Audrina, is something wrong?" asked the teacher.

"No, ma'am," I lied, ashamed to say what was wrong in front of the boys.

"If you need to be excused, the girl's room is at the far end of this wing. Turn left as you leave the room."

Blushing and miserable, I jumped to my feet and ran. I left the whole classroom laughing. When I came back, I was too embarrassed to enter. "Come in, Audrina," called Miss Trible. "The first day in a new school is always somewhat traumatic, but you'll soon find out where everything is. What you don't know, ask." Then she was tapping her pointer on the blackboard, calling for attention.

Somehow I managed the first terrifying days of school. I did what the other girls did, fading into their shadows. I smiled when they smiled, laughed when they did, and soon I was feeling completely false. Some of what those girls whispered in the restrooms shocked me. I didn't know girls talked like that. Little by little I found out what made Vera the way she was. She conformed. I couldn't. I didn't know how to laugh at jokes that seemed gross and not funny. I didn't know how to play the game of tease the boys and then run, for I had too many visions of the First Audrina's rainy day in the woods. I made one friend, the girl who sat in front of me.

"It's going to be all right," she told me when the long first week of school was over. "But don't try to out-dress the rich girls from the city . . . unless you, too, are rich." She gave me a troubled look. "You are rich, aren't you? There's something different about you. Not just the clothes you wear, and your hair, which I think is the prettiest hair I've ever seen, but you seem to come from another century."

How could I tell her I felt like I came from another world? The nineteenth-century world, old and antiquated as the house I lived in.

My class wasn't large like Vera had predicted, but small. My school was a private school. That made Vera dislike me even more, since her school was a public one.

Faithfully I attended music classes every day after school. Someday I would be a fine pianist if I kept on as I was. Lamar Rensdale treated me with special kindness.

"Are you grateful you're in school? Do you wish now I'd minded my own business?"

"No, Mr. Rensdale, I'll forever be grateful for what you did, for I'm beginning to feel real, and I never did before. I owe you for that."

"Goodbye, good luck and may your music live on forever," he called as I ran out the door, hopping into the old car Billie had bought for Arden.

My teachers seemed to be very careful with me, and I appreciated that. They smiled encouragingly and gave me the books I took home each day. After two months in school, I found there was some hidden source of knowledge within me that made it seem I had been to school before. Maybe I had really absorbed all the First Audrina's memories, or else my mother and my aunt had taught me very well while I sat at the kitchen table. Those other tutors that Papa kept saying he'd hired (and I couldn't remember) must have contributed, too.

For the first time, Arden was allowed to visit and sit down at our table on Easter Sunday. I'd pleaded and begged and cried and threatened, wanting Billie, too, but Billie had refused. "Come to see me after your dinner. We'll have that chocolate mousse you say your aunt doesn't know how to make right for dessert."

Easter Sunday dinner was a miserable meal because Papa kept questioning Arden about who his father had been and what his occupation had been, and why he had left his wife and son. All through the meal Vera flirted with Arden, batting her long eyelashes, twisting and turning to show off her breasts that clearly showed she didn't wear a bra. Arden seemed awed by the size of my home. He glanced around uneasily, as if thinking he'd never be able to afford anything half as grand.

When summer came, Arden and I spent every spare minute together. He taught me how to swim in the River Lyle, really swim like he did. The river bottom was muddy and layered with oysters and crabs; mullets swam, jumping and frolicking mostly during

234   V. C. Andrews

the twilight hours. Their little splashes came to me in dreams, waking me sometimes so that I'd drift to the window and gaze down on the glittering moonlit water. Something wonderful was happening inside me this summer, making me eager to wake up and escape the house; but try as I would to leave Vera behind, she always came trailing after.

Vera was demanding that Arden teach her how to drive his old car. I was hoping he wouldn't want to, but he did teach her to drive the country roads without much traffic. One day, after such a lesson, we hurried back to the river and tore off our outer clothes. All of us wore swimsuits beneath our shorts. The temperature was soaring near a hundred degrees. I turned to see Arden staring at Vera in her skimpy bikini. The three little triangles were bright green and very flattering to her hair color. Her pale skin had tanned to a light copper shade, and even I had to admit she looked extremely pretty. Already she'd developed a woman's figure, with high, full breasts that jutted out that little-nothing green bra. My chest was still flat as a pan bottom.

Vera strolled closer to Arden with a lighter green towel thrown casually over her shoulder. Her hips undulated. Apparently the fascination of watching them move like that made Arden forget all about me. "I'm terribly tired after all that driving, and the long hike here. Arden, would you mind helping me down the incline?"

He hurried to assist her down the gentle slope, which I knew she could manage perfectly well. For some reason he couldn't seem to let go of her waist or arm. His fingers on her upper arm just brushed the swelling contours of her new bosom. I flushed with anger when she smiled up into his eyes. "You grow more handsome each year, Arden."

He grew nervous, flushed, then snatched his hands away and looked guiltily at me. "Thank you," he said with difficulty. "You seem prettier each day yourself."

My eyes widened as I watched Vera lie on her stomach in the bright sunlight. Arden hovered above, seemingly unable to move away. "Arden, would you mind smoothing on some of my suntan lotion? With my kind of light-sensitive skin, I have to be very careful or I get a terrible burn."

She had the palest skin I'd ever seen. Even as I stared at her pretty copper tan, I was wondering when she'd acquired it. Then, to my amazement, Vera was asking him to untie her bra in back. "I don't want pale string marks. Stop glaring at me, Audrina. I won't show anything if I don't move too quickly. Not that Arden hasn't seen naked boobs before." She grinned when he jerked away and looked surprised—and guilty. Still he knelt down to untie her bra, and even if he looked embarrassed and awkward, he managed to smear some of that oil on her back—and a darn long time it took him to do it, too.

It was taking too long. I thought his hands lingered unnecessarily long in certain places. He appeared so excited his hands trembled. Furious with him, with Vera, I jumped up and ran all the way home, hating them both.

Hours later Vera limped into my room, flushed and happy looking. "What a silly prude you are," she said as she fell into my best chair. "I'm not interested in your boyfriend. I've got my eyes on someone else."

I didn't believe her. "You leave Arden alone, Vera. To get him you'll have to kill me first."

It might have been better if I'd never said that. Her dark eyes lit up. "Ohh, if I really wanted him, he'd be easy enough to take," she purred like some fat cat. "But he's just a boy, too immature for me. But maybe he's more mature than I thought and I owe him another chance. The next time I'll let him apply the oil—all over."

"Papa would kill you."

She threw a bare leg over the velvet arm of my chair, exposing so much I had to look away. "But you won't tell him, Audrina, his sweet Audrina, for you've got a great big secret. You're taking lessons from the Don Juan of Whitefern Village. Lamar Rensdale has seduced every virgin within a radius of twenty miles."

"You're crazy!" I shouted. "He's never done anything . . ."

She leaned over the opposite arm of the chair so that her hair dangled to the floor. The tiny bikini top rode up so high I saw she had tanned her breasts, too. "But Papa won't believe that," she answered smugly, shaking her hair to free it of sand. "Papa will believe anything the villagers tell him. So you'd better be nice to me, Audrina."

I felt sick as she got up, went to the mirror and took off her bathing suit, showing me what she had and I didn't. Then, still naked, she sauntered out of my room, leaving her wet suit on my rug.

Now I was nervous about my music lessons, afraid now of the man I'd trusted before. I cringed when he leaned above me, and shrank when his hand accidently touched mine. His handsome face showed puzzlement as his eyes tried to meet mine and failed. "What's wrong, Audrina?"

"Nothing."

"I hate it when someone says that, when obviously something is very wrong. What made you stop trusting me?"

"I guess I've heard a few things," I whispered with my head bowed. "I'm afraid I can't come here again."

"So," he began in a bitter way, "you're going to be like all the others and believe the worst of me." He jumped up from the bench and paced his small living room. "You happen to be the only student who keeps me tied to this hick town. I keep telling myself even if I'm not good enough for Broadway, I am contributing a fine musician to the world."

I felt sorry for him, for me, too, for there wasn't another qualified teacher except in the city thirty miles away, and I had no way to reach the city. "Mr. Rensdale—" I tried to begin.

"Lamar—why can't you call me by my first name?" he shot out angrily, locking his long fingers together and flexing them back and forth.

"I can't call you by your first name. Papa has warned me not to do that, for it's the first step . . ." Here I hesitated, beginning to feel very hot and uncomfortable. "Vera talks a lot, remember that. If she ever told Papa about your reputation, he'd come after you. Papa is huge, and it's not his way to stop and listen to reason. He'd believe anything Vera told him . . . and she hates me. He knows she hates me, and still he'd believe what she says, for he doesn't trust any man around young girls. If he didn't believe me so chaste and pure in mind, he wouldn't have let me come in the first place."

"I'll speak to Vera when she comes for her next lesson." He stopped pacing and stood before me. "She's wasting her time with me, and your father's money. She has no musical ability at all, yet she insists on trying. She's competing with you, Audrina. She wants everything you want. She wants your young man, she wants the love your father gives you and not her. She's jealous of you, and dangerous, too. Beware of Vera."

Slowly my eyes lifted to meet his. He lightly touched my hair, then my cheek where the tear had slid. "Are you crying for me, or for yourself?" he asked softly. "Who will teach you the piano when I'm gone? What will you do with your talent then? Bury it under the dishes you wash and the babies you bear, like your mother did?"

"I'll come back," I whispered, terribly afraid of repeating my mother's frustrations. "I'll risk Vera's telling Papa, but you be careful of her, too."

His smile came thin and crooked as he wiped away my tears. It was a smile very much like Vera's.

Each day I played better and better. At her piano I felt like Momma, enthralled by the music I created and somehow disappointed in the life I led. Something was missing, and I didn't know what it was.

I stood that winter staring out at the softly falling snow, wistful and needing, and I allowed myself to believe it was Sylvia I needed for fulfillment. Once I had Sylvia home with me, where I could give her all the love and mothering she must desperately need, I'd feel happy. I wondered as I'd wondered a thousand times just what was wrong with Sylvia. Was it so awful Papa was sure the truth would deliver such a blow to my "sensitivities" that I might not recover? Was I really that sensitive? My aunt ridiculed the notion so often that I felt both she and Papa shared the proof of my hidden weakness.

The snow danced in the wind, whirling around like tiny ballerinas, bouncing up, drifting down, floating sideways, making pictures, telling me, always telling me that I was never, never going to be free, anymore than Momma had been free.

Vera came bounding through my bedroom door, the cold air clinging to her heavy coat as she threw it down and stained yet another delicate chair. "Guess what I've been doing!" she exploded, hardly able to contain herself. Her eyes were lit up like black coals. The cold had made her cheeks red as apples. There were red marks on her neck. Marks she pointed out to me. "Kisses made those," she said with a smirk. "I've got those marks all over me. I am no longer a virgin, little sister."

"You're not my sister!" I flared.

"What difference does it make, I might as well be.

Now, sit down and listen to what's going on in *my* life, and compare it to the dull stuffiness of yours. I have seen a naked man, Audrina, a real one, not just a picture or illustration. He is so hairy. You'd never suspect just how hairy by looking at him fully clothed. His hair travels from his chest down past his navel and runs into a point and keeps on going and getting bushier until—"

"Stop! I don't want to hear more."

"But I want you to hear more. I want you to know what you're missing. It's wonderful to have all those nine inches stabbing into me. Did you hear me, Audrina? I measured it . . . almost nine inches, and it's all swollen and hard."

I ran to the door, but she was up and blocking my way. With surprising strength she threw me to the floor, then straddled my body. I thought about kicking her out of the way, but I was afraid she'd fall and break another bone.

She put her shod foot on my chest, which was just beginning to swell. "He's got a marvelous body, little sister, really a fantastic body. What we do would shock you so much you'd scream and possibly faint . . . and I love every second of what we do together. Can't get enough, never can get enough."

"You're only fourteen," I whispered, truly shocked at the loony way she looked and the disgusting way she talked.

"Soon to be fifteen," she said with a hard laugh. "Why don't you ask me who is my lover? I'll tell you, gladly tell you."

Aunt Ellsbeth looked up from washing the dishes. What I saw in her dark eyes startled me. They were glowing radiantly, as if she'd looked all her life and had at last discovered something to be joyful about. No longer did she call Papa cruel and callous as once she had. He no longer called her a walking beanpole, tall, lean and mean, with the tongue of a shrew.

"Audrina," she began, and in her voice I heard a bit of warmth, "you've got to be very careful not to let your father dominate your life. He'll never do that to Vera because she doesn't care what he thinks of her. Because you do care, you make yourself vulnerable. He's self-serving to the point of being cruel enough to rob you of what you need. He lies; he cheats and deceives. He's devilishly clever and likable but, I'm sorry to say, completely without honor or integrity. If he can possibly manage it he will keep you here with him until the day he dies and never allow you to have a life of your own. I can tell that you love him. In some ways I commend you for your loyalty and devotion. But blood ties are not supposed to be chains. You don't owe him, or Sylvia, your life."

Oh, what did she mean?

"He's bringing Sylvia home this spring," she said in that flat monotone that sent chills down my spine. "Once she's here you won't have time for music lessons, or time to do anything but wait on her."

I was thrilled to know that at last Sylvia was coming, but the joy of that was shadowed by her words and her expression. "Sylvia was two years old last

September, Aunt Ellsbeth. Doesn't that mean she's past the time of being a troublesome baby?"

She snorted. "Your father doesn't want me to discuss Sylvia. He wants you to grow very attached to her. I'm warning you, don't let that happen."

I stared at her, completely bewildered. Wasn't I supposed to love my own sister? Didn't Sylvia need me to love her?

"Don't look at me like that. I'm thinking of you, not her. Nothing can help Sylvia, and that's too bad, but you can be saved and that's what I'm trying to do. Keep yourself detached. Do for her what you can, but don't love her too much. In the long run you'll thank me for saying this now and not when it's too late."

"She's deformed!" I cried out, horribly distressed. "Why didn't Papa tell me, Aunt Ellsbeth? I have the right to know. What is wrong with Sylvia, Aunt Ellsbeth, please tell me. I need to be prepared."

"She's not deformed," she said in a kind way, looking at me with such pity. "Indeed, she's a beautiful child, and in many ways she looks very much as you did at her age. Her hair is not colored as remarkably as yours, but then, she's hardly more than a baby, and it may change and become exactly like yours—and your mother's. I only hope that someday she will look exactly like you. Lord God above, if that happened, perhaps he'd set you free from playing those silly dream games he believes in so much. For an adult man with a high degree of intelligence, he can sometimes be as superstitious as any moron. I've seen you swing that ring on a string over the stock lists you make, so I give you credit for being clever. Be clever enough to save yourself when the time comes."

What did she mean?

"Audrina, heed my advice and stop what you're doing. Don't try to help him. Try, instead, to see him for what he is, someone determined to keep you tied to him in as many ways as he can dream up. He's convinced himself that you are the only female in the world worthy of his love and devotion, and to you he will give everything he possesses, never realizing he's stealing from you the best the world has to offer."

"But I don't understand!"

"Think about it, then. Think of how afraid he is of growing old and infirm so he'll be put away in some old-age home. It's like a phobia with him, a sickness, Audrina. We all have to grow old. There's nothing we can do to stop it."

"But, but . . ." I sputtered. "Why are you trying to help me, when I didn't know you even liked me?"

"Let me try to explain," she said, folding her work-reddened hands primly on the slight lap she made. "When I came back here to live with my daughter, I was made into a servant. I was afraid to let myself feel anything for you. I had Vera, and Vera had nobody but me. The trouble was, Vera adored Lucietta and soon grew to despise me for being a slave, when I had to be that or get out. I had my reasons for wanting to stay. And I was right to stay on . . . for it worked out just as I knew it would if I had the patience."

My breath caught. "Tell me more," I whispered.

"In the beauty race your mother always won, so naturally I was envious of her in all ways. I was jealous of her figure, her face, her talent and, most of all, of her ability to make men love her exceedingly well." A tightness came into her voice. "There was one man I loved, only one—and then he saw her. Once he saw her, it was all over for me. It hurts to lose, Audrina, hurts so badly sometimes you wonder how you can live with it. But I did live with it, and perhaps one day I will even win one race by default."

It hit me then, hard, why my aunt had always been so jealous of Momma, and why Momma had always flung back at her sister that *she* always got what she wanted and my aunt never did. Aunt Ellsbeth had been in love with my father! Despite the fact that she argued with him, disapproved of him, still she loved him. It seemed that way back in my mind I'd guessed this long, long ago and tried to tuck it away into one of my memory holes.

"Aunt Ellie, do you love him even when you know he cheats and deceives and has no honor and no integrity?"

Alarmed, her eyes fled from mine. "I've talked enough for one day," she answered shortly, stalking into the dining room with a fresh tablecloth. "But you take heed of what I said, and be aware that things are not always as they seem to be. Put your trust in no man, and, most especially, discard any dreams that disturb you."

Sylvia

Time had slowed down for me. Now I could retain my memories and store them in the safest places in my brain. With the help of my daily journal, I read over my memories daily to deeply implant them. The rocking chair was helping in more ways than one. I had hold of peace now. I had a refuge now, a sanctuary where I could find Momma's image floating on the clouds.

I was eleven years and eight months old that May when Sylvia came home. My aunt had confirmed this, and I believed she was telling me the truth this time. She also confirmed Vera's age as being three years and ten months my senior. Nothing, I told myself, would ever make me forget my age again. I wouldn't allow the gray mists of forgetfulness to come again and obscure important events. I looked in my mirrors and saw small, hard breasts swelling out my sweaters. I wore my sweaters loose, hoping Arden wouldn't notice, but already I'd seen him looking there and trying not to let me see him when he did. I saw other boys in school taking interested surveys on how my figure was improving. I ignored them and concentrated on

Arden, who was still in the same school Vera attended. What I had under my sweaters was small in comparison to what Vera displayed by wearing the tightest sweaters she could squeeze into.

Papa never objected to Vera's tight sweaters. Vera was allowed to date and go to movies and school proms. She belonged to half a dozen clubs, or so she reported when she came home very late sometimes. I never had time to socialize. I had to hurry to Mr. Rensdale every day after school, but I was uneasy with him now. I couldn't help but think of what Vera had told me about what she did with him. Half the time I thought she lied; half the time I thought maybe she didn't. One day he had his sports shirt open at the throat, and his chest was very hairy, just as she'd said. She had described his naked body to me in such detail it was almost as if he wore transparent clothes. I couldn't look his way.

The girls I met at school asked me to their slumber parties, but Papa always refused to let me go. He wanted me home with him, listening to him, watching him shave, hearing of his trials and tribulations at work. While he shaved and I still perched on the edge of his tub, I learned how to short stocks, what buying long meant. I heard about wash sales and municipal bonds, and tax shelters, and percentage rates, and hedging, and tax loopholes. The stock market was a crazy gambling game for the very rich. Only the ones with millions were sure to profit—unless they were somehow "intuitive."

"And you are," said Papa with a wide smile as

he wiped off the excess shaving lather. "Audrina, the rocking chair did help, didn't it?"

"Yes, Papa. Can I go now? I want to call Arden and make plans to meet him tomorrow. There's a movie showing I'd like to see."

"I'll take you to the movie."

"Vera goes to the movies with boys. Why can't I?"

"Because I don't give a damn what Vera does."

I'd argued this out before and lost; I was sure to lose again. Then Papa smiled at me. "Well, my love, my impatient one, you are soon to have *again* what you want most. Tomorrow morning early, I'm taking off to drive to where Sylvia has lived since she left the hospital. I've already called and made all the necessary arrangements. Sylvia will come home with me tomorrow morning."

"Oh, Papa!" I cried happily, "thank you, thank you!"

How strange his sad smile, how very strange.

Early the next morning, long before Papa was out of bed and was ready to drive to Sylvia, I raced through the woods to the cottage on the other side. The woods were lush and green, full of the beauty of spring. I was hoping to catch Arden before he rode off on his bicycle to deliver the morning papers. His old car had "conked out" and was now just junk to clutter the yard as he tried to repair it again.

Robins and purple martins were on the grass, paying little attention to me as I ran to the cottage door and threw it open without knocking. Straight on into the kitchen I ran, only to pull up short and gasp.

There was Billie wearing shorts and a red tank

top. For the first time I was seeing her without all those long, full skirts that made it seem she did have two legs hidden somewhere underneath. Her hair was loose and waving, and the knit top revealed a remarkably voluptuous bosom, but all I could see were the little eight-inch stumps thrusting out from the legs of her short shorts. They seemed like fat sausages that slimmed down quickly so they could be neatly tied at the ends. Faint radiating lines made folds like wrinkles from where the excess skin had been drawn and somehow fastened. I shrank away.

It was so pitiful, those stumps where her beautiful legs used to be. I glanced toward the living room where she had all those photographs of herself in costume. I choked back a cry of distress, when I hadn't wanted to show pity. I had wanted to see them, and not remark, or even seem to notice.

To my surprise, Billie began to laugh. She reached to touch my cheek, then tousled my already windblown hair. "Well, go ahead and stare all you want to. Can't say I blame you. They're not pretty to look at, are they? But remember that once I had two of the most beautiful, skillful and creative legs any woman could desire. They served me well when I had them, and most people will never have what I did."

Again I was left without words.

"People learn to adjust, Audrina," she said softly, refraining from touching me again as if afraid now I wouldn't want her to. "You're putting yourself in my place and thinking you couldn't stand to live with my handicap, but somehow, when it's your own, it isn't nearly as horrible as it seems to someone else. Then again, as contrary as we humans are, I can look around and think, why me and not her, or him? I could throw myself into an abyss of self-pity if I wanted to. Most of the time I don't even think about the loss of my legs."

I stood there, all gangly and awkward, feeling humbled. I could almost see her legs that weren't there. "Arden told me he sees you with your legs. He never sees the stumps."

"Yes," she said, her eyes shining, "he's a wonderful son. Without him I probably would have given up. He saved me. Having Arden forced me to carry on and teach myself to do everything. And Arden would do anything for me. Somehow because we had each other, we've managed. None of it has been easy, and yet because it was difficult we have more to be proud of. Now, darlin', enough said about me. What are you doing over here at such an early hour?"

She went on with her canning as I hesitated. Her high stool on rollers was placed so she could scoot from here to there with hardly any effort, just by shoving or pulling with her hands. Then it happened quicker than I could wink—she slipped from the stool and fell to the floor with a thud. She lay at my feet for a brief second like half a large doll.

I started to help.

"Don't help," she ordered, and in no time at all she had used those strong arms to heft herself back onto the stool. "Audrina, look in the pantry and you'll see a little red cart I use when I want to really speed around.

Arden made it for me. He wants to paint it a different color each year, but I won't let him. I like red best. Nothing shy about me, darlin'."

Weakly I smiled, wishing I could be as brave. Then I asked if Arden had already left.

"Yep, he's gone. If that lousy, stingy husband of mine would send more money, my son wouldn't have to work himself to death." She turned and smiled brightly and asked again, "C'mon, tell me what you're doing over here so bright and early?"

"Billie, Sylvia's coming home today. My aunt's told me she isn't normal, but I don't care. I feel so bad that a poor little baby never had a mother, and no family but Papa to love her. That's not enough, especially when Papa only visits her once or twice a month—if he does. You can never tell when my father tells the truth, Billie," I said with some shame. "He lies, and you know he's lying; and he knows you know he's lying, and still he doesn't care."

"Your father sounds like a real dilly."

"I told Arden yesterday that Sylvia *might* come home today. Knowing how Papa is I wasn't really sure, but I eavesdropped and heard him talking on the telephone last night. He is bringing her home. He also called his office and told them not to expect him in today. Did I tell you he's manager now?"

"Yes, darlin', you've told me at least two dozen times. And now I'm going to tell you something perhaps you don't know. You are very proud of your papa. Even when you think you dislike him, you dislike him regretfully. Darlin', don't feel bad about loving and hating your daddy. None of us is all good or all bad. People come in all shades of gray. No out-and-out devils, and no true angels and saints." She smiled. "Honey, you go right on loving your papa even if he is straight from a cake. Arden feels the same way about his father."

Two hours later, with my heart lodged somewhere in my throat, I stood on the front steps of Whitefern with my aunt beside me and waited to see my baby sister for the first time. I looked around, knowing I had to remember this special day so that later I could tell my little sister just how it had been when she first came home. The sun was out bright and full. Not a cloud was in the sky. Some haze hung over the woods and muffled the cries of the birds. Dampness from the dew, I told myself, only that. The warm breezes from the River Lyle stirred my hair.

The spacious lawn had been mowed by a man from the village; he'd trimmed the shrubs, weeded the gardens, swept the front walk. The house had been re-painted white, and its roof was new, too—red as dark as congealed blood, like the blinds at the windows. We were dressed in our best to welcome Sylvia home. Vera was there, too, seated lazily on the swing, a small secret smile curving her lips and making her dark eyes sparkle wickedly. I suspected she knew far more about Sylvia than I did, as she knew more about everything than I did.

"Aud . . . dreen . . . ah . . . ," she chanted, "soon you're going to see . . . see for yourself. Boy, are you gonna be sor . . . reee you kept pleading to have your baby sister—because I disown her. For me, Sylvia Adare just does not exist."

In no way was I going to let Vera kill my excitement or my happiness. I suspected Vera was jealous that it was my mother's baby and not my aunt's.

"Audrina," said my aunt, "are you really as happy as you look?" She could seldom keep from frowning when Sylvia's name was mentioned, and this was obviously no happy day for her.

"Look, look! Here they come!" I cried excitedly, pointing to Papa's Mercedes ducking in and out of the thick rows of trees that lined our curving drive. I edged a bit nearer to my aunt, who straightened her spine and stood taller. For a brief second her hand reached for mine, but she didn't take my hand, as she'd never taken it.

Behind us Vera tittered as she swung to and fro, to and fro, chanting her "You'll be sorry" tune.

The shiny black car drew to a stop before our entranceway. Papa got out and strolled around to the passenger side, opened the door—and for the life of me I couldn't see anyone in there. Then Papa reached inside and lifted from the seat a very small child.

Papa called to me, "Here's Sylvia." He beamed a broad smile my way and then put Sylvia on the ground.

That's when the creaking of the wooden slab swing stopped. Vera rose reluctantly to her feet and drifted closer. I glanced to see her eyes fixed on me, as if she were only interested in my reactions and didn't care about Sylvia at all. Not once did she look at my sister. How odd.

Despite Vera, and my aunt's grim expression, I was so happy as I stared at that pretty little girl who was my sister. In another second I was seeing her as not just pretty, but beautiful. She had a bright head of chestnut-colored curls, reddish blond where the sun highlighted, and how marvelously shiny they were. I saw her sweet little dimpled hands that reached pleadingly toward Papa, wanting him to pick her up. He had to stoop to catch hold of her hand, yet he did that and began to guide her toward the steps. "One step at a time, Sylvia," he encouraged. "That's the way it's done, just one step at a time."

How dear were the little white shoes she wore. What fun she was going to be, a living doll of my very own to dress and play with. Too excited for words, I stepped down lower, just one step—and then paused. Something . . . something about her eyes, about the way she walked, the way she held her mouth. Oh, dear God—what was wrong with her?

"Come, Sylvia," urged Papa, tugging on her miniature hand, which must be lost in his. "You come too, Audrina. Step down to our level and meet the little sister you've been dying to have. Come closer so you can admire Sylvia's aquamarine eyes that tilt so charmingly upward. See how widely spaced they are. See Sylvia's long, curling, dark lashes. See all the beauty that Sylvia possesses—and forget everything else."

He paused, looked at me and waited. Vera giggled and moved for a better place from which she could observe my every reaction.

Frozen, I thought at that moment that all of nature stood still waiting for my decision and my judgment of Sylvia. It was my move now, but I couldn't move and couldn't speak.

Grown impatient, Papa spoke. "Well, if you can't come to us, then we'll come to you." Undaunted as always, he flashed me a charming smile that made his teeth flash in the sunlight. "You have been pestering me for more than two years to bring home your baby sister. Well, here she is. Aren't you delighted?"

Step by tortured step, Papa had to assist Sylvia to walk. She couldn't lift either foot with any degree of skill. She shuffled her feet along, making them slide over obstacles. Even as she did this, her head lolled to the right, then to the left; it fell forward; it jerked and fell backward as if she stared at the sky. Then back again, and the ground would draw her attention—if that nothing stare could be called attention.

Sylvia's bones seemed made of rubber. Before she'd taken five small steps, she'd scuffed her new white shoes, fallen to her knees three times and been hauled up by Papa. Easily enough Papa tugged her up the steps by lifting her by one frail arm. As they advanced, I backed up the stairs, not even realizing I was retreating. Still Sylvia was coming closer and closer so I could see details. Her lips never met but gaped so that she drooled, her eyes never focused.

I trembled, feeling sick. Papa, it was all his fault! He was responsible for Sylvia's condition! All those arguments, the times he used his belt for a whip.

I sobbed then for Momma, who had done her bit, too, when she drank that hot tea laced with bourbon, even when Papa told her not to.

Coming closer every second was the end result of all this abuse, this lovely little girl who looked absolutely moronic.

I backed up until I felt that house hard behind my back. Relentlessly Papa pursued, dragging my sister along. Then he swooped to pick her up, and in the cradle of just one of his arms, he held her so she was at my eye level.

"Look, Audrina, see Sylvia. Don't turn your head aside. Don't close your eyes. See how Sylvia drools and can't focus her eyes or even make her feet move correctly. She'll reach for what she wants a dozen or more times before she can figure out how to grasp it. She'll try to shove food into her mouth and miss, though eventually she'll find a way to eat. She's like an animal, a wild thing—but isn't she beautiful, charming and terrible, too? Now that you see, perhaps you'll understand why I kept her away for so long. I was giving you freedom and not once did you thank me. Not once."

"Sylvia is a crazy . . . a crazy . . . a crazy . . ." chanted Vera softly in the background. "Now Audrina's got a nutty . . . a nutty . . . a nutty . . ."

Papa roared, "Vera, get in the house and stay there!"

For some reason, Vera paled. She stalked closer to where Papa stood with Sylvia. "You'd rather have that idiot little girl than me, wouldn't you?"

screamed Vera, glaring at him and Sylvia, too. Something tortured twisted her mouth and made her look old and ugly. "There will come a time when you'll want me more than you've ever wanted anyone else—but I'll spit in your face before I'll help you when you need it!"

"You are not telling me anything I don't already know," said Papa coldly. "You are like your mother— free with your hate and spite, stingy with your love. I don't need your help, Vera. Not now, and not in the future—I have Audrina."

"You have nothing when you have Audrina!" yelled Vera shrilly, striking out at him. "She hates you, too, only she doesn't know it yet!"

Easily Papa continued to hold Sylvia as his free hand shot out and delivered such a hard slap to Vera's face that she fell to the porch floor. Crumpled there she screamed wildly, almost insanely. Sylvia began a loud wailing.

"Damn you for hitting her!" cried my aunt. "Damian, all that girl wants is a little show of affection from you. You've never given her anything but indifference. And you know who she is—*you know!*"

"I don't know anything," Papa said in a voice so deadly cold I shivered with fear. He riveted his dark, menacing eyes on my aunt, almost visually ordering her to keep her mouth shut or perhaps he'd knock her down, too.

Panic was taking me over. Vera crawled to where she could use the screen door to pull herself up. Then, still crying, she disappeared into the house. And I was left still staring at Sylvia, who couldn't focus on anything or anyone.

What kind of eyes did she have? Vacant eyes. Nowhere eyes. Though their color was striking and her long lashes were dark and curling, what difference? What difference when there was no intelligence behind that void stare.

I swallowed over that aching lump that came again to thicken my voice and sting my eyes with tears. My fist balled and I swiped at my tears, trying not to let Papa see.

Papa was staring at me. "No comment, Audrina? Come, now, you must be thinking something."

My eyes lifted to meet his. His smile came then, slight and cynical. "Why can't Sylvia close her mouth and focus her eyes?" I asked in a weak voice. "And why can't she walk as well as other children almost three years old?"

"Leave us," said Papa to my aunt, who appeared rooted to one spot. I could still hear Vera's cries rebounding down the stairs. Though our huge house was cluttered with dark and massive furniture, when someone screamed as Vera was screaming now it seemed a hollow house, ghostlike and full of echoes.

"Why should I leave, Damian? Tell me that."

"Nobody's influence should come between Audrina and her sister. Ellsbeth, take that disapproving scowl from your face. It's not becoming."

Without another protest, my aunt entered the house and slammed the door. Papa put Sylvia on the porch and released her hand. Immediately she began to wander about, aimlessly heading this way, then that, turning to clumsily bump into a wicker rocker, to upset a potted fern placed on the white wicker stand, so that the fern tumbled off the stand before it, too, fell over.

Oh! "She's blind, isn't she, Papa?" I cried, all of a sudden realizing why her eyes were void and couldn't focus. "Why didn't you tell me that a long time ago?"

"It would be better if she were blind," said Papa sadly. "Sylvia may look blind, but she can see almost as well as you or I—only she can't control the muscles of her eyes and make them stay in focus. Her doctors thought soon after she was born that she had one of those nerve diseases and they tested her for those. She's been through every examination known to modern medicine to find out what's wrong with her. She can see, and she can hear, but still she doesn't react to anything as she should. Now, go ahead and ask how the doctors know, and I'll go into great boring details to explain all the tests they gave her as soon as they suspected something was wrong."

"Tell me," I whispered.

"If you watch carefully, you'll see that she will bump into chairs and knock things over, but she will not fall down the stairs." He had his eyes on me, and not Sylvia, who really needed watching. "If you call her name repeatedly, she will respond eventually. She may walk right by you, but she'll come. I wanted to leave her with the therapists for another year. I hoped in that time they might have succeeded in teaching her how to control her body functions." He saw the look on my face and said softly, "Audrina, Sylvia wears diapers like many other children her age, but unlike other children, Sylvia will no doubt have to wear diapers the rest of her life."

Oh, how awful! I stared at Sylvia disbelievingly.

Papa went on. "If what her specialists say is true, Sylvia is permanently and severely retarded. I don't like believing that, yet I have to accept the fact. Still, some little part of me keeps thinking that maybe Sylvia will one day be normal if given the right care—that is, if any of us know just what normal is."

I'd prepared myself for anything but this. Blind, deaf, lame I thought I could handle—but not this. I didn't need a retarded sister to complicate the rest of my life.

That's when I turned to see that Sylvia was dangerously near the steps. Rushing forward, I grabbed her just in time. "Papa, you said she could see!"

"She can see. She is also very intuitive. She wouldn't have fallen. She's very much like a wild creature that lives by its instincts. Love her a little, Audrina, even if you can't love her a lot. She needs someone to love her and if you love every stray cat and dog and nurse every wounded bird you find, then you can love your retarded sister and care for her as long as she needs you."

I stared up into his full, handsome face just beginning to show a few lines. A bit of silver softened the dark hair at his temples. I wasn't twelve years old yet, and he was putting me in charge of a child that would stay a perpetual baby.

Many times Papa had told me I was smart, that I could do anything I set my mind to. Soon he was saying I'd have Sylvia potty-trained in no time at all. Love could do more than professional expertise. I continued to stare at him with wide eyes as he went on to say I'd also teach her how to focus her eyes, control her lips, how to walk properly, talk well. I couldn't stop watching Sylvia awkwardly backing down the five steps on her hands and knees. Then she got up to wander about in the yard. Several times she made an attempt to pull a camellia from the bush. The color seemed to attract her, and when she finally had it in her small hand, she tried to hold it to her nose and sniff. She didn't know exactly where her nose was, or if she did, she didn't know how to aim precisely. I was touched, horrified and full of pity. In the short time she'd been here, she'd managed to dirty her dress and scuff her shoes beyond repair, and her pretty hair was hanging in her face.

I was in turmoil. I pitied Sylvia. I wanted her and I didn't want her. I loved her, and maybe I was already beginning to hate her a little, too. Weeks later I was to suspect that if given a choice at that moment, before she had a chance to seize my heart, I would have sent her back to where she came from.

But Sylvia was here and she was my responsibility. Maybe I didn't want her or need her, but for my beloved dead mother I would take care of Sylvia, even if it meant denying myself the freedom I might have had if she'd never been born.

As I stood at the age of almost twelve watching her, something tender and loving came and hurried me along the path toward maturity. I rushed down the stairs so I could snatch her up into my arms. On her round chubby cheeks I planted a dozen or more kisses. I cupped her small head in my hand and felt the soft silky baby hair.

"I'll love you, Sylvia! I'll be your mother. You'll never be mistreated from now on. I'll teach you one day how to control your bladder and how to use the toilet. I'll save you, Sylvia. I'm not going to believe you're retarded, only physically undertrained. Each morning when I wake up I'm going to tell myself to find new ways to teach you what you need to know. There is a way to make you normal, I know there is."

Sisters

That very same evening Papa held me on his lap for the last time. "You're growing up, Audrina. Each day sees you more and more a woman. I see the changes taking place in your body, and I certainly hope your aunt did a good job of instructing you on how to handle certain situations. From now on I won't be able to cuddle you like this. People often presume ugly things—but even if I don't hold you, it won't mean I don't love you."

His hands were in my hair as I pressed my face against his shirt front. At that moment all I felt was his love.

"I'm proud and very glad you promised to take care of Sylvia," he went on in an emotional voice, as if at last I was proving myself to be very like his First and Most Beloved Audrina. "It is your duty to take care of your unfortunate sister. You must agree never to put her in a mental institution where she'll be abused by other patients, and by the attendants who are not honorable when it comes to pretty young girls. And she will be beautiful; even now you can see it. She won't have any mental capabilities, but men won't care. She'll be used by them, abused by them. By the time she reaches puberty some boy will steal her virginity, perhaps make her a mother. And God help her child, which will then become your responsibility, too. Don't look at me like that and think I'm putting my burden on your young shoulders. Sylvia will outlive me, just as you will. I'm preparing you for the time when I'm gone and your Aunt Ellsbeth is, too."

I sobbed on his shoulder, thinking of the heavy cross Sylvia was.

Papa carried me up the stairs for the last time and tucked me into bed, and maybe for the last time he kissed me good night. Vague images came of all the times he'd put me to bed and kissed me good night, and heard my prayers, and taken me to the First Audrina's room to rock and dream. He was telling me as he stood in the doorway, looking at me sadly, that from now on he expected me to be an adult.

"It's all right, Papa," I said in a strong voice. "I'm not afraid to walk the halls at night now. If Sylvia cries out in her sleep, I'll run to her and you won't have to bother. But you love her, too, and do for her all that you did for me. I'm not even afraid to sit in the rocking chair anymore. When you don't stay outside the door, I *do* become the empty pitcher that fills to overflowing with everything beautiful. The boys in the woods don't bother me now, for I've learned not to fear them like I used to. Thank you, Papa, for helping me overcome my fear of boys."

He stood there silent for long, long moments. "I'm happy to hear your empty pitcher has filled."

"When I rock in the chair now I can find Momma and talk to her . . . is that crazy, Papa?"

Some shadow came to darken his eyes even more. "Stay out of the rocking chair, Audrina. It's done all it can for you now."

What? How surprising. I knew now I wasn't going to give it up. Papa was protecting me from something he didn't want me to know, and that very something was what I *had* to know.

He left me then and closed the door and I was alone. I lay so still in the gloom I could hear the house breathe, and the boards of the floors whispered, conniving a way to keep me here forever.

In the dimness of my shadowed room with all the ghosts of previous Whiteferns murmuring, I heard the creak of my door as it opened and softly closed. It seemed a wraith straight from hell came through. Its hair stood on end. The long white garment it wore trailed on the floor. I almost screamed!

"Audrina . . . it's only me . . . Vera."

My heart pounded so fast from the fright she'd given me that my voice quivered when I asked what she wanted. Weak and faltering her words came to dumbfound me. "I want to be your friend . . . if you'll have me. I'm tired of living in a house where everybody hates me, even my own mother. Audrina, I don't have anybody. Teach me how to make people love me like they love you."

"Your mother doesn't love me," I choked.

"Yes, she does. At least, she loves you more than she loves me. She trusts you with the best china and crystal—and that's the real reason she lets you take on most of my chores. I'm not good enough to be a kitchen slave. Audrina, have you noticed how often she throws that into Papa's face? It's her weapon to beat him with, like she knows it hurts him when she says that. For that's what he made your mother—his kitchen and bedroom slave."

I didn't like this kind of talk, it seemed disloyal. "My mother loved him," I said defensively. "When you love I suppose you give up what you want for yourself."

"Then give up something for me, Audrina. Love me as you are willing to love Sylvia, and she's retarded and stupid, even if she is little and pitiful and kinda cute. I'll be your best sister. I will. From now on, I swear never to be mean or hateful to you again. Please be my friend, Audrina. Please trust me."

Vera had never come near me before without making some attempt to harm me or my possessions. She trembled as she stood near my bed, seeming pathetically vulnerable in her long white nightgown with her strange hair that rose straight up and made her look frightful. Yet I couldn't help understanding. It was terrible to be unloved by your own mother . . . and if she wanted my love, I'd give it a try.

Less than eagerly I allowed her to crawl into my bed, and, locked in each other's arms, we were soon fast asleep.

I never questioned why, on the very day that Sylvia came home, Vera decided she needed me. I was only grateful.

Soon Vera and I were very close and having so much fun together it seemed impossible that a short while ago I'd felt she was my worst enemy. Though she studied with Mr. Rensdale once a week, she began to come with me every day to my music classes. Very proper and subdued, she'd sit on his sofa and listen to me play. Arden whispered that he was happy that Vera and I were friends at last. "That's the way it should be with sisters—or first cousins. Families should stick together."

"It's all right to say she's my sister. Everybody thinks she is anyway."

Now that I was seeing Vera and my music teacher together, I thought I could judge from their behavior just what lies, or truths, Vera had told me. Were they really lovers? One hot summer afternoon Vera wore nothing but a brief white piqué bra with her bright green shorts. I had on a white blouse and skirt that Papa approved of for music lessons. The way Vera was dressed (or undressed) he'd think was indecent—for me.

As I earnestly tried to play with the sensitivity of a promising artist, Vera sprawled in one of Mr. Rensdale's chairs, one leg thrown over an arm. Her fingers indolently traced circles over her breasts to define her nipples, which were already protruding. Mr. Rensdale couldn't keep his eyes from wandering her way. No matter how beautifully I played, or how many mistakes I made, he didn't notice. What good had eighteen hours of practice on one piece done when Vera was there to distract him? Thoughtlessly, Vera would hug herself, caress her thigh, her arms, jiggle her breasts as if to shake crumbs out of her bra. It was amazing how she kept so busy doing things to her body.

"Vera, for God's sake, what's wrong with you?" snapped Lamar Rensdale.

"A bee stung me in the most embarrassing place, and it hurts," she wailed, looked at him beseechingly. "I need to pull out the stinger, but I can't see it. It's on the bottom side of my—"

"I know where it is," he said shortly. "You've been trying to pull it out for half an hour. Audrina, go into my bathroom and help your sister pull out the stinger."

Mr. Rensdale had his back turned to her and was looking at me pleadingly. Behind him Vera was violently shaking her head, telling me no, she didn't want *my* help. I got up anyway and went into the bathroom to wait for Vera. Minutes passed. "Hurry up, Vera. Soon Arden will be coming back to take us home."

"It's all right," sang out Vera cheerfully. "I just now managed to pull out the stinger myself." As I came back into the living room, she smiled and tugged down her brief bra. "All I needed was a good magnifying mirror. Thank you for letting me use your tweezers, Mr. Rensdale."

Why was he looking so red-faced? Then I saw Vera's smug look and guessed she'd pulled up her bra, and in front of him had pulled out the stinger—if there had been one there in the first place.

From that day forward I began to notice the little exchanges between them. For my sake, it seemed, he wanted to show decorum, but for my sake, too, Vera wanted to reveal just what their relationship was. When it was her time to play at the piano, she struggled to produce some childish tune that made him wince . . . and yet her halter top would come untied, or her tennis dress would show her panties. She flirted with her eyes, with her gestures, with the way she sat carelessly, invitingly, telling him in all possible ways that she would be free with herself—if and when he wanted. I began to dislike her again. She told jokes that made me blush, and he sat with his eyes downcast, seemingly very tired. Always he looked so tired. "It's the heat," he explained when I questioned. "The mugginess drains me of energy."

"Oh, save a little, Mr. Rensdale," crooned Vera. "Save just enough for the sake of pleasure."

He said nothing, only got up and handed me my assignments. "I hope your house isn't as humid as this one."

He didn't assign anything to Vera, but they exchanged some secret message with their eyes.

"The downstairs rooms are wonderfully cool," chimed up Vera, "but upstairs it's just as hot and muggy as this. I'd go naked all the time if Papa and my aunt didn't have a fit."

I stared at Vera. Once in a great while, during a long hot spell, our upstairs was stuffy, but seldom so hot anyone would need to stay nude.

As the summer days stretched long and sultry, the beach was an occasional treat with Arden beside me and Papa keeping a watchful eye on what we did together. Vera refused to go anywhere with Papa, and my aunt had too much to do to have any time for fun. Sylvia toddled on the sand, looking pitifully different from other children her size and age. She couldn't fill her sand bucket, though she tried diligently; she didn't have enough sense to run from the waves that could have caught her in the undertow and carried her out to sea. It was Arden and I who ran to save her time and again. Papa sprawled under a huge, colorful umbrella, eyeing all the pretty girls.

Soon I learned that Sylvia would eat anything, even grass. She crawled outside the house, inside the house, got up to stumble around, bumping into things. Miraculously, after the first day she never broke anything. Left alone in the garden for only a few seconds, she meandered off and became lost. Once, after an hour of frantic searching and calling, I found her sitting under a tree eating wild strawberries, looking as innocent as a cherub without sense. She screamed during the nights, proving she did have active vocal cords and could one day speak if ever I could activate her dormant brain. She fed herself by clumsily picking up her food after many fruitless attempts, then shoving whatever it was in her hand toward her mouth. Unfortunately she never managed on the first try and would miss at least twice before she centered her hands on her mouth.

Each meal ended with Sylvia looking a dreadful mess, with food plastered all over her face, in her hair, in her nostrils. A bib did no good at all. She dropped, she spilled, she threw up often, especially after eating grass. Worst of all—worse than anything—she still had no control over her body's elimination functions.

"She's not three years old yet," encouraged Papa when I put away an old potty seat in disgust. "Even you weren't out of diapers at her age."

"Yes, she was," disagreed my aunt. "Audrina was always painfully aware of being messy. She trained herself as Lucietta read nursery rhymes and showed her pretty pictures and rewarded her with cookies when she performed well."

Papa scowled disapprovingly, then proceeded to ignore her. "And you will have to keep her cleaner, Audrina, or she'll end up with a red, raw bottom that will be the devil to heal—that's why she cries out in the night. That diaper rash hurts."

"Damian! Stop it! You cannot expect a young girl like Audrina to take full responsibility for a retarded child. Put her back in that place or hire a nurse."

"I can't afford a nurse," added Papa sleepily, yawning and stretching out his long legs, ready to nap on the porch chaise. "I've got you, Ellie, and that daughter of yours to support. That takes all my cash."

I stared at Papa, hating the way he could take the truth and twist it.

Half an hour later I tried the potty seat again, tying Sylvia to it so she wouldn't wiggle off. For an hour I read to her from Mother Goose, but to no avail. The moment I had Sylvia dressed again in clean diapers with plastic panties over them, she was soiled. Vera came in just in time to see me change her again. She laughed scornfully. "Boy, I'm glad she's not in my charge, or she'd stay filthy."

"A fine nurse you'll make," I said angrily. Then I snapped my head around to glare at her. "Where've you been?" Sometimes when I thought Vera was in her room reading, she wasn't there at all. She wasn't anywhere where I could find her. Usually she'd show up just before six, when Papa was due home.

Yawning sleepily, she fell into one of my bedroom chairs. "I hate summer school. I hate winter school. I know school ends at twelve, but I do have a few friends in the village, even if you don't . . ."

Smiling and mysterious looking, she tossed a Hershey bar my way. "A gift. I know you like chocolate."

Something was going on in Vera's life, but I didn't pry. Though she no longer openly tormented me, she still didn't help with the housework, or the dishes, or with Sylvia. "I'm pooped, Audrina, really pooped." She yawned and curled up in the chair like some slinky, sensuous cat. I could almost hear her purring.

As my aunt and I prepared the meals and cleaned the house and changed bed linens together, some kind of closeness developed between us as we worked, doing all the many things Vera refused to do. Occasionally, now, she even let me call her Aunt Ellie. Oh, how she struggled to cook as well as Momma had cooked. It was her desire (though she never said this to me, I sensed it) to cook even better than my mother. She wanted Papa to have all his favorite dishes.

Sometimes it was two o'clock in the morning before she went to bed.

Perhaps it was six months after Sylvia came before finally one day Papa smiled after he wiped his mouth and put down his napkin and said, "Well, Ellie, you really outdid yourself this time. No one could have done better. That was a superb meal, really superb."

Who would have ever thought I'd be happy to hear him say my aunt could match my mother in anything? I appreciated his compliment so much that tears came to my eyes—perhaps because they came to hers, too.

A different kind of life developed for me. A frantic life that stole my summer; stole three afternoons a week from taking music lessons, leaving me little time for Billie and Arden. In the fall it forced me to race home from where the school bus let me off, arriving to search breathlessly for Sylvia, who had the worst habit of wanting to hide herself away somewhere.

It was a thankless task I'd set for myself, truly an impossible task to try and train Sylvia in the same way you would a child of normal intelligence. Her attention span was exceedingly short. She couldn't sit still. She couldn't focus her eyes or her mind on anything but movement. The worst of it was that no sooner did Papa drop Sylvia into my lap than he forgot her existence. Desperately I turned to my aunt and pleaded for help. "All right," she agreed reluctantly, "I promise to do what I can while you're in school, but the moment you come home and on the weekends and school vacations, Sylvia is yours—all yours."

Many times I rescued Sylvia from some horrible

punishment my aunt felt perfectly justified in delivering. "No!" I yelled, racing into the kitchen and throwing down my schoolbooks, "don't use that switch on
Sylvia! She doesn't know it's wrong to pull up all the
chrysanthemums. She thinks they're pretty, and she
likes pretty, colorful things."

"Don't we all?" asked my aunt acidly. "I like to
put them on the table for your father. What's more,
Sylvia trampled down my vegetable beds, too! Everything ready to harvest she's ruined. Sometimes I think
she's deliberately trying to drive me as crazy as she is."
Tears of self-pity made her eyes sparkle.

Sylvia's room was like a padded cell. In that small,
pitiful room was a small low bed from which she
could fall to the floor without injuring herself when
she hit the thick carpeting. Truly, sometimes it seemed
my aunt was right: Sylvia should never have been
born. But born she was, and there wasn't much I could
do about it and still like being me.

Sylvia was three years old now, and unlike other
children who liked to play with building blocks and
balls and small kiddy cars, Sylvia wasn't interested.
She didn't know what to do with herself but roam
about endlessly. She liked to climb, to eat and drink,
to prowl, to hide away, and that was all. I didn't know
how to begin her education when pretty picture books
couldn't capture her attention and toys were meaningless objects to her. Even when I tied her in a chair, she
could still loll her head about and avoid seeing anything I tried to show her.

Then one wonderful day when I was rocking in the

chair in the First and Best Audrina's playroom, I had a vision. I saw a little girl who looked somewhat like me or the other Audrina playing with crystal prisms, sitting in the sunlight and catching sunlight, to refract it on the walls, into the mirrors that shot the colors back again, and all the room turned into a kaleidoscope. On the toy shelves of the playroom I found half a dozen beautifully shaped crystal prisms, two like long teardrops, another like a star, one a snowflake and another like a giant diamond. I gathered them together, then opened the draperies wide, tore back the sheer curtains and sat on the floor to play with the prisms myself. It was Sylvia's habit to follow me around when I was home, such a close shadow that often when I turned abruptly, I bumped into Sylvia and knocked her down.

The sunlight through the prisms shot rainbows about the room. I saw in my peripheral vision that Sylvia was interested in the colors. She was staring at the rainbows that danced about the room. I played them over her face, made one cheek red, the other green, then briefly flashed the light in her eyes. It dazzled her and blinded her, and for some reason she cried out. Stumbling forward, she moaned as she grabbed for the prisms, wanting them for herself.

I'm sure to Sylvia the things in my hands were hard, iridescent flowers. She took them and went to crouch in a corner, as if to hide from me, and there she tried to make the colors dance. They wouldn't. I watched her, mentally telling her to move into the sunlight. Only in the sunlight would the colors come alive.

Over and over she turned the prisms, grunting in frustration, a wailing noise coming from deep inside her, and then she began to crawl with a prism clutched in each hand until she was in the largest patch of sunlight. Immediately the crystals came to life and filled the room with beams of color. For the first time I saw her eyes widen with surprise. Sylvia was making something happen. She knew it. I could see her joy as she made the colors move about the room.

I sat up to hug her close. "Pretty colors, Sylvia. All yours. I give to you what used to belong to *her*." A faint and fuzzy smile visited her gaping lips. It seemed those prisms might never leave her hands now that she'd found one thing she could do easily.

"Oh, God, take those things from her," complained my aunt the next morning as Sylvia sat in her high chair and dropped one prism in her cereal even as with another she beamed rays of light to dazzle everyone in the kitchen. "Did you have to give her those?"

"Leave her alone, Ellie," said Papa. "At least she's found something to do. She's fascinated by the colors, and who knows, maybe they'll teach her something."

"What?" asked my aunt cynically. "How to blind us?"

"Well," said Papa thoughtfully, buttering his third slice of toast, "how to keep her fingerprints off the walls and furniture, at least. She's holding on to those things like they'll run away if she lets go . . . so leave well enough alone."

While I cared for Sylvia and Vera continued to be sweeter than sugar to me, I tried like crazy to find time to practice at least once a day on my mother's piano. Sylvia didn't like me to practice on the piano. She sat in the sunlight and threw colored beams on my sheets of music, and if I shielded them in some way, she beamed the lights in my eyes so I couldn't read the music.

I continued my lessons with Lamar Rensdale, even though I didn't have much time to practice. I knew he was preparing to go to New York. This time he was planning to stay to teach music at Juilliard. "It's better than eking out an existence in a place that treats any artist with scorn," he'd explained. He'd called to tell me his good news the night before, sounding terribly excited. "I'd rather you didn't tell anyone of my appointment, Audrina. And you must swear to go on with your music study. Someday I know I'm going to sit in an audience and say to myself that I was the one who started Audrina Adare on the road to fame."

I hadn't told a soul except Arden, that I'd decided to drop by Mr. Rensdale's to say goodbye. In my pocket I had a small farewell gift, a pair of gold cuff links that had belonged to my maternal grandfather.

Once Lamar Rensdale had seemed the neatest man possible. A place for everything, and everything in its place. Now his once impeccable lawn and garden was untended and cluttered with junk. The grass needed mowing, the weeds needed pulling, and beer cans were rolling in the wind. He hadn't even raked the leaves or torn down the old bird nests over his door. I started to knock at the back door, but at the slight touch of my knuckles, it swung open, helped by the strong gust of wind that blew in behind me.

Whenever I entered his home I'd hear him at the piano, and if he wasn't there, he'd be in the kitchen. Since the house was very quiet, I presumed he'd gone into the city. I decided to just leave my gift with a note and then sit on the porch and wait for Arden to come round and pick me up. I began to scribble a note on his kitchen memo pad.

"Dear Mr. Rensdale," I'd written when I heard a noise coming from the living room. I parted my lips to call out when I heard a familiar girlish giggle. Stiffening, I shuddered to think that all those lurid tales Vera had told me might be true. I tiptoed to the kitchen door and eased it open just a bit. Mr. Rensdale and Vera were in the living room. A lively log fire was crackling in the fireplace, spitting sparks up the chimney. November had just turned cold enough for fires. This afternoon was dreary, but with the fire it seemed very cozy and cheerful in that small room as Lamar Rensdale moved to put a record on the player. Sweetly it filled the house with Schubert's "Serenade," and now I knew I was secretly witnessing a scene of seduction.

I stood there, unable to decide what to do. It would be an hour or more before Arden came for me. It was such a long walk home and the highway was dangerous on foot. I couldn't be so foolhardy as to hitchhike. No, I'd go sit on the back porch, despite the cold. Instead of moving, I debated back and forth as a good reason to watch what was going on in the living room.

"You see," said Lamar Rensdale, "you can dance just fine. I told you your limp is hardly noticeable.

You make too much of it, Vera. When a girl is as pretty as you are, and has your kind of figure, no man is going to notice one small flaw . . ."

"Then my limp is a flaw? Lamar, I was hoping you'd see me as perfect." Her voice had a plaintive, sweet tone, reproachful yet touching. Did she really love him? How could she? She'd only just turned sixteen last week.

"Really, Vera, you are very pretty, and very appealing, and very seductive. But you're too young for a man my age. For two years we've had wonderful times together and I hope you never regret one moment. But now I'm leaving. You should find a boy your own age, a boy who'll marry you and take you away from that house you seem to hate."

"You said you loved me, and now you're talking as if you don't," wailed Vera, tears beginning to streak down her cheeks. "You never did, did you? You just said that so I'd go to bed with you . . . and now that you're tired of me, you want someone new. And I love you so much!"

"Of course I love you, Vera. But I'm not ready to get married. You know I need that professor's assignment. I told them I wasn't married, and they liked that. They thought I'd be more devoted to teaching. Vera, please remember that I am not the only man in the world."

"For me you are!" she wailed louder. "I love you. I'd die for you. I gave myself to you. You seduced me and swore to me you'd always love me, and now that I'm pregnant, you don't want me!"

Deeply shocked, I cringed backward.

Mr. Rensdale forced a controlled laugh. "My dear girl, you cannot possibly be pregnant. Don't try that old trick with me."

"But I am," she wailed. When this seemed to have no effect, she moved, pouted, then snuggled closer in his arms. She pressed against him so tightly they seemed welded together. "Lamar, you do love me, I know that you do. Make love to me again, right now. Let me prove again how much I can thrill you . . ." I gasped to see how she ran her hands all over his back, then down to his buttocks even as she parted her lips and kissed him with such wild passion I felt giddy just watching. She did something then that I couldn't see while the music still played, and the fire still burned.

"Don't . . ." he pleaded as she became more aggressive and tugged at the zipper of his trousers. "Audrina mentioned something last night about dropping in to say goodbye . . ."

"Are you teaching her what you've taught me?" asked Vera in a sultry low voice. "I'll bet I'm ten times better, better than—"

He grabbed her then and shook her by her shoulders as he shouted, "Stop saying things like that! Audrina is a lovely, innocent girl. The Lord alone knows how the two of you could turn out so different."

As he continued to scold her, Vera lifted her green sweater to show her naked breasts. They bobbed as he kept shaking and she kept laughing. Even as he shook her, she unfastened her skirt and let it fall to the floor. In another second her thumbs were hooked inside her panties and off she snatched them. Lamar Rensdale couldn't resist staring at her nudity. It seemed silly for her to keep that sweater pulled up under her armpits as she taunted. "You want me, want me, want me . . . so why don't you take me—or do I have to do what I did last time . . . *Mr. Rensdale?*"

Oh! She was imitating the way I spoke. Suddenly he seized her in his arms and kissed her ruthlessly hard, bending her backwards until I thought she might break. They both fell to the floor, and there they wrestled and kissed, breathing hard with passion, even as they said ugly things to one another. Over and over rolling . . .

Petrified, as if seven years old and trapped in the rocking chair again, I watched until their violent sexual act was over and Vera was lying naked on top of his long, very hairy body. Tenderly she stroked his cheeks, caressed his hair, kissing his eyelids and nibbling on his ears as she murmured with a certain vicious tone, "If you don't take me to New York with you, I'll tell everyone you raped me—and Audrina. The police will throw you in jail, for I'm only sixteen and Audrina is only twelve. They'll believe me, not you, and never again will you find a decent job. Please don't make me do that, Lamar, for I love you. Really love you so much it hurts to even say mean things like that to you." With those words she sat up, turned and began to play with the most intimate parts of his body. His moans of joy followed me out the back door, which I closed softly behind me.

Outside I breathed the cold November air

deeply, trying to cleanse my lungs of the musky odor of sex that permeated all those small rooms. I was never going back. No matter what happened, I was never going back.

Silently I sat next to Arden all the way home. "Is everything all right?" he asked. "Why aren't you talking to me?"

"Everything is fine, Arden."

"Of course it's not fine. If it were you'd be babbling away, telling me about Lamar Rensdale and how wonderful he is. But you're not saying any of that—why not?"

How could I tell him what I was thinking? Vera had boasted only the other day that she'd had sex with Arden, too.

That very evening Vera jumped on me. "You were there, Audrina! You spied on us. If you tell Papa you'll pay—I'll see that you pay. I'll tell him you do the same thing with Arden, and with Lamar, too!" She hurled the gold cuff links I'd left for Mr. Rensdale at me. "I went into the kitchen and found these where you left them on the kitchen table." Menacingly she limped closer. "I'm warning you right now, if you dare to tell Papa I'll do something so dreadful you'll never want to look in a mirror again!"

I hated and despised her so much then that I wanted to hurt her as she threatened to hurt me. "You wanted to be my friend. What a wonderful friend you make, Vera. With you for a friend I don't need any enemies, do I?"

"No," she said with a slow smile that lit up her dark eyes with a sinister glow. "With me for your friend you have the best of all possible enemies. I wanted you to love me, Audrina, so you'd be hurt more when you realized how much I hate you! How much I've always hated you!"

The vehemence of her shrill words left me quivering. "Why do you hate me so much? What have I done to you?"

She spread her hands wide, indicating the entire house and everything in it. She told me I'd stolen everything that was rightfully hers. "You idiot! How can you be so blind? Can't you look at me, at my eyes and see who's my father? *I* am the First Audrina, not *you!* Your papa is my father, too! I'm the eldest and I should come first, not you! Papa dated my mother before he even knew your mother, and he made my mother pregnant. Then he saw your mother, who was younger and prettier. But he didn't say one word to my mother until she told him she was pregnant with me. He refused to believe he was the father and forced my mother to leave town. And that stupid mother of mine did just what he wanted. And all the time she kept thinking that when she came back and he saw me and how pretty I was, he'd want to marry her then. I was only one year old and she had me all fixed up so he'd be impressed—but he wasn't impressed, for he'd married your mother in the meanwhile. Oh, Audrina,

you just don't know how much I hate and despise
him for what he did to both of us. I was just a baby
and rejected by my own father. He has never given me
any of the things that are rightfully mine. He plans to
leave you this house, and all his money, too. He told
my mother that—and it belongs to me! Everything
here should belong to me!" She sobbed and struck
out at me. Quickly I dodged and sprang away. Whirling around, Vera, in her insane rage, hit out at Sylvia.
Down flat on her face Sylvia sprawled, screaming at
the top of her lungs.

That's when I ran to tackle Vera, yelling as I did,
"Don't you ever hit Sylvia again, Vera!"

I was on top of Vera, holding her down as she
writhed and kicked and tried to scratch out my eyes.
She fought me wildly, trying to rake my face with her
long, sharp nails. Sylvia was still screaming. I sprang
to my feet and ran to pick her up. Using a chair to pull
herself up, Vera was finally on her feet. She stumbled
toward the bedroom door and the hall outside. She
didn't notice a small prism that Sylvia had been playing with. She stepped on it, lost her balance and fell
again to the floor.

Sylvia howled in great distress, but it was Vera who
screamed the loudest. When I looked, I was amazed to
see great pools of blood on the floor.

With Sylvia in my arms I ran for my aunt. "Aunt
Ellsbeth, come quickly! Vera is bleeding all over my
bedroom floor!"

Indifferently my aunt looked my way, flour smudged
on her chin.

"She's really bleeding, and the blood is running down her legs . . ."

Only then did my aunt stride to the sink to wash the flour from her hands. She dried them on her spotless white apron. "Well, come along. I may need your help. There's a wild, destructive side to that girl, and no doubt she's managed to get herself in trouble."

We arrived in time to see Vera crawling on the floor, drenched with her own blood by now and still bleeding as she pawed through the congealing pools of blood, crying out, "The baby . . . I've lost my baby . . ." Wild and distraught looking, she raised her head when we entered the room. I hugged Sylvia closer.

"Were you pregnant?" asked my aunt coldly, doing nothing to help her daughter.

"Yes!" screamed Vera, still feeling around in the blood. "I've got to have that baby! I've got to! I need that baby! It's my ticket out of this hellhole, and now it's gone. Help me, Momma, help me save my baby!"

My aunt glanced down at all the blood. "If you've lost it, better so."

Demented looking, Vera's eyes went wild and her fingers curled around one huge clot of blood that she hurled at her mother. It struck my aunt's apron and fell to the floor with a sickening clomp. "Now he'll never take me with him," Vera wailed.

"Clean up the mess you've made, Vera," ordered my aunt, seizing me by the hand and trying to drag me away. "When I come back I want to see this room as spotless as it was this morning. Use cold water on that rug."

"Mother," cried Vera, looking weak now and ready to faint. "I've just miscarried—and you worry about the rug?"

"The Oriental is valuable."

Closing the door behind us, my aunt shoved me in front of her as Sylvia continued to whimper. "I should have known it would happen this way. She's no good, like her father." She paused, seeming to reflect before she added, "And yet he made other children without her flaws . . ."

Feeling sick, I still managed to find a voice. "Is Vera really Papa's child?"

Without answering, my aunt hurried back to the kitchen, where she immediately washed her hands again, scrubbing them with a brush. She hurled her soiled apron into the laundry sink, which she filled with cold water, and then took a fresh apron from a cabinet drawer. The apron was white with sharp, ironed creases. Once she had the apron strings tied, she began to roll the pie pastry she'd abandoned.

"You look paler than usual," Papa said to Vera at the dinner table. "Are you sick with a cold or something? If so, you should eat in the kitchen. You should know better than to spread your viruses around."

The look Vera gave him was so thick with hatred it could have been sliced with a knife. She got up and left her dinner unfinished. I felt sorry for her as I watched her stumble weakly from the dining room. She always limped worse when she was tired. "Vera, is there anything I can do to help?" I called.

"You can stay the hell away from me!"

Vera didn't even make an effort to clean my rug of all that blood. She just left it for me to do. For hours and hours that night before I went to bed, I scrubbed on my hands and knees at the bloody stains that refused to leave the deep woolen pile. My aunt came in and saw what I was doing, left to return shortly with a second pail and a hard brush. Side by side we both worked on the rug. "Your father has gone to bed," she said in a low tone. "He must never know about this. He'd skin Vera alive. Audrina, tell me what he's like, this music teacher of yours. She told me he's the father."

How could I tell her when I knew absolutely nothing about men? To me he'd seemed a fine, kind and noble gentleman who would never seduce a young girl—but then, what did I know?

But the rocking chair knew. Knew everything that Papa knew about how evil men were, and the terrible things they did to girls.

"Where's Vera?" asked Papa when I carried a clean and sweet-smelling Sylvia down into the kitchen the next morning. I strapped her securely into her high chair, tied a huge bib under her chin and gave her the prisms to play with until I had her breakfast ready. Finally he looked up from his morning paper and saw me.

"What's wrong with your face? Were you in a fight? Audrina . . . who hit you in your eye and scratched your cheek?"

"Papa, you know I sleepwalk sometimes. I did that last night and fell."

"I think you're lying. I noticed your face looked red last night, but Vera made me so damned mad that I didn't pay much attention to you. Now you tell me the truth."

Refusing to say more, I began the bacon that Papa ordered. Again he picked up the newspaper and began to read. Until lately the newspapers had never been delivered to our house but had been mailed. I frowned as I gave this some thought. "Papa," I said, dropping bread into the toaster, "why do you need the morning paper now, when you didn't want it before Momma died?"

"It is just something to do, love, besides argue with your aunt."

His words brought my aunt striding into the kitchen. The moment she saw what I was doing, she shoved me aside and took over turning the bacon.

Breakfast was over before my aunt said one word, then quietly came her information. "She's gone, Damian."

"Who's gone?" he asked blandly, turning the newspaper before he neatly folded it so he could read the next page.

"Vera's gone."

"Good riddance."

My aunt paled. Her head bowed for a moment, and then she pulled a folded note from her apron pocket. "Here," she said, handing it to him. "She left this for you on her pillow. I've already read it. I'd like you to read it aloud for Audrina to hear."

"I don't care to read it, Ellsbeth. She's your daughter, and I'm sure she's said nothing that will make my day happier."

Instead, Ellsbeth handed the note to me. Tears came to my eyes as I read what she'd written.

"Wait a minute, Papa," I called as he stood to pull on his jacket. "You need to hear this for the good of your own soul."

For some reason he paused, looking ill at ease as he shifted his weight from one leg to another. He kept his face in profile as I read:

Dear Papa,

You have never allowed me to call you Papa, or Father, but this time I'm going to disobey and call you Papa as Audrina does. You are my father and you know it, my mother knows it, Audrina knows it and I know it.

When I was very young all I wanted was for you to love me, even just a little bit. I used to stay awake at nights plotting all the good things I could do to make you notice me and say, "Thank you, Vera." But I was never able to win your affection, no matter how hard I tried, so soon I gave up.

I used to watch your wife so I could learn to be like she was—soft-spoken, always well dressed and smelling of perfume, and you spanked me for using her perfume, and spanked me for wearing my good clothes when I played. You spanked me for any reason at all. So I stopped trying to please you, especially after you had "your sweet Audrina," who could do no wrong. She was the one who pleased you in all ways.

No doubt at this moment as you read this you are glad to be rid of me, since you never wanted me in the first place. I'm sure you'd be happy to see me dead. But you can't get rid of me so easily. For I'm coming back, Damian Adare, and everybody who made me cry is going to cry ten times more than I ever did.

I won't give away any secrets in this letter, but there will come a day when all your secrets will be dragged out in the open for all to view. Count on that, dear Papa. Dream about that at night. Think about my dark eyes, which are just like yours, and wonder just what I've got in store for you and yours. And remember most of all, you brought it all on yourself by being heartless and cruel to your very own flesh and blood.

Without love now, I am the daughter who will serve you best . . . and serve you longest.

Vera

Slowly, slowly, Papa turned around and stared at me. "Why did you want me to hear that? Audrina. Don't you love me either?"

"I don't know," I answered in a small, uncertain voice, "except I thought you owed her a great deal she never got. Vera's gone, Papa—and she told you the truth. You didn't listen when she talked. You tried not to see her. You never spoke to her except to order her to do this or do that. Papa, if she is your daughter, don't you owe her something? Would a little kindness and a little love have been too much to give?"

Papa squared his massive shoulders. "You've heard Vera's side of it, Audrina, not mine. I'm not going to defend my actions. I say this one thing: Beware the day when Vera comes back into our lives. Go down on your knees tonight and pray that she stays away. But for your aunt I would have had her put in some distant boarding school a long, long time ago. There are some who should never have been born."

Unwaveringly, he looked my aunt in the eyes. I seemed to hear their dark eyes clashing with the sound of swords. It was she who lowered her eyes first, then her head bowed so low her long, straight part showed. Her voice was small and thin when she spoke. "You've said enough, Damian. You were right and I was wrong. But she is mine, and I had hopes she'd turn out differently."

"We all had hopes, didn't we?" With those words he left the kitchen.

Solving Dilemmas

Alone with Aunt Ellsbeth, I didn't know what to say. She sat on and on at the kitchen table staring into space. Quietly I cleared the table and filled the dishwasher. Then I lifted Sylvia out of her high chair, washed her face again and took her upstairs with me while I dressed for school.

I tore off my robe, realizing I might be late for the school bus, and searched my drawers for the sweaters I washed each Saturday. Only my old and too small sweaters were in the drawers. Every good cashmere was gone. All the pretty blouses, too, the ones Papa brought home for me from time to time, all gone. Vera must have taken my best clothes that fit her. I ran to the chest of drawers to see what else might be missing. She didn't want my underwear, all that was there, but when I opened the jewelry case that had once been Momma's, everything of real value left to me by my mother was gone. Even the cuff links and tie clasps meant for my future husband, gone. I cried when I discovered my mother's engagement ring and wedding band had been stolen, too. How ugly and hateful to rob me of things I treasured so much. All the fine jewelry Momma had inherited from her ancestors had no doubt been hocked in some pawnshop. The only thing left of any value was the tiny birthstone ring I always wore on a chain about my neck and the quartz rose that Arden had given me. It's a wonder she hadn't tried to take those off while I slept.

When I returned to the kitchen with Sylvia in my arms, I found my aunt still sitting at the table. "Vera took all my good sweaters and blouses, and the jewelry Momma left me."

"She took what jewelry I had, too," said my aunt in a flat voice, "and also my best coat. I only bought that coat last winter. The first new coat I've had in five years, and Lord knows when I'll have another."

"Papa will buy you another." But I wasn't so sure he would.

All day long, while I tried to concentrate on what the teachers said, I kept thinking of Vera and how she'd slipped away in the night like a thief, not caring whom she hurt. As soon as the schoolbell rang at the end of the last session, I was out the door and running to plead a ride with a friendly girl I knew.

The little cottage where I'd studied music for three years looked deserted. I stood on the front porch and pounded on the door as the wind behind me whistled and tore at my hair. "Hey, you, kid," called the lady next door. "Won't do you no good to keep hitting the door like that. He's gone. Heard him drive off in the middle of the night. Took some woman with him."

"Thank you," I said, turning away and not knowing what to do now. Arden would be home from his school by this time and preparing to deliver his papers, but I didn't have a dime to call him and tell him where I was. I hadn't asked my aunt for change when I left home, since her purse had been emptied by Vera.

With my stomach growling, I began the long fifteen-mile trek to my home. It began to rain long before I reached home. The wind whipped the trees along the roadside and tore at my wet hair, and soon I was so cold, despite my heavy coat, that I began to sneeze. Men slowed their cars and offered me rides. I felt wild with panic as I pretended not to hear them. I speeded my steps. Then a car pulled to a stop and a man got out as if to catch me and drag me into his car. Wild with terror, I screamed as I raced on. It was like a rocking chair nightmare.

A hand grabbed my arm and spun me about. Screaming still, I struck out at him. Then he had my other arm, and I was captured even as I continued to kick and struggle. "What the devil's wrong with you, Audrina?"

It was Arden who had me. His amber eyes came closer as he pulled me into his arms. His hair was pasted down on his forehead. "You're all right. It's only me. Why are you trembling? You shouldn't be out here on the highway, you know that. Why didn't you call?"

My teeth chattered so that I couldn't speak. What was wrong with me? It was only Arden. Why did I feel like I wanted to slap him? Shaking his head in puzzlement, he led me to his car. I huddled on the front seat, cringing to the far side, not wanting to be near him. He turned up the heat so high that he soon said he felt he was cooking—but I was having chills.

"You're going to be sick," he said as he glanced my way. "You're already feverish looking. Audrina, why did you go to the village? I heard in the village that Mr. Rensdale left last night for New York."

"He . . . he . . . did." I sneezed, then told him about Vera. "I think she's the woman he took with him. Papa's going to throw a fit. He knows she's run away, but he doesn't guess she ran away with my music teacher." I shivered and felt all the goose bumps on my arms under the coat.

"Take care," said Arden as he let me out. Swiftly, he leaned to brush a kiss over my cheek. That kiss made me want to scream again. "Don't you go worrying about Vera. She knows how to look out for herself."

I was sick in bed with a terrible cold that gave me four days to think about nothing much but Vera and Lamar Rensdale. "Do you think he'll marry her?" I whispered to my aunt one night soon after dinner.

'No," she said with authority, "men don't marry girls like Vera."

The new year started, and though Vera was gone from our lives now, she was far from forgotten. "Damian," began my aunt one morning, "why don't you ask about Vera? Do you miss her? Do you worry about where she is and what's happening to her? She's only sixteen. Don't you feel any concern for her?"

"All right," said Papa, neatly folding the morning paper and putting it beside his plate. "I don't want to ask about Vera because I don't want you to tell me something I might not want to hear. I don't miss her. This house is a much nicer place to come home to now that she's gone. Nor do I worry about her, or feel concern for her. She's given me just cause to despise her. If she did what I think she did, what I have a very good reason for believing she did, I could take her neck and gladly wring it. But you protected her even then, and tried to convince me she couldn't have been that cruel. I was a fool to have let you protect her. Now pass the butter. I think I'll have another English muffin and another cup of coffee."

I wanted to ask what Vera might have done that made him want to wring her neck. But already I'd learned that neither he nor my aunt ever answered questions, except by asking me questions about what I remembered. I couldn't remember Vera when she was younger than ten, or twelve, or whatever age she'd been when my memory began again.

"No doubt she ran off with that good-for-nothing piano player," said Papa with his mouth full. "Rumors are all over the village, speculating on the woman who left with him in the middle of the night." He gave me a quick surveying glance, then smiled approvingly. "Audrina, I know you know what can happen when you fool around with boys. And if you never believe another word I say, believe this—you'd better not try the same trick. I'd follow *you* to the ends of the earth to bring you back where you belong."

In some ways life was much better without Vera in the house. Still, I wondered how Vera was faring with a man who hadn't wanted her.

Every day I asked my aunt, "Have you heard from Vera?" Every day she told me the same thing. "No. I don't expect to hear from her. I made the worst mistake of my life the day I came back here. But now that I've made my bed, I'm going to make the most of it. That's the winning attitude in life, Audrina, remember that. Once you decide what you want, stick with it until you have it."

"What is it you want?"

She didn't answer, just plodded about the kitchen in floppy shoes that made slip-slop sounds—shoes that she took off before Papa came home. An hour before he was due, she raced upstairs, bathed, dressed, arranged her hair, which she'd had trimmed so it hung loose sometimes. She looked years younger, mostly because she'd found a smile to wear.

Without Vera our lives took on a certain sameness, an unexciting routine that was comforting. I turned thirteen, then fourteen. Sylvia grew but did not progress. She took up all my spare time, but still I saw Arden every day. Papa had resigned himself to Arden, confident I'd see so much of him that I'd soon be bored with the sameness. I was filled with sadness when Arden told me that next fall he'd be going away to college. I didn't want to think of life without Arden.

"Oh, Audrina," cried Arden suddenly, picking me up by my waist and swinging me around so my white skirt flared wide. His amber eyes were on a level with mine now. "Sometimes when I look at you and see how lovely you've become, it makes my heart hurt. I'm so afraid while I'm gone you're going to find someone else. Audrina, please don't fall in love with anyone else. Save yourself for me." Somehow or other my arms had gone around his neck, and I was clinging to him. "I wake up in the night," he went on, "thinking of how you'll look when you're fully grown, and I think as your father does then, that you'll feel toward me like a brother. That's not what I want. I've heard my mom say she changed her mind about boyfriends three times a week when she was your age."

Suddenly I was very conscious of being in his arms, and I squirmed until my toes were on the ground, though he still held me. "I'm not your mother." How serious I felt, how adult and wise, when I wasn't adult or wise.

Something soft and wonderful happened in his eyes, making his pupils enlarge, grow darker. The light that grew in them told me even before his head inclined that at the tender age of fourteen I was going to be kissed by the only boy I'd allowed into my life. How tender his lips were on mine, so tentative and light I felt shivers both hot and cold race up and down my spine. Joy and fear combined as I tried to decide if I liked that kiss or not. Why should I fear? Then he kissed me again, a bit more passionately, and I was filled with apprehension as the rainy day in the woods came back to haunt me. It belonged to the First Audrina, that awful day—why was it tormenting me, and punishing Arden?

"Why are you trembling?" Arden asked, looking hurt.

"I'm sorry. I just couldn't help but be a little alarmed. I've never been kissed like that before."

"I'm sorry if I shocked you—but I just couldn't help myself. A million times I've held back . . . this time I couldn't."

Then I was sorry. "Oh, Arden, isn't it silly of me to be scared when I've wondered what was taking you so long." Why had I said that? It sounded like something Vera would say, and all along I'd been scared to death.

"Are you going to be a pushover? My mother was like that. I was hoping you'd be different, and that would prove to me that what we have now might last forever. Maybe Mom hasn't told you, but she's been married more than once. She was only seventeen the first time, and it was over in a few months. My father was her third husband, and, so she claims, her best. Sometimes I think she says that just to make me feel good about him."

Three times? "I'm no pushover," I said quickly. "It's just that I love you. Puppy love, Aunt Ellsbeth tells me. I never tell her anything. She just looks at me and says it's more than just being outside so much that makes my eyes shine and my skin glow. Even Papa says I never looked healthier or happier. But I think it's you, and I think it's because I've learned to love Sylvia so much. And she loves me, too, Arden.

When I'm not around she crouches in a dim corner as if she doesn't want anyone to notice her. I think she's terrified of Aunt Ellsbeth. Then when I come into the room, she comes over to me and she tugs on my hand, or on the hem of my skirt, and her small face tilts backward . . . and she makes me the center of her life."

He looked uncomfortable, refusing to turn and look at Sylvia, who was always with me—if not in sight, somewhere close by. She made him uneasy, yet he never said this. I think she embarrassed him with her odors, her messy habits, her inability to talk or focus her eyes.

Not too far away Sylvia crawled on the ground, following a long string of ants to their hole in the ground.

"Stop looking at Sylvia looking at the ants," he teased, "and look at me." Playfully he slapped at me when I refused to look at him. I shoved him away, and he shoved back, and then we both fell on the ground and wrestled around before his arms encircled me and we were soulfully staring into the eyes of the other. "I do love you," he whispered hoarsely. "I know I'm too young to feel this way, but all my life I've been hoping it would be like this, while I'm young, with the kind of girl you are—special, clean, decent."

My heart began its nervous throbbing as his amber eyes traveled slowly downward from my face to my neck, my bosom, my waist. Then he was looking to a lower place that made me blush. Staring into my eyes, and even looking at my breasts had made me feel beloved and beautiful, but to look there sent shivers of recognition darting through my memory, stirring up the nightmares of the rocking chair and all that had been done to the First Audrina, who had died because all three of those boys had looked there, despite her frantic efforts to kick them away. Shame filled me. Quickly I moved my leg to a concealing position. What I did made Arden blush.

"Don't be ashamed of being a girl, Audrina," he whispered with his head turned away. All of a sudden I began to cry. *She's* made me ashamed. All my life I'd been tortured because of her. *I hated her!* I wished she'd never been born, and then maybe I'd feel right and natural, instead of wrong and unnatural.

Still I kept on shivering, even more violently. What feet were walking on my grave? Hers?

"I'm going home now," I said stiffly, getting up to brush off my slacks.

"You're angry with me."

"No, I'm not."

"It's half an hour before twilight. Plenty of time before dark."

"I'll make up for it tomorrow." I ran for Sylvia and seized her small hand, pulling her to her feet before I turned to smile weakly at Arden. "Just stand where you are and don't walk us to the edge of the woods. If anything bad happens, I'll call for you. I need to do this, Arden."

The sun was in his eyes, preventing me from reading his expression. "Call out when you reach your lawn to let me know you're all right."

"Arden, even if sometimes I act strange, and I pull

away and tremble, don't pull away from me. Without you I wouldn't know how to get through the woods, or the days." Embarrassed, I whirled around and tried to run. But Sylvia didn't know how to run. She stumbled on tree roots, tripped on sticks, fell over her own feet, and soon I had her in my arms. She was six years old now and getting heavy. The crystal prisms she carried in her pockets everywhere she went made her heavier. Soon I put her down and slowed my hurrying feet. Home before dark, I kept saying to myself. Home before it rained.

"I'm here, Arden!" I called. "Safe in our own yard."

"Go inside . . . and good night. If you dream, dream of me."

His voice from the woods sounded very close, making me smile sadly. He'd followed us, as if he knew what had happened to the First Audrina and wanted to save me from her fate.

Arden had been in college one year when I had my sixteenth birthday. He made top grades, but it was a dull year for me, lonely in the house, and even lonelier when I ran through the woods, hauling Sylvia with me when I visited Billie. The cottage seemed half empty without Arden, without its heart. I marveled that Billie could stay there alone and still manage to smile. Over and over again she read his letters to me, as I read bits and pieces of his letters to me to her. She'd smile when I skipped some little endearment, for in his letters he dared much more than he did in person.

High school pleased me more than grammar school, but the boys there were much more persistent. Sometimes it was hard to concentrate solely on Arden, whom I saw so seldom. I was sure he was dating other girls he never wrote about, but I was faithful, dating no one but him when he came home on school vacations. All the girls were envious that I had a college-age boyfriend.

Taking care of Sylvia filled my life, stole every spare moment when I could have made friends with girls my own age. I didn't have time for any of the social activities they enjoyed. Every day I had to rush home as quickly as possible in case I had to rescue Sylvia from the switch my aunt liked to wield—and out of pure indifference my aunt made Sylvia suffer unnecessarily, waiting for me to tend to her physical needs.

I spent my afternoons with Billie, and in the years Arden was away, Billie taught me to cook, to sew, to can. Every once in a while she'd tentatively try to teach me just a little about men and what they expected from their wives. "A physical relationship is not everything, but it's very important as far as men are concerned. A good sex life makes the best cornerstone for a long and happy marriage."

The Christmas after I turned seventeen, a card arrived from New York, showing the city as seen from the Hudson River, all pastel and bluish with snow sprinkled over with glitter. My aunt had grunted at the message inside. It said only, "You'll see me again, never fear," and was signed Vera. It was the first we had heard from her in three years.

"At least she's alive, and for that I should be grateful. But why did she address the card to Damian and not to me?"

A week later, I suddenly awakened in the wee hours of the night. Since Sylvia came into my life I'd developed some alert sixth sense that made me aware, even when I was asleep, of the passage of time, of events going on that needed me there. My first thoughts were of Sylvia when I heard the loud voices again. In a flash I was out of bed and racing to her room, only to find her deeply asleep.

A thin line of light came from under my father's bedroom door, and to my utter amazement, my aunt's voice was coming from there. "Damian, I want to go to New York. Yesterday Vera called. She needs me. I'm going to her. I've done all I can for you, and for your daughters. You can always hire a maid to cook and clean, and you do have Audrina, don't you? You've managed to tie her hand and foot to Sylvia. It's not fair what you're doing. I know you love her, so let her go to college. Set her free, Damian, before it's too late."

"Ellie," he said placatingly, "what would happen to Audrina if she left here? She's too sensitive for the world out there. I'm sure she will never marry that boy, and he'll find that out once he tries something. No man wants a woman who can't respond, and I doubt if she'll ever learn how."

"Of course not!" she yelled. "You've done that to her. When she told you the rocking chair gave her those visions, still you made her use it."

"To give her peace," he said wearily, while I froze in panic. Why were they fighting over me? What was my aunt doing in his bedroom at three in the morning?

"Now listen to me, Damian," my aunt went on, "and hear some common sense for a change. You like to pretend that Vera doesn't exist, yet she does. And as long as she is alive, neither you nor Audrina nor Sylvia is safe. If you allow me to go to her, I can talk some sense into her head. She's constructing her entire life around you and her revenge. If she comes back, she could destroy Audrina—let me go, please. Give me enough money to make the trip and tide me over until I find a job. I need to be with Vera, and you do owe me something, don't you? That girl in New York is just as much your flesh and blood as Audrina and Sylvia, and you know it. You said you loved me."

"It's over and done with, Ellie," he said wearily. "There's more to life than regretting the past. Let's get on with today, and the here and now."

"Why did you say you loved me, when you didn't!" she screamed.

"You had your charms then, Ellie. You were sweeter then."

"I had hopes then, Damian," she said bitterly.

"Ellie, tell me what Vera is threatening to do if she comes back. I'll kill that girl if she does one more thing to hurt Audrina."

"Oh God! You made her what she is. Behind every evil thing Vera did was frustration and pain from feeling rejected by her own father. You know what Vera's threatening. When first you and Lucietta told me what you planned to do about Audrina, I thought the two of you fools, but still I sat back and said nothing, hoping it would work. I gave up trying to please you long ago, for I don't know how to subjugate myself to your whims. It's Audrina I want to save. There was a time when I thought that girl a weakling, but she's proved she is not. I thought she had no spirit, no fight, but I applaud each time she slaps back at you. So sit there and glare those damn black eyes at me, I don't give a damn, but tell Audrina the truth— before Vera does."

"There's a fortune in this house, and part of it could be yours," he said to her in a cajoling voice. "But none of it will be yours if ever you or your daughter say one word to Audrina." The persuasion left his voice and it turned colder. "How could you go anywhere without money, Ellie? Who would want you but me?"

"You don't want me!" she yelled with so much anger I fell upon my knees and put an eye to the keyhole, just as Vera used to do so many years ago when Momma fought with him. "You use me, Damian, as you use all women."

Ohhh . . . there was my prim and prissy aunt pacing my papa's bedroom, dressed in nothing but a filmy peignoir that had once belonged to my mother. She was naked underneath. To my amazement she looked better without clothes than with them. Her breasts weren't large and full like Momma's had been, but smaller, firmer and very high. My aunt's nipples were wine-colored and very large. How old was she, anyway? For the life of me I couldn't remember my mother telling me her age, and she'd been vain enough not to want her birth date carved on her tombstone. Many times I'd heard her tell Papa not to let the newspapers publish her age.

It wasn't the first time I'd realized that no one's birthday was nearly as important as mine.

My aunt's long, dark hair was loose and flowing, fanning out as she spun around. I stared at my aunt, wondering why she hadn't found another man after losing Papa to my mother? As she was now, she seemed very exciting, and challenging, especially if I could judge from the way Papa's eyes lit up even as he yelled at her and tried to talk her out of going to New York.

Suddenly he lunged, grabbed her by her waist and dragged her kicking and fighting onto his lap. She struck at him time and again as he laughed and ducked and then managed to crush his lips down on hers. All the fight went out of her then as her arms hungrily embraced him, and she held his head to hers, moaning as his lips began to explore all the crevices and hills of her body. I watched, shocked, as he kissed her breasts while his hand fondled beneath her peignoir.

"You're wrong, Ellie," he muttered, his face flushed with passion as he stood and carried her to his bed. "I do love you in my own way. Just as I loved Lucky in a very special way. It's not my fault if I can't keep love after the object of it is dead. I have to go on, don't I? And if you think I love myself more than I love anyone else, then I haven't tried to deceive you, have I? At least respect me for being honest, if you can't respect me for anything else."

Now I knew for a certainty, with no more guilty speculating, just who the man was my mother had stolen from her half-sister. I also knew definitely my father was also Vera's father. The more I thought about it, the more uncomfortable I became about my mother. Had she deliberately stolen her older sister's lover?

Standing, I left them on the bed. Now my aunt and my father were lovers again. Strangely, after more hours of thought, I wasn't as shocked as once I would have been, or as distressed. Perhaps fate did work in mysterious ways to see that all things worked out equally. It also occurred to me that perhaps the two of them might have been lovers even when my mother was alive—right in this house, under her own roof. Certainly there were enough unused rooms that would have given them the place and opportunity. My memories went flittering back to "teatimes" when Aunt Mercy Marie's photograph was on the piano, and in my head the echoes of all the harsh words exchanged between my mother and her sister resounded. Not once had my aunt showed one indication that she was anything but jealous of my mother. No, I decided, Aunt Ellsbeth had too much respect for herself, and scorn for Papa than to have had a clandestine affair with the man who'd rejected her once when Lucietta Lana Whitefern was still alive.

After I labeled their relationship as Papa's need and my aunt's reward, I put away their secret and determined never to let them know I knew. It was a long time before my aunt ever mentioned Vera again.

The Christmas I was seventeen, Arden put an engagement ring on my finger, then pulled me into his arms. "Now you can stop fearing any year with a nine. When you are nineteen, you'll be my wife and I'll take care to see that nothing bad ever happens to you."

That June I graduated from high school. I still wore the engagement ring Arden had given me around my neck on the chain that used to suspend my little birthstone ring. I began to notice a steady change in my aunt, who didn't seem as contented as before. I'd never thought of her as happy until I faced her unhappiness. She seldom went anywhere. Other women her age belonged to bridge clubs and attended coffee klatches, but my aunt didn't have a single friend. What clothes she wore at home were old, and the new ones she wore to go out were chosen by Papa, just as he often selected my best clothes. She didn't have one hobby other than knitting as she watched those everlasting soap operas. She had me, she had Sylvia, and Papa, and that eternal cooking and cleaning—and the reward of having a few hours to sit before her choice of new color TV sets. And I'd never realized that she needed or deserved more.

She didn't complain. There were no obvious physical symptoms to make me think she was ill, but something had changed. She often paused in her work to stare into space. She began to read the Bible, as if

looking for solace. She took long hikes alone, avoiding the woods and sticking to the shores of the river.
Sometimes I walked beside her, neither of us speaking
much. She'd stop to stare down at the ground with
undue interest. She gazed up into the trees and at the
sky with the same kind of intense curiosity, as if she'd
never taken notice of nature before and it was brand-
new to her. She stared at the squirrels that infested all
our impressive old trees. I told her I was sure they had
been here when Columbus set sail from Spain, and my
aunt had scoffed and told me I was unduly romantic
like my mother. Practicality was my aunt's virtue. Yet,
if she hadn't won Papa, why hadn't she set her sights
on another man? In no way would my "unrealistic
and romantic" mother have remained unmarried all
her life.

But how could I say any of this when I was just
beginning to understand my aunt? And with the understanding came the love that had been lacking in our
relationship before. I wanted to talk to her, but it was
difficult to communicate with a woman who'd never
learned the art of conversation. One day she surprised
me. "Do you love that young man?"

"Arden? Oh, yes, of course I do. He makes me feel
so safe, and beautiful, too. He tells me all the time how
wonderful I am, and how much he loves me." My own
words gave me pause—it was like I was letting Arden
convince me I had to love him because he loved me.

Frowning, my aunt glanced my way briefly, then
looked away. "I hope you'll always feel that way about
him. People change, Audrina. He'll change. You'll

change. You'll see each other differently because of
new perspectives. You may not love him at twenty as
much as you do at eighteen. You're a beautiful young
woman and could pick from the best the world has
to offer. But you have even more, something far better than beauty, for that won't last. You think it will,
pray that it will, but it goes sooner or later. The more
beauty you have the worse it hurts when it's gone. In
one thing your father is right—you *are* special."

"No, I'm not." My head bowed in embarrassment.
"I have no special gifts. My dreams are only ordinary."

"Oh, that," she said as if she'd known all along.
"What difference does it make how you achieve your
goals? At least your father leaves you alone now at
nights, and you no longer scream out. I've always considered him a monster for forcing you into that room
when you didn't want to go there—but that's beside
the point. Without you, Damian wouldn't have fared
so well, so don't let him take credit for all his good
fortunes. You motivate him, and give him reason for
accumulating wealth. To travel life's road alone isn't
easy, and no one knows that better than I. Damian
could never have survived your mother's death without you. Men are strange creatures, Audrina, remember that. So stand up for your rights and demand a
college education. Don't let him talk you out of what
you want. He'll try to keep you from marrying, from
ever leaving him—don't let him succeed in chasing
Arden away."

"He couldn't do that, or else Arden would have
disappeared a long time ago. I know Papa's tried.

Arden's told me he's tried to make him stay away from me."

"All right, then. But when you see your chance to escape, seize the opportunity and flee. You don't need to live near those woods, and in that house filled with all its unhappy memories. Why, it would even be better if you moved into that cottage with his poor crippled mother . . ."

I gasped. "You know about Billie? I didn't think anyone knew."

"Oh, for heaven's sake, Audrina. Everybody knows about Billie Lowe. There was a time when her face was plastered on every magazine cover, and when she lost one leg, and then the other, that made the headlines. You were too young at the time to notice. Besides, your father only allowed you to read the financial pages." She paused, as if ready to say more, but seemed to think better of it. "Don't you realize your father has been coaching you about the stock market since the day you were born? Audrina, use your knowledge and benefit yourself, not him."

What did she mean? I asked, but she refused to explain. Still, I loved her for trying to help me, never suspecting that maybe she was waiting for me to try and help her.

Later that night I decided she was depressed because Papa didn't marry her, depressed because she hadn't had but one Christmas card and one telephone call from Vera in five years. How hateful of Vera to treat her mother as if she'd never existed. I had to have a talk with Papa soon, very soon.

But Papa was seldom home, and when he was, my aunt was there and I didn't want her to know I was going to urge him to marry her.

How complicated everything was. Those were almost the first words I said to Arden when he came home for a weekend. "My aunt knew all about your mother's condition."

He smiled, kissed me four or five times, held me for long, long moments so hard I felt every muscle in his strong young body. I felt something else, too, making me draw away and glance downward. That bulging hardness clamored the wind chimes in my head, filled me with frightened panic so I felt weak and ready to run. He noticed and seemed hurt, then embarrassed so much he held his topcoat to cover what betrayed his excitement. Lightly he said, "Well, I did what I could and she did what she could, and I'm sure you did what you could, but secrets will out, and maybe it's for the best."

He went on to speak of our marriage soon after he finished college, and that was only weeks away. Again panic visited and told me I needed more time. We were in the woods again, on the way to my home, when he embraced me, much more passionately than ever before. Until he grabbed me I'd heard the little birds overhead singing, but the moment he touched me the birds turned off. I froze and became stiff from one too intimate caress. I jerked from his arms and turned my back, clamping my hands over my ears to shut out the clamor of the wind chimes, which I shouldn't be hearing way out here.

Tenderly Arden slipped his arms about my waist and pulled me back against him. "It's all right, darling. I understand. You're still very young, and I've got to keep remembering that. I want to make the rest of your life happy to reimburse you for . . . for . . ." and there he stumbled, making me yank away again and whirl to confront him. "Reimburse me for what?"

"For all the things that shadow your eyes. I want my love to erase your fears about everything. I want our child to respond to your care as Sylvia never has."

Child, child, child. I didn't need another child. Arden seldom spoke Sylvia's name, as if he, too, wanted to pretend she didn't exist. He did nothing to harm her, but nothing to assist her, either.

"Arden, if you can't love Sylvia, then you can't love me. She's part of the rest of my life. Please realize that now and tell me if you can accept her, or else let's say goodbye before this goes on any further."

He glanced to where Sylvia was winding round and round the tallest tree in the woods. Her slender arm was outstretched so her fingers could lightly trail over the bark as endlessly she circled. I told myself she was trying to communicate with the tree by feeling its "skin" and there was some sense in what she did. That's the way she was, always active, never still while she was awake, always doing something that was essentially nothing.

Right to the edge of the woods Arden escorted me

and Sylvia. I was feeling right enough by this time to exchange happy plans with him for that evening and the next day.

My father and aunt were in the kitchen arguing. The minute they heard me enter the house, their voices stilled and I heard that unnatural quiet that comes to announce that you've interrupted something private.

I hurried up the stairs with Sylvia.

Arden returned to college for his last semester, and I settled down to helping Papa turn this house into better than new. Now that Papa was noted for making everything he touched turn to gold, Aunt Ellsbeth liked to tell him acidly that soon his head would be too large to come through the double front doors.

Literally thumbing his nose at her, Papa ordered workmen to tear down walls, to make some rooms larger and others smaller. He had bathrooms added to his rooms and to mine, and two more as well. He decided he needed two large walk-in closets to accommodate his many suits and dozens of pairs of expensive shoes. My own room was enlarged and a dressing room was added, and with my private bath, I felt splendidly decadent with all those crystal and gold fixtures and electric lights framing my dressing mirror. In the end it seemed we'd have a home not equal to but surpassing what it had been. Papa searched until he found all the genuine antiques the Whiteferns had sold years ago, proving that all that my aunt had thrown in my mother's face about the "fakes" in our house was true. Even that grand bed Momma had believed was the real thing proved to be just a reproduction.

I listened with incredulity to all he planned to do. He had such miserly ways about petty things, and such extravagant ideas when it came to this house and his clothes.

To everyone in the financial world he was the "messiah" of the stock market. That gave him so much confidence he began to write a stock advice newsletter in his spare time. He listed the stocks to buy, to short, to sell and then sold what he told others to buy long the day his newsletter was delivered. He covered his shorts when others went in too short. He bought what he told his clients to sell. In a few hours of trading, he'd end up with thousands of dollars in profits. It seemed unfair, and I told him this. But he replied by saying that all of life was unfair. "A battle of wits to survive, Audrina. The victories in life belong to those who move fastest and most cleverly—and it's not cheating. After all, the public should have better sense, shouldn't they?"

Papa sent this stock advice letter to a friend who lived in San Francisco, and this friend had a publishing business, and all such "friends" were willing to collaborate in the fraud.

Then came that wonderful day when Arden was due "home from college, having received his diploma. Papa had been so heartless as not to allow me to attend his graduation ceremonies.

Unknown to Papa, who'd have me always dependent on him, Arden had taught me to drive years ago. Therefore it was easy to "borrow" one of Papa's older cars while he was at work, and with Sylvia dressed in her best, I headed for the airport terminal to wait for his plane to land. The moment was at hand. I was foolish enough to think I was ready for anything.

A Long Days' Journey

Arden came running to me in the airport. Soon I was so tightly embraced and so fervently kissed that I pulled away, overwhelmed with his emotions. Frantically I looked for Sylvia, who'd disappeared the moment Arden seized me in his arms. After an hour's search, we found my small sister staring at the colorful magazines. She was completely disheveled by this time, and I'd wanted Arden to see how pretty she was when she was fresh and clean. To make matters worse, someone who'd meant to be kind had given her a chocolate ice cream cone. Half the ice cream was on her face, part in her hair and in her nostrils, and very little of what was left was finding its melting way into her mouth. I took it from her grasp and held it for her to lick. Worse than anything was the stench that came from her diapers. I had managed to half toilet train Sylvia, but she still had enough accidents that I kept her in diapers.

There was little Arden and I could talk about on the way home, when every move Sylvia made was an embarrassment to both of us. "I'll see you later this evening," he said as I let him out on his corner. He tried not to wrinkle his nose when Sylvia clawed at him for affection.

No sooner were Sylvia and I inside the house than I heard the loud voice of my father. A terrible argument was going on in the kitchen.

I paused in the doorway with my arm protectively around Sylvia's thin shoulders. Aunt Ellsbeth was dashing about, frantically preparing another of those troublesome gourmet meals that Papa loved so much. She wore a new dress, a very pretty, feminine dress that might well have been taken from my mother's closet where all her clothes still hung, growing old and musty smelling. Aunt Ellsbeth wielded a huge cleaver so ferociously I wondered why Papa didn't fear for his life when she glared at him with that thing in her hand. He didn't seem afraid as he bellowed again, "Ellie, what the hell is wrong with you?"

"You need to ask?" she yelled back, slamming down her knife and whirling to confront him. "You didn't come home until five-thirty this morning. You're sleeping with someone. Who?"

"It's really none of your business," he answered coldly. I shuddered from his flat tone. Couldn't he tell she loved him and was doing the best she could to please him?

"None of my business, hey?" she stormed. Her long, handsome face flamed redder. "We'll see about that, Damian Adare!" Her dark eyes furious, my aunt seized up the large bowl full of her chopped vegetables and quickly dumped them down the garbage disposal. Then she was emptying all the steaming pots and pans into the sink.

"Stop that!" roared Papa, appearing beside himself. "That food cost me good money! Ellsbeth, behave yourself!"

"To hell with you!" she screamed back at him. She tore off her apron and hurled it in his face, then shouted, "I need a life of my own, Damian! A life far from here. I'm sick of being your housekeeper, your cook, your gardener, your laundry expert, and, most of all, I'm sick of being your now and then bed partner! I'm also sick of taking care of your idiot daughter—and as for your Audrina—"

"Yesss?" drawled Papa, his eyes narrowing, his voice taking on that deadly, silky tone that made the hackles on my neck rise. "What is it you want to say about *my* Audrina?"

I quivered as I drew Sylvia into my embrace, trying to cover her ears and her eyes and shield her as much as possible from this. I had to hear what they were going to say. They didn't seem to see either of us. I watched the color in my aunt's usually pale face drain away.

Nervously my aunt fluttered her hands toward him in a helpless, appealing way. "I wouldn't tell her, Damian, really I wouldn't. I would never tell Audrina anything to make her unhappy. Just let me go. Give me what is mine, and let me go."

"And what is it that is yours, Ellie?" asked Papa in that same oily voice, sitting at the kitchen table with his elbows propped there and his hands templed under his chin. I didn't trust him when he looked like that.

"You know what is mine," she said in a hard and very determined voice. "After you lost Lucietta's inheritance, you went after the little I had left. You promised to pay it back doubled in three months. What a fool I was to have believed in you. But hasn't that always been my weakness, believing in you? Now, Damian, give me back my two thousand dollars—*doubled!*"

"Where would you go if you left here, Ellie? What would you do?" He picked up the little paring knife she'd used to peel potatoes and began to clean under his nails, which were always clean.

"I'm going to my daughter, to your daughter, too, though you don't want to admit she is. She's in that huge city all alone, cast off by that man she ran away with."

He stayed her with his upraised hand, like a king who had to turn his head away from a distasteful subject. "I don't care to hear more. You're a fool if you go to her. She doesn't love you, Ellie, she just wants to take what you'll bring. I heard in the village that Lamar Rensdale killed himself. No doubt your daughter had a lot to do with his suicide."

"Damian, please!" she wailed, all her fire gone now. "Just give me what is mine, that's all I want. I'll go and never bother you again. I swear you'll not hear from me or Vera—just give me enough so I won't starve."

"I am not giving you one red cent," said Papa

coldly. "As long as you stay in my home you'll have food to eat and clothes to wear, a place to sleep and money to spend on the trifles you need. But hell will freeze over before I give you money to go and live with that hellcat you gave birth to. And remember this, Ellie: Once you leave, you can't come back. Not again. Life is hard on the outside, Ellie, very hard. You're not a young woman anymore. And even if it isn't heaven here, it isn't hell, either. Think twice before you leave me."

"Isn't it hell?" Her voice rose to a shriek. "It's hell with a capital *H*, Damian, pure, unadulterated hell! What am I here but an unpaid housekeeper? After Lucietta died and you began to look my way with kind eyes, I thought you'd love me again. You came to my bedroom when you needed release, and I gave you that. I should have denied you, but I wanted you, as I've always wanted you. When you lived in this house with my sister, I stayed awake at night picturing the two of you in your bedroom—and how I envied her, and hated her. I began to hate you, too, even more than I did her. Now I wish to God I'd never come back with Vera. There was a young doctor in the hospital where I gave birth to Vera who wanted me to marry him, but I had your image engraved on my brain. It was you I wanted. God alone knows why when I knew even then what you were, and still are. Give me my money, Damian," she said, striding toward his office as I backed away, pulling Sylvia with me. She didn't see us as we crouched in a dim corner of the wide hall cluttered with furniture.

In a few seconds, while my father sat at the table, she was back, carrying my father's corporation checkbook. "Write," she ordered. "Make it twenty-five thousand. After all, this was my home, too, and I should get something for abandoning my lifetime privilege to live under this roof. Wasn't it considerate of my sister to include me in her will? It was almost as if she meant for her husband to be part of her legacy — but I don't need you nearly as much as I need the money."

He gave the blue checkbook a funny look, then took it and with precision wrote a long blue check, which he handed to her with a tight, ironic smile. She glanced at the figure, then glanced again. "Damian, I didn't ask for fifty thousand."

"Don't leave me, Ellie. Say you're sorry for all those ugly words. Tear up the check or keep it, but don't go."

Rising again to his feet, he tried to take her in his arms. She kept staring at the check. As I watched, I saw a blush of excitement heat her face.

Then Papa seized her from behind and turned her around to crush his full lips down on her thin ones. Even as she tried to struggle, the check slipped from her grasp and fluttered to the floor. Greatly to my surprise, after all she'd screamed at him, her arms slipped eagerly around his neck, and she responded to his kisses with just as much ardor as he showed. Helplessly, as if unable to resist, she allowed him to pick her up. He headed for the back stairs with my aunt in his arms.

Feeling numb and dazed, a queasiness in my stomach, I dragged my trembling sister into the kitchen. I picked up the check and stared at the fifty thousand dollars and no cents made out to Ellsbeth Whitefern. I pinned the check to the corkboard where my aunt was sure to see it in the morning, and with it she could leave—if she wanted to.

All that I'd heard and seen in the kitchen churned in my head that night like a carousel of skeletal ponies, going round and round and up, down. Lamar Rensdale had killed himself—why? How did the villagers know? Had his death been in the local newspapers, and if it had, why hadn't I seen it? It had to be that Vera had called and told my aunt, and she was so grief-stricken now she needed someone, and the only one she had was her mother. Had Vera truly loved my handsome music teacher? If so, why had he taken his own life? I sighed and heard the wind answer . . . and that was about all the answer I was likely to get.

Deep in the recesses of my mind I avoided the biggest question of all. What was it my aunt promised she wouldn't tell me? What was the secret that would make me so unhappy if I learned it?

Bad dreams woke me up early the next morning. At the top of the front stairs, with the early sun pouring through the stained glass, I stopped short and froze.

Down on the foyer floor, with the sun coming through that rich, colorful glass to throw geometric designs on the floor, my aunt was sprawled facedown and very still. I took the steps slowly, slowly, like someone sleepwalking and fearful every second of facing too many horrors. She's not dead, I kept telling myself, not dead, not dead, only hurt. I had to call an ambulance before it was too late. She very seldom used the front stairs because the back ones took her down so near the kitchen, which was where she stayed almost all day. I thought I heard a faint sound from the kitchen, like a door being carefully closed.

Tentatively I approached her. "Aunt Ellie," I whispered fearfully. I knelt to roll over the body of my aunt, and then I stared into her face. "Don't be dead," I pleaded over and over. She was difficult to move, like lead. Her head lolled unnaturally loose as I shoved and pushed and finally had her on her back. Her dark and fiery eyes gazed glassily at the intricately carved ceiling. Her skin had a sickly, greenish gray color.

Dead, she was dead. Dressed for traveling in a suit I'd never seen before, she was dead and already traveling to compare His heaven and hell with here.

There was a scream stuck in my throat. Rasping sobs kept it from sounding. I didn't want her dead. I wanted her to have that check and have the chance to enjoy herself, and at the same time I wanted her to stay on here with us. Crying freely now, I began to straighten the bow at the neck of her new white blouse. I tugged down her skirt so her slip wouldn't show, and arranged her broken legs beneath her so they didn't look broken anymore. With that huge bun at the back of her neck, her head kept falling to a crazy angle. Crying harder, I undid her figure-eight knot and spread her hair so it looked pretty. Then her head stayed in position.

Everything done now, I heard the screams. Over and over someone was screaming. It was me. Out of the kitchen heavy feet came running fast, a voice calling my name. I whirled to see Sylvia tripping awkwardly down the stairs, babbling to herself as she tried to hold on to the bannister and the prisms at the same time. She was coming to me as fast as possible, a big smile on her pretty face. And her eyes were focused! I thought she was going to speak when suddenly from behind me a voice . . .

"Who was screaming?" asked Papa as he raced into the foyer. He stopped short and stared at Aunt Ellie. "Ellie . . . is that Ellie?" he asked, pale and shocked looking. Shadows seemed to immediately darken his face. He hurried to kneel where I'd knelt only a moment ago. "Oh, Ellie, did you have to do this?" he asked with a sob, lifting her so that she was cradled in his arms and her rubbery neck stretched too long. "I gave you a check, Ellie, more than you asked for. You could have gone. You didn't have to fall down the stairs just to hurt me . . ."

Seeming to remember my presence, he paused and asked, "How did this happen?" His eyes narrowed as I pulled Sylvia into my embrace. I wanted to defend her from that hard way he was staring at those prisms clutched in her hand. Holding her head against my breasts, I faced him. "I was coming downstairs when I saw her . . . she was facedown on the floor, like she'd fallen."

Again he was staring at my aunt's dead face. "She very seldom used the front stairs. You turned her over?" How empty his eyes, how flat his tone. Was he hurting like I was hurting?

"Yes, I turned her over."

"You heard us last night, didn't you?" he asked accusingly. Before I could answer, he was picking up the purse I hadn't noticed and rummaging through it. "No check," he said as if surprised. "We did quarrel last night, Audrina, but later on we made it up. I asked her to marry me. She seemed very happy when she went back to her room . . ."

He eased my aunt back onto the floor and stood up. "She wouldn't leave me . . . I know she wouldn't do that, not after I asked her, and she wanted that, I know she wanted that . . ." Then he was taking the steps three at a time standing there.

I grabbed hold of Sylvia and forced her to run with me to the back stairs, hoping we'd reach my aunt's room first and I'd be there to see what he did with the check when he found it.

Even if his way was the longest way, he was in her room before I could drag Sylvia there. Her suitcases lay open on her bed. Frantically, he was tearing through her things, opening and closing every handbag she owned. "I can't find it! Audrina, I have to find that check! Did you see it?"

I told him then that I'd pinned it to the corkboard so she'd see it first thing in the morning.

He groaned and wiped his hand over his lips. "Audrina, run and see if it's still there."

With Sylvia beside me, stumbling along as I tried to hurry, I reached the kitchen and found the corkboard empty. I reported that to Papa. He sighed heavily, glanced again at the still form of my aunt in her crisp dark suit, then dialed the police.

"Now," he instructed before I went upstairs to dress, "you just tell them exactly how you found her—but don't tell them she was leaving. I'll put away all her clothes. I can't believe she was leaving anyway. She had such idiotic things in her suitcases, clothes that wouldn't even fit her now. Audrina, I think it would be a good idea if you took off your aunt's traveling suit and put on one of her housedresses."

I didn't want to, though I understood his reasoning, and with his help we managed to take off her jacket, blouse and skirt. Soon she was wearing a plaid cotton dress. I was trembling long before we were finished. Hurriedly I did up her hair while Papa held her in position. My fingers shook so her knot had never looked so messy. No sooner was I dressed myself than the police were jabbing at the doorbell.

Huddled with Sylvia at my side on the purple velvet chaise, I watched and listened as my father gave the two policemen an explanation of my aunt's fall down the stairs. He appeared calm, only a little distraught, with worry and sadness making him seem genuinely grief-stricken. The policemen seemed to consider him charming, very likable, and I was thinking unmercifully what an actor he was. He would never have married her. What a lie to tell me that—as if he considered me so gullible I'd believe anything.

"Miss Adare," said the older of the policemen, his

face kind and grandfatherly, "you were the one who found her? She was on her back?"

"No, sir, she was facedown. I didn't want to think she was dead, so I had to turn her over to check." I bowed my head and began to cry again.

His voice was sympathetic when he asked, "Was your aunt subject to dizzy spells?" On and on the questions came until Papa fell into a chair and bowed his head into his hands. Somehow I forgot to mention I'd heard the back door softly close. But perhaps I'd only imagined I'd heard that.

"Where were you when your sister-in-law fell?" asked the older policeman, looking directly at Papa.

"I was asleep," said Papa, lifting his head and meeting the eyes of the policeman squarely.

Even as my aunt's body was lifted and put on a stretcher, covered over and taken to the police morgue, the questions went on and on. I was numb and feeling dazed, and I was forgetful of Sylvia, who hadn't eaten breakfast. That was the first thing I did after the police left. Papa sat down to eat what I prepared, too, not saying a word to me, only chewing and swallowing automatically.

Yet, later on, when I was alone in my room and Sylvia was napping in hers, I kept thinking of my aunt and the argument she'd had with Papa. She had wanted to go to Vera, and now she was dead. The more I thought about that the more alarmed I became about my own situation. How many times had my aunt told me to escape when I had the opportunity? Hundreds of times.

Now, while Papa was off somewhere making funeral arrangements, was my chance.

Where did you go when Fate kept breaking your heart over and over again? A little voice inside me kept whispering that Papa thought baby girls were born every day just to serve his needs when they grew older. And when he was old and ugly, he was thinking money would buy them—and when even money couldn't, he'd still have me left to take care of him and keep him from those institutions he seemed to hate. Even as I thought that, behind that was another whispering menace . . . that awful thing my aunt had said to him about how he was capable of doing anything and everything to get his way. I dashed about madly, throwing my clothes into suitcases. I ran for Sylvia's room and gathered up what she'd need, too. We were leaving. Leaving before something awful happened to us, too. Now, while Papa was away and couldn't stop us.

As I pulled Sylvia along with me, we had to pass the front salon, and in the door I paused as I said goodbye to my mother's grand piano. It seemed I could see her sitting there playing her favorite Rachmaninoff melodies, one of which had been given lyrics in a popular ballad: "Full moon, and empty arms . . ."

Steel arms, that's the kind my father had. Killing arms of love.

As I stood there I think I forgot every hateful, mean thing my aunt had ever said or done to me and Sylvia. I shoved into the darkest corners of my brain all she'd said to tell me I was too sensitive and unable to cope with reality, and remembered only the good things, the thoughtful deeds. I forgave her everything.

Pulling Sylvia with me, I picked up the two heavy suitcases and began our journey through the woods to reach the cottage on the far side. Billie looked sober when I told her my plans. Arden was delighted. "Of course. What a wonderful idea. But why can't your aunt look out for Sylvia? It's not going to be much of a honeymoon if we have to drag her along with us."

With my head low and my voice, too, I told them what had happened and that it was escape now or never. I had told everything in such a way that Papa had seemed blameless. Why had I spared him?

Billie cuddled me in her strong arms. "We have to think some things are for the best when there is nothing we can do about it anyway. You've told me your aunt has acted all winter like she wasn't happy, or she was ill. Maybe she did have a dizzy spell. Now, there's no reason why you can't leave Sylvia here with me, if you truly feel you have to escape like this. I just want you to be sure you love my son enough, Audrina. Don't marry Arden today and regret it tomorrow."

"I will love Arden forever!" I cried fervently, fully believing this was the truth. Arden smiled at me lovingly. "I can echo that," he said softly. "All my life will be devoted to making you happy."

Nervously I glanced from Sylvia, who started to scream when Billie tried to touch her, to Billie, then Arden. I couldn't leave my sister with Billie, whom

she seemed to fear and dislike. I'd promised Papa a long time ago that I'd take care of Sylvia; she was my responsibility, and I couldn't leave her.

My heart seemed to stop as I waited for Arden's response after I told him Sylvia had to go with us. He blanched, then quietly agreed.

Perhaps Billie was right to look worried as she waved goodbye.

I Take Thee, Arden

In a small town in North Carolina, where the law permitted couples to be married on the same day they took out a marriage license, Arden and I were wedded by a fat, balding justice of the peace, while his plain-looking, skinny wife played atrocious wedding music on a worn-out old organ. When the brief ceremony was over, she v sang (without our request) "I Love You Truly."

Sylvia perched restlessly on what looked like a bridge chair, swinging her feet as she played with the crystal prisms and babbled incessantly to herself, as if suddenly she'd found her voice and was going to use it, even if she couldn't say meaningful words—or was she trying to sing? It was difficult to concentrate on our vows.

"In a few years we'll do it all over again in the proper way," promised Arden as we headed south toward a famous beach and a fine hotel. "You look so pretty in that violet suit. It matches your eyes. You have such wonderful eyes, so deep. I wonder if ever in a million years I will have time to find out all your secrets."

Uneasily I fidgeted. "I have no secrets."

By nightfall we were registered in the hotel. Soon we were in the dining room, where all the guests stared at Sylvia shoving food into her wide-open mouth without benefit of cutlery. "I've been working on that, too," I said with apology to Arden. "Sooner or later she'll catch on." He smiled and said that we'd both teach Sylvia how to be the perfect lady.

I was glad dinner took a long time. Only too soon would come the time I dreaded most.

Try as I would, that dark, fugitive memory of the wet woodsy day kept flashing before my eyes. Sex had killed the First Audrina, and it was my wedding night. Arden wouldn't hurt me, I said again to reassure myself. It wouldn't be awful with him. The pain and the terror and the ugliness all belonged to that crazy rocking chair dream of the First Audrina; it didn't belong in my life with a wedding certificate in my purse.

Arden was wonderfully considerate, tolerant of Sylvia as he simultaneously tried to be romantic with me — a nearly impossible task. I felt sorry for him as he tried so hard.

He'd rented a double suite of rooms with a connecting door so Sylvia could have her own bathroom, and in her bathroom I slowly, painstakingly did what I had to. When I tucked her into the wide bed I gave her strict orders to stay in bed — or else. The last thing I did was put half a glass of water on the nightstand. "Drink as little as possible so you won't have an accident during the night." I kissed her and reluctantly withdrew when she drifted into sleep, still clutching the crystal prisms.

In the bedroom Arden and I were to share, he paced the floor impatiently while I took an hour-long tub bath and shampooed my hair. Next I rolled it on curlers, used my hair dryer, creamed my face, and while my hair finished drying, I removed my nail polish and did my nails all over again, my toenails, too. Now that my hair was thoroughly dry, I had to wait for my nails to dry as well. When they seemed solid enough, I carefully took out the curlers and brushed the tight curls into loose, soft waves. I sprayed on cologne and puffed on talcum and finally dropped a fancy nightgown down over my head. Stupid, stupid, I was calling myself for being afraid to go to my husband.

I tugged at the revealing nightgown Billie had given me on my last birthday, wishing it weren't so transparent, though I guessed she'd given it to me for just this reason. It had a matching peignoir of violet, with creamy lace that wasn't placed to conceal anything. When I'd finished every last detail I could think of, I sat on the edge of the bathtub and just stared at the closed door, dreading to open it and go through.

I kept seeing Momma as I sat there, so much like I looked, only older. I thought of Papa and the belt he used for a whip. I envisioned again all that had happened to the First Audrina that awful day in the rain when she'd been found dead under a golden raintree. A child raped, it wasn't fair or right. I began to tremble, and beads of sweat came to dampen my armpits despite the deodorant I wore. I saw Vera rolling about on the floor with Lamar Rensdale, and the violent way he'd taken her, like a rutting animal. I couldn't go through with it. I didn't want to go through with it.

Standing, I began to unfasten my peignoir—I couldn't let him see me in this bit of nothing.

"Audrina," called Arden from the other side of the locked bathroom door, his voice beginning to sound angry, "what's taking you so long? You've been in there for hours."

"Give me five more minutes," I answered nervously. Already I'd promised him that two times before. I fiddled with my hair, the peignoir, taking it off, thinking about pulling on my panties or getting fully dressed again. I began to chew on my fingernails, a habit long ago abandoned. I told myself again that Arden had known me since I was seven, seen me in playclothes, in a bathing suit, in all sorts of conditions ... but he'd never seen me in a see-through nightie just before intimate relations. Yet he was my husband now. Why did I have to be so worried? I wouldn't end up dead under a golden raintree, or on the floor, nor would he use his belt ... would he?

"One more minute," reminded Arden. "I'm holding you to your time limit ... and no more excuses." His tone was so grim it scared me. He'd never sounded so harsh before. Oh, it was just like I'd heard Aunt Mercy Marie, Aunt Ellsbeth and my momma say: You never knew a man until you married him.

"I'm watching the second hand," he informed me. "You've got thirty seconds now. If you're not out when you promised, I'm coming in. Even if I have to kick down that door, *I'm coming in!*"

I shrank back against the wall, my heart pounding as I panicked. I took a step closer to the door, said a quick prayer for the soul of my aunt and asked her forgiveness for not attending her funeral.

"Time's up!" he yelled. "Stand back—I'm coming through."

He'd hurt himself if he backed up and ran forward to slam his shoulder through the door. He kicked the door twice, but it didn't budge. I heard him swear and guessed he was going to throw himself against the door next. Hurriedly I turned the lock and threw open the door.

It was his misfortune to hurl himself forward at the very second I swung the door inward. He slammed hard against the tile wall opposite the door. He crashed against it, then slid to the floor and lay there looking stunned and in terrible pain.

Rushing forward, I knelt to hover above him. "Oh, Arden, I'm sorry, so sorry. I didn't know you'd really try to break down the door."

To my surprise, he laughed and grabbed for me. He began to smother me with kisses. His words came between them. "I've heard that brides can get stage fright, but Audrina, I thought you loved me." More kisses on my face, neck, the swell of my breasts. "It's not as if we just met."

Jerking away, I rose to my feet. Painfully he stood,

too, before he leaned over and felt for broken bones. "I guess nothing is permanently damaged," he said with a good-natured grin. Tenderly he took me in his arms and gazed deeply into my eyes. "You don't have to look so scared. All this is kinda funny in a way, like a farce, but I don't want our wedding night to be a farce. I love you, Audrina. We'll take it easy, go slow, and you'll be surprised at how naturally things come about." Lightly he kissed me with his parted lips. "Your hair looked great before, you didn't have to wash it again. Yet, I've never seen you look so beautiful . . . and even if you do look terrified, you take my breath away." Again he kissed me, like he didn't want to stop. "I'll be finished in a flash," he said, reluctantly parting and entering the bathroom.

He didn't have to tell me that. I'd known all along he'd be finished in a "flash."

I'd have to endure this night, and all the nights to come if I was to escape Papa and find the physical rapport every woman was supposed to enjoy with the man she truly loved.

Pulling off the peignoir that Arden hadn't even noticed, I slipped between the sheets of that huge bed. Hardly had I arranged myself comfortably when Arden was opening the bathroom door, finished with his shower and what little else a man did to get ready for bed.

Quickly he came to the bed, silhouetted briefly before the golden light behind him. To my horror, he wore nothing but a damp bath towel swathed about his slim hips. Whatever dim light there was in the hotel room seemed to concentrate on his damp, shiny skin, forcing me to take notice of his maleness even when I didn't want to think about it. I just wanted this night over and done with as quickly as possible. I could have screamed from the casual way he took off that towel and tossed it aside. It missed the chair arm he aimed for and slid to the floor.

Oh, it was already starting, all the sloppy things neat men did after they had a wife to pick up after them. "You forgot to turn off the bathroom light."

"Because you turned off all the lights in here," he said easily, "and I like some light. I could open the draperies instead, and let in the moonlight." The scent of toothpaste was on his breath. He lingered by the bed, as if wanting me to look him over in the pale rosy night light he turned on.

"Darling, look at me. Don't keep your head turned. I've waited for this night for years and years. I've gone through all sorts of trouble to make my body muscular and attractive, and not once have you ever said anything to say that you noticed. Do you ever notice anything about me except my face?"

I swallowed. "Yes, of course I've noticed."

Smiling, he put one knee on the bed. Alarmed at what I saw briefly before my eyes took flight again, I drew into a tighter knot inside and inched farther away on the bed. "Audrina, you're shivering. It's not cold in here. Don't be frightened. We love each other. I've kissed you, embraced you, and a few times I've dared a bit more and was quickly reprimanded. There's more to making love than all that combined."

His low voice sounded worried. "You do know what this is all about, I hope . . . ?"

Yes, I knew. Perhaps too much. I stared toward the windows, sickeningly terrified. The faint and distant sound of thunder filtered into our room. With the approaching electrical storm came a new flood of terror, bringing with it visions of the dark woods overhung with leaden skies. Like it had been in the First Audrina's room, I felt the ominous threat of what lay ahead.

Rain, oh, please, God, don't let it rain tonight!

Fraction by fraction he moved closer. I could sense him in every pore. I breathed his special male aroma, felt his nakedness, felt my own vulnerability beneath my nothing nightgown. My skin seemed to wake up and turn into a zillion antennae, each almost invisible hair quivering, warning me to do something and do it quickly. Back, back, I was going back to the rocking chair when it had frightened me, before I learned how to escape the horror of the woods. I felt myself rocking, heard a childish voice singing, saw the spiders spinning, saw the eyes of the stuffed animals glinting, heard the floorboards squeaking. The wind was blowing and soon the lightning would flash and the thunder would crash.

Arden said something sweet. Why couldn't I hear clearly? "I love you," I heard him say again, his voice coming to me as if through a dream. My heart thudded so loudly that I hardly heard him above the noise of all that was happening inside of me.

Very close now, Arden turned on his side and tentatively put out his hand to lightly touch my upper arm. His fingertips brushed the left side of my breast. Don't, don't, I wanted to yell. I lay there speechless with fright, my eyes so wide they began to ache. My mouth became very dry.

He cleared his throat and moved so his flesh was against mine, hot flesh, bristly with hair. His lips, even hotter and moist, brushed over mine. I shrank into the pillow, trying to choke back a scream. "What's the matter?" he asked. "Have you stopped loving me already, Audrina?"

An excuse came to me from one hole in my memory. Momma saying to Papa she was too tired. "I'm just so tired, Arden. It's been a long day. My aunt died this morning. Why can't you just hold me in your arms tonight and tell me you love me over and over again, and then, perhaps, I won't feel so ashamed."

"There's nothing to be ashamed of," he said lightly, though I sensed his tenseness. "You're feeling like lots of brides feel, so I've been told. Since you're my first, and I hope my last, I can't speak from experience."

I wanted to ask him if I was the first girl he'd taken to bed, but I was afraid he'd say no. I wanted him to be just as inexperienced as I was; then, contrarily, I wanted him to know exactly what to do to make me like what I was sure I would hate. If I really knew he'd waited to have sex with me first, that would prove he loved me enough.

His fingers lightly trailed a pattern up and down my arm as he leaned above me, forcing me to close my eyes. Hadn't I heard my own mother say that boys were always more ready than girls for sex? Joking with my aunt at the time, with Aunt Mercy Marie, too, as she sat smiling vacuously on the piano.

Now his hands dared more, venturing to fondle my breasts before his fingers arrowed in more specifically. They began to circle round and round my nipples, which were only lightly covered by the thin fabric. I shivered, cringed away and wearily asked, "Have you ever had sex before?"

"Did you have to ask that at a time like this?"

"Is it the wrong thing to ask?"

His sigh sounded exasperated. "There are differences between men and women, some say. Maybe that's true, and maybe it's not. A woman can live out her life happily without sex, so I've heard said, but a man has a buildup of sperm that has to be released in one way or another. The most pleasurable way is with the woman he loves. Loving is sharing, Audrina. Sharing mutual pleasure, not pain, and not shame, either."

"Did Billie tell you to say that to me?" I asked hoarsely.

His too eager lips burned the hollow of my throat before he murmured, "Yes. Before we left the cottage, she took me aside and told me to be very tender and slow with you tonight. She didn't have to tell me that. I would have been anyway. I want to do everything right. Give me a chance, Audrina. Maybe it won't be as terrible as you're thinking it will be."

"Why are you saying that? Why do you think I'm thinking it will be terrible?"

His half-laugh was tight and small. "It's pretty obvious. You're like a violin with wires tuned so tight

I can almost pluck your nerve endings and hear them twang. But it was you who came running to me today, wasn't it? You did throw yourself into my arms and say, 'Let's get married,' didn't you? You wanted to elope today—not tomorrow or next week. So isn't it natural that I'd think that at last you were ready to accept me as your lover?"

I hadn't thought. I'd just acted. Escape from Papa had been all that mattered. "Arden, you didn't answer my question."

"What question?"

"Am I the first?"

"All right, if you have to know. There have been other girls, but none that I loved as I love you. Since I decided you were going to be the one I'd marry, I have not touched another girl."

"Who was the first girl?"

"Never mind," he said with his face pressed between my breasts and his hand exploring beneath my gown. I didn't stop him from doing what he wanted to. I clung to my pain. He didn't love me enough. He'd had others, perhaps a hundred. And he'd always acted like I was his one and only girl. How deceitful, like Papa.

"You're so beautiful, so soft and sweet. Your skin is so smooth," he murmured, his breath coming faster, as if all that he did to me was all he needed, and nothing I did or didn't do mattered at all. His hand was now beneath my bodice, cupping my breast, kneading it, molding it to the shape of his hand as his lips came down hard on mine. I'd been kissed by him many times before, but not like this.

Panic put me back in the rocking chair, made me a child again and terrified of that playroom where awful things came inside and filled me with shame. The lightning flashed and made my nerves jump so that I bucked upwards. Arden took that for beginning passion, for his lust sizzled more and the shoestring straps of my nightie broke as he pulled it down, baring my breasts for his lips and tongue to play with. I arched my neck and forced my head back into the pillow as I bit down on my lower lip to keep from screaming. I squeezed my eyes together and tried to endure the humiliation of everything he did. Inside I was sobbing, just like when they'd ripped off the First Audrina's pretty new dress and torn off her silk underclothes.

Crying, I was crying, and he didn't hear me or see my tears. My eyes popped open when next the thunder clapped. The lightning lit up the room enough for me to see his handsome face just above mine, rapt looking, out of himself with the euphoria he was experiencing.

All this touching, caressing, kissing was giving him pleasure while it gave me terror. I felt cheated, angry, ready to hurt him with my screams when he tugged off my nightgown and threw it away like a rag. They'd done that!

His hands were all over me, finding everything but what he seemed to be seeking. I hated where he had his hand and was glad when he swore to himself as his fingers worked madly. Then he sighed and rolled on top of me, and I felt his hardness.

Oh! The rocking chair, I was in it again, rocking

to and fro. I saw the woods, heard the obscene words shouted, heard the laughter.

But it was too late. I felt him jabbing deep into me, thick and hot and slippery wet. I fought to free myself, bucking, kicking, scratching. I clawed deep into the skin of his back, raked at his naked buttocks, but he didn't stop. He kept on jabbing, causing the same kind of shame, the same kind of pain as they had caused her. His face . . . was that Arden's boyish face with his hair plastered to his forehead, his eyes bulging as he stared before? No, no, Arden hadn't been born then. He was just another like them, that was all. All men alike . . . all alike, alike . . . like . . .

Blurrily I was drifting, losing sense of reality. Aunt Ellsbeth had been right when she said I was too sensitive. I should never have led Arden on and allowed him to believe I could be the perfect wife.

I couldn't be any kind of wife at all.

His hot ejaculations came then. Scream, scream, but the thunder overhead muffled my cries. Nobody heard, not even him. I tasted my own blood on my lips from the bite of my teeth that tried to cut off my screams. Only Arden who loved me. This was the way physical love had to be . . . and one more last heaving thrust nearly ripped me apart . . . then, spinning off, all terror and shame faded. Blackness mercifully took me, and I felt nothing, nothing at all.

Morning light wakened me. Sylvia was slouched in the corner of our bedroom playing with her prisms, her nightgown riding up to her hips. With her vacant eyes looking at nothing, her lips parted and drooling, she crouched there as limp as a rag.

My husband rolled over, came awake and reached for my breasts as if they belonged to him. He kissed them first, then my lips. "Darling, I love you so much." More kisses he rained on my face, my neck, all over my naked body, and Sylvia was there, though I'm sure he didn't see her. "At first you seemed so tight, so scared. Then, all of a sudden, you seized hold of me and eagerly surrendered. Oh, Audrina, I was hoping you'd be like that."

What was he saying? How could I believe his words when his eyes were pleading the way they were? Yet, I allowed him to fake his satisfaction, realizing that he'd had some, while I'd had nothing but pain, shame and humiliation. And far, far back in my perforated memory was the scent of blood, of damp earth and wet leaves . . . and Audrina was stumbling home, trying to hold the shreds of an expensive dress together to cover her nudity.

PART 3

Home Again

As we drove up our long curving drive, I saw Papa standing on the front porch, as if he'd known in advance this was our day to come home.

He towered there, a formidable giant, wearing a spanking new white suit, white shoes, with a bright blue shirt and a white tie with silver and blue diagonal stripes.

I quivered and looked at Arden, whose eyes met mine with a great deal of apprehension. What would Papa do?

With one hand I clung to Arden's arm, my other held Sylvia's, as all three of us slowly ascended the steps to the front porch. All the time Papa's fiery gaze clashed with mine, silently accusing me of betraying him, failing him. Then, done with me, he turned those dark, piercing eyes on Arden as if to weigh him and his strength as an opponent. Papa smiled warmly and thrust out his huge hand for my new husband to shake. "Well," he said genially, "how nice to see all of you again." He pumped Arden's hand up and down. Endlessly, it seemed.

I was proud to see Arden didn't wince. To squeeze too firmly in a friendly handshake was Papa's way of determining a man's physical strength and emotional character. He knew his powerful grip hurt, and a man who grimaced was crossed off his list and labeled "weak."

Turning to me then, he said, "You have disappointed me deeply." Casually he patted Sylvia on the top of her head, as if she were some pesty puppy. Three times he kissed my cheeks, one, then the other, but at the same time he managed to reach behind me to pinch my bottom so hard I wanted to cry out. This kind of pinch was meant to test a woman's endurance, and her reactions were noted, labeled, filed.

Let him label me as he would. "Don't you ever pinch me like that again," I said fiercely. "That hurts, and I don't like it. I have never liked it—and neither did my mother or my aunt."

"My, what a saucy bit of baggage you've become in four days," he said with a wide, mocking grin. Then he reached to playfully pat my cheek, and it felt like a slap. "You didn't need to elope, my sweetheart," he said in a soft, loving purr. "It would have been my pleasure, my joy, to walk you down the center aisle and see you wearing your mother's beautiful wedding gown."

Just when I thought nothing he did could ever surprise me, he caught me off guard. "Arden, I've been talking to your mother about you, and she tells me you've had some difficulty finding the kind of position you want with a good architectural firm. I admire you for not accepting a third-rate job in a second-rate firm. So until you find the kind of position you really want, why not accept a junior account executive position with my brokerage firm? Audrina can help teach you the ropes so you can pass the exam, and, of course, I'll do what I can to help. Though she knows almost as much as I do."

This wasn't what I wanted. Yet, as I glanced at Arden, I saw he was very relieved. This offer would solve a lot of problems. Now we'd have an income and could rent a small apartment in the city, far from Whitefern. Arden appeared very grateful and glanced at me as if I'd overexaggerated Papa's desire to keep me all for himself.

How like Papa to take a situation he disliked and turn it around to his advantage. Good-looking young account executives were much in demand, and Arden was smart and good with math.

"Yes, Arden," he expounded, putting a friendly, fatherly arm over my husband's shoulders, "my daughter can teach you the fundamentals, and the technical side, too." His voice was smooth, easy, relaxed. "She is almost as knowledgeable as I am, and perhaps even better since the market is not a science but an art. Audrina has a stranglehold on sensitivity and intuition—right, Audrina?" He gave me another smile of great charm. Then, while Arden wasn't looking, he quickly reached to pinch my bottom again, even harder. He smiled, and when Arden glanced our way again, Papa was hugging me lovingly.

"Now," he continued, "I have another wonderful

surprise for you." He beamed at both of us. "I've taken the liberty of moving your mother out of that miserable little cottage. She is now established upstairs in the best rooms we have." His polished smile shone again. "That is, the best next to my own."

It hurt to see Arden so grateful when he should have known better. Perhaps all men *were* more or less alike and understood each other very well. I raged inside that Papa was still controlling my life, even though I was married.

Cozily established in what had been my aunt's rooms, made grand in a useless effort to please her, was Billie, dressed like a stage star in a fancy lace dress that should have been seen only at a garden party.

Her bright eyes glowing, she gushed, "He stormed over to my place about an hour after you drove away and raged at me for encouraging the two of you to elope. I didn't say a word until he calmed down. Then I think he really looked at me for the first time. He told me I was beautiful. I was wearing my shorts, too, with those damned stumps sticking out, and he didn't seem to care. Darlin', you just don't know what that did for my ego."

Papa was clever, so clever. I should have expected he'd find a way to defeat me. Now he had my mother-in-law on his side.

"Then he said we should make the best of a situation that couldn't be changed, and that wonderful man invited me to come and live here, and share your lives and his. Wasn't that gracious of him?"

Of course it was. I glanced around at the room I thought should be a shrine to my aunt's memory and

ached inside ... and yet, what good were shrines when Billie was so grateful? And Aunt Ellsbeth had never appreciated anything done to make her rooms pretty. Certainly if anyone deserved rooms like these, it was Billie.

"Audrina, you never told me your father is so kind, understanding and charming. Somehow you always made him seem insensitive, conniving and abusive."

How could I tell her Papa's good looks and contrived charms were his stocks-in-trade? He used them on all women, young, middle-aged and old. Ninety percent of his clients were wealthy older women who totally depended on his advice, and the other ten percent were wealthy men too old to have good judgment of their own.

"Audrina, darlin'," Billie went on, holding me against her full, firm breasts, "your father is such a dear. So sweet and concerned about everyone's welfare. A man like Damian Adare could never be cruel. I'm sure you misunderstood if you think he mistreated you."

Papa had followed us upstairs, and until she said this, I hadn't seen him leaning gracefully against the door frame, taking all of this in. He spoke to Arden in the sudden silence. "My daughter has been raving about you since she was seven years old. God knows I never thought puppy love would last. Why, I loved a dozen girls or more by the time I was ten, and two hundred before I married Audrina's mother."

Arden smiled, appearing embarrassed, and soon he

was thanking Papa for offering him a job when no one else had—and a decent salary for someone with absolutely no training as a broker.

And so again Papa had won. Aunt Ellsbeth was dead. She had not saved me any more than she'd saved herself. Only Papa was free to time and time again hurt those he claimed to love most.

Soon Papa was talking seriously to me and Arden about giving him a grandson. "I've always wanted a son," he said while looking directly into my eyes. It hurt, really hurt to hear him say that, when he'd always claimed I was enough to please him. He must have seen my pain, for he smiled, as if I'd been tested and he found me still faithful. "Second to a daughter, I wanted a son, that is. A grandson will do just fine, since I already have two daughters."

I didn't want a baby yet, not when just being Arden's wife was traumatic enough. Bit by painful bit I was learning how to cope with those nightly acts of love that seemed atrocious to me and wonderful to him. I even learned to fake pleasure so he stopped looking so anxious and allowed himself to believe that I was now enjoying sex just as much as he did.

Even before Arden and I returned from our seashore honeymoon, Billie had taken over in the kitchen Aunt Ellsbeth had so recently abandoned. Billie had her high stool there, carried over with most of her other belongings by my own father, who detested doing physical labor. I watched him as he watched her with admiration, adroitly putting meals together without one grumble, and not much fuss, either. She smiled, laughed in response to his many jokes. She cared expertly for his clothes and ran the huge house with so little effort that Papa couldn't stop admiring her remarkable efficiency.

"How do you do it, Billie? Why do you even want to? Why don't you tell me to hire servants to wait on you?"

"Oh, no, Damian. It's the least I can do to repay you for all that you're doing for us." Her voice was soft and her eyes warm as she looked at him. "I'm so grateful that you wanted me and have welcomed my son as your own that I can never do enough. Anyway, having servants in the house steals your privacy."

I stared at Billie, wondering how a woman with her experience could be so easily fooled. Papa used people. Didn't she realize that she was saving him tons of money by being his housekeeper and cook?—and that generous offer to hire servants was all fraud, calculated to make her feel she wasn't being used.

"Audrina," said Billie one day when I'd been married about two months and Arden was still studying for his broker's exam, "I've been watching Sylvia. For some reason she dislikes me and would like to see me gone. I'm trying to think as she might think. It could be she's jealous because she sees you love me, too, and she's never had to share your love with others. When I was in the cottage it was different, but now I'm in her home and stealing your attention and your time from her. Arden is her competition, too, but for some reason, maybe because he leaves her alone, she isn't jealous of him. It's me she's jealous of. What's more, I don't believe she's nearly as retarded as you think. She mimics you, Audrina. Whenever you turn your back, she follows you. And she can walk just as normally as you do—when she knows you can't see her."

Whipping around, I caught Sylvia just behind me. She appeared startled and quickly her closed lips parted, and her focused eyes went vacant, blind looking. "Billie, you shouldn't say things like that. She can hear. And if what you say is true—although I don't believe it is—she might understand and be hurt."

"Of course she understands," said Billie. "She isn't brilliant, but she's not beyond the pale."

"I don't understand why she'd pretend . . ."

"Who told you she's hopelessly retarded?" Sylvia had drifted out into the hall tugging Billie's little red cart along with her. As I watched, she sat upon it and began to shove herself along in Billie's fashion.

"Papa didn't bring her home until she was more than two and a half years old. He told me what her doctors had told him."

"I admire Damian a great deal, although I don't admire the way he's burdened your life with the care of your younger sister, especially when he could afford to pay for a nurse to care for her, or, better, a therapist to train her. Do what you can to teach her skills, and continue with your speech training. Don't give up on Sylvia. Even if those doctors gave what they thought was an honest evaluation, mistakes are often made. There is always hope and a chance for improvement."

In the months that followed, Billie convinced me that perhaps I had misjudged my father after all. She obviously adored him, even worshipped him. He ignored her legless condition and treated her with such gallantry he surprised me and pleased Arden. Papa even had a special wheelchair custom-made for Billie. He hated her little red cart with a passion, though the fancy "our kind" of chair with concealed wheels didn't speed around fast enough for her. She never used that chair unless Papa was around.

Arden worked like an Egyptian slave in the day, then studied half the night, trying to remember all he needed to know for his broker exams. It was what he said he wanted, but I knew his heart wasn't in it.

"Arden, if you don't want to be a broker, give it up and do something else."

"I do want it—go on, teach."

"Now," I began when he was seated across the table in our bedroom, "they will give you several kinds of tests to judge your reading ability and comprehension of the written word. Then comes your verbal agility, and you'll have to understand what you're saying, which goes without saying." I smiled at him and shoved his roving foot away from my leg. "Answer, please, would you rather paint a picture, look at a picture or sell a picture?"

"Paint a picture," Arden answered quickly.

Frowning, I shook my head. "Second question. Would you rather read a book, write a book or sell a book?"

"Write a book . . . but I guess that's wrong. The right answer is sell a book, sell a picture—right?"

After three failures came the passing exam, and my husband became a Wall Street Cowboy.

One day when my work was through, I wandered into the room where my mother's piano was. I smiled ironically to myself as I pulled out Aunt Mercy Marie's photograph and set it on the grand piano. Who would have ever thought I'd do such a crazy thing on my own? Perhaps it was because I was thinking about my aunt and how I'd missed her funeral. To make up for that, I went often to the graveyard to put flowers on her grave, and on my mother's grave, too. Never, never did I bring any flowers for the First Audrina.

In memory of them, I began my own "teatime." As I began the routine once performed by two other sisters, Sylvia crept into the room and sat on the floor near my feet, staring up into my face with a look of bewilderment. A weird sensation of time repeating itself stole over me. "Lucietta," said the fat-faced woman I was speaking for, "what a lovely girl your third daughter is. Sylvia, such a beautiful name. Who is Sylvia? There used to be an old song about a girl named Sylvia. Lucietta, play that song again for me, please."

"Of course, Mercy Marie," said I in a good imitation of how I remembered my mother speaking. "Isn't she beautiful, my sweet Sylvia? I think she is the most beautiful of all my three girls."

I banged out some tune on the piano that was pitifully amateurish. But, like a marionette controlled by fate, I couldn't quit once I'd begun my act. Smiling,

I handed Sylvia a cookie. "And now *you* talk for the lady in the photograph."

Jumping to her feet with surprising agility, Sylvia ran to the piano, seized up the photograph of Aunt Mercy Marie and hurled it into the fireplace. The silver frame broke, the glass shattered, and soon the photo in Sylvia's hands was torn into shreds. Finished, and a bit scared looking, Sylvia backed away from me.

"How dare you do that?" I yelled. "That was the only picture we had of our mother's best friend! You've never done anything like that before."

Falling down on her knees, she crawled to me, whimpering like a small puppy—and she was ten years old now. Crouched at my feet, Sylvia clawed at my skirt, allowing her lips to part, and soon spittle wet her chin and dribbled down on her loose, shiftlike garment. A small child couldn't have looked into my eyes with more innocence. Billie had to be mistaken. Sylvia couldn't focus her eyes but for a second or two.

In my dreams that night while Arden slept peacefully at my side, it seemed I heard drums beating, natives chanting. Animals howled. Bolting awake I started to wake up Arden, then decided the animals' howling was only Sylvia screaming again. I ran to her room to take her into my arms. "What's wrong, darling?"

I swear I think she tried to say, "Bad . . . bad . . . bad," but I wasn't truly sure. "Did you say bad?"

Her aqua eyes were wide with fright—but she nodded. I broke into laughter and hugged her closer.

"No, it's not bad that you can talk. Oh, Sylvia, I've tried so hard, so hard to teach you and at last you're trying. You had a bad dream, that's all. Go back to sleep and think how wonderful your life is going to be now that you can communicate."

Yes, I told myself as I snuggled up close to Arden, liking his arms about me when he wasn't passionate, that's all it was, a bad dream Sylvia had.

Thanksgiving Day was a week away. I was more or less happy as I sat with Billie in the kitchen and planned the menu. Yet I still treaded the long halls like a child, still taking care not to step on any of the colorful geometric patterns the stained-glass windows cast on the floor. I'd stop and stare for long moments at the rainbows on the walls, just as I had when I was a child. My memories of childhood were still so hazy.

As I left the kitchen and started for the stairs, with the notion of visiting that playroom and evoking the past, challenging it to reveal the truth, I turned to find Sylvia trailing me like a shadow. Of course, I'd grown accustomed to her being my constant companion, but what surprised me was the way she managed to catch a random sunbeam with that crystal prism she clutched and flash the colors directly into my eyes.

Almost blinded, I staggered backward, for some reason terrified. In the shadows near the wall I dropped the hand I'd used to shade my eyes and stared toward the huge chandelier that caught all the colors already on the marble floor. The mirrors on the walls refracted them back to Sylvia, who directed them again at me, as if to keep me from the playroom.

Dizzy and unreal feeling, visions flashed in my head. I saw my aunt sprawled facedown on the hard foyer floor. What if Sylvia had been downstairs in the foyer and had used that prism to blind my aunt's eyes with sunlight colors? Could that have made my aunt dizzy enough to fall? Was Sylvia trying to make me fall, too?

"Put that thing down, Sylvia!" I yelled. "Put it away. Never flash those lights in my eyes again! Do you hear me?"

Like the wild thing Papa compared her to, she ran. Stunned for a moment I could only stare after her. Feeling frightened of my own violent reaction, I sat on the bottom step and tried to pull myself together—and that's when the front door opened.

A woman stood there, tall and slender, wearing a smart hat of many shades of green feathers. A mink cape was slung casually over one shoulder, and her green shoes matched her very expensive-looking green suit.

"Hi," she said in a sultry voice. "Here I am, back again. Don't you recognize me, sweet Audrina?"

A Second Life

"What are you doing?" called Vera as, much in the manner of a very young child, I began to back up the stairs without standing up. "Aren't you a bit old for such childish behavior? Really, Audrina, you don't change at all, do you?"

Striding into the foyer, Vera hardly appeared to limp. But when I checked I saw that the left sole of her high-heeled shoes was an inch thicker than the right sole. Gracefully she approached the stairs. "I stopped off in the village and they told me you really did marry Arden Lowe. I never thought you'd ever be adult enough to marry anyone. Congratulations to him, the fool, and my best wishes to you, the bride who should have known better."

The trouble was, what she said could very well be true.

"Aren't you glad to see me?"

"Your mother is dead." How cruelly I said that, as if I wanted to even the score and dish out pain for pain.

"Really, Audrina, I know that." Her dark eyes

were cold as she looked me up and down, telling me in her own silent, eloquent way that I was no competition for her. "Unlike you, sweet Audrina, I have friends in the village who keep me posted as to what goes on here. I wish I could say I was sorry, but I can't. Ellsbeth Whitefern was never a real mother to me, was she? Your mother was kinder."

She turned around slowly and exhaled a long withheld breath. "Wow! Would you look at this place! Like a palace. Who would have ever thought dear Papa would be idiot enough to fix up an old house like this. He could have bought two new ones for what it cost to restore this monstrosity."

Standing midway up the stairs, I tried to regain some lost composure. "Did you come back for some reason?"

"Aren't you happy to see me?" Smiling, she cocked her head to one side and scanned over me again, then laughed. "No, I can tell you aren't. Are you still afraid of me, Audrina? Afraid your boy husband might find a real woman twice as appealing as a modest, shy bride who can't really give him any pleasure? Just looking at you in that white dress tells me you haven't changed. It's November, little girl. Wintertime. The season for bright colors, parties, good cheer and holidays, and you wear a white dress." Mockingly she laughed again. "Don't tell me your husband is no lover at all and you are still Papa's pure little darling."

"It's a wool dress, Vera. The color is called winter-white. It's an expensive dress that Arden selected for me himself. He likes for me to wear white."

"Of course he does," she said even more mockingly. "He indulges your need to stay a sweet little girl. Poor Audrina, the sweet and chaste. Audrina the pure and virginal. Dear Audrina, the obedient little darling who can do no wrong."

"What do you want, Vera?" I asked, feeling very cold. I sensed danger, felt Vera's threat. I wanted to order her out of the house. *Go, leave me alone. Give me time to grow up, to find the woman that's hidden somewhere in me.*

"I've come home for Thanksgiving," said Vera smoothly, in that same sexy voice she must have copied from someone she admired, as she'd tried once to talk like a TV actress. "And if you're nice to me, *really* nice, as a family member should be, then I'll stay on for Christmas, too. It's really not very hospitable of you to keep me standing in the foyer while my bags are on the porch. Where's Arden? He can carry in my luggage."

"My husband is working, Vera, and you can bring in your own bags. Papa won't be happy to see you. I suppose you must know that."

"Yes, Audrina," she said in that smooth, hateful voice. "I know that. But I want to see Papa. He owes me a great deal—and I intend to have what belongs to my mother, and what belongs to me."

A small scuttling sound made me look toward the back hall to see Billie shoveling along on her little red dolly cart. As if she'd just seen a mouse, Vera jumped backward and nearly lost her footing because of that thick sole. Her gloved hand reached to smother her cry. Her other hand stretched forward as if to ward off contamination. I watched her struggle to gain her composure as the small half-woman, twice as old and three times as beautiful as Vera, looked at her appraisingly and with a great deal of self-composure. I admired Billie for holding her own.

Then, to my amazement, Vera smiled brilliantly at my mother-in-law. "Oh, of course. How can I have forgotten Billie Lowe. How are you, Mrs. Lowe?"

Cheerfully Billie greeted Vera. "Why, hello there. You're Vera, aren't you? How beautiful you look. How nice you've come home for the holidays. You're just in time for lunch. Your old room is clean, and all I have to do is put on fresh linens and you'll feel right at home." She looked upward to give me a special warm smile. "Well, Audrina, that itchy nose of yours really did herald a visitor after all."

"Do you live here, too?" asked Vera, rather taken aback. Someone in the village didn't know everything that went on in Whitefern.

"Oh, yes," gushed Billie happily. "This is the most wonderful house I've ever been lucky enough to call home. Damian has been absolutely marvelous to me. He's given me the rooms that used to belong to"— here she hesitated, looking a bit embarrassed—"your mother." Her appealing look at Vera touched my heart. "At first I thought it was wrong to take such a grand suite of rooms when Audrina might want them, but Audrina hasn't said a word to make me feel I'm usurping anyone's place. What's more, Damian carried over all the things I wanted from the cottage himself. He did that the very day Arden and Audrina eloped."

Billie gave me another loving smile. "Come, darlin', it's time for lunch. Sylvia is already at the table. There's plenty for all of us."

"Help me bring in my luggage, Audrina," said Vera, abruptly turning to head toward the porch, as if tired of responding to all the warmth and good cheer Billie showed her. "I'll be leaving in a few weeks, so you don't have to look so bothered. I don't want your husband."

"Because you have your own?" I asked hopefully.

Laughing, she half turned to grin at me with Papa's own cunning. "You'd like that, wouldn't you? But no, I don't have my own. Lamar Rensdale was a miserable failure who took the easy way out once things got rough. What a coward he proved to be. No talent at all once you took him away from the provinces. Do you still play the piano?"

No, I didn't practice on the piano anymore. There was too much to do. But as I helped Vera bring in her three bags, carrying two while she carried one, I vowed that when I had the time I'd find another music teacher and pick up where I'd left off. "Vera, I'd like to hear more about Lamar Rensdale. He was very kind to me, and I'm sorry he's dead."

"Later," said Vera, following me up the stairs. "After we eat, we'll have a nice long talk while we wait for Papa to come home and rejoice at seeing me again."

On the way to her room we found Sylvia riding Billie's cart, shoveling along with some expertise.

"Sylvia, take Billie's cart back to the kitchen. You have no right to use it even when she isn't. Any moment she may want to hop down and her cart won't be there." I reached to pull Sylvia from the dolly. If there was one thing that made Sylvia stubborn and hateful, it was taking from her that little red cart she wanted for her own.

"Good God," exclaimed Vera, staring at Sylvia as if at some creature in a zoo, "why waste your breath on an idiot? Why not just shove her off and be done with it?"

"Sylvia is not as retarded as Papa led us to believe," I said innocently enough. "Bit by bit she's learning to talk."

For some reason Vera turned to stare at Sylvia with narrowed, suspicious eyes, distaste clear on her face. "God almighty, this house is full of freaks. A legless woman and a stammering moron."

"As long as you're in this house, you will not refer to Sylvia as a moron, idiot or freak. And you will treat Billie with the respect due her, or else I'm sure that Papa will kick you out. And if he doesn't, then I will."

Appearing surprised, Vera smiled weakly, then turned her back and strode on into her old room to unpack.

I was silent at lunch as Billie did her best to welcome Vera home. Vera looked sophisticated in the lovely beige knit dress she'd changed into. The soft color flattered her complexion, which seemed not as sallow as it had once been. Her makeup was expertly applied, her hair styled to perfection while mine was windblown and wild appearing. My nails were short and unpolished since I had to help Billie with the housekeeping. Every one of my imperfections rose up like mountains as I stared at Vera.

"I'm sorry about your mother, Vera," said Billie. "I hope you don't mind if Audrina told me all about that. She is like my own daughter, the one I always wanted to have."

Gratefully I smiled, happy she wasn't going to abandon me for Vera, who seemed to have become the epitome of glamour. I knew Billie admired all that Vera now represented. Pretty clothes, long polished nails and the kind of jewelry Vera wore—that's when I realized it was my mother's jewelry, my aunt's jewelry she was wearing. The stolen jewelry.

Jewelry that she took off and stashed somewhere before Papa and my husband came home together.

We were seated in the Roman Revival room. The sun had just settled down behind the horizon, leaving a bloody trail of fire clouds, when Papa threw open the door and strode inside with Arden at his heels.

Papa was talking. "Damn, Arden, how the hell can you forget when you make notes? Do you realize your mistakes are going to lose several good clients? You have to list all the stocks each client owns and call them when dramatic changes occur, or, better, before they occur. Anticipate, boy, anticipate!"

That's when Papa saw Vera. He stopped in the middle of another chastising remark and stared at Vera with loathing. "What the devil are you doing here?"

Billie winced. Papa had disappointed her. Arden threw Vera an uneasy glance, then came to kiss my cheek before he settled on the sofa beside me, putting his arm about my shoulders. "Are you all right?" he whispered. "You look so pale."

I didn't answer, though I did snuggle closer to him, feeling safer with his arm about me. Vera stood up. With her high heels on she was still about five inches shorter than Papa, but on those stilts she managed to look formidable even so. In the corner of the large room, Sylvia squatted down on her heels and rolled her head about idiotically, as if she were deliberately going to undo all the progress we'd both struggled to achieve.

"I had to come home, Papa, to see my mother's grave," said Vera in a small voice of apology. "A friend called and told me when she died, and I cried all night and really wanted to come for her funeral. But I was on duty and couldn't get off until now. I'm a registered nurse now. Also, I didn't have enough money to get down here, and I knew you wouldn't send me the money to come. It comes as such a shock when someone healthy dies in an accident. That same friend sent me the newspaper obituary. It arrived on the day of her funeral."

She smiled then, tilting her head to one side in a charming manner, separating her feet so she stood staunchly, with her arms akimbo. Suddenly she appeared not so sweet, but defiant, masculine, taking up almost as much space as Papa did when he spread his legs wide and prepared himself for assault.

Papa grunted and glared at her. He seemed to recognize her challenge. "When will you be leaving?"

"Soon," said Vera, casting down her eyes, gone

dovelike and demure as she tried not to appear hurt. But her feet stayed apart, and that betrayed her put-on expression of meekness. "I felt I owed it to my mother to come as soon as I could."

Arden leaned forward to better watch her expression, dragging me along with him as he forgot his arm about me.

"I don't want you in my house!" snapped Papa. "I know what went on here before you left."

Oh, dear God. Vera threw Arden a nervous, warning look.

Immediately I pulled free from Arden's casual embrace and moved to the far side of the sofa. No, I tried to tell myself, Vera was deliberately trying to involve Arden and ruin my marriage. But Arden looked guilty. I felt my heart crack. All along he'd claimed I was the only one he loved. And Vera must have told the truth a long time ago about sleeping with Arden.

"Papa," appealed Vera in her seductive, throaty voice, "I've made my mistakes. Forgive me for not being what I should have been. I've always wanted to win your approval and be what you wanted, but nobody told me anything. I didn't know what Mr. Rensdale wanted when he kissed me and started petting. He seduced me, Papa!" She sobbed as if with shame and bowed her smooth cap of shining, orangey hair. "I came back to pay my respects at my mother's grave, to spend Thanksgiving Day with the only family I have, to renew our family ties. And I also came to collect what valuables my mother left me."

Again Papa grunted. "Your mother had nothing of

value to leave you after you ran from here and stole what jewelry she had, and what jewelry my wife left Audrina. Thanksgiving Day is a week away. Pay your respects at your mother's grave today and leave tomorrow morning."

"Damian!" said Billie reprimandingly. "Is that any way to talk to your own niece?"

"It's exactly the way I talk to this one!" stormed Papa, pivoting about and striding toward the front stairs. "Don't ever call me Papa again, Vera." He glanced back at Billie. "It's our night out on the town, have you forgotten? The movies after dinner in a good restaurant. Why aren't you dressed and ready to go?"

"We can't leave the house on the day your niece comes home," Billie said in her calm way. "She thinks of you as her father, Damian, regardless of what you call your relationship. We can always dine out and go to the movies. Damian, please don't embarrass me again. You've been so kind, so generous—I'd be so disappointed if you—" There she broke off, looking at him with tears in her eyes.

Her tears of distress seemed to affect him greatly. "All right," he said, turning then to Vera. "I want to see as little of you as possible, and the day after Thanksgiving you leave. Is that understood?"

Vera nodded meekly. Bowing her head, she sat down to lock her legs together and form a lap on which she could demurely fold her hands, a well-trained, modest young woman. And modesty was something Vera had never possessed. "Anything you want, Pa—Uncle Damian."

I turned my head just in time to see Arden gazing at her pityingly. From one to the other I stared, sensing it had already begun. The seduction of my husband.

In no time at all Vera and Billie were fast friends. "You dear, wonderful woman, to take on all this housework all by yourself when my father could easily afford a maid and a housekeeper. I marvel at you, Billie Lowe."

"Audrina helps a great deal," said Billie. "Give her credit, too."

I was in the powder room down the hall from the kitchen, tediously trying to untangle Sylvia's wild mop of chestnut curls. Pausing, I waited to hear what else Vera had to say to Billie. But it was Billie who again spoke.

"Now, if you'd do your bit and run the vacuum in the two best salons, I'd really be grateful. Be sure to use the attachments on the lamp shades, furniture and draperies. It would help Audrina. She really has her hands full trying to teach Sylvia how to talk and move correctly, and she's succeeding, too."

"You're kidding." Vera sounded surprised, as if she was hoping Sylvia would never talk. "That kid can't really talk, can she?"

"Yes, she can say a few easy words. Nothing is clearly enunciated, but understandable if you listen closely."

Holding Sylvia by the hand, we followed Vera to watch her enter the Roman Revival Salon, where she pushed the vacuum without enthusiasm. I loved Billie for putting her to work without asking, as if she assumed Vera would be willing. Not to be willing would spoil Vera's game. At least, I thought it was a game. Vera pushed and pulled the vacuum, but all the time her eyes were on the many treasures. While the machine idled, she pulled out a notepad and began to write. Very quietly, leaving Sylvia in the hall, I slipped up behind her to read over her shoulder.

1. Vacuum, dust, use furniture polish.
   (Mirrors, huge, gold leaf, worth a fortune.)
2. Pick up newspapers, arrange magazines,
   neatly. (Lamps, Tiffany, Venetian, solid
   brass, priceless.)
3. Should make beds before coming
   downstairs. (Genuine antiques everywhere
   now, oil paintings, originals.)
4. Help with laundry. Don't use bleach
   on towels. (Oriental and Chinese rugs,
   bric-a-brac of porcelain and blown glass,
   especially birds.)
5. Run for the mail early. *Never* forget!
   (Checks stored in his office safe. Never saw
   so many checks come in the mail.)

"What an interesting way to list your chores," I said when she sensed my presence and whirled around, looking startled. "Along with the valuables, you want to run for the mail. Are you planning to rob us, Vera?"

"You little sneak," she snarled. "How dare you steal up on me and read over my shoulder!"

"One always watches a cat who becomes very quiet. Is it really necessary to list everyday ordinary chores? Don't they come naturally to you? As for the rest, most of it was here before. Everything has been refurbished and upholstered, that's all. Papa hunted up some of the older Whitefern antiques that had been sold. Since you weren't impressed before, why be impressed now?"

For a moment it seemed she might slap me. Then she sagged limply into a chair. "Oh, Audrina, don't fight with me. If only you knew the horror of being with a man who doesn't want you. Lamar hated me for forcing him to take me with him to New York. I kept insisting I was pregnant, and he kept insisting I couldn't be. When we reached New York, we moved into a boardinghouse, and he went to teach at Juilliard. He was always throwing you in my face, saying he wished I was more like you, and then maybe he could have loved me. The fool! What man could enjoy a woman like you?" Then she flashed me a strange look and allowed tears to trickle from her eyes. "I'm sorry. You are very beautiful in your own way." She sniffled, then went on. "While Lamar taught, I started my student nurse training. The pay wasn't enough to feed a parakeet. In what little spare time I had, I did some modeling for an art school. I told Lamar he could do the same thing in his spare time, but he was too modest to take off his clothes. Models don't wear a stitch. I've always been proud of my body. Stupid

Lamar was too modest to do that, and too proud. He hated me more for showing myself to all those men in the classes. Every time I modeled I'd come home to find him dead drunk. Soon he was drinking so much he didn't have any job at all. He lost his touch at the piano, forcing us to move to a slum area where he taught music to poor kids who never had the money to pay him—that's when I left. I was fed up. The day I graduated as a registered nurse, I picked up the newspaper to read that Lamar had drowned himself in the Hudson River." She sighed and stared into space. "Just another funeral I had to miss. I worked the day they buried him. I was glad his parents came to claim his body, or else he might have ended up one of the cadavers in the hospital where I worked." She grimaced before she looked downward. A heavy silence filled the room.

I bowed my head, weighed down with sorrow for a man who'd wanted to help me and had fallen innocently into the trap Vera had set. I knew who'd done the seducing.

"I suppose you're thinking I helped kill him, aren't you?"

"I don't know what to think."

"No, of course you don't!" she cried scornfully, jumping up and beginning to pace the room. "You've had it easy, staying on here and being taken care of. You've never had to face the real world and all the ugliness out there, and all the things you have to do in order to stay alive. I've done it all, Audrina, the whole can of worms. I came back to help—and you don't want me." Sobbing, tears beginning to course down her cheeks, she fell onto the sofa.

Disbelievingly I watched her cry. Billie, who must have been listening, came scooting into the room. In a flash she was on the sofa beside Vera, trying to comfort her.

Instantly, Vera bolted. A short hysterical scream escaped her lips. Then she paled. "Oh . . . I'm sorry. It's just that I don't like to be touched."

"I understand." Billie lowered herself onto the dolly and disappeared.

"You've hurt her feelings, Vera. And you promised that as long as you're in this house, you would never say or do anything to hurt Billie or make her feel unwanted."

Vera said she understood. She was sorry, and never, never would she pull away again. It was just that she was unaccustomed to being touched by a legless woman, a cripple. I stared down at her shoe with the inch lift, perversely enjoying the way she blanched.

"You can't notice my limp now, can you?" she asked. "We all have small idiosyncrasies, such as yours for forgetting."

Soon Arden was telling me whenever we were alone, usually not until we were in bed, what a wonderful help Vera was, taking so much work off his mother's shoulders—and mine. "We should all be glad she's back to help."

I turned on my side and closed my eyes. To turn my back was my way of telling him to leave me alone. Quickly he turned me against his front so that my back was fitted into the warm curve of his body. Our breathing coordinated even as those uncontrollable hands of his began to search out the curves he wanted to trace again and again.

"Don't be jealous of Vera, darling," he whispered, moving so he could rub his cheek against mine. "It's you I love, only you."

And once more, I had to let him prove it.

Thanksgiving Day came and went, and Vera stayed on. For some odd reason Papa stopped ordering her to leave. I reasoned he saw how much help she was to Billie while I taught Sylvia how to talk, to walk, to dress herself, to comb her own hair, to wash her own face and hands. Slowly, slowly, Sylvia was emerging from her cocoon. With each new skill she mastered, her eyes came more into focus. She began to make a real effort to keep her lips together and not let the drooling begin. In some ways it was like finding myself, as I taught her all she needed to know.

In the First and Best Audrina's playroom, she seemed to learn best. On my lap while we rocked together, I'd read to her from Mother Goose and simple books for very young children of two or three. With the dolls and stuffed animals on the shelves for schoolmates, we sometimes sat at the small tea table and ate our lunch, and it was there that Sylvia picked up a tiny spoon and stirred the bit of tea in her miniature cup.

"And one day very soon, Sylvia is going to pick up her own knife and fork and she will cut her own meat."

"Cut meat . . ." she repeated, trying to pick up the fork and knife and hold them as I was demonstrating.

"Who is Sylvia?"

"Who . . . who ess . . ."

"Tell me your name. That's what I want to hear."

"Tell me . . . yer name . . ."

"No. What is *your* name?"

"Nooo . . . what esss yer name . . ."

"Sylvia, you're doing wonderfully well today. But do try to think about the reasoning behind what I tell you. Everyone and everything must have a name, or else we wouldn't know what to call one another, or how to know a chair from a lamp. Take me, for instance. My name is Audrina."

"Mah . . . name . . . esss . . . Aud . . . dreen . . . na."

"Yes, *my* name *is* Audrina. But *your* name is Sylvia."

"Yesss . . . mah . . . name . . ."

I picked up the hand mirror the First Audrina had on her small dressing table, held it before Sylvia and pointed. "See, in the mirror, *that* is Sylvia." Then I held the mirror so my face was reflected, and again I let her look so she could see what I was trying to impart. "*That* is Audrina in the mirror." At the same time I pointed to myself. "Audrina." I pointed to myself, then put the mirror so she could see her own face. "That is Sylvia. *You* are Sylvia."

Some flickering small light lit up her lovely aqua eyes. They widened and focused on the mirror. She grabbed for it and stared at her reflection, holding it so close her nose was mashed against the glass. "Syl . . . vee . . . ah. Syl . . . vee . . . ah." Over and over again she said it, laughing, jumping up and dancing awkwardly around the playroom. Hugging the mirror hard against her small chest, she glowed with happiness. Finally, after many repetitions, she said it right. "My name is Sylvia." I ran to hug her, to kiss her, to reward her with the cookies I'd hidden in a drawer.

I turned with the cookies to see that all happiness had fled from Sylvia's eyes. Sylvia was frozen. Her eyes unfocused, her lips gaped and the spittle ran. Once more she went mute.

Vera stood in the doorway.

She wore the expression of an angel, so pious as she looked us both over. Lambs for the slaughtering, I thought irrelevantly.

"Go away, Vera," I ordered coldly, hurrying to protect Sylvia. "I've told you before not to come up here when I'm teaching Sylvia."

"Fool!" she snapped, striding into the playroom and sitting down in the rocking chair. "You can't teach an idiot anything. She's just repeating what she hears you say, like a parrot. Go help Billie in the kitchen. I'm so damned sick of preparing meals and cleaning house. My God, it seems nobody does anything in this house but eat, sleep and work. When do you have fun?"

"When the work is finished, Vera," I answered angrily. I caught hold of Sylvia's hand and started for the door. "Rock in the chair, Vera. I'm sure nothing I've seen there would make you scream—for you've known it all, the whole can of worms."

Screaming like a demon straight from the pits of hell, my small sister ran to hurl herself at Vera. She tore into her, scratching, kicking, and as Vera tried to ward her off, Sylvia clamped her teeth down on Vera's arm.

Violently Vera slammed Sylvia to the floor. "You screwy little idiot! Get out of here! I've just as much right in this room as you have!"

I ran to save Sylvia from more harm as Vera raised her foot to kick, aiming for Sylvia's pretty face. But before I could reach her, Sylvia rolled out of harm's way. In so doing her shoe caught behind Vera's foot and threw her off balance. Vera crashed to the floor like a felled tree. Then came the howls of pain.

Even before I knelt to check, I could tell from the grotesque position of her left leg that Vera had again broken it. Damnation! The last thing we needed was an invalid to wait on.

Fretting and fuming, I paced the Roman Revival room as Arden and Papa came home carrying Vera with another cast on her broken leg. Her black eyes met mine, challenging me as one of her arms encircled Arden's neck. The other was around Papa. They supported her on the cradle they made with their arms.

"Audrina," said Arden, "run for pillows to stack behind Vera's back. She'll need others to raise her leg above her heart level. She's got to wear that thing seven to eight weeks."

Slowly I gathered several pillows from other sofas and stuffed them behind Vera's back. Arden tenderly lifted her heavy casted leg and put four more pillows under it. Her red toenails wiggled like little warning flags as he tended to her.

"How did Vera fall, anyway?" asked Billie that night as I helped her prepare dinner.

"An accident. I heard Vera tell you that Sylvia deliberately hooked her foot behind her ankle, but I was there and it was an accident."

"It was not an accident!" screamed Vera from the other room. "The brat did it deliberately!"

"Audrina, I hope that's not true." Billie threw Sylvia an uneasy glance. Once again Sylvia was riding on the little red cart, speeding down the slick waxed floor of the back hall.

"You know, Billie, both you and Arden find it very hard to believe anything I say about Vera. I don't mean to be overly critical, but it was the first real breakthrough for Sylvia. I saw her eyes light up with understanding . . . and then Vera had to show up at the door."

I heard Sylvia singing as she raced up and down the back hall on that red cart. "Just a playroom . . . safe in my home . . . only a playroom . . ."

I almost dropped the spoon in the steaming gravy. Who had taught Sylvia to sing that song?

"Are you all right, darlin'?" asked Billie, pulling herself along by grabbing the countertops.

"I'm fine," I answered out of habit. "But I can't remember teaching Sylvia to sing any song. Did you hear her singing, Billie?"

"No, darlin', I didn't hear her singing. I thought that was Vera's voice. She sings that song a lot. It's like a child's song of reassurance—rather pitiful. It makes me hurt to think that Damian didn't show Vera more kindness. And she's trying so to make him appreciate her."

Silently I poured the gravy into its bowl, then carried it into the dining room. On the way back I pulled Sylvia off the cart and scolded her thoroughly. "How many times do I have to tell you to leave that cart alone? It's not yours. Go ride the tricycle Papa gave you. It's red and pretty."

Pouting her lower lip, Sylvia backed away from me. I pushed the cart with my foot into the kitchen.

That evening Papa and Arden picked up the purple chaise with Vera still lying there like an orange-haired Cleopatra and she ate with us in the dining room.

I hated seeing her on Momma's purple chaise, but there Vera lay day after day, reading those same paperback novels she had read years and years ago.

Sylvia retreated into herself, refusing to enter the playroom and be taught again. Because Papa had to have gourmet meals and no longer could Billie be given relief by eating in restaurants with him, she did nothing but cook. I did all the housework, all the laundry, though Arden did what he could after he came home from work. Papa was always too busy, or too tired to do anything but talk or watch TV.

A month after the New Year had come and gone, I led Sylvia again into the playroom to continue our lessons. "I'm sorry I've neglected you, Sylvia. If Vera hadn't broken her leg, I'll bet you'd be reading by now. So let's go back to where we left off. What is your name?"

We had reached the playroom door, and to my

surprise, and Sylvia's, too, Billie was in the rocker. She blushed when we caught her. "It's silly, I know, but if there's magic in this chair, I want a little of it myself." She looked very girlish and pretty, then she giggled. "Don't laugh. But I've got a dream, a wonderful dream that occupies most of my thoughts. I'm hoping this chair will help my dream come true." She smiled at me tremulously. "I questioned your father and he said anything is possible, if you believe, so here I am . . . and I'm believing." She smiled and held out her arms. "Come, Sylvia, let me hold you on my lap. Be my little girl today and tell me what your name is."

"Noooo!" wailed Sylvia, loud enough to bring Vera hobbling down the hall on the crutches the doctor was allowing her to use now.

"Baaaad!" yelled Sylvia, pointing at Vera. "Baad!"

Sylvia would not sit on Billie's lap, but on another day Papa found us both there rocking and singing together. "Just you, my love," he said, looking at me and never at Sylvia. "Rock alone, become the empty pitcher that fills with everything wonderful."

I ignored him, thinking him a fool on that particular subject. I turned to Sylvia, wanting to show her off in front of Papa. "Darling, tell Papa your name." Only a moment ago she'd said it, before we started singing. "Tell him my name, too."

My small sister on my lap made her beautiful but sometimes terrible eyes vacant, so that they looked straight through him, and some babbling nonsense came from her lips. I wanted to cry. I'd worked so hard, and denied myself many trips into the city with

Arden to stay home and teach Sylvia. Now she refused to give me the reward I felt I needed.

"Oh," said Papa in disgust, "you're wasting your time. Give it up."

My husband seldom came home before nine or ten at night. Often he missed dinner, explaining this by saying he had so much paperwork to do, so much technical data to read, he had to study in order to keep up.

"And there are so many distractions at home," he said in an evasive way. "Now don't jump on Damian. It's not his fault but my own. I just don't catch on as quickly as I should."

The very next night Arden came home with even more papers to read. Financial reports, financial advisory services, technical stock charts, tax shelters to evaluate—more work than Papa had ever assigned to him before. At two in the morning, I awoke to see Arden still at our small bedroom desk, reading, making notes, his eyes tired and bloodshot.

"Come to bed, Arden."

"Can't, honey." He yawned and smiled my way. As exhausted as he was, he still didn't lose patience with me, or with Papa. "Today your father took off somewhere and left me in charge of the firm. I couldn't take care of my own affairs when his are more important—and now I have to catch up." He stood up and stretched, then headed for the shower. "Cold water will wake me up."

In another moment he was back at the bathroom

door, beginning to tug off his clothes as he said in a troubled way, "Well, there I was in Damian's office, in charge, and I knew damn well he was expecting me to make every mistake possible so he could shout and humiliate me again in front of everybody. It was a quiet day, and as I sat behind his massive desk and waited for the telephone to ring, I started looking for something and discovered the drawers were very short. I couldn't understand why such a large desk had such short drawers. So I fooled around, and soon found several small secret compartments way in the back of the drawers."

Fully out of his clothes now, he stood there naked, as if he wanted me to look at him, something I could never do without quivering and blushing. Though he said nothing sexual to me or indicated he wanted me to do more than listen, I sensed a certain kind of expectation.

"Audrina, I'm not an expert bookkeeper, but when I found a ledger in one secret compartment, I couldn't resist leafing through it and doing a little calculating. Your father 'borrows' money from his more dormant accounts, uses it to invest in his own account, and when he's made a nice profit, he puts the money back in months later. His clients never know the difference. He's been doing it for years and years."

Blankly I stared at him.

"That's not all he does, either," Arden went on. "Just the other day I heard him telling one of his wealthiest clients that the stock certificates she found in her attic were worthless except for framing. She mailed him the certificates to frame and hang in his office—a little gift, she told him. Audrina, they were Union Pacific stocks that have split time and time again. When she gave him that little gift, she gave him hundreds of thousands of dollars—and she's eighty-two years old. Rich, but old. He probably thinks she's got enough and doesn't need it nearly as much as he does, and he must figure she's too old to find out he's cheated her."

He yawned again and rubbed at his eyes, and again he seemed boyish and very vulnerable. For some reason I was touched. "You know, for the longest time I wondered why he collected old stock certificates. Now I know why he wants them. He sells them on the West Coast. It's no wonder he's so rich now, no wonder at all."

"I should have known he had to be doing something dishonest to have so much cash to invest, when only a few years ago we couldn't even afford meat on our table. Oh, how dumb not to have guessed years ago!" I looked at him anxiously.

Something sweet, young, wistful and yearning was in his eyes that pleaded for me to come to him. And this time I felt the stirrings of sexuality in my own body, responding to his call. Alarmed by my surprising arousal, I whirled around to leave. I couldn't let Arden distract me. I had to confront Papa with his thieving ways.

"Arden, you didn't say anything to Papa about his embezzling funds, did you?"

I heard his sigh. "No. Besides, when I checked

the secret compartments in his desk later, they were empty." He looked toward the windows, his lips tightening, as if he gave up in trying to entice me by doing nothing aggressive, and he said nothing to keep me with him. "I suppose Damian thinks of everything and had some way of detecting when those papers and ledgers were tampered with."

"Go to bed. I'm going to Papa."

"I wish you wouldn't. He'll wonder how you know."

"I won't say anything that will let him know who told me." I waited for him to protest again, but he turned and headed for the bed. I leaned above him and kissed him good night.

"Audrina . . . ?" he murmured. "Do you really love me? Sometimes in the night I wake up and wonder why you married me. I hope it wasn't just to escape your father."

"Yes, I love you," I said without hesitation. "It may not be the kind of love you want. . . but maybe one day soon you'll be surprised."

"Let's hope so," he muttered before he fell into exhausted sleep.

If only I'd stayed in bed that night and given to Arden what he needed. If only I hadn't thought I could always set everything right.

I expected Papa to be asleep at almost three in the morning. Certainly I didn't expect to see the thin line of yellow light under his closed bedroom door, any more than I expected to hear his laughter and a woman's smothered giggle. I stopped short, not knowing what to think or do. Had he been so insensitive as to bring home one of his "playmates," as Momma used to sarcastically call them?

"Now you stop that, Damian," said a voice I couldn't help but recognize. "I've got to go now. We can't risk letting the children find out about this."

Not for one second did I stop to consider what to do once I knew who it was with him, nor did I think of the consequences of my impulsive actions. I threw open the door and stepped into the dimly lit room that Papa had redecorated since Momma died. Red-flocked wallpaper, with gold-framed mirrors everywhere, made his room seem an opulent eighteenth-century bordello.

They were in bed together, Arden's legless mother and my father, playing intimately with each other. When they saw me, Billie gasped and snatched her hand away. Papa quickly yanked up the covers to conceal them both. But I'd seen enough.

There was such a red rage in my brain I wanted to scream out every word I was to think of later but not now. All I could do was yell at her, "You whore!" Then at him I hurled, "You filthy son of a bitch! Leave my house, Billie! I never want to see you again! Arden and I are leaving you, Papa, and taking Sylvia with us."

Billie began to cry. Papa slipped discreetly from the covers and pulled on a red brocade lounging robe. "You silly little girl," he said easily, not appearing embarrassed at all. "As long as Billie wants to stay she will."

Insulted, feeling Billie had betrayed me and Arden,

too, I whirled about and raced back to my room to find Arden had gotten up from bed to resume his work. However, it had done him little good. He was slumped over on his desk, fast asleep on his papers. Sympathy rushed to erase my anger, and gently I woke him up and helped him off with his robe. Then, with my arm about his waist, I assisted him to the bed, and in his arms I lay as he fell asleep.

All night long I fretted before I reached my conclusion. It wasn't Billie's fault—it was Papa's. He'd seduced her with his gifts, with his charm and good looks, so he could have the kinky thrill of having sex with a legless woman. I couldn't drive Billie out. It was Papa who had to leave so we could all live decent lives.

And now I had the perfect weapon to force him to go. I'd threaten to expose him for the fraud and embezzler he was. Even if he had hidden the incriminating ledgers, I had all the information I needed about his illegal stock advisory firm in San Francisco—and that alone would be threat enough.

However, it wasn't to be that way.

Billie came to me early the next day, soon after Arden and Papa had left for work. Her eyes were red-rimmed and swollen and her face seemed very pale. I turned my back and continued to brush my hair.

"Audrina . . . please. I wanted to sink through the floor last night when you stormed into his room. I know what you think, but it wasn't that way, really it wasn't."

Viciously I tore the brush through my hair.

"Listen to me, please!" she wailed piteously. "I love Damian, Audrina. He's the kind of man I always wanted but never had."

Spinning around, my eyes blazed as I tried to scream out all my anger, but for some reason her tears stopped me. The colors in her eyes made me feel strange, as too many colors always did. She had a habit of always wearing bright clothes: crimson, scarlet, magenta, electric blue, emerald green, purple and bright yellows. Colors flashing . . . colors and the tinkling wind chimes when trouble came. I put my hand over my ears and closed my eyes, turned my back and refused to hold the gaze that pleaded for my understanding.

"Turn your back and close your mind as well as your ears, but I think he loves me, too, darlin'," she went on. "Maybe you think because I'm crippled he can't love me. Still, I think he does, and even if he doesn't, I'll just be grateful he gave me a little of what I always wanted—a real man. Compared to him my three husbands were little boys playing at being men. Damian would never have left me, I know he wouldn't have."

I had to look at her then, to see if she truly believed her words. Her beautiful eyes pleaded, just as her hands reached out to me. I stepped farther away.

She rolled closer to me. "Listen to what I say. Put yourself in my position, and maybe you'll understand why I love him. Arden's father walked out on us the day I lost my second leg. He was a weak man who expected me to support him with my skating. When

I couldn't, he sought out another woman who could.
He never writes. He stopped sending child support
long before Arden came of age. I had to earn what I
could, and you know yourself that Arden has worked
like a man since he was twelve, and even before
that . . ."

Don't! I wanted to yell. What you do with him is
ugly, unforgivable, and you should have known better.
We were bound to find out, bound to . . .

"Your father is the kind of man who needs a woman
in his life, just as my son is. Damian hates being alone,
hates doing anything alone. He likes to come home and
smell good food cooking. He likes someone to run his
home, to keep it clean, to take care of his clothes, and
I'd gladly do all that for him, even if he never marries
me. Audrina, doesn't love make it not ugly? Doesn't
love make all the difference . . . doesn't it?"

I didn't believe Papa loved her. Standing with my
back to her, I stiffened and wanted to scream.

"All right, darlin'," she whispered in a hoarse
voice. "Hate me if you must, but don't make me leave
the only real home I've ever had, and the only real
man who's ever loved me."

Pivoting to confront her, I said sarcastically, "Perhaps you'd be interested to hear that my aunt Ellsbeth
loved him as much as you say you do, and he claimed
he loved her in return, too. Regardless, he soon tired
of her, and night after night, after she'd slaved all day
to prepare his meals and keep his house clean, and
take care of his children, he still had other women. She
ended up just his slave. That's what she used to call

herself—his kitchen and bedroom slave. Is that what you want for yourself?"

I paused, gasping for breath as I heard the TV in Vera's bedroom giving the morning news. Lazy, lazy Vera, who seldom got up until noon.

"There will come a day when he will stop loving you, Billie. A day when he'll look at you and say such ugly words you won't have any ego left. He'll have some other woman he'll say he loves like no other before, and you'll be only another notch on his belt with many notches of conquest."

She winced as if I'd slapped her. Fresh tears came to shine her blue, blue eyes. But perhaps she'd cried too many times before to let them spill because of anything I could say.

"If a kitchen slave is all I'll ever mean to Damian, or just another conquest . . . even so, Audrina, I'd be grateful, even so." Her voice lowered. "When I lost my legs I thought that never again would a man want to hold me and love me. Damian has made me feel like a whole woman again. Tell me that I smile and act cheerful, Audrina, but that's the facade I wear, like a pretty dress. The ugly dress I wear is the fact that I hate the way I am now. There's not a day goes by when I don't think of the way I used to be, graceful and strong, with the agility to do anything, and when I walked down the street I pulled all admiring eyes my way. Damian has given me back the pride I used to feel. You don't know what it's like to feel half a woman. To be restored and complete again, even if only temporarily, is better than the bleakness I faced before."

She opened her arms wide and pleaded with her eyes. "You are just like my own daughter. To lose your respect hurts so much. Audrina, forgive me for disappointing you and giving you pain. I love you, Audrina, as I've loved you since you were a child and you came running to me through the woods as if you'd found a second mother. Please don't hate me now, not now when I've found such happiness . . ."

Unable to resist, I fell into her arms, forgiving her anything, crying as she cried. And praying that when the time came, Papa would be kinder to her than he had been to Aunt Ellsbeth—and Momma.

"He'll marry you, Billie!" I cried as I embraced her. "I'll see that he does!"

"No, darlin'. . . not that way, please. I want to be his wife only if he wants that. No force, no blackmail. Just let him decide what's the right thing to do. No man is made happy by a marriage he doesn't want."

A small snort of disgust in the doorway made me look. There stood Vera with the cane she had to use until that lame leg strengthened. How long had Vera stood there eavesdropping?

"What wonderful news," said Vera drily, her dark eyes hard and cold. "Another freak to add to the Whitefern collection."

"I've never seen my mother happier," Arden commented a few weeks later as we ate breakfast together in the refurbished solarium. Hundreds of beautiful plants surrounded us. It was April and the trees were leafing out. The dogwoods were in bloom, and the azaleas made a riot of color. This was one of the rare occasions when we had the chance to be alone. Vera was on a side porch lounge chair wearing a brief little bikini, pretending to be sunbathing. Arden took great pains not to notice she was there.

Sylvia was on the floor with a stuffed cat taken from the playroom upstairs. "Kitty," she said over and over again. "Pretty kitty," and then, dropping the cat, her attention span always short-lived, she picked up one of the crystal prisms and began to hold it in such ways as to throw rainbows everywhere. She had gained considerable skill at directing the rays, and it seemed she wanted to dazzle Vera's eyes. Vera, however, wore sunglasses.

Feeling uneasy, I glanced away. Sylvia stepped on all the refracted colors that I avoided—what was that Arden was saying?

"Mom said last night that this is the way she always wanted to live, in a wonderful house, with people she loves. Audrina, has it occurred to you my mother might be falling in love with your father? We can't expose his fraud. It would ruin him, and destroy her. I'll speak to him privately and tell him he has to stop."

Gathering up his papers, Arden neatly bumped them on the table to even the edges, then stashed them in his attache case before he leaned to kiss me goodbye. "See you around six. Have a good time with Sylvia down by the river. Be careful, and remember, I love you . . ."

Before he left he had to steal a glance at Vera, who had taken off the top of her bikini. I glared at him, but he didn't turn to see me. Her breasts were medium-sized and firm—very pretty breasts I wished she'd keep covered.

"Come along, Sylvia," I said, getting to my feet. "Help me put the dishes in the washer."

Papa came into the kitchen as I finished putting everything away. "Audrina, I've been wanting to talk to you about Billie. You've avoided me since that night you caught us. Billie says she talked to you and you understood. Do you understand?"

I met his eyes squarely. "I understand her, yes, but not you. You'll never marry her."

He seemed thunderstruck. "She wants me to marry her? Why, I'll be damned . . . it's not such a bad idea at that." He grinned and chucked me under my chin as if I were two years old. "If I had a wife again who adored me, I wouldn't need daughters at all, would I?"

He grinned again as I stared at him, trying to see if he was serious or only teasing. He said goodbye and hurried out to ride to work with Arden.

"Come along, Sylvia," I said, catching hold of her hand and guiding her to the side door. "We're going to have a lesson on nature today. The flowers are all in bloom, and it's time you knew how to name them, too."

"Where are you going?" Vera sang out as we passed her. She'd put her bra back on now that Arden had gone. "Why don't you ask me to go with you? I can walk now . . . if you don't go too fast."

I refused to answer. The sooner she left, the better.

Trotting at my heels, Sylvia tried to keep up. "Going to see the fish jump," I called to her. "Going to see the ducks, the geese, the squirrels, rabbits, birds, frogs and flowers. It's spring, Sylvia, spring! Poets write about spring more than any other season because it's the time for rebirth, for celebrating the end of winter—and, hopefully, the departure of Vera. Summer comes next. We're going to teach you how to swim. Sylvia will soon be a young woman, and no longer a child. And by the time she is, we want Sylvia to be able to do everything other young women her age do."

Reaching the riverbank, I turned to look for my ten-year-old sister. She wasn't behind me. I glanced back at the house and saw Vera had carried a blanket down onto the lawn and was sunning herself out there as she read a book.

A small sound from the edge of the woods made me suspect that at last Sylvia was going to play a hide-and-seek game, something I'd been trying to teach her to do for months. "Okay, Sylvia," I called. "Ready or not . . . here I come."

Nothing but silence in the woods. I stood there looking around. Sylvia was nowhere in sight. I began to run. The paths here were faint and randomly made. Unfamiliar paths that soon had me befuddled and very anxious. Suddenly a golden raintree loomed just ahead of me, and beneath it was a low, grassy mound. I froze and just stared. They'd found the First and Best Audrina lying dead on the mound under a golden raintree, killed by those terrible boys. I began to back off. The woods were usually alive with the sounds of birds claiming their territory, with insects making perpetual hums and buzzes. Why was it so quiet? Deadly quiet. Even the leaves on the trees didn't move. An unearthly stillness visited as my eyes stayed glued to that mound that had to be the one.

A drum began to pound behind my ears.

Death.

I could smell death. Whirling around, I screamed Sylvia's name again. "Where are you? Don't hide now, Sylvia . . . do you hear me? I can't find you. I'm going back to the house, Sylvia. See if you can catch me!"

Near the house I found a stem of pink sweetheart roses that had fallen to the ground. They gave me a hint. There was only one place where they grew—near the cottage where Arden and Billie used to live. Had she made it there and back in such a short time? It had been Sylvia's habit, since the first day she came, to always pull the prettiest flowers and sniff them. Again I looked around, wondering what to do next. The rose I now had in my hand was warm, the tiny blossoms crushed, as if held too tightly in a small hand. I stared up at the sky. It was cloudy and looked like rain. I could see Whitefern, though it was a good distance away . . . but where the devil was Sylvia? Home, of course. That had to be the answer. All the time I'd skipped along the trail to the river, thinking Sylvia was directly behind me, she must have headed for the cottage, thinking that was our destination. She'd pulled the roses, changed her mind and headed home. She did have an animal's instinct about storms.

Yet I didn't want to leave her if she was still in the woods. All these years I'd waited for Sylvia to do something independent of me except steal Billie's red cart . . . and she had to choose this day to wander off alone. Maybe Sylvia had even gone down to the river to find me, and when she reached there, I'd been in the woods staring at that raintree.

A chill wind whipped up to beat the branches of the trees so that they fanned and struck at my face. The sun became a sly fugitive, racing to escape the wind, ducking behind the dark clouds that came rushing over the tree-tops like black pirate ships. I looked for Vera on the lawn, hoping she could tell me if she'd seen Sylvia. Vera wasn't there. I again raced for home. Sylvia had to be there.

Inside the door in the nick of time, I heard the first terrible clap of thunder sound directly overhead. Lightning sizzled and struck something down by the river. The rain beating at the windows seemed likely to break them. It was always dim in our house but for the brief moments when the sun could shine through the stained-glass windows. Without the sun it was almost dark. I thought about finding matches, lighting a kerosene lamp. Then I heard a cry. Shrill! Loud! Terrifying!

Something clattered down the stairs. I cried out and ran forward to catch whatever it was. I collided with a chair that was out of place—and both Billie and I were always careful to put every chair in the same dents it made in the soft rugs.

"Sylvia . . . is that you?" I called in distress. "Have

you fallen?" Or had Vera done it again, and we'd have to wait for another bone to heal before she left?

Near the newel post I stumbled over something soft. I fell to my knees and began to crawl around in the dark, feeling with my hands for whatever had made me fall. My right hand slid on something wet, warm and sticky. At first I thought it was water from one of the fern pots, but the odor . . . the thickness of it . . . blood. It had to be blood. More gingerly I reached with my left hand. Hair. Long, thick, curling hair. Strong hair that I knew from the feel was dark blue-black.

"Billie . . . oh, Billie. Please, Billie . . ."

Far away in the high cupola the wind chimes tinkled. Pure crystalline notes that shivered down my spine.

Gathering Billie's shortened body in my arms, I cried and rocked back and forth, comforting her as I would Sylvia. Even as I did, silly thoughts flitted in and out of my brain. How did the wind get in the house? Who had opened one of the high windows in the cupola that nobody but me ever visited?

Over and over again, the same ringing notes. Easing Billie's dead weight to the floor, I crawled to where an oil lamp should have been and felt in a table drawer for matches. Soon the beaded shade allowed a soft mellow glow to brighten our foyer.

I didn't want to turn and see her lying dead. I should call a doctor, an ambulance, do something just in case she was still alive. I shouldn't believe she was already dead.

Aunt Ellsbeth, Billie, Aunt Ellsbeth, Billie . . . confused, time repeating itself. . .

With great difficulty, I managed to stand. Leadenly I approached the still figure of Billie on the floor, her eyes staring up at the embellished ceiling, just as my aunt's eyes had stared.

I hovered above Billie. Too late for a doctor to save her, her glazed eyes told me that. I panicked then, felt weak and faint, though I wanted to scream. On and on in the flickering, struggling gaslight I stared down at the beautiful doll without legs, lying at the bottom of the stairs. Six feet away was the little red cart she must have been riding before she misjudged her positioning, or maybe she'd been coming down the steps with the cart in tow . . . to turn *on the* lamps?

Time was trapping me in deja vu . . . Aunt Ellsbeth . . . Billie, over and over again the two women changed places. My hands rose to feel my face, which felt numb. Tears slipped between my fingers. That was no princess doll on the floor, wearing bright blue with no legs, no feet and no shoes. This was a human being with black mascara smearing her cheeks with tears only recently shed. Who had made Billie cry when Papa was gone? What had smeared Billie's scarlet lipstick when Papa was gone?

Frozen in shock, I was brought back to myself by a familiar sound, the metal roll of small ball-bearing wheels on the hard marble floor. Ready to scream, I spun around to see Sylvia shoveling along on Billie's cart, which had splintered but was still usable. "Sylvia . . . what did you do? Did you push Billie down the stairs? Did you have to have that cart so much you would hurt Billie? Sylvia, what have you done?"

In the same old way, as if I hadn't spent a good portion of my life trying to teach her how to hold her head high, Sylvia's head lolled on a rubbery neck, rolled from side to side as her eyes went unfocused and her lips gaped. She grunted, quivered, tried to speak, but in the end nothing came out that could be understood. She seemed just as stupid as when she'd come home for the first time.

Immediately guilty and feeling ashamed, I hurried to take her into my arms. She shrank away. Her vacant eyes appeared huge in her pale and frightened face.

"Sylvia, forgive me, I'm sorry, sorry . . . even if you didn't like Billie, you wouldn't hurt her, would you? You didn't push her down the stairs . . . I know you wouldn't do that."

"What's going on here?" Vera called from the top of the stairs. A lilac towel was wrapped about her naked body, another swathed about her wet hair. She held her hands away from her as if she'd just finished a manicure and didn't want to smear the wet polish. "I thought I heard someone scream. Who screamed?"

With teary eyes I stared up at her and then pointed down at the floor. "Billie fell," I said weakly.

"Fell . . . ?" said Vera, coming slowly down the stairs, holding on to the bannister. Reaching the bottom step, she leaned to peer into Billie's face. I wanted to shield Billie from that kind of cruel curiosity. "Oh . . ." sighed Vera. "She's dead. I know the look, seen it a hundred times. First time I saw it, I could have screamed myself. Now sometimes I think some are better off dead. When I was in the tub, I could swear I heard Sylvia screaming, too."

My breath caught. I looked at Sylvia, who was again riding on Billie's little red cart. With a rapt look of intense enjoyment, as if knowing that the cart was hers forever now, she rolled happily along, softly singing the playroom song to herself. I felt almost sick. "What else did you hear, Vera?"

"Billie, shouting something at Sylvia. I thought she was telling Sylvia to leave her cart alone, but, as you know, Sylvia can't seem to leave it alone. She wanted it—now she has it."

When I looked again, Sylvia had disappeared. I ran to search the house and find her, as Vera called Papa's office.

What had Sylvia done?

Breaking Through

Sylvia was nowhere to be found. Hysterical, I ran outside in the rain, searching for her. "You come out! Don't try to hide! Sylvia, why did you do it? Did you shove Aunt Ellsbeth, too? Oh, Sylvia . . . I don't want them to put you away, I don't . . ."

I tripped and fell to the ground and just lay there crying, not caring anymore. No matter what I did, or how hard I tried, everything went wrong. What was wrong with me, with Whitefern, with Papa, with all of us? It was useless to try to find happiness. Whenever I had it just within my grasp, it slipped from my hand and shattered.

It just wasn't fair what had happened to my mother, to my aunt, and now to Billie. I beat at the ground and screamed at God for being unmerciful. "Stop doing this to me!" I yelled. "You killed the First Audrina—are you trying to kill me, too, by killing all those I love?"

A small touch on my arm brought me back to myself. Through my tears I turned to see Sylvia above me, pleading with eyes that had focused again. "Aud . . . dreeen . . . naaa," she said in her slow way.

I sat up and with relief pulled her into my arms. On the wet grass she slumped against me. "It's all right," I crooned, "I know you didn't mean to hurt Billie."

Gently I rocked her back and forth, thinking, despite myself, of her dislike for Billie and how she coveted that red cart. Several times she'd shone the colors the prisms made into my own eyes. An accident? Deliberately? Of course, whatever Sylvia had done, it had to be done without intent to kill. She'd shoved Billie off the cart, and when she had, both Billie and the cart had clattered down the stairs.

But not deliberately planned—for Sylvia couldn't think ahead.

Sylvia started to speak, but speech didn't come easily to her. As she struggled to say the right words, with the rain soaking us both to the skin, Arden came running to me.

"Audrina, Vera called. What's wrong? What are the two of you doing out here in the rain?"

How could I tell him? Thank God Vera hadn't made the effort. Death seemed as nothing to her, an everyday occurrence that made her only curious, not sad.

"Let's go inside, darling," I said as he helped me to stand. Holding fast to Sylvia's hand, I guided him to the side door and into the hall that led to the dining room. I stood and allowed him to dry my hair with a towel taken from the powder room behind him. I saw my pale reflection in the mirror.

"It's your mother, Arden," I said falteringly.

"What about my mother?" Immediately he was alarmed. He ran a nervous hand through his hair. "Audrina, what's wrong?"

"Sylvia and I went down to the river . . . or at least I thought Sylvia was behind me . . ." I floundered, and then I had to let it gush out. "When I went back the storm had started. The front hall was dark. Something came crashing down the stairs. I stumbled on whatever it was. Then, Arden . . . it was . . . it was . . . Billie. She fell down the stairs. The cart came with her. Arden . . . it's just like what happened to Aunt Ellsbeth . . ."

"But, but—" he said, dropping the towel and searching my eyes. "Your aunt died . . . Audrina . . . Mom . . . she's not . . . not dead?"

My arms went around him as I pressed my cheek against his. "I'm so sorry, Arden, so sorry to tell you. She's gone, Arden. She fell all the way to the bottom. I think she broke her neck just as my aunt did . . ."

His face crumpled. His eyes went void with pain he didn't want me to see, then he pressed his face into my hair and cried.

Just then a loud roar jolted us both. Papa's voice screamed at Vera, "What are you saying? Billie can't be dead!" His heavy steps came running down the hall. "Billie can't have fallen down the stairs! Things like that don't happen twice."

"They do when Sylvia is on the loose!" yelled Vera, limping to where we were. "She wanted Billie's red cart—and shoved her so she fell down the stairs. I was in the bathtub. I heard the screams."

"Then how do you know it was Sylvia?" I yelled. "Can you see through walls, Vera?"

In the foyer, Papa knelt beside Billie's still form and tenderly took her into his arms. Her dark head lolled backward, much in the way Sylvia's did. "I was having artificial legs made," he said in a flat way. "She told me she couldn't ever use them to walk, but I thought she could have pretty legs just for showing off when I took her into town. They would have fit over the stumps and looked good. Then she wouldn't have had to wear all those long, hot dresses to . . . oh, oh, oh . . ." He sobbed. Carefully he put Billie back on the floor, and then he jumped to his feet and made a grab to seize Sylvia. "Damn you!" he screamed as he came at me to get to her.

I shoved Sylvia behind me and heard her whimper of fright. "Wait a minute, Papa. Sylvia was with me all the time. We went down to the river, and when we came back, Billie was dead on the floor."

"But Vera just said—" he shouted, then stopped, looking from me to Vera.

"You know what Vera is, Papa. She lies."

"I did not lie!" yelled Vera, her pale face very white, her apricot hair flaming like wildfire. "I heard Billie yelling at Sylvia, and then I heard Billie scream. Audrina is the liar!"

Papa's eyes narrowed as he tried to guess who was telling the truth. "All right, both of you tell different tales." He sniffled and wiped away his tears, shrugged and turned so he couldn't see Billie. "I know for a fact that Vera is a liar, and I also know that Audrina would do anything to protect Sylvia. Regardless of how Billie died . . . I cannot bear to look at Sylvia now. I am going to have her put away so she can never harm anyone else."

"No!" I screamed, pulling Sylvia into my arms and holding her protectively. "If you put Sylvia away, then send me with her! Whatever happened, it was an accident."

His hard eyes became slits. "Then Sylvia was not with you all the time?"

Something came to me then and lifted a burden from my heart. "Papa, Sylvia would never go near Billie. She refused to let Billie touch her, and never would she willingly touch Billie, even to get her cart. Her way was to sneak Billie's cart from her when Billie wasn't looking."

"I don't believe you," said Papa, looking at Sylvia with loathing. "I only hope for your sake that the police will. Two deaths from falls down the same stairs is going to be rather difficult to explain."

It was Papa who called the police, and by the time they arrived, we'd all gained some control of our emotions. With Billie photographed a dozen times first, the police ambulance drove her away.

Pacing before the ornate fireplace covered by tooled leather, Papa made a formidable, impressive opponent for the detective who came with the same two policemen who'd investigated my aunt's death. He told his story straight.

Then it was Vera's turn. I marveled at how protective she was of Sylvia, never mentioning the shouts or the screams she'd heard. "I was taking a bath, shampooing, doing my nails, and when I came out I heard my cousin down in the foyer crying. When I went down, I saw Mrs. Lowe at the bottom of the steps."

"Wait a minute, miss. You are not Mrs. Lowe's sister?"

"We were raised as sisters in this house, but we are really first cousins."

Papa scowled darkly but at the same time seemed to breathe a sigh of relief.

It was then my turn to repeat what I knew. I weighed each word I said carefully, doing my utmost to shield Sylvia, who crouched in a distant corner with her head hanging so low her long hair completely concealed her face. She seemed like a small puppy cowering in the corner after misbehaving.

"My mother-in-law had a way of lowering herself down the stairs one step at a time. As she went, she'd take the cart with her, putting it on the next lower step first. She went up the stairs in the same way. Her arms were very strong. She had a splinter in one finger. She must have put too much weight on that hand and lost her balance and fell. I can't be positive, for I wasn't there. I had taken my sister Sylvia down to the river with me."

"The two of you stayed together all the time?"

"Yes, sir, all the time."

"And when the two of you came back, you found your mother-in-law dead on the floor?"

"No, sir. Soon after we came in the door, before I

had the chance to light the lamps, I heard her falling down, and the cart, too."

Vera was watching the younger policeman, about thirty, who kept staring at her. Oh, my God! She was flirting with him, crossing and uncrossing her legs, fiddling with the neckline of her half-open robe. The older policeman didn't seem nearly as interested but rather disgusted. "Then that means, Miss Whitefern," he said quietly, "that you were the only one in the house when Mrs. Lowe, senior, fell."

"I was taking a bath," repeated Vera, throwing me a hard glare. "I sunbathed this morning, and that made me feel hot and sticky. I came inside to wash my hair, and, as I always do, I soaked and did my nails. Did my toenails, too," she said. She thrust forth her expertly manicured nails. Her gleaming toenails peeked through her sandals. "If I had struggled with Mrs. Lowe, I would have smeared my nail polish."

"How long does it take for nail polish to dry?"

He asked me this, not Vera.

"It all depends." I tried to remember. "One coat dries in a hurry, but the more coats you use the longer it takes to dry. I try to be careful with my nails for at least thirty minutes after the last coat."

"Exactly!" said Vera, looking at me gratefully. "And if you know anything at all about nails you can see I put on five coats, counting the base coat and the top sealing coat."

The policemen seemed lost in the complexity of feminine toiletry.

In the end, it was decided our front stairs were highly dangerous to everyone, especially after they were examined and a loose place in the carpeting was found. "Easily that could have tripped her up," said the younger officer.

I stared down at the red carpeting, trying to remember how that could have happened when our house had been refurbished from top to bottom and new carpet had been laid on the stairs. How could a woman with no legs trip, anyway? Unless somehow she'd started to move her hand and it had snagged beneath the loose place, or her clothes had caught on something . . . or a prism was flashed in her eyes to blind her. But the hall had been dark after the sun went away.

Maybe we all looked too grief-stricken to be murderers, or Papa had strings he pulled, for again another death at Whitefern was called accidental.

I was uneasy in Sylvia's presence now. She hadn't liked Aunt Ellsbeth, either. I began to watch her covertly, again realizing, but with more impact, that Sylvia resented anyone who might be a threat to her place in my heart. It was in her eyes, in her every reaction, that I was the only one who mattered in her life, and to me she was going to cling. I had done that to her myself— with a little urging from Papa.

The day of Billie's funeral I was deathly sick with the worst cold of my life. Feverish and depressed, I lay on my bed as Vera tended to me, seeming happy to show off her professional skills. Tossing and turn-ing, burning with fever, I hardly heard her when she spoke of how handsome Arden had become. "Of course, he was always good-looking, but when he was a boy I thought him weak. He seems to have taken on a little of Papa's strength and personality . . . have you noticed?"

What she said was true. Arden was as ambivalent about my father as I was; he loathed him and admired him. And, bit by bit, he was picking up Papa's man-nerisms, his walk, his firm, resolute way of talking.

Dreamlike, I saw Billie behind my eyes sitting at the cottage window, passing goodies out to Arden and me when we were children. I saw her as she'd looked the last week of her life, radiant with happi-ness because she was in love. But why had Billie tried to use the front stairs when the back ones were so much closer to the kitchen? Just like Aunt Ellsbeth, who had also spent most of her days in the kitchen. Could it be that because the front stairs led straight down to the marble floor, without the sharp turns and carpeted landings of the back stairs, they were the only "deadly" stairs? Then that meant someone had delib-erately pushed both my aunt and Billie.

I lived that day of Billie's death over and over again, hearing her scream, then the clatter and thuds of both Billie and the cart crashing down the stairs.

"Stop crying!" ordered Vera harshly as she thrust a thermometer in my mouth. "Remember when my mother told you that tears never did any good. They don't, never have, never will. You take from life what you want and don't ask permission, or else you get nothing."

As sick as I was I cringed from the harshness of her loud voice when there was no man around to hear her speak. She threw Sylvia, who was crouched in the corner, a malicious glance.

"I despise that little monster. Why didn't you tell the truth to the police and rid yourself of her? She's the one who killed my mother, just as she killed Billie." She strode over to stand in front of Sylvia, making me shove up on my elbows to try to prevent what might happen next. "Get this, Sylvia," shouted Vera, prodding Sylvia with her foot. "You are not going to sneak up behind me and shove me down the stairs, for I'll be on my guard—and it's not going to happen, understand?"

"Leave her alone, Vera." My voice was weak, my vision fuzzy, but it seemed Sylvia was more terrified of Vera than Vera was of her . . . so terrified of Vera that she crawled under my bed and hid there until Papa and Arden came home.

Life went sour after Billie died. Perhaps because all of us (but Vera and Sylvia) missed her so much, perhaps because I was suffering a double loss now that I doubted and mistrusted Sylvia. I gave up on Sylvia and no longer bothered to try to teach her anything. Often when I turned suddenly I caught Sylvia staring at me wistfully, a yearning in her expression. It was not so much in her eyes as it was in her attitude as she tried

to catch hold of my hand and tried to please me with
wildflowers she brought in from the woods.

My cold lingered and lingered, keeping me cough-
ing through most of the summer. I was nineteen still
and looking forward to that birthday that would make
me twenty. I'd feel safer then, with no nine to curse
me. Life seemed too cruel, taking both my aunt and
Billie in only one year. And Vera was still with us, taking over the household chores with a willingness that
both surprised and pleased Papa.

I lost weight and began to neglect my appearance.
My twentieth birthday came and went and the relief of
escaping a year with a nine in it didn't bring me happiness. I clung more to the shadows near the wall and
eyed all colors with fear. I wished now my memory
still had holes into which I could drop my anguish and
my suspicions of Sylvia. But the Swiss cheese memory
belonged to my childhood, and now I knew only too
well how to hold on to that which grieved me.

Another autumn passed, another winter. There
were nights when Arden didn't come home at all, and
I didn't care.

"Here," said Vera one spring day, near the anniversary of Billie's death, "drink this hot tea and put some
color in your cheeks. You look like death warmed
over."

"I like iced tea better," I said, shoving the cup and
saucer away. Angrily she shoved it back at me. "Drink
the tea, Audrina. Stop behaving like a child. Didn't
you just say a few minutes ago you had a chill?"

Obediently, I picked up the cup and started to put

it to my lips when Sylvia came running forward. She hurled her full weight against Vera, who fell forward and grabbed for me. In so doing she knocked the cup from my hand. It fell to the floor and broke and both Vera and I tipped over in the chair.

Screaming her rage, with pain twisting her face, Vera tried to punish Sylvia . . . but she'd sprained her ankle. "Oh, goddamn that moron! I'm going to talk to Papa about having her put away!"

Blinking my eyes and trying to pull myself back into focus, I picked myself up and out of habit pulled Sylvia into my arms. "No, Vera, not as long as I live will Sylvia be put away. Why don't you leave? I'll take over the housework and the cooking. We don't need you any longer."

She began to cry. "After all I've done to help you, and now you don't want me." She sobbed as if her heart were broken. "You're spoiled, Audrina, spoiled. If you had a backbone at all you'd have left this place a long time ago."

"I thank you for taking care of me, Vera, but from this day forward I'll do for myself."

One day in summer Arden came storming home from his office very early. He ran into our bedroom and yanked me from bed.

"Enough is enough!" he yelled. "I should have done this months ago! You cannot throw away your life and mine because you're not mature enough to face facts. Death is all around us, from the moment we're born we're on our way to our graves. But think of it this way, Audrina," he said as his voice softened and he pulled me into his embrace. "No one really ever dies. We are like the leaves of the trees; we bud out in the spring of our birth and fall off in the autumn of our lives, but we do come back. Just like the leaves of spring, we do live again."

For the first time since that awful day Billie fell, I really saw my husband's fatigue, the small lines etched around his tired, red-rimmed eyes. Eyes that had sunk deeper into his skull, like mine. He hadn't shaved, and that lent him a raffish, out-of-character look, like a stranger I didn't know and didn't love. I saw faults in his face I'd never noticed before.

Pulling away, I fell back on the bed and just lay there. He came to kneel and bow his head on my breast, pleading for me to come back to him. "I love you, and day by day you are killing me. I lost my mother and my wife on the same day—and I still eat, still go to work, still carry on. But I can't continue to live this kind of life—if this can be called living."

Something in me cracked then. My arms slid around him and my fingers curled into his thick hair. "I love you, Arden. Don't lose patience. Keep holding on and I'll come your way . . . I know I will, for I want to."

Almost crying, kissing me with a passion almost crazy, he finally drew away and smiled. "All right. I'm willing to wait—but not forever. Remember that."

Soon he was in the bathroom showering and Sylvia had risen from her place in the corner to stand at the foot of my bed. Pitifully she tried to focus her eyes. Her small hands reached for me pleadingly, begging

me to come back to her, too. She had changed. I hardly
knew her.

At twelve years of age, Sylvia had developed almost overnight (or while I wasn't looking) a woman's
figure. Someone had brushed her hair and tied it
back in a pony-tail with an aqua satin ribbon that
matched the lovely outfit I'd never seen before. Totally
surprised, I stared at her beautiful young face, her
shapely young body that the form-fitting cotton dress
revealed. What a fool I was to have suspected Sylvia
could harm anyone. She needed me. How could I have
forgotten Sylvia in my apathy?

I stared at Sylvia, who had moved to the dimmest
corner and crouched with her knees pulled up so the
crotch of her panties showed. Pull your dress down,
I thought, and watched her obey without any sense of
power or surprise. A long time ago Sylvia and I had
developed a rapport between us.

Mothers and aunts could die, daughters and sons, too,
yet life went on and the sun still shone, the rain still
fell, and the months came and went. Papa began to
show more definite signs of aging as he also showed
faint signs of mellowing.

I knew that Arden was seeing a great deal of Vera
away from Whitefern. Even under my own roof I
often glimpsed them in some room that was seldom
used. I closed my mind and my eyes and pretended
I didn't notice Arden's flushed face and the way
Vera had to smooth down her tight sheath dress that

seemed painted on. She smiled at me smugly, mockingly, telling me she'd won. Why didn't I care anymore?

Late one evening when I no longer expected to see Arden enter my room, he opened the door and came in to sit on the edge of my bed. To my utter amazement, he began to tug off his shoes, then his socks. I started to say something sarcastic about Vera, who'd been bitchy all day, but I said nothing.

"In case you're interested," he said in a stiff way, "I'm not going to touch you. I'd just like to sleep in this room again and feel you near me before I make up my mind what to do with my life. I'm not happy, Audrina. I don't think you're happy, either. I want you to know I've talked to Damian, and your father no longer embezzles money from his dormant accounts. He's honest now about old stock certificates that have great value. He was surprised I'd caught on and didn't deny anything. All he said was, 'I did it for a good cause.'"

He gave his information in an indifferent way, as if the words were spoken only to bridge the gap between us. Now that Arden was assistant vice president of my father's firm, he'd stopped talking of someday returning to his first love, architecture. He put away his draftsman's tools, the drawing table Billie had bought for him when he was sixteen, just as he put away the other dreams of his youth. I guess we all did the same thing. Fate dictated the paths we trod. Yet it hurt to see those things carried up into the attic, for so seldom did anything come back down.

I watched him put his creative ability away like

something useless, and I felt disappointed to see he'd developed Papa's craving for money, for power and then more money.

Though I tried time and time again to find concrete evidence that he was Vera's lover, I guess I didn't really want to know, or easily enough I could have caught them.

And time, once so fast, then so slow, speeded up again from the very monotony of everydayness, and I was twenty-two. Another spring and summer would soon disappear into the void I'd created for myself.

Just for something to occupy myself with, I seriously began cultivating the rose garden Momma had started long ago. I bought books on how to grow roses, and attended garden club meetings, taking Sylvia with me and introducing her for the first time to outsiders. Though she said little, no one thought her anything but shy. (Or at least they pretended to think that.) I dressed Sylvia in pretty clothes and styled her hair becomingly. She was always frightened and seemed relieved to come home again and put on her old garments.

One hot Saturday in late May, I was down on my knees in Momma's rose garden, lightly scratching the ground with a hand rake before I added fertilizer. Tuberose bulbs were nearby, and soon I'd have them in the ground. Sylvia was inside the house taking a nap, and Vera had driven with Papa into town to shop for new clothes.

Suddenly a long shadow threw cool shade above me. I tipped back the brim of my straw hat and stared up at Arden, whom I'd believed was off playing golf with his buddies. A small part of me thought he and Vera could very well have arranged to meet in town.

"Why are you wasting your time out here and forgetting your music?" he asked harshly, kicking at the bag of fertilizer by my garden tools. "Anybody can grow flowers, Audrina. Not everybody has the potential to be a great musician."

"What happened to your dream of making all American cities beautiful?" I asked sarcastically, thinking that as soon as I won prizes with my new breeds of roses and tulips, I'd go on to cultivate orchids in a greenhouse I'd ordered. And once I was bored with orchids, I'd find another hobby to keep me going, until one day I, too, ended up in the Whitefern cemetery.

"You sound bitter, like your aunt," said Arden as he settled down beside me on the grass. "Don't we all have dreams when we're very young?" His voice and face took on a certain wistfulness. "I used to believe that you would never find anything as fascinating or absorbing as me. How wrong I was. No sooner did we marry than you were locking doors to keep me out. You don't need me like I thought you would. There you are on your knees with canvas gloves on your hands, and you keep that damned hat on your head to shade your face so I can't even see you. You don't lift your eyes to meet mine and you've stopped smiling when I come home. You treat me as if I've become a stuffy piece of furniture to clutter up the neatness of your days without me. Don't you love me anymore, Audrina?"

I went on feeding the roses, plotting the tulip beds, thinking about the orchids, wondering how soon Sylvia would wake up. Arden reached to put his arms about me. "I love you," he said in such a solemn way I was alerted enough to stop what I was doing. His arms about me knocked off my wide-brimmed hat. "If you can't love me, Audrina, then let me go. Set me free to find someone who will love me as I want and need to be loved."

I forced myself to say indifferently, "Vera . . . ?"

"Yes," he bit out, "Vera. At least she isn't cold and unresponsive. She treats me like a man. I'm not a saint or a devil, Audrina, just a man who has desires you won't satisfy. I've tried for almost three years—oh, how I've tried. But you won't yield and now I'm tired of trying. I want out. I'm going to divorce you and marry Vera . . . unless you can love me physically as much as you love me in other ways."

I swiveled around on my knees to stare into his face. He really did love me, it was in his eyes. I saw love for me shining in his eyes, and a terrible sadness was there. Divorcing me and marrying Vera wouldn't make him truly happy . . . not nearly as happy as my physical response would.

Confused thoughts raced through my mind. Puppy love, my aunt and father had called what I felt for Arden . . . and they'd been right. Adolescent love that wanted nothing more than hugs, small kisses and hand-holding.

Now he was leaving me for Vera . . . and in the end he'd be just another Lamar Rensdale. Vera didn't love him. She'd never love any man more than she loved herself, or maybe because she couldn't love herself, she couldn't love anyone.

I shook my head, wondering if at last I was finally growing up. Was the mature side of me going to burgeon forth at this very moment? I felt a rising excitement and none of the fear I'd experienced on our wedding night. He could have gone and never said a word to warn me. He could have taken Vera and I wouldn't have contested our divorce, and he knew that. Still . . . he was giving me another chance . . . he did love me . . . it wasn't pity . . . he did love me.

His eyes delved into mine as his hands gripped my shoulders and his voice filled with urgency, as if he sensed what was going on within me. "We can start all over," he said in an excited way. "This time we can start off right. Just you and me, without Sylvia in the next room for you to fret about. I have physical feelings for Vera, but I love you in all the sweet, romantic ways that seem silly with someone as unromantic as Vera. You touch my heart when I come home and I see you sitting near a window, staring out. I stand and I see the way the light falls through your hair and makes it a halo and your skin seems translucent, and I'm filled with wonder that you are my wife. Vera never makes me feel I have anyone special, only someone any man could have. I used to think when I was younger that when I won you, I won a princess who would love me forever, and happily we'd grow old together, and hand in hand we'd face old age without fear. But it hasn't worked out that way. I can't go on this way, loving you but taking Vera in your place. You drain me dry, Audrina. You take my heart and wring it, forcing me to run to Vera for solace. When it's over, I find only physical satisfaction but no spiritual sustenance. Only you can give me that. How can you expect me to go on wanting you when you don't want me in the same way? Love is like a fire that needs replenishing often, not just with tender smiles and light touches but with passion, too. Let's do it again, our honeymoon night, without doors between us to hide behind. Without shame, make love to me now. Right now. Out of doors, here where we are. Damian is in town. Vera is gone. Sylvia was in that damned rocking chair singing to herself before I came out here, and she's likely to stay there until she falls asleep . . ."

He was touching my heart, caressing me with his eyes and stirring my blood as he'd never done before. His amber eyes burned, even his hand seemed hot when he touched my face lightly. Quickly he withdrew his hand as if my flesh felt as hot as his.

"Darling, marriage needs to grow, become adventuresome . . . do something that you've never done before. I don't care what. Make love to me this time. Don't wait for me to start."

No, I thought, I couldn't do that. It was a man's duty to make the first overture. It would be cheap and unladylike to touch him first. But his eyes were imploring, lit up with desire. I didn't deserve him—he should leave me alone, for in the end I'd fail him. Still, I wanted him. Something was telling me to do as he said, regardless of what Papa had said about men and their evil desires that shamed the women who did as they wanted. Papa had brainwashed me long ago, I told myself . . . and this time I was going to override all the signals that flashed evil, dirty, nasty . . .

It wasn't easy to drown out all that shouted shame. I didn't even think I could initiate anything unless he kept on looking at me as he was now. He made himself vulnerable, put his hands behind his back and resisted his urges to touch me first. I fought the small voices instilled by Papa and his teachings . . . no, he was my husband, and I did love him, and he really did love me.

"I'm scared, Arden . . . so scared of losing you to Vera."

His eyes were warm, soft, encouraging me. Deep and passionate eyes that kept urging me to go ahead and it wouldn't be his lust, only my own desire, and for some reason that seemed to make a great difference. What I did would be what I wanted to do—and if it was evil, then let it be evil.

Arden needed me. He loved me and not Vera. Tentatively I cupped his face between my palms. He didn't move. His hands stayed behind his back. I kissed him lightly on his cheeks, his forehead, his chin, and, finally his lips. They stayed soft, but not too soft, and parted only a little. Again I kissed him, with more passion, and still he didn't respond. He was like someone I could do anything with and he'd never harm me. I dared another kiss that was deep and long, even as my hands curved around him and began to stroke his back right down to his buttocks. Something was coming alive in me as he allowed me to do what I wanted, without his doing anything to me or requesting or hinting.

Passion such as I'd never felt before began to swell deep and hot and demanding in me. My breasts grew larger and peaked with demand as I ached to have his hands on my flesh, needing his body, wanting him inside me. My breath began to come faster, his, too, but still he didn't reach to drag me down or pull off my clothes. I was the one who tore at his shirt. Off with his belt, too, then I unzipped his trousers and threw them aside. Shamelessly I pulled down his briefs—and even then he didn't touch me, though he rose up on his knees to allow me to rid him of all that he wore and fell on his back so I could pull off his shoes and socks. He seemed so eager he was impatient, but it seemed ridiculous to me to keep on shoes and socks.

Not a word did he say as I fell upon him to kiss him everywhere and fondle everywhere, until at last I could wait no longer.

Under a clear blue sky, with the hot sun beating down, I guided his penetration. This time, this marvelous first time, I really allowed myself to enjoy the feel of him inside me, lifting me with him into the kind of paradise I'd read about but never experienced.

And when his arms finally clasped me, I groaned from the pure ecstasy of having made him one with me at last.

"You're crying," he said when it was over. "It was so wonderful. I've finally reached you, Audrina. After trying so long, I've broken through that barrier you put up a long time ago."

Yes, he was right. A barrier that Papa had constructed to keep me always bound to him.

"Sometimes I thought it was because you just didn't love me as a man, only as a companion."

"And still you kept right on loving me?" I asked with wonder.

"I could never stop loving you, no matter what." His voice was hoarse, gritty with emotion. "You're in my blood, part of my soul. If you never let me touch you again, I'd still want to wake up and see you asleep beside me. I said what I did only to shake you up and make you fear you might lose me to Vera. Audrina, there are times when you seem so remote and aloof, almost as if you're in a trance, or caught in a spell."

Quickly I leaned to kiss him, to stroke where I'd never wanted to touch before. He groaned with the joy and held me tighter. "If ever I should be so unfortunate as to lose you, I'd look the world over until I had another Audrina—so that means I'd go to my grave still searching. For there will never be another you."

"Another Audrina? Did you know another Audrina?" I asked with a shiver that raced up and down my spine. Why had he said that?

His hands were warm on my skin, his eyes warmer. "It's just my way of saying I have to have you and no one else."

It was sweet to hear him say that and I easily shook off the sudden chill of apprehension and forced some

leaden weight away from my soul, from my heart
and conscience. Young and joyous as I'd never been,
I laughed and turned to him again. I teased him with
kisses and small touches, and wantonly I explored his
body as many times he'd explored mine. For I loved
him so much then that I could have died for him. And
once I'd thought all this so sinful and evil. Damn Papa
for making me think that, for spoiling what could have
been like this all the time.

Twilight flooded the sky with its rosy farewell to
the day, flaming the cloud bottoms crimson, streaking
violet shot through with saffron. Folded in his arms,
I watched the sun sink into the bay beyond the river. I
watched as Arden fell fast asleep. For the first time after
making love, I felt clean, and worthy of staying alive.

Unlike Papa, who loved the First Audrina best,
Arden loved me for what I was, not for what he
wanted me to be. I wrapped him in my arms as I
watched the colors reflected on the water, different
from the colors in the house. I lay there and began to
think I hated all that stained glass, all those Tiffany
lamps and shades, all that art deco and other false,
man-made colors that gave me false fears. What did I
have to fear now?

In the middle of the night I awakened. I thought I
heard Sylvia calling my name. "Aud . . . dreen . . . naa."
Softly, repeatedly, my name called like that.

I'm coming, Sylvia, I thought-waved to her, as I
often did, and somehow my messages seemed to reach

her. First I had to lift Arden's arm from my waist, then carefully I shifted from the heavy weight of his leg thrown over both of mine. When I was free I bent above him and stroked his cheek, kissed his lips.

"Don't go . . . where are you going?" he sleepily asked.

"I'll be back in a few minutes," I whispered.

"You'd better be," he murmured sleepily, exhausted from hours of making love. "Need you again . . . soon . . ." and then he slept.

Sylvia was deeply asleep, curled up on her side, looking angelic in sleep as she always did. I kissed her, too, feeling full of love for everyone. Asleep she had never looked anything but beautiful and normal.

On the way back to where Arden slept and waited, I thought I heard my name called again. It seemed to come from the playroom . . . *her* bedroom. Was she jealous because now I'd found a man who loved me more than anyone had loved her?

I had to go to the playroom. I had to go and face up to her terror, which had always prevented me from enjoying Arden as I should have. It was in that rocking chair that I'd seen the three boys assault the First Audrina, and that had been the first step to force me away from normalcy. The second step to take me even further away from ever enjoying sex was Papa and all the things he'd done to Momma, and said to me. And the third step, taking me miles and miles away, was Papa's indifference to how he hurt my aunt. But it wasn't my horror, I told myself. It was Papa's, it was hers, too, that first daughter who'd died before I was born.

Again Upon a Rainy Day

What compulsion had driven me to the First Audrina's room and forced me into this chair where I sang foolishly? As I rocked, an ingrained terror of this chair that had tormented my childhood stole over me and made me a child again. Something whispered and told me to get out and leave before it was too late. *Go back to Arden,* said a wise part of me. *Forget the past that can't be changed, go back to Arden.*

No, I said to myself. I had to be strong. I had to overcome my fears and the only way to do it was to deliberately evoke the rainy-day scene and make it happen again . . . and this time I'd stay with it until she died—and cast her memory forever from my life.

As I'd done before as a child, so I did again as a woman. I rocked and I sang and soon enough the walls softened and became porous before the molecules divided and I was inside the First Audrina's memory again.

I saw my mother as she must have been when the First Audrina was alive, looking so young and pretty as she warned, "Audrina, promise you will never take the shortcut through the woods. It's dangerous for young girls to go there alone."

She was wearing one of her lovely watercolor printed voile dresses that fluttered in the breezes cooled by the river. All her favorite colors and mine were in that dress. Shades of green, blue, violet, aqua and rose. Her beautiful hair was loose and bannering out. Even as I thought all of this, I was planning to disobey and take the shortcut home.

Momma stooped to kiss my cheek. "Now, obey me, even if you are late for your own birthday party. It can't start until you arrive anyway. Just forget the shortcut and ride the schoolbus home."

But Spencer Longtree rode the school bus with his gang of roughneck buddies. They said such nasty, ugly things to me. I couldn't tell her the awful things they said.

"U . . . G . . . L . . . Y . . ." shrilled Spencer Longtree, who hadn't taken the school bus home. Risking the woods wasn't sparing me his awful presence. "Audrina Adare has got ugly hair . . . spelled — "

"I already know how to spell ugly, Spencer Longtree," I threw over my shoulder, "and that's a description that fits you just F . . . I . . . N . . . E."

"I'll get you for that . . . and maybe when you've been had, you won't feel so high and mighty just because you're one of the Whiteferns who live in a fancy big house."

Time to run, to skip, to hop and have fun in the woods where all the little animals hid. Look at the rainclouds overhead. They hid the sun and made it dark. Would the storm reach me before I reached home? Ruin my dress? Frizz my curls? Momma would throw a fit if I didn't look prettier than any other girl at my party—and this silly kind of dress water-spotted and shrank, too.

The rain came down.

I took the faint and winding path at full speed, feeling the silky whisper of my ruined dress as it clung to my legs. Yards ahead I thought I saw the bushes by the path move. I paused, ready to spin around and flee.

The thickness of the leaves above made a kind of canopy that caused the rain to fall in exceedingly large drops. They splashed down on the dirt before me, making dark polka dots that swiftly blended until all the dirt went dark and muddy.

Some people whistled when they felt afraid. I didn't know how to whistle. I could sing. Happy birthday to me, happy birthday to me . . . happy birthday, dear Audrina . . . happy bir—

I broke off my song and froze. A definite movement in the bushes ahead. A muffled giggle. I turned to run the other way, then glanced back and saw three boys jump out from behind those thorny bushes that lined the faint path. Scratches bloodied their faces and made them seem fearsome. Yet they also seemed silly. Stupid, silly boys. Did they think they could catch me? I could run faster than Aunt Ellsbeth, who had boasted she could outrun anybody as a child.

Just when I thought I'd outraced them, one boy bounded ahead and seized me by my long hair. He almost ripped it from my scalp, it hurt so much. "Stop that, you beast!" I screamed. "Let me go! It's my birthday—let me go!"

"We know it hurts," Spencer Longtree's raspy voice snarled. "We're glad it hurts. It's our birthday gift to you, Audrina. Happy ninth birthday, Whitefern girl."

"You stop pulling my hair! Take your filthy hands off me! You're ruining my dress. Leave me alone. You just dare to do one thing to hurt me and my papa will see all of you put in jail and burned!"

Spencer Longtree grinned. His buck teeth seemed fit for a horse. He thrust his long face full of pimples closer to mine. His breath smelled bad. "Do you know what we're going to do to you, pretty face?"

"You're going to let me go," I said defiantly, but something in me quivered. Sudden fear made my knees weak, made my heart beat faster, made my blood sink into my heels.

"Nooo," he growled, "we're not going to let you go . . . not until we're finished. We're going to rip off all those pretty clothes, tear off your underwear and you're going to be naked, and we're going to see everything."

"You can't do that," I began staunchly, trying to be brave. "All the Adare women born with my color hair can put the curse of death on those that harm them. So beware of your life when you harm me, Spencer Longtree Spider-legs. With my violet eyes I can burn you with the fires of eternal hell while you still live!"

Sneering, he shoved his face so close his nose touched mine. Another boy grabbed my arms and pinioned them behind me. "Go on, *witch*," he said, "do your worst!" The rain plastered his hair to his forehead in a fringe of spikes. "Curse me now and save yourself. Go on, do it, or in another few seconds I'm going to take off my pants, and my buddies are going to hold you down, and each one of us will have our turn."

I screamed it out: "I curse you, Spencer Longtree, Curtis Shay and Hank Barnes! May the devil in hell claim all three of you for his own!"

For a moment they hesitated, making me think it was going to work. Looking from one to the other gave me the chance to run . . . but just then *a fourth* boy rose up from behind the same bushes they'd used to hide, and I froze and stared at him. His dark hair was wet and glued to his face, too. I swallowed and grew weak. All my blood turned to rainwater. Oh, no, not him, too, not him, too, never him. He wouldn't do this. He'd come to save me, that's why he was there. I called his name, pleaded with him to save me. He seemed in a trance, staring blindly ahead. What was wrong with him? Why didn't he pick up a stick, a stone, hit them? Batter them with his bare fists . . . do something to help!

This wasn't the way it was supposed to be. He was my friend. He stood there more petrified than I was. I cried out his name . . . and he turned and ran!

My mouth opened to call him back, but a dirty rag was stuffed inside.

"I was wrong, Audrina. You really are a pretty thing."

They ripped off my clothes. My new dress was torn from neck to hem and hurled away to land on a bush under the golden raintree. Next my pretty petticoat with the Irish lace and the hand-embroidered shamrocks was ripped off and trampled in the mud. I fought like crazy when rough hands tried to pull down my panties, kicking, screaming, twisting, turning, trying to tear violating eyes from their sockets.

Then the lightning flashed, the thunder rolled. I was terrified of being outside in an electrical storm. I screamed again.

It happened fast, but not mercifully fast enough. My pretty underpants were yanked down and torn off. My legs were spread wide as one boy held me under my chin . . . and every one of those three participated in my desecration. Even as I was being despoiled I kept thinking of him. That coward who'd turned and run! He could have stayed to fight even if he lost, for then I could forgive him. Maybe they'd have killed him, like they were really killing me . . . better that than this . . .

I came back to the rocking chair in the playroom. My eyes were wide, so wide they hurt. I'd seen him again with the rain pasting his hair to his face. *Arden!* That was the name she'd called . . . and he'd run. Oh, the lies they'd told me to shield me from knowing just who Arden was. Oh, no wonder Papa had warned me against all boys, and Arden most of all. Papa knew him for what he was—a coward, as bad as the others, maybe worse, for she'd known him, trusted him, thought him her friend, and then he'd turned to me . . . years later?

He'd been there! Through me he was redeeming himself!

Oh, oh, oh . . . now I knew why my memory was full of holes. I'd seen him before in visions, many times, and had made myself forget that he'd been there when those boys had raped, then killed her, just because she was a Whitefern and all the villagers hated Whiteferns.

Papa had lied to me when he said the First Audrina was nine years older! Vera had told the truth!

And Papa had put me in the rocking chair so I could capture contentment and peace. He'd taken my empty pitcher and filled it with horror so that never again could I trust anything male.

I sobbed, knowing I'd betrayed her, too, and married the friend she'd hoped would protect her and fight for her . . . and he'd run. I jumped from the chair and ran from the room. Oh, if only I'd known before I would never have gone to his cottage! This day would never have happened. Papa, why didn't you tell me all the details about your first daughter? Why did you hold back so much? Didn't you know the truth always serves the purpose better than a lie?

Lies, so many lies . . . and to think Vera had told me the truth all the time when she said she'd known the First Audrina, who was so much better than me— prettier, smarter, more fun . . .

As I ran toward my room, determined to wake Arden and face him with the truth, a gas lamp came on. Next a flashlight was shone directly into my eyes. Blinded by the lights after the darkness of the hallway,

I barely made out the vagueness of a hand that dangled a crystal prism before the beam of strong battery light. Colors refracted in my eyes. I staggered backwards, throwing up my hand to shield my eyes from the light. Then I turned to run. Someone followed. I heard the thump of footfalls. I screamed, whirled around and shouted, "Arden, have you come to finish what they started? What are you trying to do to me?"

More lights came on. Strung down the main upstairs corridor were hundreds of crystal prisms, catching colors, sparkling, stabbing and blinding me, threatening me. I spun about, confused and disoriented, unable to find the direction of my bedroom. Then the hands . . . hands that struck me on the shoulders from behind. Hard, strong hands that sent me pitching forward into space . . . and down, down, down . . . hurting all the way until my head struck . . . and then blackness.

Whispering, whispering, on the shallow waves of evening tide voices drifted. They called. Forced me back from a place I couldn't name. Was this me, this tiny pepper dot in the sky? How could I see above, below, behind and before? Was I only an eye in the sky seeing everything, understanding nothing?

Whose name was that I heard spoken so softly? Mine? Whose room was this? Mine? On a narrow bed I lay, staring up at the ceiling. Fuzzily I made out the dresser across the way with its wide mirror that reflected what was in back of my bed. My vision cleared more so I could see the white chaise longue that Arden had wanted me to have. Whitefern, I was still in Whitefern.

In the adjacent room Vera's voice drifted to me as she spoke softly to Arden. I cringed, or tried to. Something was wrong with me, but I didn't have time to dwell on that. I had to concentrate on what Vera was saying.

"Arden," she continued in a stronger voice, "why do you keep objecting? It's for your own good, for hers, too. Certainly you know she'd want it that way."

What way?

"Vera," answered the unmistakable voice of my husband, "you have to give me time to make a decision like that—an irreversible decision."

"I've had about all I can take from you and from her," said Vera. "You have to decide just who you want, her or me. Do you think I'm going to hang around here forever waiting for you to choose?"

"But . . . but . . ." stammered my husband, "at any moment, any day, maybe today or tomorrow, she could pull out of the coma."

Coma? I was in a coma? I couldn't believe this. I could fuzzily see, hazily hear. That had to mean something, didn't it?

"Arden," said Vera's deep and sultry voice, "I'm a nurse and I know about things you've never heard of. No one can stay in a coma three weeks and pull out of it without irreversible brain damage. Think about that for a while, a long while. You'd be married to a living vegetable to burden the rest of your life. When Damian is dead, you'd have Sylvia, too—don't forget her. With the two of them to care for, you'd be praying to

God that you'd done as I suggested, but then it would be too late. I'd be gone. And you, my dear, would never have the courage to do it alone."

Courage to do what?

The two of them were coming closer. I wanted to turn my head and watch them enter my room. I wanted to see Arden's expression, and watch Vera's eyes and see if she really loved him. I wanted to swing my feet to the floor and rise. But I couldn't move, not anything. I could only lie there, a stiff, still thing, feeling only mental anguish and an unbearable sense of loss. Again and again I was flooded with panic. Drowning in panic. How could this have happened? Wasn't I the same as earlier today, last night, yesterday? What had made me this way?

"Vera, my darling," said Arden, now sounding even closer, "you don't understand how I feel. So help me God, even as she is, I still can't help loving my wife. I want Audrina to recover. Every morning before I leave for work I come in here and kneel by her bed and pray for her recovery. Every night before I go to bed, I do the same thing. I kneel and wait for her eyes to open, for her lips to part, for her to speak. I dream about seeing her well and healthy again. I'm in hell and I'll never be free of hell until she's herself again. Just one sign of life and I'd never . . . never consent . . ." He paused, sobbed, choked out, "Even as she is, I don't want her to die."

But Vera did. I knew now that somehow Vera was responsible for this situation, as she was responsible for the most disastrous events in my life.

"All right!" shrilled Vera. "If you still love Audrina, then you cannot possibly be in love with me. You have used me, Arden, used me! Stolen from me, too! For all I know I may be carrying your child again—as I carried your child once before and you didn't know it."

"One time between us then, Vera, only one. You don't know that I was the one responsible. The odds against it were too great. You came to me, too, and let me know you wanted me, and were willing to do anything, and I was young, and Audrina was still a child."

"And she will always be a child!" Vera shrilled. Then her voice dropped an octave as she continued to persuade. "You wanted me, too. You took me and you enjoyed it, and I had to pay the price."

Oh, God, oh, God . . . on and on all of us kept paying prices, I thought, my mind going in circles as I tried to grasp at something stable.

"But if you love her, Arden, then you keep her. And I hope her arms will give you comfort when you need it and her kisses will warm your lips and her passion will satisfy your desire. Lord knows I've never known a man who needs a woman more than you do. And don't you stand there and think you can hire another nurse to take my place. You may not know this, but Audrina needs me. Sylvia needs me, too. Somehow, despite all you've said about Sylvia not responding to anyone but your dear wife, I've managed to make Sylvia trust and even like me."

"Sylvia doesn't trust or like anyone but Audrina," Arden said.

I stared at Vera. Her shining apricot hair peaked out below a starched white cap. Every strand was perfectly in place. Her pale complexion appeared as soft as putty, but even so, she was very pretty wearing white, with those glittering black eyes of hers. Hard, cruel, spider eyes, I thought.

Just as I used to do, she cupped Arden's handsome face between her hands, resting her long, crimson fingernails on his cheeks. "Sweetheart, there are many ways to know when Sylvia is trusting. I'm beginning to know her . . ."

Oh, God! Sylvia shouldn't trust and believe in Vera! Of all people, not Vera!

As if she heard me speak, Sylvia shuffled forward into view. I sensed she must have risen from her perpetual crouch and realized, too, that she was desperate now that I could no longer protect her. In her meandering way she advanced toward my bed as if to shield me. Poor Sylvia, all I wanted was to keep her safe, and now she had to keep *me* safe.

Her aquamarine eyes stared at me blankly, as if she saw through me, beyond me, and into some far, far distance.

Sylvia, Sylvia, what a burden she'd always been. My cross to bear for the rest of my life. Now I was the cross for someone else to bear. I tried to swallow the self-pity I felt and found I could barely manage to make my throat muscles move. I went on thinking of that far ago day when I was eleven and Papa had brought Sylvia home for the first time. My baby sister, who was nine years younger and born on my very birthday. Cursed, the Whitefern girls, each born nine years apart . . .

Or was that why my Aunt Ellsbeth had always said, "Odd, so odd," and she'd looked at me as if to give me a clue. And, of course, it was odd. My life was built on lies. That older Audrina had not been nine years my senior.

Why was I thinking as I was? Something was in the back of my brain, something that had happened in the playroom . . . something that made me hate Arden . . .

"Goodbye, Arden," Vera said, breaking into my reverie as she moved toward the door, leaving my husband staring after her with a stricken expression. Suddenly all that the rocking chair had revealed came back, and I remembered what he had done to the first, dead Audrina. Still I ached for his terrible dilemma— to keep me, now a nothing thing, and to keep Sylvia, a mindless, wandering creature, or to leave and take what happiness he could find—or steal.

"Don't go!" cried Arden. His voice was deep and hoarse, as if the words were torn from his throat against his will. "I need you, Vera. I love you. Maybe not in the same way I love my wife, but it's love never-theless. I'll do what you want, anything you want. Just give me a little more time. Give Audrina a little more time—and promise you won't harm Sylvia."

Vera came forward again, all smiles, her spider eyes sparkling. Her voluptuous figure swayed from side to side as she glided into my husband's eager open arms. Together they melded, to move in rhythm to silent music as their earthy lust began right before my eyes.

Sometimes nature was kind. My vision fogged. I began to drift away, but etched deep on my brain was the thought that I had to save Sylvia and rid Arden of a woman who would ruin his manhood in the end. Still, why should I care? He'd failed the First Audrina, too, when she needed him most. . . and that's when I knew. Arden was mine to punish, not Vera's.

I had to stay alive for Sylvia, to save her from an institution. Papa had to be somewhere—I had to save him, too, from Vera. But how, when I couldn't move or speak?

As the monotonous days slowly passed, I began to really know Vera as never before, by the cruel words she said to me. Thinking I couldn't hear, she always spoke the truth.

"I wish you could hear and see me, Audrina. I'm having sex with your beloved Arden. He calls it making love, but I know what it is. He's going to pay for everything I've been through to win him. He's going to give me the world, this house, Papa's fortune, and everything this monstrosity holds will be sold at auction. As soon as I have everything in my name, I'll get rid of Sylvia . . . and Papa, too." She laughed cruelly. "Arden is so appealing in some ways, so dependent on women for his happiness. A man is a fool to allow that to happen. I admire a man who always keeps his wife in her proper place—but I'll be the man in our family. Sooner or later Arden will be mine, never doubt that."

Her long nails scratched as she brutally rolled me

over on my side to change the sheets. She'd placed me so precariously near the edge I almost fell to the floor. By my hair and one bare leg I was seized and yanked back to safety. She delivered a hard slap on my bare bottom, as if I'd purposefully tried to roll off the bed. Next she moved me from my side over onto my back, came around to the opposite side of my bed and finished tucking in the clean sheet before she stared at my naked body in an appraising *way*.

It was so awful to be naked and vulnerable and un-able to help myself—and her eyes were no kinder than those ravishing eyes of the boys in the woods.

"Yes, I can see why he loved you once. Nice breasts," she said, pinching my nipples so I felt a dull pain. Pain . . . that meant I was going to recover—if she gave me time. "Slim waist, too, flat stomach, nice, very nice. But your beauty is leaving, Audrina darling, leaving fast. All those rich young curves he loves will soon be flabby flesh to hang and droop, and he won't want you back then."

I lay staring at the ceiling high above. Where was Papa? Why didn't he visit me?

In the corner Sylvia leaned forward, her aqua eyes in focus as she studied Vera intently. Warily she was inching closer and closer, too. I could barely see the drift of her long hair in the dimness of the large room. Yet, I kept willing her to do something to help. *If you don't want to be put away in one of those awful places, help me, Sylvia! Help me! Do something to save my life and your own, too!*

Sylvia had inched forward enough to find a spot of

random sunlight that fell on her hair and turned it copper. In her hand she turned the crystal prism constantly, like a baby watching the colorful light rays sparkle myriad rainbows about the room. One ray of scarlet and orange she beamed directly into Vera's spider eyes.

"Stop that!" yelled Vera. "That's what you did to my mother, wasn't it? You did it to Billie, too, didn't you?"

Crablike, Sylvia sidled back to her place in the shadows, keeping a watchful eye on me, on Vera.

On and on Vera rambled as if I were her confessor and when she put me in the ground I'd take her secrets with me and never again would she be haunted by any of the awful things she'd done.

"You know something, dear sister, there are times when I think Arden believes it was me who shoved his mother down the stairs. When he thinks I'm sleeping, he rests on one elbow and stares down into my face, and it makes me wonder if I talk in my sleep and say things he hears. *He* talks in his sleep. He says your name, trying to call you back from wherever you are. And if I wake him up, he turns from me unless I want to make love. I sense that's all he wants from me. In many ways I don't think he trusts me, and doesn't really love me, only needs me now and then. But I'll make him love me more than he loves you. Ten times more than he loves you. You were never a real wife to him, Audrina. How could you be after what happened?" Brittle as thin glass her laughter tinkled, like the wind chimes in the cupola. "Wasn't it a nice birthday present those boys had for Audrina?"

Arden came into the room just then. He seized Vera by the shoulders. "What are you saying to her? She might be able to hear! Her doctors tell me sometimes a patient in a coma can see and hear and think and no one knows it. Please, Vera, even if she dies, I want her to die believing in me and loving me still."

Again she laughed. "So it is true, you were there, and you did nothing to save her. What a boyfriend you turned out to be. You ran, Arden, ran! But I can understand, really I can. They were so much older and bigger, and you had to think of yourself."

Confused, I tried to put all this together—at last I knew the secret of the First Audrina, who had not been nine years older. But why had Papa told me such a silly lie? What difference would it have made just to tell me the truth? That meant Vera must have played with the First and Best, and truly she did know her and had liked her so much I could never take her place. But then I must have known her, too! My head began to ache. Lies, my whole life constructed on lies that really didn't make any sense.

Day after day Vera tended me with loathing, looked at me with disgust, brushed my hair ruthlessly so that much of it came out. With unsanitary methods she inserted a catheter, even when Arden was in the room. Thank God he had enough respect for me and the decency to turn away.

But often when Vera was somewhere else in the

house, my husband came to me and talked softly as he gently moved my arms and legs.

"Darling, wake up. I want you to recover. I'm doing what I can to keep your legs and arms from becoming atrophied. Vera tells me it won't do any good, but your doctors say it will. She doesn't like for me to talk to them unless she's there, too. For some reason they seem terribly reluctant to say anything; perhaps Vera has been trying to protect me from knowing too much. She nags me every day to pull your life support system. She doesn't have the nerve herself. Oh, Audrina, if only you could save yourself and save me from doing something that will ruin the rest of my life. She tells me I'm weak . . . and maybe I am, for when I see you day after day like this, I think perhaps you would be better off dead. Then I think, no, you'll recover . . . but Audrina, if you grow much thinner, you'll wither away to nothing, even if Vera and I do nothing."

He was weak. He'd failed her, and he'd failed me. Despite all his declarations of love, he still went to Vera every night.

Then one day when I'd just about given up hope, Papa came into my room with tears in his eyes that fell onto my face like warm summer rain. I tried to blink my eyes to let him know I was conscious, but I had no control over my eyelids. They popped open or closed without my will.

"Audrina," he cried, falling down on his knees and clutching at my thin, slack hand, "I can't let you die! I've lost so many women in my life. Come back, don't leave me alone with only Vera and Sylvia. They're not what I need or want. It's always been you I've counted on to last. God forgive me if I've put a burden on you by loving you too much."

I was tired of Papa, too.

If Papa came to me again, I wasn't conscious. The next time I woke up it seemed weeks later. But I was now as I had been as a child; I had no sense of time, so how could I know? Again I was in the bed. My room was empty but for me. The house was so quiet; it felt so huge and empty all around me. I lay there paralyzed and tried to think of what I could do to escape while Vera was occupied elsewhere.

The door opened and Arden and Vera came in together. She was talking to him in an irritated tone. "Arden, sometimes you are more of a boy than a man. There must be some legal way we can force Damian to leave you his money when he dies. Certainly he must realize Audrina can't outlive him and wouldn't benefit from his millions."

"But Sylvia will always need care, Vera. I don't blame Damian for looking out for her. If, or when, Audrina should die, he's having it drawn into his will that if Sylvia is put in an institution, or dies, my share that would come from Audrina's will be cut off. He's putting it in a trust fund so it will be doled out monthly. I don't care if he leaves me anything. I can always earn enough to keep us fed, clothed and housed."

"Fed, clothed and housed? Is that all you want out of life? There's a world of glamour and pleasure beyond the walls of this museum. Go after it. If you don't,

I will. Arden, look at me. I'm twenty-five, one year younger than you are. Life moves so swiftly. Soon we'll both be thirty. It's now or never. What good does lots of money do when you're too old to enjoy it? What good are beautiful clothes and expensive jewelry when your figure is gone and your neck is wrinkled? I want it now, Arden, now! While I'm still pretty enough to feel good about myself. Decide, Arden. Decide what you want. Do something positive for once in your lifetime. You've allowed guilt to rule you because you failed that day in the woods . . . and in a way you failed again when you were stupid enough to marry Audrina. Say it now, that you take me and not her. I want out of this miserable situation—today!"

Appearing torn by indecision, Arden glanced at me, at Vera, then stared at Sylvia, who shambled into the room. She meandered over to my bed and tried with clumsy hands to brush my hair even as she tried to say my name. But Vera was there, and she couldn't even make her hands stop trembling. Appearing deeply troubled and frustrated, she slowly turned around and spread her arms wide as if to protect me.

"Whenever she can, Sylvia sneaks up on me and jumps me. She clamps her teeth into any part of my body she can grab hold of. I hit her, kick her, stomp on her toes and pull her hair to make her stop, but she hangs on like a bulldog! She's crazy."

On and on Arden stared at her without speaking. Then he turned his eyes on me lying like a stick of wood, my eyes half open, my lips slack. The IV dripped its solution into my veins, and my hair lay in limp, dull strings on the pillow. I knew I couldn't appeal to him now.

"Yes," he said heavily as the mists began to form around him and Vera, "I guess you're right. Audrina would want to die rather than live on as she is now. She's so young to have suffered so much. Isn't it a terrible pity that I've never been able to help her, when all I ever wanted to do was save her from more suffering. Oh, God, if only I could have done differently, then maybe none of this would have happened."

His head bowed. The last I saw of him this time he was kneeling by my bed, his hand clutching mine, and on our clasped hands he rested his cheek that was wet with his tears.

And just barely, before I floated to that nowhere they called sleep, I felt the warmth of his face, the wetness of his tears. I tried to speak, to tell him I wasn't going to die, but my tongue stayed frozen and all I could do was drift away.

Last Rites

On what I was to find out later was a clear summer day it came to me as in a dream that my death was at hand.

The purposeful way Vera strode into my room that morning told me so much. She came to my bed and stared down into my face. I kept my eyes almost closed, knowing my lashes would give me the appearance of being asleep. Her cold hand touched my forehead to feel its warmth.

"Cool," she said, "but not cool enough. Are you recovering, Audrina? Your skin looks better today—why, you almost look half alive. I do believe you've put on some weight. Though I'm sure Arden won't notice that." She giggled. "He seldom sees anything but your face, even when he sneaks in here to move your arms and legs. Papa does that, too, and his eyes are always so full of tears he can't see anything, either. The two of them are so burdened down with guilt it's a wonder they can still get up in the mornings and go to work."

She glanced at Sylvia, who'd taken to sleeping on the floor near my bed. "Get away from there, idiot!"

She made some movement that I took to be a kick. Sylvia squealed in pain, then jumped up and staggered over to her favorite dim corner. There she crouched down to keep a suspicious eye on Vera.

"Last bath time," sang out Vera. "Wouldn't want the coroner to think I neglected you. 'Gonna wash that man right out of your hair,'" she sang gaily, "gonna paint that face and make you look pretty . . . but not so pretty he'll cry too long."

Like a musical farce she was making my death, as she came toward me bearing a basin of warm water and several towels. Quickly she disconnected the IV and eased me around so my head dangled off the side of the bed into the basin of water. She used several pitchers of warm water to rinse off the lather. Next I was moved back onto the bed, bathed, and over my head she tugged one of my prettiest nightgowns. She seemed to notice some difference in the flexibility of my body. She looked disturbed, hesitated, then shook her head and began brushing and arranging my dried hair.

Several times she used her thumb and forefinger to spread my lids and peer into my eyes. "Did I just see you move? Audrina, I could swear I saw you move. You winced, too, when I pulled your hair. Are you only pretending to still be in your coma? Well, I don't give a damn. Keep the game up and pretend long enough and in your grave you'll find yourself. Already you've pretended too long, Audrina. You're so weak now you can't do a thing to help yourself. Too weak to walk, too weak to talk, and Papa and Arden have gone away on a daylong conference in Richmond. They won't be home until late. Soon I'll be rushing off to the beauty parlor in Arden's car, and our new maid named Nola will be instructed to look out for you."

Every sense I had quickened, became sharper.

My survival instincts came alive as I quivered with apprehension, wondering how she planned to kill me and what I could do to save myself.

Seconds later Vera used my dressing room to apply my makeup to her face. I caught the whiff of my own French perfume, smelled my own dusting powder. Then I heard her fumbling around in my closet. Finding what she wanted, she came into view wearing my best summer suit.

"It's August, Audrina. August in Paris, what a honeymoon that's going to be. Before this month is over Arden Lowe will belong to me . . . and he's got enough evidence on Papa to have him locked away in jail. He doesn't want to use it, for dear Papa has reformed and no longer cheats and embezzles. Your noble Arden made him quit. I don't really want Papa in jail anyway. I want him where I can put my hands on him and make him pay, and pay, and pay. And when I have all his money, into an old folks home goes dear Papa, and dear little Sylvia will get her just rewards, too. I think it's very romantic for you to die in the summer. On your grave we can lay all the roses you love. Remember that first box of Valentine candy Arden sent you? And I ate every piece? I hated you for attracting him even then, when I was more his age. You've been unconscious three months . . . do you know that? I pray you *can* hear. According to your husband, you and he finally 'found each other' just before your fall down the stairs. Really, Audrina, you do know all the right ways to mess up your life. Too many people fall in this house. Someone should have Sylvia locked up before somebody else takes a tumble. You shielded a killer, Audrina. But you won't have to worry about anything after today. I'm driving to the village, making a big show of myself. While I'm gone . . . the job will be done. I'll come home to find you dead." She laughed and then turned to look hard at Sylvia.

The clickety-clack of her high heels on the floor sounded ominous as she went out the door.

I was alone now, except for Sylvia.

I tried to speak, to call, and though I made some gurgling, throaty noises, nothing coherent came out. *Sylvia,* I willed, *come to me. Do something to help me. Don't let me be here when Vera comes back. Please, Sylvia, please . . .*

In her corner Sylvia played with several prisms, using them to send separate light rays that crossed. Looking up every once in a while, she vacantly stared my way. I had to find my voice. Desperate need gave me the strength to speak. **Sylvia . . . help me . . ." It came out as little more than a moan, but Sylvia heard and understood.

Sluggishly she rose to her feet. Excruciatingly slowly she wandered not to my bed but to the dressing table, which was not reflected in the mirror over the dresser. But I could hear her fiddling around with the pretty jars and bottles. She squished the perfume atomizer, wafting to me the scent of jasmine.

Sylvia, I moaned again. *Help me. Take me away. Hide me. Please, please... Sylvia ... help Audrina.*

Something had her attention. Now I could see her reflection in the dresser mirror. She was looking my way. Startled, almost scared appearing. Inch by slow inch she ambled toward my bed. In her hand she carried my silver hand mirror, and from time to time she glanced at her own reflection, as if fascinated by the pretty girl in the glass — and no wonder. When she held her head high and threw back that tangled mop of hair, she was breathtakingly lovely.

I found my voice again, weak and trembling. "Billie's cart, Sylvia . . . the little red cart — find that cart. Put me on it."

Slowly, slowly, she came to gaze with unfocused eyes into my face. Then she looked in the hand mirror. I could tell what she must be seeing. She looked more like me now than I must look like myself.

"Please . . . Sylvia . . . help me," I whispered.

The door opened. My heart almost stopped beating. Vera was back so quickly. What had gone wrong? Then I saw her reason for coming back. She held a plastic bag full of cookies. The very kind of cookies that Sylvia had such a passion for.

"Look, Sylvia," charmed Vera in her sweetest voice. "Pretty Sylvia hasn't had a treat like this in years and years, has she? Mean Audrina won't let you eat cookies, but nice Vera will. Come, pretty Sylvia, eat your cookies like a good girl and I'll bring you more tomorrow. See where your half-sister puts your cookies . . . under the bed."

What was she up to?

In another few moments Vera was on her feet, picking up her purse, which was really my purse, and, softly chuckling to herself, she headed once more for the door.

"Goodbye, Audrina, goodbye. When you get to heaven say hello to your mother for me. If my mother is there, ignore her. Dying won't hurt much. Your food supply will stop, that's all. The machine functioning for your kidneys will shut off . . . it won't hurt. Maybe when the respirator stops you'll just stop breathing . . . it's hard to tell, but you can't last long. All that grieving for Billie helped run down your health long before your fall. And did you know I contributed a little drug to your tea? Just a little to keep you in a constant apathetic state . . ."

Bang! She slammed the door.

No sooner had she closed the door than Sylvia was on her knees and under the bed. When next I saw her she was munching on a handful of cookies—and in her free hand was the single plug that connected all my machines to the outlet. Good God! Vera must have fastened the cookies to the plug with the picture wire I saw dangling from Sylvia's hand. Sylvia plucked the wire from the cookies, threw it down, then stuffed her mouth again. I felt strange, really strange. Sylvia was growing fuzzy, fuzzier . . .

I was dying!

Do you want me to die, Sylvia? Desperate now, I

concentrated every last bit of willpower I had on controlling her. Determined to live, I fought the drowsiness that tried to take me down, down.

As if consolidating her strength, trying to focus her eyes and keep them that way, my younger sister touched the tear that slipped from my right eye. "Aud . . . dreeen . . . naaa . . . ?"

She loved me. The bread cast upon the waters of Sylvia was coming back a thousandfold. "Oh, Sylvia, quickly." Vera could come home sooner than I think. And Sylvia was so slow . . .

Excruciatingly slow. It seemed like hours passed before Sylvia came back with Billie's little red cart that had splintered badly when it had clattered down the front stairs. "Baaa . . . ad Vera . . ." mumbled Sylvia, tugging on my arm and trying to lift me off the bed. "Baa . . . ad Vera . . ."

Panting, gasping, I managed to make a small sound that sounded like, "Yes," and then I willed Sylvia to try to pick me up. Certainly I couldn't weigh much. But her strength was so minimal that she couldn't manage to do more than tug and pull on one arm and one leg. She succeeded in pulling me off the bed so that I landed on the thick piling of the soft carpet. The jolt sent rippling waves of shock throughout my body. Ripples that reached every nerve ending.

"Aud . . . dreeen . . . na . . ."

"Yes, Audrina wants you . . . take her away . . . Down the hall to a safe place."

I was difficult for her to manage. When she had my buttocks on the cart, my head and upper body were

off, and my legs dragged. Sylvia studied me with a
puzzled look. Then she leaned to shove up my knees,
and since that seemed to work, she gave a grunt of
pride and with struggling efforts pushed me into an
upright position. But when she let go, I fell sideways.
Again she shoved me back on the cart, then looked
around.

I slumped over on my pulled-up knees and tried
to latch my fingers together to keep my legs in position. My head lolled heavily, jerkily, when I wanted to
lift it. Every small movement I made was so difficult,
so painful that I wanted to scream with the agony
of doing what used to come so easily. Desperation
made me frantic, yet it lent me an unexpected spurt of
strength. I managed to lock my arms together with my
fingers in such a way that I kept my legs from straightening out. I was like a crudely wrapped package.
Wringing wet with perspiration, I waited for Sylvia to
begin pushing me out of the room.

"Syl . . . vee . . . ah, Aud . . . dreen . . . na," she happily murmured as she got down on her hands and knees
and began to shove. Fortunately she'd left the door
open when she came back with the cart. Talking all the
time in her mumbling way about me being her baby
now, she mentioned again that Vera was baaa . . . ad.

The grandfather clocks in the lower hall began to
chime in all their myriad voices. The clocks on the
mantles joined in, the clocks on the tables, dressers
and desks tolled the hour of three. Someone had finally synchronized all our clocks.

The thick carpeting down the halls, meant to

soundproof and give privacy, made it very difficult for Sylvia to shove me along. The little wheels dug deeply into the pile and resisted. No wonder Billie had asked Papa to have the carpet taken up when she used the corridors. But now it was back to hinder my escape. Where could Sylvia put me?

Tediously Sylvia shoved, panting and heaving and talking gibberish. She stopped to rest often, to take her prisms from the huge pockets of her loose, shiftlike garment.

"Aud . . . dreeen . . . na. Sweet Aud . . . dreen . . . na."

Weakly I turned my head. I moved spastically. I managed to look over my shoulder to see Sylvia's rapt expression of pleasure. She was helping me, and happy to be of use. Her eyes were glowing with joy. To see her like that flooded me with strength enough to manage a few more halting words. "You . . . said . . . my name . . . just . . . right."

"Aud . . . dreeen . . . na." She beamed at me and wanted to stop and play, or talk.

"Hide me . . ." I managed to whisper before I half fainted.

Everything began to move in on me then. The walls came closer, then receded. Bric-a-brac on the hall tables moved, figurines loomed up hugely. The swirling patterns on the rug snaked around me, trying to choke me as I fought off the blackness that wanted to claim me again. I had to stay awake and in control or I would fall off the cart. Hours and hours of Sylvia crawling behind and pushing. Where was she taking me?

Suddenly the front stairs were just ahead. Nooo! I wanted to yell, but I was mute with terror. Sylvia was going to shove me down the stairs!

"Aud . . . dreeen . . . ah," she said. "Sweeeet Aud . . . dreen . . . ah."

Gently and slowly, the cart curved away from the stairs and headed toward the western wing where the First Audrina's room was.

In and out of consciousness I flitted, feeling pains stabbing from time to time. I began to silently pray. Downstairs I heard the front door slam.

Speeding up just a fraction, Sylvia made the turn into the playroom.

No, no, no, was all I could think as Sylvia shoved me into the room where all my nightmares had begun. The high bed loomed ahead. Straight under it Sylvia pushed me as I released my hold on my pulled-up knees and fell backward to avoid being knocked out, and just in the nick of time, too. The old-fashioned coil springs, coated with years of layered dust, met my stare. Sylvia peeked under the dust ruffle and then let it drop.

Sylvia's slow steps faded away. I was alone under the bed with the dust—and a huge spider was spinning a dainty web from one coil to another. It had eyes as black as Vera's. Seeming aware of my presence, it paused in its chore, looked me over, then went on to complete its half-finished design.

Closing my eyes, I gave in to whatever fate had in store. I tried to relax and not worry about Sylvia, who might forget where she'd hidden me. Who would ever think to look for me under the bed in this room no one used anymore?

Then I heard Vera screaming. "Sylvia! Where is Audrina? Where is she?" There was a crash, as if something had fallen, then another cry, closer this time. "I'll catch you, Sylvia, and when I do you'll regret throwing that vase at me! You idiot, what have you done with her? When I catch you I'm going to rip the hair from your scalp!" I heard doors opening and closing as the race to catch Sylvia went on. I didn't even know Sylvia could run. Or was it Vera running as fast as she could to check every room before Arden and Papa came home?

She was searching in such a hurry that it didn't seem she could be doing a thorough job. There were so many rooms, so many closets and antechambers.

Then I heard her enter the playroom.

The dust ruffle cleared the rug about half an inch. Painfully, I turned my head, unable to resist, and I saw her navy blue shoes come closer. One had a very thick sole. She was approaching the bed.

The rocking chair began to make those familiar squeaking noises. "Get out of that chair!" snapped Vera, forgetting to look under the bed as she hurried to haul Sylvia away. Vera yelled as Sylvia scampered out of the room. She started to give limping chase.

Just barely I could see her shoes receding. I think I fainted then. I don't know how long it was before I heard footfalls, and once more Sylvia was peeking under the dust ruffle.

Again Sylvia was tugging on my arm. I tried to help, but this time I was in too much agony. Still, somehow she managed, and later I came back into fading daylight to find myself seated in the calla-lily rocking chair. Sylvia lifted each of my arms so I could grip the chair arms. I screamed. I didn't want to die! Not here, in *her* chair!

Sylvia closed the door behind her.

I began to rock. Had to rock now to escape the pain and horror of what was happening.

Easily my full pitcher of woes emptied to hold more. I had no resistance to protest anything that happened. I saw again Vera as she'd been in her early teens, and she was teasing me about not knowing what men and women did to make babies—but you'll find out one day soon, she whispered.

The rainy day in the woods came again. The boys chased and caught me as always in visions I was the First Audrina, and she made me suffer her shame. It was Arden this time who ripped off my clothes that were her clothes, and Arden who fell on her who was me, and was the first to ravish. I screamed, then screamed again, over and over.

"Audrina," came my father's voice from a far, far distance, just when I'd called for him. This time not God, but Papa heard my cries . . . and in the nick of time.

"Oh, dear God in heaven, my sweet Audrina has pulled out of her coma! She's screaming! She's going to recover!"

Feeling like they weighed tons, my lids parted enough for me to see Papa running to me. A few steps behind him was Arden. But I didn't want to see Arden.

"My darling, my darling," sobbed Papa as he took me into his strong arms and held me. "Arden, call an ambulance."

I gasped as I shoved off Arden's hands that tried to take me from Papa. "The dream, Papa, the First Audrina . . ." My voice came raspy from disuse, funny sounding.

He sighed and held me closer, though I was fading away. I saw Arden run off, presumably to call the ambulance.

"Yes, my darling, but that was a long time ago, and you're going to be just fine. Papa will take care of you. And the rest of my life I'll go down on my knees and give thanks for God sparing you, just when I thought there was no more hope."

I don't remember what happened after that. But when I woke up I was in a hospital room with pink walls, and red and pink roses were everywhere. Papa was sitting in a chair near the window. "Let me talk to her," he said to the nurse, who nodded and told him not to take too long. "Mr. Lowe wants time to see his wife, too."

Sitting on the bed, Papa tenderly took me into his embrace and held me so I heard his heart thudding. "You've had a trying ordeal, Audrina. There were times when neither Arden nor I thought you'd pull through—and that was long before today. Today was a special kind of hell for both of us. We paced outside while the doctor worked on you—and now it appears you'll be all right."

But there was something I wanted to know, had
to know. "Papa, you've got to tell me the truth this
time . . ." My throat hurt when I spoke, but I made
myself talk. "Was Arden there when your First Audrina died? I saw his face in my dreams. He was there,
wasn't he? The First Audrina tried to warn me against
him, and I paid no heed, no heed."

He hesitated and looked toward the door that
Arden had opened. He stood there looking as distraught as I'd ever seen him, except when he was a boy
in the woods who had no courage whatsoever.

"Go on, Damian," said Arden, "tell her the truth.
Tell her, yes, I was there, and I ran! Just as I'm going to
leave now, for I see by your eyes that you hate me. But
I'll be back, Audrina."

In the torturous days that followed, I refused to
allow Arden into my room. He came with flowers,
with candy, with pretty nightgowns and bed jackets,
but I sent them all back to him.

"Tell him to give them to Vera," I said to Papa,
who looked solemn as he saw the tears roll down my
cheeks.

"You're being very hard on him, although I can
understand why. But you must hold on there, girl,"
ordered Papa when I wanted to sleep. "Since the night
of your fall, Arden and I have been through hell. I
admit I never wanted you to marry Arden Lowe, yet
you did, and his mother made me understand something I hadn't understood before. And both you and I
owe his mother a great deal. And if you owe her, you

owe her son even more. Give Arden a chance, Audrina. He loves you . . . let him come in . . . please."

I stared at him disbelievingly. Papa didn't know that Arden had been planning to kill me and run off with Vera.

A gray-haired nurse opened my hospital door and stuck her head inside. "Time to go, Mr. Adare. I'm sure Mrs. Lowe will want to have a few minutes to spend with her husband."

"No!" I said firmly. "Tell him to go away."

I couldn't see Arden yet. He'd been unfaithful with Vera. And he'd failed my dead sister when he might have saved her . . . and there was something else I had to figure out. Something elusive that kept evading me even as it whispered that I still didn't know the whole truth about the First Audrina.

Days came and days went. I grew stronger as I was fed vitamins and high-protein food. Papa came to visit twice a day. I still refused to see Arden.

I was given physical therapy treatments to strengthen my legs and arms, and lessons on how to control all the muscles that had been so long unused. I was taught to walk again. In the three weeks I was in the hospital, not once did I allow Arden into my room. Then Papa came to take me home. Sylvia sat beside me.

"Arden wanted to come with us," said Papa as he turned off the main highway. "Really, Audrina, you can't put him off forever. You've got to talk this out with him."

"Where's Vera, Papa?"

He snorted in disgust. "Vera fell and broke her arm," he said indifferently. "Egg-shell bones if ever I heard of any. Lord, the hospital bills I've paid to keep her whole."

"I want her gone from our house." My voice was hard. What happened between me and Arden depended on what happened between Vera and Arden.

"She'll leave the day the cast comes off." His voice was as hard and determined as mine. "I think Sylvia made her trip. Sylvia's got a real hatred going for Vera." He shot me a shrewd glance. "You really can't blame Arden for what he did with her. Many a morning at breakfast, even before Vera came back, I noticed how unhappy he seemed. He'd smile when you were looking his way, but when you turned your head I could tell his nights with you left much to be desired—and it pleased me. I confess that."

It pleased me, too, that I'd made him unhappy. I hoped Arden never lived long enough to have another happy hour. Ugly thoughts welled up out of me as we approached that tall, splendid and restored house. Whitefern. What a laugh to have been so proud that my ancestry was dated back to those who'd come ashore to settle in The Lost Colony.

With Papa supporting me on one side and Sylvia on the other, we slowly ascended the porch steps. Arden threw open the front door and came rushing out. He tried to kiss me. I jerked away. He then tried to take my hand. I snatched my hand from his and spat, "Don't touch me! Go to Vera and find your solace—as you found it while I was in that coma."

Pale and miserable looking, Arden stepped back and allowed Papa to guide me inside. Once we were inside, I fell onto the purple velvet lounge, now with its golden tassels and cording bright and new and all its stuffing covered over.

Now came the moment I'd dreaded, when I was left alone with Arden. Wearily I closed my eyes and tried to pretend he wasn't there.

"Are you going to lie there with your eyes closed and say nothing? Won't you even look at me?" Then his voice grew louder. "What the hell do you think I'm made of? You were in a coma and Vera was there, willing to do what she could to help me survive. You lay on that bed stiff and cold—and how was I to know that day by day you were gradually getting better when you never indicated in any way that you were?"

He got up to pace the room, never striding its full length but stalking back and forth the length of the chaise I lay on. With some difficulty I rose to my feet.

"I'm going upstairs. Please don't follow me. I don't need you anymore, Arden. I know you and Vera planned to kill me. I used to have such faith in you, such trust that I'd found the one man in this hateful world who would always be there when I needed him. But you failed me. You wanted me dead so you could have her!"

His face turned white and he was so shocked that his voice ran away and left him speechless, when he'd learned to be as garrulous as Papa. I used that opportunity to head for the stairs. In another moment he rushed to stop me, catching me easily since I moved so slowly.

"What's ahead for us now that you hate me?" he asked hoarsely. Without answering I passed on by the room we'd shared, though when I looked in there I saw my regular large bed was back, and the narrow one had been carted away. Everything had been refurbished, so there was nothing left to remind me of all those dreadful days when I'd lain there unmoving and waiting to die.

"Where are you going?" he asked.

What right did he have to ask me anything? He didn't belong in my life now. Let him have Vera. They deserved each other.

Painfully, but gaining strength with each step I took, I headed for other stairs that soon took me into the attic. Arden started to follow. I whirled around and flared at him in a hot burst of temper.

"No! Let me do something I've been trying to do most of my life! When I lay on that bed and heard you and Vera plotting to end my life, do you know what bothered me most? Well, I'm going to tell you. There's a secret about me that I've got to find out. It's more important than you, than anything else. So leave me alone and let me finish something that should have been finished a long time ago. And maybe when I see you again, I can bear to look at your face . . . for right now, I don't think I ever want to see you again."

He drew back and stared at me bleakly, making my heart ache as I saw him again as a boy, when I'd loved him so much. I thought of Billie, who'd told me once everybody made mistakes, and even her son wasn't perfect. Still, I headed for the attic, for the spiraling iron stairs that would take me into the cupola where even now I could hear the wind chimes tinkling, tinkling, trying as they'd always tried to fill the empty holes in my memory bank.

The Secret of the Wind Chimes

Laboriously I managed to climb the iron stairs that had led me away from Vera so many times. The sun was shining brightly through all the stained-glass windows, and on the patterned Turkish rug they threw myriad confusing patterns, turning this room as the sunlight did into a living kaleidoscope. And I was the center of all the colors, making everything happen, as the colors caught in my chameleon-colored hair and made it a rainbow, too. My arms were tattooed with light, and in my eyes I felt the colors that patterned my face as well. I looked around at the scenes my childish eyes had loved so well and saw high above the long slender rectangles of painted glass suspended on their faded scarlet silken cords.

I looked around, trembling as I did, expecting childhood memories to rise up like specters and scare me off, but only soft memories came, of me all alone, wishing, always wishing to go to school, to have play-mates, to be allowed the freedom other children my age had.

Had I made so much effort to gain no new knowledge? "What is it?" I screamed at the wind chimes high above. "Always I hear you blowing and trying to tell me something—tell me now that I'm here and willing to listen! I wasn't willing before, I know that now! Tell me now!"

"Audrina," Papa's voice came from behind me, "you sound hysterical. That's not good for you in your weakened condition."

"Did Arden send you up here?" I yelled. "Am I never to know anything? Must I go into my grave with my mind full of holes? Papa—tell me the secret of this room!"

He didn't want to tell me. His dark, fugitive eyes quickly dodged away, and he started talking about how weak I was, how I needed to lie down and rest. I ran to him to batter his chest. Easily he caught both my fists and held them in one hand as broodingly he stared down into my eyes.

"All right. Perhaps the time has come. Ask me what you will."

"Tell me, Papa, everything I need to know. I feel like I'm losing my mind by not knowing."

"Okay," he said, looking around for something to sit on, but there was nothing but the floor. He sat down and leaned back against a window frame and managed to pull me down with him. Holding me in his arms, he began to speak in a heavy voice.

"This is not going to be easy to say, nor is it going to be pleasant for you to hear, but you're right. You do need to know. Your aunt told me from the beginning you should know the truth about your older sister."

With bated breath I waited.

"The vision you had when first you went into the rocking chair, where the boys jumped out of the bushes—I'm sure now you realize that those three boys raped my Audrina. But she didn't die as I told you."

"She's not dead? Papa . . . where is she?"

"Listen and hear, and don't ask more questions until I'm finished. I told all those lies only to protect you from knowing about the ugliness that could have spoiled your life. That day when Audrina was nine, after the rape, she staggered home clutching the remnants of her clothes together, trying to hide her nudity. They had humiliated her so, she had no pride left. Muddy, soaking wet, bruised and scratched and bleeding, she was filled with shame, and in the house twenty children were waiting for the birthday party to begin. She came in the back door and tried to steal upstairs without anyone seeing her, but your mother was in the kitchen, saw Audrina's shocking state and raced to follow her up the stairs. Audrina was able to say only one word, and that was 'boys.' That was enough for your mother to realize what had happened. So your mother took her in her arms and told her it would be all right, that those awful things did happen sometimes, but she was still the same wonderful girl we both loved. 'Your papa doesn't have to know,' she told Audrina . . . and what a mistake that was. Those words clearly told Audrina that I would be ashamed of her, and that what those boys had done had mined her value for me. She started screaming that she wished the boys had killed her and left her dead under the golden raintree, for she deserved to die now that God had deserted her and failed her when she had prayed for Him to help."

"Oh, Papa," I whispered, "I know how she must have felt."

"Yes, I'm sure you do. Then your mother made her second mistake, an even worse one. She took Audrina into the bathroom and filled the tub with scalding hot water, then forced my girl into that hot water. With a hard brush she began to scrub off the contamination of those boys. Already she was sore and cut and bruised, and her body had endured shock enough, but Lucietta went wild with rage and wielded that harsh brush with no mercy, as if she was ridding the world of all filth, all boys, never realizing what she was doing to her own daughter. It was degradation your mother was trying to remove, and if that brush took off a great deal of Audrina's skin, she didn't seem to notice.

"Downstairs, the kids who had come for the party were clamoring for ice cream and cake, and Ellsbeth dished it out, and told the guests that Audrina had come down with an awful cold and she wouldn't be attending her own party. Naturally this didn't go over very well, and soon the guests departed. Some left their gifts, others took theirs back, as if they thought Audrina was slighting them.

"Ellsbeth called me at my office and told me briefly what she thought had happened. My rage was so huge I felt I might have a heart attack as I ran to my car and drove home so fast it's a wonder the police didn't stop me. I reached home just in time to see your mother pulling a white cotton nightgown down over Audrina's head. I glimpsed that small raw body, so red it seemed to be bleeding all over. I could have killed those boys and beaten your mother for being so cruel as to use that damned brush on that tender skin that had already endured enough. I never forgave her for doing that. I had little mean ways of throwing it back in her face later on. When she scrubbed Audrina down with that brush, she implanted the idea in her head that the filth would never come off, that she was forevermore ruined in my eyes, in everybody's eyes. Then your mother went to the medicine cabinet and came back with iodine . . . not the kind we use nowadays, but that old-fashioned kind that stung like fire.

"I screamed at Lucietta, 'No more!' and she dropped the iodine, and Audrina broke away from her mother. She seemed terrified to see me, the father she'd always loved so much, and on bare feet she went flying up to the attic. I chased behind her and so did your mother. Audrina screamed all the way, no doubt from pain as well as from shock. She ran up these spiraling stairs to this room we're in right now. She was young and fast, and when I came into the cupola she was standing on a chair and had managed to open one of those high windows."

He pointed to the one. "That's where she was, and the wind was howling in, and the rain, and the thunder was cracking, the lightning was flashing, and the colors in here were mind-boggling with the brightness the lightning caused. The wind chimes were beating frantically. It was pandemonium up here. And Audrina on that chair had one leg outside the window and was preparing to jump when I raced up and seized hold of her and pulled her back inside. She fought me, clawed at my face, screaming as if I represented to her all that was evil in every male, and if she harmed me, she'd succeed in harming them . . . the ones who'd stolen her pride when they ravished her body."

I twisted about to stare up at the wind chimes that hung so still on their silken cords, yet I thought I could hear them faintly tinkling.

"There's more, darling, much more. Do you want to wait for another day when you feel stronger?"

No, I'd waited too long already. It was now, or it was never. "Go on, Papa, tell it all."

"I told your mother time and again she shouldn't have given Audrina a bath. She should have comforted her, and later we could have gone to the police. But your mother didn't want her shamed and humiliated by more men who would have asked her all sorts of intimate questions a child shouldn't have to answer. I was so enraged that I could have killed those boys with my bare hands, wrung their necks, castrated them, done something so terrible no doubt they would have put me in prison for life . . . but my Audrina wouldn't name them . . . or else she couldn't name them for fear of their reprisal. Maybe they threatened her, I don't know."

And Arden had been there, too. Arden had been there and she had pleaded to him for help—and he'd run away.

"Where is she, Papa?"

He hesitated, turning me so he could look into my

eyes, and up above the wind chimes began to clamor more, and I knew instinctively they'd keep on doing that until I knew the secret.

I stood in the circle of Papa's powerful arms in the middle of the Turkish rug, where he'd pulled me so I wouldn't stand too near the glass. "Why did you pull me from the windows just now, Papa?"

"The sky. Didn't you notice the dark clouds? A storm is brewing, and I don't like being up here when storms come. Let's go downstairs before I tell you the rest."

"Tell it now, Papa. This is where she always came to play. I always knew those paper dolls were her dolls."

He cleared his throat, as I needed to clear mine. It was constricting, making me breathe too fast, making me feel panic was soon to make me scream. It was like being in the rocking chair again when I was seven, and I was scared, so scared.

Papa sighed heavily, releasing me long enough to put his large hands to his face, but only briefly, as if afraid to let go of me for too long. "I loved that girl, God how I loved her. She gave so much to those she loved, gave so much trust to me. She was really the only female who ever trusted me fully and I promised myself I'd never disappoint her. And it wasn't only that she was an exceptionally beautiful child; she also had the ability to charm everyone with her warmth, her friendliness, her sweetness. She had something else, too, some indefinable quality that made her seem lit up from the inside with happiness, with a contagious exuberance for living that so few of us have. To be with her made you feel more vitally alive than you felt with anyone else. A trip to the beach, the zoo, the museum, a park, and she'd light up your life and make you feel a child again, too, seeing everything through her eyes. Because she saw wondrous things, you saw them as well. It was a rare gift worth more than anything money can buy. The least little present and she was delighted. She loved the weather, the good and the bad. Such rare qualities she had, so very rare." He choked then, lowered his eyes briefly and met mine, then quickly looked away.

"Even your mother was happy when Audrina was near, and God knows Lucky had reasons enough to be unhappy; Ellsbeth did, too. I loved both of them. And I tried for both of them to be everything they needed. I don't think I ever succeeded in making either happy enough." His voice faded small then as his eyes swam with unshed tears. "But she should have obeyed our instructions. Time and time again we told Audrina not to take the shortcut . . . she should have known better."

"Don't stop now," I said nervously.

"After your mother washed away all the evidence of the rape, we thought we could keep Audrina home and the secret would stay in this house. But secrets have a fast way of leaking out no matter what you do to keep them hidden. I wanted to find those boys and smash their stupid heads together. As I said before, she wouldn't tell us who they were, nor would she return to school, where she might see them again. She didn't want to go to any school. She refused to eat, to leave her bed, nor would she look in a mirror. She got up one night and broke every mirror in this house. She'd scream when she saw me, not as her father anymore but as another man who might harm her. She hated anything male. She threw stones and drove her poor cat away. I never allowed her to have a cat again, fearful of what she might do if it was male."

Numb, I stared at him incredulously. "Oh, Papa, I'm so confused. Are you trying to tell me that Vera is truly the First Audrina, the one I've envied all my life? Papa, you don't even like Vera!"

The strange light in his eyes frightened me. "I couldn't let her die," he went on, his eyes riveted to mine, pinning me to him like butterflies were pinned to a board. "If she died, part of me would have died, too, and she'd take that gift of hers into her grave and never again would I have known one second of happiness. I saved her. Saved her in the only way I knew how."

Like water sinking into concrete, something was trying to filter into my brain, some knowledge that hovered on the brink of being born. "How did you save her?"

"My sweet Audrina . . . haven't you guessed yet? Haven't I explained and explained and given you all the clues you need? Vera is not my First Audrina . . . *you are.*"

"No!" I screamed, "I can't be! She's dead, buried in the family cemetery! We went there every Sunday."

"She's not dead, because *you* are alive. There was no First Audrina, because you are my first and only Audrina—and if God strikes me dead for telling a lie, then let him strike me dead, I'm telling you the truth!"

Those voices I heard in my head, those voices that said, *Papa, why did they do it? Why?*

It's only a dream, love, only a dream. Papa will never let anything bad happen to his Audrina, his sweet Audrina. But your older dead sister had the gift, that wonderful gift that I want for you now that she doesn't need it any longer. Papa can use the gift to help you, to help Momma and Aunt Ellsbeth.

God wanted the First and Best Audrina dead, didn't he? He let her die because she disobeyed and used the shortcut She was punished because she liked feeling pretty in expensive new dresses, wasn't she? That First Audrina thought it was fun for the boys to run after her and she could prove to them she could run faster than Aunt Ellsbeth. Faster than any other girl in school. She thought they'd never, never catch her, and God was supposed to be looking out for her, wasn't he? She prayed to him and he didn't hear. He just sat up there in his heaven and pretended everything was just fine in the woods, when He knew, He knew. He was glad another proud Whitefern girl was being assaulted because God is a man, too! God didn't care, Papa!— and that's the truth of it—isn't it?

God is not that cruel, Audrina. God is merciful when you give him a chance. But one has to do what's best for oneself when He has so many to take care of.

Then what good is He, Papa, what good?

I screamed and tore myself from his grasp. Then I raced headlong down the stairs at breakneck speed, not caring if I fell to my death.

The First Audrina

Out into the stormy, threatening afternoon I ran to escape Whitefern. I ran to escape Papa, Arden, Sylvia, Vera, and, most of all, I ran to escape the ghost of that First Audrina, who was now trying to tell me I didn't exist at all.

The rape had happened to her, not me! I sped like a crazy woman, afraid all her memories were chasing after me, wanting to jump into my brain and fill all the empty Swiss cheese holes with her terror.

I ran, trying to run fast enough and far enough to escape what I was, to escape everything that had tormented me most of my life. Lies, lies, running to where they couldn't exist, and at the same time not knowing where I was going to find such a place.

Behind me I heard Arden call my name—but that was her name, too! Nothing was my very own.

"Audrina, wait! Please stop running!"

I couldn't stop. It was as if I were a spring-wound toy, twisted for years and years until now finally I had to let go or break.

"Come back!" Arden called. "Look at the sky!"

He sounded desperate. "Audrina, come back! You're not well! Stop acting crazy!"

Crazy, was he telling me I was crazy?

"Darling," he gasped as he continued to chase me, sounding almost as panicked as I felt, "nothing can be as bad as you think."

What did he know about me? Me, like a fly caught in Papa's sticky web of lies, spinning round and round me, wrapping me in a cocoon so my life could be drained dry of pleasure. I threw my arms wide and screamed at the sky, at God, at the wind that rose up and tore at my hair and whipped my skirt wildly. The wind screamed back and came at me more forcefully, so fierce I felt I might fall. I yelled again, defying it to harm me. Nobody, nothing was ever going to tell me what to do, or what not to do, not ever again would I believe anyone but myself!

Suddenly my arm was seized. I was whipped around by Arden. I struck at him with both fists, battering his face, his chest, though as easily as Papa had, he caught both my hands in his and perhaps he might have dragged me back to the house—but fate was with me this time. He lost his footing and let go of my hands. I was free to run on.

The white marble headstones of the Whitefern cemetery came into view, stark against the gloomy, menacing sky. Lightning flashes in the distance heralded a big storm. Deep and ominous thunder grumbled beyond the treetops near the village church steeple. I was terrified of storms when I was outside Whitefern. Out here, God help me, for He hadn't helped her, and probably wouldn't help me, either.

Terrified, yet needing to find the truth, I whirled about and began to search for something to dig with. Why hadn't I thought to bring a shovel? Where did the person who tended the graves leave his equipment? Somewhere I had to find something for digging.

Our family plot consisted of about one-half acre that was enclosed within a low crumbling brick wall with four entranceways. Red ivy crept along those walls, trying to choke the life from the masonry. Even in the winters when Papa had forced us to come here at least once a week, preferably on Sundays, rain or shine, sick or not, it had been a dreary, bleak place, with the trees clawing at the sky with black bony fingers. Now in September, when the trees were brilliant elsewhere, in the cemetery the leaves chased along dry and brown on the ground, sounding like ghosts tripping lightly back to their graves.

Stopping to look around, I began to tremble. I saw the grave of my mother, of Aunt Ellsbeth, and Billie. There was a space next to my mother's grave where one day my father would lie, and beside him was the grave of the First and Best Audrina. Irresistibly she'd drawn me here. Inside her coffin she was now calling to me, laughing at me, telling me in all ways possible that I'd never equal her in beauty, in charm, in intelligence, and that her "gifts" were hers alone and never would she relinquish one to save me from being ordinary.

It was her tombstone that glittered the most. Rising up tall and slender and graceful, like a young girl itself, that single tombstone seemed brighter than all the others, catching all the ghostly light there was in the cemetery.

I told myself that we always saw what we wanted to see, and that was all. Nothing to be afraid of, nothing. Stiffening my resolve, I strode straight to that headstone.

How many times had I stood right where I was standing now and hated her? "And here is the grave of my beloved," I imagined Papa intoning as I hesitated. "Here my first daughter sleeps in hallowed ground. In her place by my side, when the good Lord sees fit to take me."

Oh! No more, no more! I fell on my knees and began to paw at the dying grass with my bare hands. My nails broke; soon my fingers were sore and bleeding. Still I dug on and on; at long last, I had to know the truth.

"Stop that!" roared Arden, rushing into the cemetery. He ran to pull me to my feet. Then he had to wrestle me to keep me from falling again to the ground and doing what I felt I had to do. "What the devil is wrong with you?" he shouted. "Why are you clawing at that grave?"

"I've got to see her!" I screamed. He looked at me as if I were crazy. I felt crazy.

The wind whipped up into a real gale. It tore more frantically at my hair, at my clothes. Frenzied, it beat the limbs of the trees so that they snapped almost in my face. Arden had me by my waist, trying to wrestle me into submission, when out of the sky came a

deluge of hail pelleting down on both of us with stinging force.

"Audrina, you are hysterical!" he bellowed at
me, sounding like Papa. "There isn't any body down
there!"

I screamed back, the wind deafening us both so we
had to shout, even though our faces were only inches
apart. "How would *you* know? Papa lies, you know
that! He'll say anything, do anything to keep me tied
to him!"

Appearing to consider that briefly, Arden then
shook his head before he shook me again. "You're
talking nonsense!" he shouted. "Stop behaving like
this! There is nobody in that grave! There isn't any
older sister and now you have to face up to that!"

Wild-eyed, I stared at him. There had to be the first
dead Audrina, otherwise my whole life would be a lie.
I screamed again and fought him, determined to defeat
him. Determined, too, that I would dig down into the
grave and drag out her "gifted" remains. Yes, I told
myself as I struggled with Arden, Papa was a liar, a
cheat and a thief. How could anyone believe anything
he said? He had constructed my whole life on lies.

My foot slipped in the mud then. Arden tried to
keep me from falling. Instead, we both tumbled to the
ground. Still I fought on, kicking, scratching, bucking
and trying to do what that other Audrina hadn't been
able to do when she was nine. Hurt him!

Arden fell flat upon me, spreading his arms to pin
mine to the earth. His legs twined around my ankles
so I couldn't even kick. His face hovered over mine,

taking me back to *her* day when Spiderlegs had tried to kiss her in the woods against her will. I butted my head up with such force against his jaw that he swore when his teeth bit through his lower lip.

Blood on his face now—like it had been on theirs.

Rain beat down on my face. Rivulets streamed off him and onto me. I flashed in and out of that day in the woods, seeing him as Spencer Longtree . . . seeing him as all three of those boys, seeing him as every boy or man who'd ever raped a girl or woman—and this time for the First Audrina, for every woman since time began, I was going to get even and win.

I heard the rip of my blouse as I fought. I felt my violet skirt ride up to my hips, but I only cared about my revenge! Blood from my scratches streaked his face, too, and the wind was in his hair and in mine. All around us beat the fury of nature gone insane, driving us both into more and more violence.

He slapped me twice. Like Papa had slapped Momma for the least little thing. He'd never done anything like that before. It made me even angrier, but I never felt the pain. I hit him back. He grabbed my hands again, seeming to realize that he couldn't risk letting go of my wrists again.

"Stop it! Stop it!" screamed Arden above the shrieking wind. "I'm not going to let you do this to me, or to yourself. Audrina, if you have to see what's in that grave, I'll run back to the house for a shovel. Look at your hands, your poor, poor hands."

Already he had my hands captured, but even so I tugged them free again, wanting to rake his eyes from his skull. Then he had them again and was pressing my filthy hands to his lips as his eyes turned soft and gazed down into the fury of mine. "You lie there, glaring hatred up at me, and all I can think is how much I love you. Haven't you had revenge enough? What else do you want to do to me?"

"Shame you, hurt you, like you shamed and hurt me!"

"All right, go ahead!" He released my hands and crouched above me, putting his hands behind his back. "Go ahead," he yelled when I hesitated. "Do what you want to. Use those ragged, dirty nails on my face, and jam your thumbs into my eyes, and maybe when I'm blind you'll be satisfied!"

I slapped him repeatedly with my open palm, first with one hand and then with the other. He winced as his head was rocked from side to side from the force of my hard blows. My strength seemed that of a man from all the rage I felt. Adrenaline pumped through my body as I screamed and hit at him. "You beast! You cowardly brute, let me go! Go back to Vera— she's the one who deserves you!"

As fiercely angry as I was, his amber eyes seemed to sizzle as they blazed down at me. Above us the sky split apart. Bolts of lightning zigzagged downward and struck a giant oak that must have sent its roots into every Whitefern buried in this cemetery. The tree split open and fell with a tremendous crash just a few feet away, then began to burn.

We didn't even turn our heads to watch the giant die. I kept on beating on his face and chest with my fists, which were raw and bleeding and beginning to weaken and hurt. Appearing so wild now, completely out of himself, Arden ruthlessly threw his weight flat down on me again, almost burying me in the soft and mushy ground. My arching back again tried to throw him off, but I was tiring. He cursed as I'd never heard him curse before, then lunged to crush his lips down on mine. I turned my head to the right, then the left, then right again, but try as I would, I couldn't escape the brutal kiss that bruised my lips and caused my teeth to bite down into the tender flesh inside my mouth.

Then his ravishing hand was inside my torn blouse, unfastening my front-hook bra. Seeing his animal lust made me want to kill him. I writhed, twisted, turned and screamed as his hands ripped off my blouse and bra and threw them both away. In the end, every conflict between a man and woman came down to this. I hated him! Hated him with such a passion I wanted to kill him.

Even as I fought him, something just as ravenous as what had hold of him betrayed me and caught fire. I fought on, but between my blows I responded to his kisses, parting my lips even as my fists stopped flailing, and my arms suddenly grabbed him and drew his head down to mine. I bit his lip, daring him to draw away, but he kept on with that kiss until I, too, was kissing back, stroking him, loving and hating him, ripping off his wet clothes, too, until we were both naked on the grave of my dead sister.

In his arms, on that grave, while the storm beat

into a wild crescendo, I surrendered to the greatest passion of my life. Not sweet, tender loving as it had been that one time, but brutal passion that devoured and demanded. Gasping and panting, I came back to reality time and time again to find myself jerking with one orgasm after another. Then he rolled off and came at me in a different way, making me into the animal he seemed. His hands reached beneath me and cupped my swollen breasts. He moaned.

Then it was over and we were both locked in each other's embrace. Even so, we kept kissing, and I returned kiss for kiss, as if we hadn't had enough and would do it all over again and never stop until we were both dead.

On shimmering hot waves of smoldering desire to do it all over again, out here in the storm when the world could end any second and no sin would matter, I drifted back to being me. Furious to find I'd lost again. I hadn't meant to surrender.

"I won't leave this place until I see her body," I said as I rose to my feet and began to pull on my sopping wet, filthy, torn clothing . . . like hers, just like hers . . .

"If that's what you want and need to convince you," he said in an angry way, "I'll run back to the house and get a shovel—but wait until I'm back!"

"All right. But run fast."

Zipping his trousers as he ran off, Arden soon disappeared into the day that had turned into night. Perhaps it was six o'clock and twilight should have had the sky full of vibrant colors, but the night was black as tar, and the storm raged on full force, and I didn't seek any shelter, just fell flat on the ground and cried.

In what seemed only a few minutes, Arden was back. He yelled at me to get out of the way, then put his foot on the spade and savagely shoveled down into the soggy earth. He heaved and panted as he threw out shovelfuls of dirt. Then he was gasping, "This ground is only six feet above sea level. The law insists on a concrete burial vault . . . so I should be hitting it soon."

The rain had me almost blind. I crawled closer to where I could look down and see *her* vault. On and on Arden dug, until there was water in the deep hole. On my knees on the very edge, the mud began to slide. I yelped and grabbed for something to cling to as I slipped, unable to stop my momentum. Arden yelled, "Get back!" just as I fell on top of him and both of us slid down into her empty grave.

Bleakly I stared down into his eyes. "Arden . . . does this mean I really am the First, the Best Audrina?"

Sorrow was in his deep voice. "Yes, darling." He threw out the shovel and embraced me. "Your father didn't lie. He told you the truth."

All the strength I'd felt before vanished. I went limp in his arms, drowning in the realization that it had been me who had been gang-raped when I was nine years old, and my entire family—Momma, Papa, Aunt Ellsbeth and even Vera—had connived to deceive me. What did they think I was, a weakling who couldn't cope? Putting me in that damned rocking chair to gain peace and contentment, to find that special something they had called her "gift" when all along it had been me? I was the First, the Best Audrina, and to this grave they'd brought me, and forced me to put flowers into the urn that was really mine. Oh, God, they were the ones who were crazy!

Somehow Arden managed to hoist me out of the grave first, then he scrambled out of the hole. He wanted to carry me back to the house, but that would show Papa and Vera, again, that I just wasn't strong enough. Devastated and wrung out, still I managed to walk beside Arden as the rain pasted our clothes to our bodies, our hair to our heads. Like war victims, we stumbled blindly forward, making that long trek back to that house of deceit. By the time we reached there, the rain had washed us both free of mud.

Once we were inside the house, Arden hurried me into the downstairs powder room and dried my hair. He stripped off my wet clothes as I stood there shivering, my teeth chattering, goose bumps rising up on my arms. He rubbed me down with a fresh towel before he pressed his face between my thighs. I jumped with the electrical thrill of his kiss put there—why hadn't he kissed me there before?

"You've never allowed me to do anything like this," he said as he took a white terry cloth robe from the linen closet and held it for my arms to slip into. His lips brushed over my shoulder before he pulled the robe on more snugly. "Don't pull away from me again. Scream and yell and fight back, but don't freeze me out. I don't know how to cope with you when you go silent and cold. Tonight when you fought and screamed, it seemed to me you were fully alive, and for the first time you had control of your life, and even if you thought you went down in defeat, you were the victor. You have made me see how wonderful our lives could have been, and how wonderful our lives will be from now on."

I couldn't decide anything now. I had to find Papa and confront him. I had so many questions. I'd force him to answer if I had to. I pulled from Arden's embrace. "I need to see Papa, and then we'll talk about us."

Impatiently I waited for Arden to dry his hair and change from his wet clothes into a robe similar to mine, and then, with him beside me, I went to find Papa.

Papa went on, following me with his troubled eyes. "You are the only Audrina. There never was another. After you were . . . after what happened, I had a grave dug and a tombstone put there to convince you that you had an older, dead sister. It was my way of saving you from yourself." His voice had turned very flat.

Had I known all along and hidden from the truth? The question badgered me. Had I known I was the first but no longer the best? I sobbed, feeling myself coming apart. Into my mind came a fleeting memory of staggering home that day, knowing the house was full of birthday guests, their cars had been parked in the drive . . . and inside the back door Momma had grabbed me, and in that scalding hot water she'd made me sit while I screamed, and she used that stiff, hard brush to scrub where already I was bleeding and hurting so much. My own mother hurting me worse than the boys had. Making all my skin raw and ready to bleed, trying to cleanse me of their filth, and at the same time letting me know I'd never be cleansed, for she couldn't reach inside my brain and scrub there . . . and Papa wouldn't want me now . . . wouldn't want me . . .

Whirling, I confronted Papa again. "What did you do to make me forget? How did you do it?"

"Stand still and let me tell you then," he said, his face going red. "And I'm going to confess something I've tried to hide from myself . . . I didn't think you could cope with that gang-rape . . . because *I* couldn't cope with it. To save myself and to save my love for you . . . I had to make you over into that same chaste little girl who'd never known an ugly deed. When you wouldn't go back to school, and wouldn't eat, and refused to look in a mirror because you didn't want to see the face of a girl who'd been so brutally used, I took you to a psychiatrist. He tried to help you, but in the end he decided the best thing to do was give you electric shock treatments. I was there the day they strapped you down. You screamed as you were buckled down and a leather strap was put between your lips so you wouldn't bite off your tongue. Inside I was screaming, too. Then they fired that electricity into your brain . . . and your back buckled up as you tried to scream. It came out a horrible gurgle that I can hear to this day . . . and I screamed, too. I couldn't stand for them to do that again. I took you home, and decided that in my own way, I could do the same thing without all that torture."

I stopped pacing and stared down at him. "But Papa, I do remember some things. My cat named Tweedle Dee . . . and I remember visiting the First Audrina's grave . . . and I was seven then, Papa, only seven!"

Cynically he smiled. "You were a clever little girl I had to outsmart. But as clever as you were, you were only a child. It's not difficult for an adult to tell a child anything and make her believe. And I wanted you to retain a few memories, so I planted them in your head piecemeal. You were seven the first day you met Arden; I let you keep that memory. I took you on my lap and as I sat in the rocking chair, I talked to you and told you about your older sister, and I remolded you, reshaped you into what you'd been before—clean and pure, sweet and loving. Yes, it was I who planted a great many notions in your head. I considered you an angel too good for this world where innocence is abhorred. You were to me everything that was sweet and feminine, and to have you raped was an abomination I couldn't live with. I did what I did for myself, too, to convince myself that it wasn't my daughter who'd been raped, not my beautiful, gifted, innocent child. And I did make you well, didn't I? I did save you from thinking you were ruined, didn't I? If I hadn't done what I did, what would have become of you, Audrina? What?

"All your pride in yourself had vanished. You cringed in the shadows. You tried to live in them. You wanted to die, and die you might have if I hadn't reconstructed you. I told you the good things about your life, and forced you to forget all the bad . . . all but a few. We need a few bad experiences to appreciate the good. You weren't stupid; perhaps in your own way you were very clever."

I nodded, almost absently, reliving it all over again, how he'd done his best to take away the horror of what those boys had done to me on that awful day in the rain.

"Didn't I wash it from your memory?" he pleaded, his eyes shiny with tears. "Wash it clean away? Didn't I build for you a fairy-tale castle to live in, and around you I put only the best? Not for your mother, Audrina, but for *you* I stole and cheated, to give you everything to make up for what had been stolen. Didn't I do enough? Tell me what I didn't do." He swiped with his fist at his tears of self-pity, as if he'd suffered more than I.

"Day after day I held you on my lap and told you over and over again, it hadn't happened to you but to your older sister, and they killed the First Audrina and left her on the mound under the golden raintree. I even tried to make her death pretty. *Not you*, I said over and over, *it was the other Audrina, the one dead in the grave.* After a while you did seem to forget, and in your own mind you did something that surprised even me. You forgot the rape, and made it seem something mysterious had killed the First Audrina in the woods. On your own, you banished the knowledge of the rape from your memory."

I shivered, then looked away from Papa, who was still talking. "I rocked you, cradled you in my arms and told you it was all a nightmare and you stared at me with those huge, tortured eyes, so hopeful, so wanting to believe it hadn't happened to you. I guessed I was on the right track so I kept it up, day after day . . . in my own way I did for you the best I could."

The best he could, the best he could . . .

"Are you listening, darling? I made you into a virgin again. Maybe I confused things for you a bit, but it was the best I could do."

The rain on the pointed copper roof of the cupola made a loud steady staccato beat, drumming into me acceptance, telling me time and again that deep inside me I'd known all the time.

"Was it easy to shift time about, Papa, and make me forget even my right age?"

"Easy?" he asked hoarsely, rubbing at his tired eyes. "No, it wasn't easy. I did everything to erase time, to make it unimportant. Because we lived so far from others, I could fool you. I had all the newspapers stopped. The newspapers that came were old ones that I stuffed in the mailbox. I made you two years younger. I put away all the calendars and told your aunt not to let you look at her television set. I set all the clocks in this house so they told different times. We gave you tranquilizers for your headaches and you thought it was only aspirin, so you slept often. Sometimes you woke up from a nap and you'd think it was a new day, when only an hour had passed. You were confused, and ready to believe anything I said that would give you peace. I made Vera swear she'd never tell you the truth or she'd be punished so severely that she'd never want to look in a mirror again—and not one red cent would she inherit if she betrayed what I was doing. Your mother and your aunt held Tuesday 'teatimes' twice a week so you'd think time really did move along swiftly. Always you kept asking what day it was, what week, what month. Even what year. You wanted to know your age, why you didn't have birthday parties, why Vera didn't have them. We lied and told you anything to make you unaware of time. Then a week later we'd convince you months had passed. And in seventeen months we convinced you there had been an older sister who died in the woods—that's all the time it took. And your aunt and your mother tutored you and kept you up with your schoolwork, though I'd told you you'd never been to school at all. It seemed safer that way. When you went back, we sent you to a new school where no one knew your history."

Tears were in my eyes. No First and Best Audrina, only me.

"Go on, Papa," I whispered, feeling very weak, very strange, riveting my eyes on him as if to pull every speck of the truth from him while I had him.

Telling it was like reliving it, and none of it was pleasant for him, either. "Audrina, I lied and deceived only to spare you suffering. I would have told any lie, done anything to turn you back into that wonderfully self-confident, friendly girl who feared nothing. And if you wonder now about certain incidents you can't remember, remember you were suicidal, trying to destroy yourself. In my own way, I think I saved not only your life but also your sanity."

My heart was pounding. Something was going on in my body, but the revelations coming at me like blows kept me asking questions when I should have guessed what was wrong. I had stood at the grave of the First and Best Audrina, and I'd envied her because he'd loved her first, and better than he'd ever love me. I had wanted to be her, just to have known that kind of love. It seemed wild and insane that I *had been* her all the time, the first, the best . . . not the second, the worst.

Tears coursed down my cheeks as I crumpled to my knees where Papa could gather me into his arms.

As if I were that ruined nine-year-old girl, he rocked me back and forth.

"Don't cry, my darling, don't cry. It's all over and you're still the same sweet girl you always were. You're not changed. Nothing dirty can touch some people. You're that kind."

Still, up there in the cupola I felt nine years old again, ravished, degraded and not quite human.

Only then did I look toward the opening in the floor to see Vera standing there. Her dark, glittering eyes showed such hatred, such malice that it made her lips quiver. Her strange orange hair seemed alive with electricity as she glared at me. Bits and pieces of the past began to flash behind my eyes.

That look of envy on Vera's face . . . the way I'd felt when I thought about the First Audrina. Gladly Vera would see me dead, as I'd been glad the First Audrina was dead. Now I remembered my ninth birthday. I remembered that morning, getting ready for school. I hadn't finished dressing. Vera and I used the same bathroom to bathe and dress for school. Vera kept glancing at me as I stepped from the tub.

"Wear your prettiest petticoat today, Audrina. The one with that handmade lace and the little shamrocks that you love so much. Wear the matching panties, too."

"No. I'll put those things on after I come home. I hate school restrooms. I hate Momma forcing me to wear my best dress to school when all the girls will be jealous and hate me for doing it."

"Oh, silly, it wasn't Momma's idea, it was mine. It's

time the village girls know just what kind of beautiful clothes you have. She thought it was a wonderful idea to show them the Whitefern girls still do wear silk dresses—and everything else."

On the porch I stood and watched as Vera headed for where the school bus would pick her up. She twisted around and called back, "Enjoy your pedestal for the last time, Audrina. For when you come home you're going to be just like the rest of us—not so pure anymore."

I jolted with that memory and stared at Vera with new awareness. No, I tried to convince myself, Vera wouldn't have set those boys on me . . . would she? She was the only one who knew which paths I always used. There were many vague meandering paths in our patch of woods that spread for hundreds of acres.

It was those dark eyes that betrayed her, the cunning way she looked me up and down, smirking, laughing at me silently inside, as if she'd get the better of me no matter what I did.

"It was *you* who set me up, wasn't it, Vera?" I asked, trying to keep my voice calm, my thoughts rational. "You hated me, and envied me so much you wanted Papa to hate me, too. I cried with my head in Momma's lap, thinking something I'd done had made those ugly boys think I was wicked. I blamed myself for teasing them. I thought I'd done some innocent thing that gave them evil ideas, when I couldn't remember anything I'd said or done to make them think I wasn't the nice kind of girl Papa wanted me to stay. It was *you* who told them which path I took!"

Despite myself my voice was rising, taking on an accusatory tone. I stood, then took several steps closer to her.

"Oh, stop it!" she yelled. "It's all over and done with, isn't it? How could I know you'd disobey and use the shortcut? It wasn't my fault—it was your own!"

"Wait a minute!" bellowed Papa, jumping to his feet and hurrying to my side even as Arden came closer, too. "Many times I've overheard whispers in the village drugstore about someone in this house who betrayed my daughter. I thought it was the boy who used to trim our shrubs and mow our lawn. But, of course, it had to be you! He wasn't of this house, or in this house . . . we bred a viper in our midst. Who else here would want Audrina harmed more than the unwanted child who didn't know who her father was!"

Appearing terrified, Vera backed away more.

"May your soul rot in everlasting hell!" roared Papa, stepping forward threateningly as if he'd finish off Vera and she'd never breathe again. "I thought at the time it was too much of a coincidence. On her birthday—but your mother kept saying you were innocent. Now I know. You arranged with those boys to have my Audrina raped!"

Vera put her hand to her throat and tried with her broken arm to feel behind her. There was terror in her large dark eyes so much like Papa's.

She screamed at him, "I'm your daughter and you know it! Deny it all you want, Damian Adare, but I am like you! I'll do anything to get what I want—the same as you will. I hate you, Damian, really hate you! I hate that woman who bore me! I've hated every day I've lived in this hellhole you call Whitefern! You gave my mother a check when she wanted to come to New York and be with me . . . and it was no good. A damned no-good check to pay for all those years when she was nothing but a slave in this house."

Papa took another threatening step closer to Vera. "Don't you say one more word to me, girl, or you'll regret the day you were born! You've been nothing but a burr in my side since the day your mother brought you here. And you were the one who came and volunteered the information that Arden Lowe had been at the scene of my daughter's rape, and he had done nothing to save her. You laughed when you told me he'd run away. You gloated then, Vera. If you hadn't reminded me just now, I might have forgotten." Papa's eyes narrowed dangerously.

Like a tigress Vera sprang forward to confront Papa, seeming to forget her broken arm, forgetting she was a woman and he was a huge, powerful man who could be merciless when it came to her.

"You!" she spat. "What the hell do I care what you think? You gave me nothing after Audrina was born. You treated me as if I didn't exist once sweet Audrina came home from the hospital. I was shoved out of the pretty room you'd had fixed up for me, and it was turned into a nursery for her. It was sweet Audrina this, and sweet Audrina that, until I could have vomited. Not one kind word did you ever say to me. The only time you took notice of me was when I was sick or injured. I wanted you to love me, and you refused to love anyone but Audrina . . ."

She sobbed then and hurried to press her face against Arden's chest. "Take me away from here, Arden . . . take me away. I want to feel loved. I'm not bad, I'm not really bad . . ."

Papa roared then like a bull and charged. Screaming, Vera released Arden, wheeled around and ran for the stairs. But she'd forgotten she wore those shoes with the lift, and never should she have run in those shoes. The built-up sole on her left shoe caused her ankle to turn over. She lost her balance and started to fall . . . and the opening of the spiraling stairs gaped like a huge square mouth behind her.

Like a doll caught in a time-lapse film, she fell headlong down the spiraling stairs. Her screams ripped the air in short, horrible spurts. First her shoulder struck against one side of the iron balustrade, then she ricocheted to strike the opposite side.

Turning over and over, striking again and again against the hard metal until her last scream was cut off in mid-air and she thudded to the bottom and just lay there.

In a flash Arden tore down the stairs to her side, kneeling there as Papa, Sylvia and I hurried down, too. She lay there, stunned, her dark eyes unfocused and already beginning to glaze as she stared toward Arden, who held her head on his lap.

"Take me away, Arden," she croaked in a small

whisper. "Take me far from this place where everyone has always hated me. Take me from here, Arden . . . take me—"

She lapsed into unconsciousness then. Arden eased her head to the floor, and without a glance my way, raced to call an ambulance to rush Vera to the hospital . . . again.

Hours passed before I heard a faraway door bang shut, telling me Arden was back from the hospital emergency room. I dimmed the gas lamp by my bed and closed my eyes, hoping he'd go away and not bother me with tales of all Vera's broken bones that would heal. I was afraid to hear his sympathy for her, afraid he'd agreed to take her far from here.

Like a child still afraid of total darkness, without some light I felt defenseless. Yet total darkness was what I wanted when he came to me with his news. Softly my bedroom door opened and closed. Arden's scent wafted to me.

"I've just spent some time with Damian, telling him about Vera . . . may I talk to you now about her?" he asked, coming to perch on the side of my bed. His tired eyes moved my heart to compassion. Unwanted sympathy tried to steal my determination not to let him dissuade me from what I'd determined to do. What I had to do.

"No need to shrink away," he said with weary impatience. "I don't plan to touch you. Vera died about two hours ago. She had too many internal injuries to survive; just about every bone in her body was broken."

I began to tremble. Some part of me had always strived to reach out to Vera and make her my sister.

"I know what you're feeling," said Arden wearily. "Some part of us always seems diminished when someone dies. Vera gifted us with something before she died, Audrina. Three deaths from accidental falls in this house caused the police to raise some eyebrows, and they were there questioning me when Vera whispered she'd tripped and fallen . . . and it was her own fault."

I turned on my side, my back toward him, and began to quietly sob. In the darkness I sensed he was starting to undress, with the notion of holding me all night, but quickly I spoke.

"No, Arden. I don't want you in my bed. Go to another room and sleep until I have time to think this out. If Vera said she was to blame for her fall, she was, wasn't she? Nobody pushed her . . . but it was she who pushed me, and as I think about it more and more, and remember the door that closed softly soon after I found my aunt dead . . . it had to be Vera who pushed her own mother down the stairs and took that blue check from the corkboard where I pinned it. And then there's Billie, who fell, too. She and Papa might have married, and that would have given Papa another heir to his fortune, for all along she must have planned to do away with me."

There was no answer from him, except when he closed the door.

Only then did I get up and pull on a robe before I went to check on Sylvia. But she wasn't in her room.

I found her in the playroom that had once been mine. Gently she was rocking to and fro, singing her strange little ditty. I knew that now as I looked around with new insight and recognized the dolls Papa had won at many a carnival from shooting the moving ducks. And all those stuffed, plushy animals, more prizes that he'd won for me.

I stared at Sylvia's pretty young face, innocently singing like one of the witches from Papa's tales of his ancestors. Those tales that had once made me shout a witch's curse to stop boys who weren't afraid . . .

Little dolls appeared in Sylvia's hands, apparently taken from the pockets of her loose garment. Tiny dolls I myself had bought to please her. Neutered dolls of no sex, but somehow they seemed more boyish than girlish.

Arden had come in behind me and stood there watching. Sylvia hung back, staring at us, then slowly shuffled out of the room.

"*Sit down,*" Arden growled, pulling me into the playroom and shoving me into the rocking chair. He went down on his knees beside me and tried to capture my hand. I sat on them to keep them from him. He sighed and I thought of Billie and all the little hints she'd tried to give me to tell me her son wasn't perfect. But I'd wanted him perfect.

Perhaps that was in my eyes as I glared at him, and accused him now, outraged and devastated at how he'd failed me when I needed him most. Sadness and guilt shone in his eyes so that I could almost read his thoughts. He'd put up with so much from me to make up for that shameful day. Even now I loved him, even as I scorned his weakness.

"This is the moment I've dreaded since that day of your ninth birthday. I was hurrying home, planning to race on to your house and be there for your party. I'd never been inside Whitefern, and it was a big day for me. On the way through the woods to the cottage, three boys hailed me and told me to hang around and enjoy some fun. I didn't know what they meant. Time, what I had of it, was spent working, and having fun with older boys was something I'd never done. It pleased me that finally I was being invited to be one of them, so I joined them when they told me to crouch down behind the bushes. Then you came skipping along the dirt path, singing to yourself. No one said a word. When they jumped out and ran to catch you, and I heard them yell out all they planned to do to you, it was like a nightmare. My legs and arms went numb . . . I didn't know what to do to stop them. I felt sick with fear for you, and weak with hatred for them . . . and I couldn't move. Audrina, I forced myself to stand up . . . and you saw me. You pleaded with me with your eyes, with your screams before they stuffed something into your mouth . . . and shame for being paralyzed made me even weaker. I knew you'd despise me for doing nothing, as I still despise myself for doing nothing but running for help. That's why I ran, for I didn't stand a chance of winning in a fight against them. One to one, I might have had a chance, but three . . . Audrina, I'm sorry. It's not enough to say, I know that. Now I wish I'd stayed and tried to defend you—and then you wouldn't be staring at me now with so much scorn on your face and in your eyes."

He paused and reached to gather me into his arms, and with his kisses perhaps he thought he could build another fire like he had in the graveyard, and I'd be his again, and forgiving.

"Forgive me for failing you then, Audrina. Forgive me for failing you every time you've needed me . . . give me another chance, and you'll never need to forgive me for failing to act when I should."

Forgive him? How could I forgive him when I could never forget? Twice he did nothing to save me from people who wanted me destroyed. I didn't want to give him a third chance.

The Last Spin of the Web

On a fine sunny day we laid Vera to rest beside Aunt Ellsbeth. Strange that I'd be at this funeral, when I'd missed Aunt Ellsbeth's and Billie's. I had loved those other two, yet it was Vera's coffin that I saw lowered into the ground. As I said goodbye to Vera, I understood her. Maybe in understanding someday I'd forgive her and remember only the moments of love I had for her.

We came home from the funeral, and immediately after I helped Sylvia out of her funeral garb, Papa suggested a game of ball in the yard would help us overcome the depression that seemed to lay on us like a thick blanket of fog, oppressive, gloomy. I had hardly spoken to Arden since the night Vera died, and now, three days later, I made my plans, while Papa sprawled in a chair across from mine and tried as always to discover my innermost secrets.

When Sylvia entered the foyer trailed by Arden her shuffling gait seemed much improved. Fresh air and sunshine were giving her a bit of color, and those lovely aqua eyes scanned to find me before she smiled.

I left before Arden had the chance to appeal to me again, and hurried up the stairs. In my bedroom I sat on my bed, trying to think ahead so I could do the right thing for myself and for Sylvia. Papa came to the door and stood there, pleading for me not to leave him. Could he read my mind?

"You promised, Audrina, you promised. All your life you've sworn you'd stay with me. And what about Sylvia? Are you going to set her back and take from her the one person who's stood by her?"

"I'm going, Papa," I said tiredly. "I promised not to leave you when I was a child and didn't understand what you wanted from me, but I can't stay. There's something wrong in this house. Something rules here that keeps everyone from being normal or happy. I want out."

"Think of Sylvia," cried Papa. "Though she's better, she'll never speak with confidence or fluency. She'll never be normal enough to perform any difficult mental tasks—how is she going to survive if I die?"

I didn't plan to leave Sylvia here, but I didn't want to tell him that. Not yet.

"How will Sylvia survive when you're gone?" His dark Arab eyes sparkled with what I took for cunning. "And so you did lose the gift, after all. They killed that specialness in you, that ability to love selflessly, the sensitivity that would always call you when someone needed you. You are no longer that special girl with the rare and precious gift."

I said with hard scorn, "There is no gift, Papa. I don't believe you anymore, Papa. It's the process of sitting and rocking and sort of hypnotizing yourself into believing anything. I pity the girl I used to be for believing so wholeheartedly in you."

"All right," he said. Another of those long, penetrating looks he gave me, forcing me to cast my eyes downward. Then he got up to leave, staring at me from the doorway with such sadness I had to turn my back so I wouldn't yield to his unspoken pressure.

Now it was even clearer . . . I had to leave this place.

He left and slammed the door shut behind him. I fell on my bed and stared at the ceiling. To sleep, I thought, never to dream again. That's the way I wanted it to be. I didn't need Arden now. I had Sylvia and that was going to be enough. Yet all night long Arden flitted in and out of my nightmares so that in the morning I woke up fuzzy-headed, thick-tongued. At the breakfast table Papa didn't speak. Usually he entered the kitchen talking and went out the same way. *No talent but for running his mouth all day long,* I heard my mother's ghostly whisper say. Most of the time he was full of good spirits, always undaunted by tragedy, always a winner, but I had managed to bring him low.

Finally he spoke as Sylvia shoved food into her mouth, and Arden ate silently, without appetite. "Vera must have been there the night Ellie and I had our last argument. It was Vera who dressed her in that traveling suit, and Vera who threw those clothes into the suitcase to make us think Ellie planned to leave me."

His head bowed down into his hands and for a

moment his wide shoulders drooped, as if tragedy could touch him after all.

"I knew Ellie would never leave me. I could have given her a million dollars and still she would have stayed on. To live for years in one place puts roots deep into the ground, even when you don't want that to happen. One day Ellie would tell me she'd be happier somewhere else, but whenever she tried to leave, she found she couldn't. She used to say she made the biggest mistake of her life when she came back here."

He didn't look my way again, but I knew what he was trying to do—brainwash me into thinking I couldn't exist outside of this house, away from his tender loving care. Telling me how he needed and wanted me to stay on, without saying it directly.

The many clocks in the house ticked away the time, each clock face now synchronized with all the others.

The kitchen faucet dripped-dropped, dropped-dripped . . .

Sylvia finished eating and took out her prisms and the colors flashed and the chimes in the cupola began to tinkle, tinkle, tinkle.

I shook my head to rid it of the mesmerizing spell being cast, not only by the colors but also by the familiar sounds. Papa had ruined my life by considering me a weakling unable to cope with the truth, when it was he who wasn't able to cope. He'd lied to brainwash himself as much as me.

And he'd ruined Vera's life as well by disliking her

from the beginning because she filled him with guilt every time he looked at her black, conniving eyes so like his own. But I was going to prove to him what I was made of.

In this house I still clung to the shadows near the walls, and still avoided the colorful patterns on the floor. Still a child, arrested at the age of nine. I'd prove to Papa and to Arden that I could yank up my roots no matter how much it hurt, and from this house I'd flee. I forced myself to pull the suitcases from the closet shelves and with mad determination I began to run about, flinging garments into the bags open on my bed. I didn't fold anything neatly, just hurled in sweaters, skirts, blouses, and I packed for Sylvia, too.

Heedlessly I threw in my underwear, stuffed in stockings, shoes, handbags, cosmetics . . . just like Aunt Ellsbeth had done. The clock on my night table read ten after ten, and I set my watch by that. By noon I'd be on my way with Sylvia.

"Audrina," said Arden, coming into my room to stand close at my side, his arms trying to enfold me, "don't turn from me." He pulled me against his chest and tried to put his lips on mine. I moved my head to avoid his kiss. "I love you," he said fervently, "I've always loved you. Terrible things, worse things happen to many people and still they stay together. They find happiness again. Help yourself, Audrina. Be brave. Help me. Help Sylvia."

But I didn't want to help anyone if it meant staying on.

I didn't need Arden now. He'd failed me twice, and it stood to reason he'd fail me a third time, and would perhaps always fail me when I needed him most.

Sobbing, I jerked free of his arms and pushed him away. "I'm leaving you, Arden. I think you are no better than Papa. Both of you should have known better than to try to base my life on lies."

No words from him this time. Nothing to say as he watched me finish packing. One suitcase full, I struggled to close and lock it. A bit of blouse sleeve showed, but I didn't care. Arden did nothing to help me as I bore down with all my strength, trying to force it to close. Finally I had it locked. I locked all my bags, five of them. Arden sighed heavily.

"So now you plan to run off to God knows where. You don't ask me what I want. You don't care what I want. You won't listen to reason or explanations. Do you call that justice? Or do you call it spite? Or revenge? Your love is a capricious thing, Audrina. Don't you owe it to me to stay and see if our marriage can't be salvaged?"

I didn't look his way. "I can't let Sylvia stay here. There's something strange in this house that holds all memories and makes them part of the future. This house contains too many sorrows to ever let any of us have any joy. Be glad I'm leaving you. Tell yourself each day of your life that you escaped by the skin of your teeth from becoming exactly what my father is, a fraud, a cheat out to steal even from his own daughters."

He gave me a long, hard look, turned from me and stalked to the door. From there he had to say one last painful thing. "I could say right now that Damian did try to help you, but I guess it's too late to say that."

I picked up an expensive paperweight and hurled it at his head. It missed and fell to the floor. He slammed out of the bedroom door.

Minutes later the door opened slowly. Quietly, on poky pussycat feet, Sylvia slipped inside the room and stood silently watching me.

"Yes, Sylvia, I'm leaving and taking you with me. I've packed your clothes, and I will buy you new, pretty clothes when we get to where we're going. This is not a healthy house for you to live out your life in. I want to give you school days, parks to play in, friends your own age. Momma left us both a share of this house, so if ever we wanted to leave Papa would have to give us our share or sell the house. So, let's happily say goodbye to Whitefern, and hello to much better lives elsewhere."

Her aqua eyes widened as she inched away from me. Violently she shook her head. "Nooo," she breathed, putting up her hands as if to ward off an enemy. "Sta . . . stay here. Home."

Again I spoke to her about leaving with me, and just as violently as before, she told me in all ways possible without speaking that she would never, never leave Papa, or Whitefern.

I backed away this time. I wouldn't let her devotion to Papa undermine my determination to go my own way for the first time in my life. Let her stay on with Papa in Whitefern . . . perhaps they deserved one another, too.

"Goodbye, Papa," I said an hour later. "Take good care of yourself. Sylvia is going to need you even more after I'm gone."

Tears coursed down his full cheeks and fell onto his clean shirt.

Papa's voice followed me as I moved toward the door. I carried only one small bag. I'd come back for the others. "All I ever wanted out of life was one woman to see me as fine and noble. I thought it would be you. Audrina, don't go. I'll give you all I possess, everything . . ."

"You have Sylvia, Papa," I answered with a tight smile. "Just remember this when I'm gone from this house. You made Vera what she was, as you made me what I am, as you've also shaped Sylvia's destiny. Be kind to her, Papa. Be careful what trail you put her feet upon when you begin to tell her tales. I'm not truly convinced—" Here I bit down on my tongue, hesitating when I saw that Sylvia had come to pause in the foyer, just outside the Roman Revival Salon.

Terror lit up Papa's dark eyes for a brief second. As if he knew Sylvia had mimicked me just once too often, and rocked in that chair many more times than I would let him force me.

Now *she* had the gift—whatever it might be, and if it could be.

"I'm going to drive your Mercedes, Papa. I hope that's all right."

Numbly he nodded. "Cars mean nothing to me now," he mumbled. "My life is finished when you go." He stared over my shoulder at Sylvia, who came to stand in the doorway. Something in her now formidable stance reminded me of Aunt Ellsbeth. There was a hint of Momma in her faint sardonic smile.

Oh, my God! My head began to ache, as I feared it would always ache in this house of spindles, bobbins and knobs, with its gold and brass gleaming, with its myriad colors confusing my thoughts and taking me away from other much more important things.

We were all a strange lot, the Whitefern girls. Daring to be different in the oddest ways. Words I'd heard Aunt Ellsbeth say to Momma and to that portrait of Aunt Mercy Marie that had made Tuesday teatimes a memorial service not to be enjoyed.

As I prepared to leave Arden and never see him again, Papa was pleading with his dark, dark eyes, even as he tried to deny Sylvia the right to take my place. Let him suffer the consequences of making her what she is . . . and God alone knew if it was Vera or Sylvia who hated Papa more. I suspected Sylvia would destroy any woman but me who came into Papa's life when I left—if ever he wanted another woman.

"Good luck and goodbye, Sylvia. If ever you need me, I'll come to take you home with me—wherever my home may be."

Again I nodded to Papa, who sat on, glumly grim. I refused to look at Arden, who came down the stairs, dressed and ready to leave for his office. I thanked Sylvia again for being there when I needed her.

Some kind of strange wisdom was in her eyes as she nodded without trying to speak. Then she turned and nailed Papa to his chair with her penetrating stare.

I shivered with the suspicion that Papa was not going to enjoy his youngest daughter who, with the flashing prism lights, controlled the destinies of those who tried to dominate too much.

With great reluctance, his face showing his misery, Arden carried my bags to the car and carefully stacked them in the trunk while I sat behind the wheel and prepared to go. "Goodbye, Arden. I'll never forget all the fun we used to have when I believed you loved me. Even if I didn't respond sexually the way you wanted all the time, I loved you in my own way."

He winced from the pain of my casual parting before he said bitterly, "You'll come back. You think you can say goodbye to me, to Whitefern, to Sylvia and to your father, but you'll come back."

My hands gripped the steering wheel more forcefully, thinking that this was Papa's last, and most expensive gift to me. I looked around to see the three-day storm was over and the sky was washed clean and bright. All the world seemed to smell new, fresh, inviting. I breathed deeply and felt suddenly very happy. Free, at last, free.

Free of that stale wedding cake house with its cupola empty of the bride and groom. It was the dimness inside that house that made the colors too dominating. Some place far from here I could make it on my own and become a real kind of person who knew what she was.

What commanded me against my will to turn my head and have second thoughts about leaving? I didn't want to stay!

Slowly, slowly, my head was forced to turn so that soon I was facing the house. My eyes lifted to that window on the second floor—that room I'd always presumed was *her* room, and through the cloudy glass I saw a pale small face staring out—a face that looked so much like my own I gasped. Framed in a mop of thick hair of an uncertain color that could change and blend with its surroundings, her wan face neared, retreated, neared, retreated. I could see that her lips were moving, saying something, perhaps singing the playroom song. My hand shook when I looked away and tried to turn the ignition key. What was wrong with my hand? I couldn't make it obey!

NO! I screamed mentally while Arden stared at me as if I were crazy. *Don't, Sylvia! Let me go!* I did the best I could for you, gave you years and years of my life, years and years! Give me the chance to live and find myself, please!

Louder sounded the wind chimes, clamoring, making my head ache so badly I wanted to scream, scream—but I had no voice.

Behind my eyes a premonition flashed. Something awful was going to happen to Papa. When it did, they'd put Sylvia away and never would she see the sunlight again.

I let go the ignition key and opened the car door, then stepped out and hurried to Arden, whose eyes lit up as he held out his arms to embrace me. With a sob his face bowed into my hair as my arms held him just as tightly as he held me. We looked deeply into each other's eyes, then together we tugged my suitcases from the trunk of the Mercedes.

My suitcases we left on the drive.

Like Papa's love for me, I'd just done the most noble deed of my life. I was the First and Best Audrina who had always put love and loyalty first. There was no place for me to run. Shrugging, feeling sad, yet cleaner than I had since that rainy day in the woods, I felt a certain kind of accepting peace as Arden put his arm about my shoulders. Automatically my arm encircled his waist, and together we headed back to the porch where Papa and Sylvia had come out to watch. I saw happiness and relief in both pairs of eyes.

Arden and I would begin again in Whitefern, and if this time we failed, we'd begin a third time, a fourth . . .

Whitefern

For Mary and Joan Andrews,
who help keep the faith

Prologue

Papa died with my name on his lips. I would have thought his final words would be a call for my sister, Sylvia, or for Lucietta, our mother, who had died giving birth to Sylvia. For years afterward, I would think about the way he had said my name in those final moments. Was his call to me a plea for help, or was he begging for forgiveness? Was it merely pleasure at having his last thoughts be about me? Did he see my much younger face before him?

Arden, Sylvia, and I were there in his bedroom when he took his last breath. Sylvia and I were sitting beside the bed. Sylvia held his hand, and my husband, Arden, standing beside me, had his hand on my shoulder, his fingers drumming with impatience. He had been on his way out the door to go to work when Papa took a sudden turn for the worse. Of course, he'd thought it was another false alarm, but he quickly returned and saw that this time, it was very, very serious.

The ticking of the dark oak miniature grandfather's clock on the dresser seemed to grow louder and louder, impressing us with every passing moment. I imagined it was like Papa's heartbeat. I would swear that it paused when Papa took his final breath. A cloud passed over the sun, and a shadow rushed in through the windows and fell like a dark sheet over his body and his face. I felt a shawl of ice slip over my shoulders as Arden lifted his hand away.

The week before, Papa had nearly passed out going up the stairs. His eyes had closed, and he'd swayed almost at the top step. Sylvia had been following him up, just as she often followed at his heels, eager to do his bidding, and that had kept him from falling backward. A fatal accident on those stairs would come as no surprise. They'd already had too much tragic history. Sylvia's scream had brought me running. I'd seen her hands on his back. Before I could reach them, he had regained his composure, the color coming back into his pale face.

"I'm all right," he had said, but without admitting that something wrong with him had caused him to lose his balance, he also declared that Sylvia had saved his life.

"We should call the doctor," I had said.

"Nonsense, no need. Everyone loses his balance occasionally. Maybe a little too much blackberry brandy."

It was futile to contradict him or insist. Papa never changed his mind about anything once he had made it up. My aunt Ellsbeth would say, "He's as stubborn as a tree stump when he digs his roots into an argument."

Nevertheless, at his insistence, we had celebrated Sylvia as a heroine at dinner that night. I was told to make her favorite cake, vanilla with chocolate icing. We had champagne and, later, music so Papa could do a little dance with her. While I'd watched them, I'd been reminded of how he would waltz with my mother sometimes after dinner when they were young, and our world would look like a world of eternal spring. Momma's peals of laughter and joy would echo off the walls. The only one who scowled would be Aunt Ellsbeth.

Sylvia had been so happy when Papa called her "my little heroine." She'd loved repeating, "I saved Papa," every morning for days afterward; it was the first thing she'd say to me when I roused her to dress and come down for breakfast. Compliments and applause were rare birds in her nest. Perhaps she thought she could do it again the day he died, save him and keep him from falling into the inevitable grave. She clung so tightly to his hand.

Arden often called her "your father's extra shadow," but he wasn't saying that because he thought what she was doing was cute or loving. No, he thought it was both annoying for Papa and embarrassing for us, mainly for him, whenever anyone he knew from work saw this grown woman still so attached to her father, sensitive to his every move, eager to do the simplest things for him, like fetching his slippers or lighting his pipe.

"He can't even go to the bathroom without her waiting for him at the door like a puppy. Can't you make her see how foolish she looks? Do something!" Arden had demanded. "You're the one she'll listen to."

"Papa doesn't mind," I'd said in Sylvia's defense, "so you shouldn't, either."

Papa never did complain, nor did he ever criticize my sister or make her feel silly or foolish. If anything, he liked females hounding him. I had no illusions about my father. He was always a woman's man. He would always flirt, even with me when I was older. Of course, Sylvia was special. Perhaps he should have tried harder to have her become less dependent on him. A girl can love her father, adore him, but at some point, she has to step out into the world with independence, or she will not mature and enjoy what other love awaits her.

No one, including me, had much confidence in Sylvia developing an independent existence or finding the love of another man. She had been born prematurely and was mentally slow. Once everyone viewed her that way, she'd become comfortable with that image. She liked being babied so much that she never tried too hard to become a mature woman with a mature woman's responsibilities. At least, that was my theory. Everyone criticized me for it. Arden, in fact, once accused me of being jealous of my father's affection for her.

"Maybe you think he'll turn her into 'my sweet Sylvia' or create a Sylvia Two," he said, with that wry smile on his face that usually irritated me. "He thinks he's God and can change anyone to his liking."

But accusing me of jealousy wasn't fair. With the exception of my father, no one ever loved or treated my sister more tenderly than I did. She used to follow me around the way she was then following him. Perhaps that was why I didn't openly criticize her or try to get her to be less fawning. Many times, I was tempted to do what Arden wanted and tell her to stop clinging so hard to our father. *Let Papa breathe*, I wanted to say, but I swallowed back the words. She probably wouldn't have understood it, and if it was explained to her, I was afraid she would go into one of her hysterical fits of sobbing and others would accuse me of the same thing Arden had. I feared even Papa would admonish me.

So when I saw Papa die in front of us, I looked quickly at Sylvia, anticipating an outburst of sorrow from her.

But then I realized she had no idea he was gone. She still clung to his hand. She shook it softly, expecting him to open his eyes and smile at her as he had done only minutes ago.

I put my arm around her. "He's gone, Sylvia," I said, my lips trembling and tears streaming down my cheeks. "Papa has passed on. You have to let go of his hand. He's gone."

She looked at me, scowled, and then looked back at him, but she didn't move, nor did she let go of his hand. The words apparently made no sense to her. I knew what she was thinking: *How can he be gone if he is still here in his bed?* Sylvia always took everything literally, expecting the truth to be straightforward, the way children did.

I looked to Dr. Prescott. He was frustrated because he had come too late, and he sat on the other side of the bed, his hands pressed against his cheeks, his shock of graying brown hair as wild as weeds from running his thick fingers through it with frustration. He was only a year younger than Papa, but lately, he'd looked ten years younger and was far sprier. He wasn't as tall as Papa; few men were. But these last months, he had looked taller.

The kind doctor raised his head to look at us, his eyes swimming in sorrow far beyond what any doctor would experience after losing a patient. Physicians, probably more than anyone, lived with the inevitability of death. It was like dogs barking at their heels. He leaned over and closed Papa's eyes. Then he gently took Papa's hand from Sylvia's and put it over Papa's now-still chest and then his other hand over that.

"I told him he needed a stent. I finally had him convinced to go into the hospital . . . this Monday," Dr. Prescott said, shaking his head and looking down at Papa. "But I knew he would put it off again and again. Stubborn man."

He had rushed over after I called to tell him Papa wasn't feeling well and was weak and pale. I'd mentioned he was having trouble breathing. Dr. Prescott had thought we should send for an ambulance, but Papa had gotten so upset about it I had to call back and tell him that I was afraid Papa's anger would just make him sicker and that Sylvia and I had helped him to bed.

"Okay, I'm on my way," he'd replied. He was more than just Papa's doctor. He and Papa were good friends and lately had spent at least one night a week playing chess, drinking brandy, and talking about their youth. On more than one occasion, I had overheard Papa's conversation drift into a sea of guilt, on which floated many regrettable actions and decisions. Maybe it was the effect of the brandy or maybe because he was getting older, but he'd sought opportunities to confess his sins.

His biggest one, as far as he and I were concerned, was his elaborate plan to convince me when I was a child that I was the older sister of my dead sister, Audrina, the perfect little girl after whom I was supposedly named.

Back then, Papa would often have me close my eyes and rock in the first Audrina's rocking chair, supposedly to capture some of her gifts and memories, the most horrid of which was her being raped at the age of nine. He knew all the memories would return, for they were really my memories. Whether or not I wanted to believe that there were good intentions behind this deception, the result was that it gave birth to more sadness and tragedy than any family should have to bear.

Papa had known that, and the knowledge had weighed on him so heavily as he grew older that his once strong and perfect manly body began to crumble, his shoulders turning in, his back bent more and more, his walk slower and unsteady, his six-foot-five frame looking so much shorter and fragile. Gray had devastated his unique black hair, which used to appear blue in the sunlight but no longer did, and his lively, sexy, almond-shaped dark brown eyes had dulled and begun to look sleepy and forlorn.

He had started to go to work less often at the brokerage firm, finally acquiescing to letting Arden take on more and more responsibility there. Occasionally, he would argue with and discuss some of the decisions Arden had made, decisions that would drive him to return to work more frequently, often to correct them. However, during the past few weeks, it had seemed to me that my father had lost interest in almost everything. Lately, he'd spent more of his time sitting on our front porch, even when it was raining or there was a thick fog, bitterly staring out at the world as though it had deceived him. I would try to cheer him up, bring him his favorite freshly baked cookies or a cup of tea, even a brandy, but he would show little enthusiasm. Only Sylvia could bring a smile to his face during those last days. He'd pet her and stroke her, and I was sure he would be thinking of our mother. Despite how angry he could get at her from time to time, he had surely loved our mother more than he'd loved—or could love—any woman.

As Sylvia had grown, she did look more like our mother than I did. I'd spent as much time as I could helping her develop into someone who could care for herself. She was so dependent on the kindness of others, even to this day. Whenever any of Papa and Arden's clients came to dinner with their wives, the wives always brought Sylvia something pretty, whether it was costume jewelry, ribbons, or delicious boxes of candy. On those nights, there was laughter and music, and no one dared mention a single sad moment from our past. Good things still could happen in our house, but that was never enough to drown out the bad completely. Those memories refused to be forgotten or buried.

Guilt, in fact, hovered in every corner of White-fern, our family home, like invisible spiderwebs trapping every happy thought to make sure that un-happiness dominated our lives. I had wanted to run from the mansion and never set foot in it again when I learned the horrible truths that had been whirling around me all my life. The grave for the so-called "first Audrina" was in the Whitefern Cemetery nearby, a grave I was taken to often to visit and hear about this mythical sister. The grave was, in fact, empty. What an elaborate ruse. Who wouldn't want to get as far away from it all as fast as she could?

I had to find a deep well of forgiveness from which to draw the understanding and tolerance that would enable me to continue to live here, to accept Arden again, to pity my father and even my ruthless, jealous cousin Vera, who, I discovered, really was what she claimed to be, my half sister. She became one of the fatal victims in this house, along with Aunt Ellsbeth and Billie, Arden's mother. They'd all fallen down the stairway to their deaths, every one of them ruled an accident. It was as if Whitefern wanted to dole out justice or attack deception and had the power to do so. Maybe such thoughts had flashed through Papa's mind when he stumbled backward on the stairway.

It wasn't difficult to accept the idea that my fam-ily home was alive and conscious of all the intrigue and pain that went on within it. It was and remained right up to today an impressive Victorian gingerbread house. Arden had organized some restoration, having it repainted white and all the blinds redone, in addition to the outside steps. Recently, a house not unlike ours in the Tidewater region of Virginia had suffered a tragedy when two women were out on a balcony that gave way without warning. They'd fallen three stories, and both had died. This had prompted Arden to get to work immediately on ours, firming things up but adhering to Papa's orders to keep the style.

Years ago, Papa had repaired the roof. He would do what was necessary, especially when he had made more money. But there were areas now that needed refurbishing and remodeling, and Papa wouldn't give permission to do it. It wasn't all about money. Arden had insisted that much of the structure was now an embarrassment, especially because we entertained so many wealthy clients, but Papa had said he saw some of the wear and tear as contributing to the house's vintage character.

He had especially never wanted to change anything about the cupola, which had windows of stained leaded glass with scenes that represented the angels of life and death. It had held too much history for him. I remembered how pleased he'd been to see the sunlight thread through the stained-glass windows and fall in swirls like bright peacock feathers. There was even a long rectangle of painted glass in the roof. Chinese wind chimes hung from scarlet silken cords. It was still true to every original detail. This had been precious to Papa.

Actually, he had fought against changing any of Whitefern's decor, no matter what reasons Arden presented. When my husband would turn to me for support in these debates, I'd always try to remain neutral.

Despite all that Papa had done to me, I couldn't hurt him, even in the smallest way. Consequently, not a single lamp was removed, nor were stronger bulbs put in any of them, even if they didn't provide enough light. It was as if Papa had been too comfortable with the shadows and would not drive one away.

At one point, Arden had wanted to replace our art, to sell some of the older pictures to take advantage of their escalating values and invest the money in stocks. But regardless of the financial reasons, Papa had resisted that, too. Some of the paintings were startling in their depictions of women. Papa had been particularly fascinated by the picture of a naked woman lying on a chaise and dropping grapes into her mouth. It reeked of sex, I thought, and certainly intrigued every dinner guest or visitor. Even as a young girl, I saw the lust in the eyes of the men who stood before it, smiling licentiously. I couldn't imagine the wall without that painting.

Some of the furniture had been replaced simply because it fell apart, but most of it was considered antique. Papa had replaced whatever was fake with the real thing. I remembered my mother proudly describing the bed in her room as five hundred years old. Perhaps it was an exaggeration, but it certainly looked like a bed for a queen. I could never imagine selling it, and whenever Arden talked about refurbishing one room or another, I felt a pang of sadness and regret. It was like giving up old friends. When I told Arden as much, he laughed and called me a hopeless romantic. However, Papa had been happy I felt this way, which pleased me, even though it was a great disappointment to Arden when his wife was unsupportive.

Once I'd told him, "You can't change the past by changing wallpaper or furniture, Arden. You've got to stop trying. We have to live with it as best we can. It's not easy for me, especially, but we must."

And that was what we did, both of us avoiding memories stirred by any references to my mother, to the piano she played, to Aunt Ellsbeth, and also to Billie, Arden's mother. Vera's name was almost a curse word now. If there was the slightest allusion to her, Arden would blush with guilt. His eyes would flee from mine, and he would find a way to quickly change the subject.

Oh, how did this house and the people living in it bear up under the weight of such pain and horror? Surely that proved it had the foundation to continue eternally, strong enough to hold up the world, like Atlas. It was a magnet for the soul, holding us within its radius. There was always a sense of relief now whenever I returned from a trip or even a simple shopping expedition. It loomed before me, its doors and windows beckoning, urging me to get inside and feel the power of its protection against a cold and heartless world.

Sylvia was twenty the year Papa died. She was still like a child, even though she had a more than ample bosom and her body had carved into a figure most women would envy. Her hair was as pretty as mine. I often thought Sylvia had a healthier, richer complexion. She looked as if she might stay young forever, as if her mind not maturing meant that her body would stay frozen in its beauty.

Not socially mature enough, Sylvia had been kept at home during her school years rather than being sent to a place where we'd thought she would suffer at the hands of other students and also some teachers, who would be impatient with and intolerant of her. Instead, Papa and I had decided she should be tutored at home, as I had been for my first years. Maybe because of what had happened to me, Papa had wanted her to be kept close, protected.

Sometimes, when I would watch her with Papa and see the delight in his eyes, I would admit to myself that Arden was right. I was jealous of how much more Papa loved her than he loved me, even when he thought of me as the first Audrina. If I ever dared mention such a thought, he surely would deny it, of course, but anyone would have to be blind not to see the way his face lit up when Sylvia entered the room after I had.

"You must always look after your sister," he had told me often. "Promise you'll never put her into one of those homes for mentally deficient children."

I'd promised. Of course I'd promised.

But the day would come when I would question the wisdom of that, when I would blame myself for what happened.

If anyone should have known it would, it should have been I, the best and only sweet Audrina.

Darkness before the Light

Papa would rest beside our mother, both just a few feet from the false grave that bore my name. Because Sylvia was taking Papa's death worse than any of us, I spent most of my time with her during the days that immediately followed, and Arden handled the arrangements for the funeral. In the course of doing that, he suffered a big shock. He met with Papa's attorney, Mr. Johnson, and learned that Papa had recently changed his will; he had left everything to the two of us and to Sylvia, as expected, but he had given me fifty-one percent ownership of the brokerage.

Arden returned home in a rage after the meeting. I hadn't attended because I thought, as he did, that it was not going to be anything significant.

"Why did he do this?" he ranted, marching up and down in front of Sylvia and me and waving his arms as violently as if he wanted to throw off his hands. He clutched a copy of the paperwork in his right hand. "Why? Why? I'll tell you why. He knew how much I knew about his earlier dealings, the graft and corruption." He paused as he thought more about it.

"Sure, that's it. Of course. He did this to punish me for confronting him with his dishonesty years ago. How stupid to use you for his revenge."

"It wasn't revenge," I said, shocked but feeling like someone had to stick up for poor Papa. "He was worried about the way you were spending money and not concentrating on the work. All those nights you were out drinking while he went to bed early so he could greet the opening stock market."

"That's . . . an exaggeration. I was at work doing what had to be done when it had to be done. You're getting me off the point. You don't really know anything about our business."

"Papa always told me I was very smart. I knew enough to help you start, remember?"

"That was the basics that anyone would know. How can you vote on major decisions? You could count on your fingers how many times you've been there these past few years. You don't even know my secretary's name."

"Yes, I do. Mrs. Crown, Nora Crown."

He paused and glared at me. "Now, you listen and listen hard, Audrina. I want you to go to Mr. Johnson's office after the funeral and sign over everything to me. I'll call him and have the proper paperwork drawn up and ready for your signature so we can reverse this . . . this stupidity."

He waited for my response. I was holding Sylvia's hand, and we were both looking at him, surprised. Even poor Sylvia could sense it, his contempt. This was not the time to rage about anything, especially

Papa. We were in mourning. It was disrespectful to Papa's memory. Maybe I didn't know as much as Arden did about the business that Papa had built and brought him into, but I had Papa's grit and determination. I could learn anything.

"I'll think about it, Arden," I said softly. "When the time is proper."

"Think about it? Think about what?"

"Lower your voice. You're frightening Sylvia," I told him.

He barely gave her a glance. "Lower my voice? You've barely ever looked at the stock market these past years. You've probably forgotten the difference between a put and a call, selling short and buying on margin. The man was obviously not in his right mind when he had our attorney do this. If it wasn't out of some revenge, then it was because he was sick. That's it. He was sick. His brain wasn't getting enough blood, which was why he wasn't capable of thinking straight. Dr. Prescott will testify to that, and Mr. Johnson will agree."

"There was nothing wrong with Papa's mind. And you know that he spent a lot of time with me explaining the stock market when I was younger. It's not something you forget quickly. He thought it was a good way to teach math."

"Oh, boy, teaching a child math through the market. Like that makes you a broker."

"I didn't say it made me a broker. But he did take me to the brokerage and even announced that I would be his partner someday when he had his own company."

"He just wished he had a son to inherit everything. Every man wants that. I became his son. He said that to me after he married my mother. Or at least, I thought I had become his son. What father would do this to his son?" he asked, waving the papers in our faces.

"Stop it. Stop saying those things. I don't like talking about going against his orders while his body is waiting for burial."

"Against his orders? Don't make me laugh. You think you could choose stocks for our clients the way you thought you could pick winners when you were a child? Tying your birthstone ring to a string and dangling it over a list of stocks in the paper until it pointed to the right one?"

"I did that, and Papa made money on the stock. You yourself were not so very good at it in the beginning. Did you forget?"

"Please!" he cried. "I was learning, whereas all you Whitefern women were crazy with your beliefs in magic . . . hoodoo, voodoo . . . paying that psychic to predict whether your mother would have a boy or a girl."

"I'm sorry I told you that story."

"I bet. Well, hear this, Audrina. There's no magic in our business. It takes knowledge and experience. You don't really have either when it comes to the stock market, especially today. It's too sophisticated. You'd do no better than . . . than *her*!" he screamed, pointing at Sylvia.

Sylvia began to cry.

"Don't point at her like that. She doesn't understand!" I shouted back at him. That only upset her more. Anyone arguing in the house put her into a panic.

"You don't understand, either," he snapped back. "You don't understand how I feel being made a fool of like this. You can feel sorry for . . . for that," he said, pointing at Sylvia again, "but not for your husband!"

Sylvia's sobbing increased, and her body shook.

"Look what you've done!" I cried. "I've been keeping her calm. It hasn't been easy."

I put my arm around my sister and began to comfort her again. Since Papa's death, she would break out into crying jags and then howl with pain whenever there was any mention of Papa's passing. Every condolence phone call was like an electric shock. She would barely eat and wandered from room to room, expecting to find him. Every night, she called to him in her sleep, and every night, I ended up sleeping in her bed with her, her head on my breast, her tears dampening my nightgown.

"You know what? This is insane. I can't believe I'm even discussing it," Arden said, and he marched angrily out of the living room, his arms stiffly at his sides, his hands clenched in fists.

We hardly said another word to each other until the funeral. I had my hands full caring for Sylvia anyway. I was terrified of how she would behave at the service, but fortunately, she was in more of a state of disbelief than one of mourning. She even looked surprised that we were there in the church listening to the sermon and the eulogy. Every once in a while, she would gaze around the church, searching for Papa, especially whenever his name was uttered.

There were many businessmen in the Tidewater area who knew and liked my father very much. And of course, there were many community leaders who also knew him, so we anticipated a big attendance.

"Where is everyone? How can they not pay Papa the respect he deserves?" I asked Arden when I saw that no one else was coming and the service was about to begin.

He turned his amber-colored eyes on me. They were sparkling, but not with tears, the way I was sure mine were. His looked more excited than sad.

"Many of his friends and older clients have died. Besides, people always think, 'The king is dead. Long live the king.'"

"What does that mean, Arden? You're the new king, so they don't care about Papa anymore?"

"Something like that," he said. "After all, he can't do anything more for them, but I can." He patted himself on his chest.

Then he smiled, and for the first time, I realized that Arden wasn't as upset about Papa's death as I thought he should be. He was the head of the household now, and he thought he didn't need anyone else's permission to do whatever he wanted.

Then Arden surprised me by getting up to say a few words, honoring Papa for building such a successful business and promising everyone that he would do his best to uphold, protect, and further develop what

Papa had begun. The speech ended up being more of an assurance to our customers that he would keep the business successful than it was an homage to Papa.

When he was finished, he walked back to his seat beside me, his eyes searching my face for admiration and obedience, but instead, I turned away.

"You could put aside your grief for a moment and compliment me," he whispered, "especially in front of these people. I am your husband, the head of the household, dedicated to protecting you and Sylvia. I deserve respect, more respect, now."

"Today is Papa's day," I said. That was all I said, but it was enough.

He turned away and didn't even hold my hand at the grave site. I had my arm around Sylvia, who finally began to realize what was happening.

"Audrina, we can't leave Papa down there," she said when we were about to leave the cemetery.

The funeral workers would fill the grave after we all left. It was far too painful for me, and for Sylvia, to watch that. Arden had thrown the first shovelful of dirt onto Papa's lowered coffin. Although it was meant to be symbolic, it seemed to me he did it eagerly, even joyfully.

I could feel Sylvia's body tighten. She whispered, "Nooooo," but I tightened my arm around her and kept her from charging forward to stop him or anyone else from covering the coffin.

I practically had to drag her away and at one point looked to Arden for help, but he was too busy shaking hands with those who had come to the burial. He was behaving as if he was conducting just another business meeting. I even heard him mention some investment to Jonathan Logan, one of Papa's oldest clients, claiming that before he died, Papa had told him to tell Jonathan about it.

More people came to our house than to the church or the cemetery. I overheard that Arden had Mrs. Crown contact clients to give them the details of the funeral, but also to make sure they knew that if the church service conflicted with something they'd rather do, they were more than welcome to come to the house instead. He was treating it more like a party. I knew that people needed to avoid excessive grief and needed hope more than depression, but the way Arden was organizing things, I was almost expecting a band and dancing girls to show up.

Arden's boisterous conversations and continuous laughter stung. The whole thing confused Sylvia, who sometimes looked as if she might attack someone for smiling. I thought it best to get her up to her room, telling her to change and then lie down.

"You don't realize how tired you are," I said.

She looked afraid to close her eyes, but eventually she did, and she fell asleep quickly.

When I went back downstairs, I was confronted again with loud laughter and conversation that had grown more raucous. More people had arrived. Arden had arranged for a bartender and two maids to serve hors d'oeuvres. I was determined to be polite, not festive. Many of the men greeted me with quick condolences but, thinking they had to, moved instantly to assure me that my husband was capable of carrying on.

"After all, he was trained by an expert," Rolf Nestor, one of Papa's high-net-worth clients, told me. "You can be very proud of him."

Others said similar things to me, and when Arden, standing off to the side, overheard them, I could see his pleased, arrogant glare. Eventually, too physically and emotionally drained to remain, I excused myself.

"Of course, darling Audrina," Arden said, loudly enough for everyone in the room to hear. "You've done more than enough for any father to be proud of you. He died knowing you would be well cared for, and you will be," he vowed.

I saw the way the women were looking at him admiringly, and the men were nodding. It was not too different from the way they would look at Papa when he was younger and more energetic. Ironically, Arden was becoming more like Papa, the man he supposedly despised now.

I said nothing. My heart was heavy. When I went upstairs, I checked on Sylvia first. She was dead asleep. Out of habit, and maybe because I wanted to convince myself that this was not all a terrible nightmare, I opened the door to my father's bedroom and stood there full of wishful thinking. I imagined him propped up with two of his oversize pillows, his glasses slipping down the bridge of his nose, reading some economic charts or some company's profit-and-loss statement. In his final years, although he was working less, he'd kept up the research and preparation to make sure that Arden made no significant blunders in his absence, the way he had in the beginning. In fact, now that I thought about it more, I could understand why he had wanted to keep Arden from galloping off with the company and thought that perhaps having the majority of the company's shares in my favor would make Arden more cautious. Papa always chose to be more conservative with other people's money. He hated to be blamed for losses.

Of course, the room was dark, the bed was empty, and the cold reality rushed back at me. I did all I could to keep from fainting and made my way quickly to our bedroom, changed into my nightgown, and slipped under the covers. Despite my fatigue, I thought I was going to lie there for hours and hours sobbing and staring into the darkness.

Memories flowed freely around me. I could hear my mother playing the piano. I could see Papa's look of admiration and love and also jealousy at the way other men looked at her, even when she was pregnant with Sylvia. I saw him reach for me so I would rush to him and sit on his lap when I was very little. We would both listen to Momma play. Out of the corner of my eye, I saw Aunt Ellsbeth standing in the doorway, holding Vera's hand. Both looked envious but for different reasons. Vera was always jealous of the love Papa showered on me, and Ellsbeth was simply jealous of her beautiful sister, who seemed to possess everything any woman would dream of having. She was always angry that Whitefern had been left mainly to my mother and not to her.

They tried not to say unpleasant things directly to each other. I recalled how they pretended to be Aunt Mercy Marie and used their imitations of her at their special Tuesday "teatimes" to let loose all the venom toward each other that they usually held back. Aunt Mercy Marie's picture was on the piano. She looked like a queen, wealthy, with diamonds hanging from her ears. Aunt Ellsbeth would hold the picture up in front of her and change her voice to say nasty things, and Momma would do the same. I was still unsure about what had eventually happened to my great-aunt after she had gone to Africa. The family thought it was possible she had been captured by heathens and eaten by cannibals.

It was all those conflicting memories that finally drove me to the edge of exhaustion and pushed me into sleep, a sleep so deep that I didn't hear Arden come up much later. What woke me was the stench of alcohol. He was being clumsy, too, and quite inconsiderate, banging into chairs, mumbling loudly, slamming a glass down on a shelf in the bathroom, and then practically falling into the bed so that my body bounced as if I were on a trampoline.

"Are you awake?" he asked. "Huh?"

I tried to pretend I was not, but he nudged me. "What?"

"You heard them."

"Heard who?"

"Our clients. You see how important it is that the business be completely under my control now," he said, sounding sober. "We can't give anyone the impression that we're not as solid as ever. If they so much as suspected someone without real knowledge of today's market was involved in their business, they'd leave us in droves. We have to talk about this, and you must do what I tell you."

"We'll talk tomorrow," I said.

"Ah, tomorrow . . . tomorrow . . . Your father wasn't in his right mind, I tell you. Well? Well?"

I wouldn't answer him.

Finally, he turned onto his side, his back to me. I was trying to fall asleep again, but then he muttered, "Your sister was crying hysterically in your father's room."

"What?"

He didn't respond.

"What did you say?" I sat up. Still, he didn't respond. In a moment, he was snoring.

I got up and found my robe and slippers. Then I went to Papa's bedroom. The door was open again, but when I looked in, I didn't see Sylvia. I turned on a light and even looked into Papa's bathroom, but she wasn't there. Arden must have imagined it in his drunken stupor, I concluded, and I turned off the lights. Instead of returning to bed, I went to Sylvia's room.

For a few moments, I stood in her doorway and peered into the darkness. The curtains at the windows had been left open, but the sky was overcast. There wasn't even any starlight. In fact, I thought I heard the tinkling of raindrops against the glass. I stepped in and immediately saw that Sylvia was not in her bed. I checked her bathroom, and then hurried downstairs.

The living room had been cleaned up halfheartedly. Spilled drinks and bits of food were everywhere; there would be a lot of work to do tomorrow. Sylvia wasn't there.

I headed for the kitchen. Maybe she had gone down for a snack, since she had eaten nothing. There were many nights when I had found her doing just that. Sometimes Papa would be with her, and they would both be having a piece of cake or cookies with milk or tea. I assumed she'd recalled those nights and had gone to the kitchen, driven by memories.

But she wasn't there, either.

"Sylvia?" I called. I checked every room, every bathroom. Growing frantic now, I hurried up to the cupola, but that was empty, too.

The realization thundered around me. Sylvia wasn't in the house! I thought about waking Arden to tell him, but when I looked in on him, he was snoring even louder. He'd be of no help and grumpy for sure, I thought. But where was she? Where would she go?

I went to the closet in the entryway and put on one of my overcoats. Taking an umbrella, I stepped out and looked for her on the porch.

"Sylvia?" I cried. "Where are you? Sylvia?"

The rain was coming down harder, and the wind was now icy. A thick fog had blanketed the grounds and the woods. It was late October, but fall was obviously being crushed by a heavy oncoming winter. I realized I was still in my slippers, so I returned to the entryway closet and took out a pair of Papa's black leather boots. My feet swam in them, but I was able to walk out and down the stairs with the umbrella shielding me somewhat. I had no idea where to look. Over and over, I called out her name. She wasn't anywhere nearby. Where could she be? Then a terrifying possibility seemed to rush out of the bitter darkness and wash over me.

"Oh, Sylvia," I muttered. "Poor Sylvia."

I hurried down the path and through the woods as fast as I could, the rain soaking my face, but I was too frightened to feel the cold now. It was a long walk, a walk I couldn't imagine her taking, but about a dozen yards from the cemetery, I heard it—a shovel—and I broke into a run, clomping along in Papa's oversize boots and nearly falling a few times.

Finally, I was there and saw her, in only her nightgown, digging away at Papa's grave, the rain soaking her so that she looked as good as naked.

"Sylvia!" I screamed. "What are you doing?"

She paused and turned to me. "We can't leave him down there," she said. "Papa. It's cold and dark. We can't leave him, Audrina. Just like we didn't leave you."

"No . . . oh, no, Sylvia. I was never dead. Papa *is* dead. Papa needs to stay there. He needs to stay near Momma."

I reached for the shovel. She held on to it tightly.

"Please, Sylvia, leave Papa to rest in peace. You're going to get pneumonia out here. He would be very angry at you."

"Angry? Papa? At me?"

"Yes, very. And mad at me for letting you do this. He's probably screaming at us now. Come on. Come back to the house. I need to get you into a warm bath. Come on," I said, more forcefully, and I pulled the shovel out of her grip.

She stumbled, and I put my arm around her waist, threw the shovel down, and, holding the umbrella above both of us as best I could, led her out of the cemetery and quickly back to the house. It was raining even harder. It seemed to take longer to get home. A few times, she paused to turn back, but I overpowered her and warned her again that Papa would be angry.

When I finally got her inside, I helped her out of her soaked nightgown and used some towels from the powder room to dry her off. After I had taken off my coat and Papa's boots, I led her up the stairs and to her bedroom, setting her on her bed while I ran her bath. Once she was submerged in the warm water, I washed her neck and shoulders and gave her hair a quick shampoo. She was quiet now, seeming very tired.

I stood up and took off my own damp nightgown. The tub was big enough for the two of us. We had taken baths together occasionally. I ran some more hot water. She opened her eyes when I got in and sat facing her.

"Audrina," she said insistently, "you came out of your grave. Papa can come out of his, too."

I closed my eyes. How would I ever get her to understand when half the time I didn't understand myself? "Not tonight," I said. That answer would have to do for now. "Not tonight."

We sat soaking for nearly half an hour, and after

we got out and dried ourselves off, we put on new nightgowns. I blow-dried her hair and mine, and then I crawled into bed beside her.

Which was where Arden found us both in the morning, sleeping, embracing each other, probably looking like two lovers to him.

"Hey," he said when I opened my eyes. "When did you come in here? Are you going to do this every night? I'll get a bigger bed, and the three of us can sleep together."

Instinctively, I pulled away from Sylvia. "Stop it, Arden. This wasn't funny. It was terrible."

"What was?"

"What she did last night . . . and in the cold rain! It's quite a story."

"Yeah, well, I have quite a story to tell, too. I'm going to work. The stock market doesn't pay attention to personal sorrow. I'll call our attorney, and we'll talk later."

"That's disrespectful, Arden. No one expects you to be in the office so soon, and you certainly should not call Mr. Johnson today."

"Death is disrespectful," he replied, and closed the door between us.

I heard him pound down the stairs, mumbling to himself.

I hoped that strangers would see his rage as a result of his sorrow and not his ambition, not that it would matter to the people our business relied on, apparently. Our wealthy clients probably believed they could buy off death itself.

The business had changed Arden, I thought. It was almost impossible now to recall the young man who was so devoted to his mother, an Olympic ice skater who had suffered from diabetes and lost her legs. So much had happened since, and so much had changed him. Papa must have realized it, and that must have been why he put that codicil in his will.

But how could I defy my husband and bring him to his senses, even if only to obey my father, who was dead and gone?

How could Papa expect me to step into his shoes and be as strong as he was?

What had he seen in me that I had yet to see in myself?

What had he seen looming on the horizon?

What could possibly be worse than the horrors fate already had chosen to rain down on Whitefern?

The Pain of Memory

I feared I would spend most of my days immediately following Papa's death listening to echoes trapped in every dark corner. I resisted as best I could, but it was difficult to shut them out. I had done that successfully for a while when I was a little girl who had been sexually and violently ravaged. But there would be no comfort from amnesia now.

Perhaps this was why Papa had left me the controlling interest in his business. He knew this might happen to me, and he wanted me to have a path away from it all. He finally wanted me to find a life outside of this house and its dreadful memories. There were many times when he was proud of me, proud of my comments and ideas. Maybe he had come to believe that a girl could carry on her father's successes as well as a boy could. Arden simply didn't fit the bill for him.

If I didn't do something more, if I relegated myself only to household chores and caring for Sylvia, the past with all its tragedies would surely weigh me down. I'd grow old before my time, just as Papa had. I wouldn't neglect Sylvia and her needs, but I had needs, too. Arden must come to realize that, I thought. He must learn to see our marriage as more of a partnership. I must convince him that doing so would not diminish him.

He was so angry. He seemed so changed. When he was younger, living in the cottage with his mother, he was sweet and considerate. I never knew then how much of a role his guilt from witnessing and not fighting to prevent what had happened to me played until he finally confessed. Was he still burdened with that guilt? Had he grown tired of it and resorted to anger as an alternative? He did seem to have a chip on his shoulder these days. I suspected Papa never let him forget.

Of course, I had to overlook his affair with my half sister, Vera. His confessions were so heartfelt that I did blame Vera more than him. She was always there, trying to outshine me.

These memories and more drummed at the door, now that Papa had died. It was no longer necessary to avoid reminding him of the past. Death had trounced that concern. I hated the idea that I might spend my days reliving all the pain, that his death had opened the floodgates. Again, I told myself that what was important now, now that I was living in Whitefern without Papa, was finding a new sense of myself while still caring for Sylvia. I would have to be reborn yet again and become a third Audrina.

I realized that I must ignore, even bury, the fragile young woman who had seen and heard more than most could bear. There were many times when I would actually envy Sylvia for being immature and unaware of the significance of most things. How soft and comfortable was her childlike world. Most of the pain she had suffered, a great deal of it at Vera's hands, was lost to her. Back then, she greeted every new day by acting as if yesterday didn't matter. She could smile and expect good things, even from a world that had given her only bad.

Was that simply a result of her immaturity? Maturity meant many unexpected things. When you were an adult, there was no time to float about in a pond of wishes. There was only time to do, to be productive, to overcome obstacles. There were choices that once could be ignored or at least put off but now demanded attention and wouldn't sit patiently waiting for you to act when you felt like it. That childlike world was the world in which Sylvia still lived.

I thought about all this the next day, pausing only to make lunch for her and occasionally playing a board game with her to keep her from thinking. It was clear she still had not accepted Papa's death. I seriously wondered if she ever would. She kept looking at the front door, expecting him to come home and cry out, "Where's my Sylvia? Who's bringing me my slippers?" Sometimes she used to wait at the front windows for his car to appear. When he was late, she would grow fidgety and needed to be reassured that he was coming home.

"Papa told me he wanted lamb chops tonight," she suddenly said while we were playing checkers. I always let her win. I looked at the clock. It was nearly three o'clock, about the time I would plan dinner. Where that tidbit of information came from I didn't know, but it wasn't unusual for her to come up with something someone said months, even years, ago. It was as if words bounced around in her childlike mind like balloons and suddenly found voice again.

"You must try to remember what happened to Papa, Sylvia," I told her softly. "It's important. We all have to be strong, the way he would have wanted us to be. You want to be strong, don't you?"

She looked like she was going to go into one of her pouts but suddenly smiled with the burst of a new idea. "Let's go to the cemetery," she said. I had the eerie feeling that she expected we'd see an open grave and an open coffin. In her mind, Papa was capable of a resurrection, just like Jesus.

I reached for her hand. "Nothing will be different there, Sylvia. I've already asked Mr. Ralph to go there and fill in the holes you dug."

Mr. Ralph, our groundskeeper, was the most trusted servant anyone could dream of having. He bore no relationship to the Whiteferns, the Adares, or the Lowes, but he had been with my family since he was about fifteen. He was more than seventy-five now, although no one would swear to his exact age, even him, and he was a little deaf, with fading eyesight. All his friends were gone or had moved away, he said. His whole life was caring for our property. He had always been fond and protective of Papa, but I thought he was more afraid than fond of Arden.

"We'll visit the cemetery when it's right to do so, and we'll say prayers for Papa at his grave, okay?" I added quickly.

She pulled her hand back, looking angry as only she could, her beautiful eyes darkening into gray, her lips tightening, with pale spots interfering with their natural ruby tint. She liked to put on lipstick whenever I did, but she really didn't need it.

"I have a secret," she said, her body recoiling like a spring. "Only Papa and I know it. Not Arden, not you."

"Then maybe you should not tell anyone else," I said, a little annoyed at her. Her look reminded me too much of Vera whenever she tried to irritate me with some fact that had been hidden from me. Whatever Sylvia's secret was, I thought, it would be something innocuous, something Papa had told her to keep her from being sad.

She continued to look at me hard for a moment, harder than I ever saw her look at me. The thoughts were twisting and turning in her head. I could see her troubling over what she should do, whether to tell me or not. These past few years, Papa's devotion to her was very important. She didn't want to share his affection and at times hated hearing any references to anyone else he loved, including me. That was another way she reminded me of Vera. I supposed there was no way to get around it. There was a little of Vera in both of us. We shared too much blood, having had the same father.

Her eyes narrowed, and she nodded to herself.

"You're right, Audrina. Papa told me never to tell anyone, even you."

I raised my eyebrows at how adult she suddenly
sounded. The memories of the various times my father
had said something similar to me returned. Sometimes
I felt I was being buried in secrets. Someone was always whispering one in my ear, whether it was Aunt
Ellsbeth, Vera, or Papa.

Sylvia kept her gaze locked on me, waiting for
my reaction, which I thought was quite unusual for
her. I pulled back a little and wondered if Sylvia even
understood the concept of a secret. Was this some sort
of game my father had played with her when I wasn't
around?

"Do you have any secrets you can tell me?" I
asked.

She shook her head. "No. When you tell a secret,
you can't take it back. That would be like trying to put
ketchup back in the bottle," she said. I knew that was
something Papa had told her, because he had told it to
me, too, when I was a little girl.

"Okay, Sylvia, don't think about it. Keep your
secrets in your bottle of ketchup." I got up. "Let's go
make dinner now. Arden will be home soon, and you
know how hungry he is when he comes through that
door. He expects everything to be ready for him, just
like all men." I recited what I had been told over the
years, especially by my aunt Ellsbeth. "They want you
to be their cook and bottle washer and their clothes
valet and keep the house spick-and-span. And you
have to do all that and still be beautiful so they can go

about proudly with you on their arm, looking up to them like they walk on water. When a husband says, 'Jump,' you're supposed to ask, 'How high, dear?' "

I paused when I saw she was staring at me with her eyes wide. She really hadn't understood a word, especially couched in an angry tone. Maybe I sounded a little too much like Aunt Ellsbeth, someone she was not especially fond of being around. All our relatives and ancestors popped up occasionally in us, I thought. There was no escaping that.

"Oh, forget it, Sylvia. Fortunately, you won't have to worry about all this business between a husband and a wife," I added, and immediately regretted it. It was surely something Aunt Ellsbeth would have told her. "Come on. Let's be good little housewives tonight. To the kitchen," I said, and pretended we should charge like knights on horses.

She laughed and stood up quickly. Sylvia liked to help prepare the salad and, despite everything else that held her back, was meticulous about how she cut carrots, tomatoes, and onions, making perfect slices. She did have artistic talent. I had recently bought her some art supplies, and without instruction, she produced some interesting representations of our surroundings, the trees and ponds and paths. Or at least, I thought they were interesting. Arden thought her work was just a muddle of shapes and colors, more like a child's finger painting. He never really studied them and saw the way she layered her pictures so that they looked like images fading into each other. They were like dreamscapes with interesting choices of color and shades. She never tried to draw a person or a face, but sometimes I thought I saw the image of someone caught in the fog or in a cloud.

Recently, before Papa grew weaker and sicker, he and I had discussed the possibility of getting her an art teacher. When I told Arden, he said it would be a waste of money.

"How can she learn anything like that? She barely knows how to dress herself and brush her teeth."

"There are people like her who can't do well in school or even in everyday life with common activities but have specific talents, Arden."

"Then what good is it? They can't handle any money they make or go shopping for themselves. She can't even carry on a conversation. Just teach her how to clean and polish the floors and furniture. At least then she'll be of some value," he said, and went on reading his *Wall Street Journal*.

Nevertheless, I promised myself I would look into getting an art tutor once our lives resembled any normalcy. More than any of us, Sylvia needed something to distract her and take her mind off our loss. I knew how her mind worked. When she picked up a thought, plucked it seemingly out of the air like a wild berry, she turned it over and over in her mind for hours if she was left alone. This told me that she wasn't really dumb; she had deep curiosity about everything that was brought to her attention. The problem was trying to get her to think about something else once she hooked onto an idea, whether it was a dead fly she carried around all day or an old photo of Whitefern. She was that way about dinner preparations. No surgeon in an operating room had more intense concentration.

I had decided earlier in the day to prepare one of Arden's favorite dinners, angel-hair pasta and chicken in olive oil, garlic, and basil. I worked on the sauce and started heating the water for the pasta. Everything was going along fine when he called unexpectedly.

"I won't be home for dinner," he said as soon as I answered. "I have a very important dinner meeting with one of our high-net-worth clients who's worried about his portfolio since your father's death. I have to assure him that we are going to be as efficient and profitable for him as ever. Fortunately, no one but you, me, and our attorney knows about this stupid thing your father did, but the danger remains that it will be discovered. Stupid."

"My father didn't do stupid things, Arden."

"Oh. I suppose the whole ruse of creating the first Audrina wasn't stupid, or marrying my mother, a woman without legs, was brilliant. She was happy and safe where she was. I would have provided for her. There wasn't a woman within arm's length that he didn't claim, no matter what."

"You didn't complain about him back then, Arden. You were very grateful, as I remember it."

"What could I do? I didn't have a job, and my real father had deserted us." He inhaled a ragged breath. "But that's not the same as liking it," he added, his voice straining with frustration and rage. "I put up with a great deal to make him happy, to pay him back, and look what he did. That's what I call ungrateful."

"Have you been drinking?" I asked. He was slurring his words a little, and he would never say these things before my father died.

"Of course I'm drinking. You think a teetotaler could survive in this business? I have to entertain clients, Audrina, and not do things that will make them feel uncomfortable. Your father was quite the drinker. If you want to know the truth, he taught me. That's why I've been telling you that you simply do not understand the business. It all doesn't happen over the phone. People need to be reassured about things in person. You don't have the worldly experience I have. You never went to college. You were practically a prisoner in Whitefern. I've given you the important worldly knowledge you have."

I heard him take a deep breath, pausing like someone who was fighting to get control of himself.

"Everything is being arranged to correct what your father did," he said in a softer voice. "It will take two days. I'll bring you to Mr. Johnson's office to sign the paperwork. It has to be notarized."

"I'm not signing anything until I read it and think about it properly. It was how my father brought me up."

"Oh, please," he said. "How he brought you up? Do you really want to resurrect that subject?"

I heard music in the background. "Where are you?"

"I'm in a very upscale restaurant. You don't entertain clients in a fast-food joint. I'll be home late. Don't wait up for me."

"You didn't call all day, Arden, and you never asked what happened with Sylvia last night."

"Save it for my bedtime story," he said. Someone laughed near him. "Gotta go."

"Arden—"

He hung up. I looked at Sylvia. She was watching me, her face full of trepidation. She was always very sensitive to my moods and feelings and would even start to cry seconds before I did when something upset me or made me sad. Maybe there was something to the theory that people who shared blood were more aware of each other's moods and feelings than even close friends would be.

I smiled quickly. "Everything's all right, Sylvia. Arden has to work late tonight, so it will be only you and me for dinner, okay? We like it all anyway. It's not just for him that we cook."

She narrowed her eyes, looked toward the stairway, and then I thought she nodded to herself as if she had heard a whisper. I told myself her behavior shouldn't be so surprising to me. Like me, she had seen too many deaths in this house. She was in the shadow of the Grim Reaper. Vera, in fact, had tried to blame her for Billie's death when Billie fell down those stairs. Vera resented the attention Papa was giving Sylvia, just like she resented any attention he gave me. Jealousy, rather than blood, ran through Vera's veins. If she cut herself, I would expect to see the green slime of envy instead of blood.

Sylvia went about setting the table in the dining room for the two of us as meticulously as ever. That didn't surprise me. I knew her better than anyone, even Papa. I had practically been her mother all these years. When her body began to look like the budding figure of a beautiful young woman, I spent hours alone with her talking about sex, in as much of a scientific, even fantasy way as I could, especially when we discovered baby mice or a nest of hummingbird eggs and she had a child's curiosity about how they got there.

Everything became more dramatic for her when she had her first period. No matter how I tried to prepare her for it, it came as a big shock. Her scream at the sight of blood made Whitefern's walls tremble. I looked at Papa and hurried up to her. I recalled how frightened I had been when I had gotten mine, and I could handle such changes, so I appreciated what she was going through.

She hadn't forgotten what I had told her, but it was always more like a story to her, something that happened to other women. Why did it look so bad? This sort of thing happened only when you hurt yourself, and the cramps, the pain? How could this mean anything good? What did it have to do with babies?

When she questioned me time after time about it, I was thrown back to when my aunt Ellsbeth had tried to terrorize both Vera and me with biblical references, claiming that women suffered so much with their monthlies and the birthing process because of what Eve had done in the Garden of Eden.

"We're cursed!" she would exclaim, her eyes wild with rage. "Men have it so easy. It isn't fair, but think

of it as the first alarm bell. Now, sex will be dangerous. Those little sperms that come shooting out of
them and into you will make babies, babies you won't
want."

"Like you?" Vera had retorted, surprising me with
her defiance. "Making me?"

Most of the time, Aunt Ellsbeth wouldn't respond
to such an outburst of insolence, but this time, she'd
smiled coldly and said, "Exactly. Look at my burdens
now. Thank you for being born."

I remember wondering how it could be Vera's
fault. Even though she hurt me, angered me, and
teased me, I felt sorry for her. I expected she would
cry, but she simply looked at Aunt Ellsbeth and smiled
back at her with the same icy eyes. I couldn't imagine
being as hard and as emotionally insulated as Vera
could be. I was too sympathetic, especially when it
came to Sylvia.

Someday, I thought the day after she had her first
period, she would be alone or I wouldn't be there to
protect her, and some boys might come along and talk
her into doing nasty things with them. Papa had once
warned me about that. Obviously, because of my own
history, that sort of nightmare haunted me. If there
was one promise I had made to Papa without ever utter-
ing the words, it was never to let what happened to me
happen to Sylvia. I didn't have to come out and say it,
and Papa didn't have to put it into words, either. We
simply looked at her growing more and more beautiful
every day, looked at each other, and nodded with the
same thought.

Sylvia's innocent beauty wasn't a big secret. I took her shopping with me often, and people saw her at events we brought her to, especially events involving Papa's business when he was still working hard. She always drew compliments but had no idea how to respond. When she lowered her eyes and smiled, however, she looked like she was flirting or trying to because she was shy. On several occasions, young men had inquired about taking her out. Some had called to speak with her, and two different young men, college boys, had come to Whitefern to visit with her. I had turned them all away, on the phone or in person.

Once I considered letting them visit with Sylvia so they could see how immature she was, but then I thought, *Why put her through it?* Worse, what if she liked one of these young men and wanted to be with him, go for a ride or out to eat, anything? How would we deal with that? No, it was easier to shield her, to step in between her and any young man approaching her, and end it before it could begin.

A few local boys were quite persistent, and even though they learned how simple Sylvia was, their lust for her didn't diminish. If anything, I could see in their faces that they thought she'd be an easy conquest because she was unprotected, and I had no doubt that she might just be.

How long could I keep her chaste, I wondered, and should I do so for as long as I could? She had the mind of a child but the desires of a woman now. Was it fair to deny her the pleasures of her sex? Was it possible for her to find someone who would sincerely

care for her and love her and satisfy her womanly
needs? I never had the courage to bring these questions up with Papa. I certainly couldn't discuss them
with Arden. He'd make a sour face or mock the idea.
However, I was tempted to discuss these things with
Dr. Prescott. He was a trusted family friend, but I
hesitated. After all, he was also a man. I couldn't help
but feel embarrassed talking about it, and now that
there was no other woman in our home, whom could I
talk to about my own problems anyway?

I longed for a true friend or a sister who could
handle such matters. It was partly my own fault that
I was so isolated. So many terrible things had happened to us that I couldn't fathom being close to a
stranger. There would be so many questions, questions I couldn't answer or wouldn't ever want to
answer, like those about the deaths at Whitefern or
the empty grave that once had a tombstone with my
name on it.

Nevertheless, I knew I needed advice when it came
to Sylvia's problems and my own. I did come close to
confiding in Dr. Prescott when I had consulted him
about my failure to get pregnant. Arden had resisted
being tested for potency, but I did, and the result was
such that he didn't have to be tested. My chances for
getting pregnant were quite small. It didn't mean it
couldn't happen, but it was most unlikely. Back then,
Arden didn't seem to be troubled by the news. He
was happier that it was my fault, of course, and let me
know it.

"I had no doubt that a man as virile as I am would

not be the reason we're not succeeding in getting you pregnant. I don't shoot blanks," he bragged. Of course, I wondered what that meant. I knew that he'd had girlfriends when he was off at college. Did he get someone pregnant? Was there a child of his somewhere?

"How do you know?" I asked, and held my breath.

He just shrugged. "A man knows. Look at how well I make love. I taught you everything you need to know about it, didn't I? If you're not satisfied when I do it, you'll never be." He smiled slyly again. "I never had a complaint from any other girl. Anyway, let's not worry about it right now." I was practically in tears, but he smiled again and told me, "Look at all the money we'll save not bothering with birth control."

"That's not funny, Arden," I told him. Papa was still alive then, and despite what he had told me about Papa considering him his son, I knew in my heart that Papa wanted a grandson with his blood.

To my surprise, Arden did apologize. Maybe he thought I would go running to my father to tell him what he had said. We continued making love, and I continued to fail to get pregnant. He was too busy back then proving himself to Papa and taking on more responsibility. Some nights, he would begin to make love and suddenly stop, claiming he was tired. "And besides, what's the use?" he would say, and I would go to sleep with tears flooding my eyes.

All these memories and thoughts streamed through my mind as Sylvia and I sat in the dining room. I didn't want to bother eating in there. I thought we could just use the kitchenette, but she had dressed up the big table the way she always did, being a little creative with the way she folded the napkins, making little crowns or flowers. Whenever we had guests over, Papa would give Sylvia the task of creating place cards according to the way he wanted his guests to sit at the table. Most of the time, Arden, Sylvia, and I had the same places, but occasionally he wanted someone closer to him. Sometimes he wanted certain other people as far away as possible, too.

Sylvia wouldn't just write the names in her beautifully artistic script. She would color them in and often draw something to complement whatever we were having for dinner. She could draw a small hen or a funny little cow, lamb, or pig or do something interesting with fish. Everyone praised her, and when she looked at Papa and saw how proud of her he was, she would brighten and look even more beautiful. Arden might even say something nice, compliment her, but I always thought it was more to please Papa.

After dinner, again more to please Papa than anyone, I would play the piano. We'd tried to give Sylvia piano lessons, too, but she never took to it. She didn't have the patience and would rather spend her time drawing and painting in the cupola, where Papa had created a small studio for her. During the past few years, before Papa had begun to show signs of weakening, we did enjoy some peace and contentment at Whitefern. Maybe it was unrealistic to think it would last very long, but for a while, at least, it was truly like we were all finally finding some sense of happiness.

The settings at the dinner table were not modified after Papa's death. His place was still there. Sylvia and I sat where we always sat. This was really our first formal dinner since he had died. With all that went on, we'd been eating buffet style in the kitchenette. Here we were tonight, when I thought we would begin again as a family—diminished, yes, but still a family— and Arden was out with clients instead.

I tried not to be too depressed, because I was afraid Sylvia would start crying once we were at the table without Papa in his chair, and my sadness would only intensify her own. But she surprised me with how relaxed and hungry she was. I should have been happy about it, but she looked like someone who really did have a big secret. I smiled at her and asked her what she was thinking.

"I'm not thinking," she said. "I'm eating, Audrina."

That made me smile. I forgot how she could be so literal, but I was still a little curious, even a little anxious, about the way she would pause, look at Papa's empty seat, and then look toward the stairway, listening as if she anticipated the sound of his footsteps.

I had to get her to stop thinking of ghosts. Even Sylvia needed some sort of future now. Keeping her busy with household chores was far from enough. And I could see that she didn't even have the small attention span for my math and science tutoring. Even role-playing to help her be more confident in social settings wasn't working.

"How would you like me to find an art teacher to help you with your drawings and paintings?" I asked her. I had to get her thinking about something else. "He could help you do so much more. Isn't that a good idea, Sylvia?"

"Papa said you would," she replied.

"Right. Papa and I did discuss it. I'll look into it tomorrow, okay?"

"Papa said you would." She repeated it as if he had just told her.

"Okay, Sylvia."

"I'm not going to wait," she said.

"What?"

"I'm going to paint something new tonight right after I help clean up," she said.

"Oh, good. You don't have to help clean up tonight," I said. I really wanted to occupy myself as much as I could to diminish how angry I was feeling. Arden should be thinking more about us now and not clients. He should be comforting me. Papa's death was far too fresh.

"Really?" she asked.

"Yes, really."

She rushed to finish her dinner and then, remembering to excuse herself politely from the table the way Papa and I had taught her, hurried up the stairway to the cupola and her makeshift studio. I smiled to myself, happy to have some respite. She could be a full-time job, especially during these dark days.

I took my time cleaning up and putting things away. I had no idea how much time had passed, but I felt so drained and tired that when I went out to wait for Arden in the living room, I had no sooner sat back than I fell asleep. Hours went by. I was in so deep a sleep that I didn't hear Arden come home. I woke when a draft of cold air splashed over my face, and I looked up at him standing there gazing down at me, a dumb smile on his face. He looked like he was swaying a bit, too.

"Oh. I didn't hear you come in," I said, grinding the sleep from my eyes and sitting up.

"I'm happy to say that I talked Mr. Camden into putting his pension plan with our firm. While you were playing nursemaid to Snow White, I was building our net worth," he bragged.

Now that I was fully awake, I could smell the whiskey on his breath, even though we were far apart.

"Don't call her Snow White, Arden. When you do things like that, she knows you're making fun of her."

"Oh, please. She doesn't know top from bottom. Well? What do you say to what I just told you?"

"You're drinking too much, Arden."

"What? That's what you have to say? After I tell you I've just talked a millionaire into placing his pension portfolio with us? That's your comment? I'm drinking too much?"

"I'm just worried about you. That's all."

"Yes, me, too," he said, turning restrained. He ran his palms over his face. "I'm tired. There's a lot to do tomorrow." He started to turn away.

"The reason I was with Sylvia last night was that she had gone out in her nightgown to the cemetery to dig up Papa's grave," I said quickly. "And although you slept through it, it was pouring cats and dogs. She could have gotten pneumonia."

"What?" He stopped turning and smiled, incredulous. "Dig up his grave? Why?"

"She's confused. You might recall when someone else was buried and then figuratively dug up."

He stared at me, not angry and not sorry. "So what did you do when you found her in the cemetery?"

"I dragged her back, and then I had to put us both in a hot bath. You slept through it all."

"Glad I did," he said. He started away again, then stopped and turned back. "I don't know about her, about us keeping her here," he said. "This might be getting to be too much. I'm afraid to bring some of our clients here now."

"What? What else would we do? She's my sister. We won't put her in some institution."

"Well, that's why I want you to sign those papers ASAP. You'll be spending most of your time caring for a mental case," he said, shrugging. "I'm going up to bed. I need my sleep."

I sat for a while longer, thinking about him, how disappointing he could be. I remembered once talking about him with Aunt Ellsbeth when I was just seventeen and Arden had given me an engagement ring. She and I went for a walk, and she asked if I really loved him. When I said I did, she told me she hoped I would always feel that way about him, but she warned me, "He'll change. You'll change. You may not love him as much as you think you do now."

I didn't want to give her credit for ever being right about anything—she was so mean to my mother and especially to Sylvia—but not considering the things she had said as true or important was just foolish self-denial. It was also self-denial to ignore how lonely I was and how much I longed for the company of another, more experienced woman.

I went up to the cupola to get Sylvia and have her go to bed. For years now, I'd been the one who told her it was time to go to sleep and the one who woke her in the morning. I was her living alarm clock. Sometimes, even though she was very hungry, she would wait for me to tell her it was lunchtime. How would she live without me, especially in this house? If something happened to me, she would surely be sent to an institution, where Papa was sure she would be abused.

When I stepped into the cupola, she was still hard at work on her painting, so entranced by it that she didn't hear me enter and likely hadn't noticed how much time had passed. I watched her for a moment, amazed and pleased at how devoted to her art she could be. Anyone watching her would never believe there was anything seriously wrong with her. She looked so beautiful and so intense, focusing her mental abilities and talent on her work.

Slowly, I inched up behind her and looked at her picture.

I immediately felt a cold chill.

She had made a reasonably realistic likeness of the woods between the cemetery and Whitefern, and she had done a good job of creating an overlay of fog, but coming out of it was the ghostlike figure of Papa.

And the way she had drawn his face made him look like he was desperate either to get away from something or to get to something, get back to White-fern . . . perhaps to save us all.

A Flood of Emotions

There were many times before this when I thought I could drown in my own sorrow. Often after my mother's death, I had felt lost and alone in our big house. Shadows grew darker and drowned out the kaleidoscope of color our stained-glass windows would normally cast over the patterned rugs and furniture. My chameleon-colored hair, which Papa called a hat of rainbows, was dull and lifeless.

When I was younger, Whitefern was a house echoing with wishes. I wished I could go to school. I wished I had friends and could go to sleepovers. I envied the freedom other girls my age enjoyed. I read about them in books. I even wished the first Audrina was alive and well, an older sister with whom I could spend hours and hours talking, taking walks, and learning how to flirt with boys.

After Momma died, clocks were haunting with their eternal ticking, amplified by the silence around the piano Momma had once played so beautifully. Papa drifted in and out of sadness, anger, and guilt. He went from room to room mumbling to himself. Sometimes, when he stepped out of a shadow, it looked like it had stuck to his face no matter how bright the light.

Aunt Ellsbeth wasn't a great help to my father or me. Later, as talk about Sylvia increased, Aunt Ellsbeth constantly warned me about my father, telling me that now that my mother was gone, despite his permitting me to go to school, he would find ways to chain me to him and Whitefern forever. The most important way he would do that, she explained, was to make me Sylvia's caretaker for the rest of Sylvia's life.

"When she's brought home, that's what you'll be," she whispered, her eyes on fire with warning. "She'll be the chain that binds you forever to Whitefern and your selfish father."

Her warnings tempered my excitement over having a little sister finally coming home after almost two years of special care. In time, I realized her warnings about Papa came from her disappointment at his choosing my mother over her. There was still bitterness in her, a bitterness her daughter, Vera, would inherit, although many times I thought Vera didn't need to inherit bitterness from anyone. She was capable of being vicious and mean all by herself, first to me and then especially when it involved little Sylvia.

Both my aunt and Vera mocked her when she was first brought home to us. They seemed to take joy in pointing out her disadvantages and slow development. I vowed to myself and to Sylvia that I would work with her and make her as normal as I could. It was a promise I made to my dead mother, too, so that instead of feeling put upon as Aunt Ellsbeth predicted

I'd be, I felt responsibility and love. Maybe Aunt Ellsbeth was right to tell me Papa took advantage of that, but I wasn't about to stop caring for my little sister, either to spite Papa or to satisfy Aunt Ellsbeth.

I suppose I should have realized earlier that Sylvia would be attracted to art. When she was just three, I gave her my prisms, and she loved toying with the colors she could create. No one thought she could feel deeply about anything, but I began to realize that there was a real person in that troubled body struggling to have its mind keep up with it as it grew. Now I understood that she wasn't interested in art just because of her fascination with colors and shapes. Art was far more to her than a way to pass the time and amuse herself. She needed it. It was her way of talking to others, of expressing the deeper feelings inside her. Deaf mutes had sign language; Sylvia had art.

I wasn't any sort of an expert about it, but I knew that an art teacher would help her technically and show her how to explore more with the brushes and colors. He or she wouldn't change or add to what Sylvia wanted to say. That came from a place inside her, words and feelings bottled up, trapped by her shyness and inability to say outright what she felt. But if her art teacher improved her techniques, it would help those who looked at her pictures to realize what she was saying, what she was depicting and expressing, and of course, that would make her happier. She would be able to speak to more people and, in a small and different way, leave the confines of Whitefern.

Perhaps most important, art was her way of escaping from herself, because in a real sense, her undeveloped mind had become her prison. All these thoughts crossed my mind as I studied her new picture. Without instruction, she had somehow achieved more, used her colors more effectively, and drawn her outlines of people and animals more clearly. I supposed there was something to the idea that people could develop their talent naturally. Perhaps she could do much more with formal instruction, I concluded.

"Is that Papa?" I asked, studying the picture and pointing to the image of him. "Coming home?"

She turned slowly and looked at me like someone emerging from the darkness. It was as if she had been in a trance while she had worked. "Papa? Papa is home," she said, nodding.

It didn't surprise me to see her come up with this idea. Whitefern certainly had its ghosts. Relatives like Aunt Mercy Marie were referred to so often it was easy to feel they had just passed through a room. Sometimes, when I came upon Papa sitting in his favorite chair and looking like he was dreaming with his eyes open, he would glance at me and say, "You never leave Whitefern. Whitefern is part of you. Even after you die, you will be here."

I was sure he had said similar things to Sylvia, who might not understand what they meant at first, but with repetition, the idea might have taken hold. Even though these past days she looked like she was waiting for Papa or imagining him still alive, I didn't realize how deeply she believed it. Maybe Papa had specifically assured her that he would always be with her. Whatever he had told her privately he made seem like a secret. I was sure of that. So it didn't surprise me at all that the picture she was doing represented her hope. Papa would not be lost to us, to her. As long as she talked about him, painted him, and looked for him, he would never be gone.

Why discourage that? I thought. What harm did it really do to anyone, even to her? It reminded me of the play *Harvey*, the story of a man who imagined he saw a giant rabbit that was his companion and kept him happy. His sister had come to realize that taking away his imaginary friend would only make him miserable.

Besides, maybe Harvey was really there. What harm was there in believing in magic, believing in something beyond the often dull reality that our monotonous daily lives could cast over us like a net to keep us from the joy of our imaginations?

Yes, maybe Papa really was watching over us, watching over Sylvia especially. His soul, so stained with guilt for many reasons, had to cleanse itself or God would send him to hell. He had to help us in order to save himself. I could believe this. I wouldn't tell Arden my idea, of course, but I could believe it.

"It's time to go to sleep, Sylvia. You can finish working on your picture in the morning, after breakfast."

She nodded, stared at her work for a few moments as if she was looking through a window to be sure Papa was still there and wouldn't be gone in the morning, and then put away her pencils, brushes, and paints neatly in the cabinet Papa had bought for them. She followed me to her room. I watched her prepare for bed. She was quieter than usual. I sensed something different about her. She washed her face and brushed her teeth and then fixed her hair the way I had taught her, but every once in a while, I caught her glancing at herself in the mirror and smiling like someone who knew an important secret.

"Do you think you will be able to sleep alone tonight, Sylvia?"

"Yes, Audrina."

"Will you cry out in the middle of the night or go walking around the house?"

"No," she said.

"You won't go outside without me, will you?"

"No. I don't have to," she said. I knew what she meant, but I didn't want to keep talking about it. Maybe I was afraid to think about it, especially tonight. After all, I had grown up in this house with visions and voices calling to me from the deepest places in my mind born out of my rocking-chair dreams. No one could appreciate what Sylvia was thinking more than I could.

"All right. I'm going to sleep, too, then," I said. I kissed her good night and put out her lights, but I didn't close the door. I never did. She never liked the door closed. The sounds the rest of us made gave her comfort.

Arden was still awake when I got to our bedroom. I was surprised that he was sitting up and reading a folder, looking like he had quickly sobered up.

"I thought you were tired," I said.

"I am, but I remembered some work I had to get done. I don't simply work an eight-hour day, you know. Things happen before the market opens and after it closes. There's not much room for blundering, especially when it's someone else's money and your reputation depends on succeeding even with the smallest portfolios. This is a word-of-mouth business. Success breeds more success. It doesn't take many failures to sink the ship."

"You don't have to tell me all that, Arden. I watched my father work for years and saw how concerned he could be about every little detail."

"Not in the beginning," he muttered. "If there wasn't Whitefern money, what would have become of you all? You'd be out on the street, that's what. He had lots of losses."

"Why think of that now? He became a very well-respected businessman. Everyone makes mistakes, even you, especially in the beginning."

"Yeah, well, whatever . . . he didn't have to concern himself with reporting everything he did to your mother, did he?" he snapped back.

So that was it, I thought. He was putting on this show to emphasize again why he wanted me to sign those papers. He wasn't really doing anything important.

"Did it ever occur to you that I might want something more in my life, Arden? I'd like to be part of the work, the business Papa built. I'd like to do things outside of this house."

He put his papers down. "Oh, really? And just how do you propose to do that and continue to be a nursemaid for your brain-damaged sister?"

"She's not brain-damaged. Don't say that."

"No, she's just slooooow. Call it whatever you want. Well?"

"She'll be taking art lessons. I'll find other ways to keep her occupied and independent. You'd be surprised at some of the progress she's made. She's not as helpless as you think. I'll arrange for more professional tutoring in all subjects. In time—"

"In time, in time . . . what's to say she won't run out and start digging up your father's grave again? Please. You've chosen to keep her here, so you care for her, full-time. So do it. I do the work we need to keep the house and our lives going, and to do that, I need to be in total control. End of story."

He could be so frustrating, I thought. I went into the bathroom and started to wash my face and brush my teeth.

"If we had a child, you wouldn't even hesitate two seconds to do what I ask," he called. "You'd be busy being a real mother instead of a nursemaid to a woman who should be in an institution."

I felt the tears coming to my eyes and put my toothbrush down and took deep breaths. If anyone should realize how sensitive I was to sexual failure, it was Arden, and not simply because he was my husband. He knew the psychological problems I had. He had witnessed why. His own words when we were younger echoed in my mind: "Audrina, I'm sorry. It's not enough to say. I know that. Now I wish I'd stayed and tried to defend you."

Were those words all lies?

I went to the door.

"You know I want to be a real mother, Arden. You know I want that very much. We can keep trying. The doctor didn't say it would absolutely never happen."

"Sure, we can try until I dry up," he muttered.

"Men don't dry up. You were the one who told me Ted Douglas made his much younger wife pregnant, and he's seventy-eight."

"So he says," Arden muttered. "I've seen that young wife of his out and about. Who knows if he really was the one to father her child?"

"Where? Where did you see her?"

"That's not the point. The point is you should think more about being a housewife than a stockbroker. I'm the stockbroker. Get a hobby. Do needlework or join a book club, and have the women over for tea and talk like some of the other brokers' wives I know. I don't know why your father did this, this vengeful thing!" he said, slapping at his papers.

I returned to the bathroom. Neither of us said another word. He had put out his table lamp and turned over so that his back was to me, clearly telling me that he would not be trying for us to have a child tonight. I lay there looking up at the darkness and thinking. Maybe I would give in to what he wanted and just sign the papers. It would bother me for a while that I had defied Papa's final wishes, but I had my husband's wishes to consider. And I did recall my mother telling me not to be too talented, not to be better than my husband at anything: "Men won't approve if it's likely you'll earn more money than they do." Even when I was young, that sounded very unfair to me. Why were men more important than women?

I didn't want to think about it any more tonight, so I closed my eyes and tried to remember happier times, especially the early days, when Arden was so loving and devoted to me.

I dozed off dreaming about a Christmas dinner when Momma and I put up decorations, but something woke me not more than a half hour later. My eyes just popped open. There was a familiar sound in the house, a sound that belonged in nightmares. I turned slowly toward Arden, but he was dead asleep, breathing heavily with an occasional snore.

I sat up and listened harder. It was there. I was not dreaming or imagining it. The sound was hypnotizing. I didn't need anyone to tell me why. It buzzed in my brain. I rose like a sleepwalker and left the bedroom. I thought the hall lights flickered as if the house was sending warnings: *Stay back. Don't go.* The floor creaked, and the wind seemed to be scrubbing the windows. There were many cracks around frames in this old house. The wind whistled through them. Curtains danced, and above me at one point a chandelier gently swayed.

My heart began to pound. Despite all I had learned about the deception under which I had been raised, I couldn't help imagining that there was a first Audrina. For most of my childhood, I would swear on a stack of

Bibles that she whispered to me whenever I was alone. *Be me. You must be me, or I will be dead forever and ever.*

When I told my father about that once, he smiled and kissed me. "Yes," he said. "That's good. That's what we want. Listen for her always."

Practically tiptoeing now, I walked toward the first Audrina's room. It would always be called that, and it would never be used, nor would any of the toys and dolls ever be taken out of it. Arden thought that was sick and sometimes ranted about it.

"We could give all that stuff to the children of poor people. We'll make a big thing of it and have the newspapers take pictures. People will commend us for our charity, and guess what, we'll get more clients, more business. That's the reason most people announce their charitable gifts, most companies. They want more business, tit for tat."

"Just leave it alone," I warned him. At an earlier time, I would add, "Maybe our daughter will have those things."

"Daughter?" He shook his head. "Go call Santa Claus and tell him you've been a good little girl. We'll find a baby wrapped in ribbons on Christmas Day."

When I was just about at the door, I stopped. There was no doubt. I heard the rocking chair rocking. I stepped up and gently opened the door. The sound stopped. I leaned to my left and found the light switch, my heart thumping.

Sylvia looked up at me.

"Sylvia, what are you doing? Why did you come in here? Why are you in the chair?"

She smiled, unafraid, looking at me as though I was the slow-witted sister and not her.

"Papa told me to," she said. "He said whenever I wanted to talk to him, I should rock in the first Audrina's chair, because that was the way you spoke to the first Audrina."

"When did he tell you that?"

"I don't know when. I don't have a watch, and calendars are just full of numbers and days and numbers and days."

"Was this the secret you wouldn't tell me, the secret Papa told you never to tell?"

"Yes, but he said if I came here and rocked in the chair, he would tell me more secrets, Audrina."

For a moment, standing there and looking at my sister, I thought Arden was probably right. I should have emptied this room. Maybe we could erase the past, if not forever, for years and years, or at least put it so far in the back of our minds it wouldn't ruin our present lives.

"Oh, Sylvia," I said. "Poor Sylvia. Come back to bed. Come." I held out my hand.

"You can talk to him, too, Audrina. Just come here and rock," she said, starting to rise so I could take her place.

"Okay. But it's very late, so not tonight. Please, Sylvia, let's go back to bed."

"But Papa's still here."

"He'll always be here, won't he?" I asked.

That pleased her, and, still reluctant, she rose to take my hand. I turned off the light and closed the door behind us.

"Let's try not to wake up Arden," I warned, afraid she would start talking loudly. "You know how cranky he gets when he's awakened in the middle of the night."

She nodded. When we were almost to her room, she paused. She seemed very excited. I looked around. What was she seeing or hearing now?

"What is it, Sylvia?"

"I almost forgot to tell you," she said. "Papa did have a secret for you that I was supposed to tell you."

"What?" I said, so tired I had only inches of patience left for her.

"He said you'll have a baby, not to worry."

"What?"

"He didn't say girl or boy, just baby," she added, and then went into her bedroom.

I followed her, feeling dazed now. I had never mentioned to her that Arden and I had been trying to have a child. She never asked, and she was never in a room when he and I talked about it or my failure to get pregnant. I wasn't confident that she would understand any of the medical information anyway.

I tucked her in and stood there in the dim light spilling through her doorway from the hallway.

"Papa told you I would have a baby?"

"Yes."

"When, Sylvia? When did he tell you this?"

"Tonight," she said. "He was here first in my room.

I knew he was here, so I went to the rocking chair because I knew he had a new secret, and he told me," she said.

"Okay. Just go to sleep now," I told her. I tucked her in, and she turned onto her side, looking very contented. I stood there looking around her room as if I expected to hear or see something.

I went back to Arden's and my bedroom and paused outside our door. For a few moments, I actually debated with myself about returning to the first Audrina's bedroom and sitting in the rocking chair. Regardless of all I knew, despite how the deceptions were exposed, I couldn't completely disregard the power of the rocking chair. There were too many emotional memories. It called to me, not just tonight but many nights, and in the beginning, after I had learned all the lies, I still wanted to feel its power.

It took a great deal of self-control to push these feelings back, but I was in more of a daze than ever, and when I entered our bedroom, I just sat on the bed for a few moments thinking. Of course Sylvia couldn't have gotten such an idea from the spirit of my father while she rocked in the chair. I tried to be logical and decided that Sylvia was more alert than either of us knew, than anyone knew. She might be sitting and looking at pictures or playing with a puzzle, but she wasn't completely shut off from what people were saying nearby. It was wrong to underestimate her. If anyone should know that, I should.

"What the hell is it?" I heard Arden demand. His shout made me jump. He must have turned, opened his eyes, and saw me sitting up, or else he had heard me walk out and back in. "What did she do now?"

My immediate thought was *Don't dare mention the rocking chair.*

"She didn't do anything terrible, Arden. She merely had a dream," I said.

"A dream? Did she scream?"

"A little," I lied.

"Why does that not surprise me? What was the dream?"

"She dreamed I had a baby," I said.

"Oh, she did, huh? Well, that should do it. We don't even have to make love. It will be an immaculate conception. We'll call the baby Sylvia's Wish. Go to sleep, or go back to her," he ordered. "It's the middle of the night. How I do as well as I do under these circumstances is a miracle. Thank goodness I'm dedicated."

I lay back and pulled the blanket over me.

"Baby." I heard him rustling about and then heard him whisper, "Okay."

"What?"

He turned sharply and threw the covers off us as if they were on fire.

"What are you doing?"

"It's baby time. Sylvia has declared it."

"I don't understand, Arden."

"Nothing to understand," he said. "Only to do."

He reached down and pulled my nightgown up and out of his way, practically tearing it off me. I cried out, but before I could say another word, he scooped my legs up and pressed his hardness into me, so roughly I lost my breath for a moment. I was shocked at how fast and easily he could be ready. He didn't bother kissing me or touching me tenderly anywhere. Instead, he hovered above me like a hawk, pouncing.

"Baby, baby, baby," he chanted, as he pushed and prodded, twisting me this way and that so he could be more comfortable. His grunts made it sound like he was lifting a heavy weight. I couldn't stand the sight of him like this and put my hands over my eyes. On he pushed and prodded. I felt like he was tearing me up. The bed sounded like it would crash to the floor. At one point, my head hit the headboard, but he was oblivious to everything but his own animal satisfaction. This wasn't even sex to me; it was anger and revenge.

As so often when we made love, he had his orgasm before I even began to enjoy one, not that I could tonight. It reminded me of our earlier years, even our honeymoon, when he practically raped me because of my fears and hesitation.

"Men will always care more about satisfying themselves than you," Aunt Ellsbeth had told me time after time. "You've got to train them like circus animals. The best way is to insult them."

"Insult them? How can you do that and still have them want to make love to you?" I'd asked her.

"You tell them they have too many premature ejaculations. You'll see," she'd said. "They'll try to prove otherwise, and then you'll enjoy sex."

I had no idea why she thought I would be making

love to many men. Maybe she thought I would be like
Vera, who Arden once told me could go through a college football team in a week. Making love to so many
different men in a short time was terrifying to me. It
actually made me sick to my stomach. He thought that
was funny.

Sometimes I wondered if Arden had really seen
what had happened to me in the woods. How could
he have seen that and not expected me to have negative
feelings when he talked like that about sex? But then
why would he confess to his failure to help me and cry
about how guilty and small that made him feel?

One night, I'd had a terrifying thought that answered that question. What if he wasn't only a witness? He had never turned in any of the boys' names
to the police, and he never even mentioned them now.
Was he worried they would turn on him? Thinking of
that had made me throw up.

I couldn't depend on my memory to deliver the
truth about anything on that horrible afternoon. Faces
and voices were forever blurred, so I couldn't identify
any of them, either. Even the rocking chair didn't
bring it all back, but I wasn't going to complain.

When he was satisfied now, he rolled over and
turned his back on me. Then I heard him say, "There.
Baby, Sylvia's baby," and he laughed.

I lay there, still naked, my body smarting from the
way he had rubbed and pressed on me. My legs were
aching, the insides of my thighs feeling burned.

"Maybe," I said angrily, "if there was more romance in our lovemaking, it would work, and I would

get pregnant. If you would think of me as more than just a vessel in which to empty yourself, the magic of two people making a child would happen as it is supposed to happen. You once loved me that way, didn't you? Or was that a lie? Or are you going to tell me it has withered like a grape on the vine?"

He didn't answer for so long that I thought he had fallen asleep instantly, but suddenly, he turned on me. "You're absolutely right. Romance comes from love, and love comes from respect and obedience. Your father taught me that," he added. "He should have taught it to you better."

I didn't doubt it. How my mother loved my father despite his meanness and selfishness amazed me. When I asked her about it once, she smiled, stroked my hair, and said, "Love is forgiveness, Audrina. That's all it really is, constantly forgiving someone for his weaknesses and hoping that it will bring about some good changes."

Is that what she would tell me now? I turned my back to Arden and tried to think of good things about him, enough so I could find forgiveness. However, before I fell asleep, I thought I wouldn't even dream of becoming pregnant as a result of this lovemaking. There was no baby on his or her way tonight. Sylvia could rock in that chair until daylight. There would be no magic.

No, as much as I wanted to believe it, Papa wasn't whispering any secrets in Sylvia's ear. What she was hearing were my thoughts. When she was rocking in that chair, she was hearing and seeing my dreams. But what would come of it? These dreams were like soap bubbles, capturing the rainbow light for seconds and then popping and dropping like tears to the hard, cold reality beneath them.

I think I passed out rather than falling asleep. For the first time in a long time, Arden was up before me, this time so quiet as not to wake me. That was unusual for him. Normally, because he was the one going to work and I was the one staying home, my having a good night's rest wasn't as important. I could always take a nap later, but he couldn't. When I looked at the clock, I was shocked. I couldn't recall when I had slept this late. My exhaustion from his rough lovemaking must be the reason, I thought, and I got up, wondering if Sylvia had gone down for breakfast. I had taught her how to make the coffee, and there were juices and cereals she liked, but I could count on the fingers of one hand how many times she had woken, dressed, and gone down without me, and that was over years and years.

Now that I was up and recalled how Arden had attacked me, I decided I had to shower before getting dressed. My body still ached in places, and I found scratches on my thighs where he had seized me, clawing at me to mold me into a position comfortable for him. Just washing my face wasn't going to be enough.

There was a chill in the air, and I realized the temperature must have taken a dive during the night. When I glanced out the window, I saw it was raining lightly, the drops sparkling like liquid ice. The wind had stripped many of the trees in the woods of their once pretty orange and brown leaves. The branches looked like the arms of spidery skeletons. I hated this time of the year. It lasted too long for me, and we couldn't avoid it. Our house had woods on three sides.

But at least Whitefern was comfortable all year round now. A few years ago, Papa had upgraded the bathrooms and bedrooms and installed central heating in the old house, except for two unused rooms on the first floor in the rear. Before I took my shower, I put up the thermostat, and afterward, I chose warmer clothes to wear, a pair of heavier jeans and a pink cable-knit sweater. A good part of the morning had already passed. By the time I walked out of the bedroom, I felt certain Sylvia would be up and waiting for me in the kitchen. She hadn't come looking for me. She probably thought I had gone down without her.

I started down the stairs and then hesitated. It was too quiet below. I listened for the sound of the rocking chair but didn't hear that, either. She wouldn't start painting without her breakfast. I went to her bedroom. Of course, my biggest fear was that she had gone out of the house and to the cemetery again. Maybe she had been there most of the night!

I breathed with relief. She was still sleeping, but her blanket was cast aside and she was naked. How odd, I thought. Had it been that hot in here? I looked at her thermostat. She had never touched any thermostats in the house. She didn't understand them. Hers hadn't been pushed up at all, and the room temperature was a little below sixty. I picked up her blanket and put it gently on the bed. She stirred and looked up at me.

"Were you that hot last night, Sylvia?" I asked. Maybe her dreams and tossing and turning had put her in a sweat.

"Hot?"

"Your blanket was on the floor." She looked at herself and then at me, seeming very confused. Then she shook her head. She looked like she was going to cry.

"It's all right. Nothing's wrong, Sylvia. Are you hungry? Let's make a bigger breakfast this morning, omelets and toast, okay?"

"With cheese?"

"Yes," I said, smiling. "With cheese. Do you want to take a shower first?"

"Yes," she said. "Shower."

I picked out clothes for her and set out her shoes and socks while she showered. Then I sat her at her vanity table and brushed out her hair. When I stood behind her and looked at her in the mirror, I thought she was truly beautiful, angelic. For some reason, even more so this morning. Her cheeks looked rosy, her lips full, and her eyes brighter than ever.

What a dirty trick nature had played on her, to give her this much beauty but not enough mentally to have a wonderful life. She could easily attract a handsome, young, wealthy man who would devote himself to her, build her a bigger home than Whitefern and all the jewelry and clothes she could want. Every man like that would turn to look at her now, but a moment later, when he tried to speak to her, he would surely lose his enthusiasm quickly and look for a fast exit.

And she wouldn't even understand why.

"Let's go down," I said.

She put her hand on mine on her shoulder and smiled.

"What, Sylvia?" I asked, smiling back at her.

"Audrina," she said. "Baby. Coming."

A Tree of Secrets

Right after Sylvia and I finished breakfast, there was an early but quick brushing of snowflakes. The rain that had begun falling at daybreak suddenly was captured by a breath of winter. I had intended to go shopping for food but hesitated when I saw the snow. I hoped that it would soon turn back to only cold rain. It did, and the roads didn't freeze over.

Weather of all sorts fascinated Sylvia, especially snowflakes. When she was little, she loved holding up her palms and letting the flakes fall into them and melt. Papa had once told her that rain and melting snowflakes were like the sky crying. That fascinated her. Actually, she loved the surprises of all seasons and the wonder of spring flowers, rich green leaves, and the birds returning after winter. I never appreciated the abundance of nature that surrounded us as much as she did.

Aunt Ellsbeth used to say, "That girl will be a child until her dying day." When it came to her appreciation of Mother Nature, I didn't think that was such a terrible prediction. The rest of us seemed to ignore how beautiful the outside world could be, perhaps because we were so shut up inside our own. Our world was lit with the lights we cast over ourselves with our petty jealousies. Who had time to look at the stars?

Sylvia never paid much attention to what month we were in, and if told, she wouldn't remember when asked later. The poor girl couldn't even remember her own birthday. Whenever I told her it was her birthday tomorrow, she would look astonished. I knew that if I was going to help her develop, I had to work on her memory, get her to associate things. She was improving, but lately I had begun to suspect that the problem was more a question of what she thought was important enough to remember rather than the failure of memory itself.

Anyone who heard this would immediately say, "Well, my birthday is important. How could I ever be expected to forget that?"

But that memory wasn't so simple for Sylvia.

Before she died, Vera was fond of reminding Sylvia that my and Sylvia's mother had died giving birth to her. I caught her saying things like "If you hadn't made it so difficult to be born, your mother would have lived," or "You were so afraid of being born, you tried to stop it, and that killed your mother." Of course, she was right there on every one of Sylvia's birthdays, between the time Sylvia understood what a birthday was and Vera's accidental death, to ask, "How could you be happy it's your birthday? Your mother died on this day. You should spend the whole day kneeling at her grave and asking her to forgive you."

No wonder Sylvia was not looking forward to it

enough to remember it, or if she did remember, she would pretend not to, I was sure. I constantly told her that our mother's dying was not her fault. "A baby can't purposely do that," I told her, after I had shouted at Vera, and Papa told her the same thing in his way, too, although I knew now that he wasn't eager to bring Sylvia home from the hospital quickly. He made all sorts of excuses about her weight, illness, anything he could think of to keep her from being released to our care. It took him quite a while to accept that he would have such a daughter and to look at her and not think about my mother. Nevertheless, to this day, Arden insisted that Sylvia had no concept of what had happened, no matter what terrible things Vera had told her.

"To tell you the truth, I don't think she even understands the concept of death. It wasn't too long ago that I saw her beating a dead bird with a stick to try to get it up and flying again. You've seen her do things like that, too."

I couldn't help wondering if he was right, but the death of your mother was such a deep loss, even a mother you saw only in photographs. How could you not be affected by it, think about it often, and blame yourself?

"I wouldn't worry about it. You have to be an adult to feel guilty," Arden once said as a response to my fears for Sylvia. "You have to develop a conscience, and that takes a little more intelligence than she possesses."

I didn't come right out and ask him the question about him that always haunted me, but I thought it, especially then: *Was that why it took you so long to confess about witnessing what had happened to me and not stopping it or telling anyone else about it so the bad boys could be punished? Is that your excuse, that you were still a child and you didn't have a fully developed conscience yet?*

I did think there was some truth to what he was saying, however. Adults were always warning us not to be in a hurry to grow up. Maybe this was a big part of why. Growing up meant responsibility, and responsibility brought guilt as well as satisfaction. In the end, conscience would always be king.

In any case, I wasn't going to stop trying to help Sylvia grow more mature in any way I could. Educating her was a big part of it. Whether I liked it or not, I had to be as good as any special education teacher in a public school. Papa put the responsibility on me when I was young, and I naturally continued it all after his death. I was motivated by that one big fear Papa had put into my head: if something happened to me, Sylvia would find herself in some institution where she was sure to be abused. I would have let Papa down in a very big way just by dying. I wanted so much for Sylvia to be able to survive on her own, to learn enough of the basics to get by.

Ever since she was fourteen, when I looked at her and realized she had developed a woman's figure almost overnight, I knew she would need special care and protection. I realized she had a beautiful face and a shapely young body. It was then that a girl really became vulnerable and needed to know how to protect herself and what to look for in a man's face that would tell her he was lusting after her only for his own selfish pleasure. I didn't think it was possible to get her to recognize that. She had a child's trusting nature. The warnings and alarm bells simply were not hooked up inside her the way they were for most girls and women.

Of course, she knew nothing about what had happened to me. Even if Arden or Papa had made some reference to it in her presence, it was as if they had spoken a foreign language. For a moment, she might listen, but then it would pass right through her and be gone like a breeze.

Occasionally, when she was younger, Papa would warn her about being alone, especially going too far away from the house by herself. But the smile on her face would tell anyone that she had no idea what terrible things he was afraid would befall her. She would nod and go on with whatever she was doing. He would look at me with frustration but also with a warning that I'd better protect her. I should be her shadow, the way she was his.

I spent almost all my free time with her. I worked on Sylvia's writing, spelling, and math and still did even today. One of the exercises was my dictating our shopping list for the supermarket. She sat at the table and painstakingly copied down the items, sometimes looking at the boxes or bottles to get the spelling right. I was amused at how important that was to her. Lately, she had become much better at it. She had good handwriting, probably because of her artistic talent. If a cashier saw our list, he or she usually had a compliment for whoever had printed it.

"My sister does that," I would say proudly.

Nothing brought Sylvia's shyness out more than when she was given a compliment. She would always look down to hide her smile, and her face would flush with embarrassment. I would tell her to say thank you, and sometimes she did, but usually with her head lowered, afraid to look strangers in the eye.

At the supermarket today, though, she behaved differently. I didn't have to tell her to say thank you, and when she did, she looked at the person to whom she was speaking. She was also more energetic and eager to find the items on the shelves. I stood back for most of the shopping and watched her go down the list, filling our cart without my telling her where to go.

If Arden could see her today, I thought, he wouldn't ridicule her so much or belittle the work I had been doing with her all these years.

Of course, I wondered what had given her this burst of energy and new self-confidence. From the little she had said about the night before, about going to the first Audrina's bedroom and sitting in the rocking chair, I gathered that what she had imagined had made her feel more important, because Papa had come to her and not to me or to Arden. She was eager to get home, help me put away the groceries, and go back up to the cupola to finish her new picture.

"I'm going to speak to someone today to help arrange for you to have an art teacher come to the house to show you things, different techniques and ways to make your pictures more beautiful, Sylvia. You still want me to do that?"

She thought a moment and nodded.

"All right. When I find the right person, Sylvia, I would like you not to talk to him or her about Papa and the rocking chair. Papa and the rocking chair are our secret, right?"

"Yes. I'll never tell," she said, putting her hand over her heart and hooking her pinkie with mine to make a pinkie promise. Like a little girl, she obviously enjoyed the idea of having a secret with her older sister.

"Okay," I said, "our secret."

After she went up to the cupola, I called the first person who came to mind for advice about something like this, Mrs. Haider, the retired principal of Whitefern High School. She had always been very kind to me and had taken a personal interest in me when I finally began to attend the public school. Because Whitefern was a relatively small town, our school was small enough for her to know some private information about her students.

She knew I had been homeschooled, of course, and that I had lost my mother when she had given birth to Sylvia. She knew of Sylvia, but, like most people, she didn't know very much about her, because in those years, Sylvia was rarely seen. After her retirement, I had seen Mrs. Haider occasionally in the village, and she was always quite friendly and very correct about how she asked questions. I never got the impression that she was a town gossip. I had no hesitations about telling her things concerning my family. She always ended her conversations with me by saying, "I hope all goes well with you, Audrina."

Her smile was sincere. She was a pretty woman, always perfectly put together, with coordinating colors and style. Her green eyes were still vibrantly emerald and contrasted nicely with her snow-white hair layered in an attractive bob.

Mrs. Haider was a widow with three adult children, all of whom had families but lived far away, her son in New York and her two daughters in South Carolina. She had seven grandchildren and lived in a modest two-story house on the north side of Whitefern.

When she answered her phone this morning, she sounded absolutely delighted to hear from me. She listened patiently while I described Sylvia as best I could and what I wanted for her now.

"That's very commendable of you, Audrina. I think that's a brilliant idea, and I know just the person for this assignment. As it turns out, Mr. Price, one of our art teachers, retired just last year, and from what his wife has been telling me, he is quite bored. They're not travelers, and he hates golf," she said, laughing. "Why don't I call him for you and, if he's interested, give him your phone number?"

"Thank you, Mrs. Haider," I said. "That's very kind."

"Oh, indeed," she said. "I, too, like the idea that I can continue to be of some use." She laughed again.

After I hung up, I called Arden at his office.

"He's in a meeting, Mrs. Lowe," Mrs. Crown said. "Is this an emergency?"

She sounded annoyed. A woman in her forties and married to a bank teller, Barton Crown, a man Arden called an untrustworthy leech, Mrs. Crown was a little too protective of Arden, in my opinion. I didn't think there was any doubt she'd rather he was her husband. She was a plain-looking woman with one of those complexions Momma used to call "an unripe peach." Her makeup seemed to fade as the day progressed, leaving her looking bloodless, with dark brown eyes. Aunt Ellsbeth would say, "She shows cleavage in hopes you won't look at her face."

"Oh, no, but please have him call me as soon as he's free."

"Yes, I will," she said. "As soon as that's possible."

I didn't say thank you. I just hung up.

Less than a half hour later, Mr. Price called to tell me he would love to be of some assistance.

"When would you like me to begin?" he asked, sounding very eager. I guessed Mrs. Haider wasn't exaggerating when she said he was bored with his retirement.

"As soon as you wish," I said. We hadn't even discussed the cost.

"I could come this afternoon to get acquainted with the young lady. How's three o'clock?"

"Yes, that would be fine," I said. "Perhaps we should discuss the cost."

"Oh, I'm sure we'll come to a mutually satisfactory arrangement," he said. "I think it's important first that your sister be comfortable with me."

He was right. I wondered what he knew about

Sylvia and what he didn't. I didn't want any brutal disappointments to occur. I was afraid of how that might disturb Sylvia, especially if someone rejected working with her because he thought she wasn't capable of learning. Arden, of course, would feel vindicated and say something like "I told you so."

"Do you know anything about my sister?" I asked.

"I know she's been homeschooled?"

"She was born premature and had to remain in an institutional setting until she was about two and a half. If she had attended a public school, she would surely have been placed in special education. She still needs me to look after her, but she is very pleasant and courteous. However, she is quite sensitive," I added, loading my voice with warning. "She can tell when someone is talking down to her or looking down at her."

"I taught special education students," he said. "No worries at all."

"She has taken to art, loves to draw and paint. She can spend hours and hours doing it. I've been doing the best I can with other aspects of her education, but when it comes to art, no one has taught her anything formally. She doesn't have that long an attention span except when she's working on her art, but I'm not sure how she would pay attention to instruction."

"A challenge. Love it," he said.

I had to smile. He was truly a bored man. "Okay, then let's see how it works out today at three."

I immediately started up to the cupola to tell Sylvia and to talk to her about our lunch, but the phone rang before I reached the stairs. It was Arden. Apparently, telling him I had called had become possible for Mrs. Crown.

"What?" he said sharply when I answered the phone.

"What? Can't you at least pretend to be courteous, Arden, and ask how I am first?"

"I'm busy, Audrina. There is no time for small talk here. I know women feed on small talk like birds on grass seed, but it's a particularly busy day. There's been a big drop in crude oil this morning. You know what crude oil is?" he asked, raising his voice bloated with sarcasm.

"Stop it, Arden. Of course I know what crude oil is. I called to tell you I'm arranging for an art tutor for Sylvia. I'll be paying him from the household account."

"Waste of money," he said. "What about the papers I want you to sign? I'll tell you where to meet me, and . . ."

"We'll talk about that later, Arden. I'm just letting you know I have the art tutor coming at three today to meet Sylvia. Unless there's a problem the teacher sees, I will contract with him today."

"Who is he?"

"Arthur Price, a retired high school art teacher."

"How old is he?"

"He's not that old, Arden."

"I'm not worried about him being *too* old." He sighed. "All right, do what you want. I repeat, it's a waste of time and money, but I have to get back to important things."

"This is important, Arden. She's my sister, and

she's your sister-in-law. My father expected we would look after her."

"Oh, spare me. Your father expected . . . Well, I expected things, too. Women can get so emotional. It's like they have a trigger finger on their emotions, which is why they don't belong in business, especially a business like this," he emphasized. " 'Bye," he said, and hung up before I could say a word in my defense.

I was so frustrated that I wished I could strangle the phone and squeeze every last word he uttered out of the wires and out of my mind. Up the stairs I went, pounding every step as if I was stamping on Arden's face. When I entered the cupola, I found Sylvia sitting and staring at a blank sheet of paper, her pencil in her hand, poised in the air like a knife she was about to stab into something.

"Where's your picture?" I asked.

She turned to look at me, her face twisted in an expression of anger and frustration. "Done," she said, nodding to the picture now lying on a long table.

I looked at it and saw that not much more had been added to it. It still fascinated me. I put it down and turned back to her. She had returned to staring at her blank sheet.

"What are you trying to draw and paint now, Sylvia?"

She looked at me, deciding whether to answer, I guessed. "What makes a baby a boy?" she asked.

"What?"

"Boys and girls come from the same mother, so who's first? And why didn't Papa ever have a boy?"

How was I going to explain this? Explain the X and Y chromosomes? No way. "Why do you want to know?"

"Because Papa told me a baby, but he didn't tell me if the baby was a boy or a girl," she said. I nearly laughed at the way she said it. She sounded condescending, like I was dumb not to realize that.

"Why is that important right now, Sylvia? Many people, maybe most, like it to be a surprise. Except for those people who want to paint nursery rooms and choose clothes way ahead of time," I added, more for myself. "So?"

"I have to draw the baby, Audrina. If I don't draw the baby, the baby will not come," she said.

I was beginning to get a headache. How was she coming up with these crazy ideas? Maybe Arden wasn't so wrong. Maybe the time had come for me to find some help with Sylvia. After all, I did have a life of my own, or I thought I did. The truth I didn't want to face was that what was holding Sylvia back from the world was holding me back, too, as long as I was chained to her daily. For a good part of my life, I had spent most of my time inside one house. For a short while, I had broken free of it, but I was right back in it now, its walls hovering around me, making me feel cloistered. Sometimes I felt I had been swallowed. The walls seemed to quiver like the inside of its lungs.

Taking walks outside around the house wasn't enough, and our short shopping trips were all full of purpose, with little or no fun. There was nothing left to explore here but my own demons, and I was tired of that. I certainly didn't want to start down a path similar to the one Sylvia had to follow, taking in everything outside slowly, in small, careful bites, but what choice was I giving myself? I wasn't trying to make friends, and I certainly wasn't joining any organizations that would lead to making friends. Sometimes I feared that someone who didn't know us would look at us and wonder who was the slow-witted one.

"Maybe whether it's a boy or a girl will come to you," I said sharply. It was not unreasonable of me to run out of patience, especially when I chastised myself for using Sylvia to justify my being such a prisoner of Whitefern. "Forget about all that, and listen to me. I have found a good art teacher for you. He used to teach in the high school. His name is Mr. Price, and he will be here this afternoon to meet you. Do not tell him what you want to draw just yet. Let him teach you the things you have to know in order to draw and paint better, okay? He might start you drawing an apple or a banana or something like that. You do what he asks and what he tells you to do. Okay?"

She didn't look happy.

"This is what you wanted, isn't it? To learn how to do this well? I'm not going to spend the money if you don't want to do it, Sylvia. Well? Do you or don't you?" I asked, practically shouting.

"I do."

"Good. Let's have you change your clothes and fix your hair. We'll talk with Mr. Price in the living room, and afterward we'll show him what supplies you have here. We'll get you whatever else you need. I'm sure he'll give us a list, and tomorrow morning you and I can go shopping."

She looked at the blank sheet without answering me.

"Sylvia!" I said sharply. "Did you hear me? Concentrate on what I'm telling you."

I rarely snapped at her like this, but she was making me nervous. Papa, the rocking chair, babies . . . I had driven all the visions and dreams, all the ghosts and whispers, down as deeply as I could in my memory. Stirring it was like throwing rocks at the hives of hornets.

She stood up reluctantly and, with her head lowered, followed me out and down to her room.

"Now, it's important that you make a good impression on your art tutor, Sylvia," I said in a calmer, more motherly tone. "I know you don't meet many strangers, and you're very shy, but I don't want you looking at other things or letting your attention wander when he asks you questions or speaks to you," I said while laying out her fresh clothes. "Teachers think girls and boys who do that are unteachable, and you don't want him to think that, right?"

She shook her head and listened to me as I went on with instructions, but I could see her mind was still elsewhere, pulling her away every few moments to look up toward the cupola, as if she had left a half-baked new baby up there. She could be like this from time to time. Once her mind enveloped a thought or an idea, getting her to put it aside, even temporarily, was like prying open a stubborn clam.

Would she be like this with Mr. Price? He'd see immediately that he was wasting his time with her. I'd feel like a fool, and Arden would strut around with his arrogant, masculine superiority and his infuriating "I told you so" look, which he could put on as quickly as a Halloween mask.

Nevertheless, I remained hopeful. I fixed Sylvia's hair and straightened her clothes to make her as presentable as possible. I had to be ready for anything, but I had to be realistic, too. If Mr. Price thought she was unteachable, even he, a man bored with his present life, would not attempt the lessons. Money didn't seem to matter to him. I hoped he was sincere when he said he welcomed a challenge. She was certainly going to be that.

"We'll prepare some nice biscuits and tea now, okay, Sylvia? I'd like you to do most of that and bring it out when I tell you to, understand?"

"Chocolate biscuits?"

I recalled the last time we had made them and how she had gotten the chocolate all over her dress and had to be continually told to wipe her mouth.

"I think he likes the plain ones," I said. Little lies were often the glue that held more important truths together. Papa had taught me that.

Disappointed, Sylvia followed me out and down to the kitchen, where I put her to work making biscuits while I vacuumed the living room and polished the furniture to brighten things up. Then I went to the powder room to make myself presentable, too. I hated how haggard I could look sometimes. Frustration, worry, and anger were like the three witches of *Macbeth* in this house, toiling and mixing their evil brew.

Promptly at three, the doorbell rang. Being on time was probably embedded in a schoolteacher after as many years as Mr. Price had worked. Part of the daily instruction I gave Sylvia, especially in the past few years, was how to greet people who came to our door. I spent hours and hours role-playing with her to show her how to introduce herself and be courteous to guests. Papa was very proud of the success I'd had. Aunt Ellsbeth, along with Arden and especially Vera, often ridiculed my efforts and said things like "You're trying to put clothes in a closet without any hangers." I ignored them, and whenever Sylvia did perform perfectly, they usually smirked and looked away with the comment that she'd forget next time.

I stepped into the kitchen. "Go answer the door, Sylvia," I ordered. "It's your art teacher. Introduce yourself after you greet him."

She looked annoyed for a moment. I kept my stern gaze on her and was reminded of how Vera could pout and stomp when told to do something she didn't want to do. Petulant, Sylvia went to the front door. I stayed back, holding my breath.

"Well, hello," I heard Mr. Price say. "I'm Arthur Price."

"Hello," Sylvia said. "Welcome to Whitefern. I'm Sylvia."

She did that well enough, but she didn't step back, leaving him in the doorway. It was awkward.

I hurried toward them. "Oh, do come in, Mr. Price," I said. "I'm Audrina Lowe."

"Yes, yes," he said, stepping in. He was short,

barely a few inches taller than I was, with a trim, graying goatee like some French artist on the Left Bank of Paris. He was balding, the patches of gray-black hair over his temples looking pasted onto his scalp. He had a jolly, Santa Claus face with bright blue eyes and was wearing a dark blue jacket and tie.

I nodded at Sylvia to close the door behind him. The afternoon breeze was quite cool and sharp. I led Mr. Price into the living room. He looked about with great interest, like some buyer of antiques who had wandered into one of the biggest discoveries of his career.

"What an amazing house," he said. "These paintings are most interesting."

Like any man, he focused quickly on our famous naked lady on the chaise eating grapes. He glanced quickly at me.

"And the clocks and vases, all family heirlooms, I imagine?"

"Some are," I said. "Please, have a seat." I indicated the sofa Papa had redone only a year ago. Momma had loved lying on it. "Sylvia will bring us some tea and biscuits," I said, and I nodded at her again.

"Thank you," he said, rubbing his palms together. "Winter's coming earlier this year for sure. You can smell the snow."

Sylvia looked at us. "Smell it?" she asked. "Snow? It doesn't smell."

"Well, not snow, exactly," he said, smiling. "It's just . . . I mean, it feels like winter's coming."

Sylvia glanced at me as if we had let a madman into the house and then continued to the kitchen.

"What a beautiful young lady," he said immediately. "I know a lot of artists, some not so amateur, who would love to have her for a model. Those eyes, startlingly beautiful, almost exotic, and a complexion like alabaster."

"She wants to be the artist, not the model," I said, probably too sharply. It occurred to me, maybe for the first time, that I could actually be jealous of Sylvia. It made me a little ashamed. It was like envying a poor girl's single doll when you had dozens.

"Of course," he said. "So is there a special place where your sister would work? Certainly not in here. I wouldn't want to get any paint on this rug." He looked down at the Turkish rug that had been there as long as I could remember.

"Oh, yes. Before my father passed away, he established a room in our cupola as a sort of studio for her. It's two flights up, if that's all right. We don't have an elevator."

"That's not a problem." He patted his ballooning stomach. "Now that I'm retired, I've gained five pounds. My wife is always after me to do more exercise. Artists and teachers sit around too much. So going up and down stairs sounds good." He looked toward the stairway.

Despite how beautiful the balustrade was, it was difficult for me to look at the stairway and not think of it as treacherous. Surely, I thought, he knew of our history, how Aunt Ellsbeth, Billie, and Vera had died on those stairs. If he had any fear, he kept it well disguised behind his appreciative smile.

Sylvia came in carrying the silver tray with the teapot and cups.

Mr. Price stood up. "Can I help?" he asked.

"She's fine," I said. "Please. Sit."

He did, and Sylvia put the tray on the table. I wanted her to demonstrate that she was capable of basic things and could easily grow and learn.

"Biscuits," she said, more as if she was reminding herself, and turned quickly.

He smiled. "Venus," he muttered after her, and then turned to me. "How long has she been interested in art?"

"As long as I can remember her being interested in anything," I said. I began to pour the tea. "Sugar?"

"Maybe one, if we don't tell my wife. And don't tell her about any biscuits. She's got me on a strict diet."

Sylvia returned with the biscuits and put them on the table. "I like chocolate," she said, still grumpy about it.

"Chocolate?" He looked at them.

"We have plain with a touch of vanilla today," I said firmly.

"Oh, I like that." He plucked one off the dish.

"I like chocolate," Sylvia repeated.

I raised my eyes toward the ceiling.

"So, Sylvia, what do you like to draw and paint? Things in nature, people, animals?"

She looked at me. "Whatever I'm told to draw," she said.

I felt my heart sink.

"Told? Who tells you?"

"She means she likes to draw what people like to see. My father used to ask her to draw birds in trees."

"Oh, I see. Well, we'll start with going over colors and then learning perspective. How's that sound?"

"I want to draw and paint," she said.

"That's what he means, Sylvia."

"Don't worry. I'll get her to understand," he told me, chewing on his biscuit. "I spent years in the grade school before teaching junior and senior high. Say, this is a very good biscuit. Homemade?"

"Sylvia made them," I said.

"Did she? Well, if you can make biscuits this good, you can paint the *Mona Lisa*."

"Who's that?" she asked.

"Oh, it's a famous painting. I'll bring a book that has many great paintings in it so you can see all the styles in which artists have worked."

"We have art books, Mr. Price. Sylvia wants to be active. Art history is a little beyond our goals here. How often do you want to give her lessons?" I asked. "And when?"

"I can be here in the afternoon." He leaned toward me. "Probably only an hour at first. I know about attention span," he assured me, nodding. "Say, three times a week?"

"Would you like that, Sylvia? Three times a week?"

"I want to do art every day," she said.

He smiled. "Oh, you'll have homework to do every day," he said.

She looked suspicious but then nodded.

"Why don't we look at your studio and see what you have, and then I'll make a list of things you'll need," Mr. Price said. He thought for a moment and then plucked another biscuit off the dish. "Let's keep this a secret." He winked at me.

Sylvia's eyes widened instantly. "Secret?"

"He means he doesn't want his wife to know he's eating what she doesn't want him to eat, Sylvia. You won't tell her, will you?" I said, trying to insert a joke quickly.

She shook her head. "Is she coming today, too?"

"No."

Mr. Price sipped his tea. Sylvia hadn't poured herself a cup or taken a biscuit. She had yet to sit.

"Let's go show Mr. Price your studio, okay?"

"Okay," she said, and he and I stood up. I nodded at Sylvia for her to go first, and we followed.

"My sister tends to take everything said to her literally," I warned.

"I understand."

We started up behind her. "She has a little bit of a wild imagination," I added, with the same cautionary tone.

"All artists need that," he replied.

"What were you thinking of in terms of cost?" I asked. I was getting mixed messages, wondering now if I was doing the right thing. I hoped he wasn't someone who would carry tales from Whitefern. There were enough rumors about us.

"How's twenty-five dollars an hour sound?"

"It sounds okay," I said. I had no idea whether it

was fair, and I was sure Arden would have something negative to say about it.

"You can pay me every two weeks so it's not a chore," he added.

We started up to the cupola. I could hear his heavy breathing already.

"This will be good for me," he said, aware that I heard it.

"I hope it will be good for us all," I replied.

Sylvia opened the door to the cupola, and we stepped in. Her sheet of paper was on the easel, but I could have sworn it was completely blank when we had left earlier.

Right now, there was the start of a baby's head.

Voices in the Brush

I was still trembling a little when I walked Mr. Price to the door to say good-bye. Sylvia followed closely behind us and stood behind me. When I glanced at her and nodded at Mr. Price, she moved quickly to say good-bye properly, adding, "I'm pleased to meet you."

"To have met you," I prompted, and she repeated it.

"And I am very pleased to have met you, too, Sylvia. I look forward to helping you with your artwork," Mr. Price told her. He offered her his hand.

She looked at it suspiciously and then touched it as if it might be a hot stovetop and quickly stepped back.

He smiled at me and said, "She's precious."

He had dictated a list of supplies, and we had decided he would begin in two days. He liked Sylvia's studio space, his only criticism being that there was not enough light. I assured him that we would bring up two more lamps.

The sun was already losing its grip on the day. Fall twilights were much earlier, so the shadows were thicker in and out of Whitefern. Papa used to call fall the "dying season." Trees were beautiful only for a short while with their brown and yellow leaves. "It's like a last breath of beauty," he had said. "Then come the skeletons."

I waited for Mr. Price to go to his car and wave to me before I closed the door. For a moment, I stood there catching my breath. Without my asking her to, Sylvia began to clean away the tea and the remaining biscuits. She was still mumbling about chocolate being better. I picked up what was left and followed her to the kitchen.

Upstairs in the cupola, she had not said anything about the partial drawing. When Mr. Price had asked her what she was doing, she didn't respond. He had looked at me, and I'd changed the subject quickly. I hoped he hadn't seen the surprise on my face when we had first entered.

In the kitchen, Sylvia was immediately busy putting the leftover biscuits into a plastic container. She was plucking them off the plate as if they were dead insects.

"When did you go back up and start drawing the baby, Sylvia?" I asked.

She ignored me and began washing the cups and the teapot.

I drew closer. "Sylvia, I thought you said you needed to know if it was a boy or a girl before you could start to draw a baby."

She paused and looked at me like a child who had been caught with her hand in the cookie jar. "I thought if I started, Papa would tell me," she said. She returned to the cups and the teapot.

"Did he?"

She shook her head. "Not yet." Her eyes widened with a thought. "Maybe he was waiting for me to learn more art and do better."

"All right." *Enough of this*, I thought. *Why am I encouraging her wild imagination?* "So you like Mr. Price and want to learn from him?"

"He didn't say he likes chocolate biscuits."

"Forget the biscuits, Sylvia. Do you like him enough to want him to give you instruction with your art?"

"He didn't tell me anything to do."

"He's coming back for that in two days. He'll be here at the same time three times a week, remember? Is that all right?"

"Yes," she said. "But next time, I want to make chocolate biscuits, Audrina." She spoke firmly, as firmly as Papa when his mind was made up about something.

"Okay. Make chocolate biscuits, Sylvia. Make tons and tons of chocolate biscuits," I nearly screamed. Anyone could have heard the tense impatience in my voice, but she simply smiled. I wondered if it was a good thing never to realize how much someone was annoyed at you. You went on your merry way, doing whatever you were doing, not feeling guilt and rarely upset with yourself.

On the other hand, I was frustrated. I went to the freezer to take out pork chops and keep myself busy.

"We're making grilled pork chops in plum sauce tonight, Sylvia. Concentrate on that now."

"Can I do the sauce?" she asked immediately.

Gradually, I had been teaching her more sophisticated recipes. She could make a nice cheese omelet or bake cookies, biscuits, and some cakes. Last Christmas, I'd taught her how to make a turkey stuffing and marshmallow sweet potatoes. The more delicate something was, the more intense was her concentration. Ironically, the easiest things bored her.

"Okay," I said. "Get out the bag of plums."

This was another of Arden's favorite dinners. Why it was so important to please the men in this house I never knew, but if you disappointed Papa, you might expect the ceiling to fall and the walls to cave in. It was the same for Arden. As Aunt Ellsbeth often said, "Men are the sun, and we are the planets circling them and held in their grip."

I took out the ingredients for the sauce—ginger, garlic, shallots, soy sauce, and honey. It was a recipe Arden's mother, Billie, had taught me. She had tried to teach it to Vera, but Vera hated working in the kitchen. She hated all household chores. Whenever she was given something to do, she would try to get me to do it for her. Sometimes she threatened me by saying she would break something and blame it on me if I didn't do it.

The memories streamed by like the echoes of nightmares.

Suddenly, I heard the front door open and close. I rushed out of the kitchen and was surprised to see Arden home so early. When he saw me, he raised his arm to show me he was holding a big manila envelope. He waved it like a winning lottery ticket.

"I've brought it all home. Mr. Johnson understands how busy you are here with Sylvia and agreed to let you sign and put your fingerprint on the page for notarization without him being present. He doesn't do this for everyone. He's bending the law quite a bit; it's a special favor for us. Let's get right to it," he said, and sat on the settee. "I want to turn it in first thing in the morning." He put the envelope on the table and began taking out documents and the ink pad for a fingerprint.

"I told you that I want to think about it first, Arden. Why are you rushing me?"

"Why? Why?" He slapped the table with his palm and sat back, folding his arms across his chest like a boy about to go into a sulk. "I'm chasing new, high-net-worth clients, Audrina," he began, speaking with obviously forced self-control. "More than likely, these people will do their due diligence and investigate us inside and out before they place millions of dollars in our hands. They'll certainly question why your father left the majority percentage of the company to you, someone who doesn't work there and doesn't even have a broker's license. That's what we call in the business a red flag. It will drive them away."

"I'm thinking of getting my broker's license," I said.

"What? You're thinking what?" His eyes widened, and he turned red with rage.

"Don't be so shocked at the idea, Arden. I was the one who tutored you in the beginning to help you get your license."

"That was years ago."

"Nothing's changed. The stock market is still the stock market."

"Yes, a great deal has changed. There are new laws, regulations."

"I'll study up on it. You know I'm good at that. Aunt Ellsbeth and even your mother told me I should have gone to college. I was always on the honor roll in school."

He stared coldly. "I can't believe I'm hearing this." He shook his head the way someone would shake water out of his ears after swimming.

"It might be very attractive for our company to have a husband-and-wife team," I suggested. "That, it seems to me, would make new clients comfortable and be a great advertisement."

"A great advertisement? Next, you'll want to wear my pants."

"Stop it, Arden. Don't treat me like a child."

"Then don't act like one."

"At least, let's let some time pass so we can think about it."

"I should think about this? I'll tell you what I think about, Audrina. I think about why I'm doing all this, why we have all this, and why I work harder and harder. We have no children. We have a mentally slow young woman to care for. That's all. And ourselves, of course, but where's the future?"

"We could adopt, I suppose. If I don't get pregnant soon," I said.

"Soon? It's been years. When will you realize it won't happen?"

He looked away for a moment and then turned back to me, his eyes smaller. He looked like he was about to cry, like a little boy who couldn't go out to play.

"And adopt a baby? You say it so casually. What about my feelings? I'd like to have my blood passed on, too, you know. I am not excited about making someone else's unwanted child the heir to my fortune, my heritage."

"I'm sorry, Arden," I said. I really did feel sorry for him now. "Let's take a breath and give everything more thought. I'm not saying you're wrong. Papa taught me that the best decisions come after they're nurtured and turned around and around to check for cracks or dents in your thinking. Every decision is—"

"Yes, I know, like a birth. He said that so much that I felt like checking into a maternity ward."

I smiled. "I'm making one of your favorites, grilled pork chops in plum sauce. Your mother used to make that. She taught me."

He looked down at the papers and then began stuffing them back into the envelope. "I need a drink," he said.

Sylvia came to the doorway. "Sauce is ready," she announced, smiling from ear to ear.

"Sauce is ready? You let her make it?" Arden asked, astonished.

"She's good at it, Arden. You'd be surprised at what she's learned in the kitchen."

"Might be poison, for all we know. I guess I need this just in case."

He poured himself a hefty glass of bourbon. Then he looked at Sylvia, who was still standing there smiling at him. Her right cheek had a streak of plum sauce across it.

"Looks like she was finger painting with our dinner."

"Oh, she just touched herself after handling the plums. Every cook gets a little messy."

"Cook. Artist. Next she'll be CEO of our company," he said, and gulped his drink, his eyes still on her. "What happened with her art teacher?"

"I hired him. He'll be here day after tomorrow. He'll come three times a week at first, an hour each time, for twenty-five dollars an hour."

"Twenty-five dollars? Are you crazy? That's seventy-five a week to babysit. You might as well open the window and toss the money out," he said, and finished his drink.

"If it doesn't help, we'll stop it, but for now, she is happy about it, Arden. You know," I added, "her name is on the estate Papa left, too. We hardly spend any of her money on her."

"I know. I know plenty," he said, and poured himself more bourbon. He looked at us both while he sipped his drink and then turned and headed for the stairs. "I'm going to wash up and get out of this monkey suit that I have to wear every day to be sure our business is a success and I can make enough money for you to waste."

We watched him head up the stairs, pausing to sip his drink. Sylvia looked at me and then stepped toward the stairway, as if she expected she'd have to charge up and save him the way she had saved Papa from falling backward. But Arden continued on, his anger marching him the rest of the way.

"Let's set the table, Sylvia," I said.

Arden came down a half hour later. He did look refreshed and relaxed, but there was something else different about him. He wore the wry smile of someone who was carrying a secret full of self-satisfying irony. He opened a bottle of Papa's prize red wine, which was to be used only for very special occasions, and poured a glass for each of us. We usually didn't give Sylvia much alcohol of any kind. Arden knew why.

Once, years ago, Vera had gotten her terribly drunk. She'd thrown up over everything in her room — her bed, her rug, her desk. The reaction she was having terrified her, and she flailed about, crying and waving her arms. Vera was hysterical with laughter when I came upon them, and when Papa found out, he went into a rage and beat Vera with his belt until Aunt Ellsbeth stopped him by clinging to his arm so tightly he lifted her off her feet with every attempted swing.

I actually felt sorrier for Vera that day than I did for Sylvia, because Sylvia simply fell asleep after we bathed her and changed her into her nightgown. Vera was off in her room whimpering like a beaten puppy. Aunt Ellsbeth didn't show her any sympathy, despite stopping Papa from beating her to death. She went to Vera's room and told her she had gotten what she deserved. She didn't even look after her welts. Some of them were bleeding. After Aunt Ellsbeth left, I went to see Vera. She was curled in the fetal position on her bed, shivering with pain.

"You need to wash those welts, Vera," I said, "before they get infected."

"Leave me alone. You're happy this happened to me."

"I'm not happy. You shouldn't have done that to Sylvia, but I'm not happy to see you so beaten," I said. I said it sincerely enough for her to turn and look at me.

"Okay. Go get me a warm washcloth and some antiseptic gel and some Band-Aids," she ordered.

When she took off her dress, I saw how Papa had hit her around her waist and thighs. She lay back so I could wash every welt and put on the medicine and bandages where she needed them.

"You know why he hit me so hard, don't you?" she asked as I worked.

"Because you did a bad thing to Sylvia," I said.

"No. It's because he loves me the most and wants me to be the perfect Audrina, not you," she said. Then she leaned forward to whisper, "He even told me to sit in the rocking chair so I could learn her special gifts."

"No, he didn't," I said.

She smiled through her pain and lay back. "He loves me more," she insisted. I watched her close her eyes and smile, despite what must have been terrible stings and aches.

I went back to sit with Sylvia, who was asleep, and brushed her hair off her face.

"I won't let her do mean things to you again," I told her. "I won't let anyone, sweet Sylvia."

The memory drifted away like smoke, but also like smoke, it left a bitter taste in my mouth.

"A toast, then," Arden said now, raising his glass after pouring the wine. "To the baby who is coming, who is always coming."

"A boy or a girl?" Sylvia quickly asked.

"Why, a boy, of course," he said.

"Who told you? Papa?"

He looked at me and smiled. "Of course," he said. "Who else?"

He drank his wine in one gulp and poured another. I looked at Sylvia. She drank hers quickly, too quickly, and he rose to pour more for her.

"Don't," I said. "You know she can't handle it, Arden."

"Oh, a little more," he said. "To celebrate."

"Celebrate what?"

"Sylvia is getting an art teacher, and I'm getting a partner, apparently." He laughed and drank.

I served the salad, and we began to eat our first real formal dinner since Papa had died. I looked longingly toward his empty chair. Arden would never have said these things if Papa were still alive. Arden saw my gaze and read my thoughts.

"Tomorrow night, Sylvia," he said, "you set my place there. It's time we faced the reality. I'm the head of Whitefern now, no matter what our estate documents read. Is that all right, Audrina?"

"No. It's not all right," I said. "But you can sit there.

Maybe it will help you think more of yourself. No matter what happened to him or to people he loved, Papa kept his self-respect."

"Why is it that after people die, we think only good things about them and forget the bad?"

"I think about it all, Arden. Your mother told me to be that way. She knew I was proud of my father, even though there were many times I disliked him, regretfully so. She taught me that none of us is all good or all bad."

"Meaning me?"

"Meaning all of us, Arden, so yes, you, too."

"What about you, Sylvia? Do you think about all this? Do you think everyone is bad and good? Do you think?"

"Stop teasing her, Arden."

"Teasing? Am I teasing you, Sylvia?"

He laughed, and we began to eat in silence. When I looked at Sylvia, I saw how happy she was despite Arden's ridiculing her. At first, I didn't understand why. Then I thought about what Arden had said and why that would make her happy. She was already planning it, I was sure.

She could finish her drawing of the baby.

I saw it in the way she rushed cleaning up after dinner. I didn't want her to be deeply disappointed, even though I wished in my heart of hearts that it was all true, that a baby was going to come.

"You must not pay attention to everything Arden says, Sylvia," I warned her. "He likes to tease you. He teases me, too."

She nodded, holding her soft smile as if I was the one who didn't understand. I helped her finish so she could go up to the cupola to work, and then I went into the living room, where Arden was having a brandy. His face was red from all the alcohol he had consumed.

"You can leave the documents here tomorrow," I told him. "I'll read them."

He widened his eyes. "And?"

"I said I'll read them and talk to you tomorrow."

"Right. Tomorrow." He reached for the *Wall Street Journal*, but I knew he wasn't going to read anything. He was simply going to hold it up and fume behind it.

"I'm going up. I'm a little tired tonight."

I scooped up the envelope and headed up the stairs. I had drunk too much wine myself, deliberately making sure there wasn't too much left for Sylvia—or for Arden. He'd wanted to open another bottle, but I had talked him out of it.

I prepared myself for bed and then went up to the cupola. I didn't want Sylvia staying up there deep into the night. She had no concept of time, especially when she was drawing or painting. She had the outline of the baby completed and was sitting there and staring at it. She turned and looked up at me.

"Is he going to be a pretty baby?" she asked me.

"We're a handsome family, Sylvia. Everyone was very good-looking, as you can see from old photographs. Momma was so beautiful that Papa was afraid to let her out of the house."

"Why?"

"Other men would look at her and want her to be

their wife," I said. "And you're beautiful. Everyone who sees you says so."

"Am I?"

"Yes, but you have to take care of yourself. It's time you went to bed. You need sleep to stay healthy and pretty. Don't forget, we're going shopping tomorrow for your art supplies," I said.

She stood and gazed at her drawing. "I don't know what color eyes he'll have. Or hair," she said, looking frantic.

"We'll worry about it tomorrow," I told her.

She turned abruptly, the way Vera would when she became impatient with me, and marched out of the cupola and down the stairs. I followed her to her bedroom and watched as she prepared herself for bed. I remembered the early years when she could do almost nothing for herself. Papa was convinced that she was severely disabled and would be practically an invalid all her life. Every bit of progress I made with her had amazed him.

I was amused by how much care she was taking with herself right now. Usually, she did nothing with her hair, and I had to brush it and pin it back for her. Both Momma and Aunt Ellsbeth refused to go to bed without first putting Pond's Cold Cream on their faces.

"Your skin dries when you sleep," they told me. "Wrinkles wait in the darkness ready to pounce."

So I put it on, and I taught Sylvia to put it on. Vera made fun of it, but she didn't live to be old enough to see any wrinkles on her face.

Usually, I still had to tell Sylvia to do it, but she went right to it tonight, and then she looked at me and asked, "Am I really beautiful, Audrina?"

"Yes, you are," I said. I smiled, happy that she was taking a female's interest in herself. It meant she was developing a little self-respect, something else Papa had never believed would happen.

Afterward, I returned to our bedroom and waited for Arden. I believed him when he said we would try again to have a baby. He always expected that I would be in the mood for lovemaking whenever he was. Most of the time, he didn't care if I was or not. I would never forgive him for telling Vera some of the details about our honeymoon night, how I had delayed and delayed coming out of the bathroom. If there was ever a time when I wasn't ready to have sex, it was then. But he had waited long enough and demanded his conjugal rights. He actually had tried to break down the door, claiming that a man had a greater need than a woman. He claimed that there was a buildup in him that had to be satisfied and that the same was not true for women.

Those memories always haunted me, along with the horrible memories that had come to me in the rocking chair. I didn't need a psychiatrist to explain my inhibitions now. Lately, Arden had come up with the idea that I was so psychologically wounded when it came to sex that my body might actually be preventing me from getting pregnant.

"Medical doctors like Dr. Prescott don't understand the emotional power a woman can employ without herself even realizing it," he'd said. "I read up on it. Until you really, really want to enjoy sex with me, you'll never get pregnant."

I tried, fearing that he might be right. But even when I thought I wanted it as much as or even more than he did, I did not get pregnant. These thoughts tormented me. Often at night, I would toss and turn in and out of sleep, trying to throw off the haunting ideas and words. I felt like shouting, but I didn't want to make any noise and wake Arden. He'd be angry about it. He might ask why I was so troubled, and he'd repeat those claims about women and about me.

Now, as I waited for him, I wondered if it wasn't the other way around. Because he thought I was so troubled by sex, it was affecting him. He would never, ever admit that he could be affected, but deep down inside his angry heart, those feelings surely twirled about and worried him. What would bother him the most, and what did he fear other men would think about him? That he couldn't satisfy his wife, that he couldn't produce a child? Not Arden Lowe. He wouldn't stand for that.

I turned over in bed and closed my eyes. He was taking so long. How long did he expect me to wait? I fought sleep, but it was heavy tonight and easily forced my eyelids closed. I had no idea what time it was when my eyes snapped open, but I saw that the light beside me was still on, so I sat up, rubbed my eyes, and looked at the clock. It was well after one. Arden hadn't come up. Where was he? Had he started drinking again? Had he fallen asleep on the sofa? He'd be upset with himself, I thought. I put on my robe and slippers and went out.

I had just started toward the stairs when I saw him. He looked like he had fallen asleep in the living room. His hair was wild, his shirt was unbuttoned and out of his pants, and he wasn't wearing his shoes. But he wasn't coming up the stairs. He was coming from the direction of the first Audrina's room and Sylvia's room.

"What are you doing?" I asked.

"What you should have been doing," he said. "Why didn't you?"

"Do what?"

"Come and get her."

"Why?"

"Why? She was making enough of a racket in that damn rocking chair. I thought someone was cutting up the floor. She's lucky she didn't go over backward in it, the way she was rocking back and forth. I heard it above me. I didn't know she would go rocking. It sounded like animals eating away at the roof. You were dead asleep, so I went to check, and there she was, rocking away. Do you know why? She thinks your father talks to her when she's rocking."

"I know," I said, a cold chill rushing through me as I recalled my own rocking-chair memories and my childhood faith in its power to take me into another world. "I'm sorry. Where is she?"

"I got her out of that chair damn fast and practically dragged her back to her room. I imagine she's fast asleep, which is exactly where I should be," he said, and walked past me toward our bedroom.

"I'm sorry, Arden," I said again.

He paused and looked back at me. "I told you years ago that we should throw that chair out, empty that room, and give away all those toys and things. Maybe now you'll listen. I can get someone here tomorrow to take it all away."

"I can't do that, Arden. I just can't."

"Suit yourself. I'm tired, and I have to get up in a matter of hours," he said.

I went to Sylvia's room and looked in on her. She was asleep, her blanket up to her waist, but her hair was down. She always liked it up when she slept. A few times when she was younger, she got strands of her own hair in her mouth and choked on them. I watched her sleep. There was something more about her, something different, I thought, and stepped closer to get a better look at her face.

She was smiling.

Maybe she was having a pleasant dream. I wouldn't want to interrupt that. I fixed her blanket a little better and then returned to our bedroom. Arden was already curled up, clutching his pillow like a life preserver.

The funny thing was, he was smiling, too.

Shadows in the Darkness

Arden was up, dressed, and gone before I got up. I had to wake Sylvia, too. For a moment, she acted as if she didn't know where she was, but it wasn't unusual for her to wake up with a look of confusion on her face. It was almost as if she never expected there would be another morning. I wondered what sort of dreams she might have had.

Did she dream?

Sometimes I felt a little confused when I first woke up, and I imagined everyone did at one time or another. For a moment or so after you awaken, no matter who you are, how intelligent or mature you are, you can feel like a stranger in your own room, in your own house. You have to let everything you know and have gotten used to as belonging to you return, sort of fade in like a movie scene. Sunlight awakens it all, pulls it all out of the shadows, and fills your eyes and your mind with your identity. If you are pleased with who you are, you are happy, grateful, even relieved, but if you are not, you wish you hadn't woken up. You wish you had remained in your dreams being who you'd rather be, what you'd rather be.

Did Sylvia ever hate who and what she was? There were many times when I did. Did she look with envy at me, or had she felt envy toward Vera, especially when Vera had returned from her failed marriage, looking prettier and more sophisticated? Could Sylvia even experience jealousy? She never complained about one of us having more than she had. Vera used to claim that when Sylvia was very young, she was jealous of Billie's wagon, a device Billie used to get around because she had lost her legs to diabetes, but I never believed much in the things Vera would say. She was the epitome of jealousy in this house, her eyes of green envy converting anything beautiful that any of us had.

Once Sylvia realized what was happening when I woke her, she usually broke into a beautiful smile. This morning, however, she looked happier than I had seen her in a long time. She was, in fact, radiant. She wasn't groggy or sleepy and moved quickly to get out of bed. There was excitement in her eyes and an eagerness to start the day that I didn't often see, especially when Vera had come back to live with us and tormented her every chance she had.

When she stood, she stretched and looked at me as if I had just popped out of thin air.

"Hello, Audrina."

"Good morning, Sylvia. I overslept, so it's later than usual."

"Me, too. What do you want to do, Audrina?"

"Do?" I asked, smiling with amusement. She never began a day asking me that.

I remembered when I was a little girl, my mother would wake me and put me through her morning rituals. I had to stretch and then brush down my body before taking a shower so I could get rid of the dead skin cells. After I dressed and she brushed out my hair, she told me to sit before my mirror and smile at myself for thirty seconds so I could immediately think well of myself. She was adamant that I didn't put on a goofy grin.

"Because we're so behind schedule, let's go down first and have our breakfast, Sylvia. Then we'll repair our rooms, shower, and get dressed to go out and shop. We're buying your art supplies, remember?"

"Oh, yes, I need them."

"I know. Mr. Price gave us a list, remember? That's how we know what to buy."

"Is he coming back?"

"Yes, Sylvia. He is coming tomorrow afternoon. I'm going to post the schedule on the wall here in your room. For now, we have to get everything ready. Let's get a move on. It's a sunny day and not as cold as yesterday," I said. "There's much to do first."

"Much to do," she said. "Repair, repair." She repeated it as though she was making fun of me.

I looked at her with a half smile. "Yes, repair, Sylvia. We always repair."

She nodded. Although Arden certainly would be the first one to ridicule the idea, I sometimes looked at Sylvia when she wasn't aware that I was there and thought she looked brighter than she did when she was with Arden and me. She would study a painting or an object, look at pictures as if she remembered relatives she had never met, and then tilt her head as though she was hearing their voices. If I made a sound, she'd go right back to her cleaning or polishing like someone afraid she had been caught doing something wrong. I shook off the impression and told myself Sylvia was just not clever enough to put on an act and probably never would be. Of course, I told myself, she wasn't being sarcastic when she repeated "repair." It was only my imagination.

It was Aunt Ellsbeth who had first used that word to mean clean up our rooms, make our beds, and periodically change sheets and pillowcases as well as vacuum our rooms and wash our windows. The perfection in Whitefern had been broken merely by our living in it. According to her, especially after my mother had died, there was much about our home and our lives that needed mending. In the beginning, Papa had growled after every one of her critical remarks, but in time, he put up with it and made her the lady of the house. Every once in a while, I had to remind myself that I was the lady of the house now. The care and maintenance of Whitefern were my responsibility. Arden simply wasn't as devoted to it as I was. That was understandable, I guess. It wasn't his family heritage, and after all, his mother had died here tragically. Yet he knew I wouldn't live anywhere else, and neither would Sylvia.

Sylvia had more of an appetite than ever this

morning. She ate almost twice as much as I did. I rarely saw her exhibit as much energy, too. She went about our chores vigorously, cleaning up after breakfast. I imagined she wanted to get her art supplies as quickly as possible so she could do a better job on everything she drew now. I should have been happier about her enthusiasm, but I couldn't help feeling there was something wrong about it.

I chastised myself for feeling this way. Why couldn't I simply be happy for her? After all, this was what I had been hoping to see all these years and why I worked so hard to help and educate her. If I was hesitant and suspicious, what could I expect from Arden?

We went into town and bought the supplies Mr. Price had listed. I rarely took Sylvia anywhere but to the supermarket, clothing stores, and the dentist. Today I thought I would take her to a restaurant for lunch. I called Arden before we had left and asked him if he wanted to meet us at Danny's, a simple hamburger restaurant in Whitefern with booths and a long counter. It was like an old-fashioned diner.

"Are you sure you want to do that? We've never taken her to a restaurant, Audrina."

"She's very excited about the idea, Arden."

He was quiet so long that I thought he had hung up. "Arden?"

"I can't. I have to meet a client for lunch. Did you spend the morning reading the papers I brought home from Mr. Johnson?"

"I haven't had a chance yet."

"Well, *get* the chance," he ordered. Then he hung up without saying good-bye.

At the restaurant, we took a booth. Sylvia looked at everything and everyone as though she had just landed from another planet. The conversations and the laughter, the work of the short-order chef, and the music piped in had her turning every which way and gaping.

"Don't stare at people like that, Sylvia," I instructed.

"Why not?"

"They'll think you see something wrong with them, and it will make them self-conscious," I said, which was exactly how I felt when people stared at me.

"What's 'self-conscious'?"

"Aware of something that you think might be wrong with you, like your hair is messy or you put too much makeup on or that you have food on your face like a baby. Understand?"

She shook her head.

"Just look at me and think about your food." Sometimes it was easier to give up explaining something and leave it hanging in the air to be plucked again another time like an apple.

I ordered for both of us, knowing what she liked— cheeseburgers with tomatoes and lettuce and lots of ketchup, which she could have drooling down her chin.

"That man is staring at me," she said, looking toward the far end of the counter.

I turned. There were actually two men looking our way and talking. I recognized the older man. "That's

Mr. Hingen. He's a plumber. He was at Whitefern two months ago to fix our hot-water heater."

"Repair," she said.

"What? Oh. Yes, repair. Very good."

"Should we tell them it's not nice to stare?"

"No, just ignore them, Sylvia. Open your napkin and put it on your lap the way we do at home, so you don't drip anything and ruin your dress."

She did, but every once in a while, she stole another look at Mr. Hingen and the young man with him. I tried to get her attention on other things, talking about some of the pictures in the restaurant.

The waitress brought our food, and we began to eat.

Sylvia smiled after taking two bites. "Better than your hamburgers, Audrina," she commented.

"Well, thanks a lot."

"You're welcome," she said, proud that she had remembered to follow up a thank-you and, of course, missing my sarcasm. Vera was the first to tell me that talking to Sylvia was like talking to yourself. It was true, but I never let her or anyone else see that it bothered me. Most of the time, it didn't.

Before we were finished, Mr. Hingen stopped at our table to say hello, introducing the younger man as his son, Raymond. He was a good-looking, dark-haired man with light brown eyes, probably in his twenties. It was obvious that Raymond was quite taken with Sylvia and had asked his father to introduce him to us.

"How's everything at the house?" Mr. Hingen asked.

"Fine, thank you."

"My son is working with me now, so if you have any problems, just give us a call. This is your younger sister?"

"Yes."

"You're very pretty," Raymond said to Sylvia. "Where have you been hiding?"

"I don't hide," Sylvia said, indignant. "Do I, Audrina?"

"No, of course not."

"Do you go to college?"

"No, she doesn't attend college. She's at home with me."

"There's a lot to do here for a small town. You'd be surprised," Raymond told Sylvia. "Do you like to dance?"

She looked to me. "We dance, don't we, Audrina?"

I shook my head. "Not like he means, Sylvia. Thank you, Mr. Hingen, but—"

"Raymond, please." He turned back to Sylvia. "If you're not seeing anyone, I'd like to call you one day."

"I see Audrina and Arden, and I'm going to see Mr. Price tomorrow," Sylvia told him.

I wondered how long it would take him to realize whom he was talking to.

"Price?"

"He's a retired art teacher, ain't he?" Mr. Hingen asked me.

"Yes. He's giving my sister lessons. Right now, that's all she has time for. Thank you for stopping by," I said curtly.

Getting the idea, he poked his son. "Nice seeing you," he said to us.

"Yes," Raymond said. "Looking forward to the next time," he told Sylvia.

She narrowed her eyes and looked at me the moment they left. "When is next time?" she asked.

"Not ever," I said. "Forget it, Sylvia. It's just something someone says."

"Well, why do they say it if it's not true?"

"Just to make conversation. Most people hate silence. C'mon, let's finish. You need to fix up your art studio with the new things we just bought."

She nodded, but she watched Raymond Hingen leave the restaurant, and I thought she was more than just curious. His smile and the twinkle in his eyes had stirred something in her, something she might have felt for the first time. I was confident she didn't understand it. I remembered when I first had it, actually when I first met Arden. It both frightened and excited me simultaneously. I wanted to understand it, this tingle in my budding breasts, this thrill that traveled through my body, but I didn't want anyone to know about it, especially Vera or my aunt Ellsbeth.

I had brought Sylvia a long way from the disadvantaged little girl who had been treated so poorly by others in our family. Even Papa had to talk himself into accepting her as his daughter at the start. Was I wrong now to assume that she wouldn't ever be interested in young men? Was the idea of a romance, a relationship, as far off as another solar system when it came to her? If she could have a passion for art, why couldn't she have a passion for a man?

Eventually, she might have these feelings; she probably did at this moment, I thought, but no man would treat her well. And even if there was a man who cherished her now, when she lost her beauty, as we all did eventually, he would have far less tolerance for her and would surely cast her aside. Maybe it was cruel of me, but I wouldn't let Raymond Hingen or any young man date my sister, no matter how far she had come. It would only mean deeper suffering for her.

I could see that after I paid the bill and we were on our way out, she was still looking for Raymond. I tried getting her mind off him by talking about her artwork, her lessons, and what beautiful paintings she might do someday.

"We'll hang them on our living-room wall next to the expensive ones we've had in our family for years, Sylvia. Wouldn't you like that?"

She was quiet, thinking, gazing out the window as we drove home.

"Sylvia?"

"The faucet by the washing machine leaks a little," she said. "Maybe we need a plumber to fix it."

Was I astonished? Yes. But was I more fearful than surprised? Yes. "I'll look at it," I said. "Sometimes it's easy to fix."

She wasn't happy with my answer, but I did get her mind on other things when we arrived at the house and brought her new art supplies up to the cupola. She didn't mention Raymond Hingen again. I thought she might say something about plumbers and leaks when we sat with Arden at dinner that night. We had prepared a roast chicken with stewed potatoes. He didn't open another bottle of wine or make any nasty remarks. I was anticipating more about the papers Mr. Johnson had sent over with him, but he didn't mention them. Maybe he had asked someone's advice and had been told he'd get more with honey than with vinegar.

At times this evening, he reminded me of the young man who had courted me when I was a young girl. He was so sweet back then, always worried about me. He volunteered to take me on his bike to my piano lessons and was always waiting for me afterward. He was so protective. When I learned that his mother had lost her legs and that her husband had deserted her and Arden, I admired him even more for doing all that he could to make his mother happy. As insulated as I was, it was probably not unexpected that I would fall in love with the first boy who showed me so much attention and concern.

Tonight, he sounded so much like the Arden Lowe I remembered, giving Sylvia more attention than ever. Suddenly, he wasn't upset about spending money on an art teacher for her.

"You do great art without knowing anything about it. Imagine what you will do when you get all these lessons," he told her. His soft tone brought smiles to her face, even though I didn't think she understood what he was telling her.

Afterward, while she washed the dishes and put

away the food, I complimented him on how nice he was to her at dinner.

He nodded, thinking. "It's important that we bring some happiness back to Whitefern," he declared. "We have to change the landscape, as they say—as your father would say."

He poured himself an after-dinner cordial and asked me if I wanted one. I decided I did, and we sat reminiscing about some of the happier times when his mother had first moved in and taken such good care of my father.

"Sometimes you had to remind yourself that she'd had her legs amputated," I said.

"Yes. She had spirit. I hope I've inherited it."

"You have."

He looked at me with the pain of warm memories lost to time in his eyes. Nostalgia is always painful. You realize you can't bring back the smiles and laughter. In our house, reminiscences of past happiness often brought heartache. Sometimes it seemed better to forget them, no matter how wonderful they once were.

"I'm sorry I always talk about it, but we need a child, Audrina. We need someone who will strengthen our bond and give us more purpose in life. And I don't mean to blame anything on you."

That brought tears to my eyes. "I know," I said. "I want it as much as you do, if not more, Arden."

He kissed me. Sylvia came in and stood there looking at us. "I'm going up to finish drawing," she said.

"Good," Arden said before I could. We watched her go up the stairs.

That night, we made love more softly and affectionately than we had in years. Maybe he was simply testing his theory that if I welcomed sex, my body wouldn't resist fertilization. Maybe if he showed me true love, he, too, would be more potent.

There was no twisting and jerking me around to make himself more comfortable. There was more concern for my comfort and pleasure. He entered me gracefully and waited for me to accept him and open myself to him. There were kisses and caresses to accompany his strokes. I had that elusive orgasm time after time. He laughed about it and then brought himself to a satisfactory climax. Breathless but happy, we lay there holding hands. I thought he was so different tonight that it was like being married to Dr. Jekyll. I hoped Mr. Hyde was gone forever.

We fell asleep in each other's arms. I didn't even worry about Sylvia. When we woke in the morning, I was expecting him to bring up the paperwork, but he surprised me again by not mentioning it. Like the morning before, he was up early, dressed, and gone before I went to wake Sylvia. I remembered he had said he had a breakfast meeting. He was working hard, I thought. I should be more considerate. I promised myself that I would look at the papers and maybe do what he asked. When would I study to become a broker anyway? Wasn't that too much like a fantasy now? How could I leave Sylvia alone?

I was in such deep thought that I didn't realize for a few moments what Sylvia's still-made bed meant. In a little bit of a panic, I hurried up to the cupola. She wasn't there, and from what I could see, she hadn't done much more on her baby drawing. I descended and slowly walked to the rocking-chair room. As I'd feared, she was asleep in the chair. She was still dressed in what she had worn to dinner.

"Oh, Sylvia," I said, and poked her gently.

Her eyes opened, but she didn't look happy to see me.

"What's wrong?" I asked.

"The baby isn't a boy, Audrina. The baby is a girl," she said.

"Okay, Sylvia. You fell asleep here. I'm not happy about that."

She looked around and then stood up. Still very groggy, she let me lead her back to her room. I pulled back her blanket.

"Maybe you should rest a while longer, Sylvia. You want to be alert for your first art lesson this afternoon, don't you?"

"Yes," she said.

I helped her take off her dress and then had her crawl into bed and fixed her blanket. I brushed back her hair. Her eyelids fluttered, and she closed them. She was asleep in seconds. I watched her for a while and then went down to have some breakfast and debate with myself about whether I should give in to Arden's demands and get rid of the rocking chair, clear out the room, and maybe even lock the door.

Perhaps he was right about other things concerning Whitefern. Maybe if it had the makeover he had once proposed to my father, things would change dramatically. When the house you live in is changed, surely you're changed somewhat, too. Why didn't I want to wash away the darkness, brighten the rooms, erase the shadows, and replace the furniture, perhaps going more for a modern decor? We could change the floors, too, sell the rugs, and have most of the rooms tiled. And the kitchen needed new counters and new equipment, too. The stove we were using was the one my grandmother had used.

I couldn't help but recall how adamant Papa had been about not making such changes. He hadn't grown up in this house, but there was something about it that claimed him. Was it simply its history, with its variety of clocks and all its memorabilia? Was it because it held his secrets and still might, secrets he never revealed?

Of course, it wasn't only Papa who had felt something special about Whitefern. When I was no more than seven or eight, I would sit outside on the lawn and admire its grandness. For me, it was always a living thing. As I contemplated some of the changes Arden had been suggesting, I couldn't help being afraid that Whitefern would take some vengeance on us all, the way it had on Aunt Ellsbeth, Billie, and Vera. Maybe it was the wrath of our ancestors who hovered over us in sepia photographs and paintings. Seriously changing Whitefern was almost as blasphemous as disturbing the bones of the dead in ancient graveyards.

Where would the whispers go?

Sylvia surprised me by getting dressed, fixing her

hair, and coming downstairs a little less than an hour later. She said she was hungry and couldn't draw or listen to a teacher if she was thinking about eating.

"We have plenty of time yet, Sylvia. Don't worry," I said, and fixed her some eggs. She said she wanted to make breakfast for herself, but I told her, "Today, I'll be your cook and waitress. You are the artist. You must be spoiled rotten."

I then had to go into a long explanation about what being spoiled rotten meant. Afterward, she did go up and repair her room. Later, we had a very light lunch, and then we waited in the living room for Mr. Price. Sylvia had decided she would behave and warm up the biscuits we had when it was time for tea, without complaining that we didn't have chocolate ones.

Mr. Price was at the door just as our clocks, the ones that were accurate, were announcing the hour. Sylvia surprised me again by leaping to her feet and hurrying anxiously to the door. In her confused and simple way of seeing things, I thought she now must believe that Mr. Price's instructions would help her create the right baby on her canvas and thus do what Papa was telling her to do. How long could I keep Mr. Price from realizing what wild thoughts she had?

He was as jolly as ever and eager to begin. I followed them up to the cupola to be sure it all began well. He was happy with what we had bought and set up the first blank sheet on her easel. Sylvia sat in the chair, and he stood next to it with one of the drawing pencils. He glanced at me and began by explaining what he would teach her first and what was important to a beginning art student.

"I'm an art student," she said, nodding.

"Yes, you are. And I am, too, Sylvia. We are always learning. I'll learn from you," he told her.

She looked at me, astounded. I nodded and smiled, which made her even more enthusiastic.

"Here are the lessons I will use," he continued, now more for my benefit than hers, I thought. "Accuracy of size, how to use basic shapes like circles and squares, contrast and tone, stroke techniques, and pencil techniques."

She looked at me again.

"Don't worry, Sylvia. Mr. Price will explain everything so you understand."

He was patient and constantly complimented her. It was going well, I thought. Sylvia was finally doing something that would give her some self-confidence. I told them I would wait downstairs and have some tea and biscuits ready before he left.

"How kind," he said. "I do love your biscuits."

"Sylvia makes them all the time now," I said.

She was beaming with pride.

I watched for a few more minutes and then went downstairs. While I waited, I read the papers Mr. Johnson had sent home with Arden. There was no question about the end result once I signed them. Arden would have complete control of everything, even of the disposition of Whitefern, because it had been added as a company asset. If Arden made tragic mistakes, the house itself could fall into jeopardy. I knew enough about business to predict that he would leverage it to raise more money to invest in the stock market.

I would never sign this, I thought. It might bring our truce and tender loving to a quick end, but it truly was as though Papa were standing right behind me and reading over my shoulder. I could hear him whisper. *Don't do it, Audrina. Don't sign those papers.*

"Don't worry, Papa," I whispered back. "I won't."

I smiled, thinking that I should never criticize Sylvia for imagining that Papa was still here.

Maybe we were both still children of Whitefern.

Maybe we'd never be anything else.

Awakenings

Arden's upbeat temperament was unchanged for the remainder of the week. He came home from work happy and excited about the successes he was having in the stock market and the compliments he was getting from clients. He practically bounced when he walked and always charged up the stairway with a show of energy that brought smiles to both Sylvia and me. We could hear him singing upstairs while he showered and changed his clothes.

At dinner, he would go on and on about the maneuvers he had made and how brilliantly they had turned out. I had never heard Papa brag as much about his business achievements. Although he'd enjoyed making money, especially after failing so much in the beginning, he never seemed to have Arden's passion for it. Perhaps it was because Arden was younger and was surprising himself with his success, or maybe he thought it was important to impress me.

The pleasure he was getting at work spilled over into everything we were doing at home. According to Arden, our dinners had never been as good as they

suddenly seemed to him, especially some of the new
recipes I had found. He used to accuse me of experimenting on him and complain about being a guinea
pig, but now he even complimented Sylvia on her
contribution to our dinners, even if it was something
as simple as whipping up mashed potatoes or chop-
ping onions.

He would even pause once in a while, look around,
and tell me the house had never looked as well kept. I
waited for the inevitable suggestion that it would look
far better if we got rid of the old furniture and redecorated, but he didn't say that. He didn't even suggest it
by harping on the threadbare rugs.

Any compliment he gave me he shared with Sylvia.
Through the years, especially before Papa died, he
would avoid looking at her and never spoke directly to
her, only about her. According to him now, Sylvia was
surprisingly bright, even funny. Sometimes he even
gave her a hug and kissed her on the forehead when he
came home at the end of the work day.

"How are my women?" he would cry, and Sylvia
would look so pleased. "My beautiful women." It didn't
sound at all like a false compliment, and truthfully, it
couldn't be, for Sylvia was looking more beautiful.

"Those lessons must be doing her a world of
good," he declared one evening at dinner. He gazed
across the table at Sylvia, who looked as surprised as
I was. "You were very wise to arrange for it, Audrina.
What a wonderful mother you would make," he added,
but not with any note of sadness. "Oh, no," he went on
to correct himself. "*Will* make. Won't she, Sylvia?"

"When there is a baby," Sylvia said, and he laughed. I had to laugh, too, at how positive she sounded.

"That's right. You can't be a mother unless you have a child," Arden told her. "You want Audrina to have a child to care for and spoil like you've been spoiled, right?" He looked at me quickly and added, "Any woman as pretty as you two should be spoiled."

"A baby is coming," she said.

She looked at me as if she and I shared a secret, but Arden didn't seem to notice that conspiratorial expression. As far as I knew, she had never told him about her drawing, and if she had, he had never mentioned it to me. All he knew was my saying that she had dreamed about it, not that Papa specifically had instructed her to draw a baby as the way to bring a child to Whitefern.

Every time I sat with her and Mr. Price after one of her lessons, I listened carefully to see if she had said anything to give him any idea of why she had been working on a drawing of a baby. Apparently, she hadn't, because he never revealed anything remotely associated with it. He talked about her natural artistic talent and praised her for how quickly she grasped visual concepts. I went up to watch every lesson for the first week and a half and saw that he was right. He didn't have to show Sylvia something more than once. How I wished Papa had lived to see this. It occurred to me that she really was visually brilliant. How ironic, but how wonderful, I thought.

It had been so long since we had such a pleasant and hopeful atmosphere at Whitefern. I worried that it wouldn't last. Every night, I anticipated Arden's asking me about the papers, whether I had read them and agreed to sign them, and every night, he surprised me by not making the slightest reference to them. Why had something that was so important to him, something that he was adamant and angry about, drifted away? My suspicious mind began to explore the darkest possibilities. Being leery and apprehensive was not an unexpected feeling in this house. If there was one thing Whitefern was fertile with, it was the dark weeds of human wickedness. After all, I grew up with the admonition never to trust kindness or believe in smiles.

I began to consider possibilities. Would Arden have forged my signature, even my fingerprint, or could he have paid off Mr. Johnson to accept it? He would certainly feel confident that I would never take my own husband to court. I wondered if I should call Mr. Johnson to ask. Would Arden be enraged that I even suggested such a thing, especially if he didn't do what I suspected? I couldn't ask Mr. Johnson not to tell him I had called. Why would he keep my confidence over Arden's? I had met our attorney only a few times at social events in the house, and he had spent very little time talking to me. I had the sense that, like Papa and certainly Arden, he didn't think women were capable of doing well in business or even understanding it.

Could it be that Arden believed that if he didn't bother asking me about the papers for quite a while, I would lose interest in them, too, and whatever he had done would go unnoticed? I hadn't mentioned anything about my becoming a broker since I had broached the subject the first time. I hadn't even researched what I would have to do to get a license or asked any questions about it, and Arden hadn't brought it up. Maybe he was simply being cautious. Papa used to say, "If you don't ask questions about things that will upset you, you'll never get upset." He believed that just ignoring something often made it go away. If I remembered his advice, Arden certainly would, for despite how critical he was of Papa, he did respect him when it came to worldly and business knowledge.

Perhaps he was complimenting Sylvia and accepting her being tutored because he believed it meant I would be more involved in her life and, as a result, I would drop the idea of doing anything more than caring for Whitefern, Sylvia, and him. Maybe our lovemaking and talk of a baby were designed to keep me dreaming. As long as I did that, I did nothing to challenge the status quo.

However, the nicer he was to both of us, the guiltier I felt about having any suspicions. I made an effort to put them aside. With Sylvia devoting more and more of her time to her art, I really did have more to do in the house anyway. It took time to get her to prepare herself for instruction, and after the lesson was over, she was too excited to polish furniture or wash a kitchen floor, sometimes even to help with dinner. Whatever assignment Mr. Price gave her for the days in between she took very seriously and devoted all her energy to it. I didn't have the heart to pull her away for menial work.

Often now, I left her alone in the cupola and did my grocery shopping without her. I knew she didn't hear me say I was leaving; she was concentrating too hard. So I put a note on her door reminding her. I felt less insecure about it, knowing she was too occupied to get into trouble like going out on her own and wandering.

Winter, although it came roaring in like a lion, seemed to have calmed down. We had less snowfall than most years I remembered and fortunately few days of sleet and icy rain. There were delightful sunny days when the air felt crisp and fresh. Occasionally, Sylvia and I took walks, during which she was far more talkative than ever, describing her artwork and what she intended to draw and paint in the future. Before she had begun her lessons, she would never pause in the forest and look at a tree or a bush and tell me that it would look nice in her new picture.

Mr. Price, Sylvia, and I didn't have tea and biscuits after every session, but I saw how well Sylvia was getting along with him. She liked being complimented, and he never stopped giving her praise. I concluded that this was because of his experience with special education students. Who else would have such patience and understanding?

It got so I didn't interrupt the lessons by appearing anymore. Although he never said anything about it, Sylvia did. After one of Mr. Price's visits, she surprised me by telling me it was better when I wasn't looking over her shoulder while she learned and worked.

"Why?" I asked.

"You make me nervous when you're there, Audrina," she said.

I was speechless. Nervous? Had I used that word enough for her even to understand what it meant?

I told Arden what she had said, and he raised his eyebrows and nodded in agreement. "I must say, it's all quite a surprise." He thought for a moment and then added, "But perhaps a nice surprise."

I should have thought likewise, but that persistently suspicious mind of mine wouldn't hibernate, not in Whitefern. Sylvia would never before say or do anything even to suggest she didn't want me to be with her or watch her do something. Although seeing her develop some sense of independence should have pleased me, it didn't. Of course, I asked myself, did I want her to be dependent on me forever? Did it make me feel more important? Did it fill my empty moments? Had I used her as an excuse for not pursuing my own ambitions? Was I being unfair to her?

Perhaps it was Arden's continued comments about how Sylvia was changing that kept me wondering about all this. The more he said it, the more I looked at her with unreasonable and unwarranted worry. But I couldn't help it. I told myself that it was a result of my not having a passion for something the way Sylvia did. I was spending too much time thinking about her and not myself. The Vera in me was showing its envious face.

One morning on a day when Sylvia was having a new lesson, I noticed that she was taking extra care with her appearance. I no longer had to hound her about brushing her hair or wearing clothes that coordinated. Colors had become important, and she wanted to be correct about them. She was even good about the shoes she chose, and she did all of it before I had a chance to tell her or make suggestions. In fact, she was waking up on her own and three mornings in a row was up and dressed before I had arrived at her bedroom. There were times when she showed some interest in wearing a little lipstick and even a little makeup. Now that she was learning about colors and contrast and how important that was in her artwork, I could tell that she was looking at herself and thinking about it more and more. Again, I was surprised to see her do anything about her face without my instruction, but she did, and she did it surprisingly well.

When I mentioned it to Arden, he said, "Why are you surprised? Isn't that all part of art? Women paint their faces. They look in their mirrors and sometimes turn pale, homely mugs into faces a man would at least glance at. Of course, when they wash it off, you'd rather not be there." Then he leaned over to whisper, "That's why most men like to make love to their wives in the dark."

Papa would say something like that, I thought. "Then they married them for the wrong reasons," I countered, irritated.

Of course, he simply laughed and went on reading.

All of this was riling up some unexpected anger and discomfort in me. I marched about the house pouncing on things out of place or anything left on tables.

My intolerance for the smallest imperfections, like a vague stain on the kitchen floor, sent me into a cleaning frenzy, mopping and sweeping while I muttered to myself. I envisioned Aunt Ellsbeth observing and nodding with approval. "Repair, repair, repair!" she would chant. It felt like a whip.

One afternoon nearly a month later, I put on my coat and boots when Sylvia and Mr. Price went upstairs to work. I stepped out of the house and looked at the skeleton forest. I felt I had to have some air. All my worried and jealous thoughts were stifling me in Whitefern. I had no shopping to do, no friend to visit, only the outside world around our home to distract me.

It was a partly cloudy day, with the sun playing hide and seek on the forest pathways. I recalled the first time I had gone through the woods to see the new family that occupied the gardener's cottage. That family was Arden and his mother, Billie. I'd still believed there was a first Audrina back then, and as I snuck away from Whitefern, defying Papa, and ventured into the forest, I'd felt myself grow uneasy. Little butterflies of panic had fluttered in my head, and the warnings I had heard for years seemed to echo now, years later: *It's dangerous and unsafe in the woods. There is death in the woods.*

Once I'd learned what had happened to me in this forest, I understood my innate trepidation. How brave I'd been to go forward when I was so young and had been told so many terrible things. The horrible memories thundered around me, but they were blurry now. No amount of time in the rocking chair would bring back the gruesome details. It was still frightening, but it was vague.

Nevertheless, when I walked into the woods slowly, my head down, the darkness seemed to close in on me. Tree limbs devoid of leaves looked spidery, swaying and trembling in the breeze like beckoning sirens, enchanting, hypnotizing, and seducing. Death lay in wait behind cold smiles. Dried leaves between small patches of evaporating snow crunched beneath my feet. It sounded like I was walking over shards of glass. Far off, a dog howled. The scent of some animal that had died in the woods recently flowed over me, churning my stomach.

I paused and opened my eyes like a sleepwalker awakening.

I was surprised to see that I had walked far enough to be near the infamous clearing in which I had been attacked. I could feel every muscle in my body tighten, and the chilled air seeped under my coat to run up my spine.

Suddenly, as if I had been nudged, tapped firmly on my right shoulder, I turned and looked back at Whitefern. There was something in the look of the mansion that alarmed me. I felt two hands on my back pushing me forward. I broke into a run and rushed back to the house. I charged through the front door and hurried up the stairs until I was at the cupola. There I paused to catch my breath and my wits. What was I doing? I didn't want to frighten them or look foolish. Quietly and slowly, I opened the door.

But then I froze.

Mr. Price was sitting in Sylvia's chair in front of
her easel, and Sylvia was standing in front of him, her
beautiful, full breasts uncovered, her hands clasped behind her head. She wore only her skirt, but it was lowered beneath her belly button. Her eyes were shifted
so that she was looking at the ceiling.

I screamed, a scream so piercing that it knifed
through both of them. Mr. Price raised his shoulders as
if he'd been slapped on the back of his neck, and Sylvia
brought her hands down and looked at me in confusion. He rose, turned, and backed away, his hands up
and pumping the air as if he thought that would keep
me away.

"Now . . . don't get excited. I can explain—" he
said.

"Sylvia, dress yourself!" I shouted, and she hurriedly did so.

I turned to him, my eyes feeling like they were
popping and on fire. "How *dare* you."

"It's not what you think. I'm teaching her . . . all
aspects of, of art, of being an artist," he stuttered.
"She's a perfect model, you see, and I'm an artist. This
is nothing more than art, you see."

"Get out!" I shouted. "Get out of my house!" I
stepped away from the door to give him a clear exit.

He looked at Sylvia and then hurried past me,
pausing in the hallway. "I'm an artist," he insisted.
"Don't you tell anyone anything else. I can sue you,"
he warned, and then hurried down the stairs.

I turned back to Sylvia, my hands still pressed
firmly on the base of my throat.

"Is that the end of my lesson?" she asked.

I was trembling so hard that I didn't think I could speak or move, but I slipped into the artist's chair and took deep breaths. Sylvia stood there looking at me in confusion but with great interest. She had never seen me like this. I glanced at her and then looked at the canvas. He had finished the drawing and done a remarkably good job of capturing both her face and her body. I reached up quickly and ripped it off the easel, then folded it and stood up.

"Did he tell you to tell me you were nervous when I was in the room?"

She thought a moment, remembering, and then smiled and nodded.

"Get dressed and come downstairs, Sylvia," I said. "Quickly!"

I was afraid that Mr. Price was still in the house, so I descended slowly, but he was gone.

"Sit on the settee," I told Sylvia when she appeared, and I went to the phone to call Arden. That self-important Mrs. Crown had started to tell me he was busy when I screamed, "Get my husband on the phone now!"

She stammered and squeaked out a "Right away."

Moments later, Arden, irritated, said, "What is it, Audrina? You have Mrs. Crown shaking."

I rattled off the details so quickly that I was sure he didn't understand.

He was silent for a few moments. "Tell me that again," he said in a much quieter tone of voice than before.

I went through it slowly this time, even mentioning Mr. Price's threat to sue us.

"Is he gone?"

"Yes."

"And Sylvia?"

"She's in the living room. She doesn't understand what's happened, what she has done, or why I am so upset," I said, and then I started to cry.

"You didn't call the police, did you?" Arden asked.

"What? No. Should I?"

"No," he said, quickly and firmly. "That would be the worst thing for us—and for Sylvia. Can you imagine them arriving to question her? And when it got out to the public . . . oh, boy. Just do nothing until I get there."

"We can't just do nothing. I have his drawing. It's clear evidence."

"I'm not saying we will do nothing, but I'll handle it. Just keep her calm."

"She's very calm, Arden. I assure you that she has no idea why what was going on was wrong."

"Okay, okay. Just have tea or something. Wait for me," he said, and hung up.

I hung up, too, and as calmly as I could, I returned to Sylvia, who waited with the expression of a little girl, frightened but confused, wondering whether or not she had to cry.

"Oh, Sylvia," I said. I sat beside her and took her hand. "This is not your fault."

"Art?"

"No, I'm not talking about art. This man, Mr. Price, he took advantage of you."

She shook her head, not understanding.

"He asked you to do something you shouldn't have done. He was here to teach you art, not to exploit you for his own sexual needs."

I could see that nothing was making sense to her. To her, I was just raving.

"Look, Sylvia, you should never undress in front of a strange man."

"Was Mr. Price strange?"

"Not strange like that. Well, maybe, but what I mean is, he's not family. He's a stranger. He was supposed to just work for us, help you with your art. He used art as an excuse to have you undress."

I thought a moment as she worked at understanding.

"Did you do this before today?"

She nodded.

"Did you undress more?"

She nodded.

I felt a cold chill first and then a hot flash in my chest. "Were you ever completely nude?"

"Like when I take a bath?"

"Yes."

"Yes," she replied.

My heart was pounding. "Did he touch you?"

"Yes," she said.

"Where?"

"In the studio."

"No, where on your body did he touch you? Show me," I told her.

She thought about it and then nodded and put her hands on her breasts, her stomach, her thighs.

I started to breathe some relief until she put both hands between her legs. The blood left my face. I sat back.

"I had to stand right for the drawing and not move."

"Oh, Papa," I muttered. All I could think of was how angry he would be at me, not Sylvia. I had broken a promise. I hadn't protected her.

My mind was a workshop of miserable thoughts. While I had been dumbly cleaning the house, taking walks, reading, and minding my own business, Sylvia was being sexually abused, and the worst part of it was that she didn't understand. I thought about all the times the three of us sat here after the lessons and had tea and biscuits together. I should have noticed something, realized something. How conniving and clever he was. He was probably the one telling Sylvia how to dress, do makeup, and brush her hair. I had stupidly thought she was simply learning to take pride in herself. Perhaps in her limited vision and thinking, she was, but that wasn't why he was doing it. All those compliments he brushed over her, dipping her in the well of ego so that she would appreciate him and never resist his mauling of her beautiful body, now made sense to me.

"Mr. Price was simply another frustrated old man," I muttered. "I don't know why the alarms didn't go off in me. I'm simply too inhibited, too cloistered here, too out of the social world to recognize the clues. It's my fault, my fault. I'm sorry, Sylvia."

I lowered my head and took her hand in both of mine. I couldn't help it. The tears began to flow.

"I'm not mad at you," Sylvia said. "Don't cry, Audrina."

"No, you're not mad at me," I said, smiling and wiping away my tears. "You'll never be mad at me. You're the angel here, Sylvia. I'm mad at myself." I took a deep breath. "Let's have some tea and biscuits, chocolate biscuits."

She nodded and then paused. "But Mr. Price left," she said.

"And he'll never be back, Sylvia. I guarantee that."

"Oh," she said. She looked stunned, worried, and then she smiled. "My lessons are over. That's all right, Audrina. I know what to do."

"Good. That's the way to think of it. I'll try to think of it that way, too."

We went into the kitchen. I was still clinging to the folded sheet on which Arthur Price had drawn my sister half-nude. I couldn't help glancing at it every once in a while, and that made the shock of the scene in the cupola return. Finally, I put it in a drawer by the refrigerator where we had other important household papers. Then I tried to talk about other things. We had our tea and biscuits in the kitchen. Suddenly, the idea of sitting in the living room to enjoy it had turned sour. Sylvia didn't care. I kept talking—babbling, really—and then I started to plan dinner, and she quickly forgot about what had happened. I doubted that I ever would.

A little more than half an hour later, Arden came home. He looked at both of us to see if we were all right, and then he told me to follow him to Papa's office, which was now his. I left Sylvia mixing batter for a vanilla cake.

"What did you do?" I asked as soon as he closed the door.

"Where's the picture he drew?"

"In the drawer by the refrigerator."

"Get it," he said, and dropped himself into Papa's desk chair. His face was flushed with rage. I hurried out and returned with the drawing.

He studied it a moment and nodded. "This is good. I mean, it's important that we have it." He took a breath, sat back, and said, "I confronted him at his home."

"You did?"

"Yes. He tried to keep his wife out of the discussion by taking me to his home studio, but I think she was just outside the door listening. He swore up and down that he didn't mean any harm to Sylvia and that he did not sexually abuse her. I told him I didn't care. That if he came within a thousand yards of Whitefern, I'd press charges. To me, it was the same as abusing one of his students in school. He got the point quickly. He promised he wouldn't come anywhere near us, nor would he say a word. He offered to give back all the money he took. I accepted it." He showed me a check he had in his inside jacket pocket.

"I don't want his money," I said. "The money isn't the important thing, Arden."

"Of course it's important. Money is always important. Consider this to be the fine levied against him, only we didn't have to go to court to sue him and attract all sorts of prurient public interest, get Sylvia— and us—in the newspapers. Can you even imagine what it would do to our business image?"

"I'm not worried about our image. I'm worried about Sylvia."

"The two things go hand in hand," he insisted. He looked at the drawing again and then put it in his desk drawer, the one that could be locked. "We'll hold this as our insurance. Have you had a talk with Sylvia? Does she realize what's happened now?"

"A little," I said. "She's not upset with herself or him, however. She's upset that I'm upset. It's probably better if we don't talk about it anymore."

"Exactly," he said. "Over and done with. She'll be all right." He put the check back into his jacket pocket.

"I'm upset with myself for letting it happen."

"I'm sure you could never have imagined this happening. I did, but that's because I'm a man, and I can understand how the male mind and lust work. If anyone taught me that well, it was your father. So I'm not blaming you. Let's go about our lives with this stuffed away in the cellar of horrors Whitefern has accumulated." He looked at his watch. "I have some calls to make because I left the office in a rush. Fortunately, Mrs. Crown did a good job of covering it up."

"Does she know why you left?"

"Not really," he said.

I wasn't sure what "really" meant, but I was mentally and emotionally exhausted and didn't want to talk about it anymore. "I'll get back to making dinner," I said. "Although my stomach is in so many knots I don't think I can eat a thing."

"You'd better. Don't get Sylvia upset," he warned. "I know her. She'll be the one who gets sick over it."

Suddenly, he was thinking more about her welfare than I was. That made me feel even more guilty. Arden was truly more mature and sensible than I was, I thought. He should be totally in charge of our business and our lives. Look at what a mess I had made of one simple thing.

I nodded and left, telling myself I had to put on as good an act as I could for Sylvia. She asked no questions and went about our dinner preparations as if it was just another day. I wondered how well her memory did work. I knew from the way she had usually acted toward Vera the day after Vera had abused her that bad memories didn't cling to her the way they did to me—or anyone else, for that matter.

But several days after the incident with Mr. Price, she looked up at me while we were having lunch and said, "Something bad happened in the cupola."

"Yes, Sylvia, something bad happened."

She thought for a moment and then looked at me and said, "I liked it, Audrina."

"Liked what?"

She looked like she wasn't going to answer or

didn't know what to answer. I thought I knew what she meant.

"You shouldn't like just anyone touching you, Sylvia. And whoever does it shouldn't trick you into thinking he is doing something else, something you should let him do."

She looked at me and nodded, but I had no false hopes about it. She didn't have any idea what I meant, and maybe she never would.

The day would come when I would wish that this was all I had talked about until she understood.

But by then, it was too late for all of us.

Shadows Do Multiply

Despite how firmly and confidently Arden had declared that the incident in the cupola was over and should never be discussed or even thought about again, I couldn't help feeling a sense of doom about Whitefern because of it. Old demons were roused from their sleep. The devil who liked to frolic about in our lives had paid us another visit. Shadows were darker. Every face in every painting looked angry and accusatory as I walked by. Every clock ticked as though every minute, every second, was heavier in this house than anywhere else. And no matter what anyone would tell me, what had happened to Sylvia was my fault.

"You don't tend your garden, and weeds will grow. And it's not the fault of the weeds!" Aunt Ellsbeth would tell both Vera and me. Her condemning voice echoed in the hallways. "Your father gave you one important responsibility, and you failed him. You failed him!"

Vera's laughter naturally followed, resonating through the hallways in my house of memories. Sometimes I went about with my hands over my ears. But the voices were inside my head, haunting, pouncing, eager to remind me that I was all twisted and beaten down, forever poisoned by the lust of the boys who had killed the real Audrina in me, the little girl her father had cherished. No baths, no shampoos, not even sandpaper on my skin, could scrub away the disgrace. How could my father have any faith and confidence in me? Aunt Ellsbeth and Vera were always there to remind me of that question. They expected failure no matter what I did. Nothing made them happier, because it proved them right.

How did you kill ghosts?

There was nothing in Sylvia's behavior to encourage this. She didn't mope around looking lost and melancholy all the time like any victim of such abuse would. If anything, she seemed to have more energy than she had before. Absent from her psyche was any embarrassment. She was still very interested in her artwork and spent more time in the cupola experimenting with her watercolors the way Mr. Price had taught her. Nevertheless, I couldn't help it. Whenever she mentioned something about drawing and painting, I didn't react with the enthusiasm she expected. I would never ask her to stop her artwork, but it seemed contaminated in my mind now, as contaminated as I believed I was deep down inside. I knew she was surprised and upset by my subdued reactions to everything she showed me proudly. I hated flashing smiles and those terribly meaningless words, "That's nice."

At times, I thought Arden paid more attention to her at dinner and afterward than he did to me. Maybe

I was imagining it, but she seemed to become more interested in the things he said. She laughed at his jokes even if she didn't fully understand them, and when he addressed her now, she seemed to try harder to do whatever he asked. He asked nicely, too, not like before, when he would snap an order at her as if she was a pet hound. When I made a reference to his changed behavior toward my sister, he said, "We've got to do all we can to keep her from feeling guilty, Audrina, feeling like it was her fault. It'll set her back years if we don't."

"Since when did her feelings matter so much to you?" I countered, annoyed at his tone. He sounded like I was the one who was making things more difficult, like I was trying to shift the blame from myself to her.

"Since I realized I was the head of this household and responsible for your and Sylvia's welfare," he replied. "That's since when."

He sounded so sincere that I couldn't contradict him, challenge him, or accuse him of being sarcastic.

"I would have thought you, of all people, would be pleased," he added.

"I am," I said, now feeling a little ashamed. "I'm just . . . surprised."

"Happily, I hope."

"Yes, happily, Arden, happily."

I left it at that, but despite how well both Arden and Sylvia were doing after what I considered a serious and terrible event at Whitefern, I could not simply forget it and go on the way they apparently were. To them, it was as though Mr. Price had never come to instruct her and had never taken advantage of her, while it haunted me. I shuddered to remember what I'd seen when I opened the cupola door. How much further would things have gone if I hadn't made the discovery, if I had continued to avoid going to the cupola because I thought that would make Sylvia more comfortable?

Needless to say, what had happened to Sylvia revived my own gruesome memories. Were all the women of Whitefern under some curse to suffer at the hands of some man? In the days and weeks that followed, I moved about under a dark cloud. I dozed off more than usual and had no sooner finished with dinner than I announced that I was tired and would go up for a hot bath and bed. At first, Arden seemed not to notice the difference in me, but one night after dinner, he ordered me to come to the living room. I thought he was going to start on the paperwork, and I was ready to give in, but to my surprise, he was more upset about me, about the way I had been behaving.

"You've got to stop beating yourself up for what happened, Audrina. Nobody would have expected you to be suspicious of a retired schoolteacher apparently quite well liked at the school where he had taught. Don't forget, the principal recommended him to you."

"I know," I said. "But I'm sure there were clues I missed."

"What clues?"

"The way he spoke to her, admired her, smiled at her, and the little whispering I saw him do with her."

"Ridiculous." He thought a moment. "But I see how heavily your misplaced guilt is weighing on you. You're sure to get yourself sick. Maybe you should see Dr. Prescott," he suggested.

"Why? I'm not sick yet."

"There are all kinds of sickness, Audrina. You might need some sort of medication for this . . . depression. I think they're called mood enhancers. One of my clients was telling me about it the other day. His wife suffers from depression."

"Any doctor would first want to know why I was depressed. He'd want to know why, and I'd be terribly embarrassed, Arden, even with Dr. Prescott, maybe especially with Dr. Prescott. He was here sometimes when Papa told me to watch over Sylvia closely and warned me time and time again how vulnerable she was. No, no, I'll deal with it myself," I said. "Give me time."

"Time? How much more time? I pretended for weeks not to notice, hoping that you would do just as you say, deal with it yourself, but you haven't, and I fear you never will. I'm afraid to invite anyone to dinner or take you out like this," he insisted, raising his voice. "A man with a growing business like mine can't have an emotional invalid for a wife."

I started to cry.

"All right, all right," he said more calmly. "Don't worry about it. I'll see about it for you."

"I don't think I'd like—"

"Stop worrying about it, I said. I'll look after you. I made promises to your father, too, you know, and one of them was to always be concerned about your welfare. Please let me fulfill that promise I made to him."

What more could I say once he invoked my father? The next day, he came home with a prescription for me. It didn't have my name on it, but he said that was because the doctor didn't actually examine me.

"It's a common one," he said. "Harmless. Try it for a while. As you see, it's best to take it in the evening, after dinner."

I turned the pill bottle around in my fingers and shook my head. "I'm not fond of pills, Arden. You know that."

"This is not anything terrible. It's just to help you manage. It's time to do something. Sylvia is becoming affected by your dark moods, too, Audrina. She's even starting to eat poorly, and I fear she's losing interest in her art. She might be blaming herself or thinking we're both blaming her now. She'll get sickly and return to the half vegetable she was. Is that what you want?"

"No, I don't want that, of course not."

"Well, she may be slow about many things, but she's not blind. Anyone, even Sylvia, can see that you're not looking after yourself as well as you usually do. Sometimes you look like a hag, a bag lady wandering aimlessly."

"I do?"

"Yes, you do. I didn't want to say anything, but someone who saw you at the supermarket commented to me about you."

"Who? What was said? When?"

"It doesn't matter who. They were concerned because of how you looked, how void of energy you seemed. They thought you were seriously ill. Why do you think I've avoided bringing anyone here? Half the time now, you don't even put on lipstick, and I don't know if you realized it, but you wore the same dress three days in a row this week."

"I did? Why didn't you say something?"

"I didn't want to bring it up. I wasn't sure if it would do good or add to the bad, but how can we go forward and do wonderful things for Sylvia and for ourselves if you are so depressed all the time?" He pushed the pills back at me. "Take them for a week or so, and let's see how you do. Okay?"

I looked at the pill bottle again and nodded. He was right. I couldn't go on the way I was. That night, I took the first one. I felt a little dizzy and even a little silly. We had wine at dinner and an after-dinner drink, too. He said the doctor had said I could drink a little with the pills.

Arden put on music, and for the first time I could remember, he made Sylvia dance with him. She was bashful and afraid, but he showed her some steps, and then she started to do it. They both looked clumsy to me, and I laughed again. Sylvia beamed, believing she was doing something I wanted her to do and that she was bringing smiles back to my dreary face.

Arden got me up to dance, too, but I didn't have the energy to go on and on. Finally, I collapsed onto the sofa while they went back at it. I closed my eyes, my face frozen in a silly smile, and fell asleep. I had no idea how long I slept. I woke with a start and looked around. There was only a small lamp lit, and both Arden and Sylvia were gone.

When I stood up, the room started to spin, and I fell back onto the sofa.

"Arden?" I called. I looked at the nearest clock. It was two in the morning. "Arden?"

I struggled to my feet, made my way to the stairs, and started up. It seemed to take me ten times as long as usual. Every once in a while, I paused, listened, and took a deep breath before continuing. When I turned to head toward our bedroom, I felt the hallway spin and pressed my palm against the wall to steady myself. In the room, there was a nightlight on, but Arden was in bed, facedown, asleep. I stood there looking at him and desperately tried to remember what had happened. Everything was so vague.

I went to the bathroom and looked at myself in the mirror. My hair was wild, and my eyes looked terribly bloodshot. I washed my face and struggled to get undressed and into bed. Arden moaned and turned over with his back to me. I wondered about Sylvia, but I was just too tired to go check on her. In moments, I was asleep again.

The dream I had that night was so vivid that when I awoke, I questioned whether it was really a dream. In it, I had sat up in bed because I was sure I heard whispering in the hallway. I had turned to wake up Arden and realized he wasn't there. So I'd risen and slowly made my way to the doorway to listen. There was definitely someone whispering. Confused and intrigued, I'd stepped out and made my way down the hallway toward the rocking-chair room. I'd stopped when I saw Arden outside the doorway, the door half open, talking.

What was he saying?

To whom?

I'd drawn close enough to look through the doorway and had seen Sylvia in the rocking chair, half naked the way she had been in the cupola, her head back, her eyes closed, rocking.

"What are you doing?" I'd cried out.

Arden had turned to look at me, and when he did, he had my father's face.

My father was looking at me, and he was angry that I was disturbing Sylvia in the rocking chair. His face had been full of such fury that I gasped.

"Papa?"

My legs had turned to water and floated away as I sank into the cool darkness beneath me.

But when I opened my eyes again, I was back in my bed. The morning light rushed in around me, and the bedroom exploded in a kaleidoscope of colors from the stained-glass windows, the same colors that had turned Momma's and my hair into chameleon hair because it was sometimes flaxen blond with gold. There were strands of auburn, bright red, chestnut brown, and copper. And sometimes in a passing ray of sunshine, our hair looked white. Papa had loved the strange prism-like color of our hair. He loved the way the light played on everything in Whitefern. I was seeing it all this morning the way Papa would see it.

It was as if time had not passed and I was a little girl again.

I turned onto my back and looked up at the ceiling. What exactly had happened last night? When did I pass out? Why did Arden leave me there? And the dream, the dream . . .

When I looked at the clock, I was shocked to see that it was nearly one in the afternoon. I had never slept this long.

"Sylvia?" I called. I listened but heard nothing. Of course, Arden would have gotten up, dressed, and been long gone.

I groaned as I got up again, scrubbed my cheeks with my palms, and went into the bathroom. The face I saw in the mirror looked like it belonged to Rip Van Winkle, the face of someone who had slept for years. There were spidery creases in my cheeks, and my hair was like a garden of weeds growing in all directions. My eyes were gray and lifeless.

There was no point in standing there and waiting for the memory of the night before to return. I threw off my nightgown and stepped into the shower, deliberating whether to turn on cold water to jerk every sleeping muscle in my body awake. When I got back out, I felt more like Lazarus, happy to have stepped out of a grave. I quickly dried myself off, then hurriedly dressed and started down the stairs.

"Sylvia," I called. "Are you downstairs?"

At first, I heard nothing, and then I heard her answer me, but from above. She was in the cupola. I turned and went up to her. She was seated at her easel and leaning over her work. She sat back, and I saw the baby she had begun to draw now completed and painted in watercolors. Only she had painted his eyes a flaming red, so bright they looked like a fire was burning behind them. Every little detail of the baby's face was just as vivid, from the twist in his mouth that gave him a ridiculing smile to the thinness of his slightly pointed nose and the gauntness in his cheeks. She had drawn a baby, but it looked like a man in a baby's body.

"Why did you paint him like that?" I asked, my voice breathless.

"It's how Papa told me to paint him." She paused. "He's coming."

"That's not a pretty baby, Sylvia. You told me you were going to draw a pretty baby."

She looked up at me angrily. She hadn't looked at me that way for a very long time, since when she was a little girl and I would tell her she couldn't have something.

"It's Papa's pretty baby," she insisted.

"All right. All right. Draw and paint what you want. Did you have your breakfast?"

"Yes. Arden and I had breakfast."

"Arden and you? You got up yourself when he got up?"

She looked back at her picture. "I think the baby is beautiful."

"Good. Look, I'm sorry I slept so late. I don't know what happened. It was probably that pill I took," I said. She had no idea what I was talking about, but

I continued. "I shouldn't have had anything alcoholic with it. I guess I just passed out. I'm surprised neither of you woke me. You left me downstairs."

She continued to stare at her picture. I didn't know if she even heard me or if she understood why I was upset. She slowly turned and looked up at me, her eyelids narrow as she focused on her thoughts. "Babies are grown first inside you. When it's time for them to come out, God pushes them gently, and they flow out," she recited. "They have to be delivered to you. That's the man's job. Afterward, you carry the baby around like a mailman carries a letter in his pouch, and then the letter has to be opened."

"Who told you all that? Did Mr. Price tell you that? Well? Answer me. Did he?"

"Papa told me," she said.

"When? When?"

"I don't remember," she said, and looked back at her picture. "Maybe he never told you, and that's why you don't have a baby yet." She smiled. "But you will. There's a baby coming . . . see?"

"Not that baby, I hope," I said. "Did Mr. Price ever take off his clothes when he was with you, Sylvia?"

"I don't remember," she said too quickly.

"It won't be your fault if he did. Did he?"

"I don't remember," she said. She smiled again. "I made you lunch. Egg salad. Is it time for lunch?"

"Oh, Sylvia," I said, shaking my head. I glanced at her baby painting. "Yes, it's time for lunch. I hope you'll work on a prettier baby now."

Looking at the image, she simply said, "If Papa tells me."

Feeling exhausted again, I started out. She followed me, babbling about her egg salad, describing every step of the process the way I had taught her. I made myself some coffee and toast and actually ate the egg salad. It was delicious. She ate some, too, being as messy as ever.

Arden called a little while later to see how I was. "I tried to pick you up, but I wasn't exactly in a steady enough condition myself," he explained. "I figured you'd come up when you were ready. We had a good time, though. It's been long in coming. Good to hear some laughter in our house, wouldn't you say?"

"If I could remember it, yes," I said.

He laughed. "That's all right. You drank a little too much. I'll make sure that doesn't happen again."

"I don't think I want to take another pill, Arden."

"It did what it was supposed to, Audrina. Your sister was happy again. It felt good. Let's try to keep our house pleasant now. This coming weekend, I'll take both of you to Don's Steak House. It's a bit of a ride, but the food's great."

"You will?"

"Yes, I will. As long as you make an effort, too. Okay?"

I paused, thinking. Could he be right?

"Okay?"

"Yes, Arden, okay," I said.

I continued with the pills. It wasn't that they made me happy, exactly, but they kept me so subdued and calm that I didn't do or say much to change the new atmosphere Arden wanted in our home. I found myself falling asleep faster and earlier and waking up confused. What was worst of all was that dream. It returned. One time, Arden was naked, and so was Sylvia in the rocking chair. I watched the whispering and then saw Papa's face, and the dream ended.

I was afraid to mention it. I was beginning to believe that one of the side effects of the pill was nightmares. I did tell Arden that without going into detail.

"Okay," he said. "Maybe you'll do fine now without it. Put it aside for a while. Besides, I want you fully alert and hungry for our night out this weekend. Why don't you take Sylvia to buy a new dress and buy yourself one, too?"

"Yes," I said. "That sounds good. Oh, Arden, I'm sorry I've put you through so much."

"I'm not upset. Ups and downs are part of marriage, part of life. If anyone should know that, it's you, Audrina Lowe."

He kissed me, and I felt happiness surging back. I did what he suggested, went shopping for new clothes for both Sylvia and myself. I got us matching shoes, too. Despite her poorer eating habits for a while after the incident with Mr. Price, I noticed she had gained weight. She didn't look too heavy; it wasn't anything like that. In fact, she looked like she was blossoming, filling out. Even her breasts looked somewhat larger.

On our way home, Sylvia talked more than usual. She asked many questions about the stores, the other houses we saw, and people on the street. Her curiosity was never sharper. I laughed about it, and she laughed, too. We were all getting better, I thought. Arden was right about everything. But when Sylvia mentioned her picture of the baby again and asked me what name it would have, I decided I had better be firmer about it. There was too much dreaming going on at Whitefern. It was something I remembered Momma saying from time to time.

"I am not pregnant yet, Sylvia. I don't know if I will be, and unless you adopt a baby, go to an orphanage and choose one, you can't get a baby. I'm afraid the stork doesn't really bring them." I smiled. "Understand?"

She shook her head. "Baby's coming," she insisted.

Rather than upset her after such a pleasant day of shopping, I decided to drop the subject.

But to my surprise, she wouldn't. As soon as we entered the house, she turned to me and said, "Baby's inside me. He's coming."

I grabbed her shoulder. "What? Sylvia, what did you say?"

She turned, her arms full of her packages. "Baby is coming."

I thought for a moment. When was the last time I had checked on her period? Although she was good at taking care of herself once a month, I usually followed up, especially if she complained about cramps. I realized that she hadn't complained about anything.

I hurried to her as she started away and grabbed her arm so hard to turn her that she dropped her boxes. "Oh, look at what you made me do."

"Forget that, Sylvia. Did you have your period? Did you take care of it?"

"No."

"No? What are you saying?" I stood there, thinking hard, as she picked up her boxes. "Sylvia?"

"I don't remember," she said. "But I don't care. I don't like it." She walked to the stairway. "We have to get dressed up," she said. "Come on, Audrina. You said we'd do my hair, too."

I nodded and watched her walk up the stairs.

Was my heart still beating?

"I'll be right up," I shouted to her, and hurried to the telephone.

To my surprise and delight, Arden picked up instead of Mrs. Crown. "Hey," he said. "My secretary is in the restroom," he added, as if that was important. "Did you get some nice things?"

"Arden . . ."

"I'm still here, Audrina. Yes?"

"I think . . . I'm afraid . . ."

"What?"

"Sylvia."

"What about her now?"

"She might be pregnant," I said. The words seemed to burn my lips. I couldn't swallow.

"Arden?"

"Why do you say that?"

"She missed periods. I forgot to check her, and she even said she had a baby in her."

"How would she know that?"

"I don't know."

"Next thing you'll tell me is she said your father told her," he said. "Lucky this is a slow day. I'll come home early, but please be sure this isn't something imagined. I'm mentally exhausted. With both of you," he added, and hung up.

From somewhere in the shadows of Whitefern, I could hear Vera's gleeful laugh.

Truth Is the Loneliest of All

"I hope this isn't a false alarm, Audrina. You tend to get very melodramatic about everything these days," Arden said the moment he entered the house. He ripped off his scarf and took off his coat angrily. I knew he was upset about having to come home early.

The two of us went into the living room to talk. Sylvia was upstairs. He poured himself a drink quickly, claiming he needed it to settle himself down. He had rushed out of the office and left others to answer important calls.

"I'm sorry, Arden. I thought you should know right away."

"It seems to me that all we do these days is move from one crisis to another. It makes my head spin."

He turned to me with his drink in hand and took a long swallow.

I was tired of saying everything was my fault, but it was. Why didn't I check on Sylvia earlier? Why didn't I tell Arden that I had the terrible suspicion something more might have happened between Sylvia and Mr. Price?

He looked a bit calmer after the whiskey settled in his stomach. "Now, as I understand it, Audrina, women can miss periods for reasons other than pregnancy," he said, sitting in his favorite chair, which had been Papa's favorite. He continued to sip his drink and looked at me, probably expecting me to be more optimistic, too. But I wasn't.

"She's missed two periods. After I called you, I went upstairs to talk to her. I asked her questions as directly and simply as I could."

"And?" He leaned forward. "Well? What did she tell you?"

"All she talks about is Papa telling her she can bring a baby to Whitefern. That he will help."

"He will help? How's he supposed to do that from the grave?"

"Nothing she says makes sense, but she did admit again that Mr. Price had touched her when she was completely naked."

"You don't make someone pregnant by touching her," he said, leaning back and finishing his drink.

"She never complained, but her breasts are somewhat swollen and tender. As far as I know, she has had no nausea, but that doesn't always occur. I don't count how many times she urinates, and she hasn't shown more fatigue than usual, but everyone reacts differently to being pregnant. While I was waiting for you, I read up on it as much as I could. So? What should we do?"

He stared at me a moment, his eyes taking on that now familiar mix of anger and determination. "For now, I'd like you to do nothing, Audrina," he said.

"Nothing?"

"Don't say anything more to her about it. She'll just get more confused, and who knows what will happen?"

"We should at least bring her to Dr. Prescott," I said. "He can give her a full examination and tell us exactly what's happening."

"Let's wait. If it's something else, we'll only have opened a can of worms."

"And if it's not something else?"

He stared at me so long that I thought he hadn't heard the question.

"I mean, if she is pregnant, Arden . . ."

He shrugged and relaxed again. "We wanted a baby," he said softly.

"What?"

"She's your sister," he said, his gaze never wavering. "You have the same blood. It's almost the same as you having a baby."

"What?"

"Stop saying 'What?' I'm just thinking aloud."

"But it won't be our baby, Arden."

"You once suggested we adopt . . . not so long ago, in fact, didn't you?"

"Yes, but . . ."

"Well, at least you know the mother of this child. If it's a boy, he could look more like your father."

"But everyone would know."

"They don't have to know," he said. He put his empty glass down. "This is a house that has an easy time keeping secrets. What's another?"

"How do we keep this one? Eventually, she'll need real medical attention."

He smiled. "First, do you agree with me that if she is pregnant, the baby is at least half an Adare? The baby's half you?"

"It's not half me—it's half Sylvia. But yes, it does have our family blood."

"And certainly belongs here more than some strange orphan, then, right?"

"Yes, but I was thinking more about Sylvia, actually. She could never be a real mother, and people who find out about the child will assume the child is like her, with her disadvantages. He or she would have a difficult time in public school. I can't imagine other people permitting their children to play with Sylvia's."

"Let's not worry about that yet," he said. "Let's wait to confirm that this is true beyond a doubt, Audrina. I have a way of confirming it one way or another without risking any embarrassment."

"What way?"

"I know someone who will definitely keep any secret involving us, whether the secret was born in Whitefern or not."

"Who?"

"Her name is Helen Matthews. She's a retired maternity nurse. We have her retirement portfolio. It's not a very big one, but it's something. I know she could use the money, and she's very reliable. She would keep a confidence if I asked her to."

"How do you know that?"

"Let's just say I know a secret pertaining to her."

"What secret?"

"If I told you, it wouldn't be a secret, and she'd have no reason to believe I'd be reliable, trustworthy, thus she would have no reason to keep our confidence. But believe me, she does, and she will."

"How did she come to be one of my father's clients?"

"She wasn't. She became one of mine. I approached her one day and persuaded her to transfer her funds into our brokerage. That's all beside the point," he said, waving his hand at me as if he was chasing off a fly. "The point is, she was a practicing maternity nurse for more than thirty years and on many occasions delivered babies all by herself. I wouldn't exactly call her a midwife, either. She's more educated. She almost became a doctor."

"She lives in our village?"

"Not far, on the outskirts. She did once, but when her husband died and her son moved off to marry and live in New York City, she got herself a smaller home."

"But she's not a doctor, Arden. Sylvia would need real medical attention."

"Stop saying that," he snapped back at me. "I assure you that she can do whatever Dr. Prescott can do. And she has the wherewithal to do it all at my request. Can't you trust me on this? Don't you have any faith in me at all as the head of this household? Am I forever going to walk six paces behind in your father's shadow, a shadow you insist on casting over everything involving this house and us? How do you think this makes me feel?"

"It's not that. Honest it isn't, Arden. I feel so . . . overwhelmed and so stupid," I said.

He smirked, shook his head, and took a deep breath. "Audrina, Audrina, Audrina, what would you have done if you realized it earlier? Would you have taken her for an abortion?"

I looked up at him. The thought had crossed my mind.

"Of course, I thought of it, too, but regardless of the situation, the child is still your father's grandchild, is it not?"

"But . . ."

"But nothing. It's too late to sit around and ponder. Let's get a confirmation of your suspicions, and then we'll make a decision, a decision best for us all, not just Sylvia," he added. "Okay?"

"Matthews. That name is familiar."

"Her son attended Whitefern High School, but he was a grade ahead of me. Well? I'd like to get things arranged today, Audrina. I do have a business to run."

"Well, if you think she's capable . . ."

"I don't think it. I know it. Didn't you listen to anything I said?"

"All right. Then do what you think best, Arden. I feel too overwhelmed to think straight."

"Exactly." He stood and started for his office. "Where is she now?"

"She's up in her room getting herself ready for dinner at the restaurant tonight."

"You sure you'll be up for it now?" he asked.

"Oh, yes. I don't want to disappoint her. Or myself," I added.

He smiled. "Nor should you, nor should any of us. I'll make arrangements with Mrs. Matthews and come up to shower, shave, and dress. I'll think of something to celebrate," he said. He turned to start away.

"We'll wait for Mrs. Matthews to examine her, but in my heart, I feel Sylvia was right," I said.

"What?" He turned back. "About what? She didn't diagnose herself, did she? You haven't educated her that well."

"No, but if you'll remember, she was the one who predicted that there was a baby coming," I said.

He shrugged. "You're a tribe of witches. What can I say?" He laughed and walked on.

If Sylvia had even the slightest suspicion that I was worried about her now, she didn't show it or maybe even care. She was too excited about going to a restaurant for dinner. She flitted about, gazing at herself in the mirror every ten seconds, checking her hair and her makeup. I continually had to assure her that she looked pretty enough to go out. Finally, I decided to share some of Momma's jewelry with her, something I rarely wore myself.

She was stunned when I opened the case with the rectangular diamonds in a necklace and matching earrings.

"You can wear this tonight, Sylvia."

"Me?"

I plucked the necklace out and put it on her. She sat gazing at herself in the mirror. It lay just at the peak of her cleavage. She touched it, her eyes wide with more feminine pride than I ever thought her capable of having. Then I showed her how to put on the earrings. She looked at me to see if I approved.

"It all looks beautiful on you, Sylvia. Momma would have been very proud."

"But what will you wear?"

"I have something Arden bought me four years ago. Don't worry."

She turned to look at herself again and ran her fingers over the diamonds.

For a few minutes, at least, I thought maybe I could, for the evening, put aside my fears and anxiety and really enjoy myself. Helping her choose what to wear, sitting beside her at her vanity table, and doing my own makeup, I did feel as I had dreamed I would with my younger sister, two young women giggling and flirting with their images in a mirror.

Aunt Ellsbeth, Vera, and even Papa would surely be sitting up in their graves, astounded that I had brought her so far from the disabled little girl who had been brought to Whitefern and left for us all to treat as a burden. Of course, she was still a far bigger responsibility than a young woman half her age would be. Pregnancy would be terrifying for her. No matter how many times I explained things to her, she would be confused. I hoped this Mrs. Matthews would be sensitive to all that. I made a mental note to be sure Arden impressed her with just how special this patient would be.

Arden was dressed to the nines, as Papa would say.

He had never looked more handsome and successful in his charcoal-black suit and silver tie. And when Sylvia and I descended the stairs, he raved about how beautiful we were. Sylvia actually flushed with embarrassment when he winked at me and gave her a kiss before hooking his arm with hers and then with mine.

"I'll be the envy of every man there," he declared. He walked us out and then surprised me by saying, "Why don't you two sit in the back? I'll be like your chauffeur tonight."

He followed that with a look suggesting that I should stay close to Sylvia and keep her comfortable and confident. He held open the door for us, and we got into the car.

"I have the Whitefern girls," he declared. "No man could ask for more."

There was probably no one better at ignoring and avoiding unhappy thoughts than Arden. Look at how well he had done with all that had happened to me. The way he was behaving right now made it seem like everything we had discussed earlier was simply a misunderstanding. I was afraid to interfere with his joviality by asking after Mrs. Matthews, how the phone call had gone. It would wait until later, when we were alone.

After all, I had yet to tell Sylvia that I thought she was pregnant. It was probably better to wait until Mrs. Matthews confirmed it, and then the explanations would begin. How dark that tunnel through which we would pass looked to me now. *Blot it out for the moment, or you won't enjoy a second of the evening*, I told myself. I turned to my sister, who sat so still with a smile frozen on her face. The excitement in her eyes made them glisten in the glow of passing car lights. She continually touched the diamonds, maybe to be sure they were still there and she hadn't imagined them.

I realized that for Sylvia, dressing up with makeup and jewelry and going out to dinner was like going to the moon. I was more excited for her than I was for myself. Arden had chosen one of the fancier restaurants just outside of Whitefern. He explained that he often came here to take very wealthy clients to lunch or sometimes dinner. They certainly knew him well enough at the restaurant. The maitre d' fawned over him and took us to what Arden said was the best table. He sat between Sylvia and me. When I gazed around the beautiful room, with its landscapes and mirrored wall sconces, the bulbs looking more like candles, and I saw how most of the other guests were gazing our way, I couldn't help but feel the optimism Arden cherished and sought.

"Darkness seeks those who keep their candles of hope unlit," Momma once told me. I had to brighten mine.

Arden ordered a bottle of champagne. Everyone was watching when the waiter popped it open. Sylvia laughed as some of it bubbled over, but it was poured quickly into our glasses, and then Arden raised his. Sylvia looked at me to copy everything I was doing.

"To the future of Whitefern," Arden said. "May it finally become the grand home it was meant to be."

Sylvia giggled at the clink of glasses and carefully sipped hers while watching how I sipped mine.

"Should I order a bottle of wine?" Arden asked.

"I think this is all the alcohol we should have right now," I replied, nodding at Sylvia.

"Okay. I'll get my favorite red by the glass. Tonight I want to have the filet mignon." He winked. "Maybe Sylvia should have that, too."

I ordered it for her, so I had to order it for myself, even though I had nowhere near the appetite to finish half of it.

All the table manners I had taught Sylvia over the years had their first real test this particular night, because she didn't have the comfort and security her own home provided. Whenever anyone nearby laughed, she looked quickly to see if she had done something wrong. What made me laugh was the way she inspected the salad.

"They don't cut the carrots right," she said. "Some pieces are bigger than others."

"It's okay, Sylvia," I said. "They don't have someone with your artistic talent doing it, but it will taste the same."

She looked at me skeptically. Maybe it would taste the same to me, I realized, but not to her. She did like the filet mignon and especially enjoyed the chocolate soufflé we had for dessert.

While we ate, some men stopped by to say hello to Arden. He introduced us, and Sylvia recited the "Pleased to meet you" I had practiced often with her. I could see all the men were attracted to her, but she was oblivious to the looks of admiration and desire in their eyes.

Before one particular man approached us, Arden informed me that he was one of the top five investors in our brokerage firm. He looked to be in his mid-sixties, with a tanned face and beautiful blue eyes. I thought he was close to Papa's height. I recalled his name, Charles Billings, and I remembered him now from Papa's funeral. He was one of the few who had attended the church service, but he hadn't come to the house later.

"Now, how do you deserve two beautiful women, Arden, while most men here are lucky to have one?" he asked, feigning annoyance.

Sylvia's eyes widened. She looked at me to see how I was going to react.

"Thank you, Mr. Billings," I said, before Arden introduced us. "This is my sister, Sylvia."

"I can see the resemblance. You lucky dog," he told Arden.

"I married well," Arden said, sounding a little peeved at the way I had taken control.

"In more ways than one," Mr. Billings said. "Tough week in the market. I hope we see a little bull in the coming days."

"We will," Arden said, as if he had control of the stocks and bonds.

"So, what are you celebrating?" Mr. Billings asked, nodding at the champagne bottle in the bucket.

Arden looked at me for a moment with an expression

on his face that I rarely saw these days. He looked like he was fighting not to burst with pride.

"We are almost one hundred percent sure," he began, and turned to Mr. Billings, "that my wife is pregnant."

Every muscle in my body seemed to collapse with shock. I had to put my glass of water down quickly, or I thought I would drop it.

"Well, congratulations," Mr. Billings said. "Making money is great, but making a family is divine."

"Exactly," Arden said. "Thank you."

I watched Mr. Billings walk away and saw him start to tell his wife and everyone at his table what Arden had just said. Sylvia had her attention completely on the chocolate soufflé now and apparently hadn't heard a word. I stared at Arden, my eyes full of questions.

He just shook his head. "Don't look so worried, Audrina."

"Worried? Why did you say that?"

He smiled and finished his wine. Then he looked at the bottle of champagne. "A little left." He poured it into his glass and drank it.

"Arden, answer me."

"Relax, Audrina. I have a brilliant plan."

I said nothing. After he paid the bill and we started to leave, he paused at Mr. Billings's table, and Mr. Billings introduced his wife and his two friends.

"I'm so happy for you," Mrs. Billings told us.

"Me, too," Sylvia said. I hadn't noticed, but she had some chocolate soufflé on her lips. "I love chocolate."

No one spoke, Sylvia's words hanging in the air.

"Thank you, Flora," Arden said to Mrs. Billings, before turning to Mr. Billings. "Here's to a bull market."

"Amen to that," Mr. Billings said, and we walked out.

The valet brought our car around, and we got in.

"Did you enjoy your dinner, ladies?" Arden asked as we drove off.

"They could have cut the carrots better," Sylvia said.

Arden laughed loudly.

I said nothing until we had gotten home and I had Sylvia get out of her clothes and prepare for bed. Then I went to our bedroom, where he was already in bed, browsing through one of his business magazines. He looked up sharply when I entered.

"Everything is set with Mrs. Matthews. She'll be here tomorrow. I'll take a break and come home, but you had better prepare Sylvia for her."

"What were you saying at the restaurant? What is this plan you have?" I asked.

He put down his magazine and put his hands behind his head.

"Everything you said about how Sylvia's child would be treated is true, and everything you said about how difficult it would be for her to be any sort of mother is even more true. Now, no one knows that Sylvia might be pregnant. Hardly anyone knows her, while most who know us, this family, know how she is."

"And?"

"So why not have people believe the baby coming is your baby, our baby?"

"My baby?"

I knew what he wanted, but the idea of my simulating pregnancy was daunting. What if someone found out I was pretending? The embarrassment would be frightening, but it was a way to protect Sylvia. Maybe I had to risk it.

"How do we do that, Arden?" I started to take off my dress.

"Simple. We have you go through the pregnancy just as Sylvia is going through it. If anything," he added, sitting forward, "it might make it easier on her to have you mimicking whatever happens to her and whatever she has to do."

"But people will see me and—"

He put his hand up. "I have that figured out, Audrina. After about four or five months, we'll keep people from seeing you." He shrugged. "We can have something made for you to wear that makes you look pregnant. Maybe we'll deliberately let some of the weekly groundskeepers, or someone else who comes onto the property, get a look at you and be able to tell people you're pregnant."

"What about Mr. Ralph? He will see Sylvia. He's in and out of the house often to fix things."

"Mr. Ralph will do and say whatever I tell him. He sees nothing and says nothing. He's always been that way. You know that."

"And Sylvia?"

"We've kept her pretty much sheltered here. We'll

just make it more intense when the time is right. We'll keep her up in her room. You can tell her she has to stay in bed, or Mrs. Matthews will tell her."

I stood there in my bra and panties, looking at him and thinking about his plan. "This Mrs. Matthews, she'll know the truth."

"She'll just have to keep two secrets," he said, smiling. "As I've said many times, what's another secret or two at Whitefern?"

"That's a lot of trust to place in a stranger, Arden."

"It's not a matter of trust. It's a tradeoff. Don't worry about it. I have it all under control."

He picked up his magazine, glanced at it, and then lowered it again. "The best part of this, Audrina, is that you will be a mother after all. But," he said cautiously, "let's wait for Mrs. Matthews to confirm that Sylvia's pregnant."

He started to read his magazine as if I had agreed to everything. It wasn't that easy for me. For one thing, I would be pretending to be something I wasn't again. I'd have to act a part, like in a play. It was still painful to remember how I'd been convinced that I was a second Audrina. Even when I'd believed it, I had wanted so much to be myself. For another thing, this would be as much as admitting that my becoming pregnant and having my own child was truly a dead idea. It would never happen.

I felt his eyes on me as I crossed the room to the bathroom to prepare for bed.

"I hope you enjoyed our dinner otherwise," he said when I reappeared in my nightgown. "I thought

Sylvia did very well, too. That's all thanks to you. You both did look beautiful."

"I enjoyed it, yes."

"Well, if there is a baby, when he or she is old enough, we'll go out a lot more. I've always envied fathers taking their wives and children out for Sunday brunch. Just think. We can really be a family . . . finally." And as if that explained everything, he put out his lamp and lay down.

"You told Mrs. Matthews about Sylvia, right?" I asked. "She understands that she's special and needs special treatment?"

He turned. "Of course I did, Audrina. You've got to stop worrying. As I said, I have it all under control now. You will have to trust me."

After a moment of thinking, I said, "That horrible man. He shouldn't get away with this."

"Don't start that again. If we accuse him of something, we'll ruin our plan. For now, just let it go. We have more important things to occupy our attention. And if you cross-examine Sylvia about it, about how it happened, when it happened, where it happened, any of it, you'll make things worse. I know her well enough after all these years to predict she'll feel guilty and terrible and sit around crying all the time. A bad thing happened. It's done, over with. Now we have to be sure nothing else terrible occurs, like a miscarriage. You probably remember Vera's vividly enough to know what that could mean for Sylvia."

"Papa would have taken out his Civil War pistol and driven over to the Prices' and shot him," I said.

"You mean like he shot the boys who raped you?" Arden asked.

It was a cold and cruel thing to say, but I understood why he was saying it. I was implying that he wasn't doing the manly thing for Sylvia.

"Clever people handle things like this in a way that doesn't bring more pain and trouble to themselves," he continued. He looked away as if he was remembering something. "Stop thinking about it, or you'll never fall asleep."

He turned toward me again, and although there was just a glimmer of light from the moon peeking between trees, I could see his wry smile.

"Think about being a mother instead," he said.

If he meant that as a comfort, he was wrong. That kept me from falling asleep even more.

Living a Lie

Arden had said that Mrs. Matthews was scheduled to come to Whitefern at around eleven in the morning. Right after we had cleaned up our breakfast dishes and put everything away, I had Sylvia sit on the settee in the living room, and I began an explanation to prepare her for a stranger coming to our home to examine her. The way she smiled at me was eerie. It was almost as if she knew exactly what I was going to say, and, contrary to what I might think, that made her happy.

"Something is going on inside you, Sylvia," I began. "Arden and I think you might be pregnant."

She nodded. There was certainly no shock, surprise, or fear on her face. This was unexpected. Perhaps she didn't understand and was simply trying to please me.

"Do you understand what I'm telling you, Sylvia? When I say we think you might be pregnant, we mean there might be a baby forming inside you."

"Yes, I know," she said. Then she smiled and said, "Papa told me, and he said the baby would be forming in you, too, Audrina."

For a moment, I was speechless. If I ever said any-thing clever or prophetic when I was little, Momma would always smile, tenderly brush my hair, and say, "Out of the mouths of babes . . ." I felt like saying that to Sylvia. Even if she had somehow overheard the things Arden had said, his plan in particular, she would never be able to comprehend it and embrace it. However, I couldn't imagine her coming up with this idea herself. Her even suggesting such a thing gave me a chill. Out of habit, I looked at Papa's chair. So often when I was teaching something to Sylvia, he would sit there and half-listen, occasionally smiling at how hard I pursued something with her until she had grasped it. I could easily imagine him sitting there now, with a similar smile on his face, encouraging me to go on.

"This is a house that welcomes ghosts," Aunt Ells-beth had once told Vera and me. She'd hugged herself when she'd said it, and both of us had looked around, expecting to see some spirit whisk past us.

"When did Papa say this to you, Sylvia?" I asked now. It was like following someone you knew was lost, traveling down roads that led nowhere, but I had to question her.

"One time when I was in the rocking chair," she said.

"What time? When?"

"I don't know the time, Audrina. I didn't look at a clock." She looked like she was going to cry because she was disappointing me. "I don't remember."

"Okay, okay. Forget about that. There is a woman coming to see you this morning. Her name is Mrs.

Matthews. She's like a doctor. She helps deliver babies when it's time for them to come out. She will make sure you are pregnant and that you are doing okay, and then she will help us with everything that has to be done. I'll be with you all the time."

"You have to be. She has to make sure everything is all right with you, too," Sylvia said.

I closed my eyes. She was fixated on this idea. Perhaps, though, Arden was right. It would make things easier for her, and for us taking care of her, if she thought it was true and I mimicked everything happening to her.

"Right. Me, too. She'll be like Dr. Prescott, okay?"

She nodded, continuing to smile.

I still wasn't sure she understood the significance of what I was telling her. How detailed and scientific should I get? For most women, being pregnant wasn't exactly a picnic. There was expected discomfort. Sylvia, who liked to rush around the house and practically fly up the stairs, would find it a terrible burden, especially when she was four or five months along, and when she was seven or eight months . . . I simply couldn't imagine it. It wasn't only what she would look like and how confused she would be. There were dangers, too, not only to the baby but also to the mother.

However, I decided not to say too much more before Mrs. Matthews arrived. Arden's advice that morning as we dressed to go down to breakfast was to take it day by day and not obsess about it. He was the one who had warned, "We don't want to panic Sylvia or frighten her about all this. That could turn out worse."

"I know that, Arden," I'd told him. "Will Mrs. Matthews know that?"

"She's been well informed about Sylvia," he had assured me. "She is quite capable. We'll be lucky to have her. She'll make this far easier than you could imagine."

Nevertheless, I was on pins and needles until the doorbell rang. I had told Sylvia to go up to her room, change into her nightgown, and wait. She would be examined there. I wanted a few minutes alone with Mrs. Matthews before she saw Sylvia and before Arden got home, too.

When I opened the door, I found a lean woman, as tall as Arden, with dark gray hair trimmed sharply halfway down her long neck. She had a hard face, her cheeks flat, with skin so white it was almost transparent. Inky blue veins could be seen in her temples. I thought you wouldn't need an X-ray to discover if she had fractured a cheekbone. Her nose was small but a bit pointed, and her pale pink lips were as thin as string. Her eyes were coal-black with tiny gray spots. She wore a navy-blue coat over a nurse's uniform and carried a satchel that looked exactly like Dr. Prescott's, clutching it in her long fingers so tightly I could see the veins in the top of her hand. It was as if she was afraid she'd drop it or have it snatched away.

"Mrs. Matthews?" I asked. I knew it was a silly question. Who else would be at our door precisely at eleven? But I didn't want to just say hello.

"That's who I am," she said. She nodded her head

and stepped forward as a way of saying, *Please step back and let me in.*

It was a gray, cold early-February day. I retreated quickly, and she entered and paused to gaze at the house, her head bobbing from nine o'clock to twelve o'clock to three o'clock.

"It's as big as I expected," she said. "Quite cluttered. Family heirlooms, most of it, I imagine."

"Everything has some memory for us, yes," I said.

She looked at me, nodded, looked at the house again, and then turned back to me. "You are Mrs. Lowe, then?"

Did she think I was a maid?

"Yes, ma'am. Audrina Lowe, Arden's wife."

She studied me as if I really was the one who was pregnant. "I remember you when you were a little girl. You've grown into an attractive woman."

"Thank you."

"I recall your mother was quite beautiful."

"Yes, she was."

"That's a tragedy we don't want repeated," she said, the corners of her mouth drawn in.

"I hope not," I said. "The very thought terrifies me."

"As it should anyone. Well, let's get to it. Where's your sister?"

"She's in her room. I'll take you there. You understand what she's like?"

"Mentally retarded. I would hate to count how many girls like that I've delivered or assisted in delivering. Nature gave them the ability to produce offspring but left them unprotected when it comes to sexual matters, not that some of the smartest girls don't get into trouble. I've had plenty of them, too. Whenever I see that, I believe there very likely is a vengeful God."

"I wouldn't categorize her as mentally retarded. She's slow to understand things, but that's because she was underdeveloped when she was born prematurely and—"

"Call her what you want. I know what to expect."

"She's very, very sensitive, Mrs. Matthews. She has the body of a woman but the emotional development of a little girl."

She turned to me, the corners of her mouth drawn in again as she pressed her upper lip over the lower one before speaking. "I think I've been doing this long enough to know how to handle a pregnant girl regardless of her mental and emotional age. The physical aspects aren't different. Shall we get on with it? According to Mr. Lowe, you're not even certain she's pregnant, and it could be that this is all idle chatter."

"I am sure of it, I'm afraid," I said. "I don't have medical training like you do, but there are things a woman can sense."

She raised her eyebrows. "We'll soon see."

I nodded and led the way to the stairs. After I started up, I realized she wasn't following. She had paused at the bottom and stood looking up. "Something wrong?" I asked.

"Any bedrooms downstairs?"

"There are two in the rear of the house, but neither one has been used for ages, decades, really. They were meant for servants, and we've never even thought of them as part of the house. They don't have fireplaces and haven't even been cleaned for ages. Why?"

"I don't fancy climbing up and down the stairs between the kitchen and her room as many times as I might have to. If she is indeed pregnant, at one point I'll be attending to your sister closely, and it will be easier if she is down here. It's also wise to avoid any possibilities of falling when you're pregnant, and I think we both know that stairways can be deadly. If she's pregnant, you'll put her in one of the rear bedrooms," she declared with the tone of a fait accompli.

"But . . . they don't even have heat. The central heating my father had installed didn't provide for them."

"You'll get portable heaters. Really, this is not a world-shattering problem."

"It will be for Sylvia. She is very comfortable in her room. She's been there ever since she was brought home from the hospital. It's not easy for her to adjust to changes."

She made a *humph* sound. "Imagine the changes that come over you when you get pregnant. She'll have a lot to adjust to. This should be the least of it." She started up after me, glaring at me when I didn't move.

"What about her going up to her studio to do her art?" I asked.

"Are you serious? Send her up another flight of stairs for a hobby?"

"It's not a hobby for her. It's very important to her."

She sighed deeply and shook her head. "Bring her art supplies down to her room."

"But—"

"Am I to see her or not?"

"I'm sorry," I said, and continued up quickly. I led her to Sylvia's bedroom. When we entered, Sylvia was at her vanity table. She had brushed her hair and tied it with a red ribbon. Now she was putting on lipstick, too.

"What is she doing?" Mrs. Matthews asked. "We're not taking pictures for a maternity magazine."

"Sylvia, don't you remember I said Mrs. Matthews was coming to examine you this morning?"

"Oh, yes, Audrina." She smiled. "I just wanted to look nice for her."

Mrs. Matthews's thin, mostly gray eyebrows knitted, and then she stepped further into the room. "Hello, Sylvia," she said. "I'm Helen Matthews. I'm here to see what's going on with you."

"We're having a baby," Sylvia said.

"Perhaps," Mrs. Matthews said, not picking up on the "we." "Let's check you out. Just lie down on your bed, please. Nothing will hurt, I promise."

"It hurts when the baby comes out, but it doesn't last long. Papa told me that."

"Hopefully that's so," Mrs. Matthews said. She looked at me and almost, I thought, smiled.

I stood back to watch her. Sylvia watched her, too, her eyes wide with interest after Mrs. Matthews had put on plastic gloves. Sylvia's face was full of surprise, but she did not utter a sound when Mrs. Matthews had her bend her legs and spread them.

"Can you see the baby?" Sylvia asked. I brought my hand up to cover my smile.

Her innocent trust never ceased to amaze me. It was probably the main reason Papa had made me swear I would always look after her. But I hadn't done that very well, I reminded myself.

"Not yet," Mrs. Matthews said. When she stepped back, she took off her gloves and turned to me. "We can confirm it with a urine sample, but I would say she's a good six weeks along."

"Six weeks? You're sure."

"I said we'd confirm it with a urine sample, but yes, I'm sure. I've seen more wombs than Henry the Eighth," she added, which was a line I imagined she had used often.

"Hello!" We heard Arden shout from below. He had come in and was heading up the steps.

"I'll see to the urine test," Mrs. Matthews said. She turned to Sylvia. "Let's go into the bathroom, Sylvia. We have one more thing to do today."

I stepped out into the hallway as Arden turned toward Sylvia's room.

"Well?" he asked.

"She's confident it's a yes. Six weeks, probably, which makes it right when Mr. Price was giving her art lessons. She's conducting a urine test to confirm it."

He nodded, not looking as upset as I felt or as I'd imagined he would be. "Well, then, there's nothing to do but go forward with our plan."

"Your plan," I said. He looked at me sharply. "But

a plan, yes. I understand. It's just that now that it's all true, I feel a bit numb."

"You'll get over it," he said. He walked past me to the bathroom and stood in the doorway, looking in. "Hi, Helen," he said. "When you're finished here, Audrina will show you to my office downstairs, and we'll discuss the arrangements. Come quickly, as I have to get back to my office."

From the way he spoke to her, the tone of his voice, I concluded he'd been telling the truth; he did have some secret he could hold over her. Did he have such confidence in her that he didn't have to wait for a confirmation? How did he know so much about her abilities? All sorts of suspicions burst like fireworks in my mind.

He walked past me without another word and hurried down the stairs. I heard Sylvia return to her room and went there. She was sitting comfortably on the bed, her hands in her lap. She didn't look at all disturbed or upset, so I had to conclude that Mrs. Matthews did know how to turn on good bedside manner when it was necessary. But that didn't give me full confidence in how she would handle Sylvia. After all, Mr. Price's assurance that he knew how to handle special education students was what had brought us here.

"You don't have to do it right away," Mrs. Matthews said, "but prepare that bedroom downstairs. The test confirms it." She closed up her satchel methodically. "I'll look into prenatal vitamins. Of course,

I'm assuming you and Mr. Lowe want to keep the baby."

"Yes," I said. I knew I sounded weak and indecisive, but she chose to ignore it.

As she started out, Sylvia called to her, and the prickly woman turned back.

"Don't you have to do it to Audrina, too?" my sister asked. "Audrina has to pee on that little stick."

Mrs. Matthews looked at me, squeezing her nose and pursing her lips as if a whiff of something rotten had flown under her nostrils.

"She'll do it in my bedroom, Sylvia," I said. Mrs. Matthews shook her head and stepped out. "I've got to show Mrs. Matthews something first. I'll be right back."

"Pray tell, what was that about?" Mrs. Matthews asked.

"My husband will explain it, Mrs. Matthews. Right this way," I said, and started down the stairs.

She followed me, and when we arrived at Arden's office, he looked up from his desk.

"Mrs. Matthews wants to know why Sylvia thinks I'm pregnant, too, Arden."

"Thank you, Audrina," he said. He stood up and came around his desk to the door. "Why don't you go back to see if everything is all right with Sylvia while I speak with Mrs. Matthews and explain it all." He smiled with his all-too-familiar self-confidence.

I looked at her and nodded. The moment I stepped back, Arden closed the door.

Secrets had a natural life here, I thought as I went back upstairs. They were born and nurtured like precious flowers. They never died in revelation, either. They stuck to our walls and our lives.

"While I was peeing, I told Mrs. Matthews I had drawn and painted the baby," Sylvia said, as soon as I returned to her room. She was lying on her bed, staring up at the ceiling.

"Did you?"

"Yes, and told her that's why I knew the baby was coming. I told her it might be a boy, too."

"Was she surprised?"

"No. She said boys are harder. What's that mean?"

"Harder to bring up, I imagine."

"Because they get dirty and get into fights?"

"Among other things, yes," I said. "Let's get you dressed. Today we're supposed to clean the pantry, remember?"

"No."

"Well, we are. You go there and start taking everything out the way we did a few months ago."

"Is there going to be a mouse again?" she asked, sitting up and making a scrunched-up face.

"I hope not."

"Maybe there'll be one dead in the trap. Don't worry. I'm not afraid of it."

"I know you're not, Sylvia, but remember not to touch it. They can carry diseases, and you can't get sick now."

"I can't?"

"I mean you shouldn't. Not when you're pregnant."

"Then you can't get sick, either?"

"Right. Let's go."

When we went downstairs, she went off to the pantry, and I returned to Arden's office. Mrs. Matthews was already gone, and he was on the phone. He put his hand up, finished his call, and turned to me.

"It's all set," he said.

"What's all set?"

"What I described we would do, Audrina. She's fully aboard. She understood completely and will play along with your being pregnant, and Sylvia, as far as the world outside is to know, is not." He sat back, smiling. "She's even going to come up with a sort of girdle apparatus that you can wear to show the months as time goes by."

"I wish I knew why you were so confident in her, Arden."

"You'll have to trust me." He stood. "Now, I have to go back to the office."

"She wants me to move Sylvia into one of the rear bedrooms downstairs."

He nodded. "Yes. She mentioned that."

"They'll need portable heaters and more light, and we'll have to bring her art supplies down. She won't like it."

"Don't worry. We'll clean up both of those rooms and make them comfortable."

"Both? Why both?"

"What Sylvia has to do you'll have to do, right? She'll put up with it if you are doing it, too. We'll have to prepare one of the rooms for Mrs. Matthews. She'll move in after a while, Audrina. It will be like having a private-duty nurse around the clock. Don't worry about it," he said. He kissed me quickly on the cheek and started to leave.

"But why would we have a private-duty maternity nurse, Arden?" I asked, chasing after him.

He paused. "Because you will be said to have problems with the pregnancy, and that's why you can't leave the house. See? It's a perfect plan." He smiled and continued out.

I stood there thinking. I recalled one of Momma and Aunt Ellsbeth's Tuesday teatimes in which Momma, playing Aunt Mercy Marie, had pointed her finger accusingly at Aunt Ellsbeth and shouted with venom, "Lies are like rats. You give them a home, and they will devour it and everyone in it."

"Why?" Vera had asked. She always loved to sit on the floor and watch them go at each other, taking turns to be Aunt Mercy Marie.

Momma had turned to her, her eyes narrowed. "Because one lie begets another, and that begets another, and woe be to anyone who swims in that swamp."

Vera hadn't been afraid of anyone or anything, even Papa. She'd giggled.

Momma had turned to Aunt Ellsbeth and, pointing to Vera, said, "See?"

I hadn't been sure what she meant by that, but in time, I understood. Aunt Ellsbeth's whole life with Vera was born from a lie.

Now I went to join Sylvia to try to keep her busy and not thinking about what lay ahead—for both of us.

The next day, Mrs. Matthews brought Sylvia her prenatal vitamins and a bottle full of the same pills for me, telling me it couldn't hurt me to take vitamins. She checked Sylvia's vitals, blood pressure, and temperature and, with Sylvia watching, did the same for me.

"She has better blood pressure than you do," Mrs. Matthews muttered.

How could she not expect that? Sylvia was totally relaxed and trusting; I was the one who was tense and nervous. No matter what Arden had agreed to with Mrs. Matthews, I was still embarrassed by the deception.

"As I understand it, your sister performs many household duties?" Mrs. Matthews asked.

"She helps out, yes."

"At one point, we'll want to restrict her activities. I encourage walking, but you have a special circumstance here, so you'll have to restrict that after a while to inside only."

The full impact of all this subterfuge hit me, and for a few moments, I was stunned. Too often, I remembered how restricted I had been when I was growing up. Papa wouldn't let me go to school for years, and I practically never left the house, except for church and visits to "my" grave in the cemetery.

"My goodness," Mrs. Matthews said, seeing the expression on my face. "You've not been sentenced to life imprisonment. Frankly, I think your husband has come up with a very clever plan. Just think of all the nastiness you'll avoid. Believe me, people are unforgiving and eager to pounce when they have an opportunity to take joy in someone else's misery. I've seen plenty of that," she added, and closed her satchel.

"Yes, so have I," I said.

"Then you understand." She smiled, if I could call it that. Her skin seemed to fold in at her cheeks, and her thin lips stretched so that I could see tiny ripples in them. Her smile was more like a flashbulb going off, an instant of light and gone. "I've put my telephone number on the refrigerator. Call me if there is the slightest problem. You want to watch for unexpected bleeding, shortness of breath, sudden dizziness, or any swelling and pain in her calf muscles."

I didn't think Sylvia was listening. She seemed absorbed in one of my new fashion magazines. But without looking up, she asked, "Audrina, too?"

We both looked at her and simultaneously said, "Yes."

I glanced at Mrs. Matthews, realizing I had a co-conspirator.

"I'll stop by every two days for the time being and then more frequently," she said. She nodded at Sylvia and left.

"She's very nice," Sylvia said. "You were right, Audrina. She told me she gave birth to a boy."

"I can't imagine what his life was like," I muttered, and went into the Roman Revival salon to ponder the journey we were embarking on, as short as it might seem. There were months to go, and I painfully recalled how slowly time would pass when I was confined. I hated the thought that I might once again be sitting by a window, gazing out, and dreaming of going off to be with other girls and boys my age, something that should have been so natural and easy to do.

Every day now, I tried to forget all that by working harder in the house. In the weeks that followed, I prepared the two unused bedrooms in the rear. I wanted to give their walls a fresh coat of paint, but Mrs. Matthews thought the odor would disturb Sylvia. Arden brought home the portable heaters and hooked them up. He moved some lamps and even rolled one of our bedroom rugs up and carried it with Mr. Ralph to the bedroom he'd decided I would be using. I wanted him to put it in Sylvia's, but he insisted, claiming that I was the one who was making the greater sacrifice.

Although Mr. Ralph was as trusted a servant as anyone could have, he naturally was curious about why we were preparing the rooms. I heard Arden explain that I was pregnant and the maternity nurse had insisted on my not having to go up and down the stairs. There could be a lot of medical attention needed.

"Sylvia," he said, "is so dependent on Audrina, as you know. She imitates everything she does."

The explanation satisfied Mr. Ralph. Arden whispered something to him that caused him to laugh. I nodded to myself, thinking that Arden really was good at handling people. He could be charming and convincing when he had to be. In more and more ways, he reminded me of Papa. They were both comfortable with lies.

For now, he had nothing more to explain. Sylvia

wasn't showing, of course. That didn't happen until she was in her fourth month, and it was then that Mrs. Matthews brought the customized girdle for me to wear in public. Sylvia didn't have to move downstairs yet, and I was still permitted to leave the house to do basic shopping, but Sylvia was not. I had to do it while she was taking a nap or involved in her art up in the cupola. Enough people saw me and believed that I was pregnant. Arden would brag about who had been deceived and how well our plan was working.

The following week, Sylvia began complaining about lower back pain, and one day, she had some blood spotting on her panties. I called Mrs. Matthews, who came over quickly and examined her. She said Sylvia was all right, but she decided that the time had come for her to move in with us. To make Sylvia happy, I complained about lower back pain, too. Maybe it was my imagination, but I thought I actually felt it.

It wasn't until Mrs. Matthews physically moved into the house that the reality of what would happen struck me. Every moment of our day and all our waking hours at night, there would be a stranger present. The privacy we had enjoyed, even the privacy associated with our family memories, would be invaded. I was, of course, afraid of what would come out of Sylvia's mouth. Mrs. Matthews was to be there at our dinners, breakfasts, and lunches. She would hear everything Arden would tell us about the business, or as much as he would want to share. There would be real privacy only in our bedroom or if I met with him in his office. I kept telling myself that it would only be for a few months.

But if anyone knew that months could seem like years at Whitefern, it was I.

As soon as Mrs. Matthews brought her things, she ordered that Sylvia be moved downstairs immediately, which meant that I would move, too. During all the time those rooms were being prepared, Sylvia had never asked me why. When I had to tell her now that Mrs. Matthews was here and insisted that Sylvia sleep in one of those rooms, she looked as frightened as she had when she was a little girl of five or six. She retreated from me, nearly backing herself against the wall behind her bed.

"I can't go downstairs to sleep," she said, shaking her head. "No, Papa won't like that."

"Papa would want you to be safe," I said, and explained again why Mrs. Matthews required it.

Sylvia clutched the bedpost.

Would Mrs. Matthews and I have to tear her away from it and force her downstairs? I couldn't do that.

"I have to stay here, Audrina."

"It's only for a little while, Sylvia. It will be okay. I promise. Remember, I'll be sleeping downstairs, too. I'll be in the room next to yours."

She shook her head even harder. "I can't be downstairs at night."

"Why can't you, Sylvia?"

"I have to talk to Papa. I have to be in the rocking chair," she said.

"You're still going there? When do you go there?"

"When you're asleep."

It stunned me for a moment. Had Arden ever heard her doing that again?

"I won't sleep downstairs," she repeated, raising her voice. "I won't!"

"What's going on here?" Mrs. Matthews asked, entering quickly when she heard Sylvia shouting.

"I told you she wasn't going to like sleeping downstairs. Why can't I bring her things? I don't mind going up and down the stairs, and . . ."

"It's not simply bringing her things. I thought you understood," she snapped at me, then turned to my sister. "Now, you will go downstairs, Sylvia, and that's that."

Sylvia was close to crying.

"This can't be good for a pregnant woman," I said.

"Woman? Don't you mean child?" Mrs. Matthews said. "I don't have time for this nonsense. There are things to do."

"Okay, okay. I tell you what, Sylvia. I'll have Arden bring the rocking chair down and put it in your room for now. Okay?"

"Rocking chair?" Mrs. Matthews said. "This is all about a rocking chair?"

Sylvia thought for a moment, relaxed, and then nodded.

"Well, now that the nonsense has ended, let's get on with it," Mrs. Matthews said. "Let's move the things we need downstairs." She went to Sylvia's armoire to choose what she would be wearing.

"Audrina's things, too," Sylvia said.

Mrs. Matthews looked at me. I thought she smiled, although with her you could never be sure it wasn't a smirk of disgust. "Yes, Audrina's, too," she said. And then she really did smile when she added, "Maybe she will rock in the chair, too."

Sylvia widened her eyes. "Papa would like that," she said.

"Well, then, it's settled." Mrs. Matthews laughed. "We'll be able to sing 'Rock-a-bye Baby' and mean it."

Losing Track of Who I Am

"Did you know that Sylvia was still going to the rocking chair at night?" I asked Arden as soon as he had come home and I could be alone with him in our bedroom.

He paused as he changed out of his business suit and stood there thinking. "You know, there were times when I woke to the sound of her shuffling along, I think, but frankly, I was too tired to get up and chase her back to her room. Audrina, I've told you many times to get rid of that chair and everything in that room. Why do you ask?"

"She would agree to go into the downstairs bedroom only if we brought the rocking chair to the room. I told her you would."

"You told her I would? Half of the problem here is that you feed this insanity," he said.

"That's not fair, Arden. Sylvia is delicate."

"Don't blame it on Sylvia. You're still afraid to throw out that chair and empty that room. You're the one keeping the ghosts alive here, Audrina, not Sylvia."

I looked down, tears bubbling like boiling milk. I thought I heard footsteps in the hallway. Mrs. Matthews had moved into her room, which was only a little way down and across from ours. The old wooden floors creaked and complained whenever anyone walked around up here. Was she eavesdropping? How much did she know about us? How much did she want to know? There were more than ghosts watching and listening to us now. It was embarrassing to have arguments in front of a stranger. How did people in big homes with servants keep their privacy?

"Okay, okay," Arden said. "I'll bring down the rocking chair. It's not light, you know."

"I can help."

"I'll manage," he said. "Or I'll ask Mrs. Matthews to help."

"Why her and not me?"

"You're pregnant, Audrina, remember?"

"What?"

"You've got to convince yourself, or you won't act properly in front of people. And it would set a very bad example for Sylvia if she saw you carrying something heavy while she's been told not to do that. When you're taking special care of yourself, you're taking special care of her. I thought you understood that."

"I do. I just forget sometimes. You can't blame me, Arden. I'm not really pregnant."

"Well, we're doing this for Sylvia as much as for us," he said.

"I know, I know."

"Shouldn't you be moving what you need to your

room?" he asked as he started to put on more casual clothes.

"I'm just as unhappy as Sylvia is about doing this. I don't know why Mrs. Matthews is so insistent about her being downstairs. She acts like going up and down the stairs is the same as climbing a mountain. She's not elderly."

"The woman knows what she's doing, and making the right decisions is what we're paying her to do. She's been hired to make sure this all works out well for us."

"I would have hoped you would be more unhappy about my moving out of our bedroom, Arden."

What really bothered me was that our space for any sort of privacy would be even more limited once we didn't share the bedroom, but he thought I was referring only to sex. He smiled. "Don't worry. I'll keep you company until you're tired enough to sleep. I'd do more, but we have to be careful. We don't want to get a pregnant woman pregnant."

He laughed, and before I could protest that I wasn't referring to that or say that he could use birth control, he went into the bathroom and closed the door. For as long as we had been together, he hadn't used any protection. We were always supposedly trying to have a child. I didn't want to emphasize that now, because it wasn't the point I was trying to make.

Frustrated, I started choosing the clothes I would bring downstairs, and when he came out of the bathroom, I went in and gathered my toiletries without saying another word. I had to have as much in my downstairs bedroom as Sylvia did, or she would wonder why I didn't. At times, she seemed more intense about my mimicking her pregnancy than Arden, Mrs. Matthews, or I were. As it was, we were taking the prenatal vitamins together and being examined together. We were now eating the same foods, too. Mrs. Matthews explained that she didn't want us gaining too much weight. Of course, she was saying this for Sylvia and not for me, but the way she looked at me when she spoke gave me the eerie feeling she really meant it for both of us. It was as if she was so focused on her work that she forgot or ignored that I wasn't really pregnant.

"It's a tricky balance sometimes, because you have to eat enough for two, and in the case of twins, three," she continued to explain at dinner. "But I'm relying on the most up-to-date nutritional information for pregnant women."

Arden smiled and complimented Mrs. Matthews on how thoroughly she went about her work. He thought it was wonderful. He thought almost anything she did or said was wonderful. Again, I wondered how he knew so much about her abilities. What gave him so much confidence in her medical abilities, or was it simply that she was someone who would keep a secret? I would have thought that was the main reason he had any interest at all, if it wasn't for how much concern he sincerely showed for Sylvia's well-being. Whenever he could, he would cross-examine me like a nervous father.

"Are you making sure Sylvia's following Mrs.

Matthews's orders, Audrina? Are you helping to keep Sylvia calm? Are you letting her do too much when Mrs. Matthews isn't around?"

I constantly reassured him about Sylvia, but he was just as anxious about how well I was mimicking her pregnancy so that Sylvia would be happy. As time went by, he was more intense and nervous about it. If I questioned him about that, he would explode in a rant about his reputation. Any exposure would destroy our ruse.

"I can't even imagine how I would explain it," he said.

He couldn't have had a better co-conspirator than Mrs. Matthews. I had to admit that. She'd had someone she trusted create the girdle-like apparatus I wore under my clothes. It had a large zippered pocket into which we stuffed large wads of wool that Arden brought home. As Sylvia expanded, so did I. Mrs. Matthews took great pains to be sure we were the same size.

At first, I felt terribly foolish wearing it. Early on, it was almost as burdensome as a real pregnancy. I'd forget and reach for something or bend down to pick something up and practically topple. I questioned Arden and Mrs. Matthews about it, pointing out that no other part of me reflected my simulated pregnancy.

"That's why you should eat on the side," Arden suggested. "Don't follow Mrs. Matthews's diet designed for Sylvia. Gain some weight."

"That would work," Mrs. Matthews seconded.

"What? I don't want to gain unnecessary weight."

"It's not unnecessary," Arden said. "You just made a good point about your appearance. We want people to believe you're pregnant, don't we?"

"But—"

"I'll buy some high-calorie foods for you to eat," Mrs. Matthews said, nodding. "You know, cakes and cookies and ice cream."

"Is that a healthy thing to do?" I asked. "Force myself to gain weight?"

She shrugged. "You'll go on a diet as soon as Sylvia gives birth. It will make sense then that you lose weight, although I must say, I've known many mothers who didn't. There are women, you know, who won't have children because they are afraid they will lose their precious beautiful figures."

She smiled at Arden, who smiled back as if they shared her medical histories and he knew exactly the women to whom she was referring.

What if they didn't have a beautiful figure to begin with, like you? I wanted to fire back. She could be so infuriating sometimes—actually, most of the time. The part I was playing to enable Arden's plan to work sometimes made me feel foolish, but of course I understood why we were doing it. When I waddled around and sympathized with Sylvia, who really was beginning to feel the weight and slow down, complaining about her lower back pain, with me echoing about mine, I could see Arden and Mrs. Matthews off to the side watching us, smiling and whispering something that made the two of them laugh.

Sylvia was starting her seventh month, and Mrs.

Matthews really began to restrict her activities. Arden had brought down her easel and her art supplies, but she wasn't doing much with them now. The new sheet on her easel remained untouched.

"Why don't you draw something new?" I asked her finally.

She looked at the easel and shook her head. "Papa wanted me to do my art in the cupola, Audrina. I need to be in the cupola."

I had the feeling she was about to tell me that it was only there that he could tell her what to draw and when to draw it. Mrs. Matthews came around just then, and I decided not to discuss it. Without her artwork, however, Sylvia's days were longer, and she looked so lost. When she just naturally, out of habit and routine, began to clean the kitchen or attempt to vacuum the carpets, Mrs. Matthews would lunge at her and take away dust cloths and cleaning sprays and practically tear the vacuum cleaner handle out of her hands, chastising her for disobeying orders.

She complained to me. "I told you she isn't to do these things now. I can't be following her around every moment of the day. You're supposed to be part of this."

"I'm sorry," I said. "She's bored."

"Don't you have any jigsaw puzzles? It might take her months to finish one, and by then, she could go back to being your maid."

"She's not my maid; she's never been our maid. This is her house, too," I snapped back. "She takes pride in what it looks like."

Mrs. Matthews looked at me without any sign of

emotion. Any complaints directed at her were like water off a duck's back. After all, Arden had put us in a situation where even the thought of firing her was impossible.

When I was a little girl, Papa had impressed on me how important it was to keep our secrets. "When you trust someone with a secret, Audrina," he had said, "you make them your master. They can always threaten you with revealing it. Be careful about that."

Of course, he'd been talking about all the secrets involving me, but it was still very true now.

"I don't want you lifting things or pushing things now, Sylvia," Mrs. Matthews told her. Her angry tone brought tears to my sister's eyes, so I had to intercede quickly and explain that I couldn't do those things, either.

Mrs. Matthews apparently thought housework was beneath her. She wouldn't even wash a glass, much less a dish. I was permitted to do that, but only behind Sylvia's back. The house was beginning to run away with itself. Half the time, we weren't even making the beds.

I complained about it to Arden, but he said, "For a while, we'll have to put up with it, Audrina. All of us have to make sacrifices. We certainly can't hire a temporary maid and have some stranger in our home witnessing all this."

"I'd be embarrassed to have anyone see how far behind we are with the upkeep of Whitefern."

"It'll be fine," he insisted. "I have no intention of having guests until this is over. Just leave it all be."

It was easy for him to say that. He wasn't haunted

day and night by images of Aunt Ellsbeth outraged at how Whitefern was being treated. She would explode over muddy feet on a carpet or food left on a counter in the kitchen, and if our beds weren't made, she would have Vera and I make them twice just to teach us that we should care more.

Mrs. Matthews's rules and orders left me feeling armless, but what could I do but try to amuse Sylvia, who looked lost most of the time?

Consequently, I spent most of my time watching television with Sylvia, something we hadn't done that much of because I had to explain so much about what was happening that I couldn't keep up with the program anyway.

Growing tired of the chore one day, I went looking through my old things and found a jigsaw puzzle rated for children ages nine to twelve. I began it with Sylvia, and when she fit a piece in, she was very pleased with herself. Mrs. Matthews saw us doing it and nodded with that bony-looking smile of hers. This was a woman who lived to be right, I thought. I couldn't help feeling that she enjoyed wielding power over us, especially me. Sometimes when she told me to do something or criticized me for doing something, I sensed a little vengefulness, bitterness.

Was there something about her that I was missing? Did she dislike my family for some reason? I felt at such a disadvantage. I knew only what Arden had told me about her, and there was still that secret that she feared would be revealed, the secret he held over her head like a flaming sword.

When she wasn't tending to Sylvia, Mrs. Matthews would leave the house to look after her own needs. As far as I knew, she never contacted her son while she was living at Whitefern, and she never spoke about other relatives. What about friends? I wondered. Wouldn't they be asking her questions about us? About why she was living here now?

When I asked Arden about that, he said, "Don't worry about it. She can be trusted to say the right things anyway."

She was doing all our shopping now, buying what she preferred to eat and drink. After I complained to Arden about this one night in his home office, he told me to accompany her the next day when she went to the supermarket.

"You can choose what you want, if it fits the nutritional principles Mrs. Matthews has set out for Sylvia. Besides, it's a good idea for you to go with her to the supermarket this week."

"Why?"

"It's time people saw you two together and understood that I've hired her to give you special attention."

"But no pregnant woman takes a nurse along to buy groceries, Arden."

"You do, because you've had some problems, Audrina," he snapped back. "Where's that brilliant mind of yours? We're claiming now that you can't drive. Don't forget that. She or I have to drive you anywhere, as far as people in this town are to know. Remember, in a few weeks, you will never set foot out of this house," he warned. "I have to develop a believable story for our employees and clients. Otherwise, everything we're doing will be for nothing, and you'll feel like a fool."

"I feel like a fool now."

"Don't start, Audrina, not now when we're so close to the end."

I sighed, resistance smothered, self-pride practically drowned. "I'll go with her, but we can't leave Sylvia alone, especially now."

"I'll babysit," he said.

"You will?"

"Yes. We both have to make sacrifices. I'm just as much a part of this, Audrina. I've told you time and time again that I'm risking my reputation, too. I could look like an idiot if the truth leaked out. And what do you think the impact would be on our business, the faith our clients have on us? Remember, Audrina, a brokerage firm's lifeblood is trust and faith."

"Everything always seems to snake its way back to business with you, Arden. You remember people's birthdays and anniversaries just so they'll continue to invest with you. You take them out to dinners and lunches to, as Papa would say, lick their boots. You even took a client out on our anniversary last year!"

"Your father? You bring up your father? He did everything I'm doing. He's the one who taught me how to do it, why it was important to the company. He set the example for me."

"Do you have to be like him in every way? You weren't always like this, Arden. Or were you?"

He smiled.

"What's so funny?"

"You're acting just the way Mrs. Matthews told me most of her pregnant patients behave, emotionally. They're very moody. Anything can set them off like firecrackers."

"I'm not really pregnant, Arden! I'm not being moody!"

He held his smile.

It was exasperating me more. I was having the shortness of breath Mrs. Matthews had predicted a pregnant Sylvia might experience.

"I know you're not really pregnant, Audrina," he said softly, "but maybe it's like a cold or something. It's catching. Sylvia's different, so you're different."

"Of course she's different. Her life has been up-ended," I said, my voice straining. "She's confused about her body. She can't do what she's been used to doing. She's not sleeping in her own room. Yes, she's different. She was raped! And that man is getting away with it."

He lost his smile. "All right, Audrina. Don't shout. You're getting yourself unnecessarily overwrought. What do you want?"

I fumed inside, but I couldn't explain it simply. I was sure Mrs. Matthews was outside his office listening. Was I going to bring up my childhood, what it was like to be so constrained, trapped, after I had been raped?

"I don't know," I said finally. "Maybe just to get this over with."

"Exactly. It isn't much longer now, and the outcome

will please you. We'll have protected Sylvia, and there'll be a baby in our house, a child to raise, someone to inherit all we have. Whitefern won't go to strangers," he said calmly. Then he walked over to me, hugged me, and kissed me on my forehead and cheek. "Mrs. Matthews says it's all going well now. You're doing your part. As soon as we're able to, as soon as Sylvia gives birth and the baby can travel, we'll all take a holiday, okay?"

I nodded, gazing down at the floor, my heart still thumping with the frustration I felt.

"I need to finish something here, and then I'll come out and sit with you and Sylvia."

"And Mrs. Matthews," I reminded him, the bitterness undisguised.

He nodded. "Yes, and Mrs. Matthews."

"Promise me something, Arden. Will you promise me something?"

"I'll try. What is it?"

"When this is all over, you'll tell me what secret you have of hers, what you hold over her. Will you?"

I saw the reluctance in his eyes, but he saw the need in mine. "Okay," he said at last. "You're right. By then, it might not matter to her. She'll be gone from our lives."

"Good."

I turned and started out. When I reached the mirror in the hallway, the full-length one in the mahogany frame, I glanced at myself and paused. I did look pregnant, but I felt idiotic. I was a walking, talking lie. What would I say when people in the supermarket stopped to ask how I was and if I had any idea if my baby would be a boy or a girl?

"It will be neither," I whispered. "It will be a hunk of wool."

I couldn't help laughing. I was still laughing when I entered the Roman Revival salon and saw Mrs. Matthews sitting with Sylvia and helping her do her jigsaw puzzle. They both looked up, surprised, which only caused me to laugh harder. Sylvia didn't need to know why I was laughing. She began to laugh, too. Mrs. Matthews looked from her to me, astonished. I was laughing so hard now that tears were streaming down my cheeks.

"I think," Mrs. Matthews said, "that you should go to your room and gather your wits."

"Gather my wits. Yes," I said, and hurried away.

I went to bed early that night. I was as exhausted as a real pregnant woman might be. It was getting very weird, I thought. There were times when I imagined a baby moving inside me, just the way it was moving inside Sylvia, surprising, frightening, and exciting her almost at the same time. As a matter of fact, it felt like it was kicking right now.

I fell asleep dreaming that the roles were reversed. It was Sylvia who was mimicking me. I was the one who was really pregnant. And Sylvia, who was truly still a child, wanted to be like me. She always wanted to be like me.

"Let her pretend," Arden told me in my dream. "What harm could it do?"

Sylvia was even lying in the bed beside me in the delivery room, screaming with pain.

And when I gave birth to a beautiful baby, Sylvia gave birth to the baby she had drawn with eyes on fire.

The image shocked me awake. I sat up, my heart pounding. I could hear the house creaking more down here. Upstairs, I didn't hear how the wind threaded through every crack. My dream raised my worry about Sylvia, so I got up and went to her room. The door was always left open.

When I didn't see her in her bed, I began to panic, but then I saw her in the rocking chair in the corner. She was asleep. I wondered if I should wake her and get her into her bed. I recalled how often I had fallen asleep in that chair, under Papa's orders to dream and capture the imaginary first Audrina's gifts. What was Sylvia dreaming about?

Let her dream, I thought, and returned to my bed. It took me almost until morning to fall asleep again. I was afraid of returning to the nightmare that had woken me.

That morning, Arden delayed going to work so he would be home while Mrs. Matthews and I went shopping. I was almost too tired to go along, but I forced myself to do it. Ironically, if I ever complained about being tired or having a pain, both Mrs. Matthews and Arden acted as though it was expected. After all, I was supposed to be pregnant. They were both sure to do this whenever Sylvia was present.

"Try a heating pad," Mrs. Matthews might tell me. "I don't like giving medication to pregnant women."

I glanced at Sylvia and saw how that pleased her, because Mrs. Matthews surely had told her something similar. It wasn't only my movements and activities that were restricted. I even had my thoughts confined. When did I pretend to cross the line into and out of reality? How could I be defiant? I was gagged and handcuffed, trapped and imprisoned, even more than I had been as a young girl who was forbidden to tempt the evil spirits that had ravished my supposed namesake. As a result, I kept my complaints to myself and even began doing jigsaw puzzles.

Now, eager to get out of the house, I hurriedly dressed and joined Mrs. Matthews at the front door. She held her hand on the knob and looked at me as if she was deciding then and there whether to let me out.

"There are things to remember now, Audrina. You're out in public. Do not walk quickly. You're in your seventh month. No fast moves in the supermarket. For our purposes, it would be best if you looked somewhat uncomfortable. Occasionally, put your hand on your lower back. Arden and I have discussed all this," she added. "If there are many people at the market, we might decide to cut the shopping short because you're having problems. Any questions?"

I stood stunned and speechless. Then I turned around and saw that Arden had heard it all.

He nodded and smiled. "Don't mess things up now, Audrina," he warned. "Listen closely, and do exactly what Mrs. Matthews tells you to do."

"Ready?" she asked.

I nodded, and she opened the door.

"Watch yourself on the steps," Arden called from behind us. I glanced back at him. He had a wide, impish smile on his face. If I could only enjoy this as much as he apparently was, I thought. I closed the door and followed Mrs. Matthews to her car, a blue station wagon that looked like she had driven it for a decade.

It was the sort of summer day Sylvia would love, I thought as I looked at the burst of color, the soft green, olive, and emerald leaves. Wildflowers were everywhere, and the squirrels were as lively as ever, doing amazing gymnastic feats on the tree branches. I remembered how much pleasure Sylvia got from sitting and watching them for hours, one or two coming very close to her until she'd raise her hand or start moving in their direction. When she was an infant, she would crawl around on the grass, and if she found a dandelion, she would immediately put it in her mouth.

Soon, I thought, she would be able to be outside and enjoy nature again.

"Your sister is doing very well," Mrs. Matthews said as we drove along the road to Whitefern village. "I am not anticipating any difficulties with the delivery."

"I don't want her to be in too much pain."

She looked at me and raised her thin eyebrows. "Some pain is good," she said. "It's the body's way of giving us instruction. Like what to avoid."

She sounded too much like Aunt Ellsbeth. "What do you mean?"

"The pain of a burn, the sting of a bee. Pain protects us, too."

"Well, it wasn't her fault she was burned and stung."

"No, but I doubt she'll be as easy to abuse after this," she said.

I turned away and stared at the side of the road, where trees ran into trees. Houses didn't appear for miles, our nearest neighbor living twelve miles from Whitefern. I never thought much about them or any of the families farther along the way. Once, according to my mother and Aunt Ellsbeth, the Whiteferns had been the most notable family in the Tidewater section of Virginia, giving the country senators and even vice presidents. But over time, we had fallen out of favor, not just with the villagers but also with everyone in the surrounding suburbs. We were no longer as honored or, in Aunt Ellsbeth's words, "even respected."

Whitefern village, where the supermarket was located, was fifteen miles from our house. It was also where I had gone to school. I had not kept in contact with any of my schoolmates. None had ever paid a visit to my home. But I did have fond memories of my teachers.

Heads turned our way when we got out of Mrs. Matthews's car and started for the supermarket.

"Walk slower," she ordered under her breath. "Don't make it seem so easy."

I thought back to what my mother had been like when she was pregnant with Sylvia and tried to emulate her stride, putting my hand on my lower back from time to time after we got a cart and began to go down the aisles. If I chose something I liked, Mrs. Matthews would give me a sideways glance and sometimes shake her head no. I felt like a little girl with no power to choose anything.

Rounding the turn toward the meat counter, we saw Mrs. Haider, the retired principal of Whitefern High School. Mrs. Matthews didn't think anything of it. In fact, she looked like she didn't even want to say hello to her, but I stopped immediately.

"Oh, Audrina, how are you?" Mrs. Haider asked, acting as if I'd startled her. Mrs. Matthews paused and looked back at me, her eyes full of warnings. "I heard you were pregnant."

"I'm getting along, but it's been a little difficult."

"Oh?"

"Do you know Mrs. Matthews?" I asked, feeling awkward now, with her just standing there and Mrs. Haider wondering why.

"Yes, I believe so. You had a son who attended Whitefern. Philip, I believe."

"Yes," Mrs. Matthews said.

"And how is he doing?"

"Staying out of trouble," she replied. It wasn't an answer, and Mrs. Haider didn't smile or react in any way. "He's working for my brother at his paper mill in Richmond," Mrs. Matthews added.

"Not married?"

"No," she said briskly. "Audrina, we don't want to keep you on your feet longer than necessary . . ."

"Mrs. Matthews is a maternity nurse," I explained.

"Yes, I know, but I thought you were retired," Mrs. Haider said to her. She was not a woman who was easily intimidated, probably hardened by her many years as a school administrator.

"I am, but I've come out of retirement to assist Mrs. Lowe. Her husband persuaded me," Mrs. Matthews said. "She's having a difficult pregnancy. In fact, I'd rather she didn't come out of the house to do shopping, but I gave in this once." She smiled with icy lips.

Mrs. Haider nodded. "I'm sorry you're having difficulties, Audrina. I do hope it all works out well for you. How is Sylvia?" she asked, still ignoring Mrs. Matthews, who was exhibiting her impatience by pushing and pulling on the cart.

"She's well, thank you."

"I'm sorry Mr. Price took sick and couldn't continue with her art lessons," she said.

"Took sick?"

"Oh, didn't you know? I would have thought you would."

Mrs. Matthews raised her eyebrows, her face reflecting annoyance now.

This was the hardest part for me, pretending that I cared and not revealing the terrible things Mr. Price had done. I practically choked on the words. "I knew it was getting harder for him. He seemed very tired, but I thought in time . . ."

"Yes, well, I'm surprised you don't know. He had a stroke. It's left him paralyzed on his right side, and for an artist who draws with his right hand, that's devastating. Perhaps you can give the Prices a call. They'd appreciate it."

"She has to be concerned about herself right now," Mrs. Matthews said sharply. "Perhaps after the baby is born."

"Yes, when are you due?"

"A little more than six weeks," Mrs. Matthews answered for me.

"Do you know if it will be a boy or a girl?"

I shook my head. I really was having trouble breathing now.

Mrs. Haider laughed. Why was she laughing? "Well," she said, glancing at Mrs. Matthews, "my grandmother used to swear that if a pregnant woman's face turns red while you're speaking to her, she is definitely having a girl. I can't wait to see if she was right. Good luck." She continued on her way.

I looked at Mrs. Matthews.

She was smiling, and not coldly. "You really do look sick to your stomach, Audrina. I think we do have to cut the shopping short." Gleefully, she hurried along.

Ancient Voices, Forbidden Dreams

"Do exactly what I tell you," Mrs. Matthews said when we reached the front of the store after having done all our shopping twenty minutes later. "Now, lean on the cart as if to catch your breath."

As soon as I did, she hollered, "Can I get some help here?"

She was loud enough for nearly everyone in the supermarket to hear. Customers stopped and turned our way. The busy cashiers paused, and the store manager came running.

"What's wrong?" he asked, looking like he might burst into tears or throw up his breakfast. He was a short, stocky man, with thinning dark brown hair and round eyes that seemed sunken in his pudgy face like dark cherries in soft vanilla ice cream.

"Mrs. Lowe isn't feeling well. She has a very delicate pregnancy. Open a register for us." When he hesitated, she added, raising her voice, "Do you want a terrible scene played out on the floor here?"

He leaped to open the register himself and signaled for a packer, who rushed over.

The manager's assistant came over, too. He was taller and younger, with the slim physique of a tennis player. "Can I help?" he asked Mrs. Matthews.

She thought a moment, glanced at me, and then told him to take me out to her car very carefully while she finished with the groceries.

"Walk slowly," she added when he offered his hand.

His name tag read "Marv Russel, Assistant Manager." He had a boyish face and cerulean-blue eyes, and his light brown hair was cut in a short, military style. He looked more frightened than I was supposed to be, but when I took his hand, he let go and decided instead to put his arm around my shoulders. We started out. "Where's your car?" he asked, seeming afraid to look at me.

"It's that blue station wagon," I said, nodding at it.

"When are you giving birth? I hope not any minute. I once saw a woman go into labor in a movie theater. I think I came close to fainting. My girlfriend thought it was quite funny." I could hear the trembling in his voice.

"Don't faint now," I warned.

He smiled. "I won't."

"A little more than six weeks," I replied to his question, making sure to agree with what Mrs. Matthews had told Mrs. Haider. Conspirators have to dot their *i*'s and cross their *t*'s when they're telling a contrived story.

"How far do you have to go?" he asked when we reached the car.

"Fifteen miles. I live in the Whitefern mansion."

He shook his head. That had no meaning for him. "My family and I moved here recently. I don't know the area that well yet," he said apologetically.

"Do you go to college?" I asked.

He laughed. "I guess I'll never look older. I graduated three years ago. I majored in business administration. Should we rest a moment?"

"Just a moment," I said. I really did want to catch my breath, but I was also feeling bad about what I was doing to his nerves. He would surely spend the rest of the day describing me and what had happened. And it was all a lie.

"How long have you lived here?" he asked.

"All my life. My family is one of the oldest ones in the Tidewater area."

"Oh. It's nice here," he said, searching for things to say.

"Very. Are you still going with the girl from the movie theater?"

"No. She dropped me for the captain of the football team, but I have a nice girlfriend here. We're talking about marriage."

"Talking about it?"

"Planning," he said, smiling.

"Get her into the car!" we heard Mrs. Matthews shout. "I want her sitting."

"Right away," he called back, and leaped into action, taking me to the car, opening the door, and helping me in. He breathed a sigh of relief the moment I was out of his hands. "Good luck with your delivery, and stay out of movie theaters," he joked.

"I haven't been to one in years," I said.

He looked surprised at my admitting that and then stepped back as Mrs. Matthews shoved her cart of groceries toward the car as if she was delivering a missile. He rushed forward to catch it and then helped her unload and pack the car. She opened her purse to give him a tip, but he refused and backed away.

"Good luck," he called to me, and hurried back to the safety of his supermarket.

"Very good," Mrs. Matthews said when she got in. "Your husband will be pleased about how you behaved."

"How I behaved?"

She made it sound like I was a child on an outing. "You know what I mean. That principal was watching us the whole time. I'm sure she'll gossip."

"She doesn't gossip," I said.

"How would you know?"

"I just know. From knowing her in the past," I added.

"We'll see. Whatever, it's fine now. There were many others who will talk about it."

"What do you know about Mr. Price?" I asked. She was silent. "And Sylvia?" I added firmly.

"I know what your husband told me. How he and you handle this is your business. I don't have to know everything." She paused and then said, "I know enough."

I bet you do, I thought. *I bet you've had your ear to the door of Arden's office whenever I was in there.* I asked her, "Did you know he had a stroke?"

"No. Why would I want to know? It would be very unwise to show any interest in him right now, Audrina. You are such an innocent." She shook her head as if that was a sign of failure.

"Wouldn't people just think you were being considerate, compassionate, if you asked about him?" Maybe I was innocent, but why would her questioning about him cause any suspicions?

"Why have them think anything at all?" she countered. "Besides, his welfare especially is the least of our concerns. We should stay focused on the project."

"Project."

"Whatever you want to call it—fake pregnancy, switch, whatever. Choose the words you want. Anyway, after this, you'll have no trouble staying inside until Sylvia gives birth and even a little while afterward. People who saw you today or those who hear about you will question me whenever I'm out and about. I'm going to tell them you're confined to bed now. In fact, I'd be happier if Sylvia was."

I didn't like her tone, the way she was ordering me about, taking charge of everything, even Arden's and my lives. "I'll discuss it with Arden," I said.

"I've already done that. He agrees, of course. Concentrate on your sister, not yourself," she said.

"That's what I'm doing," I practically shouted back at her.

Anyone else would have realized she had insulted

me by suggesting otherwise, but not our Mrs. Matthews. She simply shrugged and drove on, not even batting an eyelash. How had she ever become a nurse, I wondered, someone who had to have extra sensitivity and compassion for others?

"You weren't a nurse in a prison, were you?" I asked, still frustrated.

"What?" She actually smiled, a real smile toying with a laugh. "Why did you ask that?"

"You seem to have the right temperament for it," I said.

Her smile quickly evaporated. "There'll come a time when you'll look back at all this and be very grateful that I had the right temperament," she said, not hiding her crossness.

Had I finally chipped the walls of that cocoon in which she dwelled? I was sure she would tell Arden. They seemed to share a lot more with each other than they shared with me these days.

Mr. Ralph was waiting for us at the steps of Whitefern. He rushed forward, as well as he could rush, to help bring in the groceries.

"Go rest," Mrs. Matthews told me. "It's obviously been an emotional morning for you."

Without comment, I went into the house. Arden, obviously anxious to leave, was dressed for work and standing like a relay runner about to hand me the baton.

"She's in her room now, resting," he said. "How did it go?"

"You'll get a full report from your chief of staff,"

I replied, and walked past him quickly to go see how Sylvia was doing.

She was lying with her eyes open but looking up at the ceiling like someone in a daze.

"Sylvia," I said, sitting on the bed and taking her hand. "Are you okay?"

She looked at me without expression and then suddenly realized it was I. "Audrina, Papa spoke to me here this morning. I kept sitting in the chair, waiting, and he didn't speak, but today he spoke."

"And what did he say?"

"He said I should stay in my room now and wait. The baby will be coming. He said I have to be extra careful. You'll have to stay in your room, too," she added.

I looked back at the doorway. How odd, I thought, that the whispering Sylvia imagined coordinated so well with the orders Mrs. Matthews gave. It was a fleeting thought, but it lingered for the rest of the afternoon, until I asked Mrs. Matthews if she had said anything to Sylvia about being confined to her room.

"I might have mentioned that the day would come when she would be. Why?"

"She thinks she has to do that now."

"Perfect. It makes my job so much easier when the patient anticipates my orders and carries them out." She flashed her usual cold smile and went into Sylvia's room.

When the phone rang, I was anticipating Arden to be calling to tell me why he couldn't be at dinner again tonight, but I was surprised and even frightened to hear Dr. Prescott's voice.

"Audrina? Dr. Prescott here," he said. "I heard the craziest story today," he continued. "One of my patients, Ceil Rubin, told me she saw you at the supermarket and that you were quite pregnant, as she put it. She mentioned that Helen Matthews was with you and there was some sort of emergency scene at the cash registers. What's this about?"

This was something neither Arden nor I had anticipated. We certainly should have, I thought. Dr. Prescott was our family doctor. Of course, he would be interested in anything involving us. My brain scrambled for the right answers. I could mess up everything, all that we had worked for these past months. I wasn't concerned as much about my efforts going for naught as I was concerned about what would happen to Sylvia. We would fail to prevent all that would follow, all that we knew would be unpleasant. Arden would be enraged for sure.

Why? I asked myself, imagining the question he would ask. Why would we not have immediately called Dr. Prescott if I was indeed pregnant?

"I'm sorry, Dr. Prescott."

"Sorry? Are you pregnant, Audrina?"

"Yes, I am," I said.

He was silent for a moment. I waited, afraid to utter another word. "Why didn't you come to me?" he asked finally.

"Arden hired Mrs. Matthews to look after me. She's full-time here now."

"Pregnant. Well, I am happy to hear it. I know that's what you and Arden wanted. I'm just surprised when you consider the odds."

"Maybe it was something that was meant to be," I offered.

"Yes, apparently so. Well, I don't mean to sound upset or anything. I'm quite pleased." He paused. It was coming. "But really, I am surprised you didn't come to see me."

"Arden was upset with the results you got from the testing and the prediction you made for us," I said. "He wanted us to handle it this way, but as soon as the baby is born, I intend to bring him or her to you to examine and care for all the time."

"Pleased to be of service," he said, but his voice was heavy with hurt. "What happened at the supermarket?"

"Oh, just a little spotting. It turned out to be nothing. I'm doing fine," I said. "I'm going to take it a lot easier for the remaining time."

"Spotting? How far along are you?"

"I'm a little more than six weeks away," I said.

"And Mrs. Matthews told you that, gave you the approximate date of delivery?"

"Yes."

"Very well. I'm aware of who she is and how vast her experience is. I'm sure your father would have been very excited about it. Good luck, and call me if I can be of any help."

"Thank you. Thank you for calling, Dr. Prescott," I said.

He hung up without saying good-bye. I held the receiver for a few moments, my heart still pounding. Dr. Prescott's voice had been full of skepticism. I didn't think he would make the leap to Sylvia immediately, but he was certainly suspicious. And I was feeling very guilty. I knew how Papa would have disapproved of our not using Dr. Prescott, but then again, how could we? It would surely be unethical, even illegal, for a doctor to do what Mrs. Matthews was doing for us.

I hung up and called Arden.

"What is it now?" he asked as soon as he got on the phone.

I told him about Dr. Prescott's call. "He was full of disbelief," I added when he was silent. "What if he starts talking to people, asking more questions?"

"He won't. A doctor's relationship with his patient is private. I could sue him if he told anyone about the tests he gave us. Don't worry about that."

"I can't help but worry. I can't imagine what we would look like in this community if the truth came out."

"You don't have to tell me that. But I said not to worry," he snapped. Then he changed his tone. "I received a call already from one of our clients whose wife happened to see you in the supermarket. They're swallowing it all out there, hook, line, and sinker. Mrs. Matthews is ingenious. Trust in her. Now, I have to get back to work. I'll soon have a child's welfare to consider, his or her education, other needs. Lots more money must be made."

"Arden, did you know that Mr. Price had a stroke? He's paralyzed on one side and can no longer do his artwork."

"No, but that's truly poetic justice," he said. "Oh," he added quickly before hanging up, "I won't be at dinner tonight. I'm taking the Allans to dinner. You were supposed to come along, but they'll understand. Another opportunity to solidify our story," he said. "Take care of Sylvia. And yourself, of course." He laughed and hung up.

When I turned around, Mrs. Matthews was standing there. "It would help the situation now if you would retire to your room. I'll bring you your dinner tonight," she said.

"What?"

"Your sister keeps asking about you. We don't want her unnecessarily disturbed. A pregnant woman's emotional health is just as important as her physical health. Calmness is the word of the month."

For a moment, I stood staring at her. I was becoming a prisoner in every sense of the word. "How would she know if I was in that room or not?"

"She could call for you and you wouldn't be there to hear her. Then she would want to get up to find you. I don't know why we're arguing about it. I would hope that you would be the most cooperative of all."

"I'm not arguing."

"Good, then do it."

It was easy for her to say. When I was confined to our house and grounds during my youth, I'd at least had my mother, Aunt Ellsbeth, Vera, despite her jealousies, and, of course, Papa to keep me company. My real entertainment came from watching all of them interact. How I looked forward to the Tuesday teas, when Aunt Ellsbeth and Momma resurrected Aunt Mercy Marie. It was major entertainment. Sometimes Vera would be nice, and we would play a game together, and I did feel like her ally when her mother punished her or scolded her for something she did wrong.

The point was that during my confinement, there were other people, their laughter bringing smiles to my face. I was even fascinated by the arguing. Now there was mostly silence in my confinement. The things I would hear were mostly the memories of old voices. I feared the flood of nightmares, forbidden dreams invading both my waking hours and my sleep. I assumed that Mrs. Matthews had no idea why I was so reluctant to cooperate. Arden could paint broad strokes of my youth for her, but he was not aware of the myriad details that I had tried to bury in the empty grave of my false self.

"Well?" Mrs. Matthews said, holding the spoon with which she was preparing our dinner. I imagined it to be a ring of jailer's keys.

"Don't you need help with dinner?"

"From now on, I'll do it by myself. I'll even wash the dishes myself," she added, and smiled her cold smile, as if that was going to make me feel better. "And yes, I'll do more to keep up the house. I know how concerned you are, but frankly, sometimes you act as if Whitefern is a national treasure, a museum. Most of what I see here would have no special meaning for anyone other than yourself."

"Which is reason enough to protect it," I snapped back. "It's a sacred obligation to care for all that your family held dear. Don't you have any heirlooms? Have you inherited nothing from your parents and grand-parents that you cherish?"

"I live for the here and now. We have museums for everything else. Besides, what I have and how I live are not the issue here. We have a job to do, and that's all that matters. You, of all three of us, should feel this the most. When this is over, it's you who will have to carry the deception forward. You'll have to be a real mother to this child, and don't forget, you'll have to convince your child that you are his or her mother, too." She paused and nodded, as though what she said made a great deal of sense. Then she added, "Consider all this as nothing more than practice for that day — preparation."

This time, she smiled with such self-satisfaction I felt sick to my stomach. Maybe I should go to bed, I thought. The episode in the supermarket, Dr. Prescott's call, Arden's glee, and now this witch of a woman's obvious enjoyment at wielding power over me all sent a dark sword of helplessness through my very soul. I wobbled for a moment as the room seemed to spin.

"Are you all right?" she asked, suddenly very concerned. After all, if something happened to me, what would she say? How would she explain what went on here, too?

It occurred to me that she was taking just as much of a risk as Arden and I were. How could she explain her behavior? She was retired from any regular work, but what sort of reputation would she have then? She might have to move away. Any friends she had, and I had trouble imagining that she had any, would certainly take a step away from her. Why, it would be like running a gauntlet to go shopping in this community because of all the looks and whispers behind her back.

"I am tired. This," I said, placing my two hands over the bundle of wool that I had to wear, even sleep in, just in case Sylvia saw me during the night, "is becoming a real burden."

"Imagine what a burden it is for truly pregnant women. Imagine what Sylvia is enduring," she said, the slight note of sympathy I thought I had heard gone. "Go lie down."

She stepped aside, and I walked out and to Sylvia's room. She was sitting up at the side of her bed, her legs dangling. She was scribbling on a pad in her lap.

"Sylvia, what are you drawing?"

"I'm writing a name," she said.

"A name?"

"When Papa told me to stay in my room, he told me a name," she said. "A name for the baby."

"He did?"

She nodded. "He whispered it in my ear and told me to practice writing it."

"But you can't pick a name until you know if the baby is a boy or a girl."

"It's a girl's name," she said.

"Okay. What is the name?"

"A-d-e-l-l-e," she spelled.

"Adelle? Adelle is my middle name," I said. She had heard it, of course, but as far as I knew, she had never said it or indicated that she remembered it. Arden and Papa often said it in her presence. If she was in a room when it was mentioned, she was usually distracted with some toy, a doll, even a piece of cardboard she had formed into something only she understood. She didn't listen to anyone but herself. In any case, I had no idea how she knew to spell it correctly.

This seemed like another thing she had plucked out of thin air. In my mind, the words of my parents, my aunt Ellsbeth, even Vera, swirled in and out of all the rooms in Whitefern. There was no silence here. Echoes never faded away. Cries, laughter, and screams of delight and pain rode in the belly of shadows. When night came and the lights were turned off, they were especially free to move about and circle me, invading my dreams.

Did Sylvia hear all this, too?

"As I said, Adelle is a girl's name, Sylvia. The baby might be a boy. We'll have to choose a boy's name, too. Did you get any ideas for that?"

She shook her head. "Girl," she insisted. "Remember? Papa told me her name. So it has to be a girl."

For now, she was so happy about it that I thought there was no point in discussing it further. "Okay. I'm going to lie down for a while. Mrs. Matthews will be bringing us our dinners."

"Because we have to stay quiet," Sylvia recited, nodding her head.

"Yes. I'll be right next door if you need me."

"Mrs. Matthews says I don't need you. I need only her."

"Did she? Well, she knows everything. I know only all the rest," I said, recalling a joke Papa had enjoyed. It was something Mark Twain had said.

I went over to her and kissed her on the forehead, the way I always did.

"She might be the nurse," I said, "and she can take care of you right now, but I'm the only one who can give you love, Sylvia. You will always need me."

She didn't react. She was absorbed in writing the name Adelle in different ways with flourishes of script.

Actually, that would be the perfect name, I thought, if I was going to be the child's mother. Maybe Papa really was whispering to her. Who was I, as someone who often heard whispers, to doubt it?

I fell asleep minutes after I lay down and woke up when I heard Mrs. Matthews come in carrying a tray.

"Are you really going to treat me like an invalid, too?" I asked. "It's double work for you."

"It's what your husband is paying me to do, what we all decided we had to do for Sylvia," she said. "He's very keen on everything going right. Don't worry. I'm being paid well. Besides," she continued, laying the tray on my lap, "the more you simulate pregnancy, the easier it will be to convince yourself that the baby is indeed your baby. It's good psychology." She smiled like she really cared. But then she added, "After all, you had good practice for something like this. A trained impersonator brought up to impersonate herself. Who could do better?" She laughed and left the room.

I felt the venom travel though my veins as I looked after her. I hoped that Arden really possessed a secret that would tear her heart in two if it was revealed.

Maybe someday I would do just that.

Almost reluctantly, I began to eat. The food was nowhere as well seasoned as when I made it, but I did have to eat, pregnant or not.

Mrs. Matthews came for the tray and dishes, nodding in approval at how much I had eaten. I looked at her as if I thought she had gone mad. She grimaced and left quickly. Even though I had slept, I was groggy again and dozed on and off.

Hours later, the sound of Arden's laughter woke me. I had started to get up to go out and see him when he appeared in the doorway.

"Good, you're awake," he said.

He was going in and out of focus. I scrubbed my cheeks with my palms and took a deep breath. "This is ridiculous. I'm not staying in this room."

"Don't do anything to mess up things now, Audrina. We are so close I can taste it. Mrs. Matthews says Sylvia had what she considered labor pains about an hour ago."

"Labor pains? But she predicted at least six more weeks."

He shrugged. "Did you forget? Sylvia herself was born premature. It could happen again."

"But complications like that would make things more difficult for us."

"Mrs. Matthews is aware of that and is giving Sylvia extra care."

"How is she now?"

"Sleeping," he said. "Comfortably."

I stood. "I want to go out and sit in the salon."

"What if she wakes and calls for you? We can't expect Mrs. Matthews to man the lookout here twenty-four hours a day. Now's the time for you to really pitch in and help. I certainly can't do it."

"But—"

"Audrina, you just made mention of it. If something happened to Sylvia now and she had to go to a hospital, there would be hell to pay, especially since Dr. Prescott called and seemed full of suspicion. We've got to take extra care of her for all our sakes. For better or worse, we started this. Now we have to carry it out to completion. I stress *we*," he added.

I sat back on my bed, weighed down by his words.

"I had a very successful day today, and tonight at dinner, I garnered another million dollars in investments. We're on a roll, and the birth of the baby will be the crowning moment." He stepped forward and kissed me on the forehead, the way I kissed Sylvia all the time. "Get some rest," he said.

"Rest? I slept all afternoon."

"You do look tired. I know this is a burden on you. Stay well, my love. I need my little mother and wife." He kissed me again on the forehead and walked out.

I lay back.

The bundle of wool on my stomach had never felt heavier, nor had any of my regrets and fears.

It was easy to fall asleep again.

After all, right now, sleep was my only escape.

Trapped in Your Own Web

During the days that followed, Sylvia's recurrent pains began to worry me, and judging by the look on Mrs. Matthews's face whenever she examined her, they were increasingly concerning to her, too. I tried to be of more help, but ever since the day we'd gone to the supermarket, I had found myself with diminished energy. I dozed on and off. I would start reading a book and after only three or four pages find myself drifting off the page. I would wake up with the book in my lap, opened to the same page, totally unaware of how much time had passed. Often, it was hours.

I made no effort to interfere with Mrs. Matthews's plans. She continued to bring us our meals, and I did nothing to help clean up. I did no household chores and wondered who was making Arden's bed and changing his linen. He never did. What's more, Arden seemed to be busier than ever with the business. According to what he told me, there were some issues with the stock market that were taking up extra time. By the time I was up and around in the morning, he was always already gone, and there were many nights when he didn't come home for dinner. I would fall asleep before he did come home, so days went by during the next month when I didn't see him at all.

"Investors are very nervous about the economy," he explained one night when he did stop by and I complained. "You have no idea how many rich people I am babysitting, comforting, and assuring. If this isn't all handled right, we could lose a lot at exactly the wrong time in our lives, Audrina. You'll have to excuse my absences. I'm running from one to the other and applying soothing balm."

"What's happening in the economy to put all this pressure on you?"

"Oh, it's too complicated to explain."

"I'm not stupid about economics, Arden. My father made sure that I was aware of what made it better or worse."

I was anticipating the debate again about signing papers and negating what Papa had done in his will, but Arden didn't bring it up. He hadn't for months, and I fell into the idea that it had lost importance for him. We were, after all, a married couple. Why would I hurt him, especially if we had a child to raise?

"I know you're quite intelligent about it, Audrina, but why have you lie around here worrying about those things, too? You need to be a real assistant for Mrs. Matthews."

"Assistant!" The mere exertion of extra effort to cry out made my head pound. "How am I any assistant to her? She does everything now. Every time I start to wander around the house, she sends me back, telling me Sylvia was asking for me. I haven't washed any clothes or changed any bedding, much less vacuumed a rug. The house is running away with itself, I'm sure."

"It's fine, Audrina. She does what has to be done, and I'm paying her more for that. So don't worry. If you do, I'll only worry about you, too." He looked sincere.

"I don't mean to complain about it. I'm happy I have the time to sit with Sylvia, of course. She's very uncomfortable."

"And crying a lot, I understand. You underestimate your contribution. Mrs. Matthews tells me it would be ten times worse if you weren't right there comforting Sylvia. Just keep up what you're doing."

I looked down and shook my head. Tears were coming into my eyes.

"What? What else is wrong?" he snapped, not hiding his impatience.

"Something's not right with me, Arden. I know you can't take me to see Dr. Prescott or have him come here, but I am so unenergetic these days. Half the time, I don't even try to get up out of bed. I don't care about what I'm wearing. I've been in this bathrobe for days, I think. That's another thing, Arden. I've been having trouble remembering things, even things I think I did the day before. I know you haven't been around that much these past weeks, but surely you see a difference in me. Surely you do!" Now my tears were free to streak down my cheeks. "Look at my hair," I cried, tugging on the loose, wiry strands. "I can't recall when

I last cared to put on lipstick. I'm turning into some
sort of hag, something you accused me of once."

He rushed over to sit next to me on the bed and
put his arm around me. "Oh, Audrina, don't cry. It
breaks my heart to see you so sad when we are on the
verge of bringing new happiness to Whitefern. The
wonderful sounds of a newborn baby's cry and laughter will drive away the shadows and dark memories
from every corner of every room. We have lived under
the cloud of sadness far too long. Both of us losing our
parents too soon and your struggle with your twisted
past would be far too much for most to bear. We have
such strength. You have such strength. Together we'll
conquer it all, Audrina. Don't cry."

I sucked back my tears and nodded. "But I'm
not feeling as well as I should, Arden. Something's
wrong."

"I know," he said, standing again. "Mrs. Matthews
told me."

"What? When?"

"Recently."

"What did she tell you?"

"She said you are suffering from intense anxiety.
She said she has seen it many times, especially with
pregnant women, so she is as familiar with the symptoms as any doctor and knows just how to treat you."

"Treat me? What do you mean?"

"First, you do agree that you have been extraordi-
narily anxious recently, especially after that last trip to
the supermarket, right?"

"I suppose so, but—"

"Well, as we've discussed time and time again, Audrina, we can't take the chance of anything happening to either you or Sylvia right now, and we can't expose either of you to the outside world. Up to now, we've been very successful convincing people that you're under special care as you draw within the last days of your pregnancy. A day doesn't go by when I don't have at least six or seven calls asking after your health. Why, even Mr. Johnson has bought it hook, line, and sinker. That's why we've put all the legal business on hold. You should be proud of yourself. You're making this possible. Just think how wonderful you'll feel with the baby in your arms, the four of us on some Sunday outing. That day is coming, Audrina, and it's coming soon."

"What did you mean when you said Mrs. Matthews knows just how to treat my anxiety?" I wasn't going to let him change the subject.

He smiled down at me. Both he and Papa always accused me of being a bulldog whenever I bit into something. "You've got to appreciate how lucky we are to have Mrs. Matthews for all this, Audrina. Imagine, someone with her medical knowledge willing to do just as we ask and not only that but do it with enthusiasm and dedication. Why, all this has become almost as important to her as it is to us."

I stared up at him, holding my expression, still waiting for my answer.

He saw that and walked to the door, peered out, and walked back to the bed. "We don't want to insult her, Audrina. That's the first thing and maybe the most important."

"Insult her?"

"Challenge her instructions or her wisdom when it comes to you and Sylvia."

"Me and Sylvia? Arden, get it through your head . . . I'm not really pregnant. I don't need a maternity nurse's tender loving care."

He laughed. "Of course you're not. I didn't say otherwise. But what I'm talking about, what Mrs. Matthews is talking about, has nothing to do with whether you're pregnant. It has to do with your anxiety. She says she has seen women as anxious as you are do rather bizarre things. Some show it with aggressive acts, sometimes hurting themselves as much as others."

"She thinks I would hurt Sylvia?"

"Oh, no. She's worried you might hurt yourself in some way, and then everything would be lost. She's only trying to make sure that doesn't happen, Audrina. It's not for long."

"What's not for long? What is she doing?"

"She's been giving you some tranquilizers to keep you calm," he confessed. "With my approval, of course. They're similar to the pills you took once before, remember?"

"Tranquilizers?" That made no sense. I took no pills. "When? How have I been taking tranquilizers?"

"She thought it would be easier to include them in your dinner. It's a very common prescription she has actually gotten for herself from time to time. It's why you sleep so well at night."

I stared at him in disbelief. "You let her do this to me without telling me?"

"It was for your own good, our own good. I'm only telling you this so you won't think there is anything seriously wrong with you, and you won't insist on going to see some doctor or rush out and do that yourself. It would be far too dangerous now."

"I'm being drugged," I thought aloud.

"Not drugged, treated. I'll speak to her about reducing the dosage, perhaps, but you should want this, too. You don't want to let your anxiety ruin things," he said firmly.

"I should have been told, have had everything explained to me," I said. "I'm not a child, and I'm not crazy. Arden, how could you let her do this to me?"

"Audrina, Audrina," he said, shaking his head as if I was a child. "Mrs. Matthews says that one of the things about people who suffer anxiety is self-denial. You have to admit that you wouldn't have accepted the diagnosis so quickly, and who knows where that would have led? And now, to really tell you the truth and add to all of this, I've been taking some of the same medicine myself. I'm not taking as much as you are, but you don't have to function throughout the day like I do. Have you any idea what it has been like for me to try to concentrate on intricate financial moves while worrying about what was happening at home and if our plan would explode in our faces? I've had great trouble sleeping. You haven't noticed?"

I shook my head.

"I know I put on a very good act for you, Audrina. I seem so strong and in control of everything, but there have been days when I was teetering on the edge of disaster. Maybe you can appreciate that now and not be so judgmental." He looked down and paced for a few moments like someone in deep thought. Then he stopped and looked up quickly. "Listen," he continued when I didn't say the words he wanted to hear—that I forgave him and Mrs. Matthews and that I understood. "I knew I needed some help to get through it, and I'm not ashamed to admit it. If someone with my ego can say that, you certainly can."

I sat up and rolled the blanket off me. "It just seems so deceitful for it to be done to me this way, Arden."

"Sometimes, as we are proving in spades, as your father would say, deceit is good. What we're doing is quite a bit more than a little white lie, I know, but look at all the good that will come of it. When it was necessary, you lied. You lied to Dr. Prescott. You lied to Mrs. Haider. You lied to everyone who saw you in the supermarket. Frankly, not a day goes by when you don't have to lie to Sylvia about something."

"And I don't feel good about any of it." I sat at the edge of the bed but still felt a little dizzy.

"But you did it because you knew it was necessary," he insisted. "So Mrs. Matthews did what she thought was necessary to protect you, Sylvia, and me, as well as herself. I admit that, but don't be angry at her and do anything that would jeopardize what we're doing, not now, not at this critical moment."

"I feel . . ."

"What?"

"Like I've lost all control of my life."

He nodded and approached me to put his hand on my shoulder. "For a while, you have, and so have I, but it will be over, and we'll have more control of our lives than ever. I'll speak with Mrs. Matthews about reducing your medicine to the amount I take. If I can take it, you can," he added, nearly growling at me like a wolf.

"I don't want to sleep all the time and lack the energy to care about myself," I said, shaking.

His hand flew off my shoulder like a frightened bird. "You won't. I don't, do I? But you'll remain calm enough for us to get through this. I'll go speak to her about it right now."

I heard him meet her outside Sylvia's room, and I rose and went to the door. They were speaking so loudly that I didn't have to listen in the hallway. Sylvia's room was right next to mine.

"Why did you tell her?" I heard Mrs. Matthews say.

"She complained about her lack of energy and wanted to see a doctor. She's a strong-willed person. You told me so yourself. It's better to be honest now. She understands why it was necessary, but you should reduce the dosage to what you've given me."

"Very well. I'm only doing what I think is required to get through this," she complained. "I don't want to be criticized for doing my job properly. I won't stand for that."

"Don't worry. She appreciates that as much as I do," he told her.

I retreated to my bed and sat waiting.

He returned. "Okay, it's all set. You will barely notice the dosage, and you'll get through this just like I will." He stepped closer and put his hands on my shoulders. "I can't stress it enough. It's very, very important now, Audrina, that you don't upset her. All we would need is for her to quit on us."

"She won't quit that fast, Arden. She would have a hard time explaining what she's done here."

"Nowhere near as hard a time as we would have and nowhere near as much to lose. Do you understand? Do you?"

"Yes," I said, feeling like my arm had been twisted.

"Good. All right. I've got to get back to some important things. Sit with Sylvia for a while. She was crying when I was in there just now. Try to think only of her."

I looked up sharply. "I don't understand why you've said that and you say it now. When have I ever thought of myself before I've thought of Sylvia's welfare?"

"I'm just trying to keep everything in perspective. It's what a good broker does, and most everything in life is in some way or another just another investment," he replied, smiling. "Another thing your good old Papa taught me."

He kissed me quickly on the cheek this time and left.

I sat there, stunned, angry, and, of course, very frustrated. I wanted to shout but knew that I couldn't. I wanted to tear the blob of wool from my stomach, tear it into shreds, and see myself as I really was again, but I knew I couldn't. I wanted to go find Mrs. Matthews and fire her on the spot, but I knew I couldn't. I felt like I was in a straitjacket and wanted to rip it off. I got up instead and went to sit with Sylvia. Mrs. Matthews wasn't in the room.

Sylvia groaned deeply and looked at me. "It hurts again, Audrina," she said. "Does it hurt you, too?"

"Yes." I hated to see her grimacing with pain. It did hurt me, too. I wasn't lying.

I put my hand on her stomach. I could feel the baby kicking and smiled in wonder.

"The baby's moving inside you, Sylvia. Feel it?"

Her stomach hardened but only for a few seconds. "Baby's coming," she said, nodding.

"Yes, soon."

"Fix her pillows behind her, and sit her up," Mrs. Matthews ordered from the doorway as she entered with Sylvia's dinner. "She hasn't been eating well. I want her to finish all of this tonight."

I did as she asked. As soon as Mrs. Matthews put the tray in front of Sylvia, Sylvia looked at me. "Audrina has to eat, too," she said.

I looked at Mrs. Matthews.

"Pull the chair up to the bed. Maybe she'll eat better with you eating beside her. I'll fetch your dinner."

"I don't want to fall asleep too quickly tonight," I said pointedly.

She looked at me, her eyes narrowing. "You won't. And you'll be doing a lot more now." She nodded at Sylvia. "There will be a lot more for both of us to do."

"How close is she?"

"I doubt we'll finish the week," she said. "Make sure she drinks all the water," she added, and left to get my food.

Sylvia was very uncomfortable. She pleaded to be permitted to lie back, but I did what Mrs. Matthews prescribed and kept her eating and drinking. She was a little more cooperative when Mrs. Matthews brought me my tray and I began to eat. I ate slowly, suspiciously, wondering if Mrs. Matthews had indeed done what Arden had asked her to do and reduced the dosage of whatever she had given me. Perhaps she wasn't putting anything in my food now. I couldn't detect it, but then again, I never did.

She returned to see how much had been eaten and nodded with approval. She took Sylvia's tray.

"I can bring mine," I said, starting to rise.

"Just stay there and keep her company. That's more important. Now you can understand why I wanted her brought down to this bedroom. I can't imagine running up and down those stairs. I hope you can appreciate everything I've asked you to do and everything I have done."

"As you've said often, Mrs. Matthews, you're being well paid," I replied with a cold tone of realism.

Her face looked even tighter than it habitually was. I thought the skin would tear at her jawbone. Then she turned and left. She didn't return for my tray for quite a while. I put it at the foot of Sylvia's bed and helped her get as comfortable as she could be. Memories of my mother during the week before she was rushed to the hospital returned. She'd been in such agony sometimes, but the furthest thing from my mind had been the thought that she would die in childbirth. Every time Sylvia moaned, I was whipped back to that day Papa returned and Aunt Ellsbeth forced him to tell me the dreadful news. I'd thought my heart had been torn from my chest.

I reminded myself now that if something so terrible was to happen to Sylvia, I would blame no one but myself. I had dropped my protective shield around her. I had provided the opportunity for this to happen. Papa would scream from his grave. Everything, everything possible, had to be done to ensure that Sylvia would not face a fate similar to Momma's. For this reason above all others, I had to placate Mrs. Matthews and appreciate all that she was doing. I shivered at the thought that something I might say or do would drive her out of Whitefern and leave us panicking over Sylvia's final moments.

When she returned, I handed her my tray. She saw the look of obedience on my face and softened her eyes into her confident smile of self-satisfaction that only someone with her ego would enjoy. I avoided looking at her and sat down again quickly.

"She's at the point where she can't sleep well," Mrs. Matthews said. "Do your best to get her to doze as much as possible. We don't give pregnant women drugs they don't absolutely need."

"Okay."

"Tell her a story, or sing to her." She shook her head. "A child giving birth to a child."

At least for the moment, she appeared to really feel

sorry for Sylvia. Perhaps I was wrong to judge her so harshly, I thought. She was simply a woman with a personality that didn't warm your heart. Maybe it was her way to get through the day, through each crisis, for her work was not work I would enjoy. Few would enjoy it. As Papa used to say, you had to have thick skin if you were going to walk among the bees.

"How old was the youngest woman you helped deliver?" I asked. I was curious, but I also wanted to be sure she thought I appreciated her and her experience.

"Woman? Hardly a woman. She was eleven," she said. "Very bloody delivery and very painful."

"Did she die?"

"No. Not in the sense you mean, but what sort of a life do you think came after that?"

"Sylvia will have a good life," I said. "I promise you that."

"As good as she might have, I expect."

"Better than she might have," I insisted. "Better."

We looked at each other. Her face did soften. There was a surge of warmth in her eyes. I looked at Sylvia. We did need to save all our compassion for her. There was enough tension without my creating any between Mrs. Matthews and myself, especially in Sylvia's presence.

"Well, I will say one thing for you, Audrina. You have an extraordinary capacity for love."

I sat back, amazed. A real compliment? From her?

"But then again," she added, "it's when we're most desperate to please others that we're in the most danger of hurting ourselves."

"Who taught you that?"

"Life," she said, and left the room.

I turned back to Sylvia and smiled. I saw no way I could hurt myself by pleasing her, not now. She looked at me curiously when I put my hand on her stomach again. Then she turned to reach toward me and put her hand on my mound of wool. I watched her face. Would she realize now that what I was doing was a bald-faced lie? Would that frighten her? Would it make her feel silly and alone?

She smiled. "She kicked," she said, and lay back. "Baby's coming."

I sat holding her hand and realized that the saying of my father's that Arden had reminded me of was true: deception was sometimes good, especially if the end result brought happiness to someone who desperately needed it, someone as fragile as my Sylvia.

She finally fell asleep. I sat quietly watching her breathe and seeing how her lips moved slightly. Somewhere in her dreams, she was talking. Was she talking to Papa? I envied her for her dreams. They were a way out of the web we were all caught in right now, at least for a few hours.

I didn't think I had been given more tranquilizers, but I did doze off. I woke when I realized Mrs. Matthews was standing beside me.

"Go to bed," she said. "I'll stand by with her. I've decided you're strong enough to contend with what is happening, and I will need your help. So get some rest, and be ready for what lies ahead."

"Her stomach gets hard for a few seconds, and she cries."

"This isn't false labor. I think she might be delivering earlier than anticipated."

"Oh," I said, the worry ringing in me like a bell.

She smiled, not coldly, not warmly, just a bland smile. "Look at it this way. It will be over sooner than we thought."

Birth, a Step toward Truth

Sylvia went into real, full-blown labor three days later. It happened late in the morning. She was screaming and crying so hard I could barely move to follow Mrs. Matthews's commands after Sylvia's water broke.

"I didn't pee!" Sylvia cried. "I didn't pee!"

"It's not pee," Mrs. Matthews said, and turned to me. "Clean it up," she ordered.

I started out for the mop and then stopped. "I should call Arden," I said.

She turned and looked at me with such disdain that I could feel the blood rushing into my face. "You want to call your husband? Will you be screaming and crying like she is but over the phone when his secretary answers?"

"Of course not."

"Then pray tell me how you intend to convey the situation we are now in. It is supposed to be happening to you."

"Oh!" I moaned. Of course, she was right. Dislike her as much as I did, I still had to give her credit for keeping her cool and never losing sight of what we had to do.

"But he should know," I offered weakly. Sylvia was crying so hard. It made me shudder.

"Clean this up. I will call him when I get a moment here. Your husband and I planned for how to handle this."

"Why wasn't I part of that planning?"

"Do you want to have a long discussion about it, or do you want me to care for your sister?"

"Okay," I said.

I ran out for the mop, and while she got Sylvia back into the bed, I cleaned the floor. I put the mop and pail aside. Sylvia looked like she was having trouble breathing. Her eyes rolled with the panic she was feeling.

"Is she all right?"

"Of course she's all right. Keep this cool washcloth on her forehead, and hold her hand. The first birth for any woman is always the most difficult. Her next one will be easier."

"Next one?"

"You never know," she said, and went to call Arden, leaving me alone with Sylvia. Now I was sorry I had even mentioned calling Arden. Sylvia was clawing at my wool belly, begging me to stop the pain.

"It will get better as soon as the baby comes," I said, and repeated it like a chant. I had read about deliveries and seen them acted out in movies, but nothing had prepared me for this. Sylvia's screams were so

loud I was sure people working on the grounds outside would hear. I had no idea what else to do. I went
to the door to look down the hall for Mrs. Matthews,
but she was nowhere in sight.

"Papa!" Sylvia screamed. "Papa!"

I returned to her side and took her hand again
while I dabbed her forehead with the cool cloth. What
if her heart stopped? I thought. Momma had given
birth too soon and died. History was repeating itself.
If she died, I wouldn't care about our precious reputation. I'd call the police and have Mr. Price arrested,
stroke or no stroke, I vowed.

As casually as she would have entered Sylvia's room
weeks ago, Mrs. Matthews returned.

"She's in too much pain," I said. "Isn't there anything else we can do?"

"We? No. There's nothing else to do but let nature
take its course."

She took Sylvia's blood pressure and then suddenly
seized her shoulders and shook her so hard Sylvia
stopped screaming.

"Now, you listen to me, Sylvia. The baby is coming. Here's what I want you to do," she said, and
began to give her instructions. She already had the
bed changed into what looked like a hospital bed now,
with something protecting the mattress. Beside it was
a pan in case Sylvia threw up. Mrs. Matthews had
moved a table and all the medical supplies she needed,
turning the room into a delivery room. I felt helpless standing by and watching her as she told Sylvia
to push. Sylvia's eyes were still wide open and wild

with fear and confusion. Her face was flushed, her forehead beaded with sweat. I continued to dab it with the washcloth. She looked at me with such pleading. I had always been there to help her, to wash her cuts and bruises, to hold her and make her feel better again, but there was nothing I could do for her now that would ease the pain.

"Why is the baby hurting me, Audrina?"

I looked to Mrs. Matthews. "It's supposed to hurt," she said sharply. "Just do what I tell you, and it will stop when the baby comes out."

Sylvia looked at me to see if I believed it. I smiled and nodded to reassure her, and for a few moments at least, she calmed.

"What did Arden say?" I asked, my heart racing with the anxiety and tension Mrs. Matthews had predicted I would experience.

"He's on his way," she said, sounding annoyed that she had to reply.

Sylvia started to scream and cry again. Mrs. Matthews gazed at her with a wry smile on her lips, reminding me of my aunt Ellsbeth, who had seemed to enjoy Vera's pain before her miscarriage. Agony was the perfect and just punishment for a woman who transgressed. I thought Aunt Ellsbeth saw herself as the voice of an angry God, enraged at the violation of one of his commandments. But Sylvia hadn't transgressed. She had been transgressed against. Yes, God had punished Mr. Price by giving him a stroke, but now, if anything, Aunt Ellsbeth's angry God should show mercy and reduce Sylvia's pain to almost nothing.

"She's not trying," Mrs. Matthews suddenly said. There was a little panic in her face. "I don't like this. It's almost as if she is deliberately holding the baby hostage in her birth canal."

"She can't do that, can she?"

Mrs. Matthews turned to me with the strangest look in her eyes. For a moment, I thought she had gone mad. It was as if Sylvia's failure to do everything exactly as she wanted reflected badly on her. "There's something else going on here," she said.

"What?"

"Take off your skirt and panties, and lie beside her," she ordered.

"What?"

"Don't you see what's happening? She's constantly watching you. She keeps waiting for you to scream in agony."

I looked at Sylvia, who was staring at me now. "But—"

"You have to give birth, too," Mrs. Matthews declared.

"Give birth, too?"

It was one thing to placate Sylvia and keep her calm all these months, to go along with her belief that I had to be as pregnant as she was and that Papa had declared it in one of those mysterious rocking-chair dreams, but to actually act out a delivery beside her . . .

The look on Mrs. Matthews's face was frightening and maddening. For a few moments, I wondered if she didn't believe Sylvia's dreams, too.

"But I can't—"

"Do it!" she cried. "It will be your baby, won't it? Deliver it!"

My heart was pounding, just as I imagined Sylvia's was. I looked at the space beside her, looked at Mrs. Matthews, who was poised and waiting, and then took off my skirt and panties and slipped onto the bed. Sylvia grasped my hand immediately. Mrs. Matthews nodded with satisfaction and then, shockingly, lifted my legs, spread them, and looked between them. I felt her fingers on the insides of my thighs.

She is mad, I thought, *as mad as a hatter*.

I looked at Sylvia. For a moment, though, she suddenly seemed to have no pain. She smiled at me and then turned to Mrs. Matthews and began to follow her orders. When she groaned, Mrs. Matthews looked at me expectantly, and I groaned, too. When Sylvia cried in pain, I did. It was a duet of agony.

"Push!" Mrs. Matthews cried. "Push! I can see the baby's head."

Suddenly, seconds felt like minutes. I felt my cheeks and realized I was breaking into a sweat. My heart was pounding. I took deep breaths. Did I feel pain? Maybe I was going mad myself, but I realized I was actually pushing. All I had read about giving birth ran through my mind. This was how it went; this was what to do. Finally, Sylvia and I let out a last, almost primeval scream, and then Mrs. Matthews lifted the baby, with the umbilical cord still attached, and placed the newborn girl, crying and covered in blood, on my stomach—not Sylvia's. Mrs. Matthews expertly cut and tied the umbilical cord. I couldn't move. Sylvia was just as quiet, watching.

"I need to suction out her mouth and nose a bit," Mrs. Matthews said.

Both Sylvia and I watched her bring the baby to the table she had set up beside the bed. After she did the suctioning, she weighed her.

"Six pounds four ounces. Being born early didn't do any harm."

She began to wash her. I was frozen, unable to move, until we heard the baby cry again.

"Adelle," Sylvia said.

Mrs. Matthews brought the baby back to me. "Newborn babies' bodies don't have the ability to control their temperature well. We want to keep her warm and dry."

She continued to dry her while the baby was lying on me. Then she put the blanket around her carefully, leaving some of her exposed skin against me.

"Your body will warm her, and this is the first opportunity to bond with your baby," she explained.

"Is everything all right with her?"

"I'll do a full Apgar assessment shortly, but I think she's just fine. Right now, I need to do some stitching on Sylvia. There are some nasty tears."

"What's an Apgar assessment?"

She looked at me, disgusted. "You clearly didn't read the pamphlet I left for you. I will judge the baby's color, check her heart rate, reflexes, muscle tone, and respiratory function. I don't just pull them out and leave for dinner," she added, and turned back to Sylvia.

I gazed at the baby. The little hair she had was similar to Sylvia's and mine. And she looked like she had Sylvia's eyes.

"What's happened?" Arden cried, rushing to the bedroom door about ten minutes later.

"Happened. A baby happened. You missed it," Mrs. Matthews said dryly, and kept working on Sylvia.

I looked up at him and smiled. "A girl, Arden. Sylvia wants her to be named Adelle."

He walked in slowly, his face full of more excitement than I had ever seen him express about anything. He was flushed from rushing, but he was so pleased that it brought tears to my eyes. He looked at me and at the baby and back at me, as if I really had just delivered her. We had pretended this for so long that we had begun to believe it. When you wanted to believe something so much, it would happen, at least in your own mind, I thought.

Arden stood gazing down at Adelle with an expression of pure joy. I couldn't say anything to contradict the way he was treating me. He would be no different if I had actually delivered her.

"Adelle is a perfect name, now that I see her, yes," he said. He smiled. "And now a surprise for you, Audrina. The nursery is ready."

"Nursery?"

"Of course. While you were down here, I redid that room. I worked on it myself at night."

"He did," Mrs. Matthews confirmed with a nod and a look of both amazement and approval. "The man lived on four hours of sleep the last week or so, because I suspected this early birth might happen."

"What room?" I asked. I knew the answer and feared hearing it, but I had to ask.

"Well, the other Audrina's room. I put new wallpaper on the walls, put down a new rug, repainted the window frames, and changed the light fixtures," he rattled off proudly. "I've been studying how to do it for months, and I had some good tradesmen give me advice. I even put together her first playpen. There's a bassinet, too, which I'll bring here."

"You did all that? Yourself?"

"We couldn't bring anyone into the house while all this was happening, as you know, so I had to rise to the task. Your father would have been quite surprised and impressed, don't you think? He didn't have faith that I could change a lightbulb."

"What did you do with everything that was in there?" I asked.

"I put it all in the basement for you to go through. Maybe now you'll throw out some of it, if not all of it. Including this damnable rocking chair."

The baby whimpered more loudly. Mrs. Matthews paused and looked at her. "Our next task," she said, "is getting Sylvia used to breastfeeding. Healthy newborns tend to be alert right after they're born. It's a good time to begin breastfeeding."

Sylvia looked very tired. She was fighting to keep her eyes open. The emotional tension had worn me out, too.

"We should move the baby over near her," I said. "Get the baby used to her."

"I thought we could avoid that," Arden said to Mrs. Matthews. "You and I did discuss it."

"I didn't say we couldn't, although I don't think it will matter much for Sylvia. Breastfeeding is a better, healthier option for the child. So many of my former-beauty-queen mothers were afraid their breasts would scar or shrivel. We have everything needed in the kitchen if you choose otherwise. I can tend to it right after this," she said.

"I think we'd prefer that," Arden said. "Right, Audrina? That way, Sylvia will be less confused. We want her to get used to thinking of Adelle as your baby and not hers."

"But we want Adelle to be as healthy as she can be, Arden."

"She'll be healthy," Mrs. Matthews said, straightening up and turning back to the baby. "Most mothers who want to breastfeed want to establish a stronger bond with their child. Obviously, that's not the case here. I'll take her now and do the evaluation and then set up the first feeding, which you can do, Audrina, perhaps in your room. Just place her on the bed with you."

"Good," Arden said quickly. "Audrina?"

"Yes, of course," I said.

"You can expect that Sylvia's breasts will leak and ache," Mrs. Matthews said. "She'll survive it, but I can imagine, having spent all this time with her, that she will be quite frightened and confused. I'll do what I can, but none of this will be my business soon."

"I'd rather we do it the way I want," Arden said. "Audrina will feed the baby." He was firm about it.

"Do as you wish," Mrs. Matthews said, sounding not so much angry as indifferent that her advice wasn't being followed. She took the baby to the table to begin her exam.

I looked at Sylvia. Her eyes were open, but she looked like she was in a daze.

"Sylvia?" I said. She didn't turn to me, nor did she speak. "Is she still in pain?" I asked.

"Some, but it will pass. I'll give her something soon," Mrs. Matthews said. "There's only one of me here."

"But are you sure she's all right? Sylvia? She's not hearing me."

Mrs. Matthews glanced at her. "A little shock. It'll pass," she said.

I sat up and kissed Sylvia's cheek. "Are you all right, Sylvia?" I patted her hand gently and kissed her again. "Sylvia?"

She didn't answer.

"Are you sure she's all right?"

"I'm sure," Mrs. Matthews said without turning back. "Leave her to rest."

"Do what Mrs. Matthews says," Arden ordered. "We hired her to handle this, Audrina."

I got up slowly and dressed, my eyes still on Sylvia, waiting for her to look at me or speak, even cry. She did nothing.

"Audrina!" Arden said sharply.

I followed him to my room. As soon as we entered, he turned to me, his face full of excitement, his eyes wide.

"We did it!" he said, holding his hands up in fists. "We did it!"

He looked like he was going to burst and waited for me to react similarly, but I sat silently on my bed, feeling like I was the one in shock, not Sylvia. What Mrs. Matthews had put me through had had an extraordinary effect on me. It would be ludicrous to say that I felt like I had truly given birth, but the mimicking had certainly given me more than simply a sense of it.

"Aren't you happy?" Arden asked when I didn't respond to his joyful outburst. "What's wrong with you?" he demanded.

"I feel so strange, like a woman who has gone through false labor and discovered there was no baby inside her."

"But there *is* a baby, damn it, get that through your head. We've prepared months and months for this."

"I know, I know, Arden. It's just one thing to plan for it and another to have it happen."

"Yeah, well, it happened, so start reading those books I brought you about being a proper mother. Mrs. Matthews recommended all of them. It's all on you from here on out as far as taking care of the baby goes."

"Adelle," I said. I wanted him to reconfirm that he would accept the name that Sylvia had suggested.

"Right, Adelle. Now, Mrs. Matthews will stay on

for a few weeks. The story is that you had a tough delivery, and she's here to help until you're strong enough."

"I'm worried about Sylvia."

"Well, stop worrying. It's all going to be fine. We've escaped the embarrassment and the damage to our name and our business. After Mrs. Matthews leaves, we'll begin inviting people over to see the baby and you. We'll have a party or something."

I nodded, but still not with the enthusiasm he wanted. I saw the unhappy look on his face hardening.

"Listen," he said, taking a softer approach. "We'll be moving you both upstairs now. You'll see how beautiful the nursery is, and you'll be too busy to think of anything else. I'm sure you'll feel a lot better then. As soon as we can take the baby out, we'll go shopping to get you new clothes. That's what new mothers do. And we'll go shopping to get the baby things, too. And yes, we'll bring Sylvia along when she's well enough and no one can tell what she's been through, and we'll buy her things, too. Okay? Okay?" he repeated when I didn't answer.

"Okay," I replied.

"All right." He brushed back his hair and fixed his tie. "I'm going to return to work and announce the baby's birth. Everyone's waiting on pins and needles at the office. I've got a box of cigars in my car that I bought months ago in anticipation. See you later for our private celebration dinner. Get yourself together, Audrina. I'm looking forward to wonderful days ahead for us all."

He walked over to kiss me on the cheek and then left. I went to the window and looked out. Mr. Ralph was trimming a tree. If I closed my eyes and imagined it, I could be back years and years ago, when I had stood by windows of Whitefern and looked out at a world I feared without realizing why. I was doing the same thing now.

I shouldn't be, I thought. After all, Arden was right. His plan was ending up just the way he wanted it to. Everything we had done was working, although it still would be strange having Sylvia think of the baby as more mine than hers. Maybe it would be enough to have her think it was ours. People who heard her say or think that aloud would surely smile and shake their heads, believing it was all part of her being a child in a woman's body. There would be nothing strange about it to them, only to me.

A little later, under Mrs. Matthews's supervision, I gave Adelle her first feeding. Despite how she had been conceived, I thought Adelle was beautiful. It was impossible to predict what her features would be like months, even years, from now, but at this moment, I thought there were very strong resemblances to Sylvia and, therefore, to me or the Adares. As soon as the baby had gone to sleep on my bed, I rose to check on Sylvia.

She was lying with her eyes open, just as before, but clearly not seeing anything. Mrs. Matthews came up beside me, looked at her, and moved to the bed and began to check her blood pressure. She listened to her heart with a stethoscope and then looked at me. "She'll be all right. Just sit here and talk to her," she ordered.

"Are you sure? Maybe she needs more medical attention. I wouldn't want anything to happen to her just because we were afraid of revealing the truth now. Really. I'm worried."

"Calm down," she snapped. "Just read her a story or something."

When she left, I sat next to Sylvia and began to talk to her.

"Our baby has been born, Sylvia. You have to help care for her, you know. You can't sleep too long. We need you. I know it was painful, but when you see her and see how beautiful she is, you will agree that it was worth it."

She blinked, but nothing else in her face moved.

"Someday soon, you'll be playing with her, Sylvia. You'll show her things, how to do things. And when she can walk, you'll take her into the woods and show her the squirrels. But you have to be strong, Sylvia. You have to be healthy and well."

I took her hand and held it. This couldn't be right. This couldn't be just a little thing. She wasn't moving or trying to speak. I lowered my head and closed my eyes. *Papa*, I thought. *Papa, help us.*

I looked at the rocking chair.

"I'm going to tell Papa about the baby, Sylvia, but he'll want you to tell him, too."

I went to the chair. It had been years since I had sat in it. It actually terrified me a little. When I sat, memories came rushing back—the visions, the voices, everything I had ever seen or heard when I closed my eyes and rocked. I glanced back at Sylvia. She looked like she had turned a little toward me. I took a deep breath, like I would if I was going to jump into the pond, and then I put my arms on the arms of the chair, closed my eyes, and rocked.

I saw Papa's angry face. The words I feared resonated.

You were supposed to protect her, Audrina. You promised.

I started to cry, crying like a little girl again. I couldn't have Papa mad at me. I couldn't.

"I'm sorry, Papa. I'm sorry," I moaned.

"Papa?" I heard, and opened my eyes. Sylvia was sitting up. "Did you hear Papa?"

"Yes." I nodded. "He's waiting for you, Sylvia, for you."

She started to get out of the bed.

Mrs. Matthews, as if she had been listening just outside the door, appeared. "You stay in that bed," she ordered, pointing with her long right forefinger at Sylvia. "I'll tell you when you can get up."

Sylvia froze.

"But it helped her," I said. "The rocking chair."

"I told you that her lethargy wouldn't last. You don't have to go through some stupid magic. She'll be fine. Now, go keep your eyes on the baby. I'll handle Sylvia. Go on!" she ordered, so sharply I winced and then got up.

"Papa," Sylvia said.

"Lie down," Mrs. Matthews commanded. "I won't have you tear those stitches and bleed all over the place. Go on. Do as I say."

Sylvia lay back reluctantly, her eyes on the chair.

Mrs. Matthews glared at me. "You'd have her up rocking in that chair with those stitches still fresh? I can see I'll be here for a while yet. Go on. Go to your room."

I wanted so much to shout back at her, but we were still trapped, trapped by the secrets. I glanced at Sylvia and then went and stood beside the bassinet, watching Adelle breathe and occasionally whimper like a puppy. Could I do it? Could I make her my baby? Could I stop thinking about who her father was and how she had been conceived? Of course, it was wrong, even stupid, to blame the baby, but it wasn't easily ignored.

I sat on my bed softly beside Adelle and picked up one of the pamphlets about caring for an infant. Hours later, Arden returned, beaming as brightly as he had before, if not more. He rattled on and on about all the congratulations he had received, the clients who had called, and how wonderful it had made him feel.

"Maybe I should have been there," I said, my voice full of bitterness.

"Now, how could you do that, Audrina? Really? If you're going to be a mother, think like an adult," he said, and looked at the baby. "Of course, like your father, I wanted a son," he said, "but for now, she will do."

"For now?"

"Maybe simulating a birth has helped make you fertile. We'll try for a son. One can hope. Of course, we can't get right to it." He smiled. "Women who give birth don't conceive days after."

What was he thinking? Women who give birth don't conceive days after? Sometimes he sounded like someone who had been through this many times. Once again, I wondered about his college years. How many secrets had he buried?

"How's Sylvia?" he asked.

"You'll have to go see for yourself. I was dismissed," I said.

"Dismissed?"

I turned back to the baby. He left and later returned to tell me Sylvia was doing well. She had even eaten something.

"A day or so of rest, and everything will be fine," he said. "I've ordered our celebration dinner. Mrs. Crown made all the arrangements. We're having lobster. You, of course, will do nothing. Mrs. Matthews is setting the table. I've bought a bottle of the best champagne. So just rest for now. Later we will move everything upstairs, and you'll be back in our bedroom, and Sylvia will be back in hers. Mrs. Matthews says we can move her later, too."

"I wouldn't go up without her."

He started out and stopped, turning back. "I'll bring the rocking chair back up if you like, but we'll put it in Sylvia's room for now. I imagine that will make her feel better. When Mrs. Matthews leaves, we can move it into the guest room or out of the house completely. Up to you," he said. "Okay?"

"Okay," I said. It would make Sylvia happy right now.

He smiled and left.

Adelle was still asleep. I lay back, keeping very close to her, and closed my eyes. I dozed off but woke when Mrs. Matthews entered. She didn't realize I was awake. I opened my eyes slightly and saw her check Adelle and then wrap her comfortably in the blanket. She picked her up and held her, smiling at her. Could this woman feel motherly? She had helped deliver so many children, I imagined, but I was certain she had never been as involved as she had been in Adelle's birth.

The moment she saw that I was awake, she stopped smiling.

"We've brought the bassinet down to be at the dining-room table," she said. "For tonight's celebratory dinner. It's what your husband asked."

"What about Sylvia?"

"It's best she remain in bed for a while longer. I'll bring her some dinner later. She's sleeping now. I gave her something to help her sleep and ease any pain."

"Okay."

She looked at me strangely for a moment. "I'm sorry you couldn't have your own child properly, but I assure you, this is a blessing in disguise. Your husband is a very smart man." She started out with Adelle in her arms. Then she stopped and looked at me. "You might want to put on something special and do your hair."

"Why is that important to you?" I asked.

"It's not important to me, but I know that the part you're playing has really just begun. My free advice is for you to get right into it."

"Somehow I doubt that advice is free," I said.

Her smug expression faded.

I wanted to be defiant, just to go out as I was, but I realized she was not wrong. The baby had been born. Sylvia would be fine. The world would know only what Arden had revealed, and we would go on, maybe even as the family Arden imagined.

After all, what other choice was there?

Our secrets begot secrets. They spun around us, tightening their grip on Whitefern.

Arden didn't realize it, I thought, but in the end, we might be in a stronger trap, and those shadows that draped themselves in every possible corner would only grow darker. They would be there for Adelle, just as they always would be there for me.

Unless, of course, I found a way for us to escape ourselves.

Pathway to the Light

There were moments during our celebratory dinner when I felt more like an observer than a participant. Arden and Mrs. Matthews talked to each other as if I wasn't even there. She had set the table, but not as nicely as I or Sylvia would. She used paper napkins, something Arden would normally criticize, and she didn't have separate forks for salad. Arden had told her to bring in some glasses for champagne, and she forgot other glasses for water. Following what I believed were her orders, Arden had placed the bassinet next to my chair. She had put Adelle in it. I started for the kitchen when the food arrived from the restaurant, but Arden told me just to sit.

"Mrs. Matthews will handle it all," he said. "Tonight you have to be a woman who just delivered a baby."

"But I didn't, Arden. I obviously can do what has to be done."

"Audrina, if you don't act like the child's mother, no one will believe you are," he said. "It has to come naturally to you. We're over the crisis, but we can still make serious mistakes. Besides, haven't you always wanted a child?"

"Yes, of course."

"Then why fight it? Enjoy it. Be the mother you've always wanted to be." He leaned toward me to whisper. "Besides, with what I'm paying her, we should let her work."

"How long will she be here?"

"Not long now. Everything will return to the way it was. Not to normal, exactly. We have a child to care for now. And you have some work to do with Sylvia, I'm sure. She'll be quite confused. I don't want her out in public too fast, although I'm sure you can ascribe anything she says to her lack of intelligence."

Before I could speak, Mrs. Matthews entered with a tray on which were three dishes crowded with food. She looked very pleased with the dinner we were about to enjoy. We had beautiful lobster tails, salad, and french fries. I had started to reach for mine when she put the tray in the center of the table, but she seized it first and brought it to me.

"Our new mother has to be treated a little specially tonight," she said. I saw the sardonic look in her eyes.

"Thank you," I replied, as if I thought she was being kind.

Arden popped the champagne and poured glassfuls for the three of us. Then he raised his and waited for me to raise mine.

"To a successful pregnancy and delivery, bringing a new child to Whitefern. Thank you for your professional care, Mrs. Matthews. To your expertise. And finally, to our new daughter, Adelle Lowe."

We clinked our glasses and drank. Adelle whimpered as if she had heard and understood it all. I couldn't help being uncomfortable, now that it had happened and Sylvia's child was to be mine. It felt very deceitful, and I wondered if it always would. Arden insisted that joy was flooding over us. In his smile, I could see that, at least for now, I had to put all my fears and dark thoughts aside. Perhaps he was right. The new days of light and happiness had arrived with the child. I didn't feel like being grateful to Mrs. Matthews, but I had to admit to myself that without her, this would not have been accomplished. A healthy child was born, Sylvia was safe, and we had not suffered a bit of embarrassment.

As we ate, Arden looked like a young boy again, his pride so bright that he seemed to glow. Rarely at any dinner since this had begun had he been as talkative as he was tonight, and he ate as if it was his first meal in weeks. I saw that even Mrs. Matthews was impressed with his glee. He rattled on and on about the changes he would now make at Whitefern, changes that were important to what he called a new family. He wanted to brighten up the house as much as he could.

"We need to repaint walls, sell off some of those old, dark paintings, and finally put in some real lighting."

"I couldn't agree more," Mrs. Matthews said. "When I first entered this house, I thought I was in a funeral parlor!"

"Precisely. That's going to change," he replied. Apparently, he had already had some important discussions with decorators and had scheduled one to visit us next week.

"Good," Mrs. Matthews said.

I looked at her. She was behaving as though she was going to be living here forever.

"Of course, nothing will be decided until Audrina confirms it," Arden said. "A husband can't make a home happy unless his wife is happy in it."

"Very true," Mrs. Matthews said. Like Arden, she was suddenly more talkative than ever. "I wish my husband had realized that."

I perked up. She never talked about her family. "What happened to him?" I asked.

"He was an alcoholic and eventually destroyed his liver. He died twelve years ago."

I wondered to myself if living with her had driven him to become an alcoholic. "I'm sorry to hear that," I said. "I wondered why you never mention much about your own family."

"Yes, well, it doesn't do us any good to belabor the dreadful past events in our lives. Look to the future. Now you have one," she added. "Be grateful, and let that gratitude drown any sadness."

"That's not always as easy as it sounds."

"It's as easy as you want it to be," she insisted. "Dwelling on disappointments and tragedies will steal away your chance for future happiness."

She always made statements that sounded like declarations from a higher power.

"Hear, hear," Arden said, and poured her and himself more champagne. "You want any more?" he asked me.

"No, thank you."

As if he was at one of his business dinners, Arden began to talk about the economy and how he would like to adjust Mrs. Matthews's portfolio.

I didn't eat half as much as they did, and when I was content with what I had eaten, I thought that one of us should go check on Sylvia. "She might have woken up and would be frightened," I suggested.

"I doubt it," Mrs. Matthews said. "I gave her enough to sleep well for a few more hours at least. She needs to sleep now. If you're restless, why don't you clear the table?"

Arden nodded in agreement. So just like that, I was back to my household duties, I thought. She looked so confident, so pleased with her power over me.

I felt my spine harden and sat back. "Would a woman who had just given birth get right back to her household duties?" I asked.

She raised her eyebrows.

I looked at Arden. "I'm simply trying to behave like a woman who just had a baby. I should get to the point where I do so without thinking, don't you agree?" I was so saccharine-sweet that I almost turned my own stomach.

"She has a point, Helen," Arden said. "Perhaps you can see to some coffee for us, too, when you clear the table. I'd like to have some with brandy tonight."

She didn't flush red, exactly, but I could see the

fury in her eyes. She rose and began to clear off the table. At that moment, I really appreciated Arden. He smiled at me, and I thought that maybe now that this was all coming to an end, we could return to being the husband and wife we had set out to be. We'd return to feeling the affection we'd had for each other when we first met, a time that felt so very long ago.

Adelle woke and began to cry. For a moment, I panicked, but then I lifted her carefully and rocked her.

"That's not what she wants," Mrs. Matthews said as she returned from the kitchen. "It's time for another feeding. Get used to it. You won't be sleeping too many hours in a row for quite a while."

"Well, you can surely help for a few weeks, can't you, Helen?" Arden asked. I listened carefully to his tone of voice. Whenever he asked her to do something now, there was an underlying threat.

"I can help a little, but if she becomes too dependent on me, it won't do you any good when I leave."

"When will you leave?" I asked, perhaps a bit too harshly.

"As soon as I can," she said. "Don't worry about that. Come with me to the kitchen. I'll fix the baby's bottle, and you can watch and know how to do it after this." She looked at Arden. "Maybe you can pitch in, Mr. Lowe, and help clear the rest of the table. I will prepare some coffee, too, as you requested."

He laughed. "Me? Clear off a table? I haven't lifted a dish off a table since—"

"Since now," she said.

I almost laughed out loud at the way the smile flew

off his face. He looked at mine and then, not hiding his displeasure, began to pick up dishes and glasses.

Later, he drank too much brandy and nearly fell asleep on the settee. I reminded him of what we had to do to get Adelle and me upstairs this evening.

"Why don't we wait?" he asked.

"You promised me, Arden. It hasn't been pleasant sleeping in those rooms, either for me or for Sylvia."

He groaned and got up.

While Adelle was sleeping, I brought up some of my clothing and then went to the first Audrina's room to see the nursery he had created. I was impressed, but not seeing the familiar toys and furniture stunned me at first. Even after I had learned the truth and Papa had faced up to the deceptions he had created, he had not wanted to disturb the room. I think there was a point where he had convinced himself that there really was a first Audrina. He had wanted her so much, as he had enjoyed her. In a way, changing the sacred rocking-chair room was like burying another part of him.

Arden came up behind me. "Well?" he asked. "You're not going to start complaining about not having those dusty things in here, are you?"

"No, Arden. You did a beautiful job. I am proud of you."

"Good," he said. "Let's finish moving everything up. I have a big day tomorrow. I've decided that I'm not moving that rocking chair up tonight. It's late, and it's heavy."

"Okay, Arden," I said. I was too tired to argue about anything.

Shortly after, Mrs. Matthews decided we could help Sylvia back up to her room. She was groggy, but the pain seemed tolerable. The two of us practically carried her up the stairs and got her into her bed.

"I'll look in on her periodically," Mrs. Matthews said. "You look after the baby. You know now how to prepare her bottle, so you'll be the one to go up and down the stairs."

Adelle was set up beside our bed on my side. The first time she cried, Arden woke with a start and groaned. "I should have left you downstairs until she sleeps through the night," he said. "I have to have my sleep. It's important that I'm alert at the brokerage, and I get up so early."

"I'm sorry, Arden." I thought for a moment and then said, "Maybe for a while, it would be better if I slept with Sylvia and the baby slept in her room with us."

"Yes," he said instantly, jumping on the suggestion. "While you get the bottle prepared, I'll move the bassinet and Adelle in there. Brilliant."

As I headed for the stairs, Mrs. Matthews stepped out of her room in her robe and slippers. "What's the problem?" she asked.

I told her our plan and what had caused the changes.

"My husband was the same way when our son was born," she said. "I've never doubted that men are the weaker sex. Go on. I'll help him."

She headed for our bedroom, and I went down to the kitchen.

I guessed it would be true, I thought. It would be

as if Adelle was both Sylvia's and mine, rather than just mine. I fed her in Sylvia's room, and she fell asleep again.

I felt exhausted, too, and was happy to lower my head to the pillow. I fell asleep in minutes, and when the sun burst in, I was shocked at how long I had slept. My first thoughts were of Sylvia. I got up quickly to get the day started. She'd barely noticed I was there. She looked dazed.

"How are you, Sylvia?" I asked, and her eyes lit with a happy glow.

"Our baby Adelle," she said, sitting up.

Mrs. Matthews appeared in the doorway, dressed. "Is everything all right?"

"Yes."

"Good. Maybe I'll be leaving sooner than we thought," she said. She looked at Adelle, still sleeping. Then she took Sylvia's blood pressure and her temperature while I got up and dressed.

"How is she?" I asked.

"She's doing fine. You'll bring up her breakfast this morning, but tomorrow I want her downstairs for all her meals. She can do a little walking later."

"Watch Adelle," I told Sylvia.

She nodded excitedly. Then I followed Mrs. Matthews down to the kitchen. Arden had apparently left more than an hour ago.

"I can make Sylvia's breakfast," I said.

Mrs. Matthews paused and smiled. "You can do everything, Audrina, but for now, concentrate on the baby only."

I wasn't in the mood to argue. I told myself this wouldn't go on much longer anyway. *You were patient and tolerant up to now. Hang on a little longer, Audrina Lowe.*

Sylvia grew stronger with every passing day. Oddly, the memory of what she had gone through seemed to drift, replaced with what she believed I had gone through. Mrs. Matthews was right about Sylvia's swollen breasts. The leakage frightened her, and she felt the pressure and discomfort for nearly ten days after the delivery. Mrs. Matthews bought a better bra for her to wear during this time and had her use some ice packs.

Mrs. Matthews was out and about more now. I took on my usual household duties, and as Sylvia grew stronger and felt better, she returned to some of her chores as if she had never stopped doing them. Most of the time, the two of us cared for Adelle and talked about every slight change we saw in her.

Arden often called during the day to be sure all was going well. He had dinner with clients only twice during the ten days after Adelle's birth. His interest in the baby amazed me. It seemed he couldn't wait to get home to see her and be sure all was well. Never once did he mention what had happened to Sylvia. I thought this was wonderful of him. He now cared more about her, talked to her more, and enjoyed how much she enjoyed Adelle. He even willingly had Mr. Ralph help him bring the rocking chair up to Sylvia's room.

"It's all turned out for the best," he said one night.

"We have seized disaster from the jaws of the devil himself. I'm very proud of you, Audrina. We could never have done this without your full cooperation and determination. I imagine even your father would be proud of us, don't you?"

"No. He would never forgive me for what I let happen, Arden. I don't think I can ever fully forgive myself. I can live with this, but I don't believe that I've compensated enough for my mistake."

"Oh, stuff that guilt, Audrina. You and your family have this tendency to hold on to every mistake any of you make forever and ever. Depressing and self-defeating. Listen to the advice Mrs. Matthews gave you."

The next morning, when I got up and went to prepare Adelle's bottle, I found Mrs. Matthews dressed and wearing her coat. Her small suitcase was at her feet. She was having a cup of coffee. At dinner, she had said nothing about leaving.

"Are you going?" I asked. I held my breath in anticipation.

"My work here is finished. Your sister is well, and you seem quite capable of caring for the baby."

"Does Arden know you're leaving?"

"Of course," she said, and put her cup in the sink. She flashed a smile and picked up her suitcase. "You are not fond of listening to my advice," she said, standing right in front of me now, like a grade-school teacher in front of a student. "But I'll give it to you anyway. Don't dwell on what happened here. Don't ask too many questions about it. Tell yourself nothing unusual occurred. A baby was born at home. It happens more often than people think it does. I have worked for families who had errant teenage daughters and kept their pregnancies secret. The girls even gave birth and returned to school a day or two later. The families gave the babies to church orphanages or such. Sometimes, couples who are having trouble having their own child adopt the baby. You live here in this mansion, fortified against the real world, and have no idea what really goes on out there. My advice is to keep it that way. You, my dear Audrina, are one of those women who are more comfortable with fantasy than reality. Your husband understands that. You're lucky. Other women like you have husbands who are far more intolerant when it comes to their refusal to face hard and ugly things. It's immature, of course, but as long as you're not out there involved in the day-to-day struggles most of us face, you'll do fine living in your own world. I wish you luck."

"You have no idea who I am," I said, shocked at her audacity.

She smiled. "Then maybe that's for the best. Your husband knows how to reach me if there are any problems."

"We'll be taking Adelle to see Dr. Prescott now. He'll handle any problems we might encounter."

"What a relief," she said, and started for the front door. I followed and watched her stop, turn, and look at the house again. "I do hope your husband follows through and gets you out of the past," she said. Then she opened the door and left.

For a moment, it was like she had taken all the air in the house out with her. Then I felt myself relax. I took a deep breath and, with renewed energy, began the new day. The odd thing, actually amusing to me, was that Sylvia didn't seem to notice Mrs. Matthews was gone. Perhaps she thought she had left to shop for us, but even later in the day, she never inquired about her whereabouts, and I said nothing to bring her to mind.

I couldn't forget her, of course, not as easily as Sylvia apparently did. Once again, I found myself envious of my disadvantaged sister. It brought a smile, which brought another and another. Later, we sat outside on the rear patio with Adelle wrapped comfortably in my arms. Sylvia laughed at the squirrels and the rabbits and pointed to them for Adelle to see and appreciate.

"When will she talk and walk?" Sylvia asked me.

"Sooner than you think, I'm sure, but not for a while, Sylvia. I remember when you first did, and I remember you crawling around out here."

"I don't," she said.

"That's all right. Everything you did, Adelle will do, and that might remind you."

She stood there smiling at the baby and me.

"What?"

"We're lucky," she said. I knew she was simply repeating something Arden or I might have said, but she said it as if she understood everything we had done together and everything that had happened. There wasn't an iota of disappointment or regret in her voice or in her smile. I wondered if she even thought now of Mr. Price.

"Yes, Sylvia," I said. "We *are* lucky."

We went in to prepare dinner. Whenever we did this now, we brought Adelle in with us. Sometimes she slept through the whole process, but often I caught her awake, listening and watching. The sounds surely made her curious, I thought. She was going to be a bright child. She would have the advantage of people not assuming she was slow-witted. Right now, with the three of us there and all of us well, I thought I was the happiest I had been in a very long time.

As soon as Arden arrived, I told him Mrs. Matthews had left. He nodded.

"Why didn't you mention it to me last night?" I asked. "I came down while she was having coffee and found her in her coat, with her suitcase packed."

"I thought it best not to say anything until she actually left. There was the slight possibility that she might stay another day," he said. For the first time in a long time, I sensed that he was lying.

"Dinner's ready," I said. The faster I forgot that woman, the better off I'd be, I thought, but there was one more thing to be discussed about her.

I waited until we had eaten and Adelle was sleeping again. Sylvia was in the kitchen finishing the dishes. Arden had gone into the Roman Revival salon and sat on the settee, smoking his pipe and reading one of his business magazines. He looked up when I entered but kept reading. I sat across from him and waited. Finally, he lowered the magazine.

"What's up?" he asked.

"She's gone. You made a promise, Arden."

"Promise?"

"To tell me the great secret you knew about her, the thing you had to hold over her that would ensure that she would never reveal ours. I want to know it. If I had known while she was here, I might not have been so intimidated by her all the time."

"Intimidated? You did what had to be done, just like I did, Audrina. And no one forced either of us. We knew it was best for Sylvia and for Adelle. Don't start moaning and groaning about how horrible it was. It's over."

"Okay, it's over. So tell me."

He looked away and pressed his lips together. "It's not an easy thing for me to tell."

"I need to know," I insisted.

"You *need*," he said, nodding. "Okay, I'll make you a deal. Now that you are obviously going to be heavily involved with caring for Adelle, there is no possibility that you will have any time for our business affairs. This wild idea of yours about becoming a broker is surely to be put aside. I'd like those papers signed properly. You'll go with me to Mr. Johnson's office, and we'll do it together. He was put off by your not signing and doing the fingerprint when I first brought it all here. Now he won't accept anything but the proper procedure. After all that is done, I'll tell you what you're asking. Do we have a deal?"

"We don't need to make a deal, Arden. You made a promise to me. First, you keep your promise, and then we'll discuss those damn papers," I said. My words pounded into his ears like nails. I stared coldly at him, challenging him to move me even an inch.

He looked so astonished that I thought he was going to stop talking and start reading his magazine again, but he surprised me. "I'm not proud of what I'm about to tell you," he said. "And for that reason, it's very difficult for me. I don't like bringing up the ugliest event of the past, both for you and for me. Yes, it's obviously uglier and more painful for you, but it's still painful for me, and it will always be. Do you still insist on knowing?"

I would readily admit that I was frightened, but I needed to know regardless of what it would mean to me. "Yes."

"Mrs. Matthew's son, Philip, was one of the boys who attacked you in the woods. As you know, I saw them do it, and I was afraid to confront them. Later, they threatened me if I said a word, and I was afraid for my mother."

"Her son?"

"Yes. I told her, so she knew that I could identify him. I promised never to mention it if she did this for us and kept our secret. If I did go to the police, they would investigate and maybe get him to confess or reveal the names of the others, which I could have done. One or more would rat on her son. She knew that. It was enough to ensure that she would never speak about what really happened here."

His words seemed to lift me up and take me to the rocking chair. I heard the screams, my screams, and heard their horrible laughter. I saw myself running through the woods, crying hysterically, and saw my mother's face.

"Audrina," he said. "Audrina!"

I seemed to open eyes that were already open.

"See?" he said, putting a hand on my shoulder and shaking me slightly. "I knew I shouldn't have told you. What difference does it make now?" His words were like icicles dripping into my ears. I felt myself shudder and tremble. What difference did it make now? How could he ask that? Did he ever have even a tiny bit of real love for me?

"She knew her son had violated me, was one of them. You would think she would have been kinder, gentler, even remorseful, but she treated me like I was spoiled and guilty myself. I was only a little girl!" I raised my fists in the air and barely kept myself from pounding his chest. How could he make any bargains with such a woman?

"I know. A lot of things have made that woman bitter, but she's good at what she does."

"How did you know that so well, Arden?" I fired back at him. When he didn't speak, a thought that had been haunting me came to the surface. I practically yelled, "You've asked for her services before, haven't you? Well?"

"Nothing ever happened after we got married," he said.

"Are you forgetting about Vera?"

"I thought we'd never mention that. It's like nothing ever happened with her. That's what we agreed on."

"All right. So what are you talking about?" I was shaking inside. I wished I hadn't asked the questions but knew I'd had no choice. It was the story of my life, scraping away the lies that disguised the ugliness and pain feeding the shadows of Whitefern and darkening my heart.

"I was a bit wild in college. I think you knew that anyway, Audrina, but what I did then has nothing to do with our lives now. You heard her. Don't force me or yourself to drag up any more of the past, Audrina. Enough! It's over," he said firmly. He sat back and opened his magazine.

I stared at him for a few moments and then got up and walked out, feeling dazed. It was as if the floor had been torn away and I was hanging on by a thread.

Adelle had woken up and was crying for her bottle. Sylvia was rushing to get it ready. I watched her and stood back to see how she would do. She was gentle and loving. And for the first time in a very long time, I realized why we were closer than most sisters, despite her mental disabilities.

We had both been violated, and we both had to bury memories the way others might bury bodies.

Truth Will Not Die

Soon after Mrs. Matthews had left Whitefern, I had to shop for groceries. For the last month or so, she had done it alone. I wanted to take Sylvia and Adelle along for Adelle's first outing but wasn't sure if I should. I called Dr. Prescott and told him I would be bringing Adelle in for him to examine her and talk to me about what her care involved now, but I was really calling for his advice about taking her out.

"I'm looking forward to seeing her, Audrina. How are you doing?"

"I'm fine, Dr. Prescott. I was wondering if it's too early to take her out with me when I go shopping for groceries."

"What did Mrs. Matthews say?" he asked. It was easy to read between the lines and hear how hurt he was at not being the doctor to deliver Adelle. "I'm sure she performed an Apgar assessment, right?"

"Yes, right away. She said it was all very good. Mrs. Matthews is no longer looking after Adelle."

"No. I don't see why she would be. Well, I see no

problem with taking her out. We're having beautiful late-summer weather. I'm sure you'll take great care."

"I will. Thank you."

"Why don't we plan on my seeing you and the baby a week from today around two p.m. Is that okay?"

"That's good. Thank you, Dr. Prescott."

"Is Arden going to be okay with that?"

"Yes," I said. Again, it was easy to hear how hurt he was that we hadn't used him to deliver Adelle and oversee my supposed pregnancy. I hadn't spoken to Arden about going to Dr. Prescott so soon, but I was determined that I should.

I called Arden to tell him about the arrangements. He was so quiet that I thought he hadn't heard me because he was concentrating on something else. He'd often do that when I called, and I'd have to repeat myself.

"It's a week from today at two. You can come along if you want," I said.

"No, that's all right. I was just thinking. You have to be careful about letting him examine you, Audrina. I'm not sure what he could tell quickly. Helen and I did discuss the eventuality of your going to him and having Adelle under his care, of course, but your breasts aren't swollen like Sylvia's. If he gets suspicious and realizes what's gone on, it could lead to complications for us."

"I don't imagine he would announce it to the newspapers, Arden. There is an obligation to keep personal information between a patient and a doctor."

"Yes, but you're forgetting that a crime was committed here, Audrina. He might feel obligated to report Sylvia's pregnancy."

"Okay, okay. I won't go through any exam. I won't undress. I'll see that he just examines Adelle," I said.

"Be sure you do that."

"We're going to the supermarket. Anything special you might want?"

"No. Whatever you get is fine. Got to get back to work," he said.

I wanted Sylvia to help, so I sat with her in the living room and discussed what we were going to do and how she should behave when people approached us to look at Adelle.

"Don't mention Mrs. Matthews, Sylvia. Don't say anything about how Adelle was born, understand? This is only for us to know."

She nodded, but I was not confident that she understood. We packed what we needed for the baby and set out. Sylvia hovered over Adelle protectively during the drive. It brought a smile to my face. *We'll be fine*, I thought. *Everything will be fine from now on.*

It wasn't too busy at the market. Sylvia pushed the cart with Adelle comfortable in her infant seat set in the top part. We had dressed her in a little pink hat, pink socks, and a pink dress. It was one of the first outfits Arden and I had bought her. Strangers stopped to speak to us, but all they wanted to know was how old she was and what her name was. Sylvia answered them all. One elderly man jokingly asked what aisle the newborn babies were in. He said he wanted to buy one for himself.

Sylvia's eyes bulged. "Buy babies in the supermarket?" she asked.

The man laughed, saw that we weren't laughing, and quickly walked away. As we rounded a turn, I saw Mrs. Haider ahead of us, studying a box of rice. I wanted to back out and go to a different aisle to avoid her, but she looked up and waved. I had no choice.

"Oh, what a beautiful baby!" she cried after rushing over. "How happy you and Mr. Lowe must be. And this must be Sylvia?"

"Yes, my sister, Sylvia. Sylvia, this is Mrs. Haider. She was principal of the school when I was there."

"And long before that," Mrs. Haider said.

Sylvia held out her hand and smiled. "Pleased to meet you," she recited.

Mrs. Haider looked at me and nodded. "And I'm pleased to meet you and your niece, too."

"Niece?"

"I'll explain it to you later, Sylvia. I really haven't gone through all that yet," I told Mrs. Haider. "You understand."

"Yes, certainly. So how is your artwork, Sylvia? Are you still drawing and painting?"

"No," Sylvia said.

"Oh?"

"Too busy taking care of Adelle," she said.

Mrs. Haider laughed, and then her expression darkened. "It's too bad about Mr. Price."

"Yes, I know," I said, hiding my real feelings about that man and his stroke.

"Did you ever get a chance to see him or speak to Mrs. Price?" she asked.

"Get a chance? No. Why do you ask?"

"Oh, didn't you know? He passed away last month. Heart failure. Probably part of the stroke. Very sad. I always admired him, and he was very popular with the students." She paused. "I wondered why I didn't see you at the funeral. I just assumed you'd be there, but with your pregnancy and all, I'm sure you were quite occupied."

"Yes," I said. I didn't want to keep talking to Mrs. Haider about anything, particularly that man. Fortunately, Adelle began to squirm uncomfortably. "We'd better move along. Almost time for a feeding," I said.

"I'll do it," Sylvia announced. "We both do it."

"That's very good, Sylvia. I'm sure you're a wonderful and helpful aunt. I'll see you again soon, I hope. Good luck with the baby, Audrina. Beautiful child," she said, and walked away.

Sylvia looked very confused, but thankfully, Adelle was taking up all her attention now. For a few moments, I stood looking after Mrs. Haider as she pushed her cart away. I replayed what she had told me. Mr. Price was dead. I should be happy about it, and I was, but I couldn't show that, and the news had caught me by surprise. I was stunned. Why hadn't Arden mentioned Mr. Price's death? Surely, he would have known. I would have thought he'd come rushing with the news, saying how just it was that he had suffered. Maybe he thought it would have disturbed me, as it was disturbing me now, and decided not to mention it.

He was right. It would have reminded me of what I'd permitted to happen, practically right under my nose.

We finished our shopping and headed for home. Adelle was crying more and was very uncomfortable now. Just as we reached Whitefern, a car that had obviously been parked in front of the house began to pull away. It slowed as we approached and then stopped and backed up.

Mr. Ralph dropped what he was doing with a lawn mower and rushed to help us with the groceries. Sylvia wanted to carry Adelle.

"Put her in the bassinet, Sylvia," I said, keeping my eyes on the strange car.

"And warm the bottle," she recited.

Whoever was in the car just sat watching us. The afternoon sun threw a blinding glare on the car's windows, but I was able to see that the driver was a gray-haired woman. She watched us enter the house. How odd, I thought. Why would anyone come all the way out here and just sit in her car?

We hurried inside, and I began to put away the groceries while Sylvia tended to Adelle. Whatever problems she had taking care of herself didn't affect her care of the baby. I thought to myself that a mother's instincts were too strong to be discouraged. Sylvia read at the level of a seven- or eight-year-old, with a vocabulary barely more advanced. She had trouble with grade-school math, and her memory was like Swiss cheese, full of gaps, but she was as focused about the care of Adelle as any new mother would be.

When I had heard about Mr. Price's death, my anger

had been revived, and my satisfaction at how much pain and suffering he experienced had been heightened. But there was irony here, too. I was so happy for Sylvia now. Adelle truly was giving her life meaning, more perhaps than she was giving to Arden's and mine. Yes, we'd be her parents. We would make all the major decisions for her from now until she was an adult herself, but the bond between her and Sylvia would be forever strong, although invisible to outsiders. In my heart of hearts, I knew that Adelle would someday realize who her real mother was.

Perhaps she would confront us and demand to know the truth, especially as she grew and her features resembled Sylvia's more than Arden's or mine. She would go to sleep at night with the question on her lips: *Who am I?* I was sure that Arden and I would argue about it. I would want to tell her the truth, and he would insist that I never do. "What difference does it make now?" he would surely say.

How could I explain it so he would understand? Could I really get him to see how difficult it had been for me being told I was the second Audrina, never as perfect as the first? How could I get him to feel what I felt as I struggled to find my own identity while being haunted by an angelic older sister whose name I possessed but whose perfection I would never realize? It would certainly never be realized in my father's eyes, the eyes that were most important to me.

I smiled as I watched Sylvia kiss and coo at Adelle. She was fascinated by her tiny fingers and toes. I told myself that I had to put aside my thoughts about what

had happened and especially not dwell on the revenge
fulfilled with Mr. Price's death. I hated to give her any
credit, but Mrs. Matthews had been right. I should not
dwell on the dark past. I should dwell on the future.

The sound of the doorbell jerked me out of my
musings. Whoever was in that parked car probably
had decided it was time to call on us. I had no reason
for it, but I began trembling. I didn't move until the
doorbell sounded again and Sylvia noticed.

"Someone's here," she said.

"Just take care of Adelle, Sylvia. I'll go see."

She smiled gratefully. She didn't want her care of
the baby to be interrupted.

Maybe it was another Jehovah's Witness or the like,
I thought, and went to the front entrance. I opened
the front door. It was the elderly woman I had seen in
the parked car. She looked like she couldn't be much
more than five feet tall. Her gray hair was thinning but
curly and trimmed at the base of her neck. She wore
a vintage-looking knee-length, embroidered, single-
breasted denim dress with a pair of very worn leather
shoes. On her right wrist was a multicolored beaded
bracelet. Arden would say she looked as if she'd been
put together in some thrift shop.

"Yes?" I said.

The woman's cheeks seemed to bubble at their
crests, and she was wearing too much lipstick and
rouge. Aunt Ellsbeth would have slammed the door.

"I'm Emmaline Price," she said. "Arthur's wife."

For a few seconds, I felt like Lot's wife when she
looked back at Sodom and was turned into a pillar of

salt. I was shot through with a stone-cold feeling that choked back my words.

Emmaline Price could see it in my face and began to speak quickly. "I know what you think of my husband, and I waited until the shadow of death left our home before coming to see you. I made him promises during his last days, and I beg you to let me come in and talk to you for a few minutes. I want nothing from you but possibly your understanding. His final days were full of such regret. I knew how heavy his heart was and how it would shatter under his sorrow. Please," she begged.

"I have no idea why you have come here. I don't know what you want from me," I finally said.

"Just your patience for a few minutes, please. When you make promises to someone you've loved with all your heart most of your life, you can't go on without keeping them. I'm sure you can understand that."

Yes, I could understand that, I thought. The promise I had made to Papa concerning Sylvia was a promise I did not keep, and this woman was at our front door precisely because I hadn't. But my rage turned quickly to empathy. I saw myself at the front door of wherever Papa had gone, pleading with him to give me a chance to explain.

Without replying, I stepped back to let her enter. She walked in quickly and waited for me.

"This way," I said, and took her to the Roman Revival salon, where I half-expected Aunt Mercy Marie's ghost to appear and begin shouting at her.

I indicated where she should sit, and I stood

watching her for a moment, deciding whether I should sit or simply look down at her with disdain. She looked at me with such desperation in her teary gray-blue eyes that I softened and sat on the settee.

"What is it you promised your husband, Mrs. Price? And how does that involve me?"

She looked up at the ceiling, took a deep breath, and began. "Arthur was not unlike most creative people—artists, writers, composers. They dream of being appreciated, succeeding in their field. They're told they have talent, and they struggle to make something of it. But Arthur was also a family man. When we first met and fell in love, we were immune to all the hardships. We had very little money. I did some odd jobs so Arthur could paint. He sold a few things but never made any real money. I know," she said, changing her tone a bit, "this is not very important or interesting to you, but I'm trying to explain enough so you will appreciate what I want to tell you."

I didn't speak. I didn't care if my silence made her uncomfortable. Her husband had brought a great deal of pain to this house and this family.

"Anyway," she said, squirming a bit, "Arthur decided to finish college and get his teaching certificate before we could think of having children and a home and all the things everyone who wants a family life wants."

"Mrs. Price," I began. I wanted to say, *I don't care. Please leave.*

But she sensed that and quickly went on. "Of course, he continued painting and trying to get noticed, but after a while, he was devoting much more of his energy to his teaching. He really enjoyed teaching. He loved young people, and they loved him. Arthur was one of the most popular teachers. I'm sure you know that. He was devoted to his students in ways most teachers are not."

"I can imagine," I said dryly. "In ways most teachers are not."

She ignored my sarcasm and went on. "He sold a few paintings, mostly to the parents of some of his students and a few to a dealer in Richmond, but he was never discouraged. Even after he retired, he worked hard at his art. When the children were younger, we traveled to see beautiful art everywhere. We went without a lot of things that other people thought were important so we could save our money for these trips. We've visited the Prado in Madrid, the Louvre, of course, the National Gallery in London, even the Hermitage in St. Petersburg."

"I still don't see—"

"What I'm trying to tell you is that Arthur was a lover of beauty anywhere he saw it. He could get inspired by a unique tree or the way an elderly man sat and stared while he thought about his life. He did a wonderful picture of that man, and a museum in Boston now has it. What I mean to say is that Arthur was a real artist, Mrs. Lowe, and not someone just amusing himself."

"What is your point, Mrs. Price?" I asked, moving to the edge of the settee, ready to stand in order to suggest that I wanted to end this conversation.

She leaned forward. "The point is that my husband really appreciated your sister's beauty, but from an artist's point of view."

"I'm sorry. I can't agree with you about that. What he did, how he touched her, was quite inappropriate." I stood and stared down at her. I didn't want this prolonged a moment more.

"He meant no harm. He was so upset over the misunderstanding," she said, dabbing at her eyes. "For days and days after your husband came to our home and screamed at him, he sat in the corner of his studio and stared at a blank canvas. He ate very little and was up often at night just walking around the house. I'm sure the stress brought about his stroke."

I took a step toward her. "My husband and I were even more upset, Mrs. Price. Do you know how my sister is, her condition, how she has been all her life?"

"I just know from what Arthur told me. I understand she's not what she should be mentally, but he said she was a very good student and very talented. He was simply taken by her innocent beauty. It overwhelmed him. He was driven to paint her. I can't tell you how many nights he described it all to me and cried and wished he could somehow get your forgiveness."

She clutched her hands together like someone about to offer a prayer. I stood there, impatient and tired. How could I care about forgiving him?

Sylvia came into the room with Adelle in her arms.

"Hello," she said, when she saw Emmaline Price. "This is Adelle."

"Your baby," Mrs. Price said to me. She stood up to get a closer look. "What a beautiful child."

"Did you feed her?" I asked Sylvia, ignoring our intruder.

"She ate a lot, Audrina."

"Good. Please put her in the bassinet now. She needs to sleep to grow, remember?"

"Yes." Sylvia paused, obviously wondering who this woman was and why I didn't do the proper thing and introduce her. This was something I had taught Sylvia she must always do.

"Go on, Sylvia. We'll have our lunch soon, too."

"Okay. I'll cut the tomatoes," she said, and after another quizzical glance at Mrs. Price, she left.

"She is a very beautiful young lady. I can see what drove Arthur to do what he did."

"Can you?" I fired back at her. My voice was so harsh she fell back into the chair. Now I stood, my temper flaring like Papa's would. "Your husband just appreciated my sister's beauty? That's all it was? An artist being inspired? That's all that went on here? Do you think I'm that stupid?" I caught my breath. "All right. You came to fulfill your promise to him. I appreciate your devotion to your husband, but this doesn't change anything, Mrs. Price. Your husband took advantage of my sister. He used art as an excuse to sexually abuse her. I'm afraid we're going to leave it at that. And you're lucky that's all we'll do."

My rage lit something in her. I could see how her body, which had been in a posture of pleading, changed. Her eyes brightened with fury. She stood, too. "I'm sorry there is no forgiveness in your soul for someone who suffered and has died. He was remorseful and sincerely in pain, a pain that killed him. His doctors confirmed that the stress was overwhelming. It took away his life when it caused his stroke. He was diminished, a shadow of who he was. Death had no struggle to take him. I'm sure he welcomed it."

She continued, "And for you, from the little I know of your family and the tragedies you've endured, to stand there and be so high and mighty . . . I feel sorrier for you now. I'm glad I came here to see who you really are. Now I can forgive Arthur for sure. The rumors about this Whitefern family have good reason." She started walking away.

Papa's rage exploded in me. "Stop!" I shouted.

She turned.

"You think I'm unsympathetic, selfish, cruel, and harsh? You blame my family? You defile my family's memory?" I stepped toward her. "Well, I'll tell you something that you don't know, that no one should know, and if you dare utter a syllable of it out there, I promise that I will destroy your husband's memory forever. And you along with it. That baby you just saw, that beautiful child in my sister's arms, that baby is her baby, not mine. Your husband *raped* my sister. How's that for artistic inspiration? Well? What do you say now? Who is the high and mighty and unforgiving one now?"

She shook her head.

"Go on, get out and leave us. We'll do fine bringing up your husband's child, a child who will never know anything about him until she can absorb such a horrible fact about herself. Maybe she'll visit you if you're still alive and make you face your husband's sin yourself. Maybe she'll visit your children and tell them they have a half sister."

She didn't move. Then she surprised me by moving back to the chair and sitting.

"Stunned?" I said. "I guess you didn't know the man you married, the man who was the father of your children, so well after all. It doesn't surprise me. He was quite good at deceiving me. Apparently, he was good at deceiving the whole community, too, especially the school community." Why was she still here?

She shook her head again. "He's not the father of my children," she said.

"What?" Now what was she confessing to? She dressed like a hippie. They probably lived with other hippies and had no morals. "I don't want to hear your confessions, Mrs. Price. Frankly, I couldn't be less interested in you. Please leave, or I'll call the police."

"All our children are adopted," she said softly.

"That's very nice, but—"

"No, you don't understand what I'm saying, Mrs. Lowe. Arthur was unable to get me or any woman pregnant. He contracted testicular cancer when he was in his early twenties. The radiation and chemotherapy stopped the cancer but led to infertility. He tested and tested and finally gave up. That's when we decided to adopt. My husband couldn't possibly be the father of your sister's child." She stood again. "If you want, I'll arrange for you to speak with Arthur's doctor. I can also send you copies of his tests and reports."

She waited for me to respond, but I couldn't. After a moment, she started out. She paused in the doorway, looked back at me, then said good-bye and left.

The door closing sounded more like a coffin being shut. I fell back onto the settee.

Sylvia returned to the living room and looked around. "Is the lady gone?"

"Yes, she's gone, Sylvia."

"I cut too many tomatoes."

"That's all right."

"Adelle's asleep," she said.

I nodded.

She looked at me, smiling, waiting for me to tell her to do something else.

A thought flashed into my mind. "Sylvia, Papa hasn't spoken to you since Adelle was born, right?"

She nodded.

"But you've been in the rocking chair; it's in your room. You haven't heard him whispering since I've been sleeping there with you?"

She shook her head. "No, Audrina. Papa has no more secrets."

I hugged myself when the chill rippled through my body. Then I put my hands over my ears.

They were all screaming at once, every ghost in the house.

Papa's Revenge

Later, when Arden called to tell me he was taking a client to dinner, I said "Hello," listened, and said "Good-bye." He didn't try to say more or ask me why I sounded like I did.

Sylvia was upstairs in the rocking chair with Adelle in her arms. We often went up there in the afternoons now. I had taught Sylvia one of the lullabies I remembered Momma singing to me. When Sylvia sang, she sounded like Momma, and sometimes I would find myself dozing off with Adelle. It made me happy. We often looked for ways to bring back something beautiful and tender from our past.

All through lunch, a lunch I didn't eat, I listened to Sylvia talk about Adelle. Since the baby's birth, a new fountain of words flowed from her lips. It was as if the traumatic delivery had jolted her ahead in years or awakened some sleeping undeveloped skills. Someone listening to her for the first time might easily assume that there was nothing abnormal about her, nothing at all.

It made it difficult for me to hate everything about

her pregnancy and certainly made it impossible to regret Adelle's birth. Look what had emerged from the darkest places in Whitefern. There sat Sylvia beside our beautiful child sleeping in her bassinet, both looking innocent and trustful. But I was once innocent and trustful, too. Something like that is sweet and pleasant to see, but in this world, it was like a door left open through which everything ugly, mean, and selfish could easily enter. It was why a loving parent must shut down her little boy or girl's childhood as soon as possible and paste those memories into albums to be remembered, though never restored.

Sylvia didn't notice how little I ate. She was too excited. She cleared the table, washed the dishes, and put everything away while I sat staring at the clock.

"Audrina," she said, "we forgot to get a baby carriage."

"What?"

She ran out and returned with a catalogue of infants' clothing and equipment. She put it on the table opened to pictures of strollers and carriages.

"Yes," I said. "We'll get one soon. She isn't ready yet, Sylvia."

"Soon," she said, nodding.

I left her and went outside for a while. I needed to be alone, and whenever I felt maudlin and even frightened, I would stroll around the grounds, in and around the woods, comforting myself with the singing of the birds and the sight of squirrels going through their bursts of gymnastics as though they were performing for me. When I was very young, I never went too far from the property. The house always held me, as if there was an invisible chain hooked to my waist.

As I paused and looked up at Whitefern, I recalled overhearing my father arguing with my aunt Ellsbeth about allowing me to leave Whitefern and go to college.

"You've managed to tie her hand and foot to Sylvia. It's not fair, what you're doing. I know you love her, so let her go to college. Set her free, Damian, before it's too late!" my aunt had cried, her voice full of desperation.

"Ellie," my father had replied, "what would happen to Audrina if she left here? She's too sensitive for the world out there. I'm sure she will never marry that boy, and he'll find that out once he tries something. No man wants a woman who can't respond, and I doubt she'll ever learn how."

Those words rang in my head, bonging like church bells. Had my father been right? Or had my aunt Ellsbeth been right to push for me to be free of Whitefern?

Was all that had happened decided the day I was born? Was Papa responsible for this now, molding me in a way that made it difficult to respond to a man, just as he had predicted? Could that justify what Arden had done, by any stretch of the imagination? Was I simply trying to find an answer that would make it possible for me to go on, blind and in denial?

There were no answers out here, no answers away from Whitefern. Whatever the answers were, they loomed inside, hovering in the corners with the secrets, waiting for me to pluck them like blackberries.

I belonged inside. Maybe I was too sensitive for the world out there, Arden's and Papa's world, in which deception and dishonesty were the currencies to buy your way to happiness. Regrets, morality, even simple compassion were obstacles, lead weights on your ankles that would only sink you in the sea of competition. Papa was right, and Arden was right. I didn't belong in that cutthroat world. As I saw too often, you couldn't leave it outside your home once you swam in it.

I went back into the house and walked up the stairs slowly. I felt like I was in a hypnotic daze. I could feel the past, with all its voices, closing in on me. It was as if I was falling back through time with every step. There was Vera smiling at me from the doorway of her room, the way she often did when something I had done made someone in the house upset or when something I asked for was denied. Her smile told me that her usually insatiable jealousy was satisfied.

There was Aunt Ellsbeth with some clothing I had not put away properly, holding it up like evidence in a murder trial. I could hear her voice cutting my ears. "Do you think your mother would be happy to see this?"

I touched the wall above my head to be sure I was not shorter, not a little girl again. Then I walked to Sylvia's room, my whole body as tight as a fist. For a while, I stood in the doorway. Watching Sylvia sing and rock intensified the rage building inside of me.

"Sylvia," I said, "I want you to put Adelle in the bassinet now."

She looked at the sleeping child and then did what I said.

"Come with me," I ordered.

She followed me downstairs and sat beside me on the sofa. I took her hands in mine. She wore her soft, innocent, and trusting smile, but she was a little frightened by my intense look. I could feel her fingers tremble.

"It is time for you to tell me a secret, Sylvia."

"Papa's secret?"

"Yes. Did he tell you to let Arden make the baby?"

I could see the wrestling going on in her mind.

"It's all right to tell now. Adelle has been born."

She nodded.

"It was Papa who told you that we would both be pregnant?"

"Papa said so." She looked like she was going to cry.

"It's all right, Sylvia. Don't worry. Papa talks to me, too."

She smiled. "I know," she said.

She wanted to go back upstairs and watch Adelle. She was never comfortable being too far from her. I poured myself some blackberry brandy and sat for a while. Sylvia came down to tell me that Adelle had woken up and that she was preparing her bottle. As if she could sense something different and important was going to happen but was afraid of it, she asked if she could take her dinner upstairs and eat alongside Adelle tonight.

I told her I thought that was a good idea. I had

no intention of eating anything myself. I drank some more brandy and looked at some old pictures. I dozed for a while, and when I woke, it was dark. The sun had gone down, and I hadn't yet put on any lights. I decided to turn on only the lamp by the sofa. It had a very weak bulb. Momma had liked it that way. She could sprawl out and fall asleep here. I thought the low illumination had comforted her. I recalled how her arm would slide off the edge, and when I was a little girl, I would crawl up to the sofa and hold her hand. Sometimes she'd wake up and smile at me, and sometimes she wouldn't wake even though I'd held her hand for quite a while.

I wished I could hold her hand now.

Hours later, I saw light from the headlights of Arden's car streak through the windows and trace along the walls before going dark. Soon after, I heard him open the front door and mutter about no one leaving a light on for him. When he first entered the salon, he didn't see me. He looked like he had drunk too much, as usual, and stood there acclimating himself to the subdued light. Finally, he noticed me and shuddered.

"Christ," he said. "You look like a ghost, and in this house, that's not an exaggeration."

"Do I? Maybe you're seeing Aunt Mercy Marie."

"Why are you sitting in the dark? And why didn't you leave lights on for me?"

"I feel like I've been in the dark for a long, long time in this house, Arden."

"Hmm," he said. "Well, you can blame your father for that."

"Apparently, I can blame him for a lot more."

"Huh?" He unbuttoned his jacket.

"We had a visitor today, Arden."

"What visitor? Did Dr. Prescott come here?"

"No, it wasn't Dr. Prescott, and it wasn't Mrs. Matthews."

"Well, who the hell was it? What's the mystery?"

"It was Mrs. Price."

"Price? Why the hell would she come here?"

"You never told me he had died."

"Yeah, well, good riddance." He saw the bottle of brandy on the coffee table. "Drinking? Good idea. A nightcap is in order," he said. "Another successful dinner to celebrate."

"Really." I watched him pour himself a glass.

He wobbled a bit and then drank half of it in one gulp. "Good stuff," he said. "So? Why did this Price woman come here?"

"She had promised her husband she would come to plead for forgiveness. She wanted to explain about him, to tell me how he was truly an artist and had only an artist's interest in Sylvia's beauty."

"Sure," Arden said, and finished his brandy. "Maybe she thought we might still press charges or something."

"She got me very angry, Arden. I wasn't going to forgive Mr. Price, and she was upset by how I treated her explanation. She said some nasty things about my family and our reputation in the community. I couldn't help myself."

"What . . ." He refocused on me and poured himself a little more brandy.

"She saw Adelle and Sylvia, and she thought Sylvia was beautiful and the baby was beautiful."

"So?"

"So then I told her we weren't only accusing her husband of groping my sister. We were accusing him of rape."

My words seemed to sober him instantly. "You told her what?"

"She was shocked and had to sit again."

"For Christ's sake, Audrina, she could go and tell someone, maybe a lawyer or someone, because she'd be afraid we'd press charges."

"Against a dead man?"

"Or discredit her in some way. How could you make such a mistake now? I don't care how angry she got you."

"What followed was very interesting, Arden. As it turns out, Mr. Price couldn't have raped Sylvia and gotten her pregnant with Adelle."

"Oh, yeah? Why not?"

"He had testicular cancer when he was younger and was made infertile. They had to adopt all their children."

Arden stood before me, blinking fast. "I'm sure that's a lie," he said. "Her way of covering up for him. She's worried about herself, that's all."

"She has the medical reports and is giving me the doctor's name. She will have him tell the truth. She's not lying."

"Yeah, well . . ."

"I had these dreams—at least, I thought they were

dreams—of you standing outside the first Audrina's room and whispering through the door while Sylvia rocked in the rocking chair. You impersonated my father and told her to do things. You told her she had to keep everything secret. It wasn't a dream, was it?"

He didn't reply. He stood there looking at me.

"You're the one who raped my sister, Arden. You're the one who took advantage of her. Did you do this for your own selfish pleasure?"

"No," he said, maybe too quickly, because he wasn't quite finished trying to deny it. "I mean . . . Oh, what are you so surprised about, Audrina? We both wanted a child, and you couldn't give me one. It worked out well, didn't it? Now we have a child who carries your father's blood and my blood. It's almost the same thing, and besides, everyone believes it. That woman won't convince anyone of anything."

"You raped my sister," I said.

"Stop saying that. I did what had to be done." He stared at the floor for a few moments and then looked up. "And maybe it will have to be done again. I want a son; you should want a son, too."

I stood up slowly. His words now and his confession, although anticipated, still struck me hard—but doubly hard when he threatened to have another child with Sylvia.

"You deceived us both, and you had me believing that schoolteacher was the rapist. It was all lies." A new thought occurred. "Did your Mrs. Matthews know the truth? Did she go along with it? Was it part of your plan? You don't have to answer. I think now that was why she was so disrespectful to me. She knew I was being a fool, and oh, what a fool you made of me."

"Now, you listen to me, Audrina—"

"No, *you* listen. You put the idea in Sylvia's mind that we'd both have to be pregnant. You set it all up, planning ahead for when the baby was born. Are you proud of yourself?"

"It was all part of the plan."

"Yes, the plan. I should have wondered more why you conceived it."

He sighed deeply and looked pathetically weak, wobbling and struggling to come up with a good response. "I did what had to be done," he said. "And yes, it was a clever plan, and I am proud of how well it was executed. Now, stop this indignation. You have a child to raise, and the world believes she's yours. You have a family. You should be thanking me."

"Thanking you? I have a family? Yes, I have a family, a family born of lies and deceit."

"That's not unusual for you, Audrina, or for Whitefern," he said, smiling. "Look at what your father planned and how well he planned it. Everyone in this house, including your own mother, followed his design. It was all a lie. They even had me and my mother believing it. To go as far as to install an empty grave with a tombstone . . . Don't try to make it look like your family was any better than I am."

"You're right, Arden. This home is hospitable to lies, but I don't intend for them to go on."

"So what are you going to do? Tell everyone Adelle is really Sylvia's baby? We both thought that would hurt the child and how she will be perceived."

"She'll remain our child, Sylvia's and mine," I said. "But someday she'll know the truth." I straightened my shoulders, just the way Papa would when he was going to make one of his definitive proposals. "I think it would be best if you left Whitefern, Arden. I don't want to share meals with you, much less my bed." I started to walk away, then stopped. "And as far as the company goes, it will remain as it is—in my control."

"What?"

"Go sleep in one of the downstairs bedrooms tonight," I told him.

"Like hell I will. And I won't leave here, either. You'll do what I say with those legal documents," he vowed, shaking his fist at me. "I'm your husband. You'll obey your husband."

"I won't," I said. "In fact, I'll be calling Mr. Johnson tomorrow and advising him of the same, so he'll know that if you try to forge anything, it will be a crime that he will be associated with, too. Good night." I started up the stairway.

"Audrina!" he screamed. "You're part of this. You can't escape it by sending me away or going to sleep or rocking in that damn chair!"

I ignored him and kept going.

"Audrina!" he shouted from the foot of the stairway. "Don't you dare walk away from me!"

Sylvia came out of her room and hurried to the

stairs. "Adelle is crying," she said, looking down at me and at Arden. "She heard the screaming."

"Yes. Well, she won't have to hear it much longer. Arden is going to move out," I said.

"Damn you!" he screamed. He rushed up the stairs. "You won't tell me what to do. And you will sign those papers."

I was nearly to the top.

He lunged at me and grabbed my arm. "I'm Papa here! I'm Papa!" he bellowed. He shook me hard.

"Stop hurting Audrina," Sylvia ordered. She sounded just like Momma telling Papa to stop hurting me or Vera.

Arden let go of my left arm to push her away from us, and I turned, freeing myself from his right hand. Before he could reach out to grab me again, Sylvia came forward with her arms out and pushed at his shoulder.

He tottered, looked at us both with surprise, and fell backward, his arms flailing out, his hands grasping air as he dropped onto his back and then flipped over, his legs flying over his torso and giving his body the momentum to flip again, this time coming down hard, his neck hitting squarely on the edge of a step. His body slid a little and stopped.

He didn't move or cry.

Sylvia and I didn't move, either.

"Arden fell," she said.

I held out my hand to keep her from following me and walked down to him slowly. As I approached, I was experiencing déjà vu. This was how I had approached Aunt Ellsbeth's body when she had fallen down the stairs. *She's not dead*, I'd kept telling myself, *not dead, not dead, only hurt*. She had been facedown, and I'd had to turn her body to look at her face. I remembered her head had lolled, unnaturally loose, and I had shaken her to wake her up, but she never did.

Arden was lying faceup. His eyes were wide open, already two orbs of lifeless glass. He had carried his expression of surprise all the way down and died with it. I knelt beside him and felt for a pulse nevertheless. There was none.

"Is he hurt?" Sylvia asked.

"Go look after Adelle," I said. I could hear the baby crying. It was the loudest she had cried yet. Maybe she sensed that her real father was gone. "Go on, Sylvia."

"Yes," she said, and walked back up and to her room. "Adelle . . ."

I stood and looked down at Arden. Perhaps I was in shock, because I didn't cry. I should have cried. I should have been screaming his name and begging him to be alive. Memories of how kind and loving he had been to me when I was young and just emerging from Whitefern were pushing away the anger and disappointment I had just felt. There had been wonderful smiles and laughter between us, too. They didn't want to be buried.

I sat on a higher step and continued to gaze at him. Sylvia came to the top of the stairs again, this time with Adelle in her arms. The baby was no longer crying.

"Did I hurt him?" she asked.

"No, Sylvia. He hurt himself."

I looked around at the dark house. Whitefern had done it again, I thought. Whitefern had exacted its revenge. The ghosts were gathered, whispering to one another and looking at Arden.

Papa, I thought. *Where are you?*

He was here; he was with us. I stood up again and stepped around Arden's body.

"Where are you going, Audrina?" Sylvia asked.

"To warm Adelle's bottle. Then I have to call an ambulance for Arden. You can wait in your room."

"I can warm the bottle," she said.

"No, I don't want you or the baby down here until this is over," I said. "Just wait in your room. Please, Sylvia."

"I'll sit in the rocking chair," she said. She said it as if that would make everything better again.

"Yes, go sit in the rocking chair," I told her, and went to put on lights in the house.

I called for the ambulance. Then I went up and handed Sylvia the bottle and let her feed Adelle while she held her in the rocking chair. It had never seemed more appropriate.

"Sylvia, the ambulance is coming, and with it will be policemen who will want to know what happened to Arden," I began.

"I pushed him," she said.

"No. You reached out to help him because you saw he was going to fall backward. Just like you helped Papa, remember?"

"Yes," she said, smiling.

"Arden drank too much alcohol, Sylvia. It made him dizzy. That's what happened, okay?"

She nodded and went about feeding Adelle. I could only hope that she would remember what I had told her to say. It would obviously be so much easier than having to explain why we had argued, how Arden had come up after me, and how Sylvia had instinctively come to my defense.

Less than half an hour later, the ambulance arrived, with a police patrol car behind it. The paramedics rushed in when I opened the door and pointed to Arden.

The two policemen looked terribly suspicious. How could I blame them? Another death at Whitefern was surely at the forefront of their thoughts.

One of the paramedics confirmed that Arden was dead. "Looks like a broken neck," he said.

"Don't move the body yet," the taller of the two policemen ordered. "We have a detective on the way." He turned to me. I was standing with my hands clasped and resting on my breasts. I was sure I appeared to be in shock. I felt I still really was.

"Can you tell us what happened here?" the shorter policeman asked.

"We were going to bed," I said. "My husband had been out to dinner with some clients. I think he had too much to drink at dinner, but he drank some more brandy when he got home. I pleaded with him to stop drinking and just go to bed, and finally we set out to do so. He was walking behind me. I thought he was okay. My sister came out. She's watching the baby in her room for me right now. She was the one who screamed that Arden was losing his balance. I turned. She reached past me to grab him, but he fell back and flipped over and over, until he landed like this."

Neither of them spoke. I gasped and tottered.

The shorter officer put his arm around my waist. "Hey, you'd better sit down."

"Yes, thank you," I said, and let him help me to the sofa, where the soft light had remained on. He went to get me a glass of water.

When the detective arrived, they told him what I had said, and then he asked to speak with Sylvia.

"My sister was born prematurely and had early development problems," I explained. "She's never been to a formal school, and she's what they call mentally challenged."

He nodded. He looked like he knew about us. When they had removed Arden's body, I went up to get Sylvia. Adelle was asleep again, so I asked the detective to come up. I thought it would be better anyway to have her questioned away from the stairway.

"Sorry to bother you," he told Sylvia, "but can you remember what happened to your . . ."

"Brother-in-law," I interjected quickly. "She's not clear on relationships."

He nodded. "Sure. Can you remember anything, Sylvia?"

"I remember things," she said with what sounded like indignation.

"On the stairway. What happened to him?"

"He fell backward," she said. "I tried to help him like I helped Papa, but I couldn't reach him . . . I was right behind Papa. I didn't have to reach him."

"She once kept my father from falling," I explained. "We made a big deal of it. I'm sure you understand."

"Yeah, sure." He looked at Sylvia again and realized she wasn't going to be much of a witness. "Okay. There'll be an autopsy, and we'll be in touch. My deepest sympathies, Mrs. Lowe."

"Thank you."

He nodded at Sylvia.

"Adelle is sleeping," she told him, as if she expected he would want to ask the baby questions, too.

He looked at me, his eyes like exclamation points.

"It's how she is," I said.

"Right. I'll call you," he told me, and left.

The silence that followed after everyone had left was the deepest silence in Whitefern that I could remember. I didn't imagine I would be able to fall asleep, so I didn't go to our bedroom, and I didn't lie beside Sylvia on her bed.

Instead, I returned to Momma's sofa, where I sat until the wee hours of the morning. Sometime before the sun rose, I did fall asleep. Sylvia woke me to tell me it was time for breakfast. She stood there holding the baby and looking at me.

"Yes," I said. I rose slowly, telling myself it was best to eat something. There would be so much to do now, so many people to talk to and repeat the same explanation.

"Is Arden coming back for breakfast?" she asked.

"No, Sylvia," I said. "Arden's never coming back."

She nodded, looking like she just wanted to hear it confirmed.

"Arden has passed away, just like Papa did," I said.

"I know," she said. "Papa told me."

Epilogue

It was a day without clouds when we buried Arden next to his mother, Billie, in the Whitefern Cemetery, exactly the wrong weather for a funeral. Everyone and everything looked too bright and alive. Arden's and Billie's graves weren't far from my parents' graves and those of Aunt Ellsbeth and Vera. Many of our company's clients and all the employees attended the service. Mrs. Crown looked devastated, as devastated as a lover of the deceased might. She cried harder than I did and needed more comfort than I did.

Sylvia stood beside me, clinging to Adelle. Onlookers thought it was one of the saddest and yet sweetest scenes they had ever witnessed. Afterward, as I had promised Sylvia many times, I took her over to Papa's grave. She read the tombstone and looked at the grave and shook her head.

"Papa's not down there, Audrina," she insisted.

"Maybe he isn't," I said, keeping my eyes on the headstone.

I had struggled through most of the day. I had

barely slept during the previous nights. I hadn't touched any of Arden's things yet. I intended to donate as many of them as I could to charity. In fact, nothing at all looked different in our home. Whitefern was invulnerable. The shadows in every corner were still there; the whispers I heard on the stairs continued. Some of the old clocks had stopped ticking, but I didn't remove them. The grandfather clocks in the halls still chimed, but I ignored them. Arden had hated them, along with the cuckoos in the wooden Swiss clocks. Now that I thought about it, he had hated anything and everything that related to my family. He had wanted to remake it all in his name.

We didn't have any sort of formal gathering after the funeral, the way we had for Papa's. Some people stopped by during the following days, people like Mrs. Haider and a few of the employees I knew. Mrs. Crown did not visit. For now, I agreed with Mr. Johnson to permit Arden's top assistant, Nick Masters, to run the firm. It took me a while to delve into real-world matters.

Arden's absence didn't appear to bother Sylvia very much. She was far too occupied with Adelle and, along with me, caring for the house. Occasionally, she would pause and look like she was about to ask after him, but then she would shake her head slightly and nod as though she really was hearing Papa.

Time closed wounds, but it couldn't prevent scars. There were so many at Whitefern. I could say we had a garden of them. Fall was rushing in. When we took walks, now with the new carriage we had bought for

Adelle, I could sense winter's eagerness. Leaves were falling faster; birds were starting to head farther south. A darker shade of blue seeped into the afternoon skies, and nights were beginning to drop with heavier darkness around us.

One evening after dinner, while Sylvia was looking after Adelle and playing some records on Momma's old phonograph, which Arden had once tried to sell as an antique, I went out and walked far enough away from the front of the house that when I looked back, I could see the entire house silhouetted against the stars.

I had been toying with the idea of selling Whitefern. We would sell the brokerage, and Sylvia, Adelle, and I would move away, to a place where no one knew us, the Whiteferns, the Adares, or the Lowes. It was a way to be reborn, I thought.

Could I do this? Could I finally leave the past, or would the voices follow us no matter where we went? It was an enormous challenge for me, even to consider it. Once, years ago, when I had tried to leave with Sylvia, she had revolted against it, and I'd had to stay. Would she revolt again? If anything, she was probably even more attached to Whitefern. It was here that she was comforted by Papa's voice.

It was impossible, I thought. Whitefern had a grip on us that even death could not break. Slowly, I walked back to the house, feeling like I was being chastised for the very thought of leaving it.

Sylvia was in the living room, cradling Adelle in her arms and dancing to one of Momma's favorite

344 V. C. Andrews

tunes. She paused when she saw me. Adelle looked comfortable and happy in her arms.

I walked to them slowly, smiling, and put my arms around Sylvia. Adelle was between us, looking up at both of us.

And we three began to dance again.

MY SWEET
AUDRINA

and

Whitefern